I0822557

Mac Town

Joseph Warren Morris

New Branch Publishing
7454 Huntwick Trail
Nashville, TN 3722
Email: newbranchpublishing@gmail.com1
Phone: 615-646-0755

Mac Town

First published by New Branch Publishing

ISBN 978-0-9988528-9-8

Book design by Jera Publishing

Printed by Lightning Source

Printed in the United States of America
Nashville, Tennessee

Acknowledgements

My many thanks to my wife Joyce Morris for her unceasing help, and Barbara Bomar Davis for her tireless editions.

As always, I am expressing my appreciation to Kimberly Martin and JERA Publishing for their flawless contribution.

Preface

This story unfolds as nearly as I can tell it, though to other eyes it may appear unseemly, hardly equating with life's experiences as they more ordinarily and likely will have evolved; and if this pen were in your hand rather than mine you might well have configured events much differently. Ipso facto. It is what it is, and has amounted to no little task on my part in recalling and piecing together those endless infinitesimal entities that turn a story into a whole.

My span of seasons on this earth have covered a lengthy course, some perhaps better forgotten but they belong in the story too. To ferret them out one by one, to recall them with the utmost of precision, and subject each to scrutiny, is to attempt an incredulous feat and must be helped along by dividing my stretch of existence into phases which begin with my very early years, then steps into the middle ones and finishes when I have attained to the age of ripeness.

Chapter 1

I WAS A mere strapling, perhaps four, maybe five, beginning the slow evolutionary process of observing the happening of events around me, old enough then to perceive that my father Charles Edward Maynard and uncle, John Eric Caldwell, more commonly addressed as John Eric, were preparing to transport a load of green tomatoes to some distant northern city for sale. They had traveled back and forth to this market site repeatedly, among others, and upon realizing that another trip loomed in the making I pleadingly asked if I could go. Picking me up into his arms my father said, not this time, but when I'd grown a little older, he'd take me along. It was particularly hot on that day, sweltering, a discharge of steam rising from the earth, the air thick and stubbornly unstirring, the hour only a tick tock away from high noon. My father and John Eric in the field at work now heard the reverberations of the old cast iron dinner bell mounted on an oaken post next to the front porch which echoed as a low but sharp clang from the strokes delivered by my grandmother, who proudly struck against it with a wooden mallet letting them know that food awaited.

"It's time to eat, John Eric," my father said, looking up at the sun, then, "ah choo, ah choo," then a third sneeze and a fourth, the last delivered with more force than the ones previous, then there was a lowering of his face. He couldn't say with certainty why looking at the sun compelled a sneeze, he declared, but that without fail it consistently did.

"Let's go eat, John Eric."

Wilted from the searing heat and humidity the men unbuckled the harness from the draft animal, a work mule, and watered and fed him then ambled over to the pump house and washed, afterwards slipping off soppy wet shirts and putting on dry ones that my mother had but an hour before gathered from the oft used clothes line that extended the full breadth of the backyard. Once seated at the kitchen table the two men driven now by the urge of hunger ravenously tore into the food, both starved and correspondingly thirsty. When finishing with the meal they made their way to the back porch where for thirty minutes my father sat in the rocker while John Eric lay prostrate on the flooring and dozed. After this it was back to the field, the heat yet intense, savage, seeming even hotter than during the morning hours.

Starting early, at six o'clock, not long after the waking sun had emerged into sight in the east and begun to spread its brightening rays over the land, they had gathered with unbroken monotony heaps of tomatoes from the heavily laden vines, laying them with supple hands into the wooden hampers situated on a cart drawn by the work mule. To minimize damage, or avert it altogether, the tomatoes were handled with the utmost of preciseness, otherwise; a lesser care likely meant that buyers on the street, often the woman of the house, would stubbornly haggle over the flaws of the merchandise and begrudge paying the top price of the marketplace.

Keeping a steady pace until the hour of four, the sun yet relatively high, they had filled some sixty odd hampers, the sum total transferred onto an A-model truck bed, then set their sights on Chicago, which could have been Detroit, or Lansing, or to wherever else the demand led them. Sometimes as close as Evansville, Indiana. But these three were the foremost among the marketplaces. I had heard them talk of such cities ever since I had begun to reason, with tall towering skyscrapers, as they told it, where a sea of people scrambled madly about and electrified streetcars and gasoline powered automobiles ran without let up in the four directions in an appearance of unchecked determination to get to where they were going. At this stage of my existence, I had gone to the small town three miles distant from our home on limited occasions with my father on Saturday afternoons where to me the one and two story brick buildings, serried and tasteless, devoid of the most meager architectural flavor, were grander and larger than any others anywhere in existence.

They would drive throughout the night, each supposedly taking turns at the wheel. My mother packed fried chicken for the trip and set in a jug of iced tea, the ice soon melting into virtually nothing, excepting water, the nightly temperatures seeing to its diminishment which registered into the low nineties. Stopping at a combination gas and grocery store now and then my father would fill the gas tank while John Eric went in for an iced drink, bicarbonate of Coca Cola or Royal Crown, liking the bicarbonate much better than tea he said. Only when there were no stores open, this due to the lateness of the hour, he opted to the tea. It was John Eric's nature to playfully joke and sometimes would laughingly embellish that he thought he had an addiction to Coca Cola. A young man, perhaps twenty, John Eric, so far unmarried, and being of an age substantially less than my father and much stronger, drove the greater part of the mileage, my father badly needing the rest. Of obvious frailty he as a lad had contracted rheumatic fever, which the old family doctor explained had seriously reduced his health. His bodily form strikingly thin he often showed signs of weariness and fatigue, working too much and too hard, but what was the option when there were four girls and two boys in the family as well as his mother; and adding to these burdens there were the misfortunes of his wife who had endured two miscarriages somewhere in the interims.

"You alert John Eric?" he asked, suddenly awakening, rubbing his eyes while attempting to distinguish a landmark on the roadside.

"I'm wide awake. You'd better go back to sleep."

No response. Not instantly, then after a lapse. "A good thing we're doing this at night. In the daytime, in the heat, you could count on one doggone blowout after another." Then he leaned back as if once again falling into slumber.

"You're right," replied John Eric after contemplating the perils of driving in daytime when the highways were seared with unforgiving temperatures. Pulling into Chicago late that morning they parked at a marked reserve for selling fresh produce at streetside with other farmers, who like themselves were anxious to peddle their wares, usually green tomatoes, but if not this, then cabbage or squash. Sometimes kale and cucumbers. There was no hindrance to clearing the truck before sundown, half the merchandise bought by avid shoppers soon after leaving their work jobs. Neither of the men left the vehicle for any length, yet once in a while John Eric absented just long enough to pick up baloney sandwiches and cold drinks at a grocery down street. By dusk, with the last of the produce gone, they cranked up the truck and started south, driving the full night and into the day before reaching home. On the return one then the other jabbered about the sultry atmosphere of the city, worse than down South said John Eric. The crossing of the Ohio River my father later described at the supper table, as we children excitedly listened, "There was a golden streak from the moon on the water and John Eric and me stopped the truck and got out and for a while just stood looking. Nature is everywhere grand, children. I wish you could have seen too what we saw." Even at that tender age his words touched me, and they are to this day unforgettable. He knew nothing of art, not in the erudite sense, but the potential to learn resided in his soul, and I have always nurtured a consummate sorrow that the doors of poverty and the lack of monetary means had deprived him of an appreciation of the masters of the Renaissance. Reaching home in midmorning they removed their clothing with the swiftness of haste and collapsed into bed, there sleeping for the rest of the day, even until the next morning. My mother saw that we children stayed quiet and the windows kept open so as to let the draft pass through the rooms where her brother and husband lay exhausted from the ordeal of travel and forced wakefulness.

Next morning, rising early, I became the second person in the kitchen, my mother the first who'd beat me there by a half hour starting to make breakfast.

"Did you want something son?"

"I don't think so. I, I,—."

"Now! What is it? There's something. Out with it."

"It's about the trip they took to Chicago. I heard daddy say to John Eric once that hauling tomatoes all the way up there is a terribly hard way to earn a living. Is it?"

"Yes it is son. Very. But let your mind dwell on something else. You are too young right now to think of matters like that."

Chapter 2

I GREW OLDER by a scant. We had continued to live on the Gilbert Yancey farm, which belonged legally to him and his wife Lillian, the childless couple infrequently driving over from a town twenty miles to the northeast to check on their property, often Mr. Yancey asking my father on these visits to accompany him across the land so as to acquire an up close view of the corn and cotton fields, the two cash crops of any consequence. He was content so far to let my father claim the proceeds from the small rather insignificant truck crops—cabbage, tomatoes, potatoes, butter beans, green peppers, onions—that were grown in the low flat periphery of the creek flowing through the heart of the farm, taking it that the cash that might have otherwise passed to him hardly amounted to more than a pittance, and wasn't worth his effort at trying to maintain an account of the sales transactions.

The Yancey's came and went, never staying for any length, most generally my father and his landlord walking the fields and looking over the barn and storage sheds where the equipment was kept, Mr. Yancey pointing sporadically at this or that which needed repair. It so happened that once when the couple came things broke unsuspectingly from the usual gist, and particularly involved myself and Mrs. Yancey. The men were away walking while she stayed on the front porch sitting in the swing talking to my mother, as was her usual custom. It was late fall, late enough that the temperatures had subsided to a comfortable level for folks of the city. She had clad herself in seasonal wear. When she and her husband paid call they followed the practice of parking their car alongside my father's A-model ford truck, something of a rickety contraption. But her car was a beautiful invention, and shortly, soiled and disheveled from playing much of the day in the yard with my sibling brother and sisters, I took especial notice of it—I think it might have been of the color blue, a very dark and shiny blue—and wandered over and put my hands on the exterior, forming traces of dust marks on the fenders and doors, unaware of watchful eyes. Lillian's had keenly followed me; and at once she rose from her seat, hastening over.

"Don't! Don't! Don't put your hands on the car Ramsey, you'll soil it," sputtering words of agitated disapproval.

"Ramsey, you shouldn't," said my mother meekly, who felt intimidated in the presence of this fine lady from the city, whose presence she painfully dreaded.

It should fall easily on one to conjecture that being so young, I in due course would have brushed the incident aside, taking it that the lady perhaps acted in a vein of naturalness and thinking no more of it, for would not have many done the same. Yet I did not, and somehow it stuck immovably in my consciousness as the years progressed. With the passage of each year the remembrance gathered added strength, the incident recurring with more acuteness than before, the scene the same without alteration. I see it still, a poor little urchin, the young son of a dirt farmer looking up at the handsome woman in the verdure of her life clad in the finest of attire, a well to do woman from the city, hackneyed that I had done something terribly displeasing in her sight. I cannot verify my age at the time. But far into adulthood I can vouch, when the image of the long ago past should have dissipated, I realized that I still greatly disliked the vision of this woman however immature it was. She could not have dreamed with all the resources her brain could muster, nor could I, that the calendar pages would turn and that in the decades which lay in store she and this young lad would at some juncture intertwine once more but, in an arena, astonishingly transformed by time, education, and experience.

The land on which we labored and lived was of meager productivity, endowed largely of poor upland clay deposits with no semblance to the deep fertile soils indigenous to the several counties to the west bordering the Mississippi River which grew cotton stalks horse back high. The Yancey's were fortunate that my parents stayed on as long as they did, gamely trying to eke out a living, who were without advanced information as to what they were letting themselves in for before moving to an unfamiliar whereabouts. They'd moved across two counties to get to where they were going, the time period in the late twenties, and in view of the advantages left behind, the decision, when looking back, appears to have been the worst of choices. My father's mother once owned 1200 acres of prime fertile river bottom soil in the county which they had left, who at some earlier stage and for no reason other than to shower her children with kindness and love, divided her land holdings equally among him and his brother and his sister. It was never fully and clearly explained to me why he later sold his fraction to his brother and his brother's wife, although some family member eventually said that it came about because my mother yearned passionately to join her brothers and sisters who had packed up and left for a community further west, successfully persuading him that they should follow. During their second year at the Yancey's place there erupted a clash between them over his sale of the land deeded to him by his mother, he contending somewhat bitterly that he shouldn't have done it, she reminding him that he shouldn't have eaten up the proceeds by "purchasing a bunch of untested milk cows and expensive farm equipment in the first place." The quarrels were helped along in large measure because of the invasion of a parching drought which struck much of the South, thereby necessitating that he sell off the milk cows and down to virtually the last piece of the equipment at abysmally reduced prices. Ashamed and bewildered he admitted to his wife, "Honey, we're broke; the money is gone from the sale of the land which my mother once passed on to me."

There was a time before this, before they moved to join my mother's relatives, that a job offer was within his grasp which came from the railroad industry, in that era the gold standard enterprise for putting middle class people to work. It was a dream job and his for the asking. It would have been that of a coachman, negotiated by his Uncle Luke who happened to occupy the position of superintendent of the massive switchyard of the region. It was an appointment of nepotism he admitted. Even though that was factual his Uncle Luke felt he qualified well for the position, for he had finished the tenth grade.

"What will you have me doing Uncle Luke?"

"Well now. Punching tickets, watching out to do as the engineers and conductor want, and seeing that the passengers feel right at home. And too, making sure that the mail sacks are properly pitched off at towns where the train doesn't stop."

"All that seems easy enough."

"Well, there are other things too.

"That's fine. The job sounds good."

"And you'd wear a nice black uniform."

"Yes sir. I'd like that."

A retreat to the sweaty draining toil of his younger years on that God forsaken farm sorrowfully arises in my conscious even now with a bitter tinge. I've wished with ever streaming remembrance that he had taken the railroad job, a grand opportunity said his uncle, and my father said it too, the deal sounding as if it were a sure thing, well on its way to being signed and sealed until my mother puffed up at the idea, complaining about the hours he'd spend on the rails traveling, too often away from home for lengthy gaps. And thus, kneeling to the pressure from his wife he turned it down, and with her set out westward. Why we moved away from the Gilbert and Lillian Yancey farm lay tied more singularly to the poor conditions of the soil than for any other reason, yet there was another which figured influentially in instigating our departure. Mr. Yancey had grown discontented with his share of earnings from the sales of cotton and corn, the major crops, proposing that he should have a better margin, and that he would happily settle if receiving a small additional cut from the tomato sales. He claimed that my father realized a very nice profit from these sales and an argument ensued, which led to the final straw.

The calendar read 1938 when we left. I am confident that I am correct because during that year my father took me along on a trip to Chicago. I sat with him and John Eric on the street throughout much of the day as they mingled with the buyers, laughing and carrying on. There was to me an unnerving wildness in the furor of city bustle—the metallic screeches and clanging of the trolleys, the rush and thunder of the automobiles, the hurried pace of the street crowds, all this very much frightening and at first I stuck as tightly as bonding glue to my father and John Eric. After a period, I became accustomed to the breathtaking whirl around me. A while past mid-afternoon John Eric decided to take me for a ride in a red and green electric trolley which traveled in a multitude of zigzagging directions throughout the city, packed bulgingly with riders, a sizeable many forced to stand. We crossed over the Chicago River and passed by the fine arts museum, to me at the time not bearing the faintest shade of purpose. I stretched my neck and gawked at the high rises towering above us. It could not have been even in the extremes of my imagination that someday when attaining to adulthood this route way would become second nature. We stayed the night with friends who'd moved to Chicago from our community down South shortly after my birth. The houses of the neighborhood were pathetically jammed together, long and narrow edifices with a few small windows. I saw early with my own eyes how middle-class industrial people lived in the city which I would read about in novels written by the nation's well-known sophisticated writers when I came of age. The lady of the house, a kind happy woman, filled bowls of food to the brim that were set out on a large rounded table covered with an oilcloth rudely disfigured by markings that seemed to have gotten engineered through the application of a sharp cutting instrument used for peeling or slicing a piece of fruit or vegetable. There was a young girl, a daughter approximating my age with curly black locks who kept looking at me. Knowing this I looked up at her with increasing quickened glances from my plate, hoping she didn't catch me, and I didn't think she had, but John Eric keenly observed it all and smiled teasingly with his eyes. It was terribly embarrassing. He and I were assigned to a bed in a back room of the house, and while I braced myself for an outpour of razzing, he said nothing of the girl before we fell off to sleep. We left early the next morning.

The year 1938 burns still in my vision, even more significant and more memorable to me than my first trip to Chicago and our leaving the Yancey place, for it brought with it something of a glimpse of my budding intellectual growth. I had begun to look at the calendar hanging on the wall above my bed, wondering what it was about. "Let me see," I pondered, "this is 1938, and next year is 1939 and after that 1940, then 1941, and I will have aged by three years." I had begun on my own to internalize the meaning of time and existence and the great obscurity of space.

Chapter 3

SO, WE moved, the distance of travel six miles in all, three miles to reach the small nearby town through which we would pass and another three miles to close the distance to our destination, the Raleigh Rafel farm. We heaped the bulk of our things onto a mule drawn wagon, the small truck not sufficiently capable of hauling a load of any size and weight. The truck would return later, picking up the left over furnishings and other pieces if necessary. I rode on the buckboard seat by John Eric who drove the mules; who'd agreed to help, seeing that we badly needed him. The furniture—chairs, tables, mattresses, and the like were stacked haphazardly into and onto one another, as if struck by a windstorm, the spindly legs of the upside down chairs appearing in the character of horribly disfigured mutations of human legs. Though young, there was something in the aura of it all that set off a feeling of degrading self realization, a disdaining embarrassment of who we were, "a caravan of gypsies," I somehow envisioned, presumably because someone in my family or in my family of relatives had told a story of these strange people of Europe and that they were of tendency to perpetually move about. When I saw the men and women on the street and at the storefront doors peering curiously at us I centered my gaze on the flooring of the wagon or turned my back to them.

The land on the Raleigh Rafel farm far excelled that which we had left, the cotton stalks growing as high as a man's shoulders and the rows long and straight, following the unbending trajectory of the creek that flowed through the middle of the farm. The land lay flat and rich in comparison to the red clay upland that my father had stuck with for years far too many and his visions of the success that he might realize from it ushered a smile to his face. The creek, sometimes swollen, leapt over its banks when heavy rains fell, which elicited from one of the older children the name The Little Nile but I recall no appreciable crop damage as a result of the flooding.

The house depicted a welcomed upgrade over the one we'd left, a much larger house with a breezeway and a front and back porch of sizeable length and width. The kitchen my mother liked a great deal, particularly impressed with its roominess which allowed the inclusion of the huge elongated dining table around which the entire family could sit without assigning some of the children to a small side accommodation. She too liked the bedrooms, plentiful in number, most fashioning spacious sized windows that let one look easily to the outside. The exterior was painted white, and my mother said the color contrasted pleasingly with the towering green cedars that populated the front yard.

Sooner or later I arrived at an age old enough to pick cotton. I believe it to have been our third year there, possibly the fourth. I did not necessarily like the work, for it was tiring and it seemed I would never reach the terminus of the cotton rows which imaginatively were without end especially in the late of afternoon when my body felt drained. As to income, we did reasonably well for awhile. The cotton sales in part restored some of the losses that my father had suffered on the Gilbert Yancey farm due to forced cattle and equipment sales and crop failures resulting from the drought. The cash which once he realized from the sale of green tomatoes to folks of the northern cities no longer remained a factor, for my father and John Eric had decided that the gains in growing and marketing the commodity were too limited in view of the sweat and trouble they had to endure. The few tomatoes we grew were used for family consumption or given away to friends and neighbors. In most major respects this period came as a time of muchly needed enjoyment, the best so far, but a less, pleasant period perked its head too, which dashed the upbeat hopes of the family and yielded more injury to my father's health. Suddenly, he fell sick, struck by an indefinable weakness, something of a debilitating malady that stupefied our old country doctor far in excess of his capability of understanding and which, starting in late spring, hung on for the full length of summer, forcing him into idleness during the absolute crucial phase of planting and plant growth. Luckily, my mother's three brothers, led by John Eric pitched in and did the ploughing and planting, though not as thoroughly and attentively as it might otherwise have gotten done. My brother, seven years my senior, and my two second cousins, some years older than my brother, shouldered a great deal of the gathering of the crops, the rest arranged for by negotiating with the cotton picker day workers to delay the receipt of their pay until after the harvest had gone to the market place and converted into cash payment. The old doctor, unable to vouch for the illness, too archaic in my opinion, unconvincingly pretended that a virus strain of unknown origin was at fault which invaded my father's system. I believe now that it emanated from hypertension, which generated the occurrence of a mild stroke or worse.

At my tender age I failed to possess the reasoning power or knowledge to suspect that my father's trouble, his sickness and worry, was at least meagerly associated with his dealings with the local banker. When years had flown away, I surmised that they indeed bore a degree of relatedness to his misfortune. Shortly before the onset of one particular spring he approached Rupert Monett the local banker in quest of a loan for purchasing seed and fertilizer for the seasonal planting. The request wasn't sizeable, barely enough to make minor purchases, but sufficient for Rupert to look up over his heavy horned rim glasses and coarsely drawl that he'd surely consider the matter. "You see me in two weeks," he directed, his sallow face hardly changing expression. At the end of the two weeks my father approached the banker again, with the reminder that he had instructed him to come and discuss the loan at the end of the period stated, to which Rupert feigned an immediate contortion of face tempered with the lamentation that it grieved him most painfully to speak that the bank stood seriously strapped for money itself and that it couldn't grant the loan.

"Do you know of some bank where I might try my luck?" my father tepidly asked, no other alternative forging through for use in negotiating with a man whose wits he knew he couldn't match. "Planting is soon upon us, you know."

"Sorry Charles. I don't. Most are like us. Strapped for money."

My mother asked if the banker viewed him as a bad risk, that he likely might not repay the loan.

"Likely. Maybe most likely. I don't know what else. I pled with him all I could without dropping to my knees."

"Thank Heaven you didn't do that"

It took some time. Going from town to town he at last found a bank—a Farmers Merchants Bank the inscription read on the window facing—that agreed to a small loan with the provision that he prepare a chattel listing, which if surviving the test of scrutiny would stand as sufficient backing for granting the amount requested. To look at the document is to wonder at the lack of shame in the man's heart. When I first glanced at the list years later, which I retrieved from my mother's trunk after her death, it ran amusedly through me that the banker might well have asked for an inventory of the family undergarments should the idea have occurred to him.

The chattel contract, crammed with the usual legalese, whereas, therefore, thereof, heretofore, aforesaid, wherefore, hereof, and so on, stated that Charles Edward Maynard, debtor, agreed to "sell and convey unto the trustee in case of default the following property to wit, (1) seven year old black horse (!) seven year old gray mule, (!) red jersey cow coming to six years old, (!) three year old fawn colored cow, (2) coming two year old heifers (one fawn colored and the other spotted), together with the increase of said cows—the unborn calves; these chattels inclusive with the entire crop of cotton grown on ten acres of land and sold during the fall harvest." Not mentioned here but appearing in the contractual enumerations were an additional eighteen items of a less tangible nature, a sizable number related to household essentials, dishes and certain cookware notwithstanding.

Chapter 4

WITHIN THE realm of two years earlier Hitler's Werchmant invaded Poland, the launching of World War II, and England and France leapt to countervail the assault which quickly spread into the Netherlands and America not long afterwards begrudgingly joined the fray. "What! Another war," people gasped. World War I had ended not many years before, at the eleventh hour on the eleventh day of the eleventh month of 1918, a war the clever dictum went, that was to end all wars.

Some of my mother's brothers and sisters dropped over at intervals for supper, there rather specifically engaging in conversation about another world wide embattlement. There suddenly loomed within me a presentiment of fear. I stretched my intellect to fathom the meaning of war, a name strange to my limited repository of knowledge, conjuring up the most horrible of scenes in my head as I listened to the adults sitting around the supper table alluding to the devastation and bloodshed of World War I, the inhumane gassing especially, but took heart when they spoke encouragingly of the strength and courage of Great Britain and Russia, two powers that until then had escaped my realization of their existence. "Great Britain and Russia!" I repeated silently. How utterly awesome these names sounded. And I concluded with the utmost of certainty that with people like that joining us America could easily defeat Hitler, although such youthful conjecture fell far from the truth. A reflection in later years told me that we ventured dangerously close to losing the war to the Axis powers.

We in the cotton fields were astonished at the giant B-17 silver bombers, nick- named flying fortresses, flying high above in formation to a destination far away that we but vaguely imagined; and daily looked forward to their towering presence. Playfully we laughed and waved wildly with a pretense that the pilot and crew saw us and waved back. With a flight ceiling greater than any of its allied aircraft contemporaries the B-17 established itself as a formidable weapons system, dropping more bombs than any other U. S. aircraft in World War II.

After a three year stay we moved again, the decision to leave stemming from two disconnected causations involving my father and his landlord. When we first settled on the Raleigh Rafel farm a Negro man known by our family as Bud Scates, approaching an advanced age and obviously of limited health, came to my father in quest of his living in a log dwelling on the back side of the farm, obscured from sight by a congestion of heavy timber growth. No one went there except hunters during squirrel hunting season. If someone hadn't told you, you wouldn't have known of its whereabouts. The roof had begun to collapse and overall the structure was in such dilapidation that on first blush it was recognized as a preposterously unfit place for human habitation; but the fireplace worked well enough and timbers in goodly supply lay on the ground for providing the old man firewood. My parents wondered what he used as furniture. Fairly early after his occupancy my mother sent over an extra bed and mattress and quilts that she had set aside to avert his dependency of sleeping on the floor. She gave them for keeps. I felt a consummate sorrow for the old black man, as did everyone in the family.

"You can have the place Bud," my father said, "it's not much. Keep plenty of wood on the fire during cold nights."

"Yah sah."

In time the landlord, Mister Rafel, learned of the old Negro's presence, arriving early one morning to our house in a ruffled attitude of temper, adamantly seeking an explanation for Bud's presence on his farm. My father went out on the porch where they began less than a pleasant exchange. An answer was given of the exact reason the old Negro had been given refuge in the dwelling, my father stressing that he acted out of the goodness of his heart, asserting that he saw every good reason why his landlord should manifest the same sentiment. Mister Rafel allowed the old Negro to stay on and my father assumed that the confrontation was sufficiently settled, but another followed, not long delayed.

The second altercation happened in the proximity of a month's passage, when Mister Rafel suddenly appeared on the front porch at noon chafing to talk, a tinge of obvious haste and nervousness in his countenance, and abruptly started the conversation without preface, awkwardly stuttering, stuttering even worse when attempting to advance the topic further, his hands darting in and out of his coat pockets. At once my father interrupted, training on the man a vehement stare.

"What is it? What is it you're saying?"

"The land. It's about the land"

"What land?"

"The lower section adjacent to the creek."

"What about it? I don't understand"

"Well I'll tell you," he blurted weakly, his voice on the brink of tremble. "You'll remember when I rented you this farm there was a piece I said I intended to reserve. I now need to exercise that part of our agreement for the coming year."

Until then, remaining with self force under control, my father affectedly lunged into arousal, and loudly asked for a clarification.

"For the coming year? I don't get it. Straighten me out."

"My son in law would like to grow cotton there; he needs the acreage and besides, there's not much of it anyway you'd have to give up." Mr. Rafel, once a wealthy farmer and subsequently an insurance executive, now shouldered too many years to manage the farm or the insurance business by himself and therefore had relinquished these responsibilities to his son-in-law.

My father grimaced. "I don't recall any agreement in the first place and in the second I would have required something in writing and signed."

"But we did agree, at least implicitly."

"No sir. We did not agree."

"We did." Saying as much came hard.

"No sir. And I won't let your son-in-law use the land."

At that, voices surged into the air, cheeks reddened, eyes flashed, the neck veins throbbing with heavy quickened pulsations, and while my father opposed generally the use of profanity, he commenced to utter one after another various exceptional descriptions, at this stage of events Mr. Rafel appearing faint and intimidated, backing away for a step or two then turning around and from there hastening to his car. Usually a calm and gentle man, calm always around his children, my father was stirred to such anger that he could not abate it anytime soon and brought it to the dinner table, where we as children sat cowering in stillness, my mother, bless her, meekly and pitiably raising her face from the table alternately, pleading with her eyes and whole face for him to calm himself. But his voice continued to rise and fall as he hammered the name of Raleigh Rafel with uncompromising heatedness.

It took days for him to recover. In a moment of his absence my mother gathered us around her to explain. "Your father was angered because he felt that Mr. Rafel, a man of land and wealth sought to do him in, thinking he could get your father to swallow his story. Forget what you heard. His anger whirled out of control, more than he could handle. That wasn't really him at all." She had been disturbed mostly by the intensity of his volatility knowing that it impacted badly on his blood pressure. She worried without let up of the condition of his physical well being. One of the children asked if we for sure were moving. I swallowed. I already knew the answer and that it brought her to tears that we were leaving a house that she'd enjoyed more than any other in which she had lived during her entire lifetime, even as a young girl growing up. "Yes we are dear," she answered with sagging spirit, "we're renting the Langstrup farm on the other side of town, close to where we used to live."

Chapter 5

A PLETHORA OF thoughts spring before me about that year, for one thing, as said, we moved again, and another, I had grown older, more sensitive and knowledgeable to things happening around me, and still another; I now faced an adjustment to a variation of teachers, possessing different attitudes, temperaments, perspectives, backgrounds, and academic training, all of them female. I liked them. This came as heartening news to my parents and especially inspired my mother to smile. Yet bad news would accompany the good, which we discovered the day of our arrival.

The Langstrup's evidently averted telling my father during the negotiations for the lease of the property of the contamination of the water well, replete with a heavy presence of sulfur, hydrogen sulfide in chemical terms, correctable provided we had the means, funds, and knowledge, but we could claim neither. "Sulfur water!" my mother exclaimed, amidst tears, discovering it first, looking over at my father with despair, he with frightened face leveled at the floor, ashamed of what he had led the family into. He weakly uttered," I'm sorry, I should have checked it out." But that, she already knew.

"No! They should have told you. The state should impose laws on landlords for lying or omitting the truth about property conditions that are harmful to renters."

In a flash he realized his calamity, stuck with unfit drinking water on his hands and helpless to do anything about it. While water of this disposition is not poisonous it is without treatment intolerable for humans to consume. One cannot fathom the taste unless first undergoing the experience. Clothes are washable in it but that is all, and yet that is not quite all, for clothes after subjection to the chemical are never entirely free of the odor and this being so we were left with the alternative of catching rain water in barrels, buckets, tubs, and other similar receptacles that flowed from the rooftop, and toting drinking water from a quarter mile distance drawn from a neighbor's well.

We had learned on the second day of our arrival on the Langstrup farm that the Phillip Stoddard family resided nearby. They were good people. We had heard that about them before moving and gathered that they had received words of commendation on our behalf from persons who were acquainted with both families. Mr. Stoddard and his chubby good natured wife Maggie and young daughter Nenia paid call to greet us. The Stoddards knew beforehand of the impurity of our well water, and after the unpleasantry surfaced generously offered to allow us to haul or hand carry from their own supply, meaning that I with buckets in hand, now grown into a sizeable strong young boy, routinely traversed to and fro between our house and theirs for fresh water. Mr. Stoddard, an aggressive and successful farmer, owned in excess of 700 acres of rich alluvial soil and pasture land that he oversaw, his son Charlie backing him up, whose task focused on seeing that the sharecroppers did as expected. There were three sharecropper families in all, several children in each family, who with their father tilled the soil and planted the seed and gathered the corn and cotton and cut and raked the hay and stored it in the gargantuan barn, more in the fashion of a colossal warehouse, erected but a short distance from the Stoddard home, and this is how they mainly earned their keep, though were expected to pitch in to help with the sheep shearing roundup, a side line business that Mr. Stoddard had gotten into. Eventually, he gave it up, but when I met him as a lad, he seriously pursued the enterprise as a newly found money maker. When the wool shearing day got there I'd know about it and go over and stand around and watch, an idleness that eventually paid off in my favor, for one day he said, "See here Ramsey. A young sprout like you can amount to a heap of use to me if you will. Why don't you help us stuff wool in these sacks? I'll pay you something. How about it?"

"Sure."

While he treated me with the utmost of respect and kindness, seeming to like me with more than usual fondness, he generally gave off a no-nonsense taciturn expression to those around him, a task master who spoke in a commanding tone to each share cropper father, insisting that his son Charlie also act in like manner. Managing 700 acres of farmland strained the old man, which I recognized despite my youth, and taking it that I could help him a great deal, but with limitations, if I set my mind to it, I gladly dove into any assignment that he asked me to fulfill. Not meaning to, I once overheard him and his wife Maggie in heated disagreement about their oldest son Gaylon, who after an angry encounter with his father promptly packed up and left.

"Phillip, you should write him. You need him back. Badly."

"I'm not writing no letter. No sir. You might as well hush up. That boy's stubborn. Needs to learn a lesson. Look at all he could have here if he'd just do as he's told."

"Who's stubborn? You should take a look in the mirror. And besides, he's not a boy. He's grown with a wife and two children."

To my knowledge, Gaylon showed up again only once, for his mother's funeral. The schism in my opinion received its birth from two persons of strong wills and fiery emotions destined never to reverse and deep down this sorely affected Mister Stoddard but he decided that he could not turn things around and finally resigned that Gaylon had gone for good.

I knew all of the sharecropper children by name, Boss, Wesley, Dick, Dimon, Marshal, Jesse, Marietta, Lattie Sue: these were the Beale siblings, with whom I was in frequent association, working among them in the Stoddard cotton fields, mere day workers; as I saw it, using our bodies for pay, only by a thread better off than the serfs of nineteenth century Russia about whom I learned when I seriously started to read the annals of its history.

I find it easy to recall one of my teachers of that era, I vividly recall her, a young thing whose parents had given her the name of Melissa, then in the vicinity of twenty, nearer eighteen or nineteen perhaps, charming and pretty—beautiful, or to say the least I saw her as beautiful—pert and lively and wore a perfume strangely fragrant and perfectly wonderful to whiff in. I refer to her as one of my teachers though I tend to forget which grade she taught, but in my senses I recall that she taught some aspect of science. I must have been ten years of age at the time; if so, that would have put me in the fourth grade. It was also a year in which my sister died, the first of my brother and sisters to pass away, her demise occurring in late fall, a season to which she repeatedly alluded as the best of the four in that she loved the golden beauty of the tree leaves which were then in their zenith. As one could expect, her passing devastated the family, more devastating to my parents than to me and more to my brother and sisters than to me because, I presume, they were older than myself and therefore more sensitive to death. Or so that is how I internalized it at the time. They cried a great amount while I didn't, hard not to do but successfully I held my emotions inside and out of sight. Well, I only partly did. It really hit me hard too; I guess especially since I was so close to her in age, and in a multiplicity of other regards. Older than me by two years she consequently became something of my guardian in school, my protector, and endowed of an aptitude to excel in academics much superior to my own she assisted me with my studies, seeing to it that I earned reasonably sufficient marks. I don't remember going through any extended grievance, that is I mean to say that I managed to keep her passing from lingering for a long while, I dealt with it, whereas my parents in particular grieved and wept openly for weeks, the sight touching me pitiably, for I had never seen anyone before affected by sorrow that engendered such an effect as penetratingly deep and crushing.

Melissa wasn't seen at the funeral, coming however to our home to pay homage; upon seeing me gathering me in her arms and hugging me and kissing my brow. For the occasion she dressed nicely and appropriately, a shade perhaps on the extravagant side, wearing a beret on her head, and clad in a furry expensive jacket that terminated at the lower portion of her waist. No one else from her family accompanied her, nor did any of the other teachers. She did it alone. She felt in her heart that she should in that she had been my sister's teacher as well as mine. She was the older of two daughters of a prominent banker in the small town, Rupert Mcylroy Monett, Mac some called him, who as well headed up the chairmanship of the local school board, a proud and ambitious man who cunningly overcame anyone standing in his way, ruthless if he chose or thought necessary, and by and large the people feared him. Sometimes, snickering with mockery, they'd guardedly reference Rupert as the Czar or Boss, or tab him as King Rupert. Whether true or not it got about that he had mandated that the common folks, people of my family's social status, were to address him as Mr. Monett, never as Mac or Rupert which a selected few did quite ordinarily. These were folks on his level, by and large old vintage families who had lived there decades before his arrival, possessing appreciable wealth, all this amounting to a very intriguing combination. These were not his competitors; they were his friends, a species of the same circle, or associates who depended on one another, separate and apart from the common folks, gatekeepers intertwined in the governance of the affairs of the community, a bonded assemblage with no outside challenge. And careful never to cross one another. Not knowing what it meant exactly, but forming a rather near idea, I once heard my father speak with a tinge of bitterness of this inner circle to John Eric.

"Rupert is the ring leader John Eric. True, the others have their say, and can do things on their own if that is their will, and often do, but he's the ramrod that draws them together They back him."

"You mean—."

"Warren, and his brother George, and the Peytons, and Douglass, and Zach and Riley Ray, stags that drink from the same watering hole."

"Not Thompson?"

"Naw. He's too old and too rich. He's akin to the tobacco chain folks you know. He has no tolerance for their shenanigans."

Madeline, Rupert's wife, bore strong and unmistakable resemblance to her husband, aggressive, clever, crafty at erecting designs to help her achieve her way, oft times seen sitting proudly by Rupert at the High School basketball games all dressed up in her furs, and no one doubted her force in the conduct of the affairs of the bank, even more forceful than her husband, who couldn't have managed nearly as surely and precisely without her. When they matured, the girls, Melissa and Melinda, the latter the younger of the two, began by slow gradient degrees to reflect traits and characteristics which tended to duplicate those of their parents. When maturing of age to work Melinda took a place in the bank as cashier full time and Melissa worked at part time intervals when not involved in teaching. Once when I had gone to the bank with John Eric she sat working from a stool, a relatively high up stool, twisting and turning her posterior now and then in full view of exploring male eyes, cutely and innocently done, which aroused a sensation in my young being that sent me to pondering the attracting power of those of the opposite gender.

Chapter 6

AS THE furor of the war approached full swing in Europe and the South Pacific, the federal government initiated serious plans to construct a munitions plant close by whose boundaries lapped over onto the Langstrup farmland by more than half. Suddenly the government instituted a condemnation proceeding and in due time submitted a purchase price under law of imminent domain, a prodigious bonus for the Langstrup's, for the offer amounted to more than five times the appraised valuation, and innervated by the magnitude of this sum the family lost no time in directing its spokesman to ask us to move. This action took place without written contract showing that we were renting the land, neither party in possession of like document, for agreements between tenant and landlord in that era were done by handshake. My father declined, contending that there had been an oral meeting of the minds which amounted to a legal and binding agreement letting him use the land and house for an indefinite period, uncertain however of the soundness of his argument in a court of law. My mother smiled triumphantly when he told her what he had done, even though a bit fearful of the actions the Langstrup's, wealthy and influential, might take against us. A certain John L. Hagman had married the daughter of Mrs. Langstrup, the aging matriarch owner of the farm, a brash loud man of heavy body physique who generally clad himself in leather boots that elevated to the knees. Some of the citizens of the town jocularly alluded to him as Mussolini junior, the deposed fascist dictator of Italy near the end of World War II. At that period of his life John L. had crossed into his thirties. He wasn't mean, nor ostentatious, nor aggressive, but as said, loud, and given to speaking his piece without the proper observance of protocol and thoughtfulness. Aware of his flaws his mother-in-law, a Christian lady, deemed it prudent to offer him a tad of coaching. "John L. I am instructing you to represent me in asking the Maynard man to vacate my property, but you must act most gentlemanly, not in any way demonstrating to him the impression that I am unkind in my heart" So John L did as told.

"Now Charles, Mrs. Langstrup has asked me to tell you as politely as I know how to move. You must leave. The law says so. You have no contract. You are aware of that I am sure."

My father perceived the full meaning of the words making entry to his ears and met them stiffly. "No sir John L. I won't do that."

John L could think of nothing readily for his use in retaliation. He had been vanquished. Yet, figured on another card to play. Deeming it unwise to extend his persuasions further the visitor on his own turned around and left, no more thereafter setting foot on our doorsteps, opting as an alternative to send tediously prepared official looking letters with wording designed to scare us on our way. The writer of the correspondence, John L or his designate, carefully skirted an offer to compensate my father for the trouble to which he had been put or might endure. Finally, though leery of lawyers, my father decided to obtain legal assistance, hiring a lawyer on condition, whose office was situated at the county seat. The case ran for three or more years during which we did no farming, only cutting trees in the lowlands next to the river for firewood. John L was likely a better man than my father originally envisioned, the proof of it surfacing some good while after we moved to the Langstrup place, without my father receiving knowledge of it, and neither did I until it reached my hearing upon attaining to manhood. The basis of the story centered upon three men in their mid to late twenties who were acquainted with John L and with him seemed to get along on the friendliest of terms. These were persons who Rupert Monett cautiously circumvented other than employing their help in the conduct of political campaigns. The persons of subject were the three Benge brothers, who had lived on the local scene for the full length of their lives, save for brief stints in prison by two. Zach, the oldest, had spent not a lengthy portion incarcerated for a felony conviction, the substance of his wrongdoing kept guardedly under wraps by the lawyers, certainly from the ears of the general public, and if someone met him face to face for the first time he'd walk away swearing that he'd met the finest of men. But his surface appearance belied the truth. Everyone knew as much. My uncle John Eric voiced his own conception. "Looking into Zach's eyes is something like looking at slow moving swamp water; it's so peaceful on the surface, but if you stick your hand down into it you may feel the sharp fangs of a cottonmouth water moccasin." Next to Zach in age there came Josephus, as opposite as night is to day from his brother, pugnacious, loud, quarrelsome, a feisty little rascal prone to igniting and engaging in brawls with more than usual regularity. But no record existed of his serving time. Then there was Fred, the youngest, his demeanor favoring that of his brother Zach, quiet, shy, and untoward, yet coiled underneath there resided a quartering of another side, a cleverness seen in the aura of his make up, if one studied him up closely, that waxed inconsistently with our system of courts and justice. The record showed that not many years in the past he had served time for furniture theft. Badly needing the money my father hired on to take the census for the government. Without cash for fueling his old truck which he would have to drive he reluctantly sought credit from John L, who from support through his mother-in-law had started to operate the Sinclair gas station situated on the main highway on the east side of town, taking over from Ode W. Kemp, and John L, realizing that my father now held a federal job, if but temporarily, agreed without reluctance to grant him an open account for purchasing any quantity of gasoline at any time. The court case went unmentioned by either man, John L figuring that he would have acted the same as my father if their positions were reversed. Soon enough the Benge brothers conjured the scheme that should my father suddenly fail to purchase gasoline for job related travel he then would cease to have a job and that the open position would pass to one of them, politics assuring as much, they assumed. It fell upon Fred, a chum with John L during and since school days, to sit with him to go over a contrivance seen as an underhanded deployment as quickly as the first few lines emerged from Fred's mouth. John L stood up from his seat, not angry but with a face of solid objection. "I can't do that Fred. You need to squash this right now. I won't do it. It's not right. And besides, we're talking about a federal job here. Both of us could go to jail"

"But I thought—."

"Naw, naw. Everything is all right with us and Charles Maynard. My mother-in- law says it is. She says he's a good honest man. She says to let him buy on credit as long as he wants to."

The last had been seen of his fraternization with the Benge brothers. It spread about that Mrs. Langstrup upon hearing of the connivance laid the law down to her son in law that she had better not hear more of it ever again. The story passed to me by one of my uncle's whose brother attended school with John L.

The census job soon played out. But it had helped. We could have farmed that part of the acreage unencumbered by the government, yet my father felt otherwise and his attorney declined to advise him to the contrary. Not farming the acreage augured to our favor. We lived in the house, planted a garden and grew food stuff, and cut trees for firewood, all this free of charge, and during this while he hired on as a carpenter in the construction of the defense plant. The family rejoiced. At last we had money. Though not without toll. We'd watch my father leave for work before daylight, tool box strapped over his shoulder, a heavy assortment of craft wear piled inside, heavy for any man, hammers, handsaws, brace and bits, framing squares, planers, hatchets, all of which when summed together indeed amounted to a burdensome strain. Which was worse, the sweaty reek of farming on this frail man, or rising each morning to a grueling day where management relentlessly cajoled workers to increase war production? The war dictated everything. "Enough," appeared nowhere in anyone's vocabulary. It was always "more." Ten hour shifts were not uncommon, the length extending to twelve whenever necessary to stay on production schedule.

One never knows when affection will spring to the surface among the young, if we may term this behavior as affection, yet in any event I began to find myself increasingly in the company of the Stoddard's daughter Nenia. I found it uncommon, if not strange, for the family of Stoddards, to me a British name, to have a daughter they called Nenia, a name of foreign rootedness I felt sure. She told me when we were alone once that in far back generations one of her forbearers traveled to England from Russia as a young girl, also named Nenia, and married a Stoddard, a union detected by Maggie in the family genealogical records many decades subsequently who determined that they should bestow it upon their daughter at her birth. I loved it at the first sound. Nenia was younger than me by a short measure and very pretty and during our stay as the Stoddard's neighbor she grew and filled out strikingly. Very soon it became habitual that we'd walk the dirt road together that ran in front of her father's farm, electing now and then to pull off our shoes and walk barefooted. Or we'd sit in the swing on the front porch. Or she'd stand by the water well while I turned the windless and drew water, then would not hear to anything less than going with me part of the way back, as far as the fence which separated the properties. It was my choosing to always set the water buckets down and crawl across and then reach and lift them up and over.

"Let me hand the buckets to you Ramsey," she'd sometimes plead. "I can do it."

"I know you can. But you'd better let me. They're too heavy for you."

It got to where if I didn't come to her house she'd come to ours, pretending to visit my younger sister, these visits starting when once I let her carry one of the lighter buckets the entire distance from her house to ours.

She didn't work; her parents wouldn't let her, not even around the house, thinking it wasn't right for their young daughter to stoop to menial labor however light, their way of keeping her to themselves for as long as they could hang on. They'd simply enjoy her, grasping to hold on more grippingly with the realization that they now were nearing old age. They had her quite late. She was a wallflower, their baby, the last at home, her sister and two brothers leaving a good many years before. She generally stayed inside studying and listening to the radio and sharing her sister's dilettantes with her mother who cared nothing at all about her older daughter's piddling with art, but if her young daughter wished to talk about the subject she'd pretend an interest. Nenia's sister's name was Thelma who lived in Saint Louis, married to a wealthy man, a stock broker. The sisters busily stayed wound up writing letters to one another. When I neared their home Nenia became aware of it and instantly dashed out, the two of us pretty soon wandering off to ourselves. Sometimes she invited me inside, leading me into one of the rooms where the shelving bulged with magazines and books, through which we'd browse for the longest and talk about with unmitigated indulgence. Her depth of reading would have caught the eyes and admiration of the most astute of scholars which very early on caught mine and it was soon commonplace that I'd ask her about the author of a book and when she told me I'd ask her to let me carry it home where I could read it too; then we'd later go over its various aspects that had attracted my interest mostly. Young as she was she became my teacher of literature. I owe her. Clearly, she had ascended out of reach of my current repository of knowledge and abilities. "What does pathos mean?" I once asked.

"It's a feeling caused by a writer who hopes to arouse pity or compassion in the reader."

"Where did you learn that?"

"I ran across it, and then I looked it up."

In all appearances Mr. and Mrs. Stoddard relished the idea of the young boy of the family nearby being around their daughter, hoping that there might emerge in my sensibilities a crush on her. I interpreted this as their feelings for I believed I especially heard it in her mother's voice whenever she saw me reaching to knock on their door. "Nenia, Ramsey's here. See what he wants dear." The Stoddards seldom were visited by company other than Charlie and his wife Arlene and their three children, but this was limited, for Arlene plainly felt uncomfortable in the presence of her father-in-law, or so people said who knew the family. I went often in the daytime to see Nenia and at night to have supper and spend the rest of my stay with her involving whatever the two of us hatched up together. As surely as I availed myself Mrs. Stoddard invariably asked me to stay and eat with them, sure that I'd always take her up on the offer and that this would bring smiles to Nenia's face. After supper we'd go into another room with her father where there sat an old time faded radio, a zenith, of preposturous height on a high narrow credenza and listen to the war news. I would have greatly preferred listening to the station that played pretty music as would have Nenia, who with no traces of timidity said as much when we were off to ourselves, but we both sat quietly and acted as if the reports of boring dullness were all consuming to our thoughts and imagination. As time passed, we began to wade in the creek together that ran through the farm, some distance away from the house, a gurgling idyllic little stream, with Nenia sometimes attired in a pretty red dress endowed of an abundance of ruffles craftily emplaced at the shoulders and wrists. Thelma bought it for her in an upscale women's and girl's clothes store in Saint Louis. She looked wonderful in it, at this stage her developing form beginning to glaringly flaunt itself. I was amazed at her increasing maturity. When we reached a certain landmark where the rocks were flat and smooth we sat down, whereon she would pull up her dress above the knees and splash her feet in the water, her legs provokingly attractive and sensual. I somewhat pretended I didn't notice. It was this exact place that she first asked me if anyone had ever kissed me besides members of the family. I said no, and so strongly did the question surprise me that I struggled without success to produce what I deemed a better answer. She then bent toward me and kissed me full on my lips. I said nothing in response, my eyes showing uncontrollable excitement and my brain reeling with dumbfoundedness at the turn of events. She laughed a little, playfully amused, and asked me if I liked it. Catching my breath I answered that I did, very much, and then she asked if I'd like another. I still sat very close to her. I said yes, and then we kissed once more and endless times thereafter on that same afternoon. When I asked if her kiss with me had been her very first she acknowledged yes and when I exclaimed that I didn't know how in the world she could have done it so well she answered that she had learned to do it vicariously, by reading life like love stories alluringly portrayed on the pages of magazines and seeing it done by actors in picture shows to which her sister had taken her.

Chapter 7

NEXT, I must tell of Leland Gurov, who may seem as a disconnected fragnment of the whole of my story, but he most definitely was not a disconnected fragment; he became an indespensible element in my life and that has held until this day. Leland Gurov wasn't American by blood, but was by birth, emerging from parents of Bulgarian heritage. His father and uncle moved to America following World War I, arriving by boat in New York harbor, their processing—the physical exams and various minutiae,—and approval for entry taking place at Ellis Island. I met Leland in grade school. He said that they had transferred to our small town from some place in New Jersey, the whereabouts by name long extinct in my power of recall. His father decided at the onset of World War II on the transfer to fill an engineer's position at the defense arsenal, the Secretary of Defense drawing him from a stockpile of rare talents throughout the nation and from around the globe.

"My father was born in Sophia, the capitol."

"The capitol of Bulgaria?"

"Yes."

"Why did they move to America?"

He answered that their country unluckily sided with Germany in the First World War and when Germany lost, his father and his uncle left, being of mind that the victors would come down hard on people like them.

"You mean hard on the Bulgarians."

"On the Bulgarians."

As it happened both his father and uncle took positions at the plant together, their presence instigated and arranged by the United States Military who previously recognized the rare technical capability of the men as mechanical and electrical engineers. They were judged vital to the country's defense and to its far reaching multiple designs for prosecuting the war. When arriving as young men in America they had taken employment with the famous Edison Corporation, rapidly infused into the scheme of things because of their knowledge of the expanding world of theoretical electronics.

Likened to his father and his uncle, Leland evinced a highly cerebreal understanding of mechanical systems, a phenomenon, as the university elite phrased it. He was born under a special star, from parents equipped with genes spilling over with innate intelligence and consequently distributed these earthly blessings to their son. Amazing to me was his propensity to see things spatially, that is, to see on the inside of a motor with no need to open it up or scan a diagram in order to grasp it in minute configuration. He could envision with precise accuracy the moving parts inside and tell to me with unalterable exactness how and why they were connected; and bowled me over with his astounding capability at designing and rigging up to build a complex structure, a warehouse for example, or lift up a stupendously heavy assemblage in the likeness of a car or truck, no matter how large and difficult the undertaking seemed to those of ordinary intellect. Leland could do everything in the sphere of things he sought to master; his father teaching him tediously well in earlier years, but seriously, I believe that given his natural bent he would have done everything I saw him do on his own without previous schooling or guidance. The rarity of his feats astounded me from the very start. I remember that day without pause, a pleasant day, the sun shining brilliantly—though a layer of dust appeared in accumulation on the roadway because of the absence of rain—when unexpectedly Leland happened along in the most unlikely of occurrence. Sitting on a tractor coming toward me he towed, I could see, a monstrously large motor assembly behind, which he had somehow mounted onto a trailer of sorts, a rickety contraption by appearance but capable apparently of carrying a weighty load. The sight was at once comedic and stunning. "Amazing!" my thoughts were telling me, "a small boy like him in control of a massive piece of machinery fifty times his weight and size."

"What do you have there," I asked when he had drawn to a stop and killed the motor?

"A transmission."

Then I knew its identity. I hadn't a moment before. "Ha! And where are you heading with it?"

"To a friend of my father. He owns a truck that's broken down."

"And this motor part you intend to install?" I pointed my hand toward it in disbelief.

"Yes. In place of the one that's unworkable."

"I see."

"Will you join me? Within an hour I will have the job finished and then we can go into town."

"All right. I will. Where am I to ride?"

"Up here by me. I'll make room" he said, scooting over in his seat.

As we jounced along, the road burdened with undulations from side to side and frontward, he mentioned that his father had incurred detainment at the defense plant and had asked him to take care of the task on his behalf, thus relieving his friend of his troubles. With no help from me of any worth, nor from his father's friend, he, when we arrived, proceeded to affix cables and pulleys to a cross beam, then with minimum waste of time and motion lowered the assemblage over the exact fittings where it belonged, inserted the holding bolts through the rounded openings in the base and tightening the capping nuts with the aid of a pneumatic tool. I had never heard of a pneumatic tool, much less seeing one. In the character of a tutor he explained that this device cost substantially less than its electric power tool counterparts, as well as being markedly safer, and added that it operated from compressed gas or compressed carbon dioxide.

After that, even though we were merely sprouts not yet in high school, we started working seriously together on tractors and cars. I watched him with glue like focus. Without my calling it as such he early on became my teacher, my tutor, my preceptor. With unfathomable patience he led me through the steps, retracing them if feeling that he'd gone too fast and that I had missed something of crucial importance. "By far," I said silently, "he exceeds the best of teachers in my school." I did not regard myself as a very apt pupil I'm afraid, conscious that the best of my comprehension fell far short of ever matching his skills and knowledge, but nonetheless studiously observed and kept notes and in the months forthcoming became sufficiently versed in what he would have me do.

"Ramsey" he'd suddenly let out, "do not conceive of yourself as a mechanic."

"Is that not what I am?"

"No. Think of yourself as an artist. That's how I think of myself."

"Ah! All right. I think I understand." I didn't understand. Not at first. Finally I caught the meaning. The flawless smooth way that he went about his work, measured, swiftly, correctly, as if he were a machine himself, seemingly guided by an invisible laser that told him with unvarying sureness of the very next step to take, soon convinced me that "yes, all this is tantamount to seeing an artist in motion." But try as I did I failed to attain to that level of sophistication, not proficient in the manner of my friend, never, not even a faint shadow in comparison. The prospect averted me then but when I advanced into adulthood some years later I would become a serious student of literature and science, more of literature than of science, and he admired me as he learned more of my interest in these pursuits. Leland, I have thought many times without number should have been guided, if only by a trifle, and if Heaven had helped but a little, would have ascended to the post of some famous corporation as chief executive officer, most singularly over the technical spheres of operation, or to a chair of research and teaching at a university institute. Instead, even when incredibly young, he delighted in the fantasy of building his own empire and the divinity of fortune placed me by his side when he started his climb.

Chapter 8

MY FAMILY would move to the outskirts of our small town within another two years, maybe three. To say more about it there is first the importance of supplying a perspective of what that small town was like at the time, in other words, to speak of the name and function of its buildings, including the configuration of the passage ways running through it, this being the railroad and the highway and mainstreet.

It was established in the mid 1800's because of the westward movement of the railroads. By appreciable degrees as the tracks were laid in that region of the South many towns similar to ours were cropping up. As the trains began to busily run at the turn of the century townspeople fell naturally into the habit of mimicking the distant woooooo woooooo of the approaching Pan American, a passenger train, or trains, which on the beginning or soon thereafter the locals and anyone living up and down the line grew to know as the Pan American, irrespective of whichever train they were speaking of, freight or passenger. These same trains were running years later when I had reached boyhood. Each day the Pan American running westward at twelve noon and eastward at four in the afternoon stopped a half coach beyond the depot for letting off and taking on passengers.

Even by several decades previous to the war's eruption our small town had evolved as the principal watering hole for the surrounding community, to which the good rural farmers came each Saturday from their weekly grind, arriving at mid morning and quite often staying until near sundown. There existed only one street, a very wide street, spanning approximately two hundred feet and extending for a length of two blocks between the highway on the south and the railroad on the north. On both sides of the street there resided a line of narrow serried buildings where the merchants, the banker and postmaster among them, tendered their wares. Northward, toward the railroad, Erwin Smith's full glass windowed store, a grocery, combined with a women's dress shop managed by his wife Emma, occupied the first position; Felix Boykin's mercantile, mostly stocked with feed stuffs, claimed position number two; Jack Fenimore's drugstore came next, then Alex Mcvector's salvage and feed store; then lastly, Jeremy Dodson's grocery, the second grocery in town, no other store rivaling its popularity. Roughly constructed oak benches bedecked the frontage around which sat the chit-chat checker players forever jabbering at one another, giving the impression they had some clever trick up their sleeve. Small gatherings of town's people, farmers more than not, stood around and watched and nodded and laughed and made non monetary bets as to a winner. The railroad ran a mere stone's throw away, thus spectators, including the checker players who temporarily ceased their foolery, were an attentive witness to the arrival and departure of passengers. It was something of a ritual.

On the street's opposite side sat the bank which opened its doors Monday through Friday at nine in the morning hour and remained open until five in the afternoon, repeating a briefer schedule on Saturday which commenced at ten o'clock and terminated when the merchantilers started to close their doors. Sam Gatby owned a hardware store which abutted the bank. Once there stood a building behind Gatby's that burned without replacement and still another which met the same fate. Doode's café stood alone immediately to the south of the highway. Billy Yonker's Shell Oil filling station faced Doode's diagonally from across the way, virtually on the highway shoulder, proudly flaunting its pumpkin yellow gas pumps. A bit further up Ode W. Kemp owned and operated a similar business. Affixed to the façade, high up where the roof line met the frontage, eleven letters of exaggerated height stood out amplifying the supremacy of Sinclair Oil. And as if this were not enough the image of a dinosaur, of immense form and power, appeared adjacent to the lettering that sought to add an extra marketing incentive to the subliminal senses of the public. The three churches of the community, the Methodist, the Baptist, and the Cumberland Presbyterian, were arranged in alignment nearby, together occupying approximately five acres of land. Huge oaks with jagged tentacles dotted the church yards. The Methodist congregation openly took pride in owning the only church bell in town, of which they required thirty minutes of tolling before service each Sunday morning. Wallace Bethune's cotton gin, built on higher ground, peered bemusedly down at mainstreet from the north, and released a persistent drone day and night for as long as cotton picking went on. One other structure, the depot, perched alongside the railroad tracks, distanced itself one half block from the cotton gin and played a dual role of providing shelter for the Pan American travelers while filling a useful cause as an assembly line for tomato packing during the peak of summer. This roughly finished edifice which consisted of an office, a sprawling wooden platform, and a silvery metal roof the people argued was the oldest landmark known to the longest remembering citizens.

This was our small town then, a simple Mecca where people regularly gathered and sold and bought and talked and shared—the substances of life's flow, a style they had known for decades and known in like manner by those that came before them. But the culture was drastically changing as the full effect of the war roared upon us.

Rupert Monett, more officially Rupert Mcylroy Monett, came to shut down the bank after the stock crash of 1929, explained Walton Burnside, a long time learned resident of the county to whom people referred as a personage known to keep abreast of happenings of a current and historical perspective and by and large accepted his commentary as fact. As it turned out he vouched incorrectly. Records spoke convincingly from some quarters that Rupert hired in as cashier of the bank a few years prior to 1929, the position accruing to him because of his marriage to Madeline Murphy, the daughter of Douglas Murphy, a businessman of the community of good if not admirable reputation. Douglas Murphy's two story home surrounded by towering lordly whiteoaks flaunted itself in striking profile on several acres of pristine land. A handsome driveway of Southern architectural charm extended beyond the portico which terminated at the side entrance. To have residence on this street translated into a position of elevated social status.

As the depression leapt across the nation collapsing one bank after another, the board of our small town bank felt persuaded to consummate a change in management. It loomed wise or opportune to Douglas Murphy, a controlling shareholder in the enterprise, to recommend as a replacement his son-in-law Rupert Monett, whom the board unanimously endorsed. Good news seemed ever scarce and bad news always plentiful in those times, the result precipitating frequent conferences between bankers and delinquent property owners. Rupert stayed busy cajoling these unfortunates to remit payment, due in full on the mortgage, reminding the debtor, sometimes subtly, sometimes with more direct frankness, that the bank held possession of the note. Since Rupert occupied the bank's highest office it fell his lot to call in the property owners, thereby giving notice that foreclosure was hardly avoidable and that in the future near at hand the bank would of necessity take custody of the property which had sunk into a serious state of indebtedness. While the phrase foreclosure overspread the county as if a specter, the people were surprisingly tolerant of Rupert's actions, except for one critical aspect of his dealings. The talk about town had it that in many instances a greater opportunity could have been granted a debtor to raise the necessary collateral for satisfying the demand, but that instead he chose the bank's advantage, and therefore his own. "Too late," he would say in a voice of feigned regret and sorrow, "the bank has extended grace as far as it can. The board cannot bend further." He believed that the people received his explanation as reasonable and as the final word. Time after time he repeated the same demand and the same explanation but was seriously unaware however that gossip now ran rampant of his taking part in an act of tarnished contrivance, rumors circulating that the banker willfully conspired with a certain wealthy individual to acquire the note and property soon after foreclosure. The accusation surfaced so often and so convincingly that his father-in-law sought to confront him about the charge which by now posed more than a wincing bother. The behavior of the young man who'd married his daughter was on the brink of causing himself and his father-in-law serious trouble. After a time, however, unsure and unconvinced of whether his son-in-law had engineered a questionable caprice, Douglas Murphy brushed the matter aside and said no more; and no more was said by the local citizenry, for they were without foundation and knew it and knew that to step forward with legal claims of wrongdoing was with certainty to prove futile. After a verbal thrashing by his father-in-law Rupert severed the umbilical cord with his shadowy investor but with great firmness of purpose and cunning continued his forward thrust to power.

Chapter 9

BY GRADUAL steps, but surely, Rupert's prominence and influence grew. He satisfactorily guided the bank to sound footing, contributed appreciably to the governor's campaign through the use of the bank's contingency fund, took the lead in the building of a new church, became the church's head deacon, headed the county tax advisory council, and at the insistence of his closest friends and associates agreed to sit as chairman of the board which directed the local system of schools.

Monett's daughters were the pride and joy of his heart. Literally he doted over them. What he and Madeline would do for them knew few limits. When once his oldest daughter, Melissa, was playing a tennis match a judge's scoring call went against her, with both parents storming forward and arguing with such cogent force that the official announced a reversal. The family owned and occupied the largest, most imposing home in town. When they were young Rupert drove his two daughters to and from school in a shiny black Chrysler, he sitting proudly at the wheel with the girls in the back seat curiously stretching their necks looking about, the scene of which an artist would have used for painting a tableau; and never did Madeline fail to dress the girls in clothes of the latest fashion bought or tailored only in the prestigious Jewish fashion stores of Memphis. They were nicely bosomed, energetic, well proportioned youngsters and wore dresses and slacks designed to make them look their ultimate best. The bulk of young girls their age wore either hand me downs or else patterned and sewn at home. The Monett girls were talkative, cheerful, outgoing, and aggressive and excelled in more than one athletic sport. Rupert and Madeline basked in their daughters' trophies ostentatiously over populating the mantle in their sumptuous living room and could not restrain themselves from alluding to these symbols of accomplishments of their beloved offspring.

"Melissa earned that trophy by winning the state tennis tournament," she would gloat. "We're so proud of her," and would not overlook Melinda by weaving in some similar compliment on her behalf. It was the impression of school peers that Melissa and Melinda sensed their opulence and delighted in flaunting it; or perhaps their demeanor got wrongly internalized by those of envy. But in any event in that day to have and wear attire that few others possessed set one apart whether or not intended. Whichever it was fellow students whispered in a vein of resentment as well as fun making about the vanity of the banker's daughters.

Before either of them had graduated from college Monett saw to it that the principal appointed each of them to a teaching position at the local school, only part time positions, but Melissa eventually finished college and became a full time member of the teaching staff. Melinda, though completing her college studies somewhat later, thereby receiving her certificate to teach, forewent teaching in favor of moving into the cashier's position at the bank and helping with a miscellany of other family enterprises.

If the bank augured as Monett's power base, his preponderant, if not ostentatious white home sweeping back from the highway served as his social showcase, to which he on frequent occasions invited his chosen guests, visitors of dignitary status, who drove shiny new cars into his exquisite driveway of pebble grain gravel and remained late into the night, sometimes staying over.

Long removed now, I recall from childhood an old home which stood on the corner next to the Monett's, decaying and falling apart which he bought and ordered demolished. It was once owned by a wealthy family of high breeding. Monett bought the home to rid himself of an eye sore the people said, but his more determined objective aimed largely at increasing his own acreage, which, through this purchase, expanded to twice its former size, the whole of his intent from the beginning, apparently, to have his residence appear in the attitude of an estate.

Walking to school with my brother and sisters each day we passed by the Monett home, a two story rectangular edifice with narrow elongated windows, meticulously trimmed shrubbery of multiple species, a pebble grain driveway, double French doors looking out from the frontage, and an elaborately styled tennis court situated on the rear portion of the yard. Two sporty bicycles generally were parked on the walkway that eventuated to a terminus near the double French doors, obviously expensive possessions, the fenders and handle bars glistening in the sun. None of us had to guess that they belonged to Melissa and Melinda Monett. Even at my young age I thought then how unfairly the joys of life are distributed. There is a connecting irony to the Monett home and another which we also passed while on our way, the other an older structure residing on the highest elevation in town featuring a portico that wrapped the full circumference around it. In its glory days, they said, no architectural design rivaled it anywhere, excepting the plantation mansions found further west and south. A mere half block removed from the Monett's, this old home had brought unrelenting distress to Monett and his wife because of its presence, an eye sore they said, and they would have bought it and ordered it torn down and hauled away but were without power to achieve their purpose.

Sometimes as we passed by this aging ornament, the time of day in the afternoon for the most part when school had turned out, we would see the strangest visitation taking place on the portico, two persons sitting convivially chatting in their rocking chairs, an elderly white lady and a Negro man of bronze color. Each time I wondered, at last asking my oldest sister, why a Negro man and white lady were sitting together.

"Oh Ramsey. That's Miss Estonia and Elizar. They're brother and sister."

It was not clear in my young limited cerebreal process how this resulted, nor was it encompassed in my thoughts to question why the people of our town were so accepting of this blending of white and Negro culture, which occurred under their very noses. I was too young and devoid of the knowledge that pertained to their genealogy and the institution of Negro slavery to have questioned it. But no one questioned it. Everyone went about as usual talking of Negroes as good folks, with little exception, internalizing deep down if the truth were admitted that Negroes ought to stay in their places. Yet such a thought was not said aloud, even to one another, with respect to Miss Estonia, nor did they say it aloud of Elizar either, her half brother who often sat with her on the frontage area of her portico. Discussions of their racial origin were scrupulously avoided, the mystery of it traceable to their father J. H. Ascension Lebranche, who upon buying massive quadrants of land in the mid-eighteen hundreds in this vicinity settled there himself, moving from the State of Mississippi. Generous in his heart and with stupendous wealth in his possession, land and money, he gave sizeable properties away to settlers aspiring to build houses and stores that would plenish a small town, and land too for building churches on the south side, and more land still for the laying of the main highway, or later laid. Not given away, but sold at an abysmally low price, land passed from his ownership to the railroad companies who had sketched blueprints ten years before for developing a line of railroad footage. They, the people, said for awhile, before they all died off of old age, that J. H. Ascension Lebranche knew of the coming of the railroad long before the tracks were laid there and as a consequence positioned himself for capitalizing on the economic progression by buying up vast acreages and selling these lands through political affiliations and deals with the railroad lawyers. Whether this happened or not the memory of the man lingered affectionately. With whispers flowing from one generation to the next, though losing accuracy with each transference, the essence of the theme remained the same. Mr. Lebranche generously bestowed favors and money on the people of his community.

I only vaguely understood who Miss Estonia and Elizar actually were, in time hearing the gossip of their origin over and over, the story deriving from word of mouth that Mr. Lebranche on his relocation from Mississippi brought with him a white wife and a Negro concubine, infusing both in moments of passion with seeds that sired a white baby girl and an off spring male of skin pigmentation a shade or two darker than that of his half sister. As I grew older I digested with fascinated ears that the wife of Mr. Lebranche held up unbelievably well to her unseemly shared marriage. The house with the portico that stood for so long is not any more there, succumbing to the blade long decades ago. Its demolishment resulted shortly after Miss Estonia died of old age and senility, not knowing at all times who or where she was. The whole town turned out for the funeral, the old and middle aged folks out of respect, the young because of curiosity. The minister in his farewell message said that she had been a tradition, now a fallen monument, and that the town owed her much, but did not mention, nor should he have even if he knew, that the town council over the past decades waived her property taxes in recognition of the charitable deeds of her father who had contributed uncountably to the town's establishment.

Chapter 10

OCCUPIED AT learning as many things as I could ingest of the mechanics of tractors I had recently slackened my visits to the Stoddards, with the exception of Nenia who I saw almost daily by joining her briefly where she waited in the morning hour to catch her bus for school. After this I'd leave for school myself and after school I would join Leland. My schedule kept me busy to the brim. Yet once I rode the yellow bus with Nenia to a much larger town than ours and stayed the day with her, joining her between classes. Her parents for some reason saw fit for her to attend this school rather than the one in which I pursued a basic education. For one thing, hers was a comprehensive facility, the offerings appreciably more diversified and richer. When the school day ended we chose not to catch the bus, deciding beforehand to stay for a picture show, likely a war movie, after which her brother Charlie picked us up in his yellow and red truck and took us home.

Again, I got around to taking supper with the Stoddards, Nenia prodding me that I should. As usual Mr. and Mrs. Stoddard acted glad to see me. On the outset Mr. Stoddard addressed my absence. "Ramsey, you've not sat with us in a while. Why is that?"

"I'm learning as much as I can learn about the mechanics of tractors sir, motors and how they are assembled and disassembled and such; I'm learning from Leland Gurov, whose father taught him."

"Oh yes, I hear that. His father is a famous man of science."

"Of electricity sir. I'm told." Suddenly it struck me that my clarification might have seemed offensive and unwisely spoken. Then it seemed not. He went on with no show of perturbness.

"Ah yes. You are correct. It's electricity. But he's knowledgeable in other things too."

"Yes sir. Of mechanical things. The things he's taught Leland."

"I'm sure. Well, let me see. You're getting into how tractors work, are you?"

"As much as I can."

"Hmmmmm. I own five tractors as you likely know. Three are down. Won't run a lick. Do you suppose your friend Leland might inspect one or two and get them in shape?"

"I'll see."

"I'll pay him something."

"Yes sir."

That worried me. I'd always felt that for the work I'd done for him his pay was too far on the chincey side and knew that Leland's father might well entertain a sensitivity to his son receiving sufficient money for his efforts. Nonetheless, the next day I talked to Leland in regard to Mr. Stoddard's need for help, stressing also that I had no idea of what he considered a fair wage in dollars and cents for the work performed.

"Don't worry Amigo. J. R. will handle that."

"Amigo! He called me Amigo," I said to myself and then openly burst into hilarity, a giggle, actually, but I knew why he had done it, the reason predicated from a movie we'd gone to see in Meadville of a few days past, catching the Pan American. It was no ordinary movie; it was a western movie featuring Texas cowboys and Mexican cattle drovers or workers where the pseudo title Amigo got frequently tossed around as decreed by the writer of the movie script. I thought it the funniest thing that a young man of far away Bulgarian decent was so fascinated with movies of the western flavor. But he was and we went on every chance to see one. He hadn't to my knowledge called me Amigo at any time before and seldom did thereafter but every once in awhile did. And that was in every respect a good thing. It meant friend or boon companion as I discovered when later looking it up in Webster's.

"Who's J. R. You haven't brought up his name before now."

"He married my father's sister, a lengthy while before they moved over from the old country."

"From Bulgaria?"

"Yes."

"Oh. What is his profession?"

"He's a lawyer."

"Well, okay, what am I to tell Mr. Stoddard?"

"That J. R. Carney will work things out with him."

I had supper with the Stoddards the next evening, expecting to find an opening in the conversation afterwards when alone with him for an instant to tell him that Mr. J. R. Carney represented the Gurov family in business agreements and favored sitting with him shortly. My opportunity would have to wait. Immediately after the meal Mr. Stoddard left for the adjoining room where the radio sat and turned it on. I went with him. And Nenia too. The voice of H. V. Kaltenborn, a newsman daily reporting on the war in Europe who seemed to delight in broadcasting the darker side of things, began, "My friends. There's bad news tonight. The Allies have suffered a grave and disturbing setback."

"Terrible, terrible," Mr. Stoddard's voice agonized a painful moan. "Hitler's going to come after us for sure."

Night after night Kaltenborn's broadcasts resounded with the same tone of news and night after night Mr. Stoddard heard it and uttered the same cry that Hitler soon would come and take us over. On recalling this scene in later years, when I was somewhat well read in the scriptures, it dawned on me with playful banter that he was a facsimile to the old prophet Jeremiah who held a gloomy pessimistic view of the present and foresaw the future as calamitous. When Mr. Kaltenborn finished and Mr. Stoddard had sunk into some degree of calm I found the courage to let him know that Leland agreed to take a look at his tractors but that Mr. J. R. Carney would talk to him of the terms of pay, that Leland preferred to leave business discussions up to a third party. He seemed in no way bothered and spoke that he looked forward to meeting with Mr. Carney.

Spring descended upon us, the plow blades soon lowered into the soil, cutting it to pieces in preparation of the first planting. Mr. Stoddard emphasized with a continuous lament that he needed all five of his tractors in action without delay. One might take it that this being the case he would have hired a mechanic a while previously to diagnose and fix the machines, but this breed of mechanic in the community by and large usually lacked the proper skill, and would have proceeded with marked slowness at completing his task. Considering that three tractors needed repair within days the only solution resided with Leland Gurov. Word of his abilities had spread. Quick and thorough they said of him and heralded that when he finished repairing a mechanical it stayed repaired. That lay at the base of why farmers literally swarmed his domain of business, bringing not only their tractors but a miscellany of machinery necessitating his skills.

Owing to the way I heard that negotiations were finalized I wished that I were privy to the exchanges between Mr. Stoddard and Mr. Carney. Mr. Carney relayed on the outset, in no manner subtle with his diplomacy, that he understood three tractors were in need of repair and that they were not in the best of condition, since they had stood idle for a while, and that the work on them would involve a lengthy tally of man hours. He ended these reductions by suggesting that Mr. Stoddard give the tractor of least value to Leland for his service, which amounted to more than a bargain to the giver, and additionally throw in two acres for Leland to lease free of charge.

"What is he to do with the land?" asked Mr. Stoddard.

"Grow cotton," answered Mr. Carney.

"Cotton! For how long?"

"Whoa! Hold your horses. The land isn't of much consequence to you, a pitiably small amount, and just think of it for a minute. The four tractors you'll have left over won't go forever without breaking down. That's the nature of a machine. Let the land use extend indefinitely, and thereby you'll have Leland around to care for them."

"I see," said Mr. Stoddard, scratching his head.

"But of course, you'll have to pay him."

"Expected, expected."

We hauled the three tractors into the old barn where we did our work and rather quickly readied them for service; from which Leland benefited by owning the one that Mr. Stoddard turned over to him, a Farmall, which as the spring began to edge through, we put to use in the preparation of the two acres of ground for planting cotton. Leland would hear of nothing less than sharing with me one half the profits and overcoming my resistance that he treated himself unfairly by doing so he gave me a half interest in the tractor. We then hired it out to Mr. Stoddard, with one or the other of us driving it for pay by the hour. That he gave in with unsuspected ease to Mr. Carney's proposal struck us with a tinge of curiosity if not with amazement, and yet, as we thought it through concluded that Mr. Stoddard viewed the transaction out of lenses completely different from our own. The tractor that he gave to Leland promised to yield nothing of value in its former condition. He could have gone for years without using it and the two acres that he let Leland have rent free were no more meaningful to him than a speck of sand to a chieftain in Saudi Arabia. Everyone therefore ended up in the happiest of spirits and I could go on accepting supper invitations with the Stoddards without feeling sheepish or embarrassed over what transpired in the negotiations.

Chapter 11

WHEN THE fury in Europe and the South Pacific gained added intensity there arose a corresponding reaction on the home front, the sprawling munitions arsenal situated a minimal distance away, a few miles, starting to buzz with human workers, machines, trucks, carrier trains, war materials and assembly lines that groaned and squeaked twenty fours hours around the clock. The stepped-up activity infused itself into our daily lives. At intervals, with narrow spacing in between, shells lifted at random from the assembly lines were taken to the testing grounds and ignited, the result immense, echoing a thunderous boom that swept across the terrain for a five mile stretch, and in the climax sending an unmistakable tremble throughout the not so strongly built narrow brick stores on mainstreet.

Defense workers swarmed upon us in smothering numbers, seeking room and board, or a house or apartment for rent, or at least a place to park a diminutive silvery trailer designed for two but accommodating a whole family of six. With the arrival of each family the local school officials were pressed to the limit to see that accommodations were provided. School rooms were overcrowded as much as the town itself; and it became consistent practice for teachers to conduct class under a great umbrella tree somewhere on the school grounds to seek momentary relief. Cheap wooden two story hotels were hastily constructed, dinky cafes shot up here and there, each with a jukebox stationed conspicuously against a side or back wall, cars choked the highways to and from the defense arsenal and merchants opened their doors early and closed late. Rupert Monett basked ecstatically. With the ground swell of the sudden population, his little bank of a several lettered name with the word "Trust" emplaced upon the frontage was now the recipient of new depositors in increasing numbers walking through its doors.

Trains crisscrossed the nation packed with young soldiers soon thrown into the war. Those scheduled to pass through our small town seldom missed stopping, taking on additional soldiers from our town and adjacent rural communities. You could see at these stoppages a gathering of ladies exerting their best to demonstrate loyalty and support to the cause by showering the soldiers with a plethora of gifts and hugs and thanks of appreciation and liberally shedding tears, all this led by a chosen beautiful local girl, Rachael Ellsworth, who was egged on by her elders that she must do it as a service to the young men of the military who would love her. Young soldiers playfully called out, as the train pulled away, that they wanted to marry her when they got back. "Goodbye Rachael," they let out by poking their heads through the windows, practically saying it at once, "I love you," and waved with jovial spirit and hilarity, yet mixed with a tinge of melancholy, and she with great energy and animation waved in return and tried to yell above the noise and furor that she loved them too.

A reporter from the Saint Louis newspaper showed up one day to gather view points as to the burden of the war on our citizenry. Contrary to what we thought he might do, he elected to interview people on the street, not anyone in particular, and we were glad, we the common folks, that he passed over those who we in our eyes saw as the socially lofty. We had no idea of the questions he might pose before us. They were fore intended as questions of uncustomary limitations we discovered. He seemed intent on doing only an abbreviated survey. A sampling. "What are your thoughts on the matter of rationing gasoline and sugar and automobile tires," he asked, and we answered that as long as the process of distribution took place fairly we'd not complain, and after this, he asked the women folks how they were coping with their husbands working the graveyard shift, most answering that they were used to it and that moreover they worked at the arsenal themselves and that half the time or more they were assigned the graveyard shift too.

"What else can one say of that small town," he wrote in the days following, "all at once transformed, exciting, vigorously alive, and bloated with humanity in no way imaginable in anyone's dreams a scant few years before. And there is money in the possession of a rural people who for a decade have been overmastered by the great depression, by a mere expectation of eking out a living and nothing more unless a part of the gate keeping circle. To have jobs and pocket change is a luxury embraced with unrequited relief and joy, with no pause to consider that the fruits of good fortune have fallen, or are falling, due to a great war certain to claim millions of lives, some being their own local sons."

Rupert Monett seemed to everyone an immovable fixture in the small town, tending to the bank and staying on top of politics; and no one could have remotely suspected what he had going on in his cunning busy mind. For a reason that baffled us all he seemed on the spur of the moment to have decided to join the United States Military and in the weeks passed originated a contrivance for getting it done. Some said they had knowledge of how he worked his plan and spread it from ear to ear, though particles of the story we took as embellishment.

There emerged a certain election where a certain politician, who, running on the one side, bore kindredness to the governor and Rupert saw it opportune to back the governor's relative.

"If the governor's candidate wins," Rupert had relayed to a confidant, "I'll receive an appointment to the U. S. Military with a rank of major. It's been promised."

His confidant spoke in disbelief. "Heavens to Betsy. You're kidding Mac."

"No kidding. It'll happen."

"But why? Why do you want to do this?"

"To serve in the armed services will put me into a very favorable light in the eyes of the people. It's the image. Serving, loyalty, patriotism. That sort of thing. Why, I might even run for governor myself one day. And the salary paid by the military is darn well incredibly good, let alone a handsome prepaid living expense"

"You'd leave the bank Mac!"

"Naw. Not exactly. I'd run it from Florida, the site of my stationing. I've got it all fixed in my head. I'll get back in town once a month to see that everything is going well. I'll set Alex Mcvector up as the officer in charge. It's true. He's done nothing more than operate a seed store and doodle with that scrap iron yard on the edge of town, but he does keep up with money pretty well. And he's loyal, stone hard loyal. He'll bend over backwards to do what he's told, and if he can't figure out what to do he won't do anything. In other words, he's unlikely to make a mistake."

"But you're forty-five years old. Will the U. S. Army take someone like you?"

"You don't get it. It's a figurehead appointment. I don't do a thing but show up for luncheons and stay in the military office that I'm assigned to. This whole thing is at the behest of the governor. And the governor's tight with Cordell Hull and Roosevelt."

Something else got spread around too, which was of doubtful substance, a bit made up, far fetched for certain somebody said, yet that is why the people were drawn to it. That night, after his candidate won the election, Rupert lay talking to Madeline in the gargantuan Victorian bed bequeathed to her by her grandmother, complete with Grecian headboard scrolls, delighting with smug satisfaction that his appointment as a major in the United States Military now approached a state of certainty and much enjoyment of living awaited them on the sandy beaches of the peninsula of Florida. Of these tales I cannot vouch personally, for hearsay is invariably skewed by the time it reaches the last ear into which it flows; yet there were portions to which I can attest. Rupert received his appointment and did go to Florida; and came home once monthly wearing a McArthur military cap and a tannish military coat that dropped below his knees. As he walked up mainstreet toward his bank—his posture regimentally erect, his strides long and confident and soldierly exaggerated—the folks stood and gawked and carried on in carefully shielded playful mockery.

"Looka there. If I didn't know better I'd swear I'm seeing the great general himself," the great general being General Douglass McArthur whom Rupert tended to copy and emulate.

Chapter 12

MELISSA MARRIED a local boy when the war was nearing an end, a nice chap that everyone liked. He seemed more like us common folks, the reason we all liked him. And it could have been attributed in some way to the fact that his father earned his livelihood as a car salesman who raked and scraped to make ends meet. In other words, Melissa's husband bore commonness to us. To her, commonness seemed not to matter. She claimed him nonetheless. As did scores of others he answered to the call of duty, going into the Army branch of service, no one knowing where he took boot camp training, but learning as time stole by that he ended up in Florida, either a slight before his father-in-law landed there or a slight later. Melissa talked incessantly to friends around town of her new husband who she said she'd recently seen and that he looked as healthy as a ripening peach because he'd spent a great deal of time in the Florida sunshine. Suddenly she quit her teaching position and joined him. To my reckoning he appeared a shade plain, considerably lacking in cultural finesse, and I found it a curious thing that a woman of her attractiveness and aloofness married him. Should I have been older and eruditely finished at the time it would have occurred to me that she had entered into a morganatic marriage, in the context of royalty a morganatic marriage meaning a marriage between two people of unequal social rank. It is sometimes referred to as a left handed marriage.

The next year Melinda married too, to Billy Mcvector, son of Alex Mcvector. Billy managed somehow to avoid the draft, a report surfacing that his excessive weight made him an undesirable candidate whereas another had it that he suffered from an ulcerated stomach, this latter account questioned more than accepted. A chubby one, which people somehow liked, as well as good natured, he easily meshed with the people which resulted in his favor. He had acquired a rudimentary knowledge of electricity and knowing this and liking him too they were easily inclined to ask Billy to come fix a light switch or electrical receptacle that ceased functioning. Repairing bicycles also fell into his repertoire of aptitudes and he began to take over his father's scrap iron yard, well on his way to adopting this and other multiple enterprises as his full time profession until hearing of the luring wage rates paid at the defense plant.

"I've just hired on at the defense plant," he said one day in elated jubilant tones as he gathered Melinda up and swung her round.

"That's wonderful Mac. You need a job like that. I'm so glad."

Melinda had called him Mac from school days onward, the name embedded in her soul. I supposed she adopted it from his family name. Most everyone in town called him Mac as well once they got to know him. It just seemed natural to them they said. But I preferred Billy and that is the name by which in almost all instances I addressed him. He landed a job at the defense plant perfectly fitting to his aptitude, that of checking tools in and out to the workers, something he could do well with his hands. The insinuation is not here intended to say that his intelligence subordinated him to a lower calling but rather to simply mention that he much better fitted hands on tasks than writing or teaching or exacting debit and credit calisthenics in the bank. As did hundreds of others he joined a car pool, an arrangement of five to the car, including himself, where the occupants rotated at driving.

While one would not ever have concluded it by a mere superficial glance, underneath Billy's façade there lurked a clever and shrewd quality at play on which he began to capitalize soon after his hiring. It began with the car pool. One of the members regretted to the others that he needed to drop out in favor of driving alone, citing that there were extenuating circumstances at home and that this misfortune now extended beyond his reach to ordinarily resolve. They all said they understood. But Billy, after a few days expired, approached him with a report that he too faced obligations at home and would he mind if he joined him in the formation of a two man car pool.

"Two are much less trouble than five. Somebody is always late when you have large numbers"

Years passed before his friend, his fellow car pooler, uncloaked to me what happened next, and the event dated so long in the past that he required no secretive pledge from me to remain forever silent. He reckoned apparently that two many years were now gone for an episode of the past to rise up and haunt him.

"Billy liked to hunt you know," my friend said, "and wore a deer hunting coat to work so long in length and so wide in breadth that it nearly swallowed him up despite his hefty mid riff. It literally shook and flopped. In the summer he wore a lesser size but not by much. It ran through me constantly why he wore such unusual clothing, especially in off season. Finally, I caught on, this happening quite by an accident one night when we were leaving the graveyard shift, twelve midnight you know. As he attempted to crawl in the car an electric drill fell from an inside enlarged pocket liner of his coat. It landed right there on the gravel. He grabbed it up in a split second. Badly embarrassed, but hoping, I am inclined to believe, that I'd think it belonged to him personally. I thought about the incident for a while, saying nothing, then it registered with me that somebody could have seen him scrambling to pick up the tool, maybe authorities, and figured that I was in cahoots with him. 'Billy,' I said, 'you're going to get caught one of these nights. You'd better quit it while you can.' I don't know whether he quit stealing or not. If he kept at it I heard no tales of his being caught and otherwise I would have heard that the authorities nailed him. Pretty soon my superiors moved me to another shift and that stopped our riding together. I don't think I alone knew of his stealing escapade because in not a lengthy stretch it had spread around town. When the war ended he bought Sam Gatby's hardware store, people kinda laughing low like and whispering that he'd stolen enough from the federal government to give him a sizeable head start. I think that helped, but I also think his father-in-law-Rupert Monett at the urging of Melinda set him up with the necessary cash."

That was the end of my friend's story. I was amazed at the knowledge he had carried in the secrecy of his bosom about Billy.

With the war over troops began to return to American soil, and suddenly the aura of things shifted back to its old self, the vibrancy of our small town all at once quiet and boring, the dinky cafes going out of business with lightning speed, the shanties in which they were housed left as an empty lifeless hull, and the two storied boarding houses with vacancy signs futilely posted in the front yards looking lost and forlorn. In this quietude there arose an irony that greatly troubled the people, who on the one hand rejoiced over the terrible world wide conflict shortly ended, yet on the other worried simultaneously that money and jobs were now on a course of extinction, or at best were in for a drastic lessening. A serious period of readjustment awaited, everyone acutely aware of it happening. My father lamented with continued downcast mood at the prospect of receiving his termination notice and therefore his last paycheck. Shortly before the war ended we had moved from the Langstrup farm to another farm near town owned by Jeremy Dodson, the grocery man. As I secretly and elatedly kept to myself my father sold his livestock, his plough mules and equipment thrown in as part of the transaction, which he began to regret the moment it happened, for now it gnawed at his insides that should he not find future work what would he do for earning a living unless going back to the farm. I did not tell him that in my opinion he acted most wisely in selling off. Keeping the animals as long as he did forged a costly drain from the paychecks he drew while carpentering at the defense plant.

The lawsuit filed against Mrs. Langstrup finally came to a settlement out of court with a payment accruing to the plaintiff in the amount of three hundred dollars, a shameful sum declared J. R. Carney who, since being a lawyer himself, gained access to the court records validating that the Lassiter Law Firm, knowing they could get away with such chicanery, kept fifteen hundred dollars out of a total figure of eighteen for their services. Jeremy Dodson heard that I maintained closeness to Leland Gurov, that I through affiliation with Leland had learned a great deal in the matter of tractor repairs under his tutelage, and that in all likelihood I'd have one to my availability for tilling his farmland. He assumed correctly; it unfolded as he envisioned. No longer did my father possess the health for enabling him to endure the grind of tilling and harvesting a farm, and Jeremy sympathetically knew of his condition, thus I became the one on whom he would depend, and this was all right with him because aside from my access to a tractor he saw in me a young strong boy who not only could do much physically but also possessed the knowledge necessary for growing cotton and corn. Leland helped me, with our using not one tractor but two that we beforehand bargained for as clunkers and converted into sound functioning mechanicals. Jeremy Dodson was assessed a fee for our use of the tractors, mainly because we tilled and harvested an increase in acreage that he year after year had let lie fallow, unable to entice anyone to put it to use. At Mr. Clary's suggestion we bargained with the man that we would grow cotton on this extra piece of land provided that full proceeds from one half of this acreage passed wholly to us, and that three fourths of the proceeds from the remaining land portion would pass to us as well. He accepted. "I suppose I'll do it boys. Realizing a few cents is better than nothing at all." He later with an approving smile on his face relayed to Mr. Carney that he was well pleased with the deal he had made with Leland and I.

Within months we bargained for some several clunker tractors and related heavy machinery, even heavy duty trucks and road graders and even hay balers and would in due course amass a sizeable grouping of these implements additionally.

While we were living at the Dodson place my father, who over this interval compiled a small savings from his work at the defense plant, acquired a few acres of ground near the railroad in town on the north side on which he decided to build a house. He gave but a pittance for the land. Of bargain basement value, land around town was easily acquired. I persuaded him that I should donate a part of my savings into the undertaking, feeling that this might alleviate his worries over running out of cash before the project's completion. He objected, but then realized that I meant from the bottom of my heart what I proposed and that accepting it was likely his best and only opportunity to see at last his dream come true. Resisting until the last minute, until he realized that his financial resources were ebbing away, as well as the amount I contributed, he approached the bank for a small loan which Rupert granted, with the provision that the bank attach the house as collateral against the debt. My father signed the note, the amount of the loan and the details of the collateral encumbrance appearing in bold italics in the beginning language. If not then, he would later regret the obligation into which he earlier maneuvered himself. A political campaign started up not many months thereafter, during which the opponent to Monett's man embarked on a strategy of passing back and forth through the area, the political district, naturally hoping to pick up a moderate count of rural votes, stopping by chance one day at our house where he and my father sat talking in the front porch swing. Someone passing by saw them and squealed to Monett, or some other person tied to his grapevine might have gladly carried the news of what appeared to them as a political conclave. Rupert kept a brigade of loyal racketys under his thumb. We never really determined the whistle blower source. On learning of the parley Monett promptly sent Alex Mcvector to pay call on my father, thereby cautioning him with a more than ordinary countenance of seriousness that Rupert was ruffled over the news coming to his hearing. Alex made no mention of the loan from the bank, likely advised to avoid the subject, but this he did not need to mention, the threat correctly interpreted and understood without further penetration. I recall my father relaying to my mother at supper that he was bowled over by the visit.

"This is the funniest, farfetched thing I ever heard. A clod hopper like me a threat to Rupert's empire."

"What did you tell Mr. Mcvector?"

"That the politician showed up out of the blue, that I merely listened to him as a courtesy. I told him that I had no intention of talking to the man again."

Leland and I promised faithfully to help my father when the house building work got underway, and delivered, performing the heavy chores ourselves, the lifting of beams and the raising of the trusses and setting in the support columns, and with Leland in the lead we wired the house for electricity and did the plumbing and trimming and painting. The savings were enormous. My mother practically walked on air. It seemed unbelievable that at last we were with electricity. It was the same to all of us who remained at home. My oldest sister married some time before and my only brother had married too following his military discharge.

Chapter 13

RUPERT MONETT returned from the military as well, people expecting him to relieve Alex Mcvector from his bank post, which did not directly materialize. Through his connections with the governor Rupert for a while occupied an office in the state capitol with the Federal Housing Agency which carried with it a handsome salary. He still came home frequently, doubly more often than during his tenure in Florida. Besides seeing in on Alex Mcvector it also helped him keep a tighter reign on local politics. Someone in the county or the region continually sought public office and Rupert with the assistance of his political associates hovered close by to ascertain that they were seated. We wondered of his next move when he returned from Florida, very quickly learning, starting with the fact that a vacancy opened up in the system of schools, the officials suddenly letting a teacher go without cause. Whereon, Monett's daughter Melissa stood ready and willing to fill the position and very soon the principal announced her addition to the faculty roster. "A mere reinstatement," the school board explained. Then we noticed too that his son-in-law, Melissa's husband, suddenly landed the job of rural mail carrier, and a short time thereafter the townsfolks learned of his promotion to the postmaster's seat of office. As a further enrichment he sat at odd intervals behind the glass enclosure of the bank interior where at his desk the plaque read "Cashier." Old enough by then I awakened to the realization that politics were exactingly real in our small town and were a dynamic force. The worst thing that struck me centered on Rupert's appointment as chairman of the school board and his complete say over its affairs. The whole town talked of his political dominance but the people were powerless to rise up in opposition, perhaps because they were excessively short of knowledge and lacking in savvy. And afraid of retaliation. Considering the good many teachers, maintenance workers, and cafeteria cooks, Rupert controlled a vast windfall of political votes, no surprise, for he had hired them and once hired it was instantaneously an imperative that the employee, his family and others related, distant or near, were to avail themselves at the polls to elect the candidate of his blessing. As chairman of the school board Rupert enjoyed governance complete over its affairs, down to the last bottom rung, where even the hiring of the cooks could only happen with his stamp of approval. Any kind soul seeking any work at all in the sector of school life found that they must pass through the doors of the bank. "You'll have to see Mr. Rupert if you expect to get a job in the cafeteria," they were told, although the exception, Wallace Bethune, sometimes filled in for Rupert in the preliminaries of the interview. With his grip on the schools and firmly occupying the seat as president of the bank Rupert sat atop the power throne and no wonder the people in mockery secretly alluded to him as King Rupert or King Mac.

It was in the realm of this period when I rode with my Uncle Sanford to a small neighboring town close by, three or four miles. We'd gone to talk to a community of black folks about hiring them to help us with work in the fields. Uncle Sanford spoke with the leader. Right off they got along. He said he knew a sizable many folks, black and white, who lived where we lived. "I sho do. I know a lot about your place. The people and all. Yeah. That's where the boss lives. That's Mac's town. You folks call him Mr. Monett over there. But over here he's known as Boss Mac."

My antipathy against the man began to grow from that moment on, stemming from his previous sullied reputation of which I had begun to be familiar, but more from an episode born some years earlier which involved my mother, who, hoping to help my father with monetary obligations, applied for work at the school cafeteria, approaching Rupert directly whether wise or not. She expressed she'd heard that a job was open and wished to apply for it. With a semblance of careful thought in his manner, raking his fingers slowly across his chin, looking belaboredly over his horn rimmed glasses, he seriously and believably proceeded through the routine of an interview, and then assured her he'd see what he could do.

"Is that a promise sir?"

"Yes, Mrs. Maynard. I'll do my best."

But within the week he hired Mrs. so and so for the job, the wife of a county road grader that Rupert maneuvered onto the state payroll for his delivery of political favors. Rupert spoke of him as his leg man or his guy. We learned that the lady hired for the job received a promise from Rupert more than a month before his interview with my mother that she could have it. Understandably, the betrayal badly wounded and insulted my mother and none of the family ever let the event slip from mind. It was not that she felt she deserved placement ahead of the other applicant, only equal consideration. But it bothered her immensely that the sly clever politics of Rupert Monett once more played its hand and that this time she ended up the victim.

A little time passed. Two years perhaps. While the Monett family now alone exacted the bank's affairs of business—Monett himself, Madeline, Melinda, Melissa, and her husband—Madeline superiorly took the lead in seeing to the particulars, part and parcel, as she had done before her marriage to Rupert and would for years thereafter. She had served as cashier before their acquaintance. A later generation could not imagine there ever being a bank in our small town without a Madeline Monett, the key ramrod, hardened, dogmatic, demanding, conniving—qualities which belied her smallness of stature. She in no manner allowed herself belovedness in the conduct of the affairs of the bank and shrank not in the least from dealing rather forcibly with poor whites and Negroes in the lending and collecting of monies, a chore that Rupert gladly relinquished to his wife. One standing in the lobby near her open office door might gain privy to the verbal lashing of a poor soul under stress because of an unpaid debt. I suspected that there were opportunities cropping up now and then when Madeline imposed an interest rate on these unknowing, uneducated folks in violation of the laws of usury. Aside from Madeline and Rupert, and likely Melinda and possibly Melissa, maybe her husband, who else would have known?

"Alice Ann, you get in heah. You heah me. You're two weeks behind. You get right in heah."

A voice at the other end pled for more time, irritating Madeline to the point of increasing her word delivery by twice fold speed, now bashing the listener with relentless intensity, her voice rising to a high tone of shrillness.

"How many times do I have to tell you 'bout pride, 'bout paying on time. I'm tired of foolin with you. You get in heah. You heah."

Still there came a plea for more time. But cut off.

"Alice Ann, you better get yourself in heah, right now. I mean it."

You could hear her spluttering to herself as she slammed the receiver into its hook, and although frustrated and angry managed not to utter profanities. "That's distressing. It surely is."

Billy stayed on at his job with the defense arsenal, even though the war had ceased by a few years, still checking in and out tools. There yet remained a skeleton crew which the arsenal management had kept in service for producing munitions for the military, as well as attending to the maintenance necessities, the arsenal then operating at less than twenty percent of former full capacity. Throughout the South the Jewish entrepreneurs were aggressively launching a sizeable complex of clothes making factories, thereby hiring many locals who otherwise were destined to go without work and there was as well a miscellany of factories of varying modes whose production operation necessitated the hiring of a sizeable count of those failing to hire on with the the clothing industries. My father lucked into landing a job at a shoe making factory as a security guard, whose job description called for his signing in and out visitors and regular workers and staff to the premises.

Since Billy McVector stayed on as part of the skeleton crew at the near idle defense plant, his hours at managing the hardware store were significantly limited and therefore

Melinda left the bank with her father's blessing to fill in for him, an exchange involuntarily natural to her, for the customers at the hardware store were largely the same as those on whom she waited at the bank. She went overboard to show friendliness, a laudable characteristic of hers; they liked her, and word swiftly traveled from the mouths of the citizens to this effect. "She's fine about helping Billy run the store. I don't know what he'd do without her." Over the course of years past the people exchanged tales of how the Monett parents groomed their daughters from infancy onward to display courteousness to others and said also that the parents were zealous when the girls were coming up through school to inculcate within them to faithfully pledge allegiance to the flag and recite the Lord's Prayer and do unto others as they would have others do unto them. "Utterances and actions of goodness and purity," my father once said, "which bears a faintness of vanity." These qualities the girls personified explicitly, qualities the people were accustomed to seeing in Melinda when visiting the bank or later when entering the hardware store to make purchase, and so understandably were taken aback when gossip spread that Melinda and a young handsome ex Navy married man allowed themselves to venture into an affair. Tall and serene in comparison to Billy, the young man showed a waistline waspy thin, and his good looks struck Melinda's heart strings with melting charm. He had married a girl of the community a year before with a good name, the daughter of a deacon of the church who owned a gas station and garage on the main highway and saw fit to take his new son-in-law on as a mechanic part time and as a gas pumping attendant for the rest. Overcome with infatuation Melinda continually began to see him daily if not several times daily, when she'd drive over to purchase gas, sitting for extra minutes, just a little longer, with her new found obsession. Sometimes he invented cause to pick up a tool specific to his mechanical needs and if not this one then one of the inexhaustible other vitals at the hardware store, knowing that he'd catch her there alone. But eyes from across the street, the switchboard operator, followed his every movement as he strolled his way to the store and it was said that she was ever alert to conveniently eavesdrop on their telephone friendliness, and therefore knew with unswerving predictability when he would show up. Only a stretch had expired when people became aware of their frequent visitations to the seclusion of the countryside, doing it with the utmost of guile. They drove separately to their preconceived tryst, he following her. The backroads were best, more secretive. And she knew them as well as a sly fox remembers his way through an entanglement of woods and undergrowth. But equipped with eyes and ears the seclusion of the rural landscape cannot guarantee secretiveness for time unlimited. And as a consequence, it happened that a lad of my age said he once saw them enter a cotton field growing on the lower quadrant of his father's farm, without their awareness of his concealment, and that after an intermission of peeking commenced to observe the cotton stalks shaking and trembling. It goes without saying that his report could have amounted to a tale told by a youth with breathless excitement over what he imagined; but I believed it with revived faith when years later, in his adult age, he retraced the story with seismographic particularity and swore that he spoke the unquestionable truth. Whether or not Rupert and Madeline picked up on their daughter's oft frequented rendezvous with her new found lover right away is not known, but Billy did, evidently, and with tears in his eyes appealed to his inlaws to intercede on his behalf to bring to a stop the romance between the couple which by this time had turned into a torrid affair. Suddenly the people missed Melinda and said so more than once, receiving the cloudy answer that she was now away for a while to finish her college degree, whereas others contended that her folks sent her away for the purpose of removing her from her new lover and thereby save Billy's marriage. Across several months she stayed away but by mid fall returned to the bank, Billy quit his job at the arsenal to tend to business at the hardware store full time and the young ex sailor seemingly disappeared forever, never seen again by anyone anywhere. Evidently abandoned, his wife moved back in with her parents.

Chapter 14

"WHAT DO you think happened between Billy and Melinda," asked Leland one day when we were alone. We were sitting in a side shed in the enjoyment of sandwiches and drink at noon, starting to rest up from a morning's work on the sprawling edifice that he had earlier conceived and now guided toward completion as our new work place. It was his wish for people to know it as the tractor factory, and thereon I issued my best compliments for his conception of the name, for taking into account the nature of the work there soon to take place the name fit perfectly. Where we were currently domiciled, a huge barn, obviously now proved insufficient in the extreme, tractors and tractor parts everywhere visible and strewn about and we thrilled at the idea of leaving it for a space incomparably more suitable for our purpose.

"What do I think happened? That's easy. A guy entered her life that she couldn't do without," I answered.

"It didn't matter at all about her husband huh?"

"Apparently it didn't. What do you think?" I rolled over and reached for another cold drink from the ice box. He waited until I'd finished and then replied.

"Well, that's the way of a woman, as I see it," he said with a touch of rhetoric interwoven with a bit of curiousity. "When they're aroused, drawn to the charms of a man, stranger or not, there's nothing that's gonna stop them, married or not, provided the right one happens along. You can see it in their eyes. If he's the right one, watch out. She'll go for him no matter who she is. She can't resist."

I rocked with laughter. He said it as if an authority on such matters. "I guess you're right. And I'll have to pretty well say the same thing."

"Pretty well? But not exactly, so—."

"Well, I'm speaking of Melinda, just her, nobody else, and I think it goes without saying that there's a seed of temptation in her somewhere. From what I've heard she's always possessed a tendency toward adventure, a trifle on the wild side. Yeah, she has a seed hidden away and it lay poised to germinate when she met that guy."

"I guess," Leland quipped, tending to agree. "It was something like that. But I have to say this, that given Billy's round pumpkin stomach, I don't see how she saw anything appealing in him in the first place. You can't blame her for taking off after somebody else, especially a good looker like that guy who breathed passion into her soul. You know what I mean?"

"Yeah. I know."

Then Leland went on, with things that were funny and sort of sad at the same time, one of which was that by and large men folks in a manner of play continually gossiped about ever since Billy's and Melinda's wedding day.

"They tell me Ramsey that Billy's penis is no more than a nub," he exclaimed, using his index finger to mark the halfway length of his thumb, "and that this, coupled with his protruding belly, probably means that not once has he ever satisfied her in the bedroom."

"Ha, ha, ha, ha, ha—-."

My response unintentionally slipped out. What else could I do but burst into laughter. I couldn't have dreamed before this moment that ideations of this making were lodged anywhere in the remotest recesses of his intellect, for by far he always seemed guided more by a temperament of straight face seriousness. But he laughed too, a sort of infectious laugh, which is indigenous of a people who greatly enjoy laughing and guffawing at a party gathering.

"Well," I finally said, "she's not at all like her sister Melissa, you know, who's uppity and reserved. A man couldn't get near her."

"No. She's not like her sister. At least on the surface she's not. But I do hear that her sister has the reverse fault. She's frigid."

"Frigid? How can you say that? She's married and has children."

"I can't say it with any real sureness. It's just what they whisper."

"I don't see her like that. On the contrary I'd have to say that she's, she's—."

"You mean sexy."

"Yep. She is."

"You noticed too."

Through the assistance of our attorney friend J. R. Carney we obtained a supply of support posts for holding up the building, the tractor factory, and more than a sufficient quantity of logs for cutting into board footage, the necessary materials for the exterior siding and decking for the roof. The timber we would take from the government owned property that once belonged to Mrs. Langstrup. We leased it. I remember walking it times innumerable, one hundred acres that extended from the river, the southern most border, on which, and especially next to the river, a growth of ash and oak stood that literally towered and were of such numerous quantity that their branches and boughs with attendant leaves admitted but menial shades of sun light which amounted to no more than a shadow when falling deftly on the forest floor. We especially sought tall straight timbers for the support columns. We had sat with Mr. Carney to go over our intentions and lay before him our designs and needs, who additionally took it on himself to confer with the attorney representing the government to see if we might lease the land for a season or two, the reputed intent being to produce farm growth, hay not withstanding. He succeeded, smiling happily when relaying that we could lease the land for a nominal sum and take from it the natural products to which a farmer is customarily entitled, this including the cutting of trees for firewood and other broadly defined purposes. We grew a limitation of vegetables, some tomatoes, and cabbage and corn and a little cotton but were more attracted to the trees by far. In reference to the trees Mr. Carney let off a mischievous grin and said with a chuckle," Well boys, I downplayed the trees to the government's attorney, taking it that he might start to get suspicious that we planned to use them for commercial gain."

"What did you say sir?" I chipped in.

"Very little of the trees. I stayed mainly on the idea of growing food stuff for the family and a little hay and corn for the few animals that Mr, Maynard presently owns."

We toured the land near the river for an entire day. Mr. Carney declined to go with us. But two new hired hands at the direction of Leland had come along. As he did with everything else Leland had begun to contemplate the wisdom of taking on a few men, two at least, to help us with the tractor business and particularly who could contribute greatly in the erection of the new building. With this utmost in his mind, he had hired them, men he'd known for awhile, brothers, Ozzie and Cavanaugh, of less than thirty years of age, stout men, who took up their work with robust energy and determination, uneducated in the book sense but much in their element at performing with their hands.

"Look at that forest will you," said Leland, "trees straight up, as tall as the sky."

"Where will we cut," asked Ozzie. "I'm confused. They all look so fine, so big and mighty, no matter where you look."

"As near the river as we can," answered Leland. "The best of the timber grows there. It's a shame to cut any of them all right. They've stood here for ages. They're like a forest now but just think of what they resembled a hundred years ago. Unbelievable. You can bet the folks ending up here had some pushing and tugging and cutting to do to make their way through."

"I'll say," I put in, and that was all for the moment, except I began to form a picture in my mind. "Back then," I said to myself, "this was at first a wild impenetrable place, untamed, uncut, unfarmed, barely dented by the surge of human progression, but drastically affected later on by the advance of the white man who came swinging axes and pulling cross cut saws in quest of driving back the wilderness, gobbling up more land for claim, and in the onslaught pushing the remnant of Indians on further west."

Ozzie threw a rock into the river from where he stood, a distance of thirty feet from the river's edge, fussing at himself for not bringing fish hooks and bait because he just knew that a school of blue channel cat were floundering on the other side at a bend where the current moved lazily slow, he said, appearing to crawl or altogether stop and added that they'd make for a tasty supper. "That's where they are. The water's deep over there."

"I don't think we can fish here Ozzie," I said, but not with serious caution.

"Why not?"

"It's government property. And we don't have leasing rights for fishing."

"I'll swear to goodness. They'll probably come get me for throwing rocks into their water a while ago."

I nearly turned inside out with laughter, and then cleared it with a smile. "That's a good one, but I don't think you'll have to worry that the government will jump on you for doing that. They are ridiculous sometimes I have to say. Always ready to tell us what we can and can't do."

"Who's the government? Who is it that can tell us them things?"

"The people we elect. The people we send to Washington. They write and pass the laws."

"I'll swear to goodness. That's something. It's really something."

"I know it sounds wrong. And sometimes turns out badly. But all the same, that's the way the country works." It struck me silently that my father used to address John Eric with essentially these very same things. "You know John Eric; the government is a make over of man himself and man is a make over of the government; give either a little power and you'll see their real character."

The next day we launched into our venture, first towing in a massive hauling truck which could transport a stack of logs a half a house high. Then Leland went to work with his inventive capabilities, devising something of a sawmill on the spot, using a very wide strapping, something likened to a leather belt not less than twelve inches in width and a half inch thick that he connected to the gearing of the truck we'd brought in. He'd gotten the truck by trading in something of slight value, a tractor he said, and had temporarily set it aside until presently needed. I watched with amusement, as always, knowing I could not do as he did even in a thousand years. But I finally suggested that we could have used a tractor instead for generating power, to which he explained that he'd turned that over a time or to but decided against it.

"Better Ramsey to use the truck motor. We can let this old contraption stay out here in the open for as long as we like and nobody will touch it. They won't think it's worth anything, so they'll leave it alone and even if they do scavenge the parts or even hall it away, we won't worry. As I say, it's not worth a hoot anyway. Besides, the truck motor is equipped with more power."

"But the strapping belt, the pulley!"

"I'm coming to that. We'll just disconnect them and take them with us when we leave each day."

With these essentials thrashed through and cleared away we began to erect the sawmill. Ozzie and Cavanaugh reacted in a snap to Leland's instructions, eager to understand and carry out what they were told. I marveled at his dispassionate dealings with men much older than himself. It was the sense of his genius that kneeled them to him, the same with all men with whom he dealt. That is the nature of genius, at once recognized and seldom challenged. With untiring patience Leland went over the technicalities of a task with Ozzie and Cavanaugh just as he unfailingly did with me, their faces and eyes immovably concentrated on the exactness of plans that were communicated and spread before them. I could tell that in return he as well placed a great amount of confidence in them. Of course, he did. That was why they were on the job.

"It's dangerous out here men. Let's all go with no exceptions by the rules of safety and no one will get hurt." he said with an energetic gesture of slapping his knee. He nurtured an inestimable concern for safety and relentlessly stayed alert to ascertain that workers at all times obeyed the rule. Starting then and never flagging for a moment he doggedly cautioned us of the essentialness of respecting the dangers of powerful equipment.

"Un hunh," we all agreed with eyes of worshipful countenance, and everyone's voice more or less in unison.

The overriding job for Ozzie and Cavanaugh dealt with the falling of trees with a chainsaw whose teeth Leland kept razor sharp, and then through the use of a tractor, towing the trees to the whereabouts of the sawmill where they were first cut into logs and then the logs were drawn onto a conveyer track and grabbed by a staggered set of metal claws that relayed them to the cutting blade, where they were cut into nice wide planking of varying dimensions. The board footage we would cut first. Logs for use as post supports for the building were cut next though not passing through the sawmill. Ozzie and Cavanaugh were to cut such logs from the trees into the specified proper lengths, again using the chainsaw.

The cutting blade of the saw mill, awesome in size, had something of a character of death about it, feared by us all and deservedly, for although not very often but sometimes, a piece of lumber flew as a missile through the air, barely missing the worker who guided the logs onto the conveyer track. Men were known to suffer injuries from like accidents, let alone death. To counter the risk Leland required that we stand aside from the trajectory of the logs destined for the blade, and then additionally improvised a shield of heavy design to protect us. "What on earth would we do without him," I thought every day we came to work.

The cutting blade was more than a cutting blade; it was a giant sized cutting blade, better than three quarters of my height in diameter. Ordinarily Leland would have stored a piece of equipment of this value and size on the interior of the barn in which we worked.

"Where did you get this Leland? I've not seen it around."

"My father has kept it in his garage. He arranged for its shipment with his other belongings when he migrated to America. This one plus three others."

"I'll declare. Why was that?"

"When he lived in the old country he worked at a saw mill in spare hours. More as a mechanic than a cutter. You know. To keep the saw mill running. He said he brought the blades with him to America thinking he might need them to help him earn a living until he got on his feet. But he left them in the shipping crates all this while. Not once removing them. Not long after his arrival he hooked up with the Edison Company and you by now know a great deal of the rest."

Chapter 15

THINGS WERE scheduled in patterns of sequence, hauling the planking away without delay taking precedence, thus when the last piece was emplaced onto a stack that measured higher than a man could reach upright loading onto the lowboys commenced and soon the tractor pulling the lowboys left for the building site. This became routine effort that ate up in excess of three days of sweat and toil.

The grind of transporting the logs to the site of our new work place necessitated once more Leland drawing upon his creative talents. The logs were of immense footage. The trailers, tethered together, were built low off the ground and were of sufficient strength and length for moving them, the excess of the logs hanging over the rear with a red flag appended to the ends for provision of safety. Once in forward motion the tractor kept going without strain from the immensity of the weight it towed. Leland worried that the chains binding the logs might break or shift and thereby let them tumble as an entangled cascade onto the roadway. But the potential for calamity failed to materialize and after a period of traveling back and forth for three days on a mid august dusty road we had stock-piled materials sufficient in amount to nearly reach Leland's projected quota. Some days later we felled additional trees for cutting into various measures of lumber, both Leland and I speculating that possibly we were exceeding the quantity allowed by the terms of our lease, therefore, as a consequence, we proceeded to Mr. Carney for his judgment on whether we might receive charges of guilt by breach.

"Well boys, you can read the agreement wording of the lease yourselves. In one place it says, among other things, for firewood and other broad purposes. Very broad indeed. Cut all you want. And who's going to the trouble of wading into that swamp to inspect what you're doing anyway? Even if they did sooner or later they'd have to abide by the provisions of the contract. Yeah, go ahead. Cut your wood." Years past, and eventually, I learned, the government sold the whole one hundred acres of land from which we'd cut our timber for one dollar per acre, the land purchased by a major state university whose officials wanted it for creating an agricultural experiment station.

I waited impatiently for the building phase to begin. As was everything under Leland's guise there were certain steps of which he required execution in the strictest of sequence. He had drawn up the diagram in long hand, the impression of a blue print more or less, though done to scale, setting down every dot and notation with tedious care. His concentration fell on Ozzie and Cavanaugh more considerably than on me, for they were the ones to shoulder the brunt of hard work, let alone climbing and working at risky heights. One early morning when the sun barely began to rise from slumber Leland asked Ozzie to position the tractor at the spots where circles of bright red paint were sprayed, the markings signifying the location of the large circular holes into which the support posts were lowered once the holes were bored. Some holes were staggered, others evenly spaced. Leland had mounted an augur with incisively sharp rotating blades onto the tractor drive train, such designed to bore and excavate the soil with astonishing efficiency and speed. By noon we were ready to lower the posts, by no means a challenge commensurate with the trouble that I expected.

"How will you drop the posts in the holes?" I asked.

"A crane. We'll need a crane."

"A crane. I figured you'd rig up with the bulldozer and cables and pull and counter pull."

"Nope. That's too difficult. That way there's no assurance of keeping the posts balanced. They're so tall and heavy. If you start lifting one up and it wiggles out of control, wham, it comes plunging down and all hell breaks loose, everything in reach smashed."

"The crane will do the job for you! And safely! But where is it?"

"Should get after lunch."

Not wishing to appear too naïve by asking from whom did he borrow the giant contraption, I didn't ask. But was confident that a heavy equipment company saw an opportunity to balance a lingering debt, and found that my reasoning was verifiable, for later Leland told me that he once spent a whole night repairing a piece of grading equipment for the firm that badly needed it the next morning at dawn. They delivered the crane; and Leland crawled up in the cab, appearing no larger than a pygmy from where I stood, the machine of monstrous size. He started the motor and commenced moving a complex of levers and foot pedals with his hands and feet, motioning to Qzzie and Cavanaugh to cross over to where a pile of logs lay, the posts, and work began, each of the brothers every minute staying busy tying the cables to them, calling out after each tie, "Take it away." By night fall the posts were in place and the bracing and counter bracing constructed and appended and after this the concrete was poured around them. Leland seemed pleased. "These babies won't go anywhere soon." After supper he introduced us to a new set of drawings, which in very exact detail showed the wall emplacements and the trusses on which the roof decking must come to rest.

"Okay men. It's time to go turn in. Tomorrow is another hard and busy day. Goodnight."

I said goodnight then set out home, but almost went back, for Leland sat motionless with his fingers to his chin, his eyes and mind tracing up and down the diagram that seconds before he'd finished explaining to us.

"No. I'd better not. He's working something out in his head. He prefers to do that alone."

The next morning, a while after we'd begun our work, a trickling of old men gathered around, curious of the visage rising before them, mostly former carpenters or builders from the old school. Leland pretended not to see the gathering. I could tell that he wished they weren't there. Without showing vexation he asked us not to talk or mingle with them lest they distract us from what we were doing; further instructing us to keep them out of range from the action of things to assure that their safety wasn't jeopardized. They stayed sufficiently back without our telling them, excitedly jabbering to one another, I imagined, that the methods they now witnessed were new to their sight and that they wouldn't have done things that way in their time. Sometimes they'd shake their heads in agreement or disagreement. But seemed constrained about voicing judgement to one another, only converged on the scene to satisfy their curiosity over the young man regarded as a wizard at repairing tractor machinery, and anything else to which he set his mind, which now centered on the erection of a structure of extraordinary design and size.

The walls were first of precedence according to the lay out design that Leland had recorded in his work plan at the very beginning of the project. But there were no walls in the usual sense, not in the manner of walls to a house. The broad and long planking that we previously cut were lapped over one another in succession and nailed to the posts. Scaffolds were built which spanned the full length of the building. Leland wasn't a believer in ladders for work done high above ground, contending that ladders employed for this purpose were too dangerous and too inefficient. "Ladders are only for handy men" he joshed, but established his point. The scaffolds were built by sections and by rungs, that is to say you could move the siding boards from left to right or upward or downward to the desired height as need be. Putting up the siding posed but minimum difficulty but lifting the trusses and balancing and appending the same necessitated a great deal of effort and skill, nor was it an easy task to lift and nail the decking to the trusses, and it proved harder still to move the sheets of tin to where they should precisely fit before someone pinned them down with roofing nails. And all this took place with the men working downward, not upward. Mostly, my job consisted of keeping the decking, the trusses, and the pieces of tin reasonably erect, the plan being that Leland would catch hold of them on the ground with the crane claws and lift them to a certain designated place where they became the responsibility of Ozzie and Cavanaugh. But additionally, Leland assigned to me a lesser job, the continued sending up of a bucket of nails to my friends on the roof by way of a pulley and draw rope. About this, he indulged in a fair share of fun. "Be patient Ramsey. Someday I'll figure out a promotion for you."

At last the day arrived when he said that we were virtually done, with the exception of cleaning up the premises and reworking a few areas which he said needed a slight change. In two weeks these tasks were fulfilled and we began to move the tractors inside. Considering that sooner than later the increase in repair demand would grow to such proportions that extra manpower would become a must, Leland, knowing he had two good ones already aboard hired Ozzie and Cavanaugh full time on the spot and began training them in the intricacies of properly repairing machinery, patiently teaching them as he once taught me and still did.

Chapter 16

OVER THE course of the past weeks I had stayed close to Nenia, seeing her at every opportunity, taking her every Saturday night to a movie at a nearby town, and in between too if I found a gap in my schedule and weren't too tired from working with Leland's building endeavor. Time had elapsed, my high school days behind me and I proudly possessed a diploma. Nenia had grown into a beauty. We still walked the back roads of her father's farm and waded in the creek and sat on the flat white rocks situated on the edge of the stream and laughed and talked. Her parents trusted me explicitly, I'm sure of that, believing or hoping that some day we'd marry, and not by any visible degree were they bothered when we returned from somewhere at or shortly after midnight. Her mother faithfully left a light burning as a means of helping her enter without unnecessary trouble. If the hour of our return was not excessively late she insisted on preparing ham and eggs and coffee for us, an offer that I readily accepted but apologetically told her that she went too far out of her way. On Friday nights, if Leland hadn't laid out work for me to complete by day's end I'd go see her, but if there was work that needed finishing, even into the night, I'd do it and for sure join her the following day, whereon we'd head out for the creek where we usually said to Maggie that we were going to fish, yet I wondered if she thought we were feeding her a dose of pretense. In any event we'd take with us a couple of lanterns and something of a pup tent, together with the conventional fishing gear. Poles and hooks and bait. We seldom fished; opting to build a fire and spread out blankets and lie and talk and look at the starlit sky. She was a lovely thing lying there beside me softly breathing in and out. I asked her if she recalled the first day she saw me, merely making small talk, but also eager to hear the answer. She smiled with artful playfulness and said she did. I then asked her if she had liked me the first day she ever saw me. She blushed, then snickered cutely and asked me if I thought she did. "I think you did," I replied, laughing, and slid over against her and kissed her lips, and she, as always, sweetly kissed mine back. Sometimes I'd touch her pretty white legs, her dress slightly raised to just above her knees, to which she offered no resistance; in fact usually snuggling closer to me or pulling me closer to her. The contour of her frame was wondrous. I don't know why I did it but I asked her if she ever revealed to her sister Thelma the intimacy in which we made love, on which she mused for a fraction and then with a nice soft smile wafting through said no, not in any detail but that she told her we loved one another's kisses. In these moments there surged within me a tendency to make love to her completely, but nurtured a fear, and she too, of the onset of pregnancy. The thought of it startled me.

"Ah," I cautioned myself. "The pain from something like that is devastating I'm sure. And the embarrassment to the parents worse than awful. And then there is a career out there somewhere, sometime, for the both of us which in a moment of ecstasy can end up literally destroyed." I think I feared more than anything else how my mother might behave toward my falling prey to such a ruinous caprice, to what I had done to a young girl, the beloved daughter of our once best neighbors.

She asked me one night when we were lying so very close if I'd like to make love to her. At this I repeatedly kissed her lips and pretty white neck all over.

"You can't imagine how much. But I'm afraid to death of doing it. But sometime. Yes. You know I would. You can tell. I know you can."

"I can tell. And I'm the same as you. I'd be so afraid. I am afraid. But must tell you that I think of us often."

"About our making love."

"Of course."

"So do I."

Given her intellectuality the next words she uttered in no way caught me unexpectedly.

"Isn't it a shame? The Lord made us as we are to enjoy one another but has imposed the possibility of great misery if we go though with it."

"The price of sin, the Bible says."

"I don't see it as sin. I see it as natural. Yet with a consequence due to the nature of our bodily system. Ah, but when we're a little older maybe we'll marry, then we won't have to worry about restraints."

She seemed more beautiful each new night we got together, her eyes so dark and alluring and melting to my heart in the lantern glow, and she was so tenderly young. I knew then, more than I ever knew, that I was in love with her and she with me. She said she loved me when but a little girl, meaning when the Maynard's first moved to the Langstrup farm. I laughed and kidded her that at such a young age the sentiment of love was surely beyond serious conception. We yearned for the arrival of Friday night, an interlude fantastic, and we returned again and again and again, but this in time would flounder to an end, for eventually there were opportunities that beckoned elsewhere which foretold of taking us on separate journeys. That remained awhile away, or so we told ourselves, yet the lessening time encroached upon our lives with deceptive haste.

It was a year later I judge that she took me inside their home to the room where she kept a montage of books and magazines, there removing a letter from her study desk, which was snugged in a corner near the window, a replica of a desk used in French styled bedrooms she said. Thelma gave it to her at age ten. She handed me the letter from her sister to read.

Dear Nenia,

I've checked things out with the university. From what I understand they'll offer you a scholarship to come and prepare for a librarian's position. See what good grades will do. They'll send you admission papers for processing right away. You should fill them out and send them back. In my opinion this is a fine opportunity for you. The pay to librarians, especially to big city library directors, is temptingly lucrative and with your ability, you'd soon move to the top.

The scholarship is nice, paying most of your fees, but you know as well as I that daddy can easily afford to pay for your expenses entirely and will if he has to.

Please write.

Thelma

I read the letter. I felt no surprise, my face apparently not mirroring any. With the talent that flowered in her veins I had reached the conclusion a long while before that she would likely pursue something academic, which might result in her relocating some distance away. Life on the farm for her offered a tenuous existence. I asked of her seriousness to attend college and if that was where she'd set her sights then when did she intend to start.

"I'm serious Ramsey. I'll enroll for the fall semester if all goes well."

"I'll miss you. And all those wonderful Friday nights." She looked pensively into my face, forging a little smile. I guess my tone echoed sadness at the idea.

"And I'll miss you even more," she tacked on, and then with optimistic emphasis continued her thoughts. "But Saint Louis is not that far. You'll have to catch the train or drive up to see me ever so often"

"Naturally I'll do that. But let us enjoy ourselves until you have to leave. We still have some time. Let's make every minute count."

"Sure. Absolutely. But by the way. What are you to do with yourself? You won't work in that tractor business always wills you?"

"No. I won't. I've thought of discussing my termination with Leland, I mean in regard to a date. But I don't want to rush things. My intention is to quit and take up college like you. He won't mind. He tells me that I should do something else more suited to my aptitude."

"Absolutely. I feel that way too."

"We'll continue talking about it."

"Good. We should."

With nothing less than full diligence I stayed tight with Leland at running the business and couldn't wait to join Nenia on Friday nights. In the meanwhile, Billy Mcvector's reputation began to show an aura of elevated importance and soon he emerged as the town's most prominent entreprenuer. It registered as no surprise when he took over the feed store across the street that his father owned, now too old to further give it proper management, appearing with the slightest glance as if drifting toward decrepitness. Soon Billy started doing away with the feed stuff and began to set in a display of furniture for sale as a replacement, an early tell tale sign that his aspirations were set on venturesome expansion. Rupert's money stood behind him, and thus he knew in advance that he faced no roadblocks in seeing to it that his new design succeeded. From time to time I dropped into his hardware store to purchase some implement or other that we needed at the tractor business, noticing right off an aggressive supplementation to his inventory, a number of items not seen before on the shelves and under the glass, and a wall had been knocked out to an adjoining space for housing extra merchandise. A newness pervaded the now expanded interior, the walls freshly painted and the floors aglitter from shellac. After this he proceeded to give the building an up to date face lift, a modern facade with his name high up in capital letters. And to add friendliness to it all had an embossment tacked up near the entrance that read "say hello to Mac." By and large folks liked the change, it was people oriented they said, and weren't slow in voicing their approval. Not long thereafter someone said he had taken over the scrap iron yard on the edge of town, buying out his father's ownership. Then they said that no buy out was in the deal, that his father deeded the property over to him carte blanche, but that whichever it was the result meant the same. Whenever I visited the store Billy unfailingly padded forth with a bright and cheerful greeting, his usual suit, and I returned the cordiality, yet invariably discovered my eyes involuntarily darting here and there in search of Melinda, who wasn't about. Billy said she'd gone on an errand. She now helped him full time in the store and had for the longest. I knew that. But the memory of the handsome ex sailor and the widely gossiped love affair lingered in my thoughts even though that happened a while in the past. "I guess they figure that people have forgotten by now or else treat the past as a stain that should have faded once and for all into obscurity." Upon concluding my purchase I turned toward the doorway and bade goodbye, adding at the last instant, "Give my regards to Melinda."

"Will do."

Chapter 17

THE EARLY fall descending on us that year failed to present its customary beauty and in turn replaced it with an atmosphere of annoying discomfort, the air dry, acrid, and oppressively hot. I recall it without hesitancy. It was one of those periods which for a reason I can't logically explain seemed vaguely strange. The dust blew in sweeps, dying down then whipping up again, and the dry offensive air parched the face and lips. The rain fell but in amounts too limited to effectively moisten the crops of the field, of which I naturally kept aware because of my job. When leaving off their implements for repair the farmers frustratingly talked of the degree to which plant life suffered. In the recent days Nenia and I had hatched up the idea of riding horseback across her father's farm until intercepting the river, then turning around and retracing ourselves. At the last minute she couldn't go, suggesting however that I do it without her. "Ride the sorrel," she urged. "He's the friendliest." I said I wouldn't, that I'd go help my mother with some things that I felt she needed to have done. Leland had traveled to another part of the state to resurrect a wheat combine that the owner wished to have repaired, without sufficient knowledge for repairing it himself, nor did he possess the means for transporting it to our shop. When Leland returned he said that we'd have to go to where the man lived and do the work on the spot. He ended up going alone, leaving me behind to tend to the affairs of the business.

I'm not superstitious, nor have I ever been so affected throughout my entire life, but on that day it seemed I sensed an omen. I supposed I had when I reached home, seeing the proof in my mothers worried face as she met me at the door, with news that they'd laid off my father at the shoe factory, that his blood pressure reading extended to seriously high levels, and that the company wouldn't allow him to work anymore.

"Where is he now?" I asked with immediate concern.

"In bed. I think he's in shock. You know how he is. A worrier. The doctor said put him to bed."

"When did this happen?"

"Yesterday. They sent him home after his medical examination."

She couldn't talk much more, or else in no way felt like it, or else didn't want to, so I would have to learn slowly all I wanted to know, and this amounted to a day or two of patiently probing her for tidbits regarding the facts. A representative of the company had telephoned before I arrived with wording identical to that which I would discover by reading that which the company had set down in print and mailed. They explained by way of letter, prepared and signed by their attorney, that company policy disallowed employment of persons suffering from his type of ailment.

"He can't work again?"

"No. That's what I'm told."

"Who told you that?"

"The director of personnel."

"Never? He can never work again?"

"Never."

"I'll be damned. Sorry mother."

"That's all right. I feel the same." Her face clouded with sorrow and anxiety she began to sob. It touched me deeply. I wished that I could have changed places with her. I tried to envision her pain. All the struggles she had endured throughout her life seemed to have migrated to a head, still forming into still a greater and more grievous agony. My anger boiled over, reasonable or not.

"Those ungrateful bastards. Just a bunch of lying, selfish Yankees. That's who they are. A man is flat of his back and instead of lifting him up they step on him."

"Well son—."

Before she ended with her line I couldn't resist butting in. "Did they say anything about insurance?"

"I asked that. They said no record existed of any. They don't cover their hourly employees. Only the higher ups."

"Damn. Ah gee. He'll worry himself to death. Well, look. I have some money saved back. Tell him not to worry. There's enough to see after the both of you for a good while."

"You don't have to do that."

"What do you mean? Yes I do. I'm supposed to. You gave life to me. You raised me. Tell him. Tell him when he's feeling better."

"Oh honey. You're such a good boy."

"Mom. Don't say that. I'm only doing what is right. And don't worry about money. Things will work out."

"It's not so much the money son. It's his health."

"What do you mean?"

"The doctor says he'll improve. To just see that he eats like he ought to. The doctor says this but he's old and I don't have, have very much faith in doctors anyway. The truth is I know your father better than anybody. And despite what the doctor says I don't think he is long due with us."

"Not long with us!" I swallowed. This was the same person that picked me up as a one year old with an ear ache and walked me around on his shoulders, the same person who had taken me to Chicago when I turned six or seven, the same person which so far as a grown young man I hadn't paused to envision someday would no longer live and walk among us. The idea didn't seem real. "But he's mortal," I reluctantly acknowledged. "He can't last much longer I know but I can't picture him dying either. I can't."

But I could. I did. And when he gathered strength enough for me to sit beside him on his bed there sprang an upsurge inside me to tell him that he would improve and that everything would turn out well. I didn't have it in me however to lie or attempt to mislead when I knew that he would see through me and smile that devastating, though weakly smile, chiding me that I shouldn't try to fool my father. Instead, I said nothing. He spoke for me. "I'm in bad shape son. You know that. But I have a mile or so left and I'll stick around as long as I can and that is all I can do. In the meanwhile, you and the other children visit me as often as your schedule will let you." We talked on a while, with him inquiring of my work with Leland and of that pretty Stoddard girl I'd been seeing. Unable to recall her first name he glanced at me as if embarrassed.

"It's Nenia. Nenia is her first name."

"That's right. It is. I forgot."

Eventually he began to tire, then began to climb further up in bed, with me helping him, and when reaching his pillow laid his head softly down and sighed and said everything felt so good, there closing his eyes and not opening them even while saying with weakened voice that he must no longer hold me up from my work and that it brought him much joy that I dropped by. I went and embraced my mother and left, deciding to spend awhile in my apartment which Leland and I shared, and after arriving plopped down in the big leather chair stationed in the corner by the wide glass window looking across at the railroad while waiting for him. I intended to relax but my father's circumstances refused to leave me, my anger not yet subsided. More than once I silently cursed the shoe company that turned him out, "the strong versus the weak, the rich and powerful pitted against the unfortunate," I said with lips of unfurled anger and swore vengeance against them if the opportunity should somehow in the years on down the line give me that chance. "The world into which we are born is preposterously unfair," I bitterly declared, "and replete with inflated high sounding phrases that spell out the rules by which we are to live with respect to our fellow man, but empty of substance when we have to face the moment of lending a helping hand. Be thy neighbor's keeper and help him overcome that which besets him and threatens to bring him down," the dictum goes, more or less, "but leaves off unless it is too troublesome to us to hold him up, then he's on his own."

Chapter 18

SITTING THERE in my chair, unmoving, contemplating, anxious, bewildered, angry; staring out the window but seeing nothing, except the railroad, the whole of my temperament and mood must have appeared as an exasperation to Leland when he opened the door and walked in, looking curiously over in my direction with no time lost in concluding that he wasn't seeing the real me. I told him of the grim news.

"Your disturbance I understand. I'm sorry. I know my saying as much hardly helps. But I truly am sorry my dear friend and I am with you in every way within me."

"Sure you are. I'm sorry for you to see me in this mood. I truly am. But it's hard for me to get over how they treated him."

"I'd feel like you."

"I assured mom not to worry with regard to money, because I have some saved back."

"And you can add whatever amount you need from my account to it. Just let me know."

"Of that I'm certain. Let's hope we don't need it. I thank you from the bottom of my heart for your generosity. No one anywhere could have a better friend than I have in you."

Leland lightly tilted his head forward in acknowledgment, as if to somehow thank me. "Does he owe anything? To the bank that is?"

"Not now. Two months ago I went in there with John Eric who needed to attend to some business. I sat down on one of the customer benches waiting for him to finish. Seeing me from her office Madeline kind of tip toed over, but pretty hurried like too, as if afraid I might leave before she could intercept me and sat down. She looked as if something bothered her, a little hyper and all, and as it turned out my judgment did not err."

"What was it that bothered her?"

"Sly like she began to edge in the importance of people paying their debts on time and when she touched on that part about the essence of pride I cut her off by asking abruptly what debt? She acted as if it hurt her to say but answered."

"Your father owes a small amount that I think he's forgotten. I thought you night like to know. But there's no rush in this matter."

"The small amount was the balance on the loan that he borrowed when he built his house. Until recently he faithfully paid the installments. She'd counted every penny in my own account not fewer than two minutes before. I'd bet my coat on that. I stunned her."

'How much?'

'Two hundred dollars.'

'Is that all?'

"My retort, Leland, plainly expressed my indignance, and that I looked upon the amount as if it were nothing, at best absurdly small."

'That's all, but there's no rush—.'

"Her anxiety level now rising she struggled to keep the conversation under control."

'What's the balance of his checking account?'

"I'm certain that my tone carried no trace of humility."

'Twenty dollars.'

"I wanted to swear, I'll be damn shooting into to mind, but I didn't. Instead, I reached for my billfold."

'I'll write you out a check for the entire amount that he owes. You want me to hand it to the cashier?'

'That's all right.'

"She expected me to plead for time. And when she saw me on the verge of making good on my father's debt a restrained, spiteful and mocking smile stole across her face. I swear it did. Lesser people weren't supposed to wash out their obligations that easily. Without thanking me she wheeled around and in little fast bird steps returned to her office, her high heels giving off a click, click, click, a short snappy popping as she hurried to her office doorway. I wrote out the check and handed it to Melinda who began to prepare the receipt and started asking of the family and making ingratiating praises about this one or that. If I failed to stare at her icily, I should have. She's a remake of her mother. She became an object of my dislike a long while ago. She cared not one damn ounce for any member of my family and I knew it."

Leland issued no comment in response, not just then, deciding to give me latitude for venting my distraught emotions. At the opportune opening he asked of my schedule for the rest of the day, with me telling him that I wanted to catch a nap and then drop out to see Nenia. He concurred with both ideas, saying that they were exactly what he would do if he were me, and pled that I shouldn't surrender to dejection, to keep my chin up, for things the next day would look better. "Above all," he advised, "forget those bastards at the shoe factory. What's done is done. You can't do anything to them anyway. But if you keep stoking your anger you'll hurt yourself."

My incomparable friend could not have fully grasped my antipathy toward Rupert Monett and his wife and offspring, for he and his parents moved too late to our small town to witness the dominant seed responsible for sprouting my discontent. There ran through me a temptation to tell him of my once overhearing my father dejectedly talking to my mother of the banker denying him a small loan when he desperately needed one, deciding however to let it pass. At least for the time being. But Rupert's refusal still lodged and burned in my craw and equated with the unconscionable actions of the shoe factory executives.

Nenia had packed a week earlier for her trip to Saint Louis, allowing room for a few articles she knew she would need sooner or later. It was apparent that her parents were taking her impending departure grievously hard. She told me in a moment of privacy that she'd seen her mother crying off and on, unsuccessfully trying to keep it from her and said her father too had been crying, but hiding it underneath his impenetrable exterior, a kind of silent weeping let me say. It was a peculiar thing, her feeling sorrow for them on the one hand and on the other experiencing a joyful euphoria at leaving. With an exceptional appetite for change and fresh adventure she daily absorbed the broad excitement from around the globe from her readings and radio and the movies, and no wonder that life on the farm had begun to lapse into a shade of dullness that she increasingly deplored. It bored her to no end. She looked with buoyed spirit to a new and provocative horizon.

I'd promised some several weeks previous that I'd ride the train with her to Saint Louis, which ignited a glow of happiness in her face. She hugged and kissed me. She said that Thelma would meet her at the train station. Nenia's mother worried without let up over her young daughter's facing the change, "only a little girl in a big loud strange city," she once said in my presence. "I worry."

"Oh Mom," Nenia countered, calm and not in any way nettled, defending herself as a grown young woman, "goodness, you speak of me as if I'm still a child."

"You are darling, in my mind," the answer came.

The day before we left we embarked on our classical walk across the farm, going until reaching the creek to which we were routinely accustomed and sat down. She leaned against me and sighed.

"We'll really miss this old hole," I said, to which she sighed once more and answered with a phrase of melancholy that she knew it and supposed we'd miss it equally.

The next day I met her on the front porch, the air nippy, the temperature registering in the low forties due to the cold spell that crept in during the night. The weather that morning is easy to remember because of the attire she wore, a gorgeous green coat with big red buttons extending from summit to knee level, a pretty brown hat that tilted slightly on her head and a pair of high heels on her feet. Underneath her coat a bright red blouse endowed of more than a plentiful array of ruffles was partially seen. the collar plainly exposed, lovely and oversized, and especially noticeable. Not on any occasion, not even when I sometimes sat at her side in attendance of church, had I seen her in dress ware so perfectly charming. But seeing her like that, beautiful and in clothes of finery, engendered a thread of discomfort if not shame, for soon I would seat her in my old car of an obviously dated age and insufficiently tidy and began to apologize. Which she perceived as hilariously funny. "Ramsey, my lands. You're acting. What's hovering over you? How many are the times I've ridden with you in that old jalopy. I know how it looks. Do you honestly think that makes a difference with me?" And then saving me from further embarrassment would burst forth with her usual wonderful adorable laugh.

Chapter 19

AS I expected Mr. and Mrs. Stoddard were still taking hard their daughter's parting when Charlie and Arlene dropped over for the send off, their faces somber like the rest, Nenia proceeding back and forth among everyone offering comfort that they shouldn't feel too downcast in that she'd return before Christmas and that Christmas was merely a snap away. Mr. Stoddard, the last she embraced, depicted something of a pathetic sight, an old man holding on to his daughter until the last moment, but in the end begrudgingly forcing himself to pull away. As we moved toward the car I glanced backward, seeing him standing perfectly upright as might a soldier at arms, trying to show bravery but fighting with hard resolve to extinguish the tears.

We crawled in, the old car untidy and a bit unclean as already intimated, and sure enough I apologized, but the words skipped over her unheard and she started to daub her moistened eyes with her handkerchief that she'd lifted from her purse. The train we were to catch passed through a town twenty five miles west of our own, requiring a driving time much less than we had allowed. She had agreed with me that an hour amply supplied more than enough leeway. But we almost miscalculated. When we arrived I hastily set her equipage along side the rail road tracks, the train not more than minutes away from departing. The ports under the engine violently discharged a cloud of whitish steam, hissing and spewing, the shrillness of the noise unnerving. She caught my arm and looked up at me. I smiled down at her. Two powerful blasts struck my ears in the resemblance of fog horns used by deep sea vessels that sometimes I saw in the movies. I leaned over and tried to tell her how the noise sounded to me but she couldn't make out what was said. She just frowned. She stayed close beside me as I edged her belongings nearer the coach that we were to board. A yard official had identified it for us. At virtually the minute we started to climb aboard there rippled across the way a yell, a frantic yell it seemed to me, "Nenia, Ramsey, Ramsey," both of us spinning around to see who it was that gave off such desperate cries. Then we saw. It was Charlie, his face reddened, who came running breathlessly to us. "You must have said a little prayer on my behalf. I almost busted a gut but I made it. Here Nenia. Daddy insisted that you have this. He started to worry that you didn't have enough."

"What is it?"

Without answering he handed her a one hundred dollar bill, and hugged her lovingly, then after tapping me on the shoulder, which of itself said, "I'll help you," began to lift up the bulk of her things and walked them hurriedly up the coach steps to the interior, leaving but a fraction for me.

"Bye sweetheart. I'll tell daddy as soon as I'm back that I caught you."

"Bye Charlie. I love you."

Suddenly as we left the depot switching yard my memory took backward flight to a time not long passed. It too had to do with a train. Nenia and I would catch the one at noon going westward, our sights set on a neighboring town to see a picture show, there arriving at one o'clock where we'd begin our walk of less than two blocks to the Ritz theatre. We wanted to see a second show at another theatre and would have but time refused to allow it. At four we'd catch the train bound eastward for home. Forced to select between the two the Ritz invariably ranked as first choice.

That was then. Now we were older, young man and woman thinking thoughts that young man and woman think, so in love, me holding her soft delicate hand in mine, and trading generously given kisses and laughing and joking and talking with abandon. Every once in a while we'd adjust our seats and lean back and listen, listen, listen to the rhythmic clatter of the rails, steel on steel, rat ta tat tat, rat ta tat tat. Sometimes she opened her eyes and looked over at me with rising excitement, "Aren't trains so romantic," very soon afterwards suggesting that we go to the diner car for coffee. Sometimes in a mood of play she would suggest something a little more bizarre. "Why don't we tell the conductor to tell the engineer just to keep on going, to not stop at all in Saint Louis?"

"Where then would we stop?" I asked in a doodle of play.

"Oh. New York. Have you ever been to New York?"

"No. But I don't think we'll make it on this trip."

I felt my eyes smiling over at her, amused a little, my thoughts being that she still had a fair share of early girlhood rummaging around inside.

She answerd. "Neither do I. But we might sometime, might we not?"

"We just might."

She did not easily remain still for long, if not suggesting that we visit again to the diner car, then tugging at my arm to share with her a magazine story that she presently scanned, and if not this, "Look, look, Ramsey," as we were racing through some town that appealed in particular to her fancy, "aren't those precious little houses over there?"

The train roared onward toward Saint Louis, near the last Nenia's excitement beginning to wane, talking hardly at all, and a little further on she sighed and reclined in her seat as far back as it would let her and there fell off to sleep. The train kept stopping at small towns to let off and take on passengers, who were forever scudding frantically to reach a seat, once finding it setting their possessions on the racking above. The coach seethed with people. I'd never seen the likes, in any event not in my train travels back home. The constant grating of shoe soles on the flooring produced an irritable unpleasantness, and I figured it might awaken Nenia, but she slept through it. I bet myself that no language anywhere was likened to that of a crowded train coach. The voices covered the full range, some coarse and heavy, some light and shrill, and all put together amounting to a mass of jumbled, unintelligible infusion. But still, somehow, they functioned and got to where they were going. The conductor in constant motion paced the isles, smiling and greeting, calling out "all aboard" when the train was on the verge of leaving for "Jefferson," or "Prairie View," or "Adamsville" and unfurling these same names when the train was making its approach to one or the other of the small towns, some if not a substantial many of the passengers preparing to disembark. Near the last the lights on both sides of the railway began to flick into view, the first of the houses, not markedly exceeding shanty size, sprinkled here and there, reminding me of the ones in the industrial district of Chicago when I tagged along with my father and John Eric as a young boy, and grew massively thicker as we chewed up more mileage, obviously on the outskirts of the city of Saint Louis and sensing as much Nenia sat up and looked over. She smiled listlessly, as if trying to awaken. And yawned.

"We're here, aren't we?"

"Just about."

The screeching of the wheels ceased. The train halted. Looking out the window Nenia released a joyful murmur at the sight of her sister standing with her husband as close to the coach steps as they dared. As soon as Nenia's feet touched the last rung Thelma gathered her into her arms, uttering, "My baby, my baby, you're here," taking on with ecstatic happiness and hugged and kissed her repeatedly. Claude, Thelma's husband, at that intermission tactfully pushed folks aside on his way to me to help with the belongings, the both of us introducing ourselves. When the women finished with their embraces Thelma turned to me and we exchanged introductions. She hugged me and I hugged her back. She said in the old, overworked cliché that my name had been uttered in the family circle so often that she felt she already knew me. I returned that I was familiar with her name too through my affiliation with the family, chiefly meaning Nenia of course, and that it pleased me greatly that they had invited me as a guest in their home. We then loaded the car with Nenia's packings, which were rather massive, together with my suitcase and climbed in and set out winding across the city, in not but a stretch reaching a residence they called home. The actual mileage proved less than it seemed. They lived in an upscale community known as Suburbia East in a fine expensive home immaculately kept and tastefully furnished. This I expected. A maid servant had prepared dinner well in advance, setting it out when instructed on an ornate table of teak wood over spread with a fabric of linen appropriately enhanced with an interesting hodgepodge of arabesque symbols, all of it being foreign to my repertoire of knowledge. At a moment of privacy Nenia explained in answer to my question that her sister imported these ornaments from the mid east and that the symbols on the table linen were Arabic in origin. In that I sat next to her she unnoticeable to the others lowered her hand to mine with little quickie grasps and squeezed, supposedly, she later told me, to lessen my apprehensiveness which surely comes to bear when one is in the presence of hosts never before seen. She read me correctly. It wasn't hard to do. My nervousness showed. After dinner Thelma led us to the drawing room where she drew out a montage of photographs of the Stoddards in earlier days. There sat Mr. Stoddard, erect and stoic and militaristic, surrounded by the family, Gaylon there too, sitting by his father, my first to see him. I judged his age at fifteen years. I didn't ask but wondered at Thelma's transcending the farm surroundings once part and parcel of her life to rise to her current state of culture and judged in the same current that she harbored a determination to see her little sister elevate to still a higher plateau. It ran through me clearly that she would in the likeness of a compass guide her in her educational pursuits. We sat looking at the photographs, many photographs, and varied, until the hour turned late, late in the sense that we were to get up early the next morning, Nenia and I, and ride with Thelma on a tour of Saint Louis University, followed by an exploration of as many of the old historic buildings and other displays of the city as time permitted.

"They're Catholic you know," said Nenia.

"I know."

"They're a great university,"

"Yeah. They are. I've read about them."

"Wish you'd join me."

"I wish too. But can't right now. Who knows? Sometime maybe."

Chapter 20

WHEN I lay down to sleep I turned my head first this way then that scanning the room, notwithanding the vaulted ceiling, settling my gaze on two objects of especial charm, first a simple but exotically sculptured pitcher fixed inside a bowl of white marble, and second, a painting of "The Beguiling of Merlin," showing Nimue, the Lady of the Lake, holding the infatuated Merlin who unwittingly had wound himself into a trap and now read from a book of spells. I encountered Merlin and the Lady in my high school studies and later readings, their undying novelties as strong as ever in this ingenious masterpiece affixed to the wall for onlookers to peruse and curiously examine. When I had laid there for awhile longer, I suddenly detected the door to my room edging slightly open and then Nenia stole through, tip toeing to my bedside in her nightgown, there bending over and kissing me fresh on my lips

"Shhhhhhh," I barely let out, putting my fingers to my mouth, urging quietness. "You'll get me in trouble with your sister."

"No I won't. You let me handle her."

And then gaining courage I reached and gathered her to me, with her letting out a tiny giggle and tapping my face with her fingers.

"Fresh. I'm going. Goodnight."

The campus appeared as most campuses, pretty, green, well kept, and depicting a varied architecture, Gothic, Colonial, French, Spanish, old English or modern American. Starting late we drove hither and yon throughout the campus, a fascinating sight indeed, but I hoped we wouldn't miss seeing the interior of the magnificent buildings, and I was not disappointed for we in a relatively short while commenced our visit of the inside of a good many.

Of notice to me on the outset a structure of colonial design jutted outward on the west side of the campus that the founders I presumed named the Dubourg House, a place of residence for students but not for Nenia. She would stay with Thelma and Claude during her first semester. The next building, truly an icon also, they called the Samuel Cupples House, a Romanesque forty four room mansion built in 1888 of Colorado purple stone, with a further adornment of twenty two fireplaces. People referred to it as a visual feast.

A statue in memory of Saint Ignatius stood mounted on the frontage near one of the main passageways. It was built of darkened stone or metal. I wasn't sure which. The Saint held a staff in one hand, a Bible in the other. Not far away from the famous statute in a grove of trees there sounded a barely audible trickle of water from a narrow man-made meandering stream. It occurred to me that the Saint might have liked this enhancement were it to have gotten built and made functional in his day.

As we passed through the information center we were given a hand book by the curator which read that Saint Louis University was a private educational Jesuit university founded in 1818 by the Most Reverend Louis Guillaume Valentin Dubourg, and that its doors opened to African Americans in 1944. Nenia said that such information conveyed nothing of consequence to her, for she'd always been integrated in her heart and likened to Sophocles the reknowned Greek playright regarded herself as a citizen of the world.

She elatedly looked forward to enrolling at the university. It made me happy for her. Their philosophy in every element seemed right for her ideals. I wished that I could have stayed and gone to school with her, but knew realistically that my wish amounted to nothing more than a half real daydream. I spoke that my train would leave the station at one o'clock, allowing us but a trifle of additional time, and after this we dropped by Thelma's for my suitcase, hurrying from there to the train station where we commenced to wait. I urged Nenia not to stay until I left. She objected. I won the debate and kissed her goodbye, and then they began to drive away. The train rolled in on schedule and as soon as it braked to a stop I climbed aboard. Within minutes there occurred a thud followed by a series of vibrations that began near the engine, which rippled through the whole line of coaches until reaching the last. The train moved creepingly forward, then gained speed and more speed, taking but minutes to leave the central core of the city and roar through the suburbs, shortly crossing into open country. I leaned back in my seat. All at once it hit me. Loneliness. Even with scores of people around me. As the fog horn discharged its moldering blast when approaching the last crossing on the southern edge of Saint Louis I began to settle in for the time consuming journey that lay ahead and almost immediately fell into randomly dwelling on a myriad of things, but mostly on the girl, my once youthful playmate of years past, that I'd left behind.

"She's wonderful in every regard. Goodness runs through her soul. She is from the finest of families, rural folks and farmers, people of steady stock. What a splendid wife she would be, what a splendid mother she would be, so settled and calm and solid of judgment. Untroubled by life's confrontations. Nothing gets under her skin. All men need a woman like her. How intelligent she is. She'll set the woods on fire at the college. And she is remarkably beautiful. So evident the first time I ever saw her. She was very young then, not yet in her teens. I know she loves me and no one else. I've not once heard her say she has an interest in someone else. But naturally she wouldn't. The guys in high school must have run persistently after her though. Who wouldn't? The guys at the college will for sure. I guess I'm foolish for thinking of love and all, and marriage too. But that is years down the road. She has to finish college, four long years of it, and I have to start considering college myself. I can't stay too much longer with what I'm doing. Leland understands. Besides, he'll transition on to something else in time. He's too gifted not to. I've heard him mention the Kaiser Company. He's thinking they're his next stop. We'll see. Well, she's there and I'll reside at home for awhile, thus, we'll have no choice but to settle for nothing more than some letter writing. Of course I'll run up to see her in between times. I'll miss all those books of hers that I've enjoyed reading but I can drop in on her parents and borrow one or two when it's handy. She's a smart girl. Really smart. Reads all the time. Deep stuff too. What is it that she's forever citing? 'For every heart there's a love.' That kinda fits us, doesn't it?"

After watching the loading and unloading of passengers until I lapsed into boredom I tried falling off to sleep, leaning back in my chair with hope of blotting out all other intrusions, the noises of the passengers and my constant thoughts of Nenia. I wasn't successful. Soon I lifted from my suit case a book and began to finger slowly through the pages, a satire by Voltaire, the title of which was Candide. The story is characterized by its sarcastic tone as well as by its fantastical fast moving plot. It was published in 1759, and since, has been widely published in English versions. Candide is the central figure in the story although his mentor Pangloss is given a prominent role as well, who forever proclaims, "All is for the best in the best of all possible worlds." When Nenia sprang into my life I fell under her regimen of reading, beginning on the average to crunch through two books of substance and depth each month. At this time I owned a substantial number on my own. I had earlier bought Candide and now it lay snug in my attaché case. I'd read through it in the few weeks past but would glance it again. I did for a while then laid it down.

I looked here and there at the people with an arousal of interest, studying their peculiarities; their faces, their clothes, their accents, their posture, their youth, their agedness, seeing that some were alike in some regards, but that most were different. "In some respects we're all alike and different at the same time. That's the way the Lord made us. Alike and different." I then returned to gazing about, centering on the massiveness of the jam packed crowd. I'd not seen that many together ever on a train down South. And then! "What is that I see there? What a pitiful looking face?" These things I asked myself when drawing bead on an old sickly man standing near the front, sickly, I say, though there was another feature which showed on his face in the character of an intermitten grimace, a cast of anger, which as soon as it appeared suddenly dissolved. I watched him with rapt attention for awhile, unvaryingly, and began to speculate. Had some one hurt him at one time or another? Had someone done him a bad deed? Did his gramacing portray offensive memories with which he now struggled? My notice had swept upon him before, when the crowds were thicker, when thereon I had felt tempted to get up and go over and offer him my seat and felt tempted still to make good on the act of kindness thar stirred in my heart. He stood close to me, near the exit door holding on to a hand rail. But just then someone with a heart of caring and compassion equal to my own or even better beat me to him. I smiled a smile at that. "Someone else has compassion too" From that moment on I began more closely to observe the old fellow, for example his dress ware, especially, a depressive slouchy coat too big for his body and white wrinkled trousers that settled as drooping folds upon the fleshless anatomy of his legs. I somehow wanted to help him. "But how? I know not one thing of him. But maybe money, a small amount any way." I nurtured an impulse to ask him of his destination, yet carefully, tactfully. "He's like all of us, all the time going somewhere. That's the way of people. Always going somewhere." Then suddenly I shifted to Nenia and Leland and myself. "We are too, but with a plan very carefully exacted in my opinion, a long range plan, and we are young, but this old fellow has none, not really, no more aim in life other than that which the welfare system has carved out for him. That's what can happen to us when we're old if we don't get ready for it, in other words saving a few bucks along the way. I hope he's suitably cared for."

These were the last of my ruminations before falling off to sleep, during which the old man left his seat and exited the train, which in my conscience I sorrowfully regretted. It had been seriously within me to sit down by him and strike up a conversation, if he were willing, and give to him a few dollars. I took it that relatives, or otherwise a responsible party, escorted him to the train when he boarded it and that others waiting at some embarking or disembarking point intercepted him upon the train's arrival, from there carrying him to his place of lodging.

Night had fallen, and soon I would step down the steps at the station frontage where my trip began, and start my drive back home.

Chapter 21

THAT MID fall, like a shot out of the blue—a shock, something remotely unexpected—Melissa Monett paid call on our place of business, at first seeming to appear there in a neighborly fashion, but showed with scant loss of time that she had more on her agenda than a mere social call. When I watched her crawl out of her shiny new Buick I deduced as much. As she neared entry to the building I met her and we spoke, this followed by her briefly glancing around at the men working and then asking if we could go inside the office. In the background Ozzie and Cavanaugh were banging on a piece of stubborn metallic of some sort, which engendered a noise not only unpleasant and distracting to her but to me as well, making it such that we couldn't converse with one another without asking for a repeat of what was said, so I gladly agreed that we should opt to the inside and upon our doing this I asked if she would excuse me briefly while I went into the wash room and cleaned my hands. At my beckoning she noticed the only suitable chair in our small not well kept office and sat down. The chair was a leather covered recliner and sizeable. When I finished washing my hands I returned and sat down on a hard wooden bench beside her. A chilly morning, she sat with her heavy black cloak pulled up about her. I asked if the cold bothered her. She said no. She had dressed nicely; her customary habit of course, the fragrance on her person sweet and pleasing as I breathed it in. It ran through me that no time in my memory did she look better. But I hadn't seen her in a while.

I wore white coveralls. Perhaps she liked them. They were clean and freshly ironed. She seemed to scan me for some reason. I didn't have an idea what because I'd heard that the item of clothing on a man catching a woman's eye the quickest started with the necktie and then the suit of clothes itself. I wore no necktie and definitely no suit. But it wasn't important to me what she saw, if she saw anything at all. As her eyes met mine she led off.

"How have you been?"

"Doing all right. Pretty well I guess I should say."

I went on, asking if she had something in mind that I could do for her, getting an explanation that she owned a tractor in need of repair, inquiring in the same breath whether Leland were around.

"No. Not today. He's not supposed to finish with a job he's doing until the weekend." Then it came to me. "She's fishing. What is she driving at?" When I put it together I surmised that she now debated whether to select me for the repair or sit it out until Leland returned.

"I badly need it fixed," she said in a voice of entreaty.

"Ah. Yeah. I see. Who owns it?" She could have said that it wasn't any of my business, no matter who owned it. But that wouldn't have been her, a lady too tactfully elevated for that. And besides, I held the higher cards. She answered courteously and brightly that she owned it and then I ventured further.

"How did that happen?"

"At my father's suggestion I took some of my savings and bought a small farm, with a tractor thrown in extra as part of the deal," the latter tempting a silent snicker on my inside. I asked if she'd gotten a bargain in the deal and she answered without wavering, "Very much."

"Hmmmmmm. Well, we can handle your trouble. What do you think is wrong with the tractor? Do you know?"

"It starts but won't run. It won't shift into gear."

"I can fix that. But I'm tied down for another three days here. By then Leland will have returned and can help me. Or do it himself."

She frowned and wrenched her hands and twisted her fingers round and round.

"What's the matter?"

"It's supposed to rain tomorrow night or the next day and hay is on the ground. All over. What'll I do?"

"I don't know. There's an outside chance that I can break loose and do the repair. But I don't know."

She lit up. Suddenly happy.

"I said I might." I had spoken tentatively. Saying that "I might" did not mean sureness. "If I do it, tonight is the only opening I'll have and quite frankly I can't think of a soul to help me. I'll need help"

"In what way?"

"First, where is the tractor?"

"It's in the field where it broke down. It's next to the Murray farm."

"I'm familiar with the Murray place and your farm land too. I just didn't realize that it recently sold."

"I bought it last year about this time." I ignored her last remark or else paid no attention when she let it out. It meant nothing to me anyway.

"It's not too terribly far out there. I could tow it here where I'd have good lighting but towing is in and of itself a hard thing to arrange. Better to do the work out there I'm supposing. But I'd need help."

"In what way?"

"Someone will have to hold the lantern and hand me tools when I ask for them. And do other things. But I don't know!" There's much more to the repair than you might think. Perhaps your father can put his finger on someone to take care of your problem. He just—."

"No, no," she protested tactifully. He says not to bother him with my farm troubles and that he told me that when I bought the property"

After a moment's silence I felt myself relenting. "I'll see what I can do. Call me in a couple of hours."

She telephoned not in two hours but in one, her voice hopeful and excited as she immediately put in that I should look no further for assistance with the repair, that she understood the troubling task of my finding someone who could truly do as I expected and that she would help me. She added moreover that attempting to track down someone else to join me would simply amount to a wasteful effort. An impulse came to me to thank her for her generous willingness to back me up. I could not help being seized by surprise and admiration at this rising spirit of bravado and by flick of mind wondered at her conjuring up a challenge so adventuresome. But I cautiously held back from brushing her offer aside. If I undertook the job I would need help; I had considered using either Ozzie or Cavanaugh, but reversed the notion, realizing from the moment she earlier pled her case that morning that they were immovably obligated to finish the work that Leland laid out for them before he left, dead set on seeing it completed upon his return. I wouldn't dare draw them off. No solution seemed forthcoming by dwelling further on the matter of securing help and in the finale I saw but one choice. It was Melissa or no one. I'd talked to two mechanics already, and struck out; "Man we're swamped," they said, which mattered but little, because I knew in advance they were ineptly versed in the intricacies of transmissions, the clear and undoubted cause of the breakdown. I'd do it myself alone, with Melissa helping in whatever way she could. I should acknowledge that I began to view her not in terms of her liabilities but for her certain strengths; she would do as asked with no talk back, as would likely have been the reverse were I to have saddled myself with an unskilled, stubbornly inclined unknown mechanic, and she brimmed with a wealth of intelligence. After all, she was a science teacher.

"All right. I'll take you on. We'll leave at five."

"Wonderful. I'll see you there on the dot. And I do mean on the dot. There's no such thing as being tardy. If you're tardy you are unpardonly tardy. And I will not let you say that of me."

"I'll bet that's so."

"What will I wear?

"Whatever you'll feel comfortable in."
"I'll decide."
"Sure."

Chapter 22

I ASKED OZZIE and Cavanaugh to give me a hand with packing the tools, two lanterns inclusive. Suspecting that the nightly atmosphere might bring with it an unfriendly chill, by far greater than that in daytime, or worse, I called Melissa to suggest that she pack extra blankets for keeping herself warm. She came to the shop at five or an inkling before, not but a slight in advance of sundown. She wore a heavy jacket and a full blown skirt, lamenting that she searched her home throughout for an army jump suit but found none, remembering that Melinda borrowed it and hadn't as yet returned it to her. The blankets she'd brought along were sufficient I adjudged. She was eager, uplifted, and ready to go.

"You act as if you're all pumped up."

"I am. Which truck are we going in? That one?"

She looked across the parking lot at several but pointed to the red pick up.

"Yep. That's it. I'm ready. Let's go over and climb in."

We pulled away. At that very same time I began an inventory in my head of the equipment and tools necessary for carrying out the work, most singularly thinking of the jacks. They were a must. I stopped.

"I need to make sure that the jacks are in the back of the truck."

"They're there. I can see them," she said, stretching as high as she could to peep out the back window, tracing the rays of her flashlight. I smiled, and she smiled back. She'd proved her alertness at spotting and remembering equipment and tools.

When we pulled into the field there was the tractor still and dead like. I crawled out and strode over to it, finding the key left in the ignition. I tried starting it and after a begrudging grunt or two, rrrrrh, rrrrrh, the motor sprang into life, smoke pouring out the exhaust spreading all over. She'd been right. The gear shift wouldn't budge when I attempted to forcibly move it in any direction. Dark began to close around us, which prompted my lighting one of the lanterns, with her anticipating that I wanted the other one lit too and did it before I asked. Then I quickly did my diagnosis. I'd done it a hundred times, or no telling, so it wasn't difficult; it was easy. A zombie could have done it I thought to myself if he were fortunate enough to have been trained under the guise of Leland Gurov. We needed a bearing replacement for the transmission and a connecting joint for the drive shaft. I told Melissa that I wasn't entirely sure which of the defects I mainly blamed for causing the trouble but that replacing both parts future breakdowns were vastly minimized. We would have to return to the shop for the parts and I now anticipated a lengthy stay in the open air for the better portion of the night. When I told her as much she chipped in that her thoughts were the same and that she'd stick with me every minute doing as I expected. When we came back from the shop we both crawled under the tractor, with her pushing by lying on her stomach and handing the lanterns to me for placement. We'd open up the transmission chamber first.

"Ummmph," the sound of an unintelligible emission, something of a grunt, a sigh, and murmur intermixed, as she edged closer to me, pushing with her legs and pulling with her arms, and flat on her stomach. She drew in a breath.

"Are you okay?" I asked.

"I'm fine."

"No need to work fast at this Melissa. We'll have to take our time."

"Unh hunh."

And there we were, on our backs looking up into the belly of the framing, the motor only slightly above us, grease and oil oozing down our hands and arms and onto our sleeves, a gummy slime not then removable. We'd have to wait for that. It seemed not to bother her. "What spunk. Looks like I've stumbled across the perfect helper. I'm amazed." When I asked for a wrench or whatever she at once lifted it from the tool box and handed it over. We said little to one another, just concentrating and working. At first she seemed careful not to touch her arms against me, timidly in avoidance, but then began to soften, less cautious. It got so that if she dropped a tool on my other side she'd hurriedly reach across me with no reservation to retrieve it. We were cramped together as if in the cockpit of an airplane, unable to move the slightest unless pressing against one another. I think I might have tried to hide my smile a little when I realized that she began to fully accept the constriction.

More than eager to please, she instantly adjusted the lantern when I asked her. I cannot begin to count them, the numerous times that I called upon her to do this or that thing. Sometimes my arms became tired to the extreme from holding a part straight upright that I'd ask her to assist me by keeping it in place while I tightened a bolt or bolts that held everything in place. Sometimes she'd have to lean across me to accomplish her assignment. Sometimes we'd rest. We had to.

The work was excessively dirty and greasy, slimey, putrid slimey, and I began to wonder how her endurance was holding up to it all. Once when I looked over at her a smudge of grease traced down her face which escaped her detection and I failed to hold back the urge to laugh.

"Why are you laughing?"

Without explaining I just drew a cloth from my pocket and gently wiped the smear away, slowly, unrushed, admittedly extending my effort to a longer duration than necessary, during which she stayed prayer time quiet and immovably still, her lips faintly open as if she actually liked it. When finished I purposely held up the cloth for her to see the oily smut that I cleared from her skin.

We were in our second rest period, after midnight I'm sure, when she mentioned that she packed sausages and biscuits for us, and that they would go quite agreeably with the hot coffee filled to the brim in the thermos that she brought along. I more than gladly agreed.

"Absolutely. What a nice surprise."

I wasn't surprised. I'd better than half counted on her packing not necessarily these eatables but others for certain, and drink. And I didn't deny my hunger. The transmission work over; the tractor would move now, and the next step called for the drive shaft correction. It seriously dawned on me that the tractor needed a new drive shaft, for the old one showed a crevice that cautioned of future breakage and not long in the making. When we finished with our refreshments, we commenced the second task. She asked if there were more grease and oil with which we'd have to contend, with me offering persuasions that she should have no concern, that she would discover that the really messy lubricants were by and large lessened. For awhile she would have to help me by applying far more physical exertion than that previously, balancing the heavy jack so as to prevent it from tilting, while I did adjustments and fitting and tightening, and if asked, which happened more times than I liked, held a section of the shaft up right. But I almost instantly stopped her. "Too heavy. You'll get hurt." She backed away. I feared that I'd let her strain herself.

"You'd better lie down for a stretch."

"All right. But only for a little."

Chapter 23

FROM THEN on I reduced her assignments to holding the lantern to an angle that admitted light on the area where needed. I'd keep the tools by my side. She wouldn't have to reach and tug anymore I assured her. She touched my arm and said something to the effect that she appreciated the tenderness in my heart to see after her. She lay there for awhile flat of her back, merely watching, the lantern on the ground by her side, which shone brightly enough for me to do my work without her holding up any tools or appliances which theretofore were crucial. From a side long view, I must confess, I from time to time caught her bosom easily rising and falling and I did not need to stretch my imagination by much to see her not as a woman at about age thirty, or a little better, but in her beginning twenties. She possessed a handsome physique. Naturally I hadn't seen it from this vantage before. But I quit looking and in the meanwhile she sank into quietness. I thought she'd fallen off to sleep. When my eyes trailed slowly over to her I discovered she hadn't, all the while peering off and on into my face, as if somehow making a study of it. She blushed, her pretty eyes dazzling, and turned away to the lantern with a pretense of adjusting the flame.

"You should pull the blankets up over yourself. Aren't you cold?" I did this to lessen her embarrassment.

"I don't need the blankets. I'm all right. I need to get back to helping you anyway."

I assured that I could do all right without her assistance at this stage, tightening the fittings and setting in place the cover plate. She insisted on helping nonetheless. I let her. She held up the lantern when asked and placed tools into my hands now and then, and as we moved along I found it convenient to turn every once in a while and glance flittingly into her pretty eyes, especially pretty in the lantern glow, large and unfathomable, seeming always as if quietly wondering something. Only Heaven knew what. I wondered too, not only with respect to what she was thinking but about something else equally mysterious.

"Why suddenly is she so different from the rest of the Monett's? She doesn't seem as if she's a part of them. And in a way she's not. More gentle, nicer, truer, a real person. A far cry from her sister Melinda. But she's clever. I know that. Yet for that I can't fault her.

It's strange that we're out here like this. Under this tractor with her pushing and pressing against me and me her. What does she think of that? Leland says that someone spoke of her frigidity. I don't see that in her at all. She's very warm and very sensual too I have to admit. I don't think that's her intention. She just is. I'm curious. Does her husband know she's out here with a young man of my age? Of course he does. I'm sure she told him. But that doesn't matter. She's the boss I hear. And he's a little on the meek side. I wonder if she loves him. Surely she does. They have two children going on nine and ten, or thereabouts.

As to age? Let me see. I don't exactly know in terms of years but I'm younger by a stretch. How can a woman like her have a straw's worth of seriousness about a younger guy? Making it worse is the fact that she once taught me in school. But just the same, I wonder. And what other man in town would she allow out here with her? I do wonder about that too. It's strange all right. Oh well. Why not forget all this? After tonight, I'm unlikely to see her again for a long while and even if I do, so what. She will have forgotten everything happening out here because there wasn't anything to it to begin with. She'll pass me on the street with nothing more offered than a hollow emotionless hello, from there going on her way with her nose skyward and sophisticated head bearing absolutely no consciousnes that I'm even alive.

But still, I can't forget. I can't possibly forget the softness and gentleness of her hands and arms as she reached across me. She couldn't have done that without at least something revolving in her head as to how that might have affected me.

Well, there's one thing that happened out here tonight for real. I'll see her in a changed light from here on. And I actually find myself liking her. That's what happens when two people suddenly are plunged close together who don't have the least bit of affinity for one another at the beginning but shortly do. But as for Rupert and Madeline and Melinda, all will remain the same.

Will she tell her husband of this night? She won't. Especially not of the moments of intimacy. She's made of a different cut. She'll keep it to herself, just as she's sure I'll keep it to myself."

When the work ended she crawled from under the tractor and stood up in the moonlight, stretching, with me following, after which I climbed into the driver's seat and started the motor and began to drive in a limited back and forth space to determine that there were no flaws which escaped my scrutiny. I heard no odd noises; all seemed well and properly working. The gears shifted easily and without evidence of binding or grating. A smile settled on my face. "Runs smoothly" I said, then jumped down and commenced to gather the tools and equipment, assuming we were soon on our way home. But she stopped me.

"Let's have another cup before we go. We're in no hurry, are we?"

I could have chuckled. We'd been there much of the night and the clearest of logic prevailed in my conscious that she was worn thin, but yet she wished to stay longer. "Fine," I said gladly, a current of warmth surging through me. We sat down side by side on the grass in that late hour and rummaged through various and sundry topics and subtopics. In forethought she placed the lanterns in front of us, and the thermos next to them. The nightly breeze had picked up in intensity. The shadows from the lanterns stole mistily across her face, trickling playfully through her hair. It was cropped in terms of style, or pixie cut, as they called it in that era, now beginning to grow out. As the conversation progressed she came to Leland and myself, expressing a widely known observation, that we were bosom friends and that we wisely pooled our intellect and energy and thereby had risen to more than just commonly successful businessmen in the community, to which I added the necessary correction that we were successful by some measures all right but that the recognition for it belonged to Leland and not to me. I further added that it indeed worked to my good fortunate that I met him at an age, a very early one, when he was about to explode into success.

"He's from the Mideast, isn't he? That's what I've always heard."

"He is pretty much. But it's more accurate to put it that his parents are from Southeastern Europe, from Bulgaria if narrowing it down to specifics. They're not from the Mideast. And Leland isn't from there either. He was born in New Jersey."

"Hmmmmm. That's revealing."

I surmised that she already knew or else would have responded with a stronger exclamation. With a minimal pause she went on to tell me that she'd heard his father planned to terminate his employment at the arsenal, that he'd fulfilled his contract and asked, "Do you know first hand about this?"

"I do. Leland spoke of it some weeks ago."

"Are they unhappy here, he and his wife?"

"Do you mean in our neighboring town? That's where they live."

"That's what I mean."

"I can't say. I'm seldom in their company. Leland says they've fretted ever since their arrival in the vicinity about the shortages of places to worship. The nearest church of their kind is nearly a hundred miles away in Memphis. Driving that distance could get badly tiring and terribly expensive. They'll welcome a return to a big city."

"Where are they going?"

"To San Francisco I hear."

The temperature had dropped appreciably by this hour prompting her to gather the blankets closer around her, noticeably tucking them tightly about her neck as well in an effort to block off the slightest vestige of the unpleasant nightly air. And after this leaned her face into the cup of her hands and yawned, looking over at me and smiling with her eyes. I guessed that she did it to feign a cover up, to shield her admittance that sleep tried hard to overcome, although her liveliness of interest in the exchange hadn't diminished, not by a spec.

"What is their religion?"

"Leland has always said it's Eastern Orthodox, which is close to the same as the Roman Catholic Church."

"I'm not sufficiently grounded in their doctrines; I have to confess. Frankly, I'm insufficiently knowledgeable of the tenets of my own church, which is the Church of Christ."

"I see. I read of it on every chance, the doctrines of the Eastern Church I should say. Not as much as I like but I do read. Leland and I get into the subject sometimes. He laughs and says in playful deference that I'm eons ahead of him. But he has it backwards."

"Tell me. In a nut shell what is it that his church advocates above all else." She appeared sincere. It showed in her countenance.

"Above all else? Goodness. Think of the immensety of your question. That would likely take a long seasoned, long bearded wise old priest the better part of a day to answer. I couldn't begin to answer you. Not sufficiently anyway. But I can briefly touch on it. They teach that they are the One, Holy, Catholic Apostolic Church established by Jesus Christ and his apostles almost 2000 years ago. Their lineage is traceable back to the apostles through the process of apostolic succession. One might easily contend that they are only by a fine thread in belief different from their Roman Catholic brethren of the West."

I'm confident that I impressed her, yet if she'd pursued further she would have discovered me rather limited, severely limited in comparison to scholars of religions of the world. But as time passed I began more avidly to dig into the scriptures as well as into a diversification of religions with far greater effort and diligence than did I currently; and had I then these studies in my repository of knowledge I would have gladly continued. But I did not. And so, with her peppering me with an onslaught of other questions, with minor input herself, we in time launched into that fertile field of good and evil, into that quarry of conflict which woman and man are ever ready to engage in banter.

"Ah! And what is good and evil?" she asked.

I did not consider that in a split second I could answer as I wanted to answer, for that reason delaying and contemplating and then, slowly, "Good and evil grew up with one another, and the knowledge of good is interwoven with evil with such extremity that their resemblances are hardly separable. They easily fall into one another's laps."

"Interwoven? Is that what you said?"

"Yes. Much likened to intermixed seeds, requiring incessant labor if they are culled and separated. Which is a terribly difficult thing."

"Why do you say that?"

"Both have to coexist. They do coexist. They have since the beginning of Adam and Eve and have dwelt amongst us ever since. And here is the divined reason I suppose. We can't know good unless there is a scale of evil against which it is assessed. What do they say? 'It was from out of the rind of one apple tasted that the knowledge of good and evil, as two twins cleaving together, leaped forth into the world. And perhaps this is that doom which Adam fell into of knowing good and evil, that is to say of knowing good by evil.'"

We could have talked on and did contuinue for an interval longer, until we both, tired and in need of sleep, called it quits, climbing into my truck and driving away. If she felt the same as I the encounter through which we that long night passed must have seemed to her of the most unexpected character, going on a course that neither of us could have dreamed at anytime before. Streaks of thin red fingers shone faintly visible in the east, dawn on its way. When she left for her car she reached her hand to mine and squeezed, with words coming from her lips that she'd stop by to see me at work sometime; I said that I'd like that.

I did not fall instantly off to sleep when I reached my apartment and tumbled into bed. Nenia suddenly hovered over me. "Why do I think of that lovely girl? I am seized by a trickle of guilt. There is none. Nothing at all took place between Melissa and me. Only slight incidental touches." Soon I rolled over and returned one last time to Melissa before lapsing into dreamy slumber. "She is home with her husband and children and the events of the night just past, now so fresh in her memory, as they are in mine, will in short while fade from her visage and mine." I lied to myself, not inclined in the faintest that either of us would forget, feeling it immensely real that the Lord and the Devil were both with us under the tractor in the course of the night and that the Lord won, but could not firmly allege to myself that He would on our next encounter.

Chapter 24

THANKSGIVING DESCENDED upon us and then Christmas. Leland invited me to his parent's home for dinner on Christmas day. Relatives from some of the large cities from abroad were there, the larger fraction flying in from native Sophia. They'd spend a week or more. Catholic icons illumed everywhere, lighted candles reverently populating the walls and fireplace mantle. In advance of the meal a religious ceremony took place which to me in my limited understanding fell only slightly short of astoundedness. It was done liturgically in Old Bulgarian, they said, and in the liturgical and scriptural language of the Orthodox Church of Slavic countries. The ceremony, lofty and mysterious, gave forth a stream of beautiful thoughts and feelings, though I did not at all comprehend them. I sensed and judged by the intonations what they meant. Most of the folks there at some time had attended the great Saint Sophia Church in the capitol city and judging from what they said about the service it was beautiful and splendid, the great choir sounding every bit angelic. Leland revealed afterwards that the ceremony to him also exceeded his grasp but that he tried to understand it in order to please his parents, above all his mother. They served the meal in the fashion of how they did it in the old country, Mrs. Gurov emphasized, hugging me to show her affections for her son's best friend, and singing followed and music and laughter and incessant jibber jabber, all unfolding in the language and social style of the Bulgarian. Mr. and Mrs. Gurov more than once thanked me for my loving kindness shown to their son. I wanted to ask when they'd leave for San Francisco. But decided not.

The scenes at the Gurov's transferred in some ways as a replica to the dinner occasion at the Stoddard's, relatives there from near and far. Thelma and Claude drove down from Saint Louis, arriving a week after Nenia had separately made her way by rail. Their home bulged with people. Once Mr. Stoddard managed to draw a smile to his usual placid face while expressing joy that I'd chosen to come and join them, departing from his usual stoicness by stretching up from his chair and patting my shoulder. Nenia said to me when we stole away from the crowd that her mother prayed every day over the last few days that Gaylon would find it in his heart to return home with his family for the Holy season. He wasn't there. The weather had stayed pleasantly mild, and thus Nenia and I slipped away one day to the south side of the farm, near the river, riding the two saddle horses, with her riding the best of the two, the sorrel, but urged that I ride him rather than she. I refused.

"Nope. That's your horse. I couldn't do that. Besides, I'm not sure he's friendly with anyone else on his back. I only joshed. The truth was however that Charlie, soon after Mr. Stoddard bought the sorrel for Nenia decided to mount up and take a short ride, with no suspicion in the least that the horse would wheel and rear in a state of dire resentment, apparently, and on doing this very thing threw his head upward with some appreciable force, thereby catching Charlie full on his cheekbone who had now leaned forward. Charlie went sprawling. "Damn," they said he said, "Get my gun I'm gonna kill that sonofabitch right now." Mr. Stoddard knew that wouldn't happen and Charlie knew it too.

The sorrel loved the presence of Nenia from the start and I think it was undebatably true that no one could handle him like her. At least at first. As time passed the sorrel's disposition changed remarkably, from cantankerousness to friendliness and calm, attributes which Nenia had taught him they said. A good many of the sharecroppers on the farm had ridden him off and on since Charlie's unsuccessful debut, and aware of their successes I wasn't leery about riding him. I just felt that he belonged to her to the bottom of her being and that he was hers to ride and hers only. It was a compelling experience to see the dignity and grace with which she sat in the saddle, erect and elitish as I easily recall, when dressed in her fox hunt outfit. "Isn't she a beautiful thing" I said underneath.

"I wish you would ride him," she urged once more.

"Nope. No can do. Your father bought that horse just for you and I can't imagine what he might think if he were to see me on him"

"Ahhh."

Once we drove over to our neighboring town to shop, two days before Christmas, a last minute effort to buy. Nothing would do her but purchase additional gifts for her brother Charlie's children. She looked terrific in her fashionable red coat and dangling locks. It struck me that she had become more sophisticated yet considered that I somewhat imagined the change. But I actually did conclude that a few months suffusion of college life had prompted at least a modicum of change however slight. She would leave before the advent of the New Year; consequently, we tried to extract the most from her short stay. We flooded the movie theatres with our presence, stopping off afterwards for hamburgers at what was then called Ted's Drive In or at some other eatery similar to his. On her return to Saint Louis she would ride with Thelma and Claude.

At my own home, it was Christmas as usual, my brother and sisters there with gifts and cookings they'd brought along, the latter prepared and supplied to save my mother from the stress of long hours in the kitchen. It uplifted my father touchingly to see us all together. I winced at his condition, plainly declining since last I saw him, a span of less than two weeks past. My mother spoke of his ailing from a bad cold and that the affliction seriously hampered his breathing. It wasn't the cold that bothered me, at least not as much as something else; it was his overall weakened appearance, and his pale grey eyes that got to me. I dared not ask how he felt. He wouldn't have welcomed the gesture. Generally, he would have inquired in an attitude of enthusiasm of my work with Leland, yet not in the faintest getting close to that on this day. The thought came to me that he hadn't because he suffered too awfully from weakness and that in his decline his lucidity and power of intellect were greatly impaired. We children spoke of his condition to one another in an air of undisguised sadness. I returned the next day, the primary intent not to see in on him, but to raise the spirits of my mother, a ritual that I began to maintain with an involuntary practice of regularity. I went not less than every two days to see them both. Two of my sisters had lived with them until recently, but one had now gone, employed by a telephone company in a large city some distance away. My youngest sister remained.

That April I caught the train to see Nenia, something I failed to do during the first semester. I arrived at mid morning. We took the trolley to the heart of the city my first day there, visiting the glitzy department stores starting at noon and taking in a Broadway play that evening, *Teahouse of The August Moon,* a story of a young military officer with the occupation forces in the South Pacific who zealously set out to teach the natives all things American. It was my first Broadway play and overflowed with humor. I'm sure I acted not altogether as she expected when we left the theatre and began to stroll slowly down street.

I led off. "What a wonderful play. Witty and truly a piece of art. Yet isn't it sad. Think of it. A lot of people in this world will never see something like that; will never know one thing about it."

"I'm afraid you're right. My parents included. They wouldn't have a clue of what I would tell them if I tried to describe it. Especially my father. All they seem to have enjoyed is hard work and a cake walk supper once a year throughout their lifetime. I don't remember them saying anything ever at all of their going to a square dance when they were young"

"You mean before they were with children to see after?'

"I mean any time. Ever. They just seem to have missed the pleasant enjoyable things in life. If they did enjoy them I never heard of it. They only knew hard work. But isn't it a fine thing beyond imagination to think that at least in one moment of their life past they saw something like we've just seen. I very much wish my mother could have. I really do. Maybe she can sometime."

"I echo that" I enjoined. "Too bad it's only a dream. Still, they're glad their children could grow up and enjoy such wondrous fineries."

"Yes indeed. That's the good side, but not enough. They should have gotten to taste a little of the fine stuff themselves."

We soon stopped at a sidewalk café, her choice, where she said they served good red wine and delicious food, neon lights flashing as fireflies on the store fronts across the street and taxi drivers tooting their horns, impatiently displeased that the car in front moved too slowly to suit. On the street front where we sat people came and went, some jabbering non stop with one another, others alone, somber, looking aimlessly ahead. I thought silently that nothing anywhere was likened to the busy unending motion and noise of the city. "Almost Parisian or New Yorkish," I said.

"Yes!" she answered with a spirit of elation.

We were especially enraptured by the things that lent themselves to romance—the agreeable cool air of the evening, our quaint little table, and the candle lights in the middle. Happiness sounded in her every phrase as she began to speak of her campus life, revealing that she intended to move into a dormitory beginning with the next school year, so that she could get involved more into things. I felt lonely and left out at the idea of not being with her, conceiving also, I must say honestly, that the guys would swarm to her in droves in an attempt to win her over, as perhaps they already had. But I didn't tell her that. The next morning Thelma left to join friends at a breakfast social which left us alone. Her kisses were warm and sweet and melting and I found it almost too much to resist the fever rushing to my brain. The threshold of making love had dared to come dangerously close.

"You are very handsome," she suddenly said, holding the palm of her hand to the back of my head, "and very tempting. Ours, my sweetheart, I must admit, is an affaire de coeur that truly tugs at our souls. Mine anyway."

But it did not happen. The taboo stood powerful and prohibitive, still very much in force.

"Women surely flock to you. Do they?"

"No." I told a little white lie. To speak straightly with the truth and hopefully free of vanity I am disposed to say that I attracted my fair share of young ladies but found or took no time to engage them. I must confess, most surely however, that in that moment the night of the tractor stirred in the back of my mind.

"I hope not."

I could only stay for a day and a night in Saint Louis. Leland needed me back. Determined not to run the risk of missing my train, scheduled to leave at one o'clock, we left more than an hour early. Nenia chose for wear a dress of light blue polka dot that foamed loosely around her bodice, like a soft rolling wave I thought, and a jacket made of black chiffon which fitted nicely on her upper portion. And I did not miss the dalliance of her locks as they trembled and jounced when touching her shoulders. She looked as a picture; and penetrated deep into my heart. A trolley ran in front of the home and stopped at the end of the block. We stood and waited and soon one happened along. The experience of her half year or more in Saint Louis paid off. I hadn't the vaguest of where we were once we were aboard. Pretty soon she leaned against me and whispered that we were close to changing to another trolley. The second trolley was the same as the first, rambling along slowly and awkwardly, the wheels screeching eerily when stopping to let passengers on or let passengers off.

"Write me," she said softly.

"I do write you."

"I know. All the same it won't hurt to remind you. You can double your effort if you like. I do love your letters. I dearly do. There's something inherent in a letter that doesn't appear in any other kind of message."

"And what is that?"

"A letter has, oh let me think, yes, mystery and elegance. That's what it has. Yes, mystery and elegance."

"You amaze me. Who could have ever contrived that idea, except you of course?"

Screeching pierced the air again, mainly deriving from the jamming of brakes. "We're here Ramsey," she looked up and said, a trace of wistfulness showing itself. Then another screech ripped the air, but not as loudly as the first, and we stopped, at once descending to the pavement and beginning to walk to the boarding zone. I asked a porter for the arrival time of my train. "It's due any minute." he cheerily informed while narrowing a glance at the face of a fine shiny watch that he'd lifted from his pocket. In another ten minutes the train rolled into view.

"Kiss me goodbye," she said, reaching her open arms. I gathered her to me, holding her as long as time allowed, and then withdrew and started up the steps.

"Goodbye sweetheart; see you this summer," she called out, half succeeding at forcing her voice to rise above the commotion.

Upon climbing aboard and settling into my seat and riding awhile the gaiety of her laughter streamed softly into my conscious, sounding as a beautiful clinging echo. I wanted to go back.

Chapter 25

BACK AT home, I soon forced the major portion of my departure from Nenia aside. We were busy beyond the bounds of normalcy at the shop, business suddenly erupting, perhaps largely due to Mr. Carney's earlier working a deal with a lawyer who owned vast acreage, in the proximity of twelve hundred acres, and owned eight tractors. It approximated a copy of the Phillip Stoddard negotiation, excepting that the land size measured to a somewhat greater capacity in terms of acreage. He complained that the tractors were down more than up, his troubles finally reaching the hearing of Mr. Carney, who persuaded the attorney to let us tend twenty acres of his land, the size of a small farm, free of cost for two growing seasons provided we kept the tractors in good working condition for the same period. Mr. Carney further set down in the wording of the contract that the man must pay for the parts essential to the repairs and throw in one aging tractor as a gift. Growing cotton that year and the year next yielded profits extraordinaire; the weather remarkably friendly and the market prices driven upward by Europe's ever pressing demand for the raw material. I earned more from a percentage view point during those two years than I earned from several years combined in my long years that followed, and this took into account my positions of professional employment in the legal industry and some quite fortunate investments.

We were barely into the month of May, the month in which the spring rains fall soothingly and the flowers blossom and bloom and the buds of the elm and the sycamore surge to life. Leland and I had signed an agreement with the lawyer for repair of his eight tractors, in addition to receiving one of the eight as a bonus as well as twenty acres of land for cotton growth, the proceeds free of hidden subtractions in the contract, Mr. Carney seeing that such chicanery did not befall us. It bowled me over that things looked as spring sometimes does, bright and fresh and with breathly promise that all will continue to go well on the impending scene. Therefore, May should have delivered to me an abundance of happiness and joy, as it did in times past and would have again but for the specter that hung on the horizon of my intuition that seemed a mite wrong and I could not put my finger on it. I felt uneasy. "Only my intuition. Yep. That's it. Just that. Quit worrying." But it became more than that which was not long in the making. I remember well that I sat in a theatre on that evening watching a movie when someone tapped me on my shoulder bearing the message that I should rush home. My father had fallen seriously ill, collapsing and crumpling to the floor, the result of a stroke, uttering these, his last words, as he lay in near unconsciousness, "Why did I have to take sick?" The ambulance soon got there, with the attendants placing him inside and speeding to the hospital in our neighboring town, Meadville. The doctors overseeing his condition were as many small town doctors back then, only limitedly informed and trained, and no better, a high percentage markedly inept if today's men and women of medicine are used as a comparative barometer. No matter who attended him, I ventured, his life will have soon run its course and that the medicine men could not save him. He lay in state at his home for one day and one night, there being no reposing facility for properly accommodating the body in our community, and even if there were my mother would have opposed taking the body to it. This house belonged to him, this house belonged to her, theirs together, and in this house he would stay in repose until they came and transported him away for the funeral. During the day when he lay for observation and the paying of respect a few trickled in, the larger number at work, yet when night descended a deluge of the town's visitors drove up the narrow half dirt road to our house and came onto the front porch and inside to view the body. Most left their car motors running, their stay intentionally brief, a choice of necessity because of the light rain that fell and the long line of waiting cars carrying folks who also wanted to pay respects. My brother stood at the doorway greeting, his responsibility more than mine I took it in that he was older. "Look at the turn out; everyone in town has come," he remarked once when I stood close by. In his view, which is a common view in a small town, the greater the show of people to look upon a man lying in state the greater the respect they held for him while he lived. Only one place would do for conducting the funeral, the old church which my parents attended since my childhood, an edifice that proudly flaunted a New England steeple surmounted by a spire towering above a sharply pitched roof, and sides and frontage and back adorned with varied colors of crab orchard stone. Melissa paid her respects, once arriving crossing softly over to squeeze my arm and embrace me, the first time I'd seen her in a while and only then at a distance. Even if I had tried gallantly to repress it I could not have; I mean to say that even with the help of Heaven I could not have succeeded at blotting out that which I ventured beyond the least of doubt stirred within her; the same as that which stirred within me.

A minister, a dignified old gentleman whose son occupied a chair next to mine in grade school, preached the funeral, reflecting on the struggles that my father endured in his poor condition of health and his bad luck with financial burdens. While funerals are a must in our lives I nurture nonetheless an aversion to them. They leave us with a wonder of death and life, each in the same capsule, neither of which we understand. Perhaps if we in some amazing way learn to understand life, that is, why we live it, why we are here, we will learn to better accept death.

At the burial site the old minister proclaimed to the family that our father now resided in better hands and that this was as far as we could accompany him. And then he read from selected scripture. When he finished, the attendants lowered the casket and the hired workers started to fill in the dirt and of all people, I thought to myself, old Sam Mcvector picked up a shovel that the workers had temporarily tossed aside and feebly began to peck and smooth the dirt that covered the casket in the form of a mound, as if this would somehow make a difference. Sam, of a ripe old age, should have been sitting down somewhere rather than paying his last respects with a shovel in hand. Yet that was his way. In his heart he felt a need to do it. "Mr. Sam, you shouldn't do that" I said as honorably and deferentially as I knew how. I could find no better words. I don't think he heard me. He gave no appearance of it. He grieved. I knew that. The last scene that I recall at the burial site took place when as the crowd began to disperse the old minister sat on the passenger side of a vehicle en route to transporting him back to Memphis where he lived in a rest home. I stood close by the driveway as the car slowly passed. He looked pitiably forlorn and sad. Over the next several weeks we children inundated my mother with our presence, exerting our best to fill the great sorrowful void in her heart.

Chapter 26

THAT JANUARY, Leland and I fulfilled our contract with the attorney. Our obligations were met. Mr. Carney assured us that they were. And then we agreed on two significant decisions that we had opened up for discussion at various times, meaning that we'd taken some few years without coming down to hard concrete realities. We weren't hasty. We'd worked up to them steadily. I had decided to begin proceedings for entering the renowned University of Chicago, and Leland had set his sights on visiting the Kaiser Corporation in San Francisco to explore opportunities with them. The Kaiser people were keen on looking at his design capabilities with heavy equipment—cranes, bulldozers, military tanks, bridges of immense span, and even airplanes—and the notion, fresh and full of promise, of transitioning into these realms appealed much to his fancy. His father, already with Kaiser, convincingly promoted his credentials to the officials responsible for hiring ultra capable people and they without much hesitation reached the conclusion that adding the young man to the corporation membership would amount to a bonus many times over. It was a done deal. And it became evident to me and to Leland that when he left for his interview, now scheduled to shortly take place, he would likely accept an offer if made, and that on his next trip to San Francisco he was leaving to stay. So I prepared myself and started looking ahead.

"What is to happen to Ozzie and Cavanaugh?" I asked when we began to focus seriously on our change.

"They can do well on their own. We'll leave everything intact. At least for the time being. They're well trained now and Mr. Carney intends to stick around for awhile. He'll help them with contracts and record keeping."

"You've covered this with them in previous talks. I know you have."

"I have. They were stunned in the beginning. But they got used to the idea. They understand." It showed in his countenance and in his voice that he grievously hated the idea of leaving them. I felt the same.

"Well, if we're going to bail out what's to happen to the building? Ozzie and Cavanaugh can't buy it."

"No. They can't. My father says that Kaiser will buy it from us."

"Wow. Good. But then what?"

"They'll tear it down and sell the materials. Then they'll sell the land to the state. Or they might give the whole thing to the town just as it is."

"Let's hope they'll do one or the other. Otherwise—."

"Don't worry. They'll buy it from us my father assures me. Taking the property off our hands is not of colossal challenge to an outfit of that magnitude. It's nothing more than a pebble in the roadway. They'll write off the value as a gift. You know, to duck taxes. But for a while at least the Kaiser people will allow Ozzie and Cavanaugh to keep on using it."

There were other discussions additionally arising, the foremost of these concerning the sizeable deposits in the bank under our names jointly, which in the end were divided, though not fairly I felt, for Leland insisted on a fifty-fifty split, a ridiculous equation to me, for the project from the beginning was of his ingenuity and risk. Yet he would have it no other way than to divide with me equally.

"Our meeting in this life, Ramsey, surely became a reality through divination. Your friendship is worth more to me than all the gold of Solomon and that won't change. You have been my happiness. Besides, in our long years to go we'll compile more wealth than we'll ever know what to do with."

Months rolled by. Maybe a year. Leland left first. I hugged him goodbye at the railroad station where he caught a train to Memphis, there taking a plane to San Francisco.

"This is not goodbye Ramsey. We'll stay close through the mail or by phone, and I'll get back to see you and you'll come to see me."

"We'll make that a certainty. But you'll have to visit me in Chicago. That's where I'm planning to start hanging my hat."

"I know. I wish you heaps of luck in your new venture in the windy city."

"Ha. Yeah, the windy city, a pseudo name. Did you perhaps hear me refer to it as such?"

"No, no. I've heard it called that for years."

Arriving too soon, his departure eventually got there. We kept repeating goodbye chit chat, the train stubbornly taking its time about being on schedule, finally rolling into the station with its usual screeching and hissing, and after an ordinary delay the engineer sounded the whistle. Leland climbed up the steps and the train began to pull away. I just stood there watching for the longest, until the fading dark configuration of coaches and caboose crossed over the rise and out of sight. Suddenly a part of my life seemed to drain out of me. Without Leland around, my dearest and best friend since grade school, all would seem lonely and strange. With an uncomfortable dread prevailing upon me I opened the door to my apartment late that afternoon, a space, aside from the furnishings and scattered photographs on the off white walls, empty and hollow, and no longer resounding with laughter and tantalizing stories we once shared with one another. I toyed with my mind. "Is this all an illusion? Did there ever exist a Leland Gurov in the first place? No, this is no illusion. It's real. It's simply one of those severe undesirable aspects of living. But perk up. You'll see him again."

Summer had turned into fall. And with it came my impending departure for the university, the University of Chicago, my friends, not excluding my mother, possessing not more than a splotch of acquaintance with that famous mill of knowledge asked, "Why there?" I begin by telling that I had heard much of Robert Hutchins, the celebrated educator and it stood at the pinnacle of widely recognized universities, especially esteemed by the educated elite. Everywhere in the journals of academia they lavishly heaped praise on its liberal arts curricula; and equally that applied to the Great Books, which Hutchins implanted or guided into the core of undergraduate studies. Over the past few years I had read a sizeable portion of the Great Books, not all, but many, since Nenia stocked a set in her home, which her sister Thelma purchased following a visit with the Dean at Saint Louis University. She emerged from that meeting convinced that nothing would suffice other than her buying a set for her younger sister, the list encompassing the names of Montaigne, Cervantes, Milton, Paschal, Kant, Fielding, Montesquieu, Gibbon, Hegel, Goethe, Marx, Chaucer, Dante, Thomas Aquinas, Tacitus, Virgil; ah, a complete list is too exhausting to offer here, and the works of these fabulous authors were in their exorbitant richness accessible to my curious expanding mind. Hutchins himself was of fascinating stature. He fascinated everyone. Not that he matched the Great Books celebrities in creativity or in their giftedness of composition and depth of thought, but rather because of his religious background and his daringness to exact change on an institution which gained prominence long before his time. I landed there at the same relative period of his administration, pervasively influenced by his sway, as were a sizeable number of other youngsters. The moment that I set foot on campus I felt the current of his thoughts and philosophical influence. Not infrequently his name arose for bantering about by students and faculty. It is with this backdrop bearing upon me that I therefore pay court to this man, infused with a consciousness that I am remiss if I fail here to take that liberty.

Robert Hutchins was an educational philosopher, dean of the Yale Law School, 1927-1929, and President, 1929-1945, and Chancellor, 1945-1951 of the University of Chicago. While President of the university Hutchins implemented wide ranging controversial reforms, among them the elimination of varsity football. Football was a distraction, he emphasized. On the heels of abolishing football he worked to eliminate fraternities and religious organizations for the same reason. The most far reaching reforms impacted the undergraduate college, which he retooled into a system of pedagogy built on Great Books, Socratic dialogue, comprehensive examinations and early entrance to college; but however grand, his plan began to fade from prominence when he resigned from his ties with the institution in 1951. His outlook on extracurricular programs, football, fraternities, and religious organizations, is seen clearly evolving in his *University of Utopia*, perhaps a work overdone, wherein he writes, “the object of the educational system, taken as a whole, is not to produce hands for industry or teach the young how to make a living. It is to produce responsible citizens,” and further held, “the educational system should have a well defined purpose of promoting the intellectual development of the people” and lambasted educators for letting universities become nothing more than a trade school and a poor trade school at that. In his several writings he dwelt on the concept of justice and I was particularly attracted to what he had to say relative to this complicated domain of legalism, although never was I certain of his descriptions of its meaning. I have to admit in the same breath however that justice is a nebulous and elusive thing to phrase into words. Some have said that it is fairness. That’s close. One prominent member of the family of penmanship has written that “when young people are asked ‘What are you interested in,’ they answer that they are interested in justice, that they want justice for the Negro, that they want justice for the third world, and if you say, ‘Well, what is justice,’ they haven’t any idea.”

The university was on the whole a school of prominence, a school on a pedestal, and that compelled me foremostly, I think, to seek its environs, yet there were other reasons, almost equally as provocative. The city itself, the windy city, the gateway to the plains, itself rich in art and culture and commerce, where my father and John Eric took me when my age numbered to less than the fingers on my hands. And let me not discount the fact that the city of Chicago borders the shoreline of one of nature’s remarkable scenes, that is to say, the great Lake Michigan, whose waters are sometimes thrown by storms into a roaring torrent whereas at others they lie tranquil in a sea of magnificent greenish hue.

A week before I left for Chicago Nenia and I had decided to spend a while, an hour or thereabouts, on the Langstrup place, or what once was the Langstrup place, with Ozzie and Cavanaugh going with us, Ozzie driving the old red pick up which belonged to the business. Cavanaugh stood or sat in back on the wooden flooring. When pilfering through the remains of the old house which a bulldozer leveled soon after we, the family, moved to the Jeremy Dodson’s farm, we found a scattering of brick from the once standing chimney poking up through the earth, and that was all, and then left for the river, in quest of that exact parcel of earth where Leland and the rest of us had set up a saw mill. There were still vestiges left over, the stakes in particular that were driven into the ground for the purpose of serving as anchor ties for stabilizing the mill. Looking upward at the magnificent stately trees we three men especially regretted that Leland wasn’t with us.

“It don’t seem right without him,” said Ozzie, looking around this way and that, unmistakably a slight lost in the strangeness of the moment.

"No indeed, it doesn't. We'll miss that guy, badly, we can count on that, I agreed with a tad of melancholy.

We then stepped over to the river for a peek at the water, which wasn't flowing enough to say it was, the flow drastically affected by the shortage of rainfall. Someone said that fall resulted early that year, that the rain fell stingily and that the dryness promised to give farmers cause for alarm because the cotton harvests were destined to fall far short of the usual output.

"I ain't seen it this dry since going way back," said Ozzie, digging the toe of his shoe into the dusty dirt.

"Yeah. I'll echo that," I answered.

"Is there a danger of fires breaking out? "asked Nenia, wrinkling her pretty forehead.

"Maybe. But doubtful," I more or less assured.

"Let's hope for rain."

"Let's hope."

"But rain too can cause trouble with the cotton picking. We don't need much. Enough, but not too much." This was Ozzie. He then spoke again on a matter that the mention of cotton had apparently set off. I swallowed hard when I figured out what he began to tell us.

"Guess Warren Bethune is gonna miss Coon."

"Yeah. How is that?"

"Didn't you hear?"

"Hear what?"

"He's moving to Saint Louis."

"He is? Ah! I can't believe it. What's got into him?"

Ozzie then began to recount that late on the previous day in Jeremy Dodson's grocery store Coon Sampson, Warren Bethune's right hand Negro at the cotton gin, sat down on one of the several seed sacks with farmer white friends who happily welcomed his presence and considered him as an indelible part of the gathering. And he, like the rest, whether at lunch or at any time, bought his baloney sandwich and cold drink and made his way to the back and sat down on the seed sacks and talked and carried on with the rest. On this day things did not fare as well, a hot head unwanted but joining them, a war veteran someone said who'd migrated to our town after the war ended with no one appearing to have knowledge of where he came from nor why. They only knew of his reputation as a rabble rouser, a radical, prone to drinking and fighting and some said they believed him touched in the head, flying explosively off the handle at the tiniest thing, his eyes wild and face turning blood red. His name was Rainey; that's how people addressed him. As soon as Coon sat down Rainey grabbed a point 22 rifle from a nearby prop, cocked the hammer and threatened to kill Coon, spewing profanities of a most insulting diminishment, and Coon, frightened, shaken, fearing for his life, ran frantically out the back door.

"My stars," Nenia excitedly let out. "That's terrible."

No one asked Ozzie if he felt sure of what he'd said. No one doubted it. You can rest assured that we were shaken. Things like that weren't supposed to happen in our small town. I looked over at Nenia and shook my head.

"I hate to hear that. That's bad, very bad. And Coon Sampson is a good man. A really good man."

I intended to drop over and say goodbye to him before he left for Saint Louis, telling him how well I saw him in my sight, and did pay call, or attempted to, finding when I knocked on the door him gone, leaving at daybreak with his family and household furnishings in a fourteen foot long bobcat truck borrowed from Warren Bethune.

Chapter 27

IT WAS next to my last day before I left that another sudden unexpected interception sprang out of no where, though looking at the occurrence with hindsight I should have anticipated something like this happening. On starting up the street I vaguely detected a car pulling alongside me, the driver lightly tooting the horn. When I drew her into finer bead Melissa began to roll down the window and beckoned with her fingers for me to get in. I opened the door and did as she asked, expressing surprise at seeing her but acknowledging my happiness at her stopping off. She'd heard folks speak of my leaving and knew why and had it on her agenda to see me and say goodbye. She asked if we could ride around somewhere.

"That's good with me."

"Fine. We'll go out to the arsenal. I haven't seen it in a while." The arsenal, the war long in the past, now lay as a secluded reserve practically devoid of human presence. As I sweepingly thought it through it dawned on me that she chose the site for that very reason.

"Neither have I."

It was no distance of any length to the arsenal and we very soon arrived, driving first here and there, seeing nothing more than abandoned aging barracks row after row, each identified by a letter taken from the alphabet, and wide concrete runways or streets in between badly riveted with potholes. She pulled over, glancing quickly around to see if anyone happened to be close by; there wasn't, and this seemed to come to her as a relief. She talked a little rapidly, nervous I supposed, a bit affected by the suddenness of our being alone together again, and I suppose I talked too fast as well for the same reason. But we moved past that hindrance and settled into an air of ease.

"We're going to miss you around town," she sheepishly said, a blush breaking on to her face that she meant to restrain.

"I'll miss everybody too."

"People are forever going away. Especially the favorites." A piquant angularity danced upon her face as she looked over with unfathomable eyes.

"I'd like to think that includes me," I said with what I considered a natural return.

"You don't need to doubt. It does. Certainly from me."

I hardly knew where she hoped to lead with our conversation, especially in view of her last remark. I surmised without knowing for sure that it carried some sort of cryptic message. I wasn't about to ask her to interpret. It struck me as a shade unordinary that she had taken me to an out of the way place but I harbored no qualms with that. In fact I enjoyed being with her. I admit it. Every word she spoke slipped over her lips with a subtlety of intrigue.

"That's nice to hear."

"Good. I meant it in that sense," she said with tender emphasis.

I hadn't been around her in a while and thought she looked gorgeous. She wore a sleeveless white blouse, with her arms and face evincing that she recently had been exposed to the sun, yet wasn't overdone. Her arms were trim and muscular and attractive beyond the ordinary, more than seen in most women I adjudged. I was affected by a tendency to touch them. She would have caught any man's notice. I couldn't help but suddenly flash back to what I had periodically thought and silently said about her since that night under the tractor. "Melissa sits on that high stool in the bank where she waits on customers sometimes and at other times is seen by lascivious eyes when going throughout town with a look of elegance and coolness, the crude old men saying what they say when they reflect on women of enormous good looks, and say also that Melissa is frigid, as Leland once ventured. Fools! Dirty old men. If they only knew what I know. Of course that will never come to pass. They could look at me until Kingdom comes and couldn't guess a pinch of the secret I have stored in my head."

She talked freely enough, but there was obvious distractedness, lingering nervousness I took it, speaking words and lines disconnectedly, which to me in no way reflected her ordinary demeanor. As we continued she would subtly touch her hand on my arm, careful to do it while talking, as if making a point, leaving it there for a length, giving a pretext of being unmindful of even a trifle of intimacy. But she knew. She once turned on the radio, though on finding no music that she thought suited us abruptly turned it off. She continuously played with her hair, letting it down and pinning it back up. She had allowed it to grow out. I wondered of her husband. "She couldn't love him," it ran through me. Even so, I dared not utter his name, lest it kill the mood of the moment which I must say in honesty that I very much relished. Is it necessary to reveal that she charmed me? What bore upon me most fascinatingly was the realization that here I sat so very close to a woman of our town, strong and powerful and glowingly attractive, who kneeled with her heart to a younger man without status or reputation, in love or smitten with him whatever the cause, and would have engaged in complete love with him should the place of their recluse been better hidden. But love or infatuation, whichever it is, can wear a strange face, can it not, and in no way explainable through the employment of logic. What is the adage that has grown old from usage? "The heart has reasons that mind knows not."

In the interval of our respite we were lucky that no one chanced upon us, lucky for her more than for me. She stood to lose everything, I not nearly as much. With the passage of but little time, and without explanation, she turned on the ignition and began to drive away in another direction, taking the back roads, eventually reaching her farm where we repaired the tractor that chilly moonlit night. I looked over and smiled and she smiled at me.

"I felt you'd like to visit here again," meaning that she was liking it and was sure that I did too.

"Looks familiar. I'm glad we came."

We got out and strolled around for a brevity, reaching a small pond close by, where she picked up some pebbles and threw them into the middle of the water, except one which she handed to me with a teasing challenge that I couldn't duplicate her accomplishment. I took it and threw it aimlessly without effort and broke into laughter. The pebble veered to the left and extended but half the distance that she'd thrown hers. And then we returned to the car. She started the motor and turned on the air conditioner. The coolness upon my skin felt good, the weather earlier in the day uncooperatively turning from comfortable to hot. We talked on a while, neither of us getting closer to a kiss or an embrace, although I believe she wanted to, no, not believing but knowing she wanted to, and in the absence of amour and conversation wearing thin she turned to my going away.

"You're going to a prestigious school. You'll do well. I've always believed that of you. Everybody says you're a scholar. It's always showed."

The laugh that escaped my lips I hoped sounded modest. "How? When I teach the Sunday school class?"

"That and more. It's the stuff you read. You're a voracious reader. I know that."

"Hmmmmm. Well, I read for sure. I always did."

"I'll keep up with you."

"Thanks. When I'm home from college I'll give you an update as to my progress."

"I'll hold you to that."

An appearance of reluctance to leave showed in her voice when she said she'd have to go. Without her saying it I saw that she felt the urge to get back to the bank, wishing she could stay longer I knew but afraid if she did those at the bank might inquire of the reason for her absence.

"I hate to but I must go."

"I perfectly understand."

She then drove me by my apartment and dropped me off, kissing me lightly on my lips as she said goodbye.

Nenia, home for two weeks from Saint Louis, saw me off on the day of my departure; I drove, and for an hour or more we sat in the car going over, among other things, what the next school year entailed, she particularly taking interest in my course of studies, to which I gave limited comment other than indicate what she already discerned, that I would for the first term matriculate in studies that fell into the realm of liberal arts. Not a great deal was said of her endeavors, except that she'd enter her last year as an undergraduate, concentrating on English all the way through, and looked forward to receiving her degree in the first week of June. Up on her age by three or four years and only beginning college as a freshman awakened me to the realization that I should have graduated by now, much less going in, and regarded by my youthful class mates as an old man when I finished, if I ever did. It was enough to send a shiver down my spine. She hinted that she might pursue studies abroad in foreign language for a year once she graduated.

"Foreign language! What for instance?'

"French and Russian."

"Hmmm. That's odd."

"Not at all. The Russians of aristocracy, more particularly in the reign of Catherine the Great, chose to speak French. They admired the culture of the French. With this as a background I think it a fitting idea to learn to speak both."

"Why did I not ever stumble across that interesting fact of the Russian culture in my many readings, largely from your library?"

"Ha. My dear boy. You apparently failed to read the right book, and moreover, I don't believe there's a single one in my shelves at home that penetrates exhaustingly into Russian history."

It was not infrequent that we kissed. Her lips were sweet and tender and as I held her close she felt wondrous. She always did. "How easy love comes when you love someone," a voice seemed to say to me. That I felt a tinge of guilt with regard to my interlude with Melissa only recently passed goes without saying. It persisted uncomfortably in my conscious during most of the afternoon. I persuaded myself that there was nothing too extraordinarily deriving from that rendezvous because nothing happened, the best of it being that a very attractive older woman nurtured a crush on me, of which I expressed silently that over the long haul if not briefer her obsession would fade from consciousness and that the affair would thereby end; and the worst being that she'd sinned against her husband, or would, yet in my heart contending that I sinned somewhat less because I wasn't married. Try as I did my conscience refused to let it stop there. I began to chastise myself for grooming Melissa to bend to adultery and that from the stance of scripture I was as guilty as she, for even though I ran free as an unmarried man that in no way could serve as my defense. I therefore promised myself that I wouldn't see her again, in any event not in seclusion, and that in Nenia, my first and only sweetheart, I had the most wonderful girl in the universe and that I would not in the slightest do anything to cause me to lose her. I added however, that I'd never tell her of my minor indiscretions with Melissa, at least not until the passage of years to come.

Chapter 28

I THINK I said goodbye to my mother for three days every day before I finally left; in other words, going over to spend a portion of time with her each day before the final one and when it descended upon us we both faced it with solemnity and tears. I found it hard in the extreme to leave her, my baby sister the only one to consistently stay with her after my departure. She put her arms around my neck and pressed her cheek to mine, her way of temporarily shielding her tears. I saw them nonetheless when she withdrew. "You take care of yourself son. And watch out for Chicago. I hear it's full of shady people."

"I'll take care of myself. And in so far as the people there are concerned, well, some are bad and some are good, but the great bulk of them are good, no different from anywhere else. They just want to harmonize with their fellowman, living their lives peaceably."

She still wasn't content, drawing the analogy between our small town and a huge city like Chicago, remarking with concern that she'd heard that Chicago ran rampant with crime, whereas our small town stood as a Holy temple by comparison, with practically no crime since she couldn't remember when. "But it's bad there son. Please take care," she repeated with a tone of worry. And then added with stunning insight a scholarly deduction that I would never have suspected existed anywhere in her, "Isn't it a shame. Crime and corruption progress much faster than the law to stop or slow it, anywhere, but more so in big cities."

"Yes mom. It is a shame. Now don't you worry. I'll watch out."

I hadn't seen Mr. Carney lately, not recently enough to bid him a final goodbye, so as I left my mother, the morning hour early, only minutes past eight o'clock, I swung by his home and said that I'd chosen him as my last stop off on my way to the university, the mention of it prompting suggestions that I should study law once I finished with my undergraduate studies and that the city of Chicago literally spilled over with night schools where I could do law studies part time and exact the duties of a full time job in daylight hours. I answered that he'd given good advice. While I clarified that law school didn't fit into my current scheme of things, I said that nonetheless I was leaving room for that possibility. What I contemplated above anything else, I explained, besides earning good if not commendable academic marks, was taking a part time job quite earlier than graduation, since by then, I feared, my savings will have dwindled to zero balance.

The sun refused to show itself during the greater mileage of the drive. It was to my chagrin a dreary dull day, the clouds hanging oppressively low, threatening to burst open and release a downpour. I viewed with relief that the rain chose not to fall and during the six hours of travel my thoughts fell not a lot on home nor on the sadness of leaving, as I expected they would, but on the fraternity house situated on the fringe of the university campus which through earlier correspondence the university officials made available to me as a place of my lodging.

When I arrived, I discovered after some minor searching the whereabouts of the house, a tall stately structure obviously built toward the latter throes of the last century. It ascended imposingly to a height of two stories. It was painted cotton white and stood glistening in the sun, because the sun had broken through, and featured a front porch that turned at the corners and ran for a distance down the exterior walls, thus forming side porches. A person of near my age introduced himself as the official in charge of affairs, a Renaldo Bertinelli, who said in a portion of his opening remarks that he originated through a line of Italian descendants and to my notion he looked it. He had attained to sophomore status at the university. A handsome fellow with a Grecian face, he could have passed indeed for someone stemming from Grecian heritage rather than from an Italian bloodline. Serving him as equally profitable as his good looking face was his coarse dark hair if it had been better groomed, but of that he apparently cared not a great deal and remarked that he didn't at some point when we knew one another better. He possessed the most pleasant persona, out of his way friendly, and often interrupted his stream of talk with laughter. And he laughed with abandon. I liked him. My room was situated on the first floor immediately off the lobby, a very large lobby, plentifully furnished with lounge chairs and sofas. A complement of side tables tastefully abutted these furnishings, each enlivened with small exotic vases into which flowers of assorted species were placed. And in addition, the side tables were enhanced with bright burning candles. A glitzy chandelier hung from the vaulting, which someone later explained to me was principally of Victorian fashion. The size prodigiously large, it ran through me that should the weight of the ornament suddenly tear it from the anchorings the result might turn out seriously devistating. I couldn't tell in what manner it was appended, unable to see the upper reaches well enough to determine. Bertinelli explained on our way to his showing me the laundry room that breakfast and dinner were served to the occupants as part of the rental assessment but for lunch everyone sought his meal elsewhere.

"On my own for lunch. Huh?"

"On your own. You have it. Excepting there is always someone looking for company at lunch and if you like you'll have plenty of ready takers."

The laundry room occupied a niche near the rear, and when there he coached me through the routine of operating the equipment, the washer and dryer. Not recalling whether he'd alluded to his chosen concentration of studies I asked him about them.

"And what did you say your major area of study is?"

"I didn't. But it's political science."

"And you're a senior I take it."

No. Sophomore. Three more to go"

"That's better than four."

"Ha. You'll make it."

Two other residents other than himself already lived in the quarters, an Aaron Stylman, he said, and a girl who they all called Darya Narvanna. "They'll return shortly. They said they were going to do shopping at the department stores then take a jaunt to the Navy Pier." Aaron, I discovered, was a Jewish boy in his late teens, bright and animated and likeable, his parents presently living in New York City, where they'd lived for years, and were involved in the plastics industry. They were mired knee deep in wealth, Bertinelli later whispered to me one night when I helped him in the kitchen, the amount elevating into the millions. Aaron, some few years younger than Bertinelli and me, was advancing to the sophomore class. Said Bertinelli of Darya, "She's a Serbian girl by blood and was born in the United States in the city of Baltimore."

The rest I cannot quote him saying exactly, but I have rememberd closely the things he said of her, and thus here treat them as a quote. "She is tall and shapely," he said further, "and strong of physique, at first not given to talkativeness as am I and Aaron, and provocatively attractive, whose carriage is erect, proper, admirable and quickly noticeable. Her hair is dark and she wears it long, down passed her shoulders. Her eyes, like her hair, are coal dark, and large, and penetrating when she talks to you. She is serious but not stilted. When she smiles it's subdued and beautiful. You will see for yourself in an instant that she belongs to the best of society."

"A blueblood."

"You got it right. A blueblood if I ever saw one."

That night as I lay in bed, I began to revolve her image round and round as it had been told so dramatically to me, not easily falling to sleep. I had something of a feeling however that I might not like her.

Upon our first meeting I discovered that amazingly she approximated a near fascimile of the description that Bertinelli had supplied. I must have looked stupefied. I ventured that the Divinity must somehow have played a hand. Little did I guess or sense, or did I, how deeply she would penetrate into my life. I would find out.

But allow me to return once more to that first day when I met her and Aaron. They had been out together exploring the city for hours, leaving that morning, one or the other declaring that the shuttle service was slow and crowded but cheap and dependable as they entered the front door, both in elevated spirit. They looked stunningly out of character alongside one another I particulary took note, she a head taller than he.

"Ramsey," said Bertinelli, as they entered into the vicinity of the lounge, "I want you to meet Darya Narvanna and Aaron Stylman, and likewise I want them to meet you." With a shade of curiosity on their faces both simultaneously glanced back and forth at one another, she at him then him at her.

"Ah! I'm glad to meet you. I'd heard you were to check in yesterday but you're here now. That's the thing that counts," she said while stepping forward with her hand reaching for mine.

"I'm glad to make your acquaintance too. Yep. I made it."

She coaxed a light soft smile to her face and appeared between my quickend glances at her to have begun looking me over. And then it was Aaron's turn.

"Hey. My pleasure." The exuberant glow in his eyes said much of him instantly.

"Same here Aaron." His hand grip belied his size; much stronger than I anticipated, but I interpreted it as a mark of his natural upbeat persona. To me it meant that there inside dwelt a kind and good soul.

While other residents were later to avail themselves, these three, as time unfolded, became for the most part my most solid friends, greatly beneficial in our joint studies and provocative discussions and debates of myriad issues late at night as we sat sipping coffee that Darya graciously brewed and served. Like all the rest who resided there, I loved the old house, warm and spirited with symbols of last century character glaringly evident everywhere I looked. And I could not resist envisioning the hundreds of young people preceding me, their intellects and personas in particular. "I wish I could have met some of them here fifty years ago. Wouldn't that have been something?" Sometimes such was my musing. Uppermost, I supposed, was the stairway, rising in a mien of charm and nobility, en route to the second tier, bordered by oaken hand made balusters of the Italian Renaissance period which of themselves were capped painstakingly with finely polished scrolls and curlicues. "Ah. This is where I'll spend my next few years. I like it, I like it very much, my new found friends not withstanding."

The meals were well prepared by the chef, drawing a lavish array of compliments, rich and well balanced and considering that I made it practice not to eat between meals nurtured a ravenous hunger whenever breakfast and dinner were served. Every one seemed equally hungry. They ate quite plentifully. Darya, the only female, beginning from the very first, usually took a seat by me at meal time. There were eight of us now, the last four, all upperclassmen, straggled in within the next few days, all living upstairs whereas Aaron, Darya, and I and Bertinelli, and a student who upon our meeting introduced himself as

Gerard Warf, resided in the lower rooms. Gerard, I gathered from the start was of German descent due to his family name, and subsequently when mutually going over our family backgrounds learned that I did not err in my assumption. He represented himself in a nice and quiet manner. While he had chosen physics as his major field of study, he as well possessed other surprising interests and aptitudes, evinced by his selection of music as a minor and playing the piano and singing as a hobby, on occasions compensated with a good rate of pay by a local club to perform.

When September rolled along and the first frost not far from coming, we sallied into the school year with fresh excitement, I with a special purpose, far more than the usual lot, who were younger and saw college life as a stage of fun and entertainment as much as they did serious study. Books and seriousness represented to me high stakes and I aimed to play the game to win. I had to win, I exclaimed to myself; I wasn't getting any younger. Pleasure would have to wait until later, but before that the objective of proving myself commanded a front row seat and I did not suffer from the illusion that things would come to me easily. But held confidently to the view that I would do well. That was a must. I sat and listened with vice like attention to the professors, took notes copiously, passed the exams with plaudits from my teachers, and from then on rather than harbor concern over whether I could meet the challenge I found myself thirsting for more and more knowledge which that intriguing world of academia plentifully offered. When I wrote Leland my first letter after he'd gone away, I humorously mentioned that my only trouble lurked its head before classes for the semester commenced. "I discovered dear friend that registration is an annoying and frustrating thing and that the catalog presents a maze of instructions, exceptions, footnotes, and directions that exceed in difficulty any text book that I will ever open. Well, it really isn't as bad as I'm making it but I can say with veritable candor that there are things I'd rather do."

I could have alluded to that day when I met the Dean in the hallway of the administration building where everyone signed up for course work, where he stepped over to greet me as a new student, leaving me baffled as to how he figured me as a new enrollee on campus. All the same, he asked if he could help.

"Yes sir you might. I'm stumped by this catalog. It's like a crossword puzzle. I simply don't understand it."

"Don't let that upset you young man. I've been here thirty years and I still don't understand it."

With that said, and with a grin of sympathy that stretched broadly across his kindly face, he adjusted his glasses and trying to act with particular compassion took the catalog from my hand and began to thumb through the pages to this or that section and in a manner of abbreviation gave off a few instructions. Though to no avail. He did it too fast. I thanked him and set out for the fraternity house where I sat down in one of the huge lounge chairs in the lobby and after an hour of aggressive digging figured it out myself.

"Any trouble?" It was Darya, who came up from behind looking over my shoulder, her big dark eyes beaming into the catalog and then at me.

I grinned a grin as if I'd recovered from near defeat. "Not much." But I urged her to check against my interpretations, discovering as she flipped the pages that she was a whiz, sorting through and verifying everything in minutes which had taken me an hour to attain to the same accomplishment. To assuage my pride I contended to myself that she'd been through the process a great deal before, rationalizing that the factor of time and experience had made all the difference. She laughed and patted me on my shoulder, handing the catalog back. "You're fine. You have it right." I complimented her quickness, which she sloughed off with a shrug of her shoulders.

"Oh Ramsey. You're way ahead of where I was when I first faced this hurdle."

In conventional play I accused her of conjuring up wording to make me feel good, and that she sought only to do that, yet said with seriousness that I most appreciated her help, and went on,to vow that I'd return the favor by helping some poor freshman in similar distress when I attained to sophomore status. I learned in the days to pass, when I had gotten to know her better and vice versa, that she was of great fun in conversation and went overboard in showing compatibility in shared studies. Sometimes, when talking, she would pause and sigh as if in contemplation of an idea she'd left unspoken. I gathered right away that the Lord had filled her head with lofty brightness, feeling that way if for no other reason because of her calmness of manner and detailed approach to the solution of a problem or the settling of issues when they arose among her companions. She now approached her sophomore year, undecided as to her major course of study, answering when asked, that more than sufficient time remained for her to make up her mind.

Chapter 29

THAT FIRST semester I sparingly journeyed into the city, staying fast with my studies, the few trips that I did take limited mainly to little quick rides on the trolley. There were exceptions. Once when I fell into the doldrums due to the constancy of my studies I drove to the heart of the city and parked and simply strolled, enthralled by the busy street life and amazed at the towering skyscrapers; and on another trip I meandered through the Chicago Institute of Art; and still on another I drove to lakeshore drive, there venturing onto that renowned roadway and traveling westward for a length then veering northward toward Wisconsin. When I reached the state line I reversed directions and drove back to the campus.

I still recall my first visit to the Chicago Theatre that I had learned reams about from Darya and from my readings in the local press advertisements. Darya joined me. I think she'd been wanting to. We rode the trolley downtown and stayed with it on its run to the Naval Academy then exited on its return to the heart of the city. There were limitless things to see and ponder. We stayed for the larger remainder of the morning gadding about, just laughing and talking and looking at the merchandise on display behind the glass windows of the magnificent store frontages, and a little later took lunch at a delicatessen before embarking on our predetermined tour, the tour led by a professional whom the theatre officials kept on retainer for guiding the crowds through, which were ordinarily of such magnitude that management scheduled a second tour for later in the afternoon. As luck would have it, the crowds had gathered near the entrance in moderate numbers for the early phase, including us. We decided to go in early, and did, from there hastening to the starting point and waiting for the tour to begin, which happened promptly at one o'clock. The tour would take time. We'd finish by three thirty.

The Chicago Theatre, the tourist guide explained, was originally known as the Balaban and Katz Chicago Theatre, a landmark, a dominant movie theatre until 1945 when the movie activity was shelved in favor of stage plays, magic shows, comedy, speeches, and popular music concerts. When it opened in 1921 it accommodated 3,880 seats. The structure ranged seven stories high the tourist guide told us and filled nearly one half of a city block and that the sixty foot wide, six story triumphal motif of the State Street Façade, an integral part of it, compared favorably with the Arc de Thriomphe in Paris. He proudly explained that the interior depicted French Baroque influence from the second French Empire, and that the grand lobby, five stories high and surrounded by gallery promenades at the mezzanine and balcony levels, was influenced by the Royal Chapel at Versailles. And lastly proceeded to report that the ecstatically glittering staircase was undoubtedly patterned from the grand star of the Paris Opera House.

This was but a smattering, the whole of everything more grand and expansive than superfluous words and lines can sufficiently describe and the only way, as I thought about it, to acquire a genuine flavor and feel of this grand old show place, or palace, hinged on a person passing through it himself, inside and out. It was marvelous in every sense imaginable, I uttered aloud, and more than well worth our going to see. She agreed. But regretted that there was no performance, a play of some sort, although we knew that none had been displayed in the tour brochure before we decided to go inside. Afterwards we caught a trolley again and rode around throughout the city, even to the suburbs, killing time and sightseeing. We switched from one trolley to the next, staying with the one we'd caught last for as long as we wished or until happening on a sight that especially catered to our fancy. I suggested once that we return home but she feigned a pout and said she didn't want to just then, that she preferred to stay out until after dark.

"Can we Ramsey?"

I wasn't about to decide against her.

"Sure."

This, I hereby report, is what we did for most of the day but there was more to come. As twilight fell softly on the city we caught a trolley out to lake side to a small café perched on the shore which she said she especially liked. It was Greek owned, with large glass windows that provided a convenience to our seeing the countless twinkling lights on the north shoreline. We sat sipping coffee for awhile, her busily chatting, me mainly listening. It was an oddity, and I wondered of it. Normally she displayed reserve and talked limitedly, but with me, when we were alone, her personality behaved to the opposite. She racked my brain with exotic imaginations and ideas, a mass of accumulated thoughts, her big dark eyes alive with animation. They dazzled and danced. She looked out at the water every once in a while and then at the lighted candles on the table and then at me. To make a point she sometimes used her hands, fluttering her fingers in the likeness of playing a piano. "She amuses me, no, amazes me" my silent processes exclaimed. As the evening began to fade the waiter dressed in a white uniform with a tall round head top approached and we ordered sandwiches and soup. I suggested that she might like to order something more diverse; "Greekish perhaps," but she said no, that what we ordered was more than sufficient and with a playful frown and a gorgeous laugh accused me of plotting to destroy her figure. "You don't want to do that, do you? I worked so hard for it."

"No indeed. Never."

But she did alter the order.

"Oh, sir. I've changed my mind. We will prefer additionally a serving of table wine."

"And your choice madame?"

"Let me see. As I was about to say, ummm, but oh, let us forget about that. My friend and I will settle on your classic La Grande Rue."

"Do you want a cut of cheese as well?"

"Yes, please. Camembert. A portion."

"Very good."

He turned and left, but virtually was back instantantaneously with the wine and drawing the cork from the bottle with a snappy pop poured full to the brim two shallow glasses, the substance now flitting and sparkling as we pressed the glasses to our lips for the first sip.

She was so easy, laughing more than I'd ever seen in her and when she laughed she did it in a low sonorous quality briefly done, as if someone in her earlier life had tutored her to do it with charm and grace. She laughed a culturally finished laugh I thought. It dawned in my senses that she had started to like me, that is, to like me very much, but held back from saying so. Not then anyway. I didn't know what I would say or do when and if she did. Skilled in the art of conversation, she tactfully selected topics on which both of us were well versed. Starting with Aaron, who evidently had lately taken up an exchange with her that centered on the field of economics, she now began, without preplanning it, to lead us into the lofty plateau of international finance.

"Did you know that Aaron's father is the chief executive officer of a plastics company in Jersey City?"

"I did. Bertinelli let me in on it. But that's pretty much the extent of what he said."

"Well he is. Aaron says his father profits enormously from his business but complains that high trade barriers vastly hinder his shipments overseas."

"Yeah, well I don't have much insight into trade barriers and doing business with countries abroad. In fact, I don't know anything at all you might say with regard to those things, other than the Marshall Plan, which helped the Jewish folks and the robber barons in this country attain to very high levels of wealth. As you know, that plan ended in 1952, supposedly" The Marshall Plan still lingered as a focal point for university professors teaching political science and economics, their lectures spawning many lively student debates over coffee at some round table on campus in the hours following. I, like everyone else, could claim only partial knowledge of the whole of the picture and realized that my input was perhaps grossly fraught with errors of logic and fact. Nonetheless, I enjoyed giving my opinion, especially if done one on one. As a rule I became somewhat reserved when members of a group began bantering with one another. On the whole I disliked heated debates.

Darya asserted that she sorely found herself lacking when delving into the ins and outs of barriers associated with foreign trade but I knew better. She read prolifically on the subject, doubtlessly well informed, and miles ahead of me. Her well of knowledge spilled over. How could I miss that? I think she pretended a lack of understanding as a ploy for picking my brain, but she faked her shortcoming, I sensed, to ascertain that I did not back down from intimidation and therefore more fully engage in the conversation.

"The Marshall Plan hunh; how did it work? I mean how did business people over here do well by it?"

"You mean make millions?"

"Exactly."

"The government sent money in steady streams to the folks overseas, you know, helping them get back on their feet. That was the idea. They then used the money for buying up stuff shipped over from our wheeler dealers."

"But did our businessmen realize a profit if the goods were bought so cheaply? They were bought cheaply were they not? How else if we were trying to help the people?"

"I doubt that they were," I answered. "Our business guys spoke of their generosity with gusto, championing honor and fair play, and proclaiming a zealousness to help their fellow man. I doubt that they sold anything abroad at a penny less than usual. Even if they did sell at a discount here's what happened. Our generous old Uncle Sam made up the difference, and the difference eventually migrated to the taxpayers. It was something like that. I'd bet on it. What a deal. The government offers a guarantee, you have inside knowledge, connections they call it. Now how can you miss? You can't. You end up with a ton."

Darya started to say something, then paused as if she perceived that I planned to add more, and seeing I wasn't tapped her fingers lightly on the table top, a subtle piquant look alighting on her face, then.

"Are they still doing it? Is our government still sending money abroad? As you said, the Marshall Plan ended some time ago."

"Sure they are. They've just subtly shifted the former funding process to a different name and gusto, now business is done pretty much as usual."

"I guess so. But I don't see how a businessman can earn a good dollar when the economy is down like it is." It sounded to me that she commenced thinking back and forth between the national and international scene. But I didn't ask her to explain.

"You may have a point. The economy is down, yet only only down for the business guy with nothing more than ordinary means. Aaron's father is well ahead of the race in that regard."

I didn't surmise that she saw the economic picture through a prism similar to mine, given that her parents, in the manner of Aaron's, were inundated with wealth, owning a major stake in a shipbuilding company in Baltimore, which she at some time before revealed. Then she changed the subject, or in any event in part. "Let's take up the matter of the President, shall we?"

"Why not? You start."

"Eisenhower is conservative, I mean too conservative, don't you think?"

"You're leading me"

"No I'm not. I don't mean to."

"That's fair enough. Hmmmm. Maybe he is. If he is all that conservative I'm surprised he's supporting the Marshall Plan concept, you know, still sending money abroad, to wherever, and in my opinion he still does and on the surface it seems like a good thing. I'll go on to say this however, that if he's too conservative and the people don't like him—because of the way he's running the country, they ought to step back and tell themselves that they shouldn't have voted him into office to begin with. And we didn't have to vote him in. Nobody twisted our arm."

"But we did have to."

"We did?"

"Sure. Absolutely." Her intensity now had begun to pick up, her eyes dancing and sparkling and she talked a slight faster than her usual custom, all this making her even more alluring. "The Americans spoke of him as the most popular man on earth, a military hero, to whom the free people of the world owed their very lives perhaps, a man destined for the Presidency irrespective of his views, which then we didn't have privy to. Not really."

"He won the office because of his image as a hero. Is that it?"

"I think so. It's analogous to an avalanche running over a snow rabbit. Heroes will demolish slogans and policies and strategies every time, if they're a great hero and he was a great hero by every definition of the word."

"Umh hunh. I guess that's right. That's the way it sometimes happens," I added. "We vote a man in because of his triumphs and personality."

She acted as if she might carry the topic further or even challenge certain aspects of it but before she did or could I let out a surprise.

"Are you a democrat?" I casually asked, and then blank faced took a sip of coffee. She held back from breaking into laughter, coquettishly looking over.

"Why do you ask? Because I'm reflecting that I'm mildly against the President?"

"Hmmmm. Not really."

"No. I'm not a democrat. My father is but I'm not."

"You're not. Then what are you?"

"Eclectic."

"What's that?"

"Don't play charade."

I managed a chuckle. "So you're a middle of the roader?"

"Somewhat. Choosing the best of the available options. The best of political strategies. You're less apt to make serious mistakes that way. If you lose you don't lose entirely."

"You mentioned slogans. Now that's an interesting propaganda technique all right. But isn't it more fitting if we allude to it as the art of public mind twisting; cause that's what it is, actually. Slogans twist minds."

"Seduce minds you mean."

"Maybe that's more like it," I let out, amused at her choice of imagery. She must have noticed my smile trying to bleed through.

"But as we've acknowledged, slogans don't always control. We weren't around when Hoover ran for his second term. 'A chicken in every pot,' he proffered, though allegedly, borrowed it from someone else. In any event it didn't get the job done. Roosevelt beat him by a landslide."

Unlike the smooth and continuous uninterrupted exchanges between myself and Darya, the majority of the small fraternity group of eight at meal time were noisy, although not loud, and eager to engage in a multiplicity of conflicting debates, particularly those spawning from inside the university classrooms. By and large the economy and politics commanded front stage. The university supplied an array of provocative speakers for the benefit of the student body as well as for the good of the community public, the speakers drawn from a multiplicity of domains, inside the nation and from around the globe, and harbored a wealth of diverse views that they unleashed upon us. In response to what they'd heard our little group evinced very closely an even balance, pretty evenly split with opinions, some severely cutting down these men of fame, knowledge, and experience and some emplacing them high on a pedestal. We had agreed that each of us would have five minutes in which to speak without interruption. I generally elected to stay out of it, passing my allotment on to someone else. No one behaved with excessive brashness or impoliteness to another, but would quickly disagree, Aaron most singularly, who kept himself well read and thrived on debate and bent everyone's ear on campus to acquire insight regarding public disputes. Invariably he chose to sit on my right, the notion eventually striking me that in some manner or other he thought of me as his older brother surrogate. Sometimes when two or more of our table associates ganged up on him in the bantering of an issue I deliberately argued his side, whether or not I innately supported the issue. I seldom concluded that he needed my alliance. I'd seen on several occasions where he more than held his own when the majority of the grouping argued against him.

Thanksgiving slipped upon us, a reminder that its big brother Christmas soon would come galloping around the corner. Bertinelli flew to New York City to take part in the celebration with his parents and sibling kin, the others of our fraternity going to their homes as well, all but Aaron and Darya and myself staying, the two of them staying because I was staying, particularly Darya. Upon learning he wasn't planning to join them over the holiday period Aaron's parents drove down from Jersey City to join him, taking a hotel suite for the short duration of their visit. Mr. Stylman and his wife on two separate occasions treated Darya and me and their son to dinner in a quaint little café, exquisitely fine I thought, looking out on Lake Michigan. Aaron picked it out in advance. He often went there. "French," said Darya smiling approvingly as our eyes met, then she turned this way and that appraising the particulars for a second time, especially the decorants appended to the walls. The water lay calm and the night air remained unseasonably warm, and these elements infused with the twinkling lights on the northward shoreline, the brightness fading proportionately as the distance increased, translated into a magical evening. I sat next to Mr. Stylman, Darya between Aaron and his mother. I tried with courtly tact to choose from the top of the line menu selections, letting the prices lead me. But I did not choose without hesitation, studying rather keenly the varied offerings presented in the quite tall colorful dinner booklets handed out by the hostess. Likely noticing my puzzlement, or so it must have struck her as such, Mrs Stylman suggested blanquette of veal for the main course and mousse au chocolate for dessert, and when we, the three guests, said that these selections met entirely with our approval Mr. Stylman ordered for us. The waiter, a very suave and dignified man dressed in a dinner jacket with folds terminating at his knees, had stood waiting and when receiving the order stored it in his head and indicated in French that he would return shortly with wine. *"Je vais revenir tout de suite avec le vin."* I've forgotten whether it was at our first or second dinner that Mr, Stylman tactfully inquired of my future vocational aspirations. I suspected he might have me in mind for something with his company someday on the strength of his son's earlier appraisal or on the plus features, if any, he may have seen in me during the brief hours of our acquaintance.

"Ramsey, Aaron has said good things on your behalf. For one thing, you're a leader. A silent one but that's the best sort to my way of thinking. I'm wondering. What are your plans after college?"

"I'm uncertain sir. It's too early to speculate seriously. I have given some thought to law, to ultimately joining a firm."

"Doing exactly what? What specialty will you pursue?"

"I don't exactly know sir. At first, after finishing college, I'll have to take a job in the daytime and study law at night. I'll teach school until I can pass the bar. And then I'll go into the profession, joining a firm that is. I have leanings toward case law. But I don't know."

"Why case law?"

"Honestly, an old friend back home suggested it."

"Not research or something related?"

"Possibly research. I can't say. I don't see myself arguing back and forth in the courtroom. Some lawyers love to argue. I don't think I would. Research, in my opinion, might fit me very well, possibly better than anything else."

"Indeed, legal research you might discover is your cup of tea. And there are scores of other professions you could pursue. But by all means don't shove law aside without first giving it careful deliberation."

The discussion ended shortly. If he entertained bringing up other inquiries or comments pursuant to what I might do after college he apparently dropped them. I gathered that he thought he'd preempted me by this time. Or he might have decided to abort his questioning because he read the countenance on his son's face. When I glanced at Aaron he seemed peeved that his father had nudged me into the conversation. From there Mr. Stylman began to ask Darya and I how we liked life on campus, our answers positively given, naturally, citing the guest speakers from near and far as a great novelty, and valuable supplements to our education; whereas Mrs.Stylman, a gentle lady, in gracious soft decorum chipped in that she hoped the sororities and fraternities were a good influence on the students and not distracting from the purpose for which they were there. I could almost feel her concern over her son in these expressions. She seemed to like both Darya and myself, and when we started to leave she tugged at my sleeve just before we passed through the doorway to the outside, letting me know that Aaron greatly relished my presence and friendship. I would have liked the opportunity to delve into detail with Mr. Stylman attendant to the structure and management of his company and believed he would have affably indulged me if the occasion had better permitted. He wished to get back to their hotel suite, once there starting into a parade of telephone calls to and from his plant superintendent, which obviously fretted his wife, because as she phrased it, they were supposed to do nothing but relax and enjoy while away from the business.

Chapter 30

WHEN MR. Stylman dropped Darya and me off at the fraternity house we entered the doorway and I without going to my room plopped down on one of the huge sofas in the lobby and began to leaf through a magazine. It was not but minutes that she joined me, bringing a receptacle of lighted candles from which she lifted three and emplaced each into a candle holder situated on the foot table. She wore a soft light night cloak. We began to return to the conversations of the evening past, to that portion particularly where Mr. Stylman sought to learn of my future professional endeavors. To this Darya lent her view that literature and history were my natural compartments of love, not law, and that these spheres were where I ought to train my sights. She'd formed an opinion sometime earlier, almost from the first week of the semester when we together enrolled in an advanced literature class. I think I impressed her, as well as the professor, by alluding to some of the Great Books, or through some of our exchanges of these sources late at night while sitting beside her in the lounge chairs. I didn't disagree with her opinion as to where my talents and interest were embedded. I deduced much the same. I truly felt in the inner corners of my thinking spheres that I wasn't cut out to perform the tasks of a lawyer, yet held correspondingly that I'd like someday to give it a whirl.

"We all have certain aptitudes," I said, Leland at that moment flashing across my brow; "aptitudes too elusive however for us to see clearly, but they're out there. Sometimes it takes a good many flippings of the calendar to sort out your niche. In my case I don't think I need to waste a lot of time searching and looking for it. I think I've found it in the fertile domain of literature."

"It's like you said the other day in class, Ramsey, singers, painters, pilots, runners, carpenters, and on and on; they all have they're genetically supplied capabilities."

"Even generals," I tacked on. I didn't know why I suddenly yanked up generals. I just did, I thought. But I did know why. It sprang from a carryover of an oral report that my literature professor had asked me to deliver to the class which concerned the imponderable Napoleon Bonaparte, whose exploits on the battlefield were among some of the most amazing accomplishments ever, his lurid love life notwithstanding, especially with Josephine, his first wife, followed by a host of other lovers. "Let's take Napoleon for example. I could choose Caesar but I'm picking Napoleon."

"And what of him?"

"He was a great general, a magnetic leader, a field tactician unmatchable, certainly by his contemporaries. He was all these things."

"He was. I grant you that" Then she looked at me with a tease in her eyes. "And a great lover too. Just ask Josephine." She said it so charmingly, with an angularity of her lips that I hadn't seen before. Her eyes sparkled.

"Hmmm." I half laughed. "Poor Josephine. Beautiful. Ah, fantastically beautiful. But she had to settle for a back seat, you know, not to his other manifold mistresses, but to the force that truly drove him with intensity far superior to that which Josephine and his mistresses could offer."

"And what was that?"

"Power, power is my only mistress," historians make it practice of paraphrasing him.

Darya implied a style of aristocracy in her relations with people in general, a natural quality for her to have in view of the opulence of her family, and it baffled me to in no small way that she had begun more and more to seek my presence. The temptation fell upon me at moments to describe to her the poor conditions of my family during my growing up years as a young boy, though in the end averting it, figuring that she wouldn't have understood because it would have been to her unseemly. She could have gained the company of any young man on campus if she had wished. I presumed she didn't because many of them were from high born families. She was anything but mercenary. Seeking advantage through the acquisition of opulence was nowhere in her. Why would she? One did not have to spend but a pittance of time in her midst to see that in her soul she disdained the aristocratic fashions. Why then did she take to me? For all she knew aristocratic blood flowed through my veins too. "But no. She doesn't see me in that light. She's figured it out. It's my simplicity that she caters to. She knows without me telling her where I come from." All at once with her dark intelligent eyes wafting straight into mine, and not far removed from mine, she leaned over and kissed me. I accepted it with warmth. What young man would have resisted? What young man would have wanted to resist? She said nothing, merely showing a lovely soft smile, acting as if nothing had happened at all, as if it were something that one would do ordinarily, this despite there being a telling blush that rose lightly from her face which betrayed the illusion.

Then with the speed of lightning Nenia flew to my awareness. A thread of guilt ran through my conscience. It was only a simple casual kiss I explained to myself yet admitted that no kiss likened to the one just implanted on my lips could happen simply or casually.

Nonetheless I justified it, mainly on the strength that every day I saw young students kissing on campus which amounted to nothing more than habitual tendency. "And besides, Nenia admitted dancing with the guys at sorority and fraternity dances back at her college. It didn't bother me when she let it out. Although sometimes I wonder if things go a bit further. Peculiar things can happen when a young bird flies far from its nest. Oh well."

I expected Darya to ask if I liked her kiss, knowing that she knew I did without obtaining verification. But she didn't ask. I anticipated another coming and I seriously betook that it teetered on the brink, with me returning it this time, when Aaron opened the door, exclaiming that his watch showed the time at nearly three in the morning and acted as if aghast that we weren't in bed by this late hour.

"How did you make it here," I asked, knowing that the flow of travel by the city buses and street cars will have drastically lessened at this hour.

"I drove my father's car."

Christmas arrived, and soon I would set out for home, being thoughtful before leaving to deliver gifts to Darya and Aaron, an attaché case for Aaron and a cosmetic set for Darya, nice and appropriate, but shameful in value balanced against the luxuriant niceties they gave me. They had done it together; forming joint decisions in the selection of two double breasted suits, one blue the other brown, plus a top coat. Darya appended a note to the latter: "It's said that Chicago is the windy city, and often is freezing cold. Hope this keeps you warm." They hadn't stopped there, placing a one hundred dollar gift certificate in my mailbox. None of us mentioned the gifts at the time of their receipt, presuming it inappropriite. But it brewed in my repertoire of felt obligations and through my sense of high principle that I thank them when I returned from the holidays.

It was later than I had counted on when setting out for home for a joyous welcome from my mother and the rest of the family; and from Nenia who already was at her parent's home. She knew that our being with one another was to amount to a very short while as her letter recently said.

Dear Ramsey,

You have been busy with your studies I am certain. You must tell me of the many fascinating things you have experienced since early fall.

Christmas is coming. It's practically here. Sorry to confirm that I can only stay at home for a length of two days. You'll recall that I went over this when talking to you by phone. As said, my drama class is taking part in a competition held in Denver over the holidays, my teacher firmly deciding that we should go and represent the university. I have to agree. I hope you'll understand. When I see you, I'll fill you in on the details. You'll have to drive to Saint Louis during the spring break and let me make it up to you.

Dying to see you this Christmas Eve.

Love you,

Nenia

In another letter of several weeks prior to this one she spoke of her election to the presidency of the drama club; thus, she could not have reasonably skirted the trip to Denver and wasn't about to resign her honored post for a few days at home. She could go home anytime. I pictured that she and the rest of the students will have received a break for spending time on the ski slopes and my sentiments were gladdened for her, yet a little grudge stirred in my heart, if not a mite of jealousy. Truthfully, I imagined myself with her. Not easily could I brush away the image of the young men swarming to her on campus seeking to win her affection, of one especially who once asked if she would remove my class ring from her finger.

"How did you answer to that?"

"Silly," she let out, putting on a frown. "You know. I gave him a polite refusal."

The more I lessened the distance to our small town the greater the urge to see her. The days had turned to Christmas Eve and the traffic on the road all the way from Chicago understandably thick. I drove first to my mother's, finding her in uplifted spirits, which I expected, for always she depicted an elevated mood during holidays. But I knew she dwelled on my father. Of course. Two of my sisters arrived and spread food and we ate. After awhile my mother asked if I'd seen Nenia to which I answered that shortly I'd leave for her parent's home.

"Yes. You should. Don't keep that very nice girl waiting." My sisters, who were fond of Nenia, echoed the same.

When I had made my way there she was not immediately in sight which happened by purposeful design, an arrangement between her and her mother. On meeting Mrs. Stoddard, Maggie, at the doorway I hugged her, and without my asking, she with her eyes and a motion with her hand let me know that Nenia waited in the next room. As I entered, there she sat by her father's tall aging radio listening to whatever, the news or music; but rising at once she came bounding into my arms with joyful laughter, her fresh beautiful lips pressing time and again against mine. I picked her up.

"Oooooh, you'll drop me."

"You're so lovely sweetheart," I heard my voice speak. "I didn't realize I missed you so much."

"Same here" she returned. "But with a major correction. I have fully realized how much I have missed you. Every day I have. I've said it in my letters."

On parsing her words I knew I had erred. I also had fully realized every moment that I missed her.

Over the next half hour we tried to cover the waterfront of the events of our lives since fall. Doing as much would have taken more than a while to complete. Finally, we settled into an attitude of usual calm and began to concentrate on the evening ahead and on the approaching of Christmas day. I excused myself momentarily to step to my car where I reached for a colorful bouquet of lilies and tulips arranged in a red Grecian vase, the perfect endearment, I had heard, for one's sweetheart. When I returned and presented it to her, she exclaimed in excited voice that they were "just really beautiful" and kissed me in front of her mother. I blushed but held in check the temptation to look to see if Maggie were getting an eye full. When I did I discovered that she was, her face and eyes beaming with approval.

In trickles the relatives gathered to the home place, all hugging me or shaking my hand or slapping my back as a conveyance that they were more than glad to see me, Nenia aglow with happiness at their going overboard to show acceptance.

"Good to see you again Ramsey," said Charlie with a voice of outward friendliness. We saw at dinner that Mrs. Stoddard outdid herself with the preparations, the cooking and all, pork and steak and chicken heaped on huge silver platters, all this supplemented with lavish bowls of salads and a potpourri of vegetables. Desserts were abundantly plentiful—cakes, pies, fruit salads and the like—a side table of sizeable circumference set in for their emplacement. Maggie objected but Nenia insisted that she help with the servings and seeing that everyone was attended to, her smooth light movements becoming the object of my gaze as she deftly circled the table waiting on everyone. When she poured tea it was exacted with the finest display of etiquette, refilling glasses as if she were attending a gathering of royalty. "Why did I not previously detect this quality of grace and charm? Well, I didn't. Has she acquired some of these finesses from her mingling with the people at the university or were they there all along, which I must have been blind not to see?" I concluded that they were there all along, though since her mother never asked her to assist with the serving of the innumerable meals that I ate with them as a boy I had no way of knowing. "Isn't it interesting," I revolved, "that the culture and quality of a person is seen more obviously at the dining table than in any other aspect of one's social mix, whether dining or serving." After a moment's contemplation I took this back. Speech, I concluded, was a greater determinant than table etiquette, or that possibly these marks of distinction were equal in importance. Whichever it was, proof abounded that she had been taught commendably well in both since her little girl years onward, much of it owing to her older sister as she increased in age. No wonder, I concluded, that she now was a young charmer at the university.

After the meal the men folks moved not to the room where Mr. Stoddard habitually sat listening to his abnormally tall aging radio, but to the living room to which Maggie asked him to take us in that it provided substantially more space. As I was on my way with them Nenia caught hold of my sleeve and whispered to me not to stay too long. She wanted us to take a stroll. "The night is alive with a star-lit sky and the temperature is mild."

"I'll cut it short."

I remember with distinctive clearness the apex of the conversation among the men folks, though a rash of topics emerged which they without me took up a little later.

"Did you hear about Doode Peyton?" Charlie asked, in a sense informing rather than asking.

"Hmmmm. What?" The expression of concern and anxiety coming from Mr. Stoddard. "What did you say?"

"Doode Peyton. They said he died in a car accident this morning. Driving back from Memphis."

"My lands! What happened?"

"As I get it, he topped a hill in his new Buick going ninety miles an hour. When he crossed the peak a road grader had stopped dead still just a slight downhill. Right in the middle of the road. Doode couldn't do a thing except plough right into it. Wham. It was all over."

"I'll declare!"

"According to what I heard his car looked like a crumpled up tin can when they dragged it away."

"Ummm. Anybody with him?"

"His girlfriend. She was killed too. Nobody could have lived through that."

"What can you say of the driver of the road grader?"

"He wasn't on it. He'd gone into the woods to take a leak. He thought he'd scotched it but he didn't do it good enough. It rolled back into the highway."

"I'll declare! And all this at Christmas. You never know, do you?"

The accident would result in endless chatter throughout the town and countryside for the next several days, speculation running rampant that Doode's divorced wife Carla Ann, who bore him two children, both girls, was soon to receive the bulk of his wealth, a hefty amount most folks contended. Some years before, Doode sold his small brick café east off mainstreet in favor of buying a plot of land adjoining the highway nearer the center of town. There he built a two story ostentatious structure, painted it cotton white, raised a flashing neon light high up on the façade, and decorated the interior with exotic ornaments and colorful advertisements supplied by the Coca-Cola and ice cream industries. The local folks were more than pleasantly impressed, and it traveled from ear to ear with growing acclaim to local and unlocal folks that Doode's place was a café of deluxe style, perhaps the foremost of the region. It was also spread, in a vein of jocularity, but true, that while he operated and managed a café business that paid exceedingly well the proceeds deriving from his bootlegging enterprise managed, guided, and manipulated from the rear quarters were even better.

You couldn't find fault with the design of Doode's grand edifice, it was compelling, but neither the structure nor the design whetted Billy Mcvector's appetite, nor Melinda's. It was the location. Not then, not on Doode's immediate death, would Billy make his move, but by biding his time he would, buying the structure and land from Carla Ann for the installation of a sporting goods store. She saw no advantage in keeping the property.

When the crowd left the Stoddards the hour hand pointed to a shade past nine, a bit late for walking but Nenia ignored my suggestion against it and hugged her mother and whispered for her not to expect us for awhile and for her and Mr. Stoddard not to wait up. We took the gravel road, once not long ago nothing but dirt, and started down the hill that gradually receded until the road crossed the creek by which there once grew a sizeable acreage of green tomatoes. From there it was but a slight furtherance that we passed by Jess Mayo's house, a mere shanty, and then English Beale's place, a family of sizeable numbers who also lived in a shanty, only a small measure larger than the one that quartered the Mayo family. Such families were long since gone, their departure to me an unknown fact with respect to where or when, and of course others eventually moved in behind them. To have asked Nenia where the old families might have re-estabilished themselves, the ones share cropping on her father's farm when I lived nearby, would have simply amounted to a waste. She wouldn't have known. I held a passionate curiosity of how life had treated them and commenced to talk to myself. "I read where an imminent sociologist wrote that there is only a meager possibility that people like the Beales and the Mayos will ever climb out of the social chasm in which they struggle. I guess he's right. With no education and no fiscal means what else? I also wonder where some of the boys of the Beale family may have gone to. I'd like to see them." And then I kept going. "When I first started to know Nenia what did her parents actually tell her of these folks, the Beales and the Mayos, that they were of a lesser class, unsuitable, by their way of judging, for her to descend into their midst. I don't know what they told her exactly. But I can vouch for one thing without hesitation. She kept her distance from them. And what's more, her parents could have said the same of me and my family too but didn't. And why was that? Ah! Very interesting. I've never dug into this very much before" So I explained it to myself. "Her parents saw a gaping distinction from the beginning. The Maynards were relatively well educated, people of good background stock, well respected and well known by neighboring families of the communities where we previously lived. My mother taught Sunday school and Bible sessions at the Methodist church for almost a ten year span and evolved into something of a saint, or in any event was a very religious person in the eyes of the rural folks and town's people irrespective of their social standing or monetary wealth."

We walked on as far as Charlie's house and turned around. Nenia insisted on going not less than this distance. On our way back we proceeded at a slower pace, caught up in the moonlight and the chilly but pleasant night air. And in no hurry to return.

At some juncture I began to dwell on the size of her father's farm, at first blush an unseemly thing but then not too seemly at that. I had walked the acreage of that farm times innumerable and it had by the process of repetition and familiarity become a being that was part of me and I a part of it. But of course, there was another aspect of it that came to me too. "Over seven hundred acres stretching to the river, and the day will arrive when her parents will have gone on to their Maker and then the probating of this massive piece of fecund earth to the heirs will begin."

"Is it in your consideration, however slight, that you'll return here someday to live?" I said to Nenia, half expecting her to reply one way or the other that she would if I would, but she didn't say that. She said no in a few lines and said it resoundingly.

"Goodness! What a question. That's a quantum distance from my aspirations. Me a farmer! You're not serious."

"No. I'm not serious. But I am when I see you in my imagination as the head of a sprawling corporation some day."

I wasn't able to see her face plainly in the moonlight but heard her voice, which sounded as if she were strong and convinced in her views of a woman's role in a changing America. "You think the time is upon us that a woman should sit at the top of the management helm. Or at least part of it. Is that right?"

"Quite right. It's apparent. After all, during the war women did a man's work on the assembly line of the defense plants, and why not now in other positions."

"Bravo. I've long held that view. No question that you are right on all you've said, if you set aside one single misstatement."

"What's that?"

"You said during the war that a woman did a man's work. Better to have said, don't you think, that a woman did a woman's work."

It was one of the best of Christmas Eves that I could recall, the sky serene and clear, or it was clear if you didn't include the jillion twinkling stars appended to it. When we came to the creek we stopped, Nenia in this moment laying her hand on the railing of the bridge while looking into the awesome zenith.

"Look Ramsey," she said in a ripple of excitment, making believe that one star especially shone the brightest, not knowing actually which. But we were alive and ecstatic with the Christmas spirit, so it didn't matter. "See it." Without naming it she meant the one that guided the three wise men to Bethlehem on the birth night of Christ Jesus.

"The night of the Magi."

"Yeah."

"That's a beautiful story isn't it?"

I only knew a smattering of the story of the Magi and welcomed her dropping the subject in favor of something else; and then we started on our way, soon reaching her parents home where there was a lighted lantern hanging from one of the porch posts, Maggie's doing, and after sitting in the front porch swing for awhile jointly decided that morning would call early and that we should catch some sleep. Her yawns had begun to pop up one after another with not a lengthy break in between. I yawned myself. She saw me and smiled. Yawns coming from others are contagious I explained. She said yes, that she had always heard that. Kissing her goodnight I left for my mother's, promising that I'd see her the next day.

When I arose from my bed the next morning, my mother still fast asleep, I found the weather nice despite the cold, the skies blue and clear except for the few wispy white clouds traveling on a northeasterly course which in my play of mind I saw as chunks broken away from a mother iceberg. When my mother asked me what I wanted for breakfast I begged off, accepting coffee, set on holding off on food until the Christmas noon meal. I knew it would amount to a feast as always. My three sisters and my brother were there, all of us happily trading talk and tales with one another, catching up on recent happenings, with them prodding me at various opportunities to report on my adventures at the university. Carefully gauging my remarks I played down academic life there, describing it as an ordinary ongoing experience, yet my mother, and my brother too, particularly swelled with proudness at what they regarded as a singular accomplishment. In their imaginative formations the University of Chicago was a grand place and silently I wholly agreed.

My mother inquired of the length of my stay, with me answering less than a week in that I needed to gain a head start on my studies for the second semester. Already I had bought my textbooks and placed them in my room at the university, doing this because I registered before I left the campus for the holidays and therefore knew of the courses I'd take up for study.

"I wish you'd stay longer son. I miss you."

"And I miss you too mother. Very much. I'll stay longer next time."

She asked as well if I'd heard of the Doode Peyton accident, assuming that someone told me of it already. In my answer I more or less repeated Charlie's explanation at the Stoddard's dinner the night before. She added that Doode in his time earned a reputation as a rascal, to which I agreed and added that just about everyone else in town was well acquainted with his questionable tendencies. I knew she held back from mentioning the tale spreading all over attendant to his military experience some few years back. For her own reason, a Sunday school teacher, she possibly just didn't want to. The tale was that the military drafted him into service soon after Roosevelt declared war on the Japanese, to fill a place along side a host of other buck privates, but in Doode's scheme of things he intended to stay for only an abbreviated length. Suddenly the town's folk saw Doode back home, everyone's curiosity peaking to learn why. Gossip arose quickly enough that he conjured in his head that the military would adjudge him as screwy if he engaged in a certain unorthodox antic, this being to stand up on his bunk in the night, under the guise of sleep, and piss all over the sheets and covers and a fellow compatriot sleeping on the bottom tier. Sure enough the scheme worked. The military, when the revolting incidents continued, issued a dishonorable discharge and ignominiously sent him home.

Who could forget Doode and his two story café on the corner of mainstreet and the highway? A chubby short fellow, he constantly bounced around at a frenetic quickened gate, with a pleasant persona on his face, and never without a sunny greeting, which the bulk of folks said lacked genuineness. No one denied his expertness at running the business that he apparently loved. It thrilled him profusely that people complimented his restaurant as the finest throughout the region. Folks whispered that a pixie Negro woman in her early twenties somehow worked her way in as his assistant and that she'd engineered herself into this position by becoming Doode's lover. They called her Dottie, a jaunty pixie person who possessed an admirable familiarity with the details of the business, perhaps more than her boss. People liked her. Upon taking the job she without delay became commendably acquainted with the patrons, greeting them cordially as Mr. or Mrs. so and so with never failing civility and was seen as an integral cog in the ongoing management of things. When Doode went away on business no one missed him; they looked to Dottie, no one offering even the least of resentment because of her origin, and pleased to have her waiting on them. Doode took time about with her at working the cash register. She was good hearted and easily and naturally drew people to her. Once when Leland and I were there repairing an electric motor she opened the ice cream storage container and invited us to pick out something to our liking, urging us to take as much as we wanted for as long as we wanted.

Chapter 31

THE PEYTON people were sizably populated in the community, certain of this strain blood related, but the relationships I have not found altogether easy to establish. Doode, and Riddick, his younger brother, were progenies of Fritz and Ventura Peyton, the latter person the daughter of Thompson Hansrote, one of the heirs to a famous tobacco conglomerate of North Carolina founded in the latter half of the 1800's. I am without knowledge that explains how and why he came to live in our small town, a good thing for certain for the Peyton's, for Mr. Hansrote brought with him an abundance of wealth. Fritz hit it lucky, occupying the right spot in space at the right time, thereby marrying Thompson's daughter Ventura. Another set of the Peyton folks lived a half block from the Monett's in an elongated brick home which distinctly lacked in architecturial style, the people said. I think they meant that it was too plain in view of the considerable sum spent on its construction. Wallace and Maudine Peyton lived there and their son Lennie lived with them until his marriage. People thought of Maudine as the finest of persons and spoke praise of her in the most respectable sense, yet anything but this about Wallace, a rogue with a mean streak running through him from head to toe. They in some manner of connection were intertwined with the other Peyton strain, Fritz's and Ventura's, whose oldest off spring Doode was small in stature as was Lennie, both equipped at birth with a devilish gambling nature. Lennie, because of his shortness of stature and petiteness in size was satirized by some of the more inventive citizens as "half pint." The people were anything but mute in the conveyance of their tales that Wallace, the father, set one fire after another to the barns on his sizeable land spreads in order to collect the insurance money; and they doubtless were flabbergasted that such reckless adventures of criminality failed to force him into a court of prosecution and conviction, but Wallace's luck, intertwined with his opulence, acted to save him from incarceration.

"We'd see a red glow in the east," said one citizen years later who'd witnessed the scene as a boy, figuring that he could speak of it with impunity because Wallace now quietly resided in the town cemetery. "That's Wallace, he's up to it again, we'd all say."

The shameful blemish on the man that comes to me more incisively than any other flows from his carousing with a young woman of appreciable beauty while his wife Maudine, a saintly soul, served deservedly as a staunch member of my mother's Sunday school class. Wearing what to me was the similitude of a panama hat, a stylish straw hat with a flat top, she each Sunday morning assumed her place in the very center of the front row of the choir and sang in a deep sonorous alto which in my impression at the time hardly was equaled anywhere. Everyone spoke of her beautiful angelic voice. By all standards of reckoning Wallace cared little for the church, nor for his wife. On late Saturday afternoon the folks would see him regaled in an all white garment, shoes and hat not withstanding, crawling into his sleek expensive roadster on his way to a rondezvous. They looked and gawked and grinned. "Yep. Wallace has his sights set on Greenfield," home to a night club, a highgrade roadhouse, of glitzy fame where a rapturous young lady waited for the arrival of her sugar daddy. The drama kept going for awhile until one night the young lady's lover of near her age unexpectedly dropped in and when Wallace challenged, he met with the utmost of whacking, such that the towns-folks noticed him on mainstreet some weeks afterward with one arm in a sling and one of his legs set in a cast. His face showed no impairment, the young man apparently acting out of pity to render no further damage. The whispers ran on for a while as they did of Melinda Monett Mcvector in her ill-fated affair with the married ex-sailor and of Doode in his well known escapades.

The Stoddards had just eaten dinner when I showed up the next day, not with any intention of food and they knew that. Nenia and I agreed beforehand that I'd not join them until after dinner. The entire family again presented themselves. I say entire family with the realization, as expected, that Gaylon wasn't there, nor were his children and wife. At a glance I missed his absence, although, even if he were there it would have amounted to seeing a stranger. I only previously met him by looking at photographs. We sat around for a while talking and engaging in high spirited goings on, joking, laughing; telling funny tales, even Mr. Stoddard stripping away his poker face now and then to join the repartee. After a stretch, things drifted into an aura of dullness and perceiving its effect on Nenia and I, Thelma suggested that she'd like to browse Nenia's collection of books and magazines, and asked if we could do it together. Thus, we rose and left. Since the book was placed near the end of the shelving Thelma easily put her finger on Hemingway's *A Farewell to Arms,* a questionable piece of literature in the eyes of the clergy and the stilted Victorians when it first appeared for public consumption. "Too sensual and immoral the critics charged. All that got changed in time as we knew it would." This was Thelma. We all three scoffed at the allegation. I really hadn't read it enough to do it justice, only scanning the pages as I leafed through it the first and only time, indicating to the others that I'd check it out at the university library and devote much more seriousness to it on my second try. Catching me momentarily alone, Thelma later on edged over and we began to talk of Nenia's leaving for France in early summer to study the French language under very rigid constraints.

"What is meant by that?" I curiously asked.

"Well, the girls—the American girls and other non-French—can only speak in French."

"Wow. That is rigid. If it were me I might starve to death before getting my order in for breakfast."

"Ha. Yeah. Claude is of the opinion that she doesn't need to study French anymore. 'What good will that do her?' he asks. "A lot of good I tell him. What do you think Ramsey?"

"The Russians did it. In my readings of Russian history and this in particular includes the Russian aristocracy during Catherine's reign, I find they spoke French more than their own language. They regarded the French as sitting atop the cultural pinnacle of all Europe, seen as a more developed nation among the European community"

"You said aristocracy. You mean? What did you mean?"

"I meant court society. The nobility. Princes and princesses and others of titles of less stature. To speak French was to add further adornments to their social stature."

Soon after this we each drifted off to others of the family for an exchange of chit chat, the kind that takes place most especially when family siblings enjoin together after an extended absence from one another. But Thelma apparently had something in mind that she didn't finish. In another moment in another area of the home she caught sight of me standing off by myself and quickly ventured over.

"Hello again."

I laughed. "Isn't she something," I whispered to myself. She was the perfect hostess and would have been on any level of society. They badly needed her in Washington it occurred to me to guide them in their illustrious fetes which were made up of the high society set, the usual politicos, and foreign dignitaries ever alert to promote their nation's cause. Taking my arm she said she was very much happy that Nenia and I were close, and asked me to make certain that I came to Saint Louis to see them before Nenia left for her stay abroad.

"Let's see. Where is it exactly? It's, it's—."

"You mean her whereabouts while in France. Calais. That's it. Calais."

"Yeah, that's right. Don't worry. I'll see her before she leaves. I've promised her I would. What time tomorrow will you and Claude start back to Saint Louis?"

"We're leaving at four in the morning. Nenia's joining us."

"You drive carefully."

At midafternoon Nenia changed into a nice pair of slacks, beautiful black shiny things, and a tan leather jacket with a large collar. Underneath she was attired in a solid white blouse, the collar of which lifted up and folded over the collar of the leather jacket. In any dress ware she looked stunning and in this one she did not disappoint. She knew that my eyes feasted upon her and smiling coyly pretended not to pay the least of attention. We decided we'd drive into town, not counting on seeing anything of consequence, not in a small town on Christmas day. We were correct in our expectations. Hardly anyone stirred, only a few young men working on their souped up cars at one of the town's two filling stations and a small gathering of folks standing in front of the Methodist church. We left and drove around for awhile, this encompassing a trip to the larger town nearby where she had gone to high school. It was lifeless too. We reversed our course and returned home.

"Let's go out by the barn and down to the creek," she suggested. "Maybe we'll catch the horses in their stalls and rub their noses and talk baby talk to them." When we got there we discovered that Charlie had let them out earlier and that they were now off pasturing.

"Let's sit on the hay," she said, taking my hand. There was a fresh stack which thus far remained untouched by the animals, bunched up as a mound in a far corner, a sight quite common to us both. When we were younger, and not very much younger at that, we'd often sit or lie down on the hay piles anywhere in the barn's interior or out in the fields which the hay baler crews left over.

"Suits me. Let's do."

Nervous as we were that someone might wander in, Mr. Stoddard more than anyone else, we nonetheless dared to go on. We sat down, then sort of leaned against one another. I knew we'd soon start kissing, but before this I began to pick up pieces of hay brittle and throw them as I would a dart at a plank in the siding of the hallway. More times than not I missed the mark. Amusedly she had watched. Or in any event I thought she had. And now she laughed.

"Why do you laugh? I didn't think I was doing all that badly." I laughed too.

"It's not that. It just occurred to me. What if our erudite friends at the universities could see us now? Wouldn't they burst with hilarity?"

"They could laugh all they want; I wouldn't care a hoot's worth," I said in a fashion of lightness. "I like it here with you. I always have. This is more or less how and where we grew up."

A sun ray had streaked through the cracks in the boarding, coming on a pathway directly to her face, and there settling upon her white gorgeous skin. I started to say something else in response to what she had said, but fell prey to distraction. It was her lovely dark eyes. Ever so subtly I pressed her a little against the softness of the hay, her kisses tender and sweet as she lifted her lips time and time again to mine, and I was intoxicated by the fire of her amour. For a little, the temptation knawed at me to try to persuade her to relent, backing away almost in the same moment because I knew even if I had tried she wouldn't have agreed to compromise. In time our kisses began to die away and she reached with delicate gentle hands and patted my face, then pushed deftly against me, a signal that the interval of bliss had reached an end.

"I'll remember this for a while, a long while" I said.

"As will I. Someday, hopefully, we won't have to remember."

That night after finishing supper with the Stoddards, Nenia walked with me to my car where with the sweetest of sayings we kissed once more and bade goodnight. I recalled that I promised to see her in the spring and again made the promise before driving away.

The next morning when I crawled out of bed I felt an empty loneliness. "By now, she's well on her way to Saint Louis." The rest of my stay during the holiday week I mostly spent driving around and staying at home with my mother. When I first arrived I decided that I wouldn't spend time visiting with the townspeople. Frankly, I didn't care to entertain the questions and comments bound to land on me, the most likely ones I could already hear in my head, "Ramsey, what are you doing in Chicago," and "How did you happen to get a job way off up there," and "We miss you boy, with all our tractors breaking down and all; you need to move back here" Likely, each and every one was aware of the city of Chicago but the University of Chicago only faintly sounded familiar and it ran in my conscience that even if they knew a smidgen of that great well of knowledge my being a part of it would have taxed their comprehension beyond natural limits to understand why and how I made my debut there. But a few commanded a relatively good understanding of it, for instance, people of Melissa's distinction and others of her intellectual level. This was not an issue of moving significance to me and so when I lay in bed that night I cast the thought aside and replaced it with something else of far steeper importance. I had decided after all that it was a good thing to go and mix and mingle with the people on mainstreet before heading north. I would the very next day; strolling here and there shaking hands with farmers and merchants and woodsmen and whomever else I ran across, sitting with those old checker players on the age worn benches in front of the store once owned by Jeremy Dodson, now owned by Billy Mcvector, and talked country talk, from which I greatly profited, for even though theirs was by and large an unschooled rural language, crude and never to undergo refinement, eons removed from the slick Chicago dialect, there were tales and fables that flowed through and from it, distinctly separate and apart from any other anywhere I might discover. I merely sat and listened to learn the lessons they were passing on, which I had not previously sought to hear and subject to the keenness of scrutiny. "I've missed much," it arose in my sphere of comprehension. "I won't do it again. On every chance I'll come back here. I wonder what my celebrated language professor at the university would think of my newborn view of an old culture that will never change or die."

Not that day but the next I drove out to stay awhile with Ozzie and Cavanaugh at the tractor place, discovering scores of things to take up, beginning with the busy hum of the facility itself, which appeared the same as always, a quay of tractors arrayed in order for admittance.

"Business still looks good Ozzie. You guys are doing all right."

"Yep. Pretty good. Yes sir. We are. Thanks to you and Leland."

"Naw. Naw. All the thanks properly go to Leland."

"You did plenty yourself."

While I sought to differ I found that he refused to listen, at the same time pulling a letter out of a metal tool box emplaced on a workbench with an intimation that I might like to read it. I knew it was from Leland as he handed it over.

Hello Ozzie and Cavanaugh,

I apologize my good friends for delaying this long. Now at last I write you these lines.

I am settled in San Francisco with the Kaiser Corporation. I'm mainly into designing machinery. It's a strange experience for me. I often wish I had stayed with the tractor business. We were doing so well. I had my reason for not sticking with it. I just felt a calling to another profession that offered an opportunity more in keeping with what I regarded as my natural abilities. We shall see how everything turns out.

Mr. Carney tells me that you are doing well and in every way I hope so. If you need me for anything just let me know. He knows how to reach me quickly if there's an emergency.

I have not heard from Ramsey in a good while. Only once since he anchored down in Chicago. I wrote him back and that was the last of our letter exchanges. We'll start up again I'm sure. Both of us have been pretty busy.

Keep up the good work and thank you for all the good things you did while you were with me.

Your very caring friend, always.

Leland.

With nothing of exceptional interest pressing upon me other than keeping my mother company and taking brief jaunts to see the folks in town, I returned twice more to visit with Ozzie and Cavanaugh, staying longer on the second visit than on the first. I even helped them assemble a motor. I preferred not to run into Melissa, principally because I suspected she might ask me if I looked at the postcard she sent before Christmas showing her husband and their two children. I'd seen some like them before. Over the years she unfailingly mailed a similar card to the people each Christmas, not of good choice on her part. Her actions were by this stage seen as a butt of mockery. "There they go again, showing off." There was another reason as well that I hoped to avoid her, such being that she might ask me to join her for a ride to some place private. Though I did not gain sight of her during the rest of my stay I nonetheless once happened to see Rupert on his way to lunch walking in the direction of his home a block away. A few years had vanished since I last laid eyes on him. It surely was him I uttered in near disbelief, blinking and looking a second time. He moved as a man recovering from the flu, shoulders slumping, gate slow and labored, and overriding these debilities there was a presence of unmistakable pallor in his face, waxy and yellowish, and lastly, he seemed as a man evidently lacking alertness to things around him. When asking my mother if she'd seen or heard reports of his condition I received that she had no awareness of poor health affecting Rupert, and later when in the company of Mr. Carney he supplied much the same answer.

A lengthy trip unraveled itself in my mind as I drove away from my mother's home for Chicago, and I had not achieved any substantial distance until beginning to ponder a range of things left undone while on my visit. They were scattered as I drew them up one by one, not in any manner sequential.

I started to fret that I should have exerted more effort to spend some time with John Eric, whom I wanted to ask if he recalled the name of the family with whom we spent the night when he and my father carried me on one of their trips to Chicago to peddle a truck load of tomatoes. I hoped that maybe the family yet resided there, and if I were lucky enough that they did I might drop by and introduce myself. I had talked to John Eric's wife by way of telephone. She said he wasn't home. I learned that he still grew green tomatoes for distribution to the locals, nothing for the Chicago market she emphasized. Finally, she mentioned that it sometimes crossed his mind to haul a load to the windy city, but that he took no time at all to drop the idea. Pretty soon John Eric vanished from my train of concentration, the weather now beginning to cause worry. The day started with a gloomy cast right from the start, the clouds hanging oppressively low that gave evidence for expecting a downpour, or worse still a tornado. The flat expansive terrain loomed as a perfect setting for a twister. Much to my relief neither the rain nor a tornado descended and while maintaining a wary eye I kept driving with relative calm. When on the verge of crossing the Ohio River I stopped and pulled over, then walked a ways across the bridge until reaching the halfway marker where I came to a halt. Gazing thoughtfully out into the water I remembered my father telling me and the rest of the children that once he and John Eric stopped in the vicinity of where I stood to drink in the serenity of the twilight, and that a bright and pretty moonbeam descended magically on the surface and that for a while they stood and watched.

What a pity, I thought. A poor laboring man taking pause for a few fleeting moments to enjoy one of nature's beautiful feats, as close as he ever came to being in a great museum of splendid art, which I doubt he ever knew existed, but why I asked, did more of the finer things not ever alight on his pathway of life, books and travel and operas and dramas and wondrous paintings: and why did the pendulum of fate not swing a little more to the left or to the right, thereby forging an opportunity, wherein, like his son, he could have found his way through the doors of a great prestigious university and thereby discover its wonders. "The pendulum did not swing to suit," I said in silence. I knew then, as I had always, that I would never quit thinking of his hard painful years while on this earth and in fantasy wished it miraculously possible to call back time so that he could start his life anew.

When I arrived at the fraternity house late that afternoon I expected to find no one there. And I was right. "Dead silence; it's just me and this big old house," I uttered upon passing through the front door. Looking curiously around I discovered a note on the kitchen table face up with my name on it. It read, "Hey buddy, you're getting back early as you said. You have a key obviously or else you wouldn't catch yourself standing where you now are. I am of course sure you don't need me. I'll see you tomorrow or the next day. In the meanwhile help yourself to the kitchen." Bertinelli signed his name at the bottom. I gladly scanned his cheery words; they lifted my spirits, and were badly needed. The house felt depressively lonely and seemed immensely larger than usual without the presence of the chatter and milling about of my college mates. I smiled upon going over the note for the second time and then laid it on the pixie round table where Darya made it practice to daily set out a Grecian vase of purple lilacs which she faithfully watered. She'd arranged with the maintenance supervisor to drop in and water them daily during her absence. I wouldn't prepare my supper, electing to patronize a small dining accommodation recessed off the street less than three blocks away that Darya and I went to once in a while. Aaron and I made our way there more often.

Immediately before retiring to bed I went and glimpsed at Darya's flowers, and poured nearly a whole glass full of water in the vase that held them. A good thing. The flowers were close to shriveling. Shortly, I crawled in bed, quite spent by now, and hoped to drop off to sleep without much delay. All was mousy quiet I kept noticing. Squeaks and gratings stemmed from every which direction, resounding more from the upstairs, to which I concluded that all big houses when you're alone are alike, replete with odd noises, and soon began to pay less and less attention to them. At last, when close to falling into slumber I reached and turned on the radio. Two or three songs played which I regarded as average, all good yet still average as judged by my taste, but the next, the fourth I think, especially touched me. I only needed to hear the first two lines; "Love letters straight from your heart, keep us so near while apart." The resonant baritone voice undulated beautifully across the airwaves.

"I'll write her a letter before I drop off to sleep." With good intentions to the contrary I dozed off before following through.

The next morning I arose with a gritty determination to "hit the books," two courses in which I enrolled before leaving for the holidays, physics and an advanced math class singularly troubling me. News had circulated that the professors who taught them were hard-nosed and strict and that earning above average marks was a target usually out of reach. Nevertheless, I rigidly challenged myself to exceed the norm and set in motion a strategy for achieving my goal, the studying of the texts upon every available hour and this included the several days before the semester commenced.

One by one my compatriots returned, Bertinelli first, the majority after New Year's Day, refreshed and happy, reporting a range of their experiences while away. The chatter and their excitedly telling of tales erupted more animatedly at the nightly meal. I particularly drew out an adjective that augured well to describe how their presence affected me. Ecstatic. Yes, that was it. Never did I realize before that they meant so much. I was even happily moved at their thoroughly corrupting the English language, everyone talking at once and every other word slang; it didn't matter, and I was amazed at how a trickle of people could pour life into a place that seemed dead and stripped of warmth during my short while alone.

Chapter 32

CLASSES BEGAN. We leapt into our studies. The fun for a while, likened to race horses nearing the final leg of the track, had started with a burst of energy but quickly ebbed away. Gradually, when everyone adapted to the new professors and began to acquire a grasp of the course work as well as the expectations that accompanied them there was a return to the vigorously past joy of debating at the dining room table, led by Aaron, but excluding me. I stayed at my predetermined task. I rose at daybreak and breakfasted early, utilizing the time saved by avoiding the group for reading and study. The same applied to supper; I ate early and retired to my room and began to cram. I seldom became involved in lengthy fraternizations with anyone. It appeared, I'm afraid, that I gave the impression of being a shunner. Darya soon called me out.

"I'm not shunning anyone," I answered. "You know I'm not. I'm in over my head with studies." I spoke the truth, explaining that I enrolled in Russian History and Philosophy for the current term, not to mention Physics and the math course, more than shouldering a heavy load, and I could have added that I shouldn't have signed up for French. I began to make it up to her. Mostly we started to go alone to some out of the way dinge for supper and after supper have coffee and indulge in a hodgepodge of chit chat. I wasn't sure why she sometimes overflowed with lighthearted laughter from some off the cuff remark that I let out which I considered less than funny. I wasn't the best at drumming up jokes or inventing clever concoctions. What I said nonetheless triggered a cord and I loved to watch her laugh. One night a guest joined us, Gerard Warf, the blond boy of German descent who asked me earlier in the day if he might tag along; and I gladly approved. We were going to Anahita's, an Iranian café nestled among a colony of plain brick retail enterprises on the edge of downtown Chicago. We caught a trolley as Darya and I were in the habit of doing. A smiling Asian waiter recommended the specialty of the evening, Noon O Kabab, a mix of ordinary American finely sliced vegetables mingled with cuts of beef and pork, a very nutritious serving. If the food tasted good to our palates the atmosphere did even better, the room filled with low burning candles and a waiter dressed as if he were serving a royal threesome. Upon pouring the wine, pretty red wine as I recall, into three imposingly tall glasses with long fragile stems he emphasized in part Iranian, part American that shortly he would return to take our order. Someone over in a remote corner of the room played a piano, playing old silent movie music, none of which I recognized by name. He played too unordinarily fast. The piano, old and ragged, the piano player and the music clearly seemed out of character, which didn't matter to us. We laughed and enjoyed it, accepting and thinking the show of it all as part of the evening package. We looked in the direction of the piano player off and on and then at each other and grinned.

I hadn't gotten to know Gerard well during the first semester. We only spoke sparingly at breakfast or dinner. I moved slowly at opening a conversation with him, waiting for a topic to spin to the surface of which I held reasonably good knowledge before plunging in. Darya, sensing my tactic, and with the propensity to converse smoothly on any topic and with anyone, assumed the lead, she and Gerard forging ahead on a spray of interests. I hoped they'd delve into literature or history which failed to materialize in that direction, at least on the outset, and I reckoned that I shouldn't have expected as much from Gerard because of his background of farming. I discovered shortly that my judgment erred rather badly. Some of the quotations that he wove in now and then evinced keenness of forethought and a background of literary classics. When the subject turned to economics and agriculture, and what subsidies meant to the small farmer, if anything at all, I asked him to reflect on his father's farm in Iowa. Leaning on my experiences with Mr. Stoddard and Leland, I skillfully guided him to the matter of tractors. He jumped immediately in.

"I've driven tractors thousands of miles," he said, "and eaten tons of dust in the undertaking. Ever since I was less than ten driving a tractor has been my lot."

"Gads. You started out young."

"Yep. Young is right. Me and my three brothers. That's the way our father raised us."

"Are your brother's still on the farm? All three?"

"They are. They say that's where they want to spend their life. My oldest brother once tacked up a board on the entry gate to our place with a painted inscription that read, all in capital letters, 'I WAS BORN TO BE A FARMER,' which is still there."

"What do you grow Gerard?" Darya broke in, well aware of what they grew, an abundance of it in the lowlands virtually contiguous to the mighty Mississippi River. She only inquired as a guise to beef up our conversation, interrupting as he started to answer. "Is it corn?"

"Ha. Corn and more corn. You never saw so much."

"How's the market for corn these days," I asked?

"Good. Good last year I should say. Gonna do better this year if my accounting is correct. The need abroad is pretty demanding. I guess I should also add that we grow cotton and soybeans. Lots of soybeans. And the demand is projected to increase."

For the most part Darya sat silently in the candle glow. She had helped us start, which I suspected had been her motive all along. Now she began to move into the flow of talk once more. She wouldn't continue the present discussion. Something else revolved inside her gorgeous head. It caught me a slight off guard.

"How was your stay back home this past Christmas?" she asked, looking at me with a gleam of curiosity. "It's been a while of course. Even so, I've not heard you say a word of what all you did. Did it go well?" Her words came so softly, her eyes measuring mine, and unconsciously, or perhaps not, she had laid her hand on mine.

"Things went quite well. Fine, fine. I didn't do much, just loitered around town seeing friends, some old, some not so old. I tried not to over eat." I avoided the rest, my being with Nenia, a part of my private sanctuary that I couldn't afford to let her invade. With good reason my most basic logic conveyed that Dary'a affections for me were real and silently vowed never to hurt her. As well, I recognized that in my heart I could easily fall in love with her, that most guys were in love with her, and that I wasn't exceedingly far from being one of them. "I have someone else," I argued, "and so I can't get attached to another. Yet Darya is so charming and beautiful that I can't possibly pretend that she doesn't exist. Gosh. Here I am emotionally drawn by two young women and it's most acutely troublesome and perplexing. Certainly that is so when they are as beautiful as Nenia and Darya and equally beautiful at that. I have to watch myself. I simply cannot allow my heart to guide me into an abyss of duplicate affections. I like Darya tremendously; I do, but I'll have to establish a limit, a line, which I cannot cross. And I won't. I won't cross it. I promise myself that." I recalled in my readings that many a young man over the ages had fallen into similar trappings and found it awesomely trying to break free from the web that bound them.

The semester rolled on, the days flew by, and we were in mid spring. It elated me to near euphoria when learning that the marks on my subjects were commendably high, all perfect, in other words A's, all but philosophy in which I earned an A minus; and even though it swept me away that I performed so well in my courses of study I floated still higher upon reading the philosophy professor's notations on my exam paper. "You'll do very well with this course if you continue to write and progress as you have during the first half." It's amazing, is it not, that a few limited words of praise from a teacher can lift a young pupil into the clouds.

I promised Nenia that I'd see her during the spring break, a promise that I did not keep, a disappointment of which she expressed in her letter, nevertheless scribbling an annotation that she understood. My reason for reneging dealt with a job which I badly needed; my cash reserves swiftly dwindling. Aaron had intercepted me only days before and told me enthusiastically that he knew of a job that I might have, good conditions and well paying, and taking into account my financial needs I more than welcomed the opportunity.

"What job? What are you saying?"

"It's one that my father mentioned."

"Oh."

"Yeah. You'd work for a law firm. I know, I know. You're one step away from pointing out that you're no lawyer. Well, don't. You don't need that kind of resume."

"I'm listening."

He proceeded from there with a slowly and carefully given description of what the work entailed. "Some lawyers need someone here to pick up depositions and deliver them to New York City and fly back on the same day."

"Did he ask you to speak to me about my willingness to try it?"

"Yeah, he did. But you won't believe what I asked him."

"What?"

"'Why can't I do it?'"

"And then what?"

"He said no, that I'm too young and immature. I agreed and said I'd speak to you and see if you're interested. I've done it. Where do we go from here?"

"I could use the money but Aaron I don't have the time."

"Yes you do. I'm familiar with your schedule. You're off at noon on Thursday. You could fly up there and deliver the materials and catch a plane back that night."

"Is that all? Anything else?"

"Yeah, there's something else. You'd have to repeat the same trip on Friday too. And before you intervene with an objection I'll remind you that you have no classes on Friday."

"Yeah. That's right. I'm free on Friday."

"Well, what do you say?

"I'll think it over."

Thinking it over happened as quickly as I could flush the idea through my brain. Which took less than a minute. Hoping to do my best at negotiating, even with Aaron, I waited an hour before again rejoining him. I hoped I didn't seem overly anxious when I gave my answer of acceptance. Aaron detailed my class schedule to his father, and his father arranged the logistics with the law firm, of which he presided as the majority owner. In a snap I became employed. I'd start the next day and work every day until classes resumed, then opt to the schedule originally approved by the law firm, working only on Thursday and Friday. A while afterwards I complimented Aaron in a spirit of mirth for his superb work as a sleuth. "You'd learned of my class schedules down to the minute. You'd already checked them out." He merely laughed and shrugged his shoulders. That was Aaron, non-chalant about everything. I knew that he felt proud of himself for helping his best friend, and was beside himself with happiness that he had. I thanked him to the extreme for paving the way to a badly needed job that fell easily into my lap. I saw Darya but limitedly and with my schedule eating up hours I only mixed briefly with the others of our fraternity. One evening the two us went to a Turkish café in the heart of the city which displayed an especial dimness of lighting to our liking and served coffee of unequaled flavor which the waiter brought to us in a gargantuan cup that featured an eagle on its surface flying over the open sea. When the two of us were alone together, as we were this night, she talked practically nonstop, shifting from one topic to another. Clearly, she showed her virtuoso capability in the use of language skills, speaking by and large English for my sake, sprinkled with miniscule doses of French and Russian as enrichments. She interpreted the Russian for me. I understood French suitably enough, enough that clarification wasn't necessary. The first day that I met her I concluded in a blink that I'd crossed paths with a rare one. Her use of words originated with the easiest of effort, as if they were preprogrammed by a machine and regurgitated through her mouth. I saw in my mind that someday she would emerge as a leading member of a filibuster team for one or the other parties of congress. Her eyes showed thoughtfulness with every expression, seemingly parsing every sentence before speaking it. Every once in a while she moved her face closer to mine, and then with her very lovely eyes telegraphing her intentions would lean even closer and plant a warm and beautiful kiss on my lips. And I returned it. But with caution. And silently instituted a rule. "Be careful not to return your kisses too lavishly. She'll think you're in love with her. You must not maneuver yourself into a corner where the truth comes out of your affections for Nenia, and therefore break her heart." I found my predicament not easy. I could not help my enamoredness with her. I was tremendously enamored with her, and would have given anything not to hurt her. Secretly I hoped that in the end the intimacy of our relations would resolve itself without hurtfulness at play. "How many millions in irretrievable love affairs have hoped for an outcome that was at least minimally harmful," I asked myself, and then began to look at things a little differently to justify my going on with her without feeling guilty. "I have three years left here after this one," I continued. "Anything can happen over that span. Why not enjoy her for the time being and quit worrying." And decided to do what I had just suggested to myself, to continue to enjoy her.

I stayed busy, how else, my flying to New York two days each week to fill the requirements of my job and attending my classes and maintaining my studies—and held these essentials together as well as my mental self. The law firm liked me, quite apparently due to my zeal and alacrity at picking up on the language of legalities and doing it with praiseworthy laudability. It soon followed that I was allowed to inscribe phrases of correction on my own by long distance telephone after first going over the narrative that might or might not need correction. The awarding of this latitude caught the attention of Mr. Stylman who proceeded to write a line or two of commendation that expressed a favorable impression of my work, and in the next line setting down that he thereby proposed that the two of us meet in New York City some Friday night when I was scheduled to fly into town. To know the contents of his agenda I could hardly wait to ask Aaron who would have no aversion to telling me, provided he knew more about the communication from his father. When I asked him Aaron didn't know, speculating in the absence of factual knowledge that it could pertain to almost anything. I then suppressed the idea as much as humanly possible and kept on with my day to day routines.

When the semester began to draw to a terminus some several of us gathered around the dining table in convivial spirit to divulge what we'd do during the summer months. Not heretofore mentioned by name or personality were a sizeable number of students that occupied various spaces in the fraternity house. Most were there at the table. By gradual process I had become their friend and they mine. Darya said rather reluctantly at breakfast one morning that she planned to return to Baltimore, casting over wishful eyes which suggested hopes that somewhere in the summer period I'd fly over and stay a few days, meeting her parents obviously a part of her design. I begged off, finding it convenient to allege that my duties at the law firm would not allow of it and that besides, I had enrolled in two courses scheduled for the forepart of the summer term and two more in the latter phase. Gerard said he'd return to the family farm to help with the planting. Aaron's plans coincided very closely with my own; sticking around, purposely I think, and mentioned later in the day that it greatly elated him that we were enrolling in a couple of classes together. But he knew that I would have stayed anyway because of my commitment to the law firm. I told no one of my itinerary to meet Nenia in Saint Louis for a stint when the spring semester ended. Likened to Aaron and myself Bertinelli would remain on campus seeing after the fraternity house, a decision of stellar importance due to the influx of a few new students who would live there during the summer months and some possibly remaining as residents for an extended length, for the whole of the next school year. Already he had begun to check them in and assign rooms. "Don't you give up my room to someone else Bert," cautioned Darya, and I think she meant it, "unless they understand they'll have to move out come the fall. I'll want it back for sure."

"I wouldn't dare."

While I kept my plans confined in my secret environs to meet Nenia, I nonetheless shared with Aaron that Darya earlier invited me to fly over to Baltimore for an abbreviated stay to meet her parents, to which he remarked he hoped it happened and followed with a show of verbal drama that I'd present myself with distinction while in their presence.

"The one serious trip that I have in mind is going to see my mother for a week but I'll delay that until the end of summer. Of course, as you know I can't go anywhere until after Clement Attlee delivers his speech. That's one that I absolutely don't intend to miss."

Aaron bobbed his head in agreement. "Ah yeah. Same here. I promised my mother that I wouldn't dare missing the great man speak. That's at the end of the summer session. Right? I think from what I hear everybody on campus is at a high peak to show up."

"Yeah. That's what I hear. We'll sit together as a fraternity if everybody likes.

"I'll spread the suggestion," he plugged in with a show of upbeatedness.

The entire campus seemed to have heard of him over the several weeks previous, the professors priming us for his appearance, unnecessary in my case for I had heard my family, largely my mother's brothers and sisters, begin to talk of Clement Attlee following the Great War. And I had read avidly of his exploits from high school onward.

Books are replete with discussions and opinions of Clement Richard Attlee, who lived from the third of January 1883 until the eighth of October 1967. I supply here only a synopsis of his service to his country and to the world stage.

Portions of the narratives that reflect on the man during his relatively young manhood years, before he ascended to prominence, give off adventures almost as intriguing as those years when he became universally acclaimed. We are always curious to learn of the beginnings of a giant. He earned his diploma at Northsaw School, a boys preparatory near Pickley in Kent, and subsequently attended Haileybury College and University College, Oxford, where he graduated with honors in Modern History in 1904, the year the Japanese/Russian war broke out; and I had acquired from other snippets that during the First World War, Attlee attained to the rank of Captain in the military, soldiering in the South Lancaster Regiment in the Gallipoli Campaign in Turkey, his decision to fight revealing something of an ideological rift between him and his older brother Tom, who as a pacifist and a conscientious objector spent much of the war in prison.

The one image of perpetual memory that I continue to harbor of the man resides on a magazine cover somewhere in the archives that I viewed while browsing the university library. The head librarian had seen fit to display the magazine on a shelving rack in the foyer, placed there I assume to draw attention from the students. The cover featured three faces common to anyone in that era that even lightly kept abreast of world affairs; Joseph Stalin, Harry S. Truman and Clement Attlee, the threesome standing in pose while in negotiations at the Potsdam Conference. I read the article in full on the spot without once sitting down. Among the peaks of his achievements, if not the peak, is his tenure as a British Labour Party politician, serving as its leader from 1935 to 1955, and as the Prime Minister of the United Kingdom from 1945 to 1951. It is not at all impractical figuring that had he and Churchill failed to combine their massive intellects and wills against the axis powers the freedom and liberty of the people of the international globe might have emerged drastically altered from its present form. Attlee's impact during the great conflict and in the sphere of far reaching politics is monumentally recorded and remembered. Aside from his proficiency as a politician one has to pay attention to his mastery at uttering passages of a rather Platonic flavor which bore his sentiments toward the unfortunate. He wrote, "Charity is a cold grey loveless thing. If a rich man wants to help the poor, he should pay his taxes gladly, not dole out money at a whim. In a civilized community, there are some persons who cannot at some period of their lives look after themselves, and the question of what is to happen to them is solvable in three ways—they may be neglected, they may be cared for by an organized community as of right, or they may be left to the good will of individuals in the community. The first way is intolerable, and as for the third: Charity is only possible without loss of dignity between equals. A right established by law, that of an old age pension is less galling than an allowance made by a rich man to a poor one, dependent on his view of the recipient 's character, and terminable at his caprice."

To this rare man we rivetingly listened to and profoundly admired as a group of aspiring students that evening in the university auditorium packed with humanity, a weighty fraction of the total comprised by our younger aged assembly. Many of us were asked to stand near the back throughout the speech and did it gladly. Once, during the speech, I consciously thought to myself that here I am, the son of a sharecropper not many years removed, in the presence of a great statesman of a foreign nation, the very man whose name I used to hear proclaimed by H. V. Kaltenborn from the radio in the early part of the evening while I sat with Mr. Stoddard, our ears grippingly attuned to the status of the war raging in Europe and Southeast Asia. That night when I sat down in my room, shortly before going to bed, I scribbled a note to my mother that I in the past few hours had received a lesson in history and political science from a master teacher, calling the former Prime Minister by name, and with firm sureness said that the lesson learned would stay with me for a lifetime.

With stealthful care I would risk no slippage to anyone of my impending trip to Saint Louis to see Nenia, my plan laid out to fly there without stopping off in Chicago when returning from one of my trips to New York; but I slipped after all when I mentioned my intentions once to my assistant supervising lawyer at the firm who generously authorized my diversion with full expenses paid. Mr. Stylman, though, deserved the credit, directing that the man and the firm support me in any way practical. When my plane reached Chicago I stayed aboard until we landed in Saint Louis, not even leaving for refreshments or attending the men's room. When we landed there stood Nenia, scrouged against the gateway, anxious in all appearances to see me. It was her smile that was of foremost attraction. It always seemed to give off a flourish of eloquence. I think we made a scene when we reached one another, the passengers nearby turning from their own preoccupancy to look upon us with amusement and admiration. The wife of an elderly couple said with barely audible intonation that she thought it wonderful to see two people of such youthful appearance in love like us and then expanded that love was wonderful at any age. "But it's a little bit better when you're young," the husband with careful softness wove in.

We caught a trolley to her apartment; she yet did not own an automobile. It was my opinion that she hadn't gone ahead and bought one because she had developed a fondness for trolleys.

"I hate to see trolley's disappear Ramsey. Do you think they will?"

"Likely. Everything does you know." The use of passenger trains of that era noticeably started to decline and after parsing through her question I said to her with conviction that

I felt certain that trolleys would in time undergo the same transition. "The City of San Francisco will hold onto theirs longer than anyone else. There, trolleys are a built in way of life." And then Leland's face shot into my thoughts. "That's where he lives. I'm ashamed of myself for not already writing him."

No longer did Nenia live with Claude and Thelma. I knew that her mother and father considered it unacceptably awful for her to live inside a quarters all by herself. In the end she won out. Dinner waited, catered in by a nearby restaurant famous locally for delivering like services. To help with the serving, she even hired a maid who had set out the food, the table immaculately embellished with a beautiful white spread. I smiled at her determination, as well as her efficiency, to see that every tedious particular now fit into place. She thought of everything and I did not fail to realize that she had done it all just to please and impress me. On the beginning of dinner we launched into catching up with the events of our lives over the past few months.

"Your trip to Denver. How was it?"

"Oh yes. Denver," she answered casually. "That's been a while. But yes. It was wonderful. I'm tremendously glad that I went. It would have been a huge mistake not to have gone."

"What was it about?" What she actually started to explain to me failed to materialize before my second question emerged. "Did it involve acting or something like that?"

"Not really. Wait a minute. In a way it did. We spent a week at intensively using proper expression, how to speak words and lines in the manner that drama coaches and linguistic teachers require. Day after day that's what we did."

"Anything else?"

"Not in that sense of things. We did as a group try our hands at skiing. Believe it or not I learned partly how. What great fun."

"You did it so quickly."

"Not really. I had the help of a tutor, who taught me the shortcuts."

"A tutor!"

"Um hum. The resort supplied a nice young man to help poor inept souls like me to learn. I tried to pay or tip him but he refused."

"I'm jealous. Still, I don't blame him. I myself wouldn't have accepted it either."

"Ha. No, you're not jealous. You should have been there. We'll have to go sometime."

I answered yes of course and that the idea appealed powerfully to my senses because I had never traveled to the great Rockies which I'd endlessly and always viewed in photographs and in paintings with unquenchable fascination.

Chapter 33

HER APARTMENT would have attracted the compliments of the most assiduous, not exquisitely decorated but tastefully done and a most enjoyable and comfortable place to live. I could see in my thoughts how she had very easily adapted to living there alone, which was partly bolstered by a steady flow of friends who muchly filled the gaps of her free time. When we first arrived, she toured me through right off, my eyes catching sight of the two bedrooms, concluding that one was for me, in which I was to sleep that night, at the same instance the idea running through me that how wonderful if I could but sleep next to her. I admired the kitchen from the first moment, dainty in size and nice and attractive, and endowed of a huge glass window with those usual little square panes running up and down and across. The window looked out onto the back patio, heavily fringed with vines and tendrils. A pale mimosa stood proudly at the western corner of the yard, a grove of beech crowding together here and there and the grass that past morning immaculately barbered. "A lovely place," I muttered. One room, the den, exhibited photographs of Mr. and Mrs. Stoddard. I looked at them and then at Nenia and nodded a smile, seeing by the pleasantness showing in her eyes that it moved her that I had promptly noticed.

"They in no way agreed to my taking an apartment Ramsey, adamantly resisting as you can imagine, but eventually caved in. Thelma argued my cause. She always has. At first I toyed with the notion of sharing space with a roommate, scuttling the idea after sorting through the pros and cons of close up daily living with another. I'm picky in matters involving housekeeping and a roommate in limited quarters day after day can easily result in cabin fever."

"You mean exploding tempers."

"Ha. Yeah."

A nudge of temptation pressed me to inquire teasingly whether she would place rather especial strictness on my untidy habits when we were married, shying away from the subject however because in my vision of the obscure future we were a long way from tying the knot, and I deemed it best not to stir up the least hint of it.

That night we started out by sitting on the divan watching television, a mechanical that hadn't attained to modern day technical standards, still consisting of perhaps an overdose of black and white imagery. Television not long before that period was birthed to the public as a rare and new invention, transformed in short while into a mode of entertainment for all ages, young, middle aged, and old, and it now augmented, yet had not replaced, the lovely songs and music played over the radio. "You know Nenia, in the olden period of our grandparents the suitor expected to ask for permission to sit with the daughter in a small room called the parlor and talk. And that was pretty well it."

"I can't imagine us doing that," she said with aroused spirit. "Terribly stifling, wasn't it. How awkward. How dry. How stripped of richness and variation. What on earth did they talk of and what did they do otherwise? Walk down by the stream with someone tagging along on their coattails as a chaperone."

I hardly expected her to comment on the social modes of the past in that manner and laughed aloud and said in agreement that way back then that's the way customs were. I chose as well to speak of a dawning new society which had burst on to the scene as a result of the war, the catalyst for producing money and televisions and cars and places to go, close and afar, and that we were prime examples of the new period and the new breed.

"Every generation is different. The next one will live by customs and behaviors that break sharply from ours, perhaps radically." The dawning of the hippies stood just around the corner to assume its station and in our wildest stretching we were unable to glean what that culture would usher forth. Whatever we chose to call it, we likely all agreed that it swept upon us much sooner than expected.

We moved at her suggestion to the patio, sitting on the chase lounges while sipping coffee which she'd brewed and served. As we sat for while, saying nothing or very little, basking in what now I allude to as a mood of virtual comfort and relaxation, just listening to the quietness of the evening or to whatever sounds the evening gives off—that is, the katydid, the tree frog, etc.—it came to me, all at once, that, "here we are, a makeover of how folks used to behave in olden times, sitting out on the back porch talking, contented and communicating in half completed sentences with worries, if there were any, a thousand miles away. "This is a good kind of living," my silent self said to me. She had dressed in a soft nice chemise, an attire of a quite thin texture, and wore as a lower piece a colorful flaring design which I took as an origin of handiwork resembling a culture of the past, the twenties or perhaps the thirties. It couldn't have been more appropriate for the occasion. I hadn't seen her before attired in clothing of this flavor. When I went to bed in the one assigned to me, she waited for a while then stole softly in. She'd changed clothing. She now fashioned a lovely gown of emerald green and had fixed her hair in a manner to keep it from falling down her back, in any event I surmised as much when she had gotten in bed with me and turned her back and asked if I would remove the pins. Raising myself I did as she asked, lifting one pin at a time, a lovely lock falling to her shoulders with each removal until I finished. She then, remaining in muted silence, cuddled into my arms as close as she could snug. We lay there for a little while without saying a word and then commenced to talk and talked for the longest of the events of the day and speculated the tomorrow to come. When the clock gonged that the hour had reached three o'clock, she said she must go, kissing me sweetly and bidding goodnight. I hated to give her up. A step before passing through the doorway she turned and said, "I'm so glad you love me Ramsey. I think of you every single night."

"I echo that sweetheart."

She started to stop but paused. Pensive like. As if forgetting something.

"What is it?"

"Sweetheart. You've never called me sweetheart before. Not ever. It warms me inside that you say that. My father used to call my mother sweetheart. Wasn't that a lovely thing?"

She bade goodnight and on inaudible little feet passed through the doorway. In truth, something inside tempted me to plead with her to stay on for just five minutes more. But she was gone. With little lapse of time I heard her yawn. She had left the door open to her bedroom and soon the loveliness of her sighs began to rise and fall.

The next morning, after the hectic commuter traffic lessened, we rented a car, an open top roadster, and drove throughout the city, starting with the roadway that traversed the banks of the great river, the Missisippi, then circled round to have a look at the breweries, famous landmarks, on which she gave a limited commentary on the matter of the Germans who, she pointed out, had migrated to the city a hundred years before with their knowledge and sophisticated skills at distilling a drink that Americans were to adopt as a favorite past time refreshment.

"Do you like beer Ramsey?"

"I can take it or leave it. Coke's are much better."

She laughed with gaiety. "Some answer."

From there we entered into our usual chit chat, light stuff, which we liked most but then again took up the Germans, becoming a bit analytical and a bit scholarly.

"The Germans are an ingenious people Ramsey; it seems they can do anything technical."

"I concur. You only have to take a casual glance at things to understand as much, tractors, bulldozers, bridges, dams, a miniscule few, and all these and more are pretty much attributable to the remarkable Germans. If not for these resourceful folks I'm afraid our illustrious progress in America might have fallen short of its present attainment. Yet there's a dark side too."

Then the story began to deepen and before we finished it had penetrated into realms that extended further by far than either of us expected or intended. But we were scholars, well read, frequently reading much of the same content, particularly if it encompassed the rich milieu of history and people; and we tended to milk a topic to the extreme.

"A dark side! Explain." She scribbled something on a note pad which I suspected challenged one of my previous remarks or else presaged a question she'd like to ask.

"The Great War. Not long ago ended. The handy work of the Germans, you know, not altogether their doing but they played a strategic role in instigating it, and the one before that."

She waited, and then. "Go on. Let me hear the rest."

I nodded okay. "My teachers in college lecture that Roosevelt and Churchill, with the war nearly over and the peace negotiations soon to get underway, entertained quite serious notions with respect to the Germans in generations that succeed us. They said that genetics and history dictated that the Germans' were warlike, aspiring toward destruction and the aggrandizement of power, a tendency running strong in their veins as far back as Caesar's time, you know, when the Roman Senate assigned him to defend against the barbarians who incessantly terrorized Gaul which is as you know now France."

To this I said I had more to add and proceeded, citing that Gibbon had written, as well as the ancient Tacitus in his weighty delineations, that the warlike Germans first were repelled but in time invaded and at length overturned the Western Monarchy of Rome, and that the German warrior, lazy by his nature, destitute of every art that might employ his leisure hours, consuming his days and nights in the animal gratifications of sleep and food and liquor, adding that this languid soul, oppressed with the weight of his own indulgences, anxiously required some new and powerful sensation; and that war and danger were the only amusements to his fierce temper. The sound that summoned the German to arms proved grateful to his ears. It roused him from his uncomfortable lethargy, and, by strong exercise of the body, and violent emotions of the mind, restored him to a livelier sense of his existence.

I said that I'd bet my last coin that Churchill had digested these lines during his many readings over time and addressed them with Roosevelt.

"What did they propose? I mean Roosevelt and Churchill?"

"I'm uncertain. The professors fell short of delving into the subject with any appreciable length, merely asserting that as far as they knew Churchill and Roosevelt seriously thrashed through the matter and I'm rather certain that they did because the leaders of the nations of the world all over were resounding concern that given latitude the Germans might break out again because it wasn't more than twenty years past when a great war ended and another had begun, the Germans at the forefront of both."

We skipped to another topic soon thereafter, not however without her taking up the concluding summation that we should practice more hesitancy in singling out the Germans, for weren't there other cultures over the centuries that demonstrated equally aggressive tendencies, the Russians, the Persians, the Mongols, the Romans, the Macedonians and Alexander the Great, "and let us not overlook the Vikings whom we should not fail to count among the worst of the terribles."

We stayed in the downtown vicinity throughout the day, gabbing, laughing, parading by my inflated estimation through a hundred stores, where once, as we happened upon one that catered to high end women's fashion, she let out a shriek at my allusion to the naked mannequin posing in the showcase frontage and covered her mouth, simply faking innocence. From time to time she would reach and take my hand or poke her hand under my arm and squeeze. When approaching a delicatessen, which she and her friends frequently patronized, she insisted that we drop in for a sandwich and coffee. We didn't stay long. But the place was nice and the patrons seemed at the peak of a good time, with an acceptable tendency toward a trickle of rowdyness. A lady with a high pitched voice kept letting out a cackle. Nenia especially noticed the extra large glass windows and the checkerboard tablecloth. After we'd finished with the sandwich and coffee we ordered a milkshake that we shared. The sandwiches were small, leaving sufficient stomach space for something additional. She looked over at me as she lifted her lips from her straw and kissed me with her eyes. Appropriately light for the season, the red frock in which she had clad herself easily ensnared my fancy, not to mention the coquettish beret, also red, pinned to her bundle of dark lovely strands. "A combination very much Parisian," it occurred to me. I teased her to watch out for those French guys, for hadn't she heard that there were forty different ways to express love in French and that some French guy might sweep her off her feet, to which she merely shrugged and cleverly downplayed the likelihood. "Don't be funny," then lowered her straw into her drink and began to sip and gleaned dapperly over at me from time to time.

Near the end of our day's excursion we left our car at a rental and caught a trolley to her home. Crowded with a bulge of people the trolley driver strove determinedly to offset his being a half hour behind schedule and after looking at my watch I asked if I understood correctly that Claude and Thelma were dropping by at seven. She verified that they were and said not to worry, that we'd make it home long before they arrived. They were there a shade after seven, fifteen minutes late. Nenia said in the expression of a hurried whisper as she started to the door to greet them that lady luck surely smiled down on her. The fifteen minutes latitude she needed for setting out pastries and coffee or iced tea for her guests. Thelma had dressed in a light grey frock and a stylish colorful hat, but small, which she handed to Nenia as she entered. Everyone referred to her as a gorgeous woman, rapturous they should have said, though not in my view as gorgeous as Nenia, but close. She kissed my cheek and hugged me. It made me feel good. It said that she affectionately received me into the family. Thelma turned her eyes this way and that, as if examining the quaintness and charm of the interior. I took it that her countenance spelled out strong endorsement.

A handsome man, Claude dressed sharply, and dapperly sported his watch and chain as usual, the chain hanging as a loop from his beltline with the watch tucked away in a niche patterned and sewn into the left folds of his trousers. His mustache was still there, which I had anticipated, and fashionably tailored to thinness in keeping with the ongoing style of modern males. It added to his cavalier looks. He had always appeared in the semblance of an actor, and I do not exaggerate in attesting that in a remarkable sense he favored the famed Hollywood actor Clark Gable, both in looks and manner. Claude received me warmly, on equal footing, man to man, not a shade condescending, and I could tell that he genuinely liked me. Once Nenia revealed that he had said to Thelma that I seemed a steady sort, a true blue, the kind that could run a big corporation and naturally that stretched my liking of him to greater extremes. I found him stimulating, well versed in an array of interests, and most particularly in his line of work, stock brokering. I had known for awhile that he served in the capacity as head broker at a prominent stock exchange in Saint Louis. Nenia casually said to me one day in private, without supplying forbidden information, that her brother-in-law owned thousands of shares in the Westinghouse Corporation.

We sat in the living room for a while, Nenia and I in the high backs which she'd moved from another room and Claude and Thelma on the divan on which Nenia and I sat the night before watching television. Since the evening presented a cool and pleasant temperature on the outside, Nenia suggested that we take seats on the patio which she had added to the rear of her home. After we had settled ourselves and begun to enjoy a second serving of coffee, Thelma let out, "We'll miss our girl," eyeing Nenia wistfully, then turning to me. "You too Ramsey."

What she actually meant left me puzzled. In my mind I heard myself saying "Absolutely, I'll miss her," and it hit me that Thelma had dropped the remark as a means of making conversation, or more seriously that she'd made a psychological slip. I knew that she wished to the depth of her soul that we would someday marry and that it would kill her if that blessed moment were derailed. Or that might not have been what she thought at all.

"I'd like to go with her. I very much wish I could. It's a tempting dream. If it weren't for my college pursuits and my work, I'd—."

"Oh! What work?" asked Claude, quickly cutting in.

Then spoke Thelma. "Claude. My goodness. You know." Her voice bordered on reproach as if he couldn't have possibly forgotten and that if he had he should feel ashamed. Nenia had conveyed to them repeatedly the nature of my work with the law firm.

In an attitude as if Thelma said nothing at all he reached his hand into the white deep bowl filled with popcorn and fed a few pieces to his mouth, then followed with a sip of iced tea. He merely smiled over at Thelma, and then clearing his throat tactfully probed into my job, asking with careful politeness what was it like. In a general sense I explained that my job had to do with delivering depositions, picking them up in Chicago at a law firm and flying them to New York City two days in a row.

"How did you end up in something like that, inasmuch as you're not a lawyer? Not a lawyer yet I'm sure."

I explained that a young man, Aaron Stylman, the son of a wealthy Jewish man approached me some few months previous with news that his father wished to offer me a job, that his father owned a significant share of the law firm.

"I think he did it as a favor. I'm on good terms with his son. You know how Jewish folks are. They're kind to you if you're kind to them. He wanted to help me because I befriended his son. The fact is Aaron and I would have stayed bound to one another irrespective of the job."

"Is the firm in Chicago or in New York City?"

"Both. They have offices in both cities."

I had sparked his interest. I could easily see that I had and then the reason why forged to the surface.

"You say you're into depositions? Well Ramsey, I've had dealings with depositions, many times, and I'm afraid I have a dim view of their use."

"How's that?" I hadn't the faintest of what view he held.

"Depositions. Hmmm. Just another device those damn sneaky lawyers employ to add to your bill and fill their coffers. Why don't they simply bypass the nonsense of that legal hokus pokus in favor of a direct trial and get it over with? They don't pay any attention to the depositions anyway once the trial begins to roll. Half the time or more they don't even read them. Period. They'll lie and tell you they do but they don't."

I had no ready answer, in fact none at all. Which I don't think he expected of me. Thelma, now bored with the job talk interrupted us before we went further.

"Your college life. Tell me about it."

A tentative thread ran through me as I muddled over where I should start, but finally I decided and from there on everything lodged into place with but minimum struggle. "To begin with, I'm loaded with course work which I like and enjoy and I like my professors, I really do. They inspire me and speaking of inspiration, Clement Attlee appeared on campus not many nights ago and I felt lucky and privileged to attend his speech. I had to pinch myself to force a realization that here I stood in the presence of the former prime minister of the United Kingdom of Great Britian."

Both uttered "wow, you don't say" and sought to pursue which portion of his speech seemed of greatest importance. I answered that everything was, also chipping in that I hoped I didn't sound curt or inept in admitting that I didn't sufficiently remember the most miniscule thing he said, or the most striking, continuing that during his speech I copiously took down as much as my capability allowed and that when I saw them again I'd have my notes with me and thereby supply them with a comprehensive report. I then chose silence.

"Is that it? Nothing else?" I suspected that she selected that question as a ploy to prod me for more. "Your social life. What's it like? And where do you live?"

"I stay at a house on campus which they call the fraternity house because a fraternity once owned it. It's not a bonafide fraternity house anymore. It's only called one. None of us residing there belong to fraternities. At least not yet, and as for me, well, I doubt that I'll ever join one. Too time consuming."

"I can well understand," Claude chimed in, then turned to the next topic stirring in his head. "How many guys live there?"

"Nine including me, but not including the girl."

"The girl! Did you say the girl?"

"I did. There's one who lives with us."

"How did that happen?"

"I don't know. I've never asked her. She lived there a year before I arrived."

"Gosh! I'm bowled over. A girl living around a bunch of rowdy boys. That's something."

"It pans out all right. She fits in. The boys are rowdy but not very rowdy. Around her they're perfect gentlemen. When they really turn rowdy it's not at the noon meal, because we don't have one at the fraternity house. It's at breakfast and at the evening meal when we are served as a group, and then they really go after one another."

"Quarreling and so on?"

"Not that. Debating. We debate everything, but there's no quarrelling, just good honest hard fought debate. We think of it as a learning process."

"I like that," said Thelma. "Does the girl participate? Does she jump in?"

"Oh yeah. She does and more than holds her own."

It was my imagination, I realized, though nonetheless I sensed Nenia's eyes cutting into my flesh as I talked of the girl and that she scrutinized every word. But I thought wrongly. Or concluded as such, for never once during the rest of my stay did she mention the girl, not even asking for her name, which I expected.

Claude and Thelma rose simultaneously, he eyeing the hour hand of his watch, Thelma announcing that they must run along; and as they hugged first Nenia then me Thelma regretted that I couldn't go with them on the trip they were taking within two days to see the Stoddards.

"It sorrows me that I can't. I would immensely enjoy seeing them." To see Mr. Stoddard once again sitting virtually against the old aging obsolete Zenith waiting for Kaltenborn to deliver the evening news would have been an amusing and refreshing experience. It seemed that Kaltenborn and Mr. Stoddard were made from the same fabric, both somber and grave in their approach to things. History was the loser when destiny refused to let them meet one another.

The formalities of bidding goodbye and goodnight went suitably well, with the exception of a peculiar aspect of the occasion which for me proved a trifle awkward, for as Thelma hugged me and wished me well it loomed that she just might entertain in her head a few negative thoughts of the young man spending that night with her sister. "Does she suspect that I'm sleeping with her young sister? Of course she suspects that." It was somewhat assuaging to know that Nenia earlier told her that I did not sleep with her and that we had committed sometime ago to this understanding; nevertheless, I still felt awkward and uncomfortable.

As they moved to the outside and started for their car Claude issued a promise that he and Thelma would in the months not far away pay me a visit, that he anxiously awaited setting foot on the campus of the famous university for the first time. I surmised that his notions were serious in that not infrequently he traveled to Chicago to attend to business at the futures exchange and while there sailing with friends on Lake Michigan.

Time was running out, the hour of my departure set for eight o'clock the next morning. My plane would leave at nine. Nenia made more coffee, which she chose to serve on the patio where we'd sat with Claude and Thelma. Within moments she turned to me with a remark from Claude.

"He likes you Ramsey; he does very much. I hope you two will form a genuine friendship"

"I like him too. Do you suppose he's serious about a trip to Chicago?"

"If he said he's coming he's coming. Count on it."

I began suddenly to contemplate how I might receive him should he really make good on his intention, and began to explore a number of venues for his entertainment. "But I'll cross that bridge when I'm closer to it," I explained to myself.

Chapter 34

THERE WAS no question that Nenia felt saddened about going away so far, her usual happy countenance gone most of the time and she did not hesitate to speak of her lowness of mood, lamenting that, "A whole year will pass without my seeing you. What will I do with myself?"

"You'll stay busy," I said consolingly, hoping that I wasn't showing downcastness too. "A year sounds like a long while but it will roll by quickly and besides you'll have your hands full with your French. You won't have time for sadness once you're there and launch into your studies. And meeting new and exciting people." She looked at me with an artificial smile without acknowlegment of my words of comfort.

It momentarily occurred to us to patronize an all night diner two blocks away, just killing time more or less, sipping coffee and listening to the juke box. Juke boxes were still widely in vogue in that era. But we decided against the idea.

Nenia asked how did my friend Leland appear to fit into the California culture, that she didn't hear me speak of him much, hardly at all. "Fine, fine" I answered. "As you know he resides in San Francisco. In his letter which I'm figuring I received two months ago he indicated they'd assigned him to the mechanical design sector, yet he aspired to move into theoretical electronics."

"Doing what exactly?"

"He didn't really bother to say. Only that he was gladdened at the opportunity. When I write him, which is right away, I'll ask him to supply more in detail." I owed him a letter. And this reminded me of something else. I urged her to give my warmest and best wishes to her parents when she visited, and to call or drop by and see my mother if she could work it out.

"You know I will. I give you my solemn promise."

We turned in at midnight. We lay there talking for an hour or more, then she rose and said she'd set the clock with assurance that she would have breakfast ready by seven. It was ready a few minutes before and not more than a half hour afterwards we were walking to the corner where we were to catch the trolley to the airport. We arrived at eight thirty, the plane not due for another thirty minutes, the alternative being that we just sat inside the terminal watching the people coming and going. They seemed only vaguely listening to the announcements booming through the public address system of arrivals and departures.

"Airports are fascinating, aren't they?" Her voice sounded vibrant, an invention to camouflage her sadness I figured.

I agreed they were, envisioning silently that within another few days she'd catch a plane at this very airport for Paris. I started to mention that in comparison to her lengthy and tiring flight, including stopovers, mine to Chicago would amount to no more than a footstep. Within another ten minutes a voice blared over the speakers that my flight would soon take off. I pulled her to me and she began to cry. The sadness of it all, seeing her cry like that, forced a lump in my throat and in the absence of better words to say I said to her to be a good girl and write and that I'd do the same. Time was up. After hurriedly kissing her lips and squeezing her one last time I made my way through the doorway to the boarding ramp.

We'd hardly gotten aloft it seemed when my plane landed at the busy Chicago airport where I promptly caught a trolley for a portion of the way to the campus, then a taxi for the remainder. By then I knew my way around the city expertly, even suggesting to the taxi driver at one stage that he take a certain street and thus gain the advantage of a short cut.

"Thanks buddy," he said, with a kind of tartness, showing no emotion one way or another, maybe not as friendly as I might have liked, but in any event wasn't too displeased at my gesture because he took the street that I designated when reaching it.

After we turned into the campus entrance and passed the Memorial Chapel there was a detectable ambience of quietness, no students of any sizeable number buzzing about, the way of life on a university campus between semesters. As I made my way through the fraternity house doorway I heard Bertinelli's cheery whistle in the area of the kitchen, as he shortly came out, striding over to give me a hug. As I had become to Aaron, I also had become to Bertinelli a close friend.

I asked if he were alone. He said he was. In a lofty mood he asked if I wanted him to fix me something to eat.

"No Bert, don't do that. I've gluttoned enough for a while. I think right now I'll camp out for a rest period in my room and read, then take a nap."

"Up late last night?"

"Late."

But then I asked where was everyone, really knowing without asking.

"They're all gone, all except Aaron."

"Where is he?"

"At the beach. He left early."

"Oh yeah. I've heard him say he liked to go over there. Guess he's having a ball among the crowd. They're at their peak this time of year come to think of it."

"Yep. They are. As thick as a bunch of bees."

Glancing at the huge window that permitted a view of a choice sector of the campus I ambled over and began to scan the serenity and beauty of the landscape. A patch of ivy clung to the façade of one of the stately halls, a scene that for decades provided impeccable distinction to the campus and always does to any campus irrespective of its whereabouts. It calls to your mind upon seeing such imagery tall stacks of books and professors and knowledge and lines of students on the threshold of graduation. Going into my room I made an instant discovery, not a surprise I should acknowledge, but neither did I expect it. Darya, before leaving for home, appended a note, a clever witticism which is common place among the academic crowd, to a side table which read, "You have a nice summer and don't forget that semesters in the summer are alarmingly short; don't drop your pencil because by the time you pick it up the semester is over."

There arose at that point a tendency within me to join Aaron on the beach, and perhaps I would have made good on the idea had I believed I could handily find him in the mass. On second thought I was dissuaded, turning instead to reading one of my favorite books on history. To this day, I recall with absolute distinction the limited paragraphs that I quickly browsed, after which I slowly re-engaged them in depth. What I read focused on the great Roman general and emperor, Aurelian, who, despite his courage and leadership in saving Rome from the Barbarians—at least temporarily—suffered annihilation at the hands of his own legions, supposedly because he succumbed to corruption for personal gain, a lie it was later ascertained. A general, Mucapor, whom he had always loved and trusted, stepped forward with the truth. Corruption walked hand in hand with the emperor's soldiers and generals, as well as those in whom he felt he could place confidence and employ for performing his appointed work; and it is this spectrum of behavior that stands out to me most acutely. The emperor's vexation with corruption and the lack of dependence on those around him is detected in a phrase of one of his private letters.

"Surely," says he, "the gods have decreed that my life is foredoomed to perpetual warfare," continuing on to lament that the workmen of the mint, at the instigation of Felicissimus, a slave to whom theretofore he entrusted the finances, rose up in rebellion, during which, or likely before, the government coin was adulterated, such that he, the emperor, felt persuaded to deliver out good money in exchange for the bad. Upon a slight reflection I equated the emperor's distress over the spoilage of the coin with the Benge brothers back in my hometown, who to my knowledge were not of record of counterfeit wrongdoing, no, not that, just a range of other vices, and in my judgment would qualify as prime candidates for counterfeiting were they in possession of the knowledge and means for impairing the public treasury. “Ha,” I let out, “even in such a small limited place the same corruption exists, or is likely to exist, as it existed in the time of the Caesars of Rome.”

A good many things happened on campus and in the city during the interval of that summer, most of which I'm afraid I have let escape me, but there are three that even now cling tenaciously with me. There were my studies, my two courses in math for which I enrolled in the first session and the course in philosophy in which I enrolled in the second term; and next, my job, the countless trips made via airplane in the delivery of depositions to New York and the transport of like documents back to the lawyers in Chicago; then there were the beaches, very crowded beaches, which drew the young in hordes as honey does flies, where Aaron and I hung out as much as my schedule allowed. The heat forced us there, I should explain, as well as the sheer pleasure of commingling with those in the proximity of our age who bunched together in flocks indulging in meaningless chatter talk oft as not and cut up and sang upbeat nonsensical songs they'd recently learned from the radio. I mainly sat and listened and amused myself, attempting to understand this urban young culture of which I physically was a part but inherently not.

My first summer in Chicago veered sharply away from what I expected, cool and breezy on the lakefront as the established citizens had attested. I found the atmosphere steamy and thick, the sun unforgiving as it rained down its scorching rays and the usual misty white clouds, now more a leaden gray than white, hung listless and glaring in the sky. But these nuisances acted not to discourage the young, so, like them; Aaron and I went back on every opportunity and baked our hides. Somewhere during this interim, near the last of summer, a letter arrived from Leland, my fingers impatiently getting in one another's way to open the envelope.

Dear Ramsey,

I see by television broadcast of the evening news that you are suffering a heat wave in your city, such bad luck. I regret it on your behalf. It was something you might well have avoided by joining me in the city of San Francisco where the temperature is more friendly. I wish every day that you were with me. Miss you terribly my dear friend.

I think of you in many regards, of you and that alluring girl with the European name, Nenia, so beautiful. You'll do well to cling to her. And I think of your beloved mother too, a Protestant Sunday School teacher, from whose classes I would have thoroughly profited, even if I am of the Eastern Orthodox faith. But after all, our separate denominations are essentially the same, both Christian.

I should not leave out saying something of my position with the Kaiser Corporation whose attitude is to move me as rapidly up the ladder as suitable—suitable to the top echelon to say the least—into the climate of electrical theory and experimentation; and I am hoping with fingers crossed that my aspirations and theirs will materialize.

In the final breath, I shall promise to avail my presence in Chicago as funds and time allow and do not forget that you have promised to pay me a visit as well. We shall see who delivers first.

Your dear friend always,

Leland

At last I left for my mother's. On my way it quite suddenly struck me that "how strange this driving; I've flown so many times from Chicago to New York and back that flying has in a sense morphed into the more natural of the two modes of travel." Flying seemed especially pleasant in comparison to the heat on the streets of Chicago that summer; the temperature at cloud level in an airplane ideally moderate, but on this day, as I journeyed southward, the sweltering conditions, every bit as intense as that in the city, continued to stay with me for the entirety of the trip. Making my discomfort even worse, the car that I drove, five years of age, lacked an air conditioner and I feared every mile that the heat from the concrete roadway might force a rupture in one or more of the tires. I said a silent little prayer every once in a while that such misfortune would not intercept me. Finally, the arrival. I walked into my mother's home, who in an aura of surprise let out a kind of yelp upon seeing me and hurried over and gathered me in her arms, squeezing relentlessly time and again and taking on in a state of profuse joy, such being her manner of expressing the love she nurtured in her heart for her youngest son whom she hadn't seen in months. She asked if I suffered badly from the unrelenting heat that I surely encountered throughout my travel.

"Not badly mom. I kept the windows rolled down and played the radio."

She laughed at this. "You've always liked the songs on the radio. I guess they played plenty for you."

"They did. All the way here."

As mothers will, she asked if I'd like something to eat, my answer conveying that I would just wait until supper, that I'd devoured a baloney sandwich and drank a Coca Cola not many miles before my arrival, meeting the insistence nonetheless that I try a piece of blackberry cobbler to which I offered no refusal. That evening my three sisters and brother showed up for supper, showering me with a rain of accolades for completing my first year at a famous university and that they were overwhelmed with the achievement of their brother. Downplaying it all, I said in a mein of casualness that perhaps good luck acted in my favor and that they should withhold their compliments in that I might not have such good fortune in the school year approaching. In truth I did not believe even a pinch of what I said, I felt greatly confident of myself, and looked with relish to the awaiting fall. Later that night I sat talking with my mother about the various events at the university during the year past, citing first some of the names of my fraternity friends, Bertinilli, Aaron, Gerard, plus a cadre of others, then at last alluding to Darya. "She's very smart. She's of foreign heritage, and her folks are of enviable wealth."

"That's a peculiar name," she wove in. "You said that she's foreign?"

I explained that I wasn't sufficiently thorough with my references to Darya, and went on to say a little bit more, that she was of foreign bloodline, dating far back, that her grandfather immigrated to America a long while ago. "She's Serbian, but genuinely American. We have a good many students from foreign countries. That's sort of the way it is at universities."

"I see. It's strange that my son is living among all those mixes of people."

"Ha! Don't worry. I won't let them contaminate me."

Coming over, she squeezed her chubby arms around me, grunting a tad, assuring in a voice of confidence that she knew I wouldn't let the people up there influence me because I was made of the right stuff to resist such things.

When at last I went to my room to turn in for the night and laid my head upon my pillow she stole softly in and hugged me. "I'm awfully glad you're home son. I've missed you greatly." A lump welled up into my throat, the sorrow in my heart difficult to bear, for I well imagined her loneliness at living by herself.

"How dreadful it is to grow old," I thought, "with your entire family of children gone whom you raised from tots to adulthood. "Life is cruel. Guess what? It's cruel to us all alike. That's the way it is. We have to learn to endure it."

"How long will you stay with me Ramsey?" she asked, a wistful cast alighting on her face as if she were hoping unrealistically that I'd say for an extended length, at the least a month. Obviously, she hadn't thought it through.

"Two weeks," I hesitantly replied.

The next morning, though the sky canvassed more than a scattering of clouds, no rain fell, not a single drop; we discovered that nature however had flushed the air with coolness which we greatly welcomed. My mother smiled at my playfulness when I told her that I had enticed it to follow me on my trip from the North.

Pretty soon after breakfast I asked her of Ozzie and Cavanaugh, with her telling me that she hadn't heard lately, figuring they were doing well with their business because John Eric had dropped by about a month before reporting nothing to the contrary.

"John Eric is all the time in touch with them. He's good about doing that. Sometimes he helps them out with common labor things. That's all he can do. He's in the dark in matters of technical machinery."

Excusing myself I exited the back door with an aim to look around, the withered garden she tended that summer catching my attraction first and foremost, then the grapevines covering the arbor that I once built. She'd gathered the grapes for making jam before the rains ceased to fall. Then there stood the old outhouse, still erect but no longer in use. Before I left I borrowed John Eric's tractor to push it down and then fill the cavity with dirt. I later burned the half rotted lumber.

That afternoon I drove down mainstreet and passed by Billy's Hardware on the right then his furniture store on the left and by Doode's two story café on the corner which featured its customary red and yellow neon lights above the windows, which Billy chose to leave as they were. He claimed the lights were a good draw for his sporting supply business. The usual citizens I in no way failed to observe standing on both sides of the street, peering, curious, pondering, the farmers dressed in overalls with hands sunk into their pockets talking the same talk as they did always, but taking particular stock of the Illinois license plate without recognizing the driver. Turning onto the highway to the east I soon passed Monett's Citizens Trust Bank on my left and a hundred yards onward the Sinclair gas station on my right, whereby a very short distance I entered the narrow gravel road that ultimately terminated at the tractor business now owned by Ozzie and Cavanaugh. I found them at work at the mouth of the huge shed building that we'd help Leland build. We saw one another at the same time. Before I could make my move they made theirs, dropping whatever tools they held in hand and with arms outstretched and beaming faces came to me at a half trot.

"Ramsey. What a shock. We didn't expect to see you."

This was Ozzie, the spokesman, the talker of the two.

"I didn't know if I'd get by to see you or not. But didn't want to miss the opportunity. I'm here on a short stay."

"But what does short stay mean."

"Maybe two weeks."

"That's good. That's good."

After this we began to take up numerous talking points, the name of Leland quickly forging into the rapidity of jabber, during which I began to look around, not seeing the assembly of tractors that should have been lined up for repair as I had anticipated, a trifle curious if activity had fallen away for some reason that slipped me.

"No need to say that you really miss that guy," I spoke, knowing they did, far more than they missed me.

"A lot. We miss him a lot. We're doing all right Ramsey, but not as easily and well as we did with him here. He could fix anything as you know, do anything, and not be long about it." Ozzie shook his head from side to side as if in disbelief and regret.

"Yep. I'll say in a second that he's the best. I have to say also that you fellows are good too. Just keep at it. You'll do well."

I don't think I believed myself, not altogether. I glanced again at the open space in the parking area where tractors were once jammed bumper to bumper tagged with number cards which were employed to signal to a certain farmer to pull his tractor into the work bay for repair. The half filled waiting lot bothered me. I'd ask Mr. Carney when I saw him for a status report. I figured on second thought that a fraction of the slack, if not more than that number, was owing to the dry weather which forced a decrease in overall farming activity. Naturally I conjectured that if the tractors weren't in use or only partially in use they weren't very often breaking down.

Upon leaving I jokingly mentioned that I might just return later in the week in my aviator outfit and help them out yet remarked in the same breath that I'd simply get in their way.

"No, no," Ozzie spoke up, "no you wouldn't. Slip on your coveralls and come on. We'd enjoy you being here man, any time you're willing."

Near the end of my first week home I decided to see in on Nenia's mother and father, the Stoddards, dropping in at mid-afternoon. I hoped to avoid an invitation to supper where I envisioned their hammering me with a deluge of questions, there finding myself striving to engage in conversations that were hardly in my zone of usual interest. The Stoddards received me warmly, and at first all three of us talked mostly of Nenia's stay abroad, an easy topic to pursue. She'd written her parents a barrage of letters and mentioned me once or twice, Mrs. Stoddard said, particularly that I came to see her prior to her leaving for France and that we'd ridden or walked throughout the Saint Louis vicinity for a whole afternoon. They said they missed her awfully, to which I remarked that I did too but was happy for her. "She's realizing an opportunity of a lifetime," I further pitched in and to this they agreed amidst faces of melancholy.

Chapter 35

AFTER AN hour's visit I stood and explained that I must run, pledging however that I'd see them once again before the end of my stay. Blocking my utterance of another word Maggie clasped my hand, looking pleadingly up into my face, insisting on my remaining for supper. She referred to the old times when I was but a young lad, smiling playfully over at me with the remark that I often ate with them, and that Nenia bubbled with happiness because of my presence at these most cordial occasions. Who could have resisted? Not I. So, I stayed, and again things seemed like old times, the heavy oaken table dotted with a carousel of foods. Mr. Stoddard energetically spoke of the crops, especially the effect of the dry weather that summer, seemingly trying not to let his distress leak through, and got around to tactfully probing into my life at the university. With skillful word choice I skimmed over most things, but purposefully cited as a highlight Clement Attlee's speaking on campus that spring.

"You don't say! And you were there for that Ramsey?"

"Oh yes," Maggie spoke up, "Thelma mentioned it in her letter. Don't you remember that Phillip?"

Nenia's absence was strange, no less. She was there and she wasn't. Her laughter echoed vibrantly in my ears when once I slipped out for a few moments and sat in the front porch swing where we'd evolve all sorts of funny things. It wasn't long until I made my way back inside. Once Maggie suggested that I look into Nenia's room where she kept her books, some of which she shipped back from Saint Louis for storage while away in France.

I asked if she wrote much, reproaching myself immediately, for I suddenly recalled that she said that Nenia frequently sent letters.

"She does. Every week. She doesn't miss."

As the six o'clock hour approached, I managed to bid goodnight, with a promise, as I had already done, to return before I left for up North as I sometimes termed it.

When first reaching home from Chicago I had decided not to pay call on the town's people to any appreciable extent, and that is precisely what I did. There were a select few that I absolutely had to see, however, one such person, an old loud talking, laughing Negro, who over the years I greatly appreciated and admired. I found him where I expected, still mounting car tires for a tire store near the once owned Jeremy Dodson grocery, a craft that he had performed for four decades, since the time of my early youth and before. I used to stand for long lengths fascinated by his workmanship which he exacted with the profoundest of ease. Before this he shod horses in addition to his tire work. I watched him do that too until the occupation of shoeing horses faded into obsolescence. He and the horses were enjoined by a natural affinity, evinced by his talking to the animals in the quietest of tone, basey, gruff but gentle too, as if he were a human speaking to another human.

"Now don't you kick me sir. We're friends. Yes sir. You don't want us to part ways do you?"

I wasn't about to miss seeing him. Recognizing me at once he laid down his handicraft and in long natural strides came over, his powerful hand squeezing mine as if he meant it from the bottom of his soul.

"Well, well young man. Glad to see you. I hear you're up North now, doing some serious studies. Yes sir."

"Yes I am. I'm home for a short stay." I felt I should have said "Yes sir," but didn't.

"Going to college I hear. That's good. I knew your daddy. He'd feel real proud of you. As are we all."

It clicked in my head that perhaps he represented the typical townsfolk feeling, that by and large they all missed me. What pricked my thoughtfulness mostly was the fact that here he was, an old Negro man who in his heart felt gladdened to see me, who had kept up with me, and seriously delighted in acknowledging my accomplishments, or what he thought they were. It touched me. Suddenly, next to my mother's feelings of me, his meant more than anyone else's in the whole community. He smiled broadly as we stood conversing; his very large white teeth glaringly dominant, his lips stretching to their extremes when he laughed. I had known him always as Bradford Cunningham, at once a commanding figure, extant anywhere you saw him. With a voice deep and coarse, people easily heard him speaking a block away unless he took precaution to subdue the volume. They always said throughout town that beginning way back he had pastored a Baptist church in the countryside. By and large they spoke of him as a gifted orator. And I have no doubt they were right. I suffer regret that I never heard him preach. Should his station in life been differently timed, his birth, he might well have sat as a senator in the capitol of our great country.

In the past I'd seen Bradford visiting with Elizar Lebranche and Miss Estonia Lebranche on her front portico. Bradford had since boyhood enjoyed a bosom friendship with Elizar and since I had just left him it struck me as something of a coincidence that as I meandered down the street I glimpsed two attractive white women climbing into an automobile whose driver was of relatively light color, bronze to a greater extent than black, and upon serious contemplation recognized the two women as Sallie and Sadie Lebranche, Elizar Lebranche's two beautiful daughters who easily drew my admiration in my growing up years, yet by now were decidedly older in appearance. I later learned from John Eric that the bronze skinned young man driving their automobile doubtless was Sadie's son.

"Where do they live now?" I asked.

"Fort Wayne. Fort Wayne, Indiana. They're here to look in on Elizar. He's not doing well. In bad shape I'm afraid."

Finally, I had caught up with John Eric on his farm where soon after the noon hour I found him earnestly at work cutting cabbage for transport up North I figured. I had it wrong. He said that the temptation often grabbed at him to truck a load to Lansing which after thinking it over changed his mind, opting to let the local broker buy the produce at a lower price who ran the packing and shipping shed situated along the railroad.

"I won't git as much pay for it but it's a whole lot of trouble to driveway up there to Lansing or Detroit. And the trip completely wears me down."

As he knew I would I rolled up my sleeves and helped him work the cabbage for the whole of the afternoon, delighted to have the opportunity, not work in the least, actually comedy with John Eric filling me in on the latest gossip of mainstreet and the irksome contrariness of one of our relatives who he didn't like and neither did I. It loomed in my imagination that my father worked beside us while listening in on our talk of the ups and downs of the people in town and the local surroundings. Rather soon John Eric struck upon asking for a snippet of my university activities, remarking before I returned a word that he knew I had done well. Everyone I met said the same thing.

"How do you know I'm doing well?" I asked.

"Your mother. She told me. She said she knew by the letters you wrote."

"That figures. Well, you know how mothers are."

"Yep. I know. But you are doing all right, are you not?"

"I am John Eric. I'm doing okay."

At some point we finished with the cabbage cutting for the day and loaded up the pickup as well as a flat bed, a trailer, attached to the truck. Just for kicks I decided I'd like to ride on the latter contraption all the way to town. To keep me from excessively jostling up and down John Eric drove slowly. When we reached the packing shed there were the dock workers cramming cabbage into sack after sack of some sort of green netted material, in the resemblance of a fish net, while heavily carrying on in a manner of horseplay and nonsense foolery. We unloaded and then went to John Eric's house in the country, a half mile away. It was nearing the hour for my departure, though dismissing myself wasn't easy because he insisted on my sitting down at the kitchen table to a freshly picked watermelon. He cut it into and pushed half of it across the table with a fork already plunged into the heart.

"Guess who I saw yesterday John Eric," I exclaimed soon after I had taken my first bite.

"Who?"

"Sadie and Sally Lebranche. I haven't seen them in years."

"Oh them. They're here to see old Elizar. He's on the edge, if you know what I mean."

"Getting old huh?"

"Yeah. Real old. They say he can hardly move his joints."

"There was a young light colored Negro man with them. Who was he?"

"Sadie's son."

"I figured as much. I haven't ever heard of him."

"No, I guess not."

"But I remember Sadie and Sally. I didn't see them much when I was growing up, but every once in a while when we passed Elizar's place on our way to school or back I'd see them on the front porch. They stood out as plain as day, so white and all. I thought they were the prettiest girls in town."

"I mean," said John Eric with an extension to his words that they were more than pretty. "Likely, that's when they'd driven in once from college, anyway from going to school somewhere up North where Elizar sent them. On back before that Ramsey, which you don't recall, and I don't either, but I remember the tale."

"When? What tale?"

"Well let me see." After collecting himself, after working it through, "Well, there was once a livery stable on the north side of the railroad tracks with a quarter acre sized pond close by, where farmers and traveling salesmen left their buggies and wagons and horses while in town to do their business. It was owned by Douglas Murphy, Madeline Monett's father. The livery stable was a low built building with a shallow loft where Douglass kept the feed stuff. The area below he set off into partitions for stabling the horses. I recall some of that, but not the part I'm coming to. The tale especially grows out of the Saturday afternoons when Sadie and Sally would pull up in their surrey, planning like everybody else to leave it and the horses for somebody to see after. Most everybody knew them, but as I said, most everybody, not everybody. When they started driving toward the stable one day, on a Saturday I take it, they were all dressed up in sparkling white clothes and somebody said they looked as pretty as a bouquet of pink roses. When they drew close enough they stopped and two young white salesmen ignorant of their being Elizar's girls rushed over to help them down and took their horses and surrey inside. Making complete arrangements for the girls. You can imagine can't you the gawkers, ignorant bastards, standing around looking on and grinning and winking and whispering to one another. As the girls left toward mainstreet across the tracks you could hear them giggling and see them holding up their hands to their mouths, beside themselves that their natural power of charm and beauty had overpowered the unknowing young white men. But the young white salesmen wadn't the only ones overpowered. The same thing happened to others no telling the times. It wadn't no trouble at all for Sally and Sadie to get away with their trickery, I guess you'd call it, cause their bloodline flowed from Elizar Lebranche, their daddy, and from their granddaddy, J. H. Ascension Lebranche, the man who a long while ago donated the land the town was founded on. But even if this hadn't been fact a good many young white men would have gone for the girls and proposed marriage if feeling they could have run away with them to some Northern city where the people wouldn't have put up such a high fuss over the mix of white and black"

"What happened after this? After this period of their lives?"

"Don't know exactly. Elizar sent them up North the word was. There's always been something going on around our little town to excite the parents to send an offspring away that's troublesome. You will have recollection of Melinda Monett and her ex sailor lover. Rupert Monett and Madeline sent her away people say to keep her away from him. You remember that don't you?"

"Who doesn't?"

My mother thrived on teaching the Sunday school class for the women of the church of which she'd long enjoyed membership, who looked upon her with veritable reverence. Some went so far as to refer to her as a kind of Saint, but meant in the references that they spoke as such because they beheld her as a splendidly good person The mind set of these women was that her knowledge of the written word of scripture went beyond their own by one hundred fold; let alone her spirituality. She threw her heart and soul into her teachings and into the reading of the gospel, switching back and forth between the Old and New Testament. They thirstily drank in every passage she uttered or read, or did a very good job of giving the indication. At the same time she took care not to gorge them, to charge that they read certain assigned scriptures and prepare well for the next Sunday's lesson, realizing that most, if not all, would not apply themselves that tediously. But I did not fit in that mold. From childhood upward she encouraged and persuaded me to join her as she combed through the Gospel from one Book to the next. Though not revealing it to her that such sittings were too often long and boring, the pattern continuing into my teens, when I attained to manhood all that changed. I began to enjoy and truly learn from those endeavors. It was when she finished leading me through one of her scriptural selections one evening that she laid the Bible down and in a gesture as if she'd almost forgotten to tell me reported that Melissa had stopped off to see me during my being out somewhere, leaving news that Rupert Monett had suddenly started ailing and that he presently received treatment at the regional hospital. She left word that she'd appreciate my driving over to the hospital to see him. She was staying at his side. My mother urged me to honor Melissa's request. I marveled at her goodness, at her power to forgive, but didn't see how she could, for I recalled with mirror transparency, coupled with never abated bitterness, how the man lied to her about the job she desperately sought at the school cafeteria, in the finale assigning it to the wife of one of his cronies. As I passed through the doorway I found Melissa sitting somberly at Monett's bedside trying to concentrate on the contents of a magazine, the sight of him at first blush conveying a man broken out with shingles on his torso and around his arms; and keenly seen also were his other defectives, his face drastically emaciated, masked with an ugly façade of yellowish pallor, lifeless, and his eyes hardly attentive to anyone deciding to visit, the portrait of much pain and suffering.

Despite the seriousness of the moment Melissa rose with jubilance and took my arm, then as she led me out into the hallway she squeezed me to her and said how deeply she appreciated my dropping by.

"I've heard you were home. I'd hoped you'd call, but I guess you were busy. And conscious of the little time you had left to spend here I'm sure."

"That's right." I avoided saying that I intended to drop by and see her, because it wouldn't have been the truth. After we'd stood and talked for a trifle she led me outside to the corridor hallway and pulled me down onto a settee beside her. I didn't know why but I began to feel glad that I came, yet succumbed to another feeling in the same breath, which was that I wasn't glad, but more glad than sad, supposedly because of her bubbly disposition and the dazzle in her eyes as she leveled them into mine. She persistently touched my arm or knee and sometimes reached her arms around me in the semblance of an embrace, all of which I confess I enjoyed. Her every manner emphasized that she was more than glad to see me. On her person she had fitted a striking pink dress that looked gorgeous upon her, and suddenly I discovered myself in backward flight to that night when she lay under the tractor with me, talking and holding up the lantern and more or less making love. Not dwelling on this reflection for more than seconds I deemed it well to ask for an elaboration on her father's condition, her gaiety swiftly vanishing.

"Not good. The doctor has diagnosed that he suffers from something worse than shingles. He's afflicted with Leukemia."

"Oh! That's too bad. I hate to hear that."

"It's awful. I think we're soon to lose him."

"Um. Um. That's too bad." I failed to discover what surely were phrases better selected.

Fairly quickly after this she took my hand and led me back into Monett's room, where to my astonishment he stirred with limited movement in his bed and with eyes that looked straight at me, but when Melissa mentioned my name I saw not the least countenance in the man's face evincing that he recognized the person standing before him. With no signs of her father displaying that he would do better than this Melissa turned to me with a suggestion that we exit to the outside and stroll about, the idea at the moment a nice thing but the hour had turned late, so I declined. "I'd better go."

"Oh! I wish you'd stay a while longer. It's unjust that you're leaving. After all it's been too long since we've spent any length together. And I hear absolutely nothing of your life while you're away up North. There's so much to talk about. And we'll have supper. I've found a small café down the street to which I'm addicted. You'd like it."

"I know I would. But I have to go." I would have relished being with her for much longer and might have stayed on except she mentioned that her mother Madeline should arrive any minute, and I did not warm up in the scantiest at the prospect of seeing her. Consequently, I begged off, yet fell prey to Melissa's plea to return the next day or day after before leaving for Chicago. Surprised at myself for consenting I nevertheless did and agreed as well when she unrelentingly insisted on walking me to my car to see me off.

I debated whether or not to return, yet when my mother urged that I should and I recalled my promise to Melissa I decided I would, arriving shortly after one o'clock in the afternoon. Rain had begun to fall when I left my mother's home, much to my chagrin elevating into sweeping torrents which refused to lessen in ferocity during my entire drive, a distance of forty miles. I sat in my car until it subsided, finally unfolding my parasol then dashing for the hospital entrance in that the downpour showed no tendency to let up. All along Melissa stood watching through the mammoth glass doorway, smiling and laughing interchangeably at the sight of my scampering to shelter. I laughed with her as I handed her my paraphernalia, looking down at my pants legs which weren't too terribly wet, but wet enough. We went to the dining nook down the hallway and sat and sipped coffee while waiting for them to dry or at least dry a bit.

"I was afraid you'd decline my plea," she said with a slight of whimper which hinted at her disappointment if I should have failed her.

I suspected that right away she'd find an opening to inquire of my activities at the university, and she did, with me answering that the academic challenges were stupendously thrilling, though hard, that I had a job traveling back and forth between Chicago and New York, and that with an opportune break in my schedule I skipped off to the operas now and then. No mention crossed my lips that Darya apt as not accompanied me in the attendance of these functions. Of course I didn't. She acted as if she entertained an impulse to pursue me in depth with respect to the few things of which I'd spoken, but a moment thereafter suggested that we drop in on her father, who to my astonishment lay alertly awake, completely lucid in all appearances, recognizing me at first sight, even calling out my name. He looked a hundred and eighty degrees better than the patient I saw in my previous observation the day before, especially in that now he lay awake and took the lead in initiating conversation. His speech rolled out slowly, in the semblance of a drawl, as he began to divulge his thoughts. I suspected that he'd suffered a stroke, even though no one else said they were of that impression.

"You've grown into a mighty fine young man Ramsey, yes you have. You're doing well I hear."

"I am, thank you sir. So far I am."

"You'll continue to. I'm sure of that. We've always known what you're made of."

"Well sir. I thank you for that." The feeling hovered over me that his daughter had built me up on a pedestal at another time, yet I did not cast aside that maybe his accolades were on the level.

Melissa smiled with elated satisfaction at the reverence that I extended to her father, and from there he proceeded, albeit slowly and feebly.

"I'm in a mess Ramsey. As you can see. It goes to show you, and while you're young you'd do well to pay it heed."

He wasn't clear. What was he driving at? "What's that sir?"

"When you have your health you have everything; nothing is more precious to a man, unless it's his family. When a man is young he dreams of money and lavish things, which, when his life is over or nearly over he realizes they amounted to no more than a thread's worth. Don't ever fall folly to such meaningless longings Ramsey. Concentrating on money is the worst of options for using your mind and talents, unfortunately like a vast many do, me among them."

I listened with riveting concentration as he rather sorrowfully laid bare his own errors and offered precautions by which man should live. In my mind I knew that his words were correct and that if anyone from past experience owned qualifications for passing out realistic advice with regard to the rules of life by which we should live I sat in the front row seat listening to his lecture. But he had waited too long for confessing regrets. Too late for anyone in his predicament. I felt for the man; as anyone with a minimum of compassion running through his emotional internals would have, yet did not attempt to extinguish my silent revolving that if he could live his life all over he might well follow the same course. So he downplayed money, the object which drives us all, and it dwelled in my being that I like him placed without reservation much emphasis on the aggrandizement of wealth and frankly hoped that one day I would have a substantial portion. How wise, and ideal, I went on musing, if we possessed the strength and wisdom in ourselves to disdain the desire for that which the Bible teaches us we should avert, concluding that the height of the bar ranged far beyond man's natural capability to reach. Then I turned in my recall to a clever and truthful line that a wise sage had once scripted, "Blessed are those who want for nothing for they shall not know disappointment."

Directly, Monett fell into sleep and Melissa walked with me to my car for the second time in two days, pulling me to her seconds before I slid into the driver's seat and kissed me on my cheek. I kissed her back and smiled as I adjusted myself into better position. I supposed I should have expected her affectionate display.

"Will you give me your phone number and address, Ramsey? I don't have them and might need to make contact with you." I didn't see why but said of course and scribbled the information on the back of an envelope that I retrieved from the glove compartment and handed it to her. She reached and touched my shoulder just as I lightly revved up the engine.

"Thank you." That she hadn't mentioned her husband during my visit was something of an oddity. Once or twice his name and image and the prospects of his availing himself invaded the environs of my curiosity. I did not pursue these aspects seriously and for any length. I supposed that her decision not to bring him up grew out of her figuring that to do so would have invited a presence of discomfort that both of us preferred to keep below our level of conscience.

Chapter 36

MY ENTIRE visit had expired, the day of my departure finding me scuttling about to discover an essential that I had overlooked, and there it was. "Whoa!" So far I had neglected to honor my friend Mr. Carney, whose office and home were situated in the town six miles away, the town where Nenia attended high school. I had risen early. Telling my mother I planned to return in the whereabouts of ten o'clock I headed for his home. When I arrived I found him sitting in his front porch swing, and upon my foot touching the bottom rung of the porch steps he arose and moved excitedly toward me with a spring in his legs, his hand outstretched. He grasped my shoulder before he hugged me. "Ramsey, my boy. Gracious! I've looked for you. When did you make it home?"

"Two weeks ago. I have to start back this afternoon. But I was hellbent on seeing you for a lengthy chat before I did."

"Heavens! I couldn't have dreamt of your doing otherwise. I'd heard you were here. It's quite good to see you. Sit down, sit down, and catch me up on what all you've been up to." He still held to my arm.

"I guess you mean around home as well as in Chicago over the year past."

"Anything you're willing to divulge," he said with a zing of excitement still in his voice.

"Not much and yet quite a bit too. I drove over to see Rupert Monett only recently, a couple of days ago. He's not doing well. I'm glad I paid my respects."

"I see. I've stayed abreast of his condition. He's in serious ill health from what I hear. The prognosis for recovery isn't favorable."

"That's what I gathered from Melissa. She was there when I went in to see him. I spent a while talking to her."

"Glad to hear you and Melissa jive. I don't think she likes for folks to see her in that light, but she seems such a stuck up thing. Aloof, if I may. But you always hit it off with her I hear folks say. And that's good."

What he said caught my undivided attention and I thought I felt my face twitch. I'm sure I blushed. Not in the slightest did I suspect that anyone in our small town associated me and Melissa in a vein of affinity. Pretending that his observation meant nothing I then turned to something else, that I studied hard at the university and together with that held down a job.

"A job on the side?"

"Yes sir"

"I'm not surprised. You were always a worker. And going on what I hear folks say you're darned smart at penetrating and learning the content of books and so I'm more than confident you're excelling in the lofty sphere of academics."

I hardly knew how to pick up on his putting me on a pedestal. I just twisted my face and bobbed my head a time or two in an effort to downplay the compliment.

"Thanks. Those are weighty words I must attest but I'm afraid sir that I don't deserve them. Truthfully though, I'm faring well, earning pretty decent marks. I intend to stay on that track."

"You will, you will."

I like it there Mr. Carney; I like it immensely. The beauty of the place is stunning, the buildings endowed of all representations of architecture. You wouldn't believe your eyes. And the people that I relate to, well, how shall I say it, well, the students and teachers migrate from all over, from a multiple mix of origins. My math teacher is German and my French teacher is French, naturally enough. Moreover, when I launch into my junior year I look forward to enrolling in some of the religious studies."

"Why that? Why study religion?"

"For many reasons, but the leading reason is tied to my nurturing a yen to listen to the precepts of the professors that delve into the deep and varied web of religious doctrines of this world. My curiosity lunged into arousal when I met Leland, who, as you know, is of the Eastern Orthodox faith, one of the subjects that we often ventured into, along with a wide array of things."

"Eastern Orthodox. I know something about that, for sure I do. My wife is Eastern Orthodox, or once was. She converted over to mine, which is Roman Catholic."

"Is that so? I didn't know that. I thought you were of Leland's faith. You are from Bulgaria aren't you?"

"Nope. I'm English. I met her in Bulgaria, and we married there."

"Is that a fact? How did you happen to wander over there from far away Great Britain."

"To begin with England isn't far from Bulgaria. And besides, Bulgaria borders on the Black Sea and the Brits with their awesome navy patrol the Black Sea and the Mediterranean around the clock given their strategic interest in the region. The Brits are almost everywhere you look, likened to money; as I say, they're everywhere. Anyway, I worked with their intelligence service after the war, quartered in Constantinople, additionally assigned to do missions in Sophia from time to time and on one of those deployments met Tatiana and you're acquainted with the rest of the story."

"Indeed I am. And what an intriguing story."

"But we weren't married on our initial meeting. It was much later, in the very late twenties. The war had ended by some measure of years."

"I'll declare." I smacked my hand on the arm of the swing on which I leaned and shook my head. "Things really happen in the most improbable ways in this life. Now, Leland wasn't born then was he?"

"No, he wasn't. Nor were you. Many a gallon of water would flow under the bridge before you two were dashed kicking and squalling onto this earth. He's about your age."

"About my age. That's right. We were in grade school together as you'll recall."

"Distinctly."

"By the way, while we're dwelling on Leland, I'll mention that I heard from him recently. He wrote me a letter."

"Good. Good. Glad to hear that." At this news, Mr. Carney substantially perked up.

"Yeah, it was good. I think he's mustering up a scheme to come see me, saving up dollars to cover the airfare."

"I hope so. And I hope he'll see me too. I'm sure he will. I'd love to see him and so would Ozzie and Cavanaugh. He means almost everything to those fellows."

"I'm aware of that. I dropped by to see them soon after reaching home, a day or two after. The first thing they asked was had I heard from him. I replied pretty much the same as I've just now reported to you, that I received a letter from him not very long ago."

I expected a quickened bounce. But he said nothing, not right then. It looked as if he were examining something in his thoughts, carefully, thoroughly, as a former British intelligence official might, or as a lawyer of rareness. I'd seen him at his work enough to discern his extra-legal capability. Then he spoke.

"Did you take it that they're doing all right with their business or were you around long enough to form a dependable opinion?"

"I guess they're doing well enough Mr. Carney. Maybe a little something is lacking. But I don't know."

"You say a little something. What does that mean?"

"The waiting line of tractors wasn't there as in the peak days. It's probable, I think I should add, that the slack might have been just for that one day, and no more than that."

"A fluke? I don't think so Ramsey. They're pretty good at what they do. But they're no Leland, who could take over a problem and solve it before it started. He was a smart one, that Leland, full of surprise quotations that sometimes left me gawking in amazement. What was it? Ah yes. 'Every solution begins with the right question,' which was one of his oft used passages. I didn't know if he snitched it from a book or heard some philosopher recite it in a speech, but it fit him well. It described his intellect perfectly. Well, so much for that. Let's get back to Ozzie and Cavanaugh. They still have customers, but competition is gaining, and they may end up in a hurting position. I know for sure that the slack is genuine. I inspect their books once each two weeks. I worry some over what I'm beginning to see. Their business is definitely slowing."

"I sure hope they turn things around."

"I do too; I hope in the strongest way they do."

I left on that note, or had gone into the motion of doing so, realizing we'd stretched this latter topic to the limit. With sad lament I bade goodbye. He had grown on me, becoming over time an endearing friend, as well as his wife, Tatiana, who as I started to leave rushed hurriedly from the inside and gave me an embrace, not immediately letting go, which bespoke a tint of sadness at my leaving.

"You will return to see us, won't you Ramsey, whenever you can," she relayed in a sweet and charming dialect of accent never to leave her.

"I will. Thank you, Tatiana."

Mr. Carney had migrated to the vicinity with Leland and his parents, electing to remain there with his wife though their relatives were gone. Great wars do incredulous things to people. They scatter them to all parts of the globe, to places where they never contemplated in their wildest they would come to and never really liked when they set foot there. Mr. Carney surely had moments of loneliness, he and his wife, she more so than him. I surmised that he stayed on as long as he did in an effort to help prop up Ozzie and Cavanaugh for whom he felt a depth of responsibility and loyalty, but that in time he'd move to San Francisco or to England or perhaps to Bulgaria where Tatiana still stayed in touch with an inkling of kin, the last we'd ever see these sweet people who once oddly dropped out of the blue and settled in as a part of us. The thought of them not there anymore tugged at me sadly. And another impression played strongly upon me too, not right then, but somewhere on the long road back to Chicago, such concerning Ozzie and Cavanaugh and their circumstance, whether they were capable of weathering the downturn, or if they should opt to the alternative of letting Mr. Carney sell the business while it looked competitively enticing. They owned only the business, not the land and building, which belonged to the colossal Kaiser Corporation and where its interest was concerned I entertained no opinions one way or another.

Those past two weeks were the most memorable of any return to my little town in the long line of years I have gone back. Perhaps the most sobering is the better term. For one thing I had gained another year of age and saw the world through a prism different from that of a year before, and secondly, the town itself had changed or I thought it had, however subtle. Or was it me? That is the way it is when you are absent for an extended length. That is the trick that time plays on you. And thirdly, I missed my friends, those my age, with whom I graduated from high school, most migrating to the large cities in pursuit of establishing a career or at the least earning a living. It fell upon me that never again would I behold the ebb and flow of my native domain as it presently existed or existed the year before when I left it. "You can't go home again," I thought to myself in melancholy, recalling the lines of prose that some clever person before my time set down as he took pen in hand. These were the machinations of my brain as I delayed at the crossing on the west side while the Pan American running late swooshed by, its eerie whistle screaming full blast. I had said goodbye to my mother and two sisters, my final goodbye upon beginning my journey northward. As the last of the coaches cleared I drove across the tracks and from there down mainstreet to the state highway and turned right.

That fall the students came back to the campus and fraternity house fully geared to plunge into their course of studies and extra curricular enticements, no one missing but two new enroolees emerged. The year would pass calmly and uneventfully aside from the ferocity of the snow storm that descended on the city and surrounding land and water masses in mid-November. Much to my fascination the lake froze over, more severely to the north of us, from the singing sands of Pere Marquette Park to the rock lined Wisconsin shore. People declared that the water of Lake Michigan froze deeper than at any time before in their remembrance. The winter produced the fourth snowiest on record, I read from the daily newspaper late the next spring, with 159 inches falling from November to May, such being among the top coldest periods in the past 116 years. There were days when all flights were quarantined and as a consequence my schedule to fly to New York City fell victim to interruption, but the missed flight time I made up by skipping classes and flying on days other than Thursday and Friday. Darya and Aaron sat through the classes for me meticulously scribbling down notes on a yellow tablet sheet, and through the use of their handiwork my absence wasn't of major hindrance.

While the city work crews manning the snowplows battled to keep the streets clear the students at the university saw the weather not as an obstacle but as an opportunity to mix and mingle and by and large relegated any serious thoughts of studies to the wind. At every chance we flocked to the open quadrangles of the campus to plunge into snowball fights and football games, the guys agreeing in conclave to behave gently when tackling the girls who insisted on playing with us. While we actively took part in the fracases Darya and I at times stole off to ourselves to sport in a private game of our own. It was always played the same way. When we'd sufficiently distanced ourselves from the swirl of activity she'd suddenly let go in something of a shriek, "I'll race you," there making a dash to playfully run away, with me giving chase, until, which was of short length, I caught up and down we went, both of us tumbling over and over, snow splattering everywhere, into our eyes and mouths and even into our clothing. She was a picture. In every way she was, I mean beautiful and charming, without let up laughing and shrieking, her eyes darting and sparkling, and the stylish red tam perched atop her head together with gorgeous long strands falling to her shoulders made her look even better. I wondered with some apprehension how without the Divinity intervening I could keep from falling in love with this enchanting girl. And then realized that I had already.

When the snow cleared, and while bracing for more to fall, Darya and I decided on a skating jaunt on the lake, a sport to which I laid no claim of mastering, yet one of which she had mastered with virtuoso capability. She was superb and patiently overlooked my ineptness—my stumbling and slipping and falling—while at the same time attempting to help me do better. She was a commendable teacher, the joy of being with her nothing less than immense. But then, a most unexpected oddity sprang from out of nowhere. It so happened that Gerard, the German farm boy skated too, very well, yet not in league with Darya. At first it did not appear peculiar that he began to wait for us on the ice each time we made our way there. Should I have been more astute to discern his purpose I would have determined on the spot that he had become substantially enamored with her, which evolved more apparently in the days to come. Little by little his courage strengthened until at last he mustered enough grit to ask her to have a turn with him, to which I in no manner objected, for in no meagre way he ranked superiorly to me in the art of skating and I felt that Darya deserved a better partner, certainly part of the time. I gladly accepted as much and honestly adjudged that they made for a handsome pair whizzing about. I felt in no way that there existed in me a growing jealousy, somewhat I suppose admitting in the days that followed that a touch of antipathy lurked a little in my subconscious that someone else with a great deal of consistency had begun to skate beside her. Nonetheless, I brushed it aside. After this however, another matter soon opened to my awareness. Darya forever made it practice to finding her way over, no matter what the meal, and sit beside me at the dining table. She adopted this pattern the first day we met. We'd often indulge in our own private agenda irrespective of what our associates around the table were taking up. One day briefly after she first skated with him Gerard began to sit down by her, whether at breakfast or supper or both. He generally sat to her right, I to her left, placing no significance on his doing as much for who was I to have jurisdiction over where he sat. Any young man could have taken a seat next to her and often did. I did not resent his attentions. I had no right to. I don't recall the conversations in which Darya and I were engaging, nor what it was that Gerard said to her or what she said to him on that day or any day following. But I saw as he continued to take his place beside her, especially by the angularity of his eyes that he had a crush on her and that in the days to pass it would grow. I said nothing regarding his persistence, and would have never brought it up with her, or gotten into a discussion of it with anyone were it not for Aaron, who, one day after Gerard's declaration to him of his affection for Darya, judged it improper that he had begun to exact a claim on someone that belonged to me. Thus, eventually he decided to address the issue when it worked out that the two of us were alone.

On the corner downstreet from the fraternity house there lodged a little cute café, a pub, more exactly described, where Aaron and I sometimes hung out to engage in nonsensical jokes and thrash through a scattering of disconnected subjects. A cozy enclosure, they called it the Cubs Nest where a fire burned each evening in winter with smoke excessively filling the atmosphere, not from the fireplace but from cigarettes. Being of exceptional wilyness he elected to delay a tad any mention of Gerard or Darya. He would wait and enter into that portion of our visit on the last. He lead off that his father had recently begun negotiations for a piece of land, with a building or two on it, on Long Island, New York City, and took up with his young son the importance of real estate holdings.

"Know what he said to me Ramsey? It was pretty catchy, so I retained it."

"What did he say?"

"Son, as you grow older always keep an eye peeled on land, land to buy. They're not making any more of it."

I could have answered that I'd heard that maxim over and over before by a good many people and deemed it very wise. I opted to remark that he should do as his father urged and that I wished to do the same whenever I had compiled enough money, either by accumulating cash or borrowing the necessary sum if I judged that borrowing wasn't too risky and likely to my advantage. We prolonged this discussion for a while, then switched to various and sundry things, though by gradual steps progressed to his real intention. He caught me off guard.

"Ramsey, Darya is the most beautiful girl on campus, don't you think?"

I must have grinned as I looked curiously across the table. Why such a sudden deduction, it ran through me. Everyone was forever saying it. But I answered, with a gist of witticism in my remarks.

"How did you guess?" I think I laughed aloud.

"Well, I could have framed it differently. She is beautiful. We all know that. And a great gal. I like her. I always have. And she likes me. I've wished with a powerful yen at times that it might have amounted to more than that. Ah! What wasted hope. What is it I once heard some guy say, a poet maybe: 'Why is something so beautiful so unattainable?' In the end I fared no better than merely being her buddy. I'm thankful that I'm at least that."

"Buddy hunh. That's good. It's the same with me. She's my buddy too. As she is to many."

"Ha, ha, ha. You stack your case with falsity my friend. How can you say she's your buddy too? She's more than a buddy to you and you know it. She's crazy over you and has been since that very first day. You know, when the two of us walked through the door and Bertinelli introduced us to you. You remember that. You'd have to."

"Yep. Sure I do."

"And there's where it all started. I saw it berthed. As I've said, she's crazy over you."

"Why are you so convinced? How do you know that?"

"Can I speak frankly?"

"Certainly."

"It shows anytime you're in her midst. She acts as if she could eat you up. Oh, it's controlled. She's reserved, subtle, not forward with it, but it's there. Always there in that gorgeous reserved face."

"You exaggerate."

"Says you. But I'm right. The question is: how do you feel about her? Don't answer that. It's obvious. You like her. You do. Admit it."

"I do admit it. She's a tremendous girl. But why are you bringing her up? And me? You're peaking my curiosity."

"I have my reasons. It's for a purpose that you wouldn't presuppose if you tried a hundred times to figure it out. I'm doing a favor for a mutual acquaintance of ours. And I guess I'll get on with it without beating further around the bush."

"Okay. Let's have it."

"Gerard, it's about Gerard."

"Gerard. How's that?"

Gerard is smitten with Darya, my friend, and has gone as far as to ask me how you felt toward her and if she might have at least some little amount of affinity for him"

"Really! But I'm not surprised he's asked you to undertake a mission on his behalf. The same as you, I've seen how he fawns over her. For that I can't blame him. Everyone does. In so far as my feelings toward her go you can relay to him that, well, they are very warm and tender and affectionate and I cou—?"

"In other words you're in love with her," he cut in before I finished.

"Yes. Truthfully, I am. And you knew without my telling you."

"Precisely."

"What message will you give him?"

"The same as you've just told me."

"That figures. Now, will you allow me to add more. He doesn't need you to ask Darya to say which of us her heart is inclined to, to him or to me. He should ask her himself. Then he will know with the straightest of sureness."

"And if there's a duel for her heart she'll have to referee?"

"I wouldn't say that. There's no duel going on, not from my vantage. I like her. I like her profoundly. But there's no duel."

"No duel. Well, I'll tell him what you have said. But what will you tell her?"

"Nothing. If she brings it up we'll discuss it. But I have no claim on her. I confess that I love being with her and I'm flattered that she loves being with me. Still, she's not bound to me. She could do as she likes."

"Not bound to you?"

No. And I can tell you now that she has no feelings for Gerard. If he will ask her she will say that she doesn't. Which naturally will hurt the guy. I'll feel sorry for him. Yet that's the way life goes. It's too bad indeed, very bad, when your heart yearns for someone you can't have."

"You have admitted with your own lips that you're in love with Darya Narvanna and I believe that you truly are. Do I have it right? I mean absolutely right."

I took my time in answering, Aaron studying my face as if reading a road map but entertaining something else in mind at the same time.

"Yes. I am very much. At first I wasn't, that is, I tried to tell myself I wasn't."

"But you are, and I will go even further if you will grant me the right."

"Please do."

"I read you well my dear friend, well enough that I've kind of figured something out. It's none of my business and if you mind please say it's not."

"As I've inferred, I don't mind."

"Okay. Is there someone else in your heart, perhaps as dear to you as Darya?"

"I won't pause, I won't delay or side step. Yes. There is someone else. Very deeply in my heart. I won't tell you the particulars of it now but will when the time is right."

"I see. Wow! She's a knockout if I'm hearing you correctly."

"She is."

"Indeed! Wow! What a situation! Two loves like that on your hands. How many fellows would like to swap places with you? Come to think of it I'm not sure I would. There is no greater predicament than to have a blessing and a curse descending on you at the same time."

"You sound a warning. How am I to take it?"

"You one day must choose, selecting one over the other or losing them both. What a torment. Have you thought of that?"

"Countless are the times."

"There's a solution you know."

"There is? Let me hear it. Whatever it is I'm sure it isn't easy. But what is it?"

"To make up your mind that it's one or the other and stick to your guns."

"You joke. That's an impossibility right at this moment."

"I'm sure of that. But what will you do?"

"Say nothing. To neither."

"And let each girl live in the dark with respect to the other."

"Yes. And hope that time and the Good Lord help me work things out."

"You said I joke. I wish I were. I'm only realistic. In the end you'll have to choose. On the other hand you'll have plenty of time for that old boy, I hope, unless you're heading to the altar before I think you are."

"No. No altar. It's a few years on down the road for that and as you indicate I'll have plenty of time."

Chapter 37

I DID NOT need for Aaron to tell me of his conferral with Gerard and that he passed on my message and presumed that he briefed him on Darya's stance as well. Gerard stopped sitting by her at meal time. In fact he failed to show up at either breakfast or supper for a while, and avoided me altogether. My heart sank because of his misfortune. I wished that things could have been different without it hurting me or him or Darya. Not surprising Darya remained her usual nonchalant self, displaying an air as if nothing had happened in the least. If she had knowledge of anything she in any event said nothing of it. Aaron later conveyed that he had revealed nothing to her and I would have vouched heavily that Gerard in no manner approached her. Surely, she wondered why he no longer sat by her at the dining table yet might have entertained the notion that his absence was of menial consequence, for as I have previously noted many a young man succeeded in finding an opportunity to take a seat beside her. I didn't mean to but one day I slipped and asked her if she knew she had become the object of Gerard's affections, to which she shrugged and replied that she knew she had by a little bit, but in so many words relayed that while he was a nice boy, affable and sociable, he shouldn't waste his time on her. I suspected that she might seize the moment to ask me of my feelings toward her. She didn't. And I didn't bring the matter up. That was something I suppose that neither of us ever addressed. Perhaps we were conscious of the other's feelings without the aid of open expression.

When the next year rolled around Gerard appeared to have overcome his setback, once again friendly and talkative. I breathed a sigh of relief, asking myself why he had made such a splash, so much of so little to begin with, yet I understood. What amounted to so little to me struck him with far greater impact. The viewpoint depended on one's position in the flirtatious undulation of striving to win some other's heart and I might not have looked at his disappointment with eyes of unaffected casualness were I to have occupied his place and he mine.

The cold period at last ended, but during the long and in some respects punishing siege many of us were deprived of leaving the campus for the Christmas holidays. When the winter finally left us the whole student body sighed a relief of good riddance, while at the same time emoting a tinge of regret, for the cold nights were perfect for certain of us from the fraternity house to join others across campus at the Cubs Nest to sip coffee and spin yarns and complain of or praise our teachers and bask in the radiant warmth of the fireplace which burned brightly from the wood that an attendant kept replenishing. Aaron, being his usual self, took front and center as the liveliest of the grouping, once sporting a red and white checkered waist jacket and a green Greek cap on his head. When jostled over his wearing such a garb, he laughed louder than anyone else and comically spun the yarn that he'd converted from Judaism to either Scottish Anglican or Greek Eastern Orthodox. A band usually showed up in the neighborhood of ten o'clock, that played loud, but well, and converted to a quieter well received ensemble when they played at other venues throughout the city. More than half the tunes they played were of a country genre. I had seldom danced with Darya, an excellent dancer, but spent a goodly portion of that evening with her in my arms on the dance floor. The space of the Cubs Nest was endowed of exceeding limitations, small to the degree that someone said the jam packed crowd reminded them of a make over of a traffic hang up bumper to bumper. Anxious to dance with Darya, Aaron tapped my shoulder off and on and stole her away, the two peculiarly unlike in the extreme, her tall and graceful and he short and lacking in athletic finesse. Well accepted was the changing of partners, and sometimes I did without Darya for at least a while to make way for a sizeable number of young men who, like Aaron, were anxious to have a turn with her. Girls were there more in numbers than guys. There was one, a lovely petite thing, who approached me once when Darya was for the moment dancing with someone else, perhaps Aaron, who took my arm and led me into the crowd. Looking up into my face with dalliance in her beautiful brown eyes she began talking at once.

"I've seen you walking by our house," she said with a cheery disposition, alive with animation in her voice.

"Which house?"

"The one next to yours, where you live."

"Oh, I hadn't noticed."

"Me or the house? You must mean me. I often sit on the front porch."

"Oh. Yeah. How ungentlemanly of me" Then I switched. "What's your name?"

"Andrea Cellus."

"Pretty name. I like it. It sounds of celebrity."

"Thank you. And yours?"

"Ramsey Maynard."

She said she came from Louisiana where her parents lived. When I asked what brought her to the university, she replied that her father enjoyed an acquaintance with Robert

Hutchins and due to the relationship decided to enroll there. It actually should have been told that she fore mostly selected the university because of her astronomically high marks in private prep school. The deans of the various colleges of the university must have beamed with electrical excitement upon scanning the paperwork of her records forwarded to them by the Director of Admissions. She'd enrolled as a freshman at the beginning of the school year, so youthful in appearance that I would have deemed her still in high school if without knowledge that spoke to the contrary. As it happened she very shortly became involved in helping me, immensely beneficial I should say, upon my ascendance into the upper sciences, into the advanced mathematics and physics classes especially. They referred to her as a math whiz, a near genius who continually reminded me of Leland. In literature and the arts as well, she soared easily to the forefront of illumination, superbly gifted with the usage of words, especially at grasping their meaning and spelling them correctly I very quickly learned. On taking one of Doctor Linskie's upper level classes she on the outset demonstrated an ability to write impeccably and while going over this attribute with a professor colleague he boasted of his star pupil, "Mercy, she can spell and use words as well as the dictionary." Only a brevity of time elapsed until her name was on the lips of a majority of the student body campus wide, not only for these rarities but for two other paramount qualities, her beauty and her friendly outgoing persona, qualities which in the semblance of a magnet attracted the eyes of a regiment of young men, Aaron as much as anyone, if not more. Later on, he asked me to speak to her on his behalf. He said he spent hours fantasizing over her, aching for a date, but when I interceded to present his wishes she replied with gracious courteous diplomacy that she liked him, that he was oceans of fun, but that her interest extended no further."

"You understand don't you Ramsey, she said. Sometimes it all hinges in the finality on the right one."

"I understand completely."

The spring, though begrudgingly slow in breaking through, made its advent and there was an uplifted mood among the student body because of the moderating weather, but they were buoyed additionally owing to the approaching end of the semester, which meant that a weighty proportion would leave for home and not return until the fall. Darya spoke that she'd be going home to Baltimore, pleading with me on her day of departure to visit her during the summer, with doubled emphasis that her parents hoped fervently that I would and that they'd leave no stones unturned in showing me around the city. That I knew, I gratefully assured her. In answer to her invitation I said I'd think it over, the best answer within me at the moment. I honestly felt that I'd lack sufficient time. Bertinelli, Aaron, and myself were staying on, I with hopes that the firm wouldn't saddle me with extra hours in the delivery of depositions. I'd counted heavily on enrolling in an elective course or two, hopefully more, during the summer term. Aaron soon put a damper on these aspirations when he handed me a message from his father who needed me on the job for five days of the week during the summer season, and that sometimes the assignment would necessitate that I take an apartment in New York for a two day span to allow for a closer affiliation with the firm's lawyers. "For your troubles," he relayed, "you will receive generous compensation," and he spoke truthfully, the size of the first check stopping me in my tracks. The firm, moreover, paid for my apartment rent, not at all unexpected, let alone locating it for me and negotiating my contract of lease. Every contingency, I must emphasize, they carefully preplanned and put in place.

Another school year now lay behind. Realizing that the schedule which Mr. Stylman had carved out for me prohibited my going home to see my mother I sat down at the small side table beside my bed one night and wrote her a letter.

Dear Mother,

The spring semester is over and a good many have left to spend their time at home during the summer. Unfortunately, I cannot. My work with Mr. Stylman is greatly important, you know, for it will provide a badly needed paycheck. I promise to visit before the fall semester starts. Please understand, and I know you do.

The winter here has treated us unkindly. You undoubtedly heard of the terrible freeze as reported over the radio. I wish you owned a television. You would have seen the mess of it all by way of live pictures. I spoke of it in one of my letters to you, which could not have done justice in terms of describing the real scene. Words can't describe something like that.

I was awfully let down to have missed Christmas with you. It couldn't be helped. Wrecks were happening all over the city. The highway patrol warned of the dangers on the state roadways. Frankly, I'm almost afraid to go anywhere in my aging jalopy, even when the weather is fair. I've set my sights on buying another, but can't say when.

I must go now. I would suggest and hope that you'll say a little prayer for me as I go off to bed, yet won't because you already have it half said in your thoughts. Please tell the others I send them my love, as I do you from the bottom of my heart. I'll write you often, more than I have so far. I promise.

Love you,

Ramsey

My stay in New York City exceeded the two days and nights that Mr. Stylman previously spelled out in his letter. Sometimes I spent a full week in the city, putting in long hours at the firm under the tutelage of two older lawyers, seniors and partial owners of the firm for many years as I discovered. Their unspoken but obvious purpose was to expose me to a regimen of vigorous training. My primary supervisor went by the name of Yazstremski, I'd heard, a man that impressed me with such thoroughness upon my meeting him face to face that I deemed it inconceivable that anyone besides Mr. Stylman could address him without the honorific Mister preceding his family name, and no one did. Mr. Yazstremski's backup officed next door, Elander Hastings, the print on the opaque half glassed door read, preferred that people address him by his first name only when meeting him face to face. I couldn't bring myself to obey; I called him Mr. Hastings. There were other lawyers situated in various sectors of the building, thirty in all I counted, though the tally did not include the three young college people my age who were introduced to me as interns, two attending Princeton and the third Yale. I pegged them as Ivy League stuck ups at the beginning, discovering once we were acquainted that my opinion was badly skewed. Within the briefest I liked them and they liked me, and they exhibited unvarying interest in my assignments, which were in no manner likened to the duties prescribed in their job descriptions. They seemed to have much free time and I none. On the outset I was guided into a mix of legal research and the editing of scores of depositions, work in which for the time being I reveled, new and fascinating, and I applied the maximum of devotion to it and the firm, such force of drive obviously discerned by my superiors. I often lingered in the office in the after hours and at times stayed until ten o'clock or later, during which I prepared the case documents—reviewing, editing, and systematically arranging them on their desks for study and analysis when they stepped into their office the next morning All this was well and good but I began to fret over my usual duties of transporting depositions to Chicago, asking my supervisor if he felt that I might have started to fall behind with my deliveries.

"I'm alive to that situation son. Don't give it a second thought. We have everything covered. You're doing very well with your present assignment and I want you to realize that I see how attentive you are to detail. You'll make a fine lawyer. And yes, I've wondered most recently. Do you prefer oral law, arguing in court shall we say, to be more descript, or researching the statutes and case rulings?"

I contemplated but a second for an answer. "The latter is more fitting to my aptitude sir, if I have any."

"Ah! You have plenty of the aptitude stuff all right, and I quite agree, that is I think I do, that you may fit into the research genre better than in the courtroom brawls."

"Yes sir. I think I lean in that direction."

Once when the hour of five arrived I discovered that no one else still hung around, all others gone home, which regularly happened, and decided to plough through some readings for a couple of hours then leave for my apartment. Yet before I followed through I would, I concluded, walk down to the corner café a half block north and sit down and sip at a cup of coffee, or order a beer, and muse and listen to the songs lilting from the jukebox. I took a seat at a table in a far corner. The tables next to me were empty. Only a trickle of people were at the bar, none anywhere else. It seemed at once very strange. Here I sat alone in New York City, one of the largest cities in the world, if not the largest, and all was so quiet. Suddenly I felt lonely, even after the friendly waitress brought coffee and smiled broadly and pleasantly traded conversation. I missed the gang at the fraternity house; I missed the winter past and the Cubs Nest, and Aaron and Darya and the image of Leland, but I did not stop there. Suddenly Nenia appeared mistily on my horizon, sweet beautiful Nenia, seemingly far back in the past, even though not long at all since I'd been with her, only slightly more than a year, and there too arose her recent letter begging me to forgive her, that she'd accepted a teaching position in Paris for six months or more and wouldn't return home until the next summer term at my university had reached an end.

"I will teach French children English, Ramsey. Isn't that the sweetest thing?"

"I must answer her," I heard myself thinking. "What a fine teacher she'll make. I'd give anything to see her going about doing what she knows how to do so very well."

In a snap I returned to Mr. Yazstremski's compliment of my work with the firm and his well-intentioned snippet that I'd make a fine lawyer. It sounded almost that Mr. Stylman clandestinely hatched up the accolade and with deliberate intention planted the idea in his associate's ear. Of course, that wasn't true. All along an impulse played in my conscious to clarify to Mr. Yazstremski that I wasn't sure I'd like the legal profession, and wasn't certain I'd choose it, opting in the end to remain silent. Good common sense told me that I should. Though young, I possessed the awareness that I worked and mixed with powerful Jewish folks who liked me and could dramatically affect my future. I averted with staunch seriousness not to make a mistake that I'd regret. "Careful, don't dig your own grave by merely opening your mouth."

Not long after taking up my new post in New York, Mr. Stylman began to treat me to lunch here and there, and sometimes to dinner at two renowned places in the city, Toots Shor's, a restaurant which specialized in chicken hash with hearts of palm and a Caesar's salad; and the Waldorf Astoria Hotel dining room, where the food on a scale of exquisiteness ranked higher than that at Toots Shor's, but the more ordinary foods were available too, eggs benedict with a salad piled high on a platter and a steak if desired, not to mention the desserts of the richest recipes with a foamy topping. Toots Shor, I learned in subsequent years was a big burly guy of Asian appearing extraction, much loved they said, with connections to an unending stream of patrons of all walks, some from the underworld. I have long regretted my misfortune of not meeting him, thinking in time that I would, for Mr. Stylman and Toots were intertwined as friends. Mr. Stylman once said to me that Toots inherited a mellow heart at birth and that he gave away more liquor than he ever sold. I have read on my own that vodka in this country in that era had begun to swell popularly to the forefront, a drink that Toots Shor supposedly helped introduce into the culture, and one may easily internalize that he played a forceful hand in the movement. People on the street tabbed his business as the "drinkingest place in town."

For the most part, we chose the Waldorf Astoria for dinner, not selected by Mr. Stylman to impress me, but to satisfy Mrs. Stylman, who joined us on every such outing, unless, as she said, there were extenuating circumstances. She missed Aaron. With tender politeness she squeezed my arm and said that I helped make up for his absence. She liked the luxury at the Waldorf and said as much, and with an obvious reason, for generally we took dinner in a reserved quiet and quaint room where only dignified conversation and educated low laughter among the guests were the expected norm. The shiny red leather chairs surrounding the dining table and the glitzy silverware emplaced on a cover cloth of the finest tapestry were a perfect match for each other. The waiters, purposely schooled, and stiff and erect, were attired in tuxedos and expensive white shirts and kept filling our wine glasses or attempting to, until Mrs. Stylman, pushing hers aside, said "No, please. I've had quite enough," and then Mr. Stylman and I followed suit.

Chapter 38

WE WERE out riding around one evening when Mr. Stylman queried if someday, I'd like to join the firm, and turning the matter over quickly I cautiously explained that school studies were a current heavy load to carry and that I found it difficult to train my thoughts on the future. Then I continued with a wrap up. "I have two years left and that seems like eons away. Earning a degree is terribly slow. Sometimes I think the end is unreachable." My intention was to express with delicate protocol that I wasn't sure I'd turn to the field of law when I graduated, that between the present and the conferring of my degree I might shift to some other interest. I half hoped that he'd read between the lines and recognize the message that I sought to relay. He wasn't swayed. I think I shot over his head. I surmised that he perceived my utterances in complete accord with his well conceived scenario and that my response corresponded in the affirmative to his question.

"You'll make it Ramsey. You'll have your diploma before you know it. And proudly, we'll smile with the broadest smiles when you do."

Likened to a blur, my experience that summer flew by, all happening with such swiftness and jammed together that I felt virtually insensible to the substance of legal subject matter and the depth of law that I had begun to acquire. My work time fell into two categories: a proportion of it performing my duties under the guidance of Mr. Yazstremski in the office and the remainder delivering stacks of depositions to Chicago and bringing back others. I discovered that I liked the intellectual challenge of legal research much better than transporting depositions and upon my making Mr. Yazstremski aware of my preference he bellowed a laugh and declared that he'd figured all along that I'd find it opportune to tell him of my choice.

"But patience Ramsey. I have a trial in the dockets on its way where I represent the plaintiff and I'll have to call on you for digging into a plethora of research that I'll need.

You'll sit tightly by my side in the courtroom, where you'll witness first hand the fruits of your labor."

"I'll look forward to that sir. When does it begin?"

"Not until sometime."

"What does it involve?"

"Inverse Condemnation. A public utility company has laid lines underneath someone's property without paying sufficiently for it. Not paying a penny up to this date."

"And the public utility company is the plaintiff; and the landowner is the defendant.

"You're stating it backwards. "

"I don't understand exactly."

"Well then, I'd better call time out and explain. Inverse Condemnation is a term used in the law to describe a situation in which the government takes private property but fails to pay the compensation required by the 5th amendment. In some states the term includes the damaging of property, as well as taking it. To receive compensation, the owner must sue the government. In such cases the owner is the plaintiff and that is why the action is called inverse. The order of the parties is reversed as compared to the usual procedure in direct condemnation where the government is the plaintiff who sues a defendant-owner to take his or her property."

"You say you are the plaintiff's attorney in the upcoming case."

"I said that."

"What government are you suing and what did they do wrongly. Or what will you charge them with doing?"

"The government is a public utility company, but about the same as the government, who has taken over a piece of land owned by a former storekeeper. The storekeeper has to sue them to gain due payment for his loss. I'm representing him."

"I see. Do you think you'll win?"

He scratched the side of his face with his long skinny fingers and squinted with a mischievous air. "That depends on how well you research the archives. No. I'm kidding, naturally. I do think I'll win. I'm well informed of the statutory laws and very well apprised of the cases of record deriving from the rulings of the courts. I've been through this controversy no telling the times. But as I said, you ought to start looking into the term Inverse Condemnation. You never know what you'll uncover and what's more you'll encounter the term for as long as you're in the practice of law, for there will always exist an intermingling of buildings and land and people, and this equation serves as fertile grounds for generating disputes and lawsuits.

"When you take on a case where there is a dispute between a corporation such as a public utility and an individual of ordinary means, does your heart favor the latter?"

"Hmmmm. Sort of. I try to remain neutral, as much as is humanly possible. In the upcoming case you might perceive the trial court as a battlefield where Goliath is to do battle with an incompetent pygmy. Personally speaking, there is lopsided unfairness in such a confrontation, easily concluded because the public utility has the funds and lawyers to stay the course as long as necessary and this sways me against them. The individual is ordinarily without this luxury. As I've said, the controversy is unfair, or in any event that's the way I see it, but what I think is fair and how the case turns out will ultimately reside in the hands of the Circuit Court judge."

"But you think you'll win."

"I do. I'll unleash on them the image thing, if I have to, the Goliath attempting to run rough shod over the common man."

"The judge has to abide by the law, to rule on the basis of law, not on emotion and biasness"

"Agreed. He's supposed to. He at the same time has latitude. But I won't have to depend on emotion or biasness or creating a negative image against the defendant. They broke the law. They clearly did. They laid a line under the ground that the storekeeper owned without securing prior approval and failed to pay him for the installation; and that's all I need in my corner. I'll beat them Ramsey. You can count on that. Now, I may use some gimmicks, especially the image contrivance, just for the heck of it if for no other reason. Oh sure, the judge and everyone else will see that I'm merely playing around and most will grin and enjoy the comedy underneath, including the judge. All court trials are given to theatrical upshots at one stage or another during a trial."

In slow progressive steps Mr. Yazstremski taught and guided me, my incomparable mentor, my teacher, so I can safely affirm that when I entered law school some few years later I knew that I strode well ahead of the majority of my classmates. In terms of knowledge I easily qualified as a practicing lawyer, at least of the junior grade, lacking only the skills and finesse gained through courtroom experience, yet claming a fair share of that too which resulted from watching Mr. Yazstremski try one case after another. No telling the times I sat by his side while he jotted down facts and ideas on a tablet sheet, turning to me all at once with a directive that I make haste and research a particular ruling handed down by the judge who presided over a previous trial which consisted of similar arguments. And another of his decisions to help my cause sticks even now firmly in my memory. He had decided to farm me out, as he put it, to the many lawyers of the firm, who were schooled in a specialty of law, each in command of a different specialty. And thereby exposing me to a great many angles of the legal profession. Mr. Yazstremski kept tabs daily on me and the lawyers to ascertain that my learning progressed to the maximum of my potential. Some of the lawyers, the younger ones, alluded to him as the kind old gentleman with an iron fist, a majority of them receiving his help and guidance when they were beginners, and revered him for it, as I too revered him.

I saw Aaron sparingly that summer, the preponderance of our interceptions taking place in the lobby at the fraternity house where we sat on the sofa and chatted and drank a beer or two and watched television. His classes were scheduled to begin at eight o'clock, early for him but he rolled out of bed for breakfast nonetheless and made it to his classes on time as far as I know. I made it a point to occasionally join him for breakfast, Bertinelli once in a while sitting down with us for a stint. But pretty soon Aaron was up and gone. Sometimes Bertinelli and I would make out for the beach and on one such outing Andrea Cellus joined us and joined us on another when we rented a sailboat and spent an afternoon on the bluish green waters of Lake Michigan. Bertinelli had gained the reputation as a skilled boatsman, such gained from growing up on the Chesapeake Bay. He kidded Andrea that she was too young to hang out with such old men, that she might pick up questionable social habits, to which she faked a pout and laughed and voiced confidently that she'd gladly run the risk. When we were alone after a day or two passed, he said that his senses told him that she liked me, or more than that, or otherwise she wouldn't have tagged along with us. I said I wasn't surprised at her wishing to tag along, for I had interpreted her feelings beforehand when she on occasions spotted me walking across campus between classes and dashed over and clasped my arm, there discharging a stream of energetic talk. I enjoyed her, I must confess I did. But held fast to a determination not to go beyond an ordinary friendship. "You have enough to deal with already, Ramsey," I counseled myself, "three women are in your life, and that's enough, more than enough. You must keep this young chicken at bay. Besides, she's just a child." At the present Andrea did not pose as a troublesome obstacle, in that many of my hours were spent in New York under the steady tutelage of Mr. Yazstremski, and those left over were minimally few in number.

But Andrea had her ways. "I'd like to participate in the breakfast and supper time debates that you and your friends have at the fraternity house? They're lively things I hear and are of an inexhaustible range. Will you invite me?"

"Sure. Why not?" I spoke too soon; suddenly realizing that Darya will have returned and visualized that some awkward moments were in the making. I cast it off nevertheless. I'd cross that bridge when I came to it. I wished Andrea might find another male friend to occupy her fantasy. Then I regretted my wish. "What will you do for a math partner of her equal if she takes up with someone else?" asked Aaron.

My professor of literature, Doctor Arthur Linskie, an aging graying gentleman, by this time my favorite teacher, who possessed a gift for intermingling history and literature, held that only a fine line separated the two fields, that they were nearly equal in their dependency on one another. I ran by to see him one day upon my return from New York. He loved European Literature, and so did I, and he nurtured an irresistible appreciation of the Russian novelists, and so did I. We swayed strongly toward Tolstoy. We both avidly read Tolstoy's novels. Secretly, there rippled through me an urge to pursue the life of a teacher, likened to my dear friend whose abilities I passionately admired. But that was not as he wished. He disdained it. Years later, when my own students circled round me in an aura of excessive reverence, I called him into remembrance. He had spoken to me in private moments that it wasn't good for the young and inexperienced to absurdly worship their professorial elders.

I would have enrolled in his class during either the first or second summer semesters were it not for my job. I explained that I sorely regretted not being a part of it and knew I will have profited immensely should my earlier intentions have materialized; and said in another breath that I was trying to take as many classes as time allowed because I hoped to graduate early. He appeared provoked at what he had heard. I had struck the quick. "Time! Hoping to graduate early! My boy! Do you realize what you have said? You're wishing your life away. The best of your existence, even if you make it to the other side of a hundred, is right here at this university where life flourishes like a bubbling spring each day, youth everywhere around with fresh and adventuresome ideas, and you wish to hurry yourself through this garden of joy and learning. You'll never again experience anything that rivals this, never. And you say you are in a hurry to get it over with. Bah."

I needed no pause to drink in his admonishment. He spoke the truth. I should have envisioned it myself. As I retrace my footsteps to those years, I am suddenly again in the fraternity house of long ago, where I hear the voices and see the faces of Aaron, Bertinelli, Balboni, Darya, Gerard, and Andrea together with others whose faces I see but whose names unveil themselves vaguely, if at all. The dining room table is encircled with youthful laughter.

"On the other hand my fine young man," my dear professor continued, "you naturally must fly your own wings, and only you can decide how fast they are to carry you. The best results, I shall add, don't always follow from the advice or preference given by others, mine included."

As it was with the previous fall, my confederation of friends returned to the fraternity house and prepared for enrollment, some new students among them, as we expected, Anthony Balboni among them, a freshman, a rather husky strong fellow, who applied for residence at the fraternity house. We accepted him. I helped review his resume. His parents were of Italian heritage, his father a building contractor in the city. When I attained to greater familiarity with him and him with me, I asked why he chose Chicago University for his schooling. He explained that it was attributable to his mother who held the university in high esteem and to a number of people who spoke to him of its prestigious Department of Economics. But he said she cared little for economics. To her, it was not much more than a term. Yet, she did have a very incisive insight into what a college education meant to a young man as he proceeded into adult years. His father lightly suggested that he study economics, if he intended to seriously study anything at all, because he said he hoped his son might take over his business someday and felt he needed a good academic background behind him that taught him about dollars and cents and taking risks.

"And these are the reasons you are here?"

"Pretty much. But mind you, I must squeeze in, it's chiefly due to my mom. She thought it a good idea that I attend a fine school like this to become finished, as she put it. She wanted me educated, just educated, no matter what the field. I don't think my father cared whether or not I attended college, not really. He'd have preferred that I join him fresh out of high school in the construction business, but that wasn't going to happen. My mom's word stood as the last word around our household, strictly obeyed."

Starting with this beginning I developed a meaningful friendship with Anthony Balboni. On the outset he showed that he grew up in a society of borderline culture; his language very pointedly demonstrating as much, which he without significant delay overcame and quickly adapted to the traditions and mores of those around him. I marveled at how he had done all this in the shortest of time.

Darya did not arrive with the majority of students that fall. She checked in a few days later. When she entered the doorway of the lobby with her encumbering luggage I stood from where I sat and she upon seeing me lowered her possessions and literally ran into my arms, spilling over with elation, but deservedly pasting me with a friendly scolding.

"You didn't answer my letter. Shame on you."

"I forgot." I half lied. "I intended to. You can't believe how busy I've been, and that's the truth." When she kissed my lips I knew that forgiveness poured from her heart.

We sat for a while trying to catch up on things, the luggage continuing to rest where she left it close by the doorway, her reminding me that I missed some very good pleasantries by not coming to Baltimore to visit. "We had a string of dinner parties all across the summer, friends and business associates of my father there, as well as my mother's close friends, and I missed you at every single one." She avoided telling me I ultimately learned, that her mother expected, or any event hoped, that I'd fly over and join them for at least a short length.' A day, or two. She hurt, not so much for herself but for her daughter. In my configuration of imaginings, I saw the occasions clearly, extravagant in the extreme, too excessively ritzy and urbane for me. I would have been completely out of place in such high born society I said to myself, a duck on land when his natural habitat is water, and from that viewpoint I breathed a sigh that I did not go. I had struggled enough with abiding by the rules of decorum in the presence of Mrs. Stylman when I tagged along with her and Mr. Stylman for dinner.

Darya brought me a gift. She always brought me gifts. She could afford it, her and her parents, who sat at the pinnacle as measured by wealth. She had brought me an attractive, and costly, blue serge, wishing that I might try it on for she couldn't wait to see me in it. I begged off for the time being. She frowned a little, but let it go at that.

"In what are you enrolling this semester," she inquired unassumingly?

"Philosophy, physics, religion. lit—."

"Oh. Religion! You'll enroll for a course in religion?"

"Yeah" Then I paused, or did something that favored a pause, a miniature stop, then kept on. "But literature, European literature, that is the real stuff."

"Oh yeah. You keep championing the European authors, insisting they have the Americans beat and I agree, but they have hundreds of years behind them in the scribbling of wit."

"Of course they have."

"Now, what's the fifth? You've named four. You are carrying a full load, aren't you?"

"I am. International law. It's an elective."

"That indeed is a natural for you, which draws me to inquire of the firm, Aaron's father's firm. How are you faring there?"

"I'm doing okay. I feel I am. There's a Mr. Yazstremski, a fractional if not equal owner of the business who is my mentor. I like him immensely. When I first met him I knew that I had fallen into a current of good fortune. On every turn he guides me and tells me as many times as he judge's necessary, I am sure, that I'm doing well. I think I'd like to work beside him for a long while."

"Ha. Very compelling. You really like him?"

"Much."

"The name is striking. What's his origin?"

"He's Polish. Polish Jewish, landing on American soil in the 1920's with his parents."

"Spell it. Can you? Ha, ha, ha."

"I can. But it took practice, a whole week of it." I spelled the name for the sake of proving that I could.

She gestured toward her luggage and I rose and went over and picked up most of the pieces, she the rest, and we delivered them to her room that Bertinelli promised he would have waiting for her when she returned from her summer's absence. As she looked around she surveyed everything, the crucials—the windows, the walls, the portraits, there emerging a glow to her face evincing that she felt pleased and happy that all appeared the same despite someone else occupying the space in her absence. We had stood for but a brevity when she pulled me to her and hugged me and kissed me again, this time when we were entirely private.

"Where'll we hang out tonight? You know we have to celebrate my homecoming."

"Not the Cubs Nest," I answered. "It's too overflowing. Somewhere we can talk and laugh as loud as we please. That's what we need."

"I hear you. Where then?"

"Koblis Kitchen. It's Japanese owned. They serve the tastiest of food, and there's the most delectable atmosphere, and I'll have the best of company."

"Guaranteed." Saying this she cutely twinkled her eyes. "But when did you learn of this place?"

"This summer. Bertinelli took me there. It's new. Some Japanese folks moved in here from California and started the business."

Koblis Kitchen, a small conspicuous eatery situated on the shoreline of Lake Michigan boasted of the best sushi served anywhere and kept their doors open twenty fours around the clock. We noticed as we entered that lighted candles had been placed on every table. Smiling from ear to ear a doorman leaned over backwards to greet us. I liked candle glow as did she, and for this reason more than for any other we were both in unison in our approval of the little café entirely new to her horizon. We were seated next to the window and talked and laughed and spun tales and munched our sushi, incredulously tasty. She agreed. I knew that when she took her first bite. She twisted her face a slight and bunched her lips, the way one does when sampling a morsel of pie or cake oozing with sugary sweetness. We both had grown hungrier by the second from the aroma of the food wafting from the kitchen.

Chapter 39

THE BARGES and frigates churning north and south on the water were vigorously active, their lights flickering from stem to stern, thus giving off an allure of magic, only matched or exceeded by those in downtown New York City at night on a holiday weekend.Yet the highlight of the evening originated with the chefs in the recesses of the kitchen who in plain view of where we sat engaged in a ritual of showmanship—I mean to say, that is, the big guy in the middle held a pan of fish over an open flame while shuffling it about as if popping popcorn. Sometimes adding to his showing off he'd unexpectedly toss the meat into the air, casting a quickie grin at the crowd in the interval, and then catch it without a single error when it came back down. Using the anterooms of the establishment we changed into attire conducive to helping us brave the much cooler air of the night, now descending upon the shoreline, and set out for the beach where we set about building a fire. A canvas of blue had affixed itself against the sky, and the evening star hung high and unmistakable among the limitless others. A whitish film appeared to radiate from it, and of all the uncanny things which it might have precipitated in my pattern of thoughts it singularly reminded me of the jasmine flower, a specimen of nature which I knew grew plentifully in southern Mississippi. I used to see it when I traveled there for a visit with relatives and for a while gathered limited facts in regard to its various aspects. When I mentioned my visit to her and the name jasmine in particular, she asked for a furtherance of what more I might say of it, with me going overboard to explain that the jasmine was a pretty white flower that springs from a genus of shrubs and vines kindred to the olive family. I added moreover that they widely cultivate it in some regions for its characteristic fragrance.

A friendly breeze blew lightly across her face and fluttered through her hair, and her eyes exuded an irrepressible lure as I looked across at her through the trickling flames. Seeing that they were on the verge of dying, dancing crazily about, we jumped up and began to refuel them with pieces of driftwood that we found and stacked into a pile close by soon after arrival. We stayed on until near morning under the blankets she'd spread on the sand. The chill would eventually drive us in. Luckily, we caught a taxi roving in our vicinity and took it back to the campus. She paid the driver. Even if of poor heritage I struggled with the notion of a female paying the fare, irrespective of her wealth, protesting that such was my obligation. But to no avail. She stubbornly insisted on footing the bill, and this encompassed any and all meals at outside restaurants.

"No, it's not your obligation Ramsey," she said as a declaration, and handed the driver five ten-dollar bills, many times over the cost of the trip. Onto this she added a tip.

Practically asleep on our feet we parted in the lobby. The pale predawn in the east sat poised to vanish and the shooting streaks of red and yellow foretold that soon the sun would surmount the earthly rim that up until that moment concealed it from view. The night stuck in my brain as a simply fantastic endeavor and I revolved it for days thereafter. I thrilled at being with her again. That, however, was our last evening together for a while. My hands were full with my travels to and from New York and at the same time I drove myself to stay on top of my course work, imposing self counsel that I couldn't simply take off for a night's adventure at any time I pleased, as I would like to have done. With determined eagerness I tore into my studies, meeting in one of the library alcoves with Andrea at selected hours to take advantage of her proficiency in math and physics and spending a disproportionate amount of intensity and time in an attempt to conquer philosophy. Many strange and complicated concepts dwelled within its framework, a body of knowledge, I will say, known as epistemology, not the most bothersome but definitely among the most bothersome. "Epistemology," our professor explained when we moved to that chapter of text dealing with the subject, "has derived from the fertile mind of Rene Descarte, 1596-1660, as well as from other geniuses that trailed him, and is a branch of philosophy which dips into the scope and nature of knowledge. It is also referred to as 'theory of knowledge.' It questions what knowledge is and how it is acquired and the extent to which any given subject or entity is knowable. Here is the question: how do we know anything, which is one of the basic questions in philosophy, the starting point for the study of epistemology."

As I have inferred the field of philosophy did not pass to me easily. I had to dog myself to master it, to pass the course, listening with strained attention to the lectures that seemed to move too fast. Epistemology is one of its most complicated branches, and I don't think I ever fully comprehended the concept or its workings, but did well if not better than the masses of the class. There were instances when a student made great sport of himself in connection with the term, inferring how out of place he was in a class of that distinction, clownishly telling how he had responded to a question appearing in the midterm exam. His name was Philpot. The question read: "Can you know and really know that you know?"

Philpot wrote this: "Yes, I don't know the answer to this question and I know that I don't know it." That night at the Cubs Nest there emerged a raft of fun and laughter over his reply.

A letter arrived at mid-fall from my mother, and then she telephoned, both communications to the effect that Rupert Monett had turned gravely ill within the week, there being no hope for recovery and that the expectations were that he would depart from this world in days not far removed. She urged me to attend the funeral and burial if I could in any way interrupt my daily affairs. I didn't, I couldn't. Mr. Stylman had me tied to a rigid schedule and I could speak the same of my studies at the university. Exam week stared glaringly from around the corner. Not long afterwards a letter from my mother confirmed that "Mr. Monett" had died, and that the burial had taken place at the Mount Pisgah Cemetery situated a mile east of town, a cemetery which originated near the beginning of the eighteen hundreds and changed with the passing of time, in keeping with the modern culture. I knew this old cemetery well. I must have walked by it countless times as a boy on my way to school and back. Near the front gate a colony of gothic tombstones stood emplaced, leaning with age, as if an old person, some quite tall, grandly designed and costly, gilded to the point of unordinary, resembling those I had seen in European paintings, where the wealthy were laid to rest, and then there were those of a more modern vintage, with little or no distinction with respect to the social or financial standing of the deceased. Here, my father lay buried.

Shortly after receiving the news of Monett's death I caught a plane bound for New York and began to narrow my focus on the man. I retraced my visits of some time back to pay my respects as he lay sick in the hospital, Melissa sitting by him when I crept deftly through the doorway, peering into his sleeping face as might a puppy looking wistfully at his master. The pallor of his complexion and his emaciated flesh were startling, which I did not mention to Melissa. I speculated on several bodily failings that took him down, stress, a heart attack, renal poisoning, or something else, in the final summary deciding that the several causes coming together delivered the fatal blow. Being inclined to curiosity I found myself guessing what the doctor might scribble in his report as to the cause of death. Almost at once I repressed these thoughts in favor of how the family members were facing up to his departure.

The body lay reposed in his two story stately white home for two days, the people paying him high honor, the whole town turning out to demonstrate genuine respect or else curiously observe and stare at the interior. The bulk of those who attended never before were seen inside. I hadn't myself but came close once when I took Melissa by who needed to stop and run in for something, with me waiting in the car.

"I'll only take a minute," she said, a little apologetically.

I was curious; I really nurtured a yen to see inside but passed up the opportunity. Had she suspected of course that I might have wished to she would have instantly seen to it.

My mother and my oldest sister attended the funeral, my mother mentioning hardly anything about it when I next saw her, yet my older sister acted to the contrary, describing the ceremony in sharp vivid detail, most of her remarks phrased in negative satire. While poor in her youth, she read widely and deeply. She stood tall and proudly. She despised Monett and his wife Madeline, disliking his two daughters even to a greater extreme and spoke of them with a caustic sting in her voice. She felt the two girls were uppity and flaunted their wealth, two high in the social order to mingle with serfs of the fields.

"They didn't even wave at us from their black shiny car, Ramsey, as they passed us on our way to school. You don't remember much of things like that but I do. It will never leave me."

I understood. We were poor, but brimmed with pride, and when my sister's eyes fell upon the Monett girls attired in fancy tailored clothing at school her resentment uncontrollably turned to flame, the same that happened to most girls her age who were largely from the rural farm sector, or if not, faring no better irrespective of the stature of the house in which they lived or their father's work.

She attended the funeral not to pay respects but to honor her mother who pled with her to go. She had said, as I recall with mirrored clarity, that the daughters bought four hundred orchids and spread them over the grave site. "But that wasn't going to wipe away his sins." Truthfully, I saw him not as a sinner, but as an unprincipled rascal, excessively given to greed, a man unresponsive to the needs of others. In no way did I ever see him as a criminal. He hadn't killed anyone nor robbed banks nor participated in a grand scheme of fraud and scandal. In some respects people saw him as an upright man. It dawned on me that likened to myself he once belonged to a family of quite common means, or could have, his parents not a great amount wealthier than my own, clawing their way up. And as my thoughts fell further upon him I discovered that my feelings were far less severe than they were during the hard times of my early youth. In fairness I forced myself to suppose that if my family had happened into richness and were unpoor, my view of him, and his view of himself, will have decidedly done an about face. "And isn't that a hell of a fact of human nature," a voice uttered inside.

Among Monett's most endearing aspirations which were well conveyed to friends before his death specified the transference of legal title of his bank to his two daughters and after their passing the bank was to be titled to their children, ad infinitum, seeing no end to the lineage. He envisioned himself as the origin of something inestimably splendid and as an eternal bearer of his name. To him the bank meant everything. He intended, they said, to change its name which bore his own coupled with the name of our small town to one which read Monett Bank and Trust Company exclusively, and although he failed to materialize the change before he died Madeline made good on his wish for him, seeing to it that the proper legal steps were taken within a month following his burial. Madeline shared equally her husband's dream. She'd been part and parcel of our small town bank before her marriage to Monett, maintaining that position for years thereafter. She zealously served as cashier before their acquaintance, younger generations harboring nowhere in their imagination that it ever functioned without her. In short, while she conveyed bank title and ownership to her daughters, exhorting them to gather in their hearts a sensitiveness to the burdens born by their parents in conducting the affairs of the business, she preached as well that they must assume this same responsibility with an air of importance and dignity—an objective which with guile and deliberation she had long groomed them to fulfill—and that the bank would faithfully sustain their high place in the community.

Crowded around a small metal table that morning shortly following Monett's burial were a gathering of men sipping coffee, smoking cigarettes, and exchanging verbiage of inconsiderable depth in Jack Fenimore's drugstore where he mainly sold nonprescription medicines and operated an ice cream parlor. A soda fountain occupied space on the left of the interior as one gained entry and a scant of magazines on the right were arranged on a flimsy showcase rack. The rack consisted of six or seven wire shelvings, the cost of a magazine denoted by a handwritten price tab affixed to the cover. A cluttered niche in the rear served as a medicinal dispensary, where medicines were made up for usage. A portion of this space he shared with his father, the old and burdensomely overweight Doctor Fenimore, who folks claimed should have quit practice ten years before. The men had gathered there twenty four or fewer hours after Monett's burial, and while in their thoughts they nurtured condolence and respect for the fallen they saw no reason for not conclaving together, as normally, to delight in one another's litany. A member of the Benge clan also occupied one of the chairs, this being Josephus. One is urged to recall that Josephus had earned the reputation as the pugnacious feisty about town whose flagrant bulliness resided in everyone's knowledge, irresistibly inclined to provoke quarrels and pick fights from which he generally emerged the better. As he usually did he sat tapping cigar ash into a half full bottle of coke, an oddity that originated further back than anyone recalled which spawned grins of amusement from those witnessing the antic. Some said that this particular additive somehow in fact enhanced the bicarbonate, verifiable by observing that when Josephus drank the mixture he invariably cleared his throat and closed his eyes as it went down.

"Who's to take Monett's place in heading the bank," someone asked, which prompted not more than a sleepy response from the man next to him.

"Yeah. Well."

"You know Madeline can't run it without help. And the girls. They're not ready yet, are they? Not ready to step in and completely take over." All this had gotten sounded by someone from across the table. And then there came an answer.

"No. I don't think they are."

"That's easy to see," said Josephus. In the keenness of his nervous eyes, which darted first on one of his associates and then on another, he gave hint that he had pre calculated the outcomes and did as much the day before Monett died, or several weeks in advance of his demise, aware, as was everyone else, that the man's condition obviously worsened by the day and that shortly he would expire.

Then someone else reinforced Josephus. "Yeah. It's a pretty natural thing that has to take place."

"You mean what will take place," said Josephus. "Not what's has to. That's what you ought to just outright say."

"That's what I meant. That's what I said."

What were the outcomes that Josephus had contemplated? Being conscious of how the Benge's kept up with news or the possible making of news would have made easy the answer. The Benge's, while not able to claim acceptance to the inner circle of the gate-keepers of the town, significantly affected many affairs that took place—much of their success owing to marriage affiliations that influenced decisions of political leverage, or due to the fact that they were involved in a welter of businesses that generally transmitted gains to someone or some several in the line of power. Josephus had said, "That's easy to see," which when translated merely meant that he saw clearly and surely the one or ones destined to fill the vacuum left by Monett. There would proceed forward one Mansford Plumber, Melissa's husband, now the postmaster and had occupied that position over the several years previous, who when not attending to his postal duties filled in part time at the bank; and thence Franklin P. Ray, the son of Riley Ray Linsford and his wife Blondell, followed closely in Mansford's footsteps. They called him Frankie around town, a sort of nickname which started in his boyhood years. We all knew that Blondell was Josephus's sister. She married Riley Ray when they were in high school, and that meant that he had then and there assumed membership in the Benge clan. He had risen to prominence as a successful cattle and hog broker for miles around; the farmers, the producers of cattle and hogs, thinking of no other name when on the threshold of selling off livestock; and hence, Riley Ray, profiting from this advantage enjoyed a goodly income, which steadily flowed as deposits into Monett's banking enterprise.

Chapter 40

THE DAYS of the calendar had turned but little when Mansford Plumber tendered his resignation from the postmaster's seat and moved into the bank as full time director, whereas Frankie soon occupied the position that Mansford left open. It occurred in the scheme of things also that there emerged a need for an assistant postmaster, and while the Benge's would likely have no bearing on this prize the grapevine flowing throughout town intimated that it would receive force and full effect through another branch of politics. Jeremy Dodson, who ran the grocery store next to the railroad until his death had fathered four sons, all of good reputation throughout the community, the second oldest the principal of the local school. They called him Lamar A., short for Lamar Austin Dodson. The whole town knew that he was inextricably tied to two persons in particular who effectively controlled certain matters that clearly belonged in the domain of his office—Rupert Monett, Chairman of the School Board whose voice spoke loudly on any and all ventures and his daughter Melissa, who spoke not nearly as loudly, but she did speak in this case and the words she spoke registered unmistakably in the ears of her principal Lamar A. His brother Lester had married a nice girl in earlier years whose origin sprang from a family looked upon with great respect and admiration. They called her Hanah. Hanah let it out only through her husband that if the job developed and applications were sought, she welcomed an opportunity to apply. She needn't have taken one step further. The position suddenly fell into her lap. People gossiped that as soon as her hopes reached the ears of Lamar A., they then flew from him to Melissa and the search there ended. That was that. The rest was easy.

In summation, when Monett departed us, three positions of employment were suddenly triggered, if not more, and three persons, not unsuspectingly, were suddenly seated in these positions. It tempted me when I absorbed this news by way of letter from my dear friend Mr. Carney to draft a term paper as part of my class fulfillment under Doctor Linskie entitled "The Intrigues of Small Town Politics," but after vacillating over the idea for not a great a length it dawned on me that such an article would not shed a particle of newness on the subject. "Even the most uninformed knows everything there is to know about small town politics," I uttered with conviction and thereby tossed the budding idea aside.

The semester swept rapidly onward. Soon Christmas. I'd see Melissa during the holidays, telling her that I deeply regretted the passing of her father, and asked her forgiveness for not attending the funeral service and the burial. She had written a letter expressing how she missed me and how better she would have fared should I have availed myself but that she understood. I felt badly, though counseled myself that worrying over a thing of the past never served anyone usefully and to suppress all thoughts of it.

In the proximity of the first week of December I became the recipient of two invitations to spend at least a fraction of time in New York and Baltimore during the impending Christmas. These of course originated from none other than Aaron and Darya. Aaron said that he knew I understood how the Jewish folks regarded the celebration and the existence of the Christ Child, but that all the same they loved holidays irrespective of their symbolic meanings and that his folks very much desired that I share some of the Christmas period with them, as would he. I begged off. "Aaron, there's no way within the realm of practicality that I can take you up on your kind invitation. It's truly nice of you. But I just can't." Darya pressed me harder. "Please say yes Ramsey. Spend at least a day or two with us. We would like so much to have you. At last you'll meet my parents and I'll whiz you about the city without let up to places you can't imagine. And we'll go sailing too" This last enticement fell temptingly on my ears. In the end I said no, pleading such a sensible and forceful case that with the exception of a few additional tries she persisted no longer. My last bit of logic had prevailed. "Darya, my mother will disown me if I don't show up for Christmas, for every minute of it. She has everything worked out. I'll bet she's written me five letters already. I can't let her down. But I'll tell you this. I'll go with you during the spring break. How's that?"

"I'll take it. And don't you forget your promise."

Due to the widespread snow storm and icy conditions of the roadways I missed going home on the last Christmas and nurtured a determination that nothing would stand in my way this time. No others except Darya and Aaron, as far as I knew, invited a friend to join them in their homes over the holidays, all of us embarking on our separate ways to where we called our home when the time came. But not before we devised our own special holiday as a grouping. It warmed me inside when I learned of it. Someone dawned upon a fun filled and enjoyable idea of a Christmas celebration at the fraternity house and little by little the idea grew into a full fledged panorama. We'd not done that before, not in my time at the university. No one had given reasons for the gathering, though as I thought it through I surmised that in some subtle way we all had the mind set that it in a sense meant good bye to those who had graduated and were long gone when the next Christmas rolled around. They were the seniors. Darya and Bertinelli and Aaron fell into that category. They will have walked the line of graduation along with a procession of others out under the giant oaks and will have said goodbye to those of us remaining, "perhaps for always" I thought. "Who knows what the future holds?"

Darya and Bertinelli led the way at pieceing the affair together and likely gave birth to the concept to begin with. Darya called a sizeable grouping together from across campus one evening after supper and laid out the scenario.

"We'll stage the festivities as well as erecting a huge evergreen here in the fraternity house, in this lobby, and our many friends from across the broader campus are invited. Some are here tonight for the brainstorming."

"Food. Will we have food?" someone asked in moderate voice from across the room.

"Food! Yes. Plenty of that. There's a compulsory fee to cover the cost but no one will mind shelling out. The food, well, we'll order it caterd in. And we'll have a band, no heavy stuff. Just soft nice music. Nothing formal in dress ware. Nice street clothes will do." She went on, touching upon everything from A to Z. That was Darya, born to take charge and seeing clearly ahead, encountering no snags that she couldn't disentangle quickly and then move forward to the next docket of business. "She's a cinch to my way of envisioning to head up a massive conglomerate someday, perhaps the one that her father will eventually pass on to her." I sat and marveled at the ease and efficiency with which she proceeded. Only one question cropped up when she finished which had averted discussion. Someone asked of the permissibility of drinks.

Turning, singling him out she answered, "Nothing stronger than strawberry punch my buddy. Or champagne."

In the days that followed we all recognized her as the central cog for ascertaining that planning got transformed into action, approaches made constantly and freely to her by those volunteering their services to help, who received concise administrative answers and clarifications from their leader.

It was within this same frame of time that I opened an envelope containing a letter from Nenia. She wrote frequently, this one lengthier than usual.

"My dear sweetheart," she began, "it's terrible that I miss you like I do in my heart. I think of you endlessly as I carry out my routines of the day. You are not ever far away and may Heaven forbid otherwise."

These were sweet endearing words which profoundly worsened the guilt that I carried within my bosom. What would this letter have been like if she somehow discovered my closeness to Darya? In the first place there would have been no letter.

"You doubtless are preparing for the holidays, as am I, and I wish every moment that we were together. Your gift is soon to arrive by separate mailing. I am practically on my way with it to the post office. Don't you wish I'd tell you what it is?

You continue to speak in your letters of your interesting work in the legal profession and that you are as busy as a bee traveling to New York City and back. On my way home at the beginning of summer my plane will land there and hopefully you can meet me and we can spend some time touring that very exciting place. Can we?

Now for a line or two relative to my work here. As you know, I finished my advanced studies in French six months ago, approximately, and then began to teach young French girls English, seventh and eighth graders. I will find it discomforting to give them up. They are perfectly delightful. The fact that I am doing this work has paid off in another regard, making possible a good many travels throughout Europe. You wouldn't believe Paris, immersed in elegance and full of life, which offers a million fascinating things to see and do. One of the things that I have especially liked is joining my friends and sitting and taking lunch at one of the colorful sidewalk cafes, for which the Parisians are noted. I have a teacher friend, her name is Danielle, a bosom travel companion, and she always insists that we take lunch at one such café in particular. I think it's because there are an abundance of young men clever at manufacturing alibis that stop by for a chat. You know how young Frenchmen are. But don't worry. They don't have a chance with me. Besides, they're only after Danielle.

Please when you are home for the holidays drop over to visit with my father and mother. Mom writes often, once a week I'd bet, and your name often pops up in her letters. Dad said tell you, by way of mom, that the house where you and your family once lived is gone, torn down by a commercial farmer who bought the farm and leased extra land for miles around for growing wheat and corn. Like everything else, agriculture is changing, going strictly big time. Dad says some of the machinery is as tall as a house. But he's known that for some time. And speaking of a house we'll have to stroll over and attempt to find where yours once stood when I'm back.

One last thing. I have a job offer at the Saint Louis Library and Archives and will accept it right away. I can begin work in July or August. Exactly when is up to me. I am purchasing the home in which I lived before I left for France and look with elation to occupying it once again.

And with this, my dear, I will bid you *Au revoir pour vn certain temps* and wish you the merriest of Christmas.

With all my love. Nenia."

I sat and stared into space after finishing the last line. Every word she scribed into print had seeped irretrievably into my heart and spun round and round. Of course, guilt coarsed all the way through me. How could it not have? And then I turned to my other self.

"Gee. What an entanglement. Two beautiful girls and you're drawn irresistibly to both. Maybe not equally but close. You've loved Nenia since your early teen years. By now she's built into your entire fabric and every letter you've gotten from her you've felt just as you're feeling now. You remember that very first kiss, don't you, the kiss of innocent youth.

There is no other kiss like the first one, is there? You remember what you said to Aaron, that you hoped things would work out. That won't happen easily. You couldn't possibly tell Nenia of Darya and you know you can't possibly tell Darya of Nenia. So there. But in the end I'm supposing you'll tell Darya that it's over, even though it will break her heart, because you wouldn't give up Nenia for anything on earth. She's too deep into the web of your soul. And she arrived there first. Then, may I ask, what are you to do? Really, what are you to do? Well, here's what. Do as you have done? Do nothing except hope. Hope that somehow all will turn out well? Maybe Darya, when she graduates and leaves here, will in the attitude of a misty cloud subtly drift away, or conclude somehow there's someone else and of her own accord elect to break it off more directly. But deep down you don't actually won't that to happen, do you?

And also, aren't you taking this to extremes? All three of you are young. Young lovers come and go. They break up and their hearts break with it. History is replete with such epical experiences. Broken hearts will mend and teary eyes will dry. Now, what will you do to lift yourself from your quandry; I mean right now? I know what you'll do. You'll continue right on shielding your secret, deep down out of sight and from sound, and in my every being my friend I hope things will turn out well for you." Nevertheless, Nenia's letter hung over me throughout the evening. I struggled to push it out of consciousness, not in any manner easy. It lingered too long.

In conjunction with a mix of other girls from across campus Darya sprang a surprise, contending that the flavor of the dinner should in some way resemble our historical past as a nation, the meal itself a duplicate of those graced by the tables of the Dutch, the Quakers, and the Pilgrims during the stressful ordeals they endured while helping to settle our country. "Let's make it as an imitation of the olden," she exuded with excitement, "like olden times. That's the theme we need to emulate. Don't you think Ramsey? We need to appreciate the old."

"Yeah," I answered, half spinning it around, with no solid opinion one way or another at the moment. But as I internalized it further, I began to see wisdom in the idea. The more I spun it the more I liked it.

We would dress in ordinary street clothes, said Darya at first, at one stage however seriously considering that we should adopt the attire of the Quakers or Pilgrims and backed away from her earlier notion. No street clothes. We'd dress as Quakers and Pilgrims. There were no gift exchanges allowed, other than the ones someone might give to another separate and apart from the current celebration. Experience had conditioned me to expect that Darya and Aaron would provide me with gifts, but separately, and far more expensive than the ones I would give them. But I did not expect a beautiful package wrapped in red crepe as I opened the door to my room the next afternoon with a large green bow appended on top. The note that accompanied it read, "I hope you like it." Andrea had scribbled her signature alongside the wording.

After the first meeting Darya asked Balboni to locate a sizeable western spruce for display in the lobby area, a mission that he carried out with dispatch. The tree nearly reached to the peak of the vaulting, the height rising a full twenty feet above floor level. I do not know how they managed the technique of standing it upright; I wasn't there. But being a rather resourceful fellow Balboni raked together a crew of young savvy men and somehow succeeded at the task of raising the tree and in accord with Darya's guidance took the lead at stringing the lights, as well as affixing an assortment of glitzy decorations to the many branches from top to bottom. The full space of the lobby glowed and sparkled.

The frenetic day of making sure that everything fell into place eventually played out and the long night of the festivity began. Small cute tables supporting a party of four, overspread with white shiny cloths, were set out at various points in the room, and we, as preplanned walked the line with our plates, filling them nearly to the rim, and then carrying them to the table bearing our names on a red rectangular card and sat down. It was not with anyone that I knew that I joined, a guy and two girls, complete strangers to me and I to them. Darya wanted to avoid seating persons together of close friendship, wisely thinking it the thing to do. Hardly were we seated when Andrea stood from her whereabouts announcing to everyone to pause for prayer, and then looked across at me with a request that I do the honors. Darya, I learned afterwards, told Andrea to ask me to. I gasped. It caught me off guard. My mother said the prayers during my growing up years, and sometimes my father. But never me. And during the whole of the time I shared a residence with Leland neither of us offered prayer. At the fraternity house blessings weren't usually said at meal time. Sometimes Darya and Bertinelli said them, the only ones to do so. Before I stood or while I had begun to stand I decided on something quick and brief, something that I could recite from memory. I'd gone over it at great length in the past and could recite without pause or error a prayer of Saint Francis of Assisi that bestowed an abiding impression upon me when I first heard it. Suddenly the prayer appeared clearly in my head, and after revealing to my audience the author of the words they were about to hear I began, "Lord, make me an instrument of your peace. Where there is hatred, let me sow love, where there is injury, pardon, where there is doubt, faith, where there is despair, hope, where there is darkness, light, where there is sadness, joy." I appended an Amen. Even though the message exited from my own mouth it nonetheless sounded to me beautiful and I gathered by the bearing on the various faces that it sounded beautiful to them too. When asked by several students where they might find this wondrous piece of spirituality, I answered that they should check with a local priest, for he would almost certainly have possession of it in his library, in that Saint Francis of Assisi was the father of the Franciscan Order, whose life ranged from 1181 or 1182 until 1226. I no longer kept a copy; over time it somehow disappeard from my files.

At the finish of the dinner the catering corps removed the food and cleared the tables of utensils, supplying in their stead a huge silver urn of coffee for each table with a flame lit underneath for continuous heating. The crowd as yet had quietly behaved, nothing loud or raucous. Dancing to the nice soft music of the band was not as active as I expected, not at all on the outset, but that would change. The students freely roamed about table hoping, evidently more content to do that than dance, sitting with friends or newly made friends in happy social exchange. The ambience of the room hummed with a mix of many and varied voices.

The band consisted of a montage of local musicians, very good musicians according to the views that spread about by the advanced publicity. I danced with a stream of girls who turned out in heavy numbers. I danced with Andrea no telling the times. She was instantly at my table when the band first started to play and said jokingly that if I didn't dance with her she'd quit tutoring me in physics and math. The two girls at my table said they were thrilled by the invitation to attend the gathering. At first blush I gathered that they were twins. They said no they weren't when asked. Soon thereafter I inquired if they perhaps finished high school together. I felt impelled to do something to initiate conversation even if of trivial tidbits.

"We did."

"Were you together all the way?"

"No. We met in the eighth grade. We've been close pals ever since."

One could not have failed to observe immediately how strikingly they were attired, "but not in the least like Quaker dress," I murmured, and how alike the attire, each wearing a snugly fitting vest of green with a red stiff collar at the neck, their nice slender arms covered in sleeves of white as they poked through the openings and a bright glittering bracelet encircled the wrist of each. But still, they were dressed agreeably with the decorum of the evening as far as Darya was concerned. They conveyed by way of expression that they were delighted to dance with me, the same as it was with Andrea, frequently, sometimes one or the other tapping me on my shoulder when I exited the dance floor with someone else.

"Could I have the next round?"

Who wouldn't have been flattered, and I was, and smiled yes and happily clasped whichever it was in my arms?

"Where are you from?" I asked.

"Evansville."

"Evansville. Down on the Ohio. The river."

"Un hunh. That's it."

"I've gone to the horse races there a time or two. Do you ever?"

"Once in a while. The last time about a year ago."

While we sat, the girls talked sparingly, for the most part waiting in anticipation of me assuming the lead with conversation, looking across through the candle glow with stunningly attractive eyes. When dancing, they suddenly came alive and talked my ears off, the reason, I assumed, because they were a tad shy of dancing cheek to cheek and attempted to overcome their embarrassment with a flow of distracting chatter. When Bertinelli dropped by he declined to sit down, only stopping long enough to lean over and whisper in my ear, "My. These girls here. Who are they? They look alarmingly young."

"They're from Evansville, Indiana. They do look young, I concur. What's the old saying? Youth is a dişability that you can't do anything about. But I'm working at it."

"How is that?"

"I'm enjoying them."

The guy who sat with us admitted that he possessed no propensity at dancing, his shortcoming throwing the burden on me to accommodate the girls, though I sufficiently broke away from them long enough to enter into a decent quantity of exchanges with him, learning that he came from Peoria, Illinois and that his father grew beef cattle. His name was Harry Lapchick. He suggested that I tag along with him one day to sight see at the Chicago Stock Yards. He also said that he'd enrolled at a private law school in the city part time, attending classes at night, hoping to complete his course work at the university at the end of the current semester but would postpone walking the graduation line until the first week of June.

"I'd like to talk to you some more of your law schooling. Would you mind giving me your telephone number?"

"Sure."

He scribbled it down on a napkin and handed it to me.

I kept dancing with the two girls, wondering if Darya were jealous. We'd only danced once but would have much more if she hadn't been too saddled with filling her obligations as hostess. Finally, she freed herself and came over, sitting down next to me, the girls looking on, and softly clasped my hand while smiling coyly. The girls pretended not to notice, half twisting around to glance at the dancers on the dance floor and at the happy persons sitting at the tables scattered across the room as if these scenes were their sole sphere of preoccupancy. When Darya left I danced with the girls a few rounds more then bade them goodnight, and Harry Lapchick as well, giving as my reason for departure some obligations necessating my presence, not defining exactly what. My obligations were actually in the singular, to drop over to where Andrea sat and very much enjoy her presence. Her eyes shone with animation as I joined her. In the meanwhile the musicians kept playing, working and sweating to keep the feet of youth flying over the dance floor. The crowd stayed late, until past midnight. When someone mentioned to the band that the gathering was nearing an end they started to play Auld Lang Syne, the words of which I had never learned altogether. Those who were familiar with the lyrics sang the song in harmony with the band and I sang fragments of the lines with them as they repeated the chorus. After the party drew its last breath Darya and I sat in the lobby for a while back-tracking to the events of the evening. Increasingly I saw sleep closing fast upon her. She'd begun to yawn, the next one arriving quicker than the one before.

"You'd better leave off for bed."

"You too."

I kissed her goodnight and offered congratulations for a job superbly done.

"It was a huge success; in every way a person can measure. You did a terrific job at meshing everything together. If not for you there wouldn't have been a party."

Chapter 41

THE NEXT morning at late breakfast Aaron slid in beside me, no one else there except Bertinelli who now stayed busy in the kitchen helping the cook. Aaron mentioned the party first. "Some fine get together that took place last night my friend. If my observation serves me well everybody had a heck of a good time."

"I echo that. It takes me back in a way to the family reunions we used to have down South. Out of the blue someone of my large family of relatives would suggest that we congregate out under some giant oak and have a barbecue cook out. And then we started to pull it together, a four-hundred-pound dressed hog soon simmering over a pit of hickory bark coals, the cooking superintended by one of my old experienced uncles, Uncle Sanford they called him, who periodically punched holes in the meat with a table fork to determine whether it had tenderized in accord with his unwritten guidelines. And that wasn't all. Someone asked us young bucks to hitch up the wagon and bring back a load of watermelons grown in one of the relatives fields, ours or someone else's, which were submerged until cutting time in the coolness of creek water that flowed nearby. Let me also mention that I remember doubly clear that there was a brand new zinc coated wash tub which my mother filled or had filled with lemonade which was cooled with ice blocks hauled in from Douglass Murphy's ice house. Those days have largely disappeared Aaron, I sorely regret. They don't do that sort of thing anymore, at least not much. It saddens me."

"How many families showed up?"

"Fifteen, maybe twenty."

"You don't say. You folks knew how to live. Take me down there with you sometime. I need to see that place."

Aaron, a New York dandy, completely without accuracy of vision of a small Southern town could only imagine the viscera of its culture, which necessitated before he had gotten very far at trying that I pave the way to helping him understand.

"Aaron, I'm from the South as you know and I am born of their mores; yet I do not wholly fit the mold."

"The mold? What do you mean by that?"

"I'm of that culture, though to you I may not demonstrate it."

"You don't at all."

"Let me say more. I'm well read, and educated, greatly educated in comparison to the usual lot of folks still residing where I originated into this world. Some, like me, are educated, very well read and educated. Some are teachers. Let me say then that I'm talking of the culture in general, not the exceptions. If you went with me there you would enjoy yourself, guaranteed, and learn much. I'm convinced of that. But you'd find yourself likened to a duck out of water, I'm afraid in many respects likened to Linsky, I am suddenly reminded, a character in the serene Puskin's poeticized masterpiece which he simply titled *Eugene Onegin*."

"And who was this fellow Linsky? I've not supplied myself thus far with Puskin's scripting."

"A suave young man from some city of Russia in the last century who had traveled to a backward farm region to visit his friend whom he earlier met. He would take lodging nearby for the benefit of assured privacy when he wanted it, and call on his friend when he chose, or go see him on occasions when invited. He would stay gone on this trip for as long as he wished. In terms of cash and property holdings his parents laid claim to more than adequate wealth and contentedly funded his sojourn."

"When did he and his friend meet?"

"I'm supposing they met while attending the university, the name of which and its exact whereabouts I'll not attempt to divulge. Because I'm unsure of the facts. In time, Linsky's friend left the university to again join his parents at tilling the soil and in additional time Linsky made good on his pledge to visit his friend when they parted. Little was Linsky aware that in this good family there lived a girl, his friend's sister, a beautiful charming thing, though finished of rural ways, whose parents upon meeting the finely attired and well mannered young man at once entertained designs of marrying her off to him. He had attained to eighteen years of age, she sixteen. The ages were of no bother. But upon his first invitation to dinner all hopes and dreams of the parents would have gotten severely dashed should they have discerned the swirling thoughts in Linsky's head as implaced there by the great Puskin."

And Linsky found the neighbors' dinner completely foreign to his taste.
He shunned their noisy conversations about their dogs and their relations,
Indeed, their sober talks of wine and crops, though shrewd and genuine,
Did not exactly blaze with wit; nor was there any poet's fire
Nor brilliancy nor keen desire nor art nor social grace in it.

"You would find me not at all critical of your people, making not the tiniest insinuations of their customs and pridefulness," Aaron softly declared, "and allow me my friend to offer that while the lines you recite from the artistic Puskin are ingenious and worthy of high acclaim they do not define my standards. I will surely like your people and hope that you will hasten the opportunity to take me there."

"In due time."

One of the last to leave for home that Christmas, I insisted that I drive Aaron and Darya to the airport to catch their planes, the day villainously cold, the wind attacking my skin as if it intended to cut to the bone. Balboni rode along with us. When we reached the airport terminal we parked and helped them with their luggage, stopping first at the waiting station where Aaron would catch his flight. Balboni said he'd stay with Aaron while I accompanied Darya to the area of her departure. When we completed the steps to where we were to wait I set her luggage down and hugged and kissed her, wishing through her a happy holiday to her parents.

"I will gladly give them such intelligence, with a special emphasis."

I laughed at her sophistication of wording. She laughed back. She had done it on purpose, just to excite a rise from me. We talked on a minute or so after this and then determining that our goodbye was over I started to leave. But instantly, she reached and caught my arm and turned me around, facing me straightaway. "Here, you'll catch a death of cold. Let me button you up." Upon this, she drew me closer and one by one fitted the buttons into the slits of my heavy gray coat. "There. That ought to do. Now, on your way. My plane is not more than minutes from lifting off." She seemed ready to pull me to her again. She gave the impression that she might. I figured wrongly. A kind of wondering wistful look spread blithely on her face, or that is how it seemed, as if she harbored an urge to say something or ask something. She didn't. Was it the sadness of saying goodbye, even for such a short while, or something else? Her beautiful pensive eyes offered no clue of what they beheld. I wouldn't keep guessing. I saw no value in that.

As Balboni and I drove back to the university we began to talk of a multiplicity of things as we always did when together. Not often, but sometimes, I spent lengthy periods meshing through things with him that were of mutual interest. This happened in the lobby of the fraternity house more apt than not. I couldn't begin to predict what he might bring up. Anything was likely. His intellect and manner did not fit into the ordinary mold, often unpredictable I had long before learned. On this day he began to mention his father and mother and without the least of reservation. I set him off I supposed by inquiring of their general well being. He dwelled on each of them about equally.

"You know Ramsey, my father is in the construction industry. He's done some pretty big jobs here in the city." He proceeded slowly, reflecting, gauging his remarks in advance.

"Tough work," I said.

"You have it right. It is. And there's more to it than nicely finished buildings that the public sees as they drive by, not the least suspecting of the human struggle that goes along with it."

"You're saying—."

"I mean some bad things go on. The gangs. They insist on their cut. And I'm talking about the unions as well. They all insist on their cut. And if you don't ante up, then you may end up with your legs being hit with a steel rod. Even as a youngster I saw some awfully bad things, and my father spoke of some I didn't see that were much worse. And he still does."

"I'll declare."

"Yeah. That's one reason I'm here. Many are the times my mom set me down and said that she wasn't about to let her son end up in the construction business, considering the nature of the people I'd have to put up with. Facing real danger and all. She's gone over this with my father time and again. I think her view has finally sunk into his brain. The truth is, I think, inside himself he doesn't want that kind of life for me either. I think he's long felt that way and one day he said so. Not too long ago. That happened when he learned I'd done well enough on my qualifying exam to enroll at the university. He didn't smile, because he never does, but he did underneath. It showed all over his face."

"Well, you're here, as you say and that must make your mom very happy and also your father."

"Sure it does. And me too."

From here the conversation led to where I anticipated it might, to his asking me to tell him of my life growing up in the South. I suspected that Aaron earlier explained something of my upbringing to him, revealing as much as he knew in any event, and that this amounted to an extension of the dialogue they'd had between themselves. He said his curiosity of my background in the South had gnawed away at him for some time, but that he nurtured a hesitancy to address the topic. I said I couldn't understand why and began to unravel a snippet of my growing up years.

"I'm the son of a sharecropper Balboni. Or very close to that. I saw after the livestock, plowed the fields, hauled hay, and chopped and picked cotton. I even trailed my uncles into the woods and pulled a crosscut saw."

It appeared in his countenance that these experiences were too extraordinary to believe. "Are you making that up?"

"No. I'm not. That's the way it was. You're not from the South. It figures naturally enough that you don't grasp easily that these things were part and parcel of my early existence."

"I'll say your'e probably right. But still I can't quite believe it. You're so educated, so smart, so smooth and level headed. Everyone here looks up to you."

"Well, I don't know. I'm just an ordinary guy. But it's nice to hear gratifying opinions."

His revelation of how he felt toward me, as well as the fact that he said others opined likewise hit me in the right spot; in other words, frankly, hearing of such evaluations made me feel good about myself. It stirred every once in a while in the labyrinths of my thoughts that others like Darya and Aaron and still scores of others on campus were better born than myself, I shamefully admit, and rich, and educated in preparatory schools of enormous advantage compared to my early growing up exposure. "Better born? No, they weren't better born," I rebuked myself, "and never should I have let such a thought see the light of day, just born with more advantage," but I had come from a Christian family abounding in virtue and values and love, and with those qualities serving as the measure, I wagered, I ran near the front of the pack. What more did I need? I had everything.

After we'd exhausted the topics and subtopics of my past we converged on a myriad of other topics, ultimately drawing to surface the names of our fraternity house associates. He adored Darya, willing at the drop of a hat to do anything for her. His liking of Bertinelli badly needed improvement, and sometimes he let his feelings spill over to me and Bartinelli vented his to me as well. I gathered that since both were of Italian heritage that the schism was somehow tied to their both being of that origin and therefore was usable as a starting point for trying for reconciliation. At the same time I deduced that I should avoid falling into the middle of their antipathies. I thoughtfully adopted the stance that I'd refuse to discuss the issues with either of them if they arose again. I did sit Balboni down once, breaking therefore my commitment, stressing that he trailed Bertinelli by a few years in terms of age and that Bertinelli made a good supervisor for the fraternity house. Going on from there I said that it seemed to me a prudent choice of behavior if he kept his feelings more in check. I think it took hold. Eventually both made a serious effort to speak to one another and stopped going childishly out of their way to purposefully avoid face to face contact.

Packing my essentials that morning before driving Aaron and Darya to the airport I was all set to head for my hometown the moment I dropped Balboni off in front of the fraternity house, telling myself that I'd better get along if I expected to make it by at least dark. I said Merry Christmas again to Balboni as I started to drive away. I'd turn right at the third street from the campus edge and set my sights southward, figuring the trip to eat up five hours or more even if I challenged the speed limit now and then. The road was heavily traveled but not clogged. I said a little prayer thanking the Lord for that.

When I reached my mother's home the proud fierce sun had begun to hide, streaks of red and gold, the only observable figments of daylight remaining. Darkness soon would follow, which descended early in the midst of winter. A current of joy surged through me as I hurriedly passed through her doorway. Glowing with happiness she gathered me into her arms, hugging me and taking on with tender motherly endearments as if she would never let go. For a fleeting moment of magical fantasy, I again was her little boy. She had cooked for a whole week in preparation, my oldest sister helping her, already there when I arrived and hugged me and fussed over me as much as my mother. Not more than a few seconds expired before my mother asked for a report on things up North, starting with the last date that I had been with her. Apparently, she confused my academic studies with my activities at the law firm, the fault of her mix up altogether mine, for I failed to write distinctly enough in my letters to clearly set them apart.

"Tell me all about what you've been doing son. Especially with your law work."

"I'm doing all right mom. I deliver documents by plane from Chicago to New York, and this is coupled with my working for an older gentleman who keeps me busy researching things for him."

"That sounds important. It really does. But will you tell me a little more, a little more detail to help me better understand?"

"There's not much to it. I just dig into the files for information concerning cases of law already tried and recorded. My job is to find out what actually happened and turn it over to Mr. Yazstremski."

"And who is that?" she asked, wrinkles gathering on her forehead.

"My boss. An older man. A fine man indeed. You'd like him. I study under him. I'm learning. I'm not a lawyer mom. I'm merely learning."

"But you will take up law someday, won't you?"

"I'm not exactly sure. I'm filling up with experiences with respect to all sorts of legal knowledge, but I'm not convinced at this stage that I'll adopt law as a life time profession."

"What will you do Ramsey? Have you considered another choice?"

"I have mom. The thought of it never leaves me."

"What do you think it is?"

"Literature. Possibly literature."

"You'd like to teach."

"I would. I would in college. The idea is strongly appealing."

"A teacher. That's an awfully good profession."

"I feel it is."

"That's what Nenia is training for. That's what Mrs. Stoddard, her mother, tells me. She says she's teaching nice little French girls how to speak English right now."

"She is. That's true. And she likes it. I actually think it's the truth however that she's dedicated to working in a big city library. She's already accepted a position in the Saint Louis Library and Archives."

"I haven't heard anyone speak of that. Did Nenia tell you of that? When did you hear from her?"

"Only recently."

"When was that?"

"The date escapes me. But recently."

"Is she coming home for Christmas? Seems Maggie said to me she was."

"No, she's not coming. She won't do that until next summer."

"I hoped she could. I'm disappointed."

It was a joyful Christmas. We largely ate. And stayed close to one another, laughing, talking, reminiscing, which we did far more than focusing on the present or speculating on the future. Retreating to old times was much more swaying. Families did that back then. They reminisced. There were gift exchanges but limited. My brother and three sisters were there, the two that were married, bringing their children with them, bouncing around everywhere as soon as they bounded through the door, squealing, giggling, running wildly through the house. Once the oldest girl wrestled her younger brother by two years to the ground pounding him with both hands to which he began yelling and squalling. Their mother rushed outside to see what it was all about, explaining as she returned that the two became entangled in an argument over who got the biggest sucker they'd taken from the candy jar that my mother kept in the kitchen for her grandchildren when they were brought to see her. The mother said that the boy had hit first and that his sister older and bigger and stronger turned on him. "He has a temper. He's bad about not controlling it. What she laid on him serves him right." Soon they were at each other again, cries and yellings and "I hate you," said by one or the other. "I can't find it anywhere in reasonable belief that I'm an uncle, going through all this," I silently generalized to myself. "It makes me feel suddenly old."

My youngest sister hadn't as yet married. She had begun to attend college at a nearby church supported institution. The temptation easily landed on me to compare our relative quietness, when the children were outside playing, to the spirited pre-Christmas festivity at the fraternity house. Afterwards, during another sitting, I casually mentioned the Christmas affair to my mother and oldest sister who began to nudge for details, some I chose to dwell upon in depth while others I carefully skirted, wary with the caution of hunted prey to avoid alluding to Darya or Andrea. If I should have slipped and mentioned the girls, even in causal passing, the antennas of both my mother and sister would have sprung abruptly skyward. They loved Nenia, they were the guardians of Nenia, they had known Nenia since her girlhood; and to them it would seem unthinkable that I might entertain the minutest interest in someone other than her.

The next day my mother relayed that John Eric dropped by during the week past with a message that he needed to hear from me the minute I set foot through the front door, or as soon as I could follow through.

"What does he want? Did he tell you?"

"He's hopeful you can join him and Sanford in a hunt in the Harts Mill Bottom." Uncle Sanford and John Eric were brothers, Uncle Sanford older than John Eric by almost fifteen years. We thought of him as the hunter supreme. The Harts Mill Bottom gained its name from a swampy marshland inundated with flood waters in the spring by a slow crawling river without adequate embankment. When the flooding ceased the waters drained away and eventually disappeared in the muddy swirls of the Mississippi.

"When?"

"Let me look at the calendar. I wrote it down." She looked and gave me the day and date. But not the hour of departure.

"What time are we to leave?"

She looked once more at the calendar. "It says here five."

"Oh my! What an hour! I'll never make it out of bed that early."

"Oh you can. He's hoping real hard you'll go with them. I think they've kind of planned it for you. Telephone him tonight that you'll meet him at his house and on time."

After groaning in mild protest, I concurred and picked up the phone and called John Eric that I couldn't under any circumstances resist joining a hunt that promised to yield barrels of fun. In no few words he went over the arrangements. We'd leave day after the next. We'd use the wagon for transport, hauling the dogs with us and the guns and some axes and a cross cut saw. Aunt Jewel, Uncle Sanford's wife, already promised to pack food, foremost among it uncooked country ham and John Eric wove in that he'd take along his oversized out of doors coffee pot and deep well frying skillets. He kept talking until I began to question whether he'd discover a stopping place. When he began to throttle down, I lunged in and assured him once again that I'd be there and with great enthusiasm. "Goodnight," he replied, with an obvious thrill in his voice.

Uncle Sanford was something of a renegade in our family, not given to holding down a work for wages job nor productively disposed to farming either. Sometimes he worked for short spurts at the cotton gin. His wife held down a job as a seamstress at a shirt factory and that largely kept bread and meat on the table. Not terribly bothered by overweightness he suffered still from another handicap of worse potential, a hernia, an aggravation the doctors elected not to correct with surgery, treating it by wrapping an elastic strap around the lower contour of his stomach and around his testicles. We all wondered whether it was the strapping or the hernia itself, or both, that were blamable for his bending a slight forward when he walked, with a frown or touch of pain emanating to his face as if in haste to relieve a biological urge.

You'd see him out with his beagles two or three days weekly hunting rabbits and as many nights with his fox hounds that he kept in separate kennels from the beagles under his front porch. Sometimes he stayed out for the greater portion of the night, the fox hounds on some fresh scent in hot pursuit, though never maneuvering their quarry to bay. That wasn't the point with Uncle Sanford. His whole delight narrowed on hearing the dogs whine and bellow as they raced tenaciously over the scented trail. Of the two leaders you could easily sort out a distinct variance in soundings, a deep mournful bellow given off by Ned, the male, and a high abject whine lifting from Betsy the female. You'd hear Uncle Sanford calling out in the wee hours, yeow, yeow, yeow, as if he were honing in on the exact whereabouts of his prize trackers somewhere in the low soggy breaks, thereby lending reinforcement from where he stood that he now had locked close into the chase with them. Sometimes he'd tilt his face toward one or the other of his shoulders, while cupping his hand to his ear, which gave the impression of his keeping pace with the entire pack foot by foot. In my years as a lad I avidly looked forward to tagging along with him, staying by his side until midnight. On some of these outings, after standing around too uncomfortably long in the marshes, fighting against the cold, I'd return to the wagon long before he quit, and there, cover up with blankets and fall off to sleep. When the chase ended Uncle Sanford returned and making sure that I sufficiently awakened before starting home gouged his stiff fingers into my back.

"Wake up Ramsey. Time we headed home. And I need a riding buddy who's wide awake."

Likened to the winters past we left Uncle Sanford's that morning at a slight after five, the shadows of darkness stubbornly refusing to lift and disappear, the wagon bouncing unrelentingly against the convoluted surface of the dirt road, with the mules moving faster than their usual gait which I supposed they did to offset the coldness of the air. A foggy mist gushed from their nostrils as they breathed out. We could have taken John Eric's pick up truck for the transport of ourselves, the dogs, and the rest and would have adopted this mode of travel except beginning at a certain distance the road gave out and from thereon the terrain lay overgrown with thickets and sedge and clogged with sloughs of backwater that we'd have to cross, dangerous to undertake because of the entanglement of growth concealing swamp holes deep enough to swallow half an automobile. We had to discover another way for circling inconveniently around these impediments. No motor powered vehicle with wheels could deal with obstacles of that magnitude and with no other options conceivably available we altered our route and lost time. Uncle Sanford kept getting up from his driver's seat and when starting to sit back down his legs sort of collapsed and he free fell to the wagon floor on his posteriori. The driver's seat consisted of a hard flat board surface with no backing against which to lean and no springs mounted underneath to counter the jolting impacts caused by the road. Finally, after we'd covered a quarter of the distance I opened the coffee thermos that Aunt Jewel had packed with the other provisions and pulled the blankets up over my body. Pouring a cup full I began to sip. When looking up I saw my two uncles smiling at one another, who had noticed, glad that their young nephew decided to tag along with them on this the kind of adventure which in their spheres of reasoning provided a life worth living. I pulled the blankets up further, propped my shoulders against the siding, and got ready to endure the rest of the journey, while my older kinfolks unaffectedly braved the penetrating chill of the early day and at the same time carried on an unbroken stream of jibber and laughter.

We unloaded the wagon by midmorning, ready, I thought, to turn the beagle hounds loose that yapped and whined and reared up on Uncle Sanford's legs, impatient of waiting longer to start tracking a fresh scent. Their master wouldn't turn them loose just yet.

"One thing about this weather," he pitched in. "It makes a man as hungry as a wolf. Gittin it ready are ye?" he kind of asked, kind of said, glancing over at John Eric.

Already John Eric had kindled a fire, moving quickly in the cold icy air to fry a batch of ham and eggs before the hunt began, disregarding the beagles that whimpered and begged Uncle Sanford to let them loose. When the smell of coffee sifted into my nostrils I rose from the log where I sat and helped myself to a cup full and sat back down. But didn't sit long. In no time I'd filled my plate with ham and eggs that I'd watched simmering in the cast iron skillet, which I could taste even before either entered my mouth. The out of doors atmosphere and the freezing temperature subtly combined to produce a voracious hunger, making every bite tastier. I then understood what Uncle Sanford meant by his allusion to the weather making him, or a man, as hungry as a wolf. I didn't tell my uncles that to me the food and the hot coffee were the highlight of the trip.

"Good, ain't it," Uncle Sanford let go, speaking to me from where he sat on the ground busily chewing a mouth full of biscuits and ham and eggs.

"Unh. hunh."

At last he called out, "Well, John Eric, it's time we turned them loose." The immortal hunt was on and the immortal prey soon in flight as the hounds leapt to the chase with a baleful cry. We'd planned not to keep up with the dogs, but rather to stand for a while in one spot until the rabbit darted away from his place of seclusion, then move about sparingly, edging closer to an opening, which consisted of no better than briar infested swampy mush where we thought he might pop into view. The beagles did the moving for us, relentlessly in pursuit, the rabbit angling in a circular fashion until exposing himself to the double barrel shotguns which required but one blast. The dogs instinctively fought through the spongy bog to retrieve the kill, the leader clutching it between gritty determined jaws until dropping it at our feet. This phase of the hunt was the fun part, the easy part, together with the stories told by my Uncle Sanford and John Eric of their growing up days as youngsters, some stretched beyond believable truth which they knew and knew that I knew. Their favorite tale pictured a panther of monstrous size that once roamed these marshes, sweeping up to some farmer's barn under cover of darkness and at will rifling corn cribs and dragging away half grown calves, never caught or stopped.

"Did they ever see him?"

"Now and then."

"But he wasn't ever caught or killed."

"Naw. They found him one day though. He'd died of old age."

The hard part of the hunt, more than anything else, definitely related to the temperature, below freezing. My hide wasn't lately accustomed to the out of doors. The savage wind unhindered and unabated shot straight up the river and onto the adjoining naked shoreline, rich alluvial soil, which once grew tall and stately gum, hickory, ash, elm, cypress, and oak, now harboring a sorrowful graveyard of dead and decaying stumps and logs.

"What killed the trees Uncle Sanford?"

"Pesticide. That's the way of them jerks over in the agriculture office. Caint leave well enough alone. Want to spray everything in sight. Bastards. I remember when nothing but big tall white oaks growed on the banks of this river as far as you could see."

I doubted his correctness of blaming pesticide for the fate of the trees, but I wasn't sure. Ecologists weren't sure themselves. I allowed it reasonable that Uncle Sanford's speculation was as credible as that of the experts.

The effects of the icy water worsened by the hour, and given the fact that even though I wore hip boots measuring to my lower waist the chill still penetrated to my legs. In time, it had begun to creep through the walls of the boots and into my skin, the discomfort eventually driving me to leave the hunt for solid ground where the wagon was left and where John Eric saw to it that the fire burned brightly just before we set out. Seeing that it had shrunk to an ember I punched it up and piled chunks of wood on the deadened coals, now still alive, but barely, with the result that very quickly small finger size flickers rose into knee high flames; and then I plumped down on a log close by and extended my half numb naked feet into the radiant warmth of the fire. As the noon hour began to pass, Uncle Sanford and John Eric slowly dragged up from the marshes with a string of rabbits tied to their belts, the dogs with tongues hanging out faithfully trailing.

"Let's eat Ramsey. You hungry?"

"Famished." Then, eyeing the pile of game they'd thrown to the ground I curiously asked how many we'd killed so far.

"Twenty four."

"Ha. A bonanza."

To my mind we outdid ourselves. I could only claim credit for four of the twenty four but no matter about that. I was there for the thrill of the trip more than for the count of game that I bagged.

Then there began the skinning and the messy evisceration, the gutting of entrails, of at least three rabbits, by now starting to stiffen. John Eric proceeded through these steps with admirable exactness and rapidity, his skilled hands taking him through the same steps hundreds of times before, beginning with his early boyhood. He could have waltzed through these exercises in his sleep. I could have done the same. I'd also had years of practice, not as many but a good many, of which he knew. I offered to help. He declined. "I'll have this done in a jiffy. You can do it next time." I merely looked on. When he finished he threw the entrails to the beagles, then dipped the raw carcass into a container of salty brine, churning it up and down until the least tint of blood altogether vanished, and then there followed the briefer chore of rinsing. He then sliced the meat into multiple pieces, the size of each as big as a chicken thigh and dropped it into a skillet of hot grease, or lard, there resulting a sharp staccato of crackling, an intense popping or fizz, as happens when a sprinkle of water falls into a substantially heated vessel of liquid, and John Eric, in an effort to avoid the dangerous splatter jumped back. Uncle Sanford fidgeted and fumbled with starting the coffee to brew, not in a modern streamlined percolator with a transparent dome but in a gallon container of heavy cast iron into which without measuring, merely guessing the right amount, he poured a ground up quantity of coffee beans. Strong and boiling hot it would taste good. It always tasted good. John Eric had timed setting the biscuits on the fire with the intent that they will have fully baked by the time the rabbit meat was fried and ready to eat.

"Okay Sanford, you and Ramsey fill up them tin plates and pour your coffee. It's time we dove in."

We were ravenously hungry. Me, more than my uncles. My stomach had begun to growl an hour before. We found a place to sit close to the fire and for the longest unforgivably stuffed ourselves with John Eric's cookings, which, I thought to myself, tasted as good if not better than any I'd ever tasted and I said as much to him. And feeling it wise not to leave him out I complimented Uncle Sanford on his making the coffee. We sat and rested for the better portion of an hour after we'd finished eating, the rabbit meat and biscuits already gone. "All the same to me," I thought. I couldn't have ingested another bite but I managed more coffee.

"Well fellas," Uncle Sanford let out, glancing at the sun nearing the mid afternoon angle in the western sky. "Let's get back to what we came for. The dogs are rarin to go again. And today the trail is hot. Rabbits are as thick as hops. What do you say Ramsey."

"Sure. Let's go."

I wasn't ready if the truth were known. Warm for the first time since early morning I would have voted in a second to pack up and head home or for a while longer lie lazily around the warmth of the fire. Besides, the temperature had dropped a slight and the wind blew more actively than it had in the morning hours. Careful not to groan in his presence, I reluctantly lifted myself up and pulled on my hip boots and we began the second phase of the hunt. Rather than wade into the water again I spotted a stump on the water's edge and sat down with my gun across my lap, Uncle Sanford and John Eric sloshing further down stream, finally electing to stand post on the periphery of the swamp. It was but minutes that a rash of yelps from the beagles ascended into the air fresh and vigorous, and abruptly, an explosion rang thunderously from the shotgun of one or the other of my uncles. Soon I learned which. Uncle Sanford yelled out, "I got im," and affectionately pampered Lucy, the she beagle, for her efforts of retrieval. Despite his age and infirm posture he still shot as well as the younger hunters who hunted with him and still killed as much of the game as he ever killed. For the next two hours, the sun descending faster than we liked, guns went off with predicted regularity, though less than during the morning hunt, until at length Uncle Sanford called it quits. When merging into my vicinity he asked for the count of game that I had taken down, "two," I said, and then he said we'd killed sixteen since lunch, making forty all told. Moving about in the attitude of a rheumatoid sufferer he started to gather the guns and the iceless ice coolers while John Eric and I loaded the rest, the sleeping bags, the axes and the rabbits we'd skinned and dressed already, and hitched the mules to the wagon and commenced our trip home. On the way back we were relatively quiet, too tired to do much talking. I rode as before on the bedding of the wagon with the beagles, whereas John Eric held the reins to the mules, while leaning akilter Uncle Sanford planted his right hand against the siding to keep from toppling over. He looked down at me and admitted what I saw in his tired and drooping face. "A full day Ramsey. I'm damn near worn out. I'm getting old."

Inside I marveled at the ruggedness and determination of my two uncles, men of the soil, their spirit firmly augured in nature, perfectly cut to have joined the early pioneers of our country in quest of charting a path for future generations. It was warmly comforting to know their brand still lived among us. They were who they were and that was that with them, not of the faintest inclination to desire more from the present or future, satisfied with the abilities and limitations the Lord had allotted them. Never could they have sat as chairman of a giant corporation, nor been a lettered minister of a big city church, nor a doctor of medicine and surgery, nor a Leland or an Andrea, budding geniuses—none of these—but they were significant in their own right, and as I dwelt more upon who they actually were I began to wonder to what degree this nation might have stopped short of its present acclaim without men of such sturdy stock. While John Eric seldom let it surface to conversation and Uncle Sanford not at all, this I knew: they were proud in the extreme of the academic pursuits of their nephew and had more than a vague notion of what it meant. My little group back at the fraternity house sometimes touched upon the lot to which man was consigned in his life on earth and what was the purpose of his being here at all. Now, I began to address this complexity alone, using my uncles as the major sources of analogy. "Why," I asked, "is it that there is such an imbalance between men, an imbalance that starts at birth? Are my uncles whom I hold dearly in my heart victims of a bad card that fate decided to deal them? Ah, but wait. Who has been dealt a bad card, you are they? Who is to say what a good or bad card is? Didn't you see how ravishingly they enjoyed themselves today? Drunk with elation and joy. It depends, doesn't it, on how you choose to look at things. To you, the pain that you endured out there, or kind of that, seemed not to have affected them an iota's worth and as a matter of fact, the wind, the cold, the near freezing swamp waters, probably gave rise to the peak of their elation. Neither Uncle Sanford nor John Eric would consider for a single minute trading places with you. Have you thought about that? It's true. You are of the same lineage as your uncles and you have always loved doing the things they do, but why did you turn out so quite markedly to the opposite? Is that not the strangest? Why is that? Well, I guess it just is. Sorry. If you are determined to know, why don't you ask the Good Lord? He's the one up there who shuffles and deals out the cards."

When we reached Uncle Sanford's home he crawled stiffly down from the wagon and waved off our offer to help with the mules and the miscellany of transports he'd need to put away. He said goodnight and then, as if to correct a near error, thoughtfully ambled over and slapped my arm, "Good to have you out with us young buddy."

After we loaded the things that belonged to John Eric in his truck he drove us to his home where he let me out and then I crawled into my car and drove to my mother's. Dark had fallen sometime earlier. She met me at the doorway.

"Good time?"

"Very good time." She smiled, showing in her countenance that she knew I had inflated the glow of my answer for her sake. "But I'm frozen stiff."

"I'll fix you some hot chocolate. That'll warm you up."

Chapter 42

I FOUND TIME the following day to look in on the Stoddards, a must in my repertoire of must do's. Elated, they swarmed me with affections and rained upon me a deluge of questions attendant to my studies and whatever else that stirred them to expression, not neglectful to mention that once a week they heard from Nenia. Maggie showed me the latest letter she'd received, underscoring the line with her finger where Nenia brought up my name.

"She's learning to ski Ramsey. Can you imagine that?"

I could but wasn't sure I wanted to. Something swelled within that I disliked Nenia learning to ski while leaning against a handsome Italian or Swedish instructor, who guided her through the training procedures time and again, introducing her to the calisthenics with no visible signs of haste, and all the while keeping his arm around her waist to which she in no way objected. No, I actually didn't believe that, yet realized in the clearest of my intellect that there were dozens of young men drawing a bead on her and would give their all to receive the attention of such a gorgeous creature. Turning away I looked out the window to avert letting them see my face and closed my eyes. And there she was, Nenia, silhouetted against the glinting snow, her hair blowing wildly against her reddened cheeks, racing faultlessly down the ski trail. I recalled her last letter, a most recent letter, which said that she'd see me next summer. Suddenly I couldn't wait. I wished in my heart that I could magically snap my finger and bingo, all at once there she stood among us now. The Stoddards in their farthest extremes couldn't have fitted in their heads the twirlings of my mind. Mr. Stoddard lamented that he'd begun to slow down in the last few years, that he'd turned over the management of his farming enterprise to Charlie, this relinquishment however not encompassing a large section of land that he'd leased to a member of the Peyton family, one of the prominent cogs of the gatekeeper circle. Not on this visit but on one soon thereafter I called again on the Stoddards and while there decided to walk over to my old home place, discovering that where the house once stood there now stood in its place the past summer's growth of skeleton corn stalks reaching higher than a tall man's head, but not nearly as high as the corn stalks grown in the soil next to the river. I looked around with wishful anticipation that I might stumble across a relic, anything, a mere meager parcel from the past, but nothing remained, the old well, the one containing that impossible to drink sulfur water, now filled and plowed over, the old weather beaten barn meeting the same fate. On the site where it stood I hoped in vain to see a decaying board or rusting plow piece or trace chain that still survived, nothing, there was nothing, only the silent inanimate cornstalks which after the spring rains would succumb to the fierce savage cutting blades, only one swift revolution, maybe two, necessary to convert them into fertilizer. From there I followed the crude bulldozed dirt road toward the lowlands of the river, where Leland and I and Ozzie and Cavanaugh once set up the makeshift sawmill. That land as well Mr. Peyton used for growing corn, the land increasingly fertile the closer the approach to the river, never before feeling the bite of the plough blade, not in a thousand years past, I wildly threw in, in any event a very long while until Mr. Peyton came along with big money and ponderous mechanicals—drag lines, tractors, bulldozers, back hoes, graders, combines. It made me sick. What, I asked, if I'd had this armada of appliances at my disposal when as a lad, the answer quickening to me that my singular choice back then was to muscle up the turning plough, or some comparable crude implement, and monotonously stare at the asses of the mules that pulled it from one end of the field to the other until sundown. In that day and time I could only dream of a brightening future, not in the least fathoming that in due time I would rub shoulders with the elitest of students in the classrooms of a great university. It entered my conscious that Mr. Peyton's birth fell into a much different millieu than my own, with family wealth and grooming to steer him. The imbalance of disadvantage hadn't previously jumped out at me as jarringly as it did now although it it had festered deep in my musings all along. "It's to whom you are born that makes all the difference. Yeah, it's that bastard's family wealth that now enables him to lease the most fecund piece of land in a three mile perimeter and convert what it produces into even greater opulence." But there was more. A sizeable plot of this land, Mr. Carney revealed to me, was offered for lease by the federal government at an alarmingly small sum to anyone with money and knowledge of the existence of a lush opportunity. With inside connections to the governor's office Monett saw an impending chance to seize the moment and secretly passed the idea on to the Peyton clan before his death, the latter acting with winged driven haste upon the messaging and paid Monett a handsome gratuity. The rich and powerful have a way of learning of lucrative nest eggs which are passionately shielded from the lower order.

But then there was, moreover, a characteristic of the land that appealed to my interest far more cogently than the aspect of financial opulence. It was its botanical nature and from there I at once fell into fanciful inquiry. Why did this land become as fertile as it is? What were the ingredients that gave rise to its stupendous growth of teeming plant life? The cornstalks there ranged three hands higher than their brethren on the upland grade. Not until I returned to the campus and consulted an agronomist did I acquire the expert explanation. Rivers carry topsoil which flows from the higher elevations, and that topsoil, or silt, contains bacteria, richly wondrous for plant growth. Such top soil, he said, is deposited at times by flooding on the banks and further outward, and that this gave the answer to why the land had acquired its enormous productive qualities. I discovered myself wishing that Leland were there with me, that we'd have ourselves an intriguing parley pursuant to this very parcel of earth where we'd once cut down trees of immense height and with razor sharp rotary blades sliced them into wide beautiful boards. I sighed and started my walk back to the Stoddards. Maggie insisted as I left for my mother's home that she'd have dinner for me the next day or the day after that, whichever, and that I must take care not to disappoint her by showing up late.

Near the end of the holidays I carved out a second visit to my friend Mr. Carney and his lovely wife Tatiana in Meadville. I partly told and partly acted out my hunting experience with John Eric and Uncle Sanford, elaborating chiefly on the agony of the biting cold and the chance once again to experience a meal of fresh rabbit meat that my uncle John Eric cooked over an open fire. He beamed as he listened and chortled as he amusedly emphasized that I failed to make an impression on him as an out of doors gamesman. As I had stirred about in the few preceding days I heard on every turn that the small town had attracted a manufacturer with the intent of employing nearly one hundred workers, rare for a refuge of its limited size. The papers were already signed the people said. The Jewish owned garment factory in the close by town of Treadwell, roughly the same size as ours in population count, will have been active at this time for some few years and the good folks there acted as if they were monumentally proud of it. Our folks ached for a factory too. Any product would do; they cared less than an iota of what it was. Jobs were a powerful unrelenting force in their mind's eye. Billy Mcvector stood as the hero amidst the excitement. He, with the backing of the Monett's together with the aid of the rest of the moneyed set, at some point attained to the seat of mayor and led in the forefront with negotiations. "Watch Billy," they said. "Whatever he says goes."

"What will they manufacture, if they bring in a factory?" I asked Mr. Carney as we sat on his front porch, confident that he would know if anyone did.

"Frankly, the whole scheme of things is in the dark. Billy's keeping the facts close to his chest, what few he has, and as of now there's a whole lot of speculation going on. They're non Jewish owned they say. I hope they don't try to put in another shirt making factory. The Jewish folks have a lock and key on the clothes making industry and will zealously block it."

"But there's something else, isn't there?" I saw already that he grasped where I had begun to lead him.

"Ha. What's that?" He grinned jestingly.

"The Jews will own that enterprise too, whatever it is. I guess Mr. Carney that not only is the South still struggling to overcome the burdens once thrown upon them, you know what I mean, they're also now under the thumb of the Northern Jewish garment overlords.

He laughed uproariously. "That bad hunh?"

"Not entirely. Some of my best friends are Jews. I should watch my lampooning, and would if I were in their company, I mean that I wouldn't talk so explicitly. But what I say carries a mild if not potent dose of truth in it. And they'd admit it privately. To me, in any event."

And then I began to silently retrace what I'd said and reproached myself. "You have to exercise more care not to expose your thoughts. I don't mean to Mr. Carney because it doesn't matter with him. It does matter in another way. You have to live with your thoughts and worse still with those that you've spoken of. As with the proverbial dog it seems you're biting the very hand, or paw, that feeds you. Now, try that on for size, and please, don't ever do it again, even in the slightest, even though you don't nurture any harm by it." I promised myself to never repeat the error.

It was here that Tatiana opened the screen door and joined us, sitting down by her husband on the settee, close also to where I sat in the porch swing. The conversation from there on covered many and sundried topics which eventually led into the subject of religion—where thereupon I seized the opportunity to ask something of her which for an extended while had prompted my bent toward discovery. Mr. Carney had casually spoken to me once or twice in the past that she made a study of religions, certainly a great deal of her own faith.

"Tatiana," I began in a tone of importance, "Leland and I used to trade thoughts on our religions, mine Protestant and his of the Eastern Orthodox denomination. Would you mind taking up this subject with me for a bit? I have an extraordinarily good reason for your doing it."

"Why not," she cheerfully added, "if that is of some value to you. What did you particularily have in mind?" and then I went on.

"Once his folks, his parents, invited me into their home to attend a Christmas dinner which was preceded by a religious ceremony, if I may allude to it as such, both of which I gratefully accepted. What I recall most poignantly from that experience was that everything to me, well, well, fell strangely on my sensibilities. While it had an aspect of strangeness about it, I should say additionally that there was something magnificient about it too. I never understood, not even remotely, that which I saw and heard unfolding before me, the litanys, the icons, the mysterious utterings, the whole of it all going beyond my capacity to drink it in. I remember Leland whispering as he leaned over that everything was done in the ritual of the Slavic. That's what he said, the Slavic. What was Slavic I asked him, which he answered but slightly, just a miniscule abbreviation, that's all, perhaps feeling the time improper for offering much in detail and that we should more politely pay attention to the proceedings of worship. At various times afterwards he has taken up the subject with me hopefully to deepen my enlightenment but which failed to effectively sink in; and now I turn to you dear Tatiana to take me to school on the matter. You will try, won't you?"

She did not pause, not mulling it over in the least. "Ramsey, I am not a scholar on Church Slavic, as it is more commonly and rightly called. You'd fare better in my opinion if you sought help from a priest. But with the admission of my short comings which I have done, I'll attempt to provide you with what little I can. You know us all as a family, Leland's family, my husband and I, together with a sprinkling of others of foreign nationality that you have met over the years, all of which are Bulgarian, excepting my husband who is British. Bulgaria, which you might not know, was once a powerful empire, then later on an empire again, great because of its political and military might but great as well because of its religious foundation that reached far and wide into the hearts and minds of many a person. Bulgaria is old; its religion is old, and very rich of substance that only time can make possible and it is with these thoughts upon me that I am persuaded to begin."

"Before you do," I interrupted, "I'd like to make an apology or at least an admission that until I met up with Leland, I had barely heard of the Slavic religion and if I have seemed to slight it by alluding to the mysterious worship taking place before the Christmas dinner I haven't meant to. It was just how I saw it. How it affected me. I acted out of ignorance. I'm Protestant Methodist as you well know."

"You owe no apology. I perfectly understand." Then looking over at me with an overpowering courteous smile, she asked with her eyes should she go on and I nodded in the affirmative.

"It occurs to me that if Leland had gone into the matter with more effort he most certainly would have had in mind the Church Slavic, which is based on Bulgarian linguistics, the language which seems to have penetrated your thoughts with a touch of strangeness if not more than that on the day of the Christmas dinner. It might be of some service to you to know that it remains the liturgical and scriptural language of the Orthodox Church in the Slavic countries."

"Slavic countries?"

"Yes. You know who they are: Bulgaria, starting first, then Russia, then Belarus, then Serbia, then Montenegro and Herzegovina and a host of others, though not a great many others. You can look them up. I know you will."

"Rest assured."

"Let me see," she said softly, touchimg her fingers to her temples," I may have overlooked something. Hold on. Oh yes. I shouldn't overlook this. Changes have evolved over time, with the Old Church Slavic giving way to the New Church Slavic.The New Church Slavic is the one I used to belong to, before I met my husband, which resorts to a conservative sacred language in the countries that I have identified for you, plus the others that I did not."

"Why the change? Why the old to the new?"

"I'll have to vaguely speculate about this, which is to say that I'm not absolutely sure I'm correct. I, I, think it happened because the people of times quite olden, centuries ago, were poorly educated and excessively illiterate. In that period, during the ninth century, two Byzantine Greek missionaries, Saints Cyril and Methodus, came and transformed the old language to correlate more in accord with the teachings of the Bible."

And then she stopped, looking over at me sweetly but quizzically, "Tell me Ramsey. What are you expecting to do with these things of which I've spoken?"

"I'll start enrolling in courses of religion pretty soon and hopefully my listening to you will help jump start me to a better and benefical understanding of what the wise professors are hopeful of teaching us pupils."

"Ha. That is clever. Getting the jump on things, the ideal way to express what you are thinking."

"Thank you. But the important development here is that you have given me a priceless lesson, thus far. Am I being too pushy to ask if there is anything else you can tell me?"

"About the Church Slavic? Yes and no. Of course, I should say yes, for there is a short tale that I might add which focuses on my grandmother whom I think will furnish a little fascination to a person of your inborn inquisitiveness. Do I have your permission? I'm afraid that by now I have over done myself."

"Heaven forbid me to even intimate that you have, for I do not feel that way in the least. How could I suggest otherwise? Please continue."

"Thank you. But mind you, to this point I have simply supplied information, facts and the narrative tie-ins.

. Now I will tell you the tale. It is preciously dear to me because it derives from an experience of my grandmother's when she was very young. She told me of it over and over until she died. It fits truly well into what I have revealed to you thus far."

"All right," I concurred softly and delicately to a very sweet person which meant please go ahead.

"As I have said, she was young then, in the realm of eleven or twelve I tend to remember her saying, when her parents sent her to a spa, a sort of religious retreat. But she referred to it as a spa. She didn't say with certainty why they sent her but supposed it was associated with further deepening her faith. It was the introduction of her mind to a new and different world, a world of the Old Church Slavic, although she didn't call it that. Yet it meant that. It was a lofty beautiful world she said, in which it was revealed to her that besides the instinctive life she had led until then there was a spiritual life, and that this life was revealed by a religion that had nothing in common with the one she had known since childhood, which found expression in the liturgy and vigils and which brought her in acquaintance with learning Slavic text by heart with the help of a priest. It was a lofty, mysterious religion she spoke of, bound up with a series of beautiful thoughts and feelings which one could not only believe but love?"

"Brain washed," I couldn't help but inject.

"No, no. Not that at all. A true magnificient religion that those of the modern era find too far transcending their reach to grasp."

At this, she stopped, because she said that was the end of the story, the end of her grandmother's tale. She hoped that I had benefited from what she had passed on to me.

"Good luck to you Ramsey in your future religious studies at the university, luck that you'll hardly need. You're a smart one. You'll do wonderfully well."

"Correction Tatiana. You are the smart one, not I."

I would take up religious studies later on when I advanced into the upper level at the university, expecting that at some stage one or the other of my theology teachers would lead us deeply into the realm of the Church Slavic.They hardly touched upon the subject. In any event I continued to read on my own and talk to Leland and learned a great deal about it, but absorbed only a scratch of the whole. Tatiana was right. I badly needed the aid of a priest.

Chapter 43

I WAS NOT in the vicinity when it happened that a manufacturer set up shop in my little hometown; they assembled bicycle parts, not a large operation, not as large as people initially hoped, employing fewer than fifty workers, but some is better than none and the townsfolk were ecstatic over an economic boost. While falling markedly short of the former war boom of the forties it called up in the memory of the older set, and those of an age not far behind them, shades of likeness to that incomparable and never forgotten era. My mother and Melissa as well had let me know of the progress of the construction stage as the plant piece by piece moved toward completion and sporadically sent me letters and news clippings depicting the human ecstasy emanating from it.

When John Eric let me out that night on our return from the hunt he said we'd have a rabbit cook in a few days and hoped I'd show up to enjoy it with everyone, everyone being some of my relatives, cousins in heavy supply, who lived in the outlying sector. They were farm people and factory workers by and large. John Eric and Uncle Sanford were the self designated chefs, using tremendously large deep well skillets for their purpose, filled with melted lard in which the meat cuts were dropped. I cringed at the thought of the intake of calories and the unhealthiness deriving from frying the meat entirely in grease but as with everyone else it terribly stimulated my palate, and I ate voraciously. Just as I did on that day of the hunt. There were more relatives that flocked to the event than I calculated might come and they seemed much gladdened to see me, not excessively inquiring of what they regarded as my new life and I appreciated the fact that they didn't. I preferred not to get cornered into laborious explanations and descriptions and repeated clarifications. I sensed that they went out of their way to behave politely and respectfully, in all probability watching what they said because my uncles purposefully cautioned them to make certain that they conducted themselves in like manner. My mother was there too and once before the reunion commenced expressed her hope that I treat my kin with the utmost of politeness. I felt I did. I'm not certain of how my relatives saw me, but in my view of them I found they were enjoyable and entertaining—and something of a study, specifically their language, which, I must attest, veered acutely from the language to which I had grown accustomed on campus. A first cousin edged over at an opportune time to join me who'd been casting glances my way from the start.

"You like up yonder?"

"Very well. Chicago is an exciting place. Have you been there?"

"Sho hadn't. I'd like too."

I tried to capture all movements and mannerisms; they were a study, as I have indicated. What I ensnared more prominently resulted from their drastic retardation of speech, and badly misused English in comparison to that of the erudite young folks with whom I now daily intermingled in a world set far apart from theirs. Such observations were unmissable, my old culture graphically returning, and likely I would never have shared them with anyone except some of my bosom friends back at the university in idle conversation, namely Darya and Aaron. It was not that I did not respect my kinsmen. I honestly and without the thinnest shade of vanity saw them in the light as described and knew then that aside from our earlier upbringing we would from there on have little in common.

Then came next to my last day, the hours running out, the last day before departing northward. That morning in the neighborhood of ten, past mid-morning in any event, Melissa drove into my mother's front yard in her shiny black Chrysler, lush and sleek, the same as the one that her mother and father drove in the era of her early teens. She opened the car door and slid out. The sight of her silken dress was enough to compel a gasp from the ordinary male, and I was ordinary, a low soft rustle emanating from it as she moved toward me. She beamed. I met her a stride or two away from the porch steps. She hugged me, first tenderly then tightly, kind of hanging to me momentarily and then stepping back, fixing a bead on my person from head to toe. Her eyes were absorbing, and happy. Her dress selection might have suggested in its elegance that she had set out enroute to a public function requiring the attire in which she was clad, but without the glitter of jewelry. Only a singular tiny spangle appeared on her lapel. This is how I saw her and she looked gorgeous. But she always did, the reason she became the foremost topic of discussion among gossipy idle old men, who strained their necks and stared fixedly when she dashed toward a store from where she parked her car. Seldom did she appear on the street and then only briefly. Something about her betold a resentment of old men who gawked at women, in particular at herself. In her eyes, such men were crude, and she treated them coldly, unless her association with them concerned the affairs of school, and had to do with their children, but even then, though cordial and professional she tended toward diastancy. She without much pause, a little timid perhaps, asked if I had time for a ride. A youthful presence abounded in her voice which I judged resulted from the excitement of meeting me. "Nervous a bit," I murmured silently. In fact I too felt nervous, but minimally. I answered, "yes, sure, why not," and in virtually the same vein of expression spoke that I'd intended to stop by and see her earlier but had gotten excessively caught up seeing relatives and hunting with my uncles and that this was why I slipped in meeting my obligation. I don't think she believed me. She forgave me just the same. "That's all right. You were planning to. No need to apologize." I excused myself for a jiffy to let my mother know that Melissa and I planned to ride around for a while, that she wished to show me something or discuss something in private. I didn't say what. I knew she would take it that our being together involved the business of school since we were both of the academic genre. She looked a shade suspicious, or so it seemed, but then as I sifted it through I concluded she wasn't. She liked Melissa, but not Melinda nor Madeline. Melissa occupied a distinct place in her heart, a name of importance, a person of decorum and dignity; and taking this into account I felt assured that she entertained no misgivings when I stuck my head inside the door and said for the second time that it was on my itinerary to get back in the vicinity of an hour, give or take a little, and then we left in Melissa's bright shiny car. We drove toward the farm. I knew where we were heading without her telling me. I recognized the landmarks. And she had thus far not given an indication of going elsewhere; so obviously she aimed for the farm. When we pulled up and stopped we crawled out and began to stroll around in an area approximate to the pond, and then around the pond, at last sitting down on the grassy embankment. The water appeared clear and nice and I remarked that it did, that and nothing more, mainly because I struggled to open a conversation common to both her and to me which might help put us at ease. It worked. She answered yes, that it was rather pretty and that it was in such fine condition due to the slack of rainfall recently which otherwise, she said, would have filled the pond with what she termed that ugly brown stuff.

When she sat on the grassy sod she crumpled a portion of her nice silk dress. "You'll soil your dress if you haven't already. Maybe there's something in the car for you to sit on?"

"I'm fine. The dress is okay. Don't bother." She knew I admired it, or in other words the way it fit upon her and that it accentuated the natural contours of her form. An assortment of leaves had attached to the waist line region and I asked that she stand and let me remove them. She obeyed. She even appeared to like obeying, standing perfectly still as I picked them off one by one. I thought of brushing them off but decided it would fare better with her if I picked them off. I remarked that it now dawned on me that a stylish beret would go well on her gorgeous head of hair, but that she in no way needed it. She smiled and blushed, pleased and surprised that I had begun to observe the details of her clothesware even to the extreme of suggesting an adornment for additional enhancement. Then the conversation suddenly shifted away from the dress and the beret and leveled on me. We were sitting once again and I had begun to break twigs and toss them into the water, to which she paid only mild attention. Other things claimed her thoughts.

"You're doing well?" It was a rhetorical question. She meant on my job and in my studies and much more.

"Good. I'm doing well, but I'm busy."

"I'm sure." She smiled into my face and playfully took away one of the twigs that I held between my fingers. I sensed that she wished to say something in particular; I tried to guess what and eagerly waited. She took only a moment at getting to the point. Already she sat close to me, close enough that I could feel her breathing. She snuggled even closer, her eyes alive and dancing, the eyes of a woman in love. Wonder spread over her face as she squeezed my arm. Her courage was bolder now.

"I've missed you. It's too long between visits. It's too bad we can't see more of each other." Her thoughts came out easily enough, but not smoothly. At sometime in the past I'd read of a French courtesan not yet twenty on her first evening out with a date, unhappy with herself as she returned to her chateau because she perceived she made an unsuitable showing at dinner and doubted that her companion would ever again seek her presence. It was true that she did not converse well. She blamed her performance on nervousness and her inability to settle into her natural self.

"Yeah. I wish. That's a very nice thought"

"To, to—.

"As you say. To see one another more often. And I'd like it too, the conversation and whatever, just as we're doing now. But things never quite work out the way you want them to or plan, do they? Still, we do see one another from time to time."

"Not enough. It's hard not seeing you as I wish. You understand, don't you?"

"Of course."

"At least we could write. Or telephone. I have written you every once in a while but you didn't answer."

"No. I guess not. Well, no. I didn't. No guessing to it. We could write. But that's not easy. We could, but, well; you know what I'm trying to say."

She laid her hand affectionately on mine and said she knew what I meant. Our cryptic language seemed to me to unspokenly center on her husband; apparent to me now that he no longer fit into her heart as her lover, that now she yearned for that duty or pleasure to fall upon me. But still, I wasn't sure. Why did she not tell me plainly what coursed through her? She didn't, not just then. She returned to the obstacles of our attempting to communicate by long distance.

"As you were saying, that's not easy. That is, I don't think you could easily write or telephone me but I can you if I have your address and telephone number."

"I see. Giving you my address is no trouble, no trouble at all, but our telephone at the fraternity house is for everyone to use. It's mounted out in the open hallway. No telling who would answer and no telling who would listen in."

"Your address will do."

I'd once given her my address but declined to bring it up. Sometime later she revealed that she'd burned it, afraid someone might make discovery and raise questions not convincingly explained. In all the while she continued to touch me, to touch my hand or squeeze my arm, pretending she wasn't conscious of such affectedness, and too, I observed a continued nervousness about her, not much but at least in barely noticeable traces from time to time. Once when she laid her hand softly on my arm she looked fawningly over and said that I looked well, very good in fact, better than she'd ever seen me, and then became even more descriptive "You have turned into a uniquely handsome man Ramsey. And may I tell you something else?" She sought reassurance, something of a preface to make easier the words that were about to issue from her lips.

"You know you can. But what do you mean?"

"Perhaps you don't realize it about yourself. It's a certain character or persona that I refer to."

"Oh. Go on."

"There is an elusive charm in your appearance and disposition which attracts a woman to you. Do you know that?"

"No. I don't know that."

"You surely do. You know you affect me in that way and other women too. I am sure. You feel quite at home among women, and like a magnet draw their sympathies."

"I, I—."

"Shhhhhhh. Let me finish. You know exactly what to say to them and how to behave. You can even go for minutes of silence in their company, as you often do with me, without their feeling the slightest discomfort."

Her revelation hit so suddenly, so unexpected, so praising, so adoring, so submissive, and yet so honestly given. So I sometimes was silent she said, yet felt no discomfort from it. I hadn't noticed but should have guessed or sensed as much. I struggled for the right thing to say in return, but the discovery of it failed me. But then.

"I'm caught breathless. You've emptied your heart to me."

"More than that. But I am yet the same. I have affections for you. And have for the longest while. Is that something of which you are completely unaware?"

Again I tried for words, for the right ones, which wouldn't come; it was then that I reached with both my open hands and closed them caressingly round her face, the narrowest of space separating hers from mine. She kissed my lips, not a lush or hungry kiss, but one of tender sweetness, as if it were the first, then drew slowly back; wondering, revolving, thinking, weighing, "Do you think ill of me; that I am a vile woman?"

"Why would I think ill of you; why would I consider you a vile woman? How can I with good conscience do either?"

"Then what do you think?"

"I think these things happen. Amour is as old as man and woman themselves; an irresistible tendency of the heart and we have succumbed to it. We saw it coming, not swiftly but slowly, by steady but sure progressions and there was nothing at our command for capably turning it back. There was nothing that we wanted to do or would do to stop it. What a wonderful kiss and knowing my heart, and by now yours, it will visit us again."

"Like now." With this said, and without uttering another word, she sighed and kissed me once more and I returned it.

"I've wanted this for the longest," she said with softness of voice, almost a whisper, her cheeks flushed. She now felt at ease.

"How long?"

"For a long while, even before that night in the field under the tractor. Does that surprise you?"

"I'm not surprised. I nurtured the same desire toward you if I speak honestly but hadn't the courage to carry it through. At one time I never thought it remotely possible."

"The same here."

I told her that I felt gladdened and relieved that we had broken the barriers and that at last there lived within me the freedom and courage to say things to her without shyness. She replied that she too was glad and would have taken amour further and quicker feeling that it fell upon her to press for it, not me, but that privacy refused to present itself easily, and that everywhere eyes lurked to see and lips of many were coiled ready to tell. She sighed and confessed that relief had settled in her heart now that our inhibitions were overcome, and that she had wondered often if that would ever come to pass. She admitted to a tinge of guilt, explaining that she no longer related intimately with her husband and hadn't for years. "I feel guilty also with respect to my children, that as their mother I have sinned against them. But I'll have to live with that." I too bore a thread of guilt, taking it that by any dissimulation of reasoning I should feel at fault in her disengagement with her husband. No matter how hard I tried to sluff it off it seemed unavoidable that by some measure I saw myself as the culprit of blame. A goodly portion of it anyway.

A period of silence fell upon us, and then she leaked out an admission of remorse which did not previously attract my notice. It caught me unsuspecting. "I have heard of people, two like us, whose lives are full of relative truths and relative falsehoods, a side of them open and visible, and another guardedly kept from view, riddled with lies in order to cover up. I don't want it like that with us. My, my." Then after letting out a little sigh she went on. "Sometimes I wish we could bring this to an end, but I cant't stand the thought of that. How could I ever learn not to love you?" For a second she dropped her face downward, her lush long hair falling around her lovely neck. A barely perceptible mist had risen to her pretty eyes, or so it seemed, but I didn't really know. Her face was now angled away from my vision. And then it lifted, "I feel as if I've sinned or am about to and that others will judge me or would like to."

"You haven't sinned, nor have I. We merely kissed. And as to others who will judge, or would like to, let me say this: they would give their all to trade places with us if only the opportunity availed itself, not for a moment hesitating if they had someone to sin with."

By degrees her gaiety returned. She lifted her face and we kissed again. She smiled as if her remorse had passed, or else now skillfully concealed. I concluded that the emotion of her feeling guilty would in time pass away and told myself that I shouldn't continue to think further of her thoughts of her husband and children and turned to what we both knew as an absolute.

"Our lives together," I said, "if they are to exist at all in this way, we must keep them inviolably secretive."

"I know. We must."

"What an uncanny twist, is it not?"

"What?"

"When I see you out publicly, at church or in a store, in the bank, anywhere, I'll glance at you and you at me, both of us perceiving the thoughts spinning round in one another's heads. And people cannot guess even if given a hundred years what they are. They'll never know."

"Never."

When she let me off at my mother's home I relayed to her my regrets for her father's passing, and that the inconvenience that blocked my attending muchly distressed me. I knew that I had taken this up with her earlier but chose to address it a second time. On parting she leaned over with her head almost out the window, pleading with me to somehow let her hear from me from time to time, knowing with unvarying certainty that I wouldn't take the chance. I presumed that due to the excitement of her departure she momentarily overlooked the danger of my sending a written correspondence. Or did she have in mind telephoning, the choice of which would have posed nearly as much risk as sending a letter.

I lay in my bed that night over and over sauntering through my mind of Melissa, such a sensual beautiful woman, a fine woman, older than me by something like ten years, striving to make sense of why she was immovably fascinated if not obsessed with a younger man, venturing that only her heart held the answer and that a woman's heart was as complicated as the universe. I knew that it would end sometime, and sensibly opined that better for it to end presently rather than later, for one thing when that happened the impact would fall upon her crushingly but would hit her less hard if our affair were now discontinued. Still, it would not end presently, for there were reasons in my own heart that I enumerated one by one which desired its continuance. She competed with the best in terms of looks and culture, a gorgeous creature and so well educated, so proud and haughty, that any man would have loved to conquer her, and I could, I had, or the same as, and truthfully in my soul I basked in the triumph, for she was the daughter of Rupert Monett and Madeline, who since boyhood I despised, because of our poorness and their richness, and to seduce their daughter, to which our present course pointed I will have as the son of a dirt farmer evened the score. Then there was an addition to all this, a natural affinity, an invisible force, that drew us to one another, admittedly fraught with wrong, and futile by every conceivable dimension, but still, as I inferred to her, there dwelled an irresistible tendency of amour in our beings.

Just before turning over I uttered a little prayer to the Lord to set things right, our errors, mine and Melissa's, and afterwards, after reflecting for a while, I advised myself to let our affair quickly pass and vowed to make certain that it did, to let it vanish into the wind. I hoped I meant it. To this my subliminal conscious called out that I lied, that I wasn't anywhere close to pushing Melissa aside, not entirely, not now. Suddenly the words written by a young poet that once my eyes swept across emerged in my recall, "I'm reminded of a flower thirsting for a drop of rain. Give it one drop and it never stops, asking for more again and again and again."

There is forever another side of the coin, as happened in this moment of mental juggling, another voice suddenly of a counseling tone, which involved more persons than just Melissa. "Why not let it die? Why not stay away from Melissa for good, never seeing her again, thereby letting this entanglement become a mere blur of the past, and thereby saving her and possibly yourself from ruin? Think of Nenia, your beautiful beloved Nenia, born of goodness, is good through and through, who lives irretrievably in your heart and you in hers. Do not spoil a love affair which is so serene that it seems born in Heaven. You think of Darya, I know you do, a wonderful girl who loves you, who adores you, who can make someone a wonderful wife and mate if that someone is right for her, which you doubt her heart will ever accept. Whether that proves true or not she is not for you; still better said, you are not for her. You are for Nenia, and no other. In the end you shall see."

Dealing with Melissa did not loom as an insurmountable obstacle as I saw it. I could simply decline to see her when I went home and not answer her correspondence nor return her telephone calls if I made up my mind to. In the instance of Darya I saw struggle, with her absorbing great hurt, and wished desperately that a miracle might zoom from out of nowhere to keep it from happening. These were the last of my complicated ponderings before lapsing into misty slumber.

Chapter 44

THERE EMERGED a feeling of surging warmth, a feeling of hominess, when I walked through the doors of the fraternity house, just as it was when I entered my mother's house at the beginning of the Christmas holiday period. "Two homes. I have two homes," I uttered to myself, "here and at my mother's." The first to return from the holidays I reached in my pocket for the key to the entrance, now serving as back up to Bertinelli, earning over time the university's trust to serve as second in administrative command. They paid me for simply carrying a key, I surmised, and for no other consideration, for I seldom did anything to deserve it. Bertinelli hardly ever called on me to do anything. Whenever I almost forcibly volunteered that I stood ready to perform any chore large or small, major or menial, that he asked of me I met with the casual reply and shrug that knowing my services were available if needed suited him just fine. A subtle feeling entered my conscious that I proved more valuable to him than for any other reason by acting as the gendarme who kept peace and tranquility among the ranks without trying.

My arriving early, by two days, sprang from my awareness that in the approaching months Mr. Yazstremski planned to assign me to researching case law and that I needed to dash ahead of this subject before meeting him to start a discussion of its substance. "What is case law?" I abruptly and curiously asked when he mentioned the topic soon after I joined the firm. With an air of seriousness, he turned his chair around to more directly face me and motioned that I should move my chair closer. And then began to drag his aging bony fingers across his chin. After the elapse of a few seconds he commenced his answer, at first talking to himself and then to me.

"Look. Well, let me see. How shall I provide an explanation? I'll start like this Ramsey. As opposed to statutes—that is, legislative acts that proscribe certain conduct by demanding or prohibiting something or that declare the legality of particular acts—case law is a dynamic and constantly developing body of law. Each case, mind you, contains a portion of knowledge wherein the facts of the controversy are set forth as well as the holding and dicta, in other words an explanation of how the judge reached a specific conclusion. In addition, a case might shed light on concurring and dissenting opinions of other judges." Seeing my brows wrinkling and I knew it, I sensed that he intended to stop, but he kept on. I hadn't intervened, I hadn't asked for a repeat. If I missed something I judged I'd straighten myself out by browsing the prolifically stocked library of the firm and there reading the material to which he'd alluded until I understood it with such thoroughness that I could recite the lines verbatim. He knew that was precisely what I would do.

"Now, and this is well worth your remembrance Ramsey, since the U. S. legal system is based on the principles of common law, higher court decisions are binding on lower courts with similar facts that raise similar issues. The concept of precedent here surges into play, or, let me say, Stare-Decisis, which means to follow or adhere to previously decided cases in judging the case at bar. It means that appellate case law is binding upon lower courts. I'll step ahead to explain by way of abbreviated summary that case law in reported decisions of courts and other courts which make new interpretations can be cited as precedents." There followed an interlude of briefness wherein he appeared as if toying with something vital that he'd left unsaid, while I tried to envision where in the firm's library I would start to research the significant subjects he'd just gone over.

"I realize this must seem frustratingly foggy, as it did to me when I'd not long set foot in my first law school classroom. Here, I'm handing you this paper with paragraphs printed out that cover the elements of law that I've just talked through with you, and much more. Read what you see until you feel you'll choke, then keep reading. Ultimately it will become as common to you as breathing in and breathing out."

When my comrades returned, straggling through the door one by one with suit cases in hand and clothes wardrobes hanging from their shoulders, I had finished a large portion of my research and met them with heart warming greetings and glad expressions for their safe journey back. Looking as gorgeous as ever Darya at once reached for my arm and buoyantly let me know that we were to go out for dinner that very evening. The hour at that juncture neared three o'clock. "They expect us at seven. I called in reservations from Baltimore." She had picked a place, a plush restaurant in the heart of downtown only open to reservationists and this at the evening hour, astonishingly glitzy with greenish tentacles and radiant flowers set in tall fat bellied urns stationed around the interior walls and when I glanced at the menu I understood why management had not the least of trouble endowing these most enticing furnishings. The prices were enough to render me breathless, and furrows would have dented my brow but for the fact that I knew she forever footed the expense. Adding to the cost, obviously, was the ensemble of Italian violinists dressed in tuxedos who approached our table once we finished dining and played for the most part a medley of instrumentals from selected compositions of the old schools of Europe. Darya arranged for their services and took great delight in watching my face, realizing that I knew who had instigated their presence. Among the tunes they played was the haunting and saddened *La Paloma*, my choice for years, and hers. I say saddened because what else might I say. It evinced in my thoughts as the lilting strains floated to me that someone had lost a lover and yearned for that lover's return. She asked them in advance to play the piece, mentioning too that she played it on her violin when at home, a bit of a shock in that in the intervals of our past acquaintance not once did she let out that she played a musical instrument, the violin, and I said to her that it gladdened me to know she'd selected the violin as first choice because I loved it more than any of all other musical instruments. Her parents hired a specialist to teach her to play beginning when she attained to six years of age.

I would find the upcoming semester "puffingly busy" as John Eric sometimes said, one of his favorite abuses of English, with my studies and law employment given precedence, let alone my social life, though limited. I tried to keep it open for Darya. I hadn't checked for my mail since my return from Christmas, and now looked in my postal bin, there spotting among the conventional assortments a letter from Leland, which hit me with such excitable force that I almost shouted.

> *Dear Ramsey, I should have prepared and mailed this sooner, before the advent of the Christmas holidays. It's always at this time of year that I think especially of you and Mr. Carney and Tatiana, and let me not leave out Ozzie and Cavanaugh. You, I am certain, dropped by when you were there.*
>
> *I write in addition to the above to inquire of your schedule this summer. I hope to visit you. If there are complications, please let me know. If not, I plan to visit you for a week's stay in mid July. It has been too long. We will have hours and hours of catching up to do.*
>
> *Your friend forever. Leland.*

"He's coming, he's coming," I let out, bowled over with the news, suddenly reliving our adventures together as we were growing up. "I wonder if he's changed, not in physique but in mood and attitude and in his general outlook on life. No, he hasn't. He's the same. Just as I'm the same. He inquired if I'd seen Mr. Carney and the lovely Tatiana and Ozzie and Cavanaugh. I can speak positively on the former but not on the latter. I let time get away. But I left Ozzie and Cavanaugh a Christmas gift each with mother. She would ask John Eric to hand their gifts to them. No doubt that she did. I'll write Leland in a jiffy to come on, that I'll have a fun packed agenda ready, that we'll tour the stockyards, and the fascinating Chicago Museum and frequent Lake Michigan for as many boating sprees as we care to indulge. We'll take Andrea with us. He'll like her and she'll make delightful company when we're out for nightly dinner meals and picture shows. By then Darya and Bertinelli and Aaron will have graduated and left the campus. I'll introduce him to my dear friend Doctor Linskie and lead him through some of the old historic buildings. And add no telling what else to the agenda as it unforeseeably surfaces."

We had traversed well into the spring semester when at the breakfast hour one morning our small group seized upon the name of Robert Hutchins, opening up his achievements for analysis at the university during his reign, not as a whole in agreement with his philosophies. We skipped classes and stayed on as the bantering heated up and began to expand. I should restress that our small group largely consisted of young folks from prominent families, rich families, extraordinarily intelligent, and superbly prepped before enrolling at the university. They were by and large conditioned with an attitude of swallowing nothing that you hear and challenging everything that you hear.

"I'm glad he's out of it, glad he's not here when I am," said Aaron, the first to ignite the issue. "As I picture the man, as I read and hear about him, the more he comes off as a snob of the cloth who climbed into the high chair of the presidency of Chicago U. with the support and promotion of the school of theology over there at Yale. His view of the required teachings here was all paramount in his head, not only here but at all colleges for that matter and he tried here to force his ivory tower ideas on the whole curriculum and pretty well succeeded. And it was a colossal mess."

"What was that exactly?" chipped in Andrea, whom we had invited some time previously for involvement in the debates, sometimes heated debates. She seemed to favor Aaron's view, and likely encompassed a more in-depth knowledge of Hutchins's background than any of us. In her question she in my opinion attempted to spawn a further rise from Aaron, which he purposely side stepped just then, moving on to further ridicule the man.

"He lambasted educators for what they taught at the other universities; with the accusation that they were no more than a trade school and a poor trade school at that."

"Wait a minute Aaron," Bertinelli intruded. "That is correct. But only partially. You have to acknowledge that he strongly advocated a curriculum of study grounded in the Great Books and the Great Books are a lot of what we still read, even now."

"That's so. Although I'll have to say this. It wasn't necessary for him to overturn the entire system just to induce us to read the Great Books. I read Sophocles before I ever heard of the Great Books."

I decided to nudge in with my views, which were eclectic more or less, a middle of the road stance.

"He did some good things, some not so good."

"Namely?" This was from Bertinelli.

"Well, he declared that an educational system should have a well-defined purpose for promoting the intellectual development of the students, who later would become the nation's citizens and leaders."

Aaron wasn't finished and entered again with a salvo of rather stinging oratory. "I think you're right on that point if you concede that there's a whole array of revelations that necessarily follow. To me he was a high-born preacher, and the son of a preacher who paraded in here with a snobbish idea of preacher influenced pedagogy and intended to install it into practice. He hadn't any more than sat down when he unraveled his designs of tearing the existing structure apart, starting with dismantling the football program and the elimination of fraternities and religious affiliates for the same reason."

I felt that we needed a greater support for parity in the debate, which up until this stage had unleashed an attack without rebuttal and spoke once again.

"Well, hold on Aaron. You may cast the man in too harsh a light."

"I don't think so."

"But you do. Perhaps. Football programs are atrociously costly; draining badly needed financial sap from the academic programs of the university."

"I can't argue against that. But am persuaded that it wasn't because of financial tightness that he wiped out football. He had this penchant in his head that you ought to entertain yourself reading Socrates on a Saturday afternoon rather than watching a bunch of guys run up and down the football field. I like football and I like to read of Socrates and his mighty wisdom, yet let me add for the sake of clarity that I've never read one line that he wrote because there is no account of his publishing anything that he thought and spoke of. He left that up to Plato."

Bertinelli then appeared to side with Aaron, stressing that the substance of Hutchins's sweeping plan must have proven unworthy of lasting validity in that the Board of Trustees abandoned it when he resigned from his university connection. The discussion had built up enough steam by this stage to drive forward for the entire course of the morning and beyond, with the bulk of the participants adopting a view against Hutchins's triumphs and dwelling predominantly on his failures; failures as far as they were concerned.

Not willing to let the forum end without her pet topic appearing on the table for scrutiny Darya alluded to the meaning of justice as lavishly propounded in Hutchins's speeches and writings. In a sense she sort of gave a speech herself, very thoroughly organized and thought through. No interruptions occurred from the beginning to the end.

"Whatever his definition of the term it's quite nebulous, given the glossy language. I find it troublesome to pin him down. What does he mean by justice, really, that he so fondly addressed? I find in one place of reading where he says schools should teach students what is right and just and somewhere else says justice is for the deprived, for the underdog, such as the Negro, and on that he's right. But who is he to proclaim that he alone has a handle on justice, what it is and what it is not, as if he's the lone voice of reason in a world of mediocrity which he is quoted as saying. Granted, he has a right to proclaim these things but must he strut so proudly when he does? He's like a host of ivory tower professors, some of whom I know, who with no practical experience in life assume with lofty oratory and slick penmanship that they have all the answers and want the world to believe they do. We all have a good idea attendant to justice, even the raggedly clad Negro in the cotton fields of Mississippi, better than any of us I wager, even if not equipped with the suaveness of language that Hutchins learned and practiced in the pastorally honed schools of his upbringing. There's a speck more and then I'm through. Somewhere he wrote that students should learn to criticize ideas in order that they might weigh and balance themselves in their own minds, boiling down arguments and synthesizing a view of their own and that in and of themselves they could learn what justice and beauty and good really are. Well, I guess so."

With this, the debate ended; the time past the twelve o'clock hour. Everyone that wished spoke freely as always. If they sounded excessively hard and vindictive, for whatever the reason, they were not alone in their criticisms, for much older critics, many alumni, prominent and rich, were plentiful to assert that the Great Books did not have one answer to what justice is or isn't, and that in fact there were many contradictory answers to this question. Sometimes when I take backward flight, I try to envision how Mr. Hutchins might have felt if from a gallery he had watched and heard our little group putting him through the wringer that morning. In my own view, I am disposed to contend as a man of academics through most of my professional tenure, that they had seated Hutchins at too young an age, thirty years old, to the presidency of one of the most esteemed universities in our land and too idealistic for the position. In the late nineteen thirties he attempted to reform the curriculum of the university along Aristotelian -Thomist lines, with the result that the faculty rejected his proposal reforms three times. It weighs upon me that he might have yearned in fantasy to emulate the ancient Greeks, an admired pure orator with ideas and thoughts of perpetual lastingness. It seems he might have been more a dreamer than an administrator. The college's financial clout, considerable prior to his tenure, underwent a serious downgrading with a decreased collegiate enrollment and a drying up of donations from the school's principal Chicago benefactors. As such, his critics viewed him as a dangerous idealist who pushed the school out of the national limelight and temporarily thwarted its possible expansion.

Chapter 45

THE SNOW fell consistently from January to the last of March, then began to taper off, leaving the impression that the last heavy spurt had gone. It was too late for another we said and set our thoughts on Easter Sunday, the university each year inviting an ecumenical minister from either the Catholic or Protestant denominations to deliver the Christian message. Students packed the auditorium, often their parents with them. We started to gather that Sunday morning an hour before service, noticing unassumingly as we proceeded toward the cathedral that tiny snowflakes had begun to swirl, not easily reaching ground, owing to the growing wind blowing from the southwest that intercepted and whipped them to pieces. This happened before they turned into a much larger and heavier size. The morning infused us with happiness, and we were energized by the briskness of the wind, with no one remotely sensing the ferocity of the weather pattern outside as we sat in our pews and sang the songs from the time worn hymnals and listened to the minister. It was warm and cozy sitting between Darya and Andrea and I smiled underneath at the peculiar situation in which I found myself. I loved their nice lilting voices. The snow had started to fall in heavy unrelenting sweeps, the beginning of a storm destined to last for two days and two nights. When we left the cathedral following the benediction, the wind struck us with cold penetrating bites, the campus grounds blanketed in a sea of white, the branches and boughs of the trees likewise. The western furs were most singularly apparent with their immense elevations and massive circumferences. Finally, we made it back to the fraternity house where, beating us there by minutes, Bertenilli had lit a fire in the fireplace and afterwards started to prepare hot soup and sandwiches for lunch. The snow stubbornly refused to let up for the whole afternoon, and pushed by the wind struck savagely against the windows and doors and exterior walls. Sizeable drifts accumulated. We stayed inside. By nightfall the wind calmed and the snow quit falling, now spread over the campus as far as you could see and with nighttime upon us the whole campus lay silent and somber and majestic and the meshing of these effects gave off an ambience that seemed Holy.

The snow covered everything, save the face and sides and the rear of the buildings, tall and grand, jutting upward as if escarpments in a domain of mountains. They too were silent. The snow wasn't like rain. The rain strikes hurriedly and leaves hurriedly, the snow more subtly, as if approaching on cat feet and stays longer. I loved the snow. I always loved it. When a boy I tramped for hours in it across our farm to the creek and back, and now suddenly as I gazed through the windows at the massive scene of white I retrieved my heavy fur coat and slipped it on and pulled down my woolen Cossack partially over my head and left through the side exit, no one with me, no one invited. I preferred to tough it alone. What I saw and thought and heard and did and said on this excursion did not fall upon me with any semblance of order, and it was in this manner by which such experiences were later set down in a booklet which I'd begun to keep in my room.

"All was silent, yet there were a thousand little things to see and hear, even in the silence. The trees, though monstrous and creature like nonetheless appeared as people. Little twinkling lights shone in the windows of the residences and somewhere close by the sound of laughter broke through, lovers out in the snow too. And in the distance, there sounded a low fading clatter of the trolley upon steel rails racing to the other side of town, unhindered by the storm. Like all else that lay flatly the campus walkways were smothered under. I had to judge tediously the exactness of my whereabouts, and where I sought to go using the buildings as landmarks. I knew all of them by name and their history. Even the donors. The wind blew less forcefully now. But it was its own boss and sometimes decided to return in gusts and then let up and for a while stole completely away. I drew my coat tighter and pulled my Cossack cap down virtually over my face. A sudden rustle nearby streamed to my ears, more laughter, more lovers lost in the magic of the evening. I remembered my past, that period when I had attained to four or five. The snow fell one Easter, the only other time in my life, which my family made much over. I begged my father to take me out in it. He said he couldn't, that if he did I might take sick from the earache. I heard music from across the way. Looking around, listening, I stopped and cupped my ears with my hands. It flowed from the Cubs Nest. Young folks were singing, not loud though, and weren't rowdy either. A sleigh appeared, a boy pulling it and a girl who rode, the girl shrieking with great delight as the boy strained and sweated and grunted. Tomorrow, I imagined, sleighs and students will flood the campus in myriad numbers. I kept walking. I loved it, everything. A little dog dashed by, obviously loving the snow too. A girl chased after him, trying to run but found it more than her ability could handle to catch up, yet in moments he scampered back and she grabbed him up into loving arns as if he were a baby or a long lost relative. All seemed once more so still and silent, except for the tiny, barely audible sounds now and then. I said to myself that nothing on earth brought human motion to a halt as thoroughly as heavy snow, unless a tornado. But tornados prompted destruction and terror, snow, man's friend, peace and tranquility. Why, I asked, did I not invite Darya? She would scold me for sure. Where have you been? she'd ask. And with a curtly tone, and only because she felt concern.

Tomorrow, the thought occurred, I will attend Doctor Linskie's class, which will be called off in advance but I'll show up anyway to see whether it was. In two days all this great compilation of white will have melted and disappeared, and then I climbed up the stairwell of one of the towering buildings. I knew my way through its corridors as easily as an engineer reads a construction blueprint. I'd attended classes there, a good many classes. The frigate lights on Lake Michigan were moving, twinkling, glistening, strobing. Even before climbing the many stepped stairwell, I knew exactly what I would see. The sailors were brave to challenge the waters when the stormy winds posed colossal danger, but storms and danger are a part of their livelihood, so they had no choice. I climbed back down, the scene below remaining the same, magical and silent, the trees monstrous and beautiful, one of nature's greatest gifts to man. I thought of Frost and Walden, lovers of nature, seekers of nature, writers of nature. Heroic names."

I began to circle back. I'd been out long enough.

"A light! Is that a light?" Someone was cutting across the campus heading toward me, the flashlight flitting crazily, and as the light began to close the distance, the beam finally transitioning from object to object to a state of steady focus, I blinked. Still unable to clearly make out what I saw.

"Ramsey, Ramsey" She ran toward me. It was Andrea.

"What are you doing out here?" I asked.

"I could ask you the same."

"I asked you first."

"Looking for you. I dropped by the fraternity house and they said you weren't there."

"Who said that?"

"Bertinelli."

"Where were Darya and Aaron?"

"Gone to pick up chocolate and marshmallows at the store. A party is in the making. Bertinelli has the fire already roaring in the fireplace."

The wind again recommenced, icy and cutting, and the snow started up all over. The bad weather had suddenly decided not to stay put. She pulled her coat up tighter and I adjusted her collar as a means of protecting her neck.

"It bites. Doesn't it. You'll freeze."

"No I won't. I'm all right."

"You shouldn't have come."

"Neither should you."

"We'd better high tail it back. This may turn into meaner stuff."

Reaching my arm around her, both of us holding one another up, we made it to the fraternity house a quarter of a mile distance, though with something of a struggle, part of it due to the wintry attire she wore, heavy floppy boots and a bearish woolen coat that dropped to the lower region of her legs. Once she slipped my grasp and fell headlong into the snow, but laughing and carrying on in an attitude of hilarity as I lifted her up. Braveness flowed through her every vein. She dared searching for a companion with nothing more than a flashlight as a guide in weather doubly tough for me much less her.

Over the next two days the snow vacillated, starting up, then taking a breather, and then returning, adhering to this fashion until finally giving way to exhaustion. During those days the professors might have wisely terminated classes, not that the students didn't attend. They attended, but not with their minds. Playing football and sledding in the snow dominated the agenda, with our group from the fraternity house claiming a fair share of the frivolity. Much of this time I spent with Darya, but once she left to fill an obligation to meet with a club on campus to which she belonged, leaving me stranded. "I've got to skidoo," she said, with inference by way of her hand to use the sled as I pleased, "Goodbye. See you this afternoon." I remember well that which followed. It was something of a replay of what Darya and I once did. The sun had suddenly broken through the overcast, though not to stay long. Little length had passed when Andrea spotted me alone and beforehand planning the cutest of schemes flitted over and rolled up a snowball and hurled it in my direction. I ducked. It missed. And laughing and shrieking to the top of her voice she turned and ran, me giving chase, the very thing she wanted, and not without strenuous effort, caught her. On succeeding, on coming abreast I grabbed hold of her arm and she mine, both losing our balance and tumbling headlong, with her ending up on her back and I on my stomach, our faces virtually touching. Snow had splattered all over us. We made no effort at getting up, just fixed there, with steamy plumes of moisture rising from our mouths, the sunrays glinting directly into her face. We breathed quickly, the result of the exertion. She had not moved. "So beautiful," I thought looking down into her face, "what wondrous eyes." Now our breathing slowed, muchly diminished. She lay so still, just looking up at me, sometimes at the sky and then back at my face, and I thought to myself, "a look of love, a beautiful look of love, that's what it is," and when she pressed her lips softly to mine she confirmed it.

"Are you shocked?"

"That's not the word. That was a lovely kiss."

She giggled girlishly, covering her face with her hands then quickly taking them away when her laugh or giggle began to fade. "That's nice to hear. I've wanted to do it for the longest."

"I didn't know."

"You lie. You could tell."

"Yeah. I could tell."

"Did you ever want to kiss me?"

"I did."

"When was that?" She excitedly anticipated the answer.

"When we were studying together. When you acted like you were seriously stymied over something, you know, like something in a book you were trying to figure out, not knowing that I stole a glance at you at every chance. I'd look at your pretty eyes and then your pretty lips and I'd feel the urge to kiss them. And who wouldn't have?"

Every feature of her face showed amusement. "Do you still?"

"Yes. Often if the opportunity is right."

"I'll remember you said that."

We didn't kiss again, not then, because if we had I would remember. We lifted ourselves up and dusted off the snow then in lightsome dalliance joined the others. The kiss engendered nothing I figured, just a kiss, done on an impulse, soon to vanish, and tended to dismiss it from mind. Nevertheless, it lingered. Things for us had changed forever. We could never go back. On the surface, as we went about campus, we tried to make it appear that nothing had happened, in any event I did. We knew better. Andrea once said shortly thereafter that Darya was to graduate at the end of the semester and that we all would sorely miss her. I supposed that she liked that idea because she would have me to herself. She planned in her tactic I presumed to remain content and wait, and did until one night when Aaron and I were at the Cubs Nest she dropped in. She accompanied a group of young girls, her friends at the house where she lived. I quickened when I saw her. She had clad herself in a lovely red sweater with a uniquely oversized white collar and charcoal black pants. "Absolutely stunning," I whispered to Aaron.

"You bet. Ravishing." He still nurtured a crush on her. "She's a precious little sweet," he said to me in something of an affectionate tone.

I knew she caught me taking peeks at her and slyly released glances at me too. Right away someone stuck a coin in the juke box to play a tune of choice, a slow one, practically everyone in the room starting for the dance floor. I delayed, allowing Aaron to waft over and ask Andrea to do him the honor, but his shyness kept him at bay. To her he was a good friend but it stopped there, which I knew she'd determined not long after they'd first met. Knowing, then, how things stood between them I rose from my seat and went over.

"If you don't mind Miss, I'd like a turn with the best looking girl in the house. Are you willing?"

"What do you think?" she replied, her big gorgeous eyes alive with excitement.

It was a nice dance, a lovely mood pervading the room; the fire trickling in the fireplace, the young folks bunched cozily together, and some girls humming along with the music. And as Andrea swayed in my arms she laid her head against my breast, her hair falling about her neck, and began to hum as well. Eyes from the males in the room fell prolifically on her, for in any quarter of the campus they knew and sought after her, much like Darya, and the larger contingent that evening recognized her at once. During the day she let the young males walk beside her as she transferred from class to class but declined to date them. I considered that atypical but said nothing to her to that effect and after the incident in the snow the remotest possibility of my doing that lodged no where within me.

The semester marched along, the usual things at the fraternity house keeping pace which as much as time and schedules spared found Bertinelli, Darya, and myself heading to the beach to cook out and bask in the wind and the sun. We'd sometimes anchor the boat a hundred yards off shore and swim over to a high place, an overlook, and with the aid of binoculars brought along in a plastic bag trace the pygmy sized sailboats with their massive rigging zipping about. Sometimes Andrea joined us, neither of the girls giving the impression of jealousy, but why should they I surmised because Darya possessed no knowledge of the intimacy once or twice involving myself and Andrea, and Andrea, I felt certain, excersised an iron will that insulated her from jealousy. They got along with the smoothest of friendliness and delighted in laughing and talking with one another. You'd think they were sisters. It held fast with me however that both were especially cautious at touching me, or squeezing my arm, when we were together, not nearly as often as when I was alone with one or the other. Beaching out ranked high among the pleasures in which we indulged; there were many, and the rest of the fraternity house residents, our fellow students, were generally part of them, which included Aaron and Balboni, to be sure, and a sizeable presence of others from somewhere on campus. The two girls from Evansville, the freshmen at the Christmas dance, joined us once when we went sailing. Aaron said they were knockouts in their bikinis, and I easily concurred. We kept on the move, conscious that the day rapidly approached when Aaron and Bertinelli and Darya no longer resided among us. It saddened me to envision their leaving. "How sorely we'll miss them."

The Cubs Nest we all saw as the central watering hole of pleasure-seeking students campus wide, but for sentimental reasons it suddenly became especially the pleasure provider for the four of us. We were there every night, no night missed. We were together incessantly, making up for good times soon to fade and never come again, at least for them. But there were other places and other things that filled our itinerary. If we were not attending an opera, then we were replenishing our intellectual recesses in attendance of a speech delivered by an invited reknown to the campus or taking a trolley across and through Chicago and getting off to see a movie or enjoy a sandwich and after that hopping on another trolley at a later hour back to campus. We even once drove over to Joliet because we had heard that the inimitable Al Capone had once made that his home. The drive up the Wisconsin coastline hardly had an equal, the trees beginning to bud, but barely, and as we drove further and turned inland the western sun had begun to drop below the city of Green Bay, famous for innumerable attributes, one, because of its quaintness and charm and two, Curly Lambeau, the celebrated illustrious coach of the Green Bay Packers once lived there. I should not leave out my trips to New York and back on which once Darya and Aaron were with me. While there, Aaron hired a taxi and asked the driver to motor us to Long Island where he treated us to a lobster feed at a place he termed his favorite café and I soon understood why; such owing to the jesting buffoonery that started between himself and the waiter the moment we entered the doorway. Aaron called him Jake, his nickname. The family name of three syllables sounded something like Grenetti. When we left, Jake and Aaron hugged and Jake called him friend and pleadingly invited him to visit again soon. He kissed Darya's hand.

"That's just like an Italian Jake, trying to put on a show of chivalry and don't know how."

"Oh Aaron. That's not nice," Darya said reproachingly. "Thank you Jake for your perfect hospitality and you will see us again, soon."

Jake smiled gratefully, favoring as I ran carefully over his face one of the Benge brothers of my small town. "It's Zach. That's who I'm trying to call up, the one with the stern piercing eyes and pock marked face, but Jake is altogether of another disposition. He smiles and that is the material difference, all the difference in the world."

We were in the last month prior to the semester's end. Darya and I had agreed that we'd catch a plane the next weekend to visit her parents in Baltimore. We were overdue. She badly wanted it to happen. I earlier promised that we'd definitely make the trip and was determined to live up to what I'd said. But a snag shot from out of nowhere, a telephone call from Mr. Yazstremski asking that I stay over from my usual trip to New York to assist him with some imperatively needed research pursuant to an impending law case. The accent of his voice conveyed seriousness and it registered in the logical environs of my thinking process that I shouldn't try to beg off. I made straight to Darya and pled my dilemma and did my best to console her.

"We'll go the following weekend, I guarantee. You can count on it. Mr. Yazstremski says I can mark it down, that he'll not need me then."

She frowned but being the steady understanding person that I knew she was, she sloughed it off with a shrug and remarked that she had no hang up with the change and would notify her mother accordingly. "By all means Ramsey, you have to do as he asks. Your job with the firm is greatly important to you and you must treat it responsibly, and besides, you should feel honored that the man has especially called on you."

Chapter 46

ARRIVING BEFORE scheduled, I showed up at the office of my dear friend in New York, who glancing up from his desk apologized for pressing me to use my weekend to give him a hand, my only days free to do as I pleased. It flabbergasted me. "Apologize to me! A man of his stature apologizing to a pup like me. I think I'm dreaming." And then I spoke. "Goodness sir, Mr. Yazsrtremski. It's an honor to me that I'm here." Then looking over rather quizzically, a mite puzzled I thought, faintly grinning, he barely ceased his study of a spread of papers before him, apparently paying little or no attention to what I'd just said. I expected him to reply but he kept on with the business that consumed him. Suddenly I caught on. He hadn't apologized at all, merely setting me at ease in his own customary unique way of being nice, a man of class.

"All right, let's get right to it Ramsey," he said after a lapse, pushing away from his desk. Let me tell you what I'm up to, and then we'll move along from there." What he said he faced in the near term grew out of a real estate controversy that the plaintiff insisted on settling by trial. Mr. Yazstremski agreed at some point to represent the defendant. The plaintiff alleged in his complaint that the defendant, who recently bought a parcel of land contiguous with his, knowingly and purposely crossed the boundary to his property and cut down a sizeable many hackberry and valuable ornamental black cherry trees. And he kept going.

"The depositions were taken a few days ago from now, which to me suggests or did when I read them, that the old guy, the plaintiff, bordered on the fringe of nuttiness, but not to the extent that it inhibited him in the shortest while to tell more lies than he had fingers and toes in abuse of the facts. Of course, such mischief stemmed from the opposition lawyer. He wrote the depositions. But the plaintiff had to tell him or lead him to what he set down in the complaint. I told the lawyer that he knew better than that. He whined around a tad, practically swearing that the substance of the deposition was what the old guy reported in good faith under oath."

"What will you have me do to help?"

"Review the depositions in addition to my own review, concentrating on both sides, what both sides have said. See if you can verify the number of trees that were actually cut down. And determine the quality of the trees. Hire a nurseryman for verification and for giving expert testimony in court if need be."

"Anything else? Any suggestion to help defuse the plaintiff's charges, to weaken his case?"

"Start with the age of the trees and how long it takes them to grow to a certain height under usual growing conditions. You may need to secure a measuring instrument, a caliper, and determine the diameter of the trunks. On the other hand, hiring a bonafide nurseryman for this undertaking is likely the better choice. We may do just that. The plaintiff says that the trees were ornamental black cherry, truly expensive trees that had grown to a height of thirty to forty feet and swears that a Mr. J. C. Berryhill set out the trees twenty years ago. See if you can determine if these allegations, which he uttered under oath, hold water. You should in short order physically visit the site and verify where the trees were standing before the cutting. And yes. Yes, yes. He insists that a certain number of hackberry trees were cut down too, but apparently places little value on them. I hear tell they're a worthless specimen, very ugly, their limbs stretching in the weirdest configurations, looking in the semblance of witch fingers.

"What is the old fella asking in terms of restitution?"

"Forty five thousand dollars."

"For crying out loud. They must think gold is stored inside those trees."

"Well don't put any stock in the price. That's the attorney's doings. They always inflate. Exorbitantly. In this case wildly."

"Any chance of the complainant settling out of court?"

"Next to none. He thinks he's on to something. Smells money, and he's not about to let us diffuse him into settling for small change. And his attorney doesn't encourage him to. It's a trial that the attorney relishes. He hopes to keep the old guy in the dispute down to the last minute. He's smelling money too. And his client, a proverbial sucker, will find out just what I mean when he receives his bill. I think the attorney is foolish for taking the case in the first place, and I'm amazed that he has because he's wealthy already, quite wealthy, and like me has a stack of past years riding on his shoulders."

"I'll jump right on this Mr. Yazstremski. How shall I obtain the address of the property where the cutting occurred?"

"The secretary has it. She has a complete package for you. I gave it to her this morning. She'll have a list of other imperatives that I'll ask you to pursue when you finish with this one. But one step at a time. Target this one first."

I subsequently caught a taxi and instructed the driver to drive me out to the scene of subject, carrying a *right to enter* paper with me and met the plaintiff's lawyer on site. We had gone from the city to the suburbs and were close on the edge of the open countryside. I revealed very little to the lawyer of that which I sought, opening up to him that I merely wished to establish a general view of where the trees once stood. I casually wandered around looking for details, observing on the outset that the bulk of trees were cut near or on the property line where a flimsy fence presently stood and were not of large diameter, not nearly enough to indicate they were thirty or forty feet in height at the time of cutting. I asked the attorney if the trees were truly ornamental black cherry. He appeared uncertain, hesitant, caught off guard by the question, to confirm that they were, referring me to the depositions where the plaintiff had said plainly and sworn to it that they were ornamental black cherry. I knew they were not. They were wild cherry, regarded by farm folks where I hailed from in the South as worthless, infested with bore worms in the early years of life and swiftly started to rot and decay after that, never reaching any substantial size. They produced some semblance of fruit, cherry's the size of a bb pellet but completely unfit for human consumption. The tree, not in any way domesticated, springs from the ground wild, hence its name, its natural habitat situated on fence rows and creek banks and thickets. With the attorney peeping over my shoulder I knelt and inspected the stubs or stumps of the trees that were cut, every last one, discovering that a good many were aged, far too old to have recently fallen by the teeth of the chain saw. When I asked the lawyer if he found this of truth he answered that such trees were likely not included in the complaint. He'd have to check that out, he said. Shortly he excused himself, with an explanation that he must leave for an appointment and that no one objected to my staying as long as I liked. After he left I then began a door to door campaign, with the intent of first asking the neighbors if they knew a Mr. J. C. Berryhill and if they were able to verify his whereabouts. The houses were thick in that vicinity, small and unsightly, and not at all a pleasant milieu in which to live. A neighbor verified that Mr. Berryhill died thirty years previous. An older person stepped forward to help and proved especially cooperative. I judged him at eighty years of age. He was the perfect one, the very one I needed, not the least hesitant to talk. I think the nice double breasted suit that I wore to some degree affected his trust. I mirrored a clean cut appearance and old people I surmised liked to see this feature when dealing with a young man.

"Mister Berryhill is not with us anymore. Is that right?"

"Not anymore."

"The trees over there on that fence row are of some interest to me sir. I'd say they are wild cherry. Are they wild cherry?" I pointed to the area where the alleged cutting took place. A good many wild cherry still stood.

"They are. Poorest kind of tree I ever saw. The ones you see are full of worms and the ones cut down full of worms too. The ones left standing look sick, as you can see."

"It was Mr. Arnold who cut down the trees. Is that your understanding?"

"It is. Louis Arnold. That's his name. Just a short while back he moved here."

"I'm representing an attorney friend of mine who has been asked by the defendant, Mr. Arnold, to plead his case in court, and asked me to make certain that anyone giving me information knew that a court case was soon forthcoming."

"A court case. Well, I'm not surprised. Old Wallace is screwy anyway, crazy in the head, made worse by his son-in-law who eggs him on about everything he can drum up."

"You know Mr. Wallace, that is, Walter Wallace the plaintiff?"

"Know him well. He's nuts. Everbody around here will tell you the same. And I know about his daughter too. She's been running around all over, specially to the corner café, spreading to folks what all kinds of money they'll squeeze out of Arnold."

"Have you talked to Mr. Arnold with respect to the trees he's charged with cutting?"

"I have. Once or twice."

"What does he say?"

"He says he cut the trees. Some of them. But not nearly as many as he's accused of cutting."

"He says that. Well, he's honest, isn't he?"

"He is. And that makes me like the man."

"Tell me this sir, if you can? Was there any chance that Mr. Arnold deliberately cut those trees down?"

"No. Not deliberately. He did it by mistake. The fence row which he thought was the boundary sagged pitifully from the overgrowth of vines and thickets. Who in the world would have known where the real property line started and stopped?"

"In your opinion were the trees worth anything that Mr. Arnold cut down?"

"Not a cent. The truth is old Wallace should have paid Arnold for clearing them out. It would have improved the looks of his property."

"Ummmmm." I elected not to say a great deal more, or else didn't figure it wise. But I did raise a question that I'd let slip me when the gentleman and I first began to talk.

"I'm curious about that white house over there sir. The one next to where the trees were cut."

"How are you curious?"

"Does it belong to Mr. Wallace?"

"It does."

"Is it worth much? Where would you place its value?"

"Bout' ten thousand dollars. Its a hundred six years old. Nobody has lived there for years. Wallace's parents lived there and died there. Crazy as he is Wallace still hangs on to the house and the furniture, every piece kept zactly in place like it was when they lived there."

"I see." I winced with aghastness. "A hundred and six years old! And that attorney is asking for restitution in the amount of forty five thousand dollars for a few worthless trees! Mr. Yazstremski must have imploded with amazement when he read this."

My investigation had been simple and quick. I thanked the man and left on my way to the firm, but stopping at the tax assessor's office to ascertain the age of Mr. Wallace's house. "It's a hundred and six years old," the clerk of records verified when he ceased dragging his finger down the list of city and county property tax records.

The case eventually wound up in court and there tried. It began with the complainant's lawyer delivering a statement of overview, then asking his client Mr. Wallace to step forward and testify. His lawyer struggled to provoke him to start answering. He appeared strangely puzzled, looking dissolutely at the judge, then at his attorney, and then at the judge, and finally began to babble. Astonishingly unintelligible I thought. Appearing somewhat unorthodox to me at the time was the the judge's decision to ask Mr. Wallace to step down in favor of his son-in-law finishing for him, the latter a brash high strung offensive man of roughly forty with a sourly dispositioned face who had lost an arm at the elbow. He had a mean streak record. He talked too close to the microphone, practically mouthing it, and as a result his words were badly distorted. When at one point Mr. Yazstremski asked the man for his occupation he caustically shot back, "That's none of your business," with Mr.Yazstremski remaining very much unfettered, and speaking softly, "But sir, I've asked you a question. You are in a court of law and you are obligated to answer,"

"Answer the question," the judge quietly ordered, but firmly.

Mr. Yazstremski with obvious determination little by little whittled away, establishing that the trees weren't set out twenty years ago, that Mr. Berryhill, who allegedly had set them out died ten years in advance of the twentieth year, implying that the plaintiff Wallace lied during the course of the depositions but not openly accusing the man. We secured the aid of a nurseryman for testimony who testified that the trees in question were not ornamental black cherry but wild cherry which sprang up wild and were of no value for any purpose other than to play host to the bore worms. The results that I obtained from the land surveyor who surveyed the boundaries verified that trees were freshly cut on Arnold's and Wallace's properties but more on Wallace's. How many on each remained on the threshold of dispute. Mr. Arnold admitted to me more than once that he cut down the trees and admitted it still once again in court while under oath. Mr. Yazstremski declined to ask for verification of the number cut down on Mr. Wallace's property because he realized that the judge already perceived without the slightest waiver that the trees were worthless and would therefore render a mild verdict, that is to say he would levy a cost against Mr, Arnold unsubstantial in amount. Mr. Yazstremski chose to accept the number set forth in the complaint. He as well asked the nurseryman to take to the stand to verify the size of the subject trees, particularly asking for the diameter at the base. The nurseryman, calm and patient, slowly and thoroughly explained that the diameter of the base of the trees vouched that they could not have attained to a height of thirty to forty feet and that they generally succumbed to worm rot at an early age. Mr. Yazstremski chose not to chide the opposition lawyer for asking such an absurd sum for restitution. But tactfully reproached him for taking the case when they were in privacy.

When he finished with his close, I knew that Mr. Yazstremski's -tactics severely weakened the complaint; "I think we let the air out of the balloon Ramsey," he jauntily whispered. Before we left the court, we heard the judge's decision who within brief interim asked the question which in my opinion should have been asked during the course of the trial, not after cessation. But the judge owns the court and has the final say.

"Mr. Arnold, the lawyers have pled their case and now the rest is up to me, consequently, I shall ask you this. Did you intend to cut down the trees; said in another way, did you do it willfully and maliciously."

"Of course not your honor."

With this, the judge called Mr. Yazstremski and the opposition lawyer to the bench to discuss the assessment of the penalty against Mr. Arnold. It amounted to less than five hundred dollars, astronomically less than the amount the opposition lawyer proposed in the complaint. As the courtroom slowly emptied I happened to glance over at the opposition lawyer and Mr. Wallace and his son-in-law huddled in an out of the way corner, the unhappy faces of the latter two depicting disappointment and frustration, as well as anger, that the judge had awarded them a shockingly low sum, a mere pittance in view of what they expected. The opposition lawyer did his utmost to console his clients, feeling himself as did they, that he in effect lost the suit.

On our way back to the office Mr Yazstremski reflected on the events of the trial and on one view in particular.

"Well Ramsey, you likely are wondering why I tried no harder to attack the plaintiff's position and completely turn the table on him for lying during the taking of the depositions. I'll tell you why. In this instance I felt it a waste of purpose and imprudent to too aggressively pursue Mr. Wallace, who at first blush was unsteady of mind, and run the risk of swaying the judge against us. I know to you this whole proceeding seemed ridiculous, that the plaintiff and defendant should have joined together and negotiated a reasonable settlement or no settlement at all, without the court settling it for them. People don't behave that sensibly, I'm afraid. That's why courts of law are imperative. But what you have witnessed, and I'm so glad you were with me, was an altercation that occurs time and time again, everyday somewhere in the American system of courts.

"Over what seems a minor disagreement," I added.

"You grasp it correctly. Except the cases are seldom minor. Land and fence rows and trees and boundary disputes. Oh boy. People rise up to complain and challenge over these things by far more than they do over anything else. Some of the most bitter and venomous disputes imaginable grow out of these situations and it always seems ridiculous and uncalled for. But it goes on happening regardless."

"If you don't mind I'd like to ask you something concerning another aspect of the case."

"You know I don't. Jump right to it."

"It comes to me a little oddly that you decided to litigate a case as trivial as this one, since obviously you saw it far beforehand as an enormously low level non moneyed suit."

"That's easy my boy. When inexperienced and starting out with a relatively unsuccessful firm on the north side I stayed busy hustling up cases in the manner of the one just litigated. In the beginning I earned my livelihood by such means. Times were slow, the economy down and people out of work, and I felt grateful and lucky to have work myself, believe me. Eventually I joined Stylman and we began to spread our wings, moving into the corporate circles, high paying corporations, and for a while, much to my shame, I set about chasing the deep pocket, corporations of great wealth. And forgot the small people cases which put food on my family's table when I needed it most. When I sat down and sifted through what I'd done I vowed to my wife not to turn my back on the folks of limited weatlh, never. If I am called upon it is now my awowed principle without fail to return to that world whenever I'm needed, even if it means declaring a hold on a lucrative contract with a corporation bulging at the seams with opulence." Suddenly there it was again, an echo of similarity, if no more than a faint resemblance, Monett's advising wisdom: "When a man is young, he dreams of money and lavish things, which when his life is over or nearly over, he realizes they amounted to no more than a thread's worth. Don't ever fall for a folly of that design Ramsey."

Chapter 47

IN THE afternoon of the week following my return from Mr. Yazstremski's, Darya and I boarded a plane for Baltimore, she euphoric, I less so, leary a little of what to expect. I already felt intimidated. But glad that at last we were going, curious to see with my own eyes the scene fertile in my thoughts which I had acquired from her descriptions and narrations over time. Once landing we caught not a taxi, which I believed we would, but rather crawled into a shiny substantially large automobile that Darya explained her parents sent to intercept us. She introduced me to the driver, calling him by his surname, rather unimpassioned it seemed to me. Not cool but neither warm. He smiled and nodded, saying nothing and began driving away. She would not admit it I think because it only ran vaguely in her conscious that she looked upon the driver, actually the valet for her parents, and therefore hers too, as belonging to the lower order. Of course, that was in fact the way it was because she was of high born society and parents who taught her by example and by years of conditioning and education to abide by aristocratic rules of conduct, which were fundamentally and deeply ingrained in her psyche. But I knew from our numerous private hours together that she opposed passionately that people might perceive her in that light.

From there we wound through the city toward the coastline, covering what I calculated as some several miles. We had traveled for nearly an hour. Soon afterwards, not of a considerable length more, we altered directions and if my senses were free of error we were moving to a rise in elevation. Not only did the terrain seem as if it were reshaping but the tree line as well, stately cypress and elm and oak populating the shoulders of the driveway leading very shortly to the starting property line of her parent's estate. It crawled and twisted in the attitude of an animal carefully threading its way over a precarious course. Off the roadside patches of gnarled undergrowth of striking beauty appeared here and there, wreathing its tentacles in serpentine resemblance around the trees, the undergrowth massively rank with vegetation and this the sun's rays found impossible to break through to the effluvium earth beneath. As we traveled further my probing nature grew exponentially and I looked about with wonder. Darya read me.

"We're almost there," she said with assurance, affectionately laying her hand on my arm. The occurrence of the next few minutes bound itself with such fascination into my senses that I made mental notes with the intention of sharing the descriptions with Doctor Linskie when I saw him again.

Eventually, within minutes, the driver slowed the car and we rolled to within near footage of a much different drive that led to her parents home not yet visible and was not because it lay a good quarter mile away. I then saw towering before me a gate of fantastic proportions standing as a bulwark to the driveway we were to enter, a structure of iron of great weight, endowed of a crown that rose gradually until reaching a climax, which resembled at the very peak the tip of a spear of amoral bearing. I knew not from what source the impulse was discharged but suddenly the gate upon some remote command slowly opened, allowing us to pass through. Now we traveled on pavement of the finest composition, aggregate rock, painstakingly cut and cultured, and laid by craftsman of selected capability. We passed around one curve and then another and then another until at length I commenced to speculate to Darya in good fun as to whether the roadway had an end. But suddenly, as we negotiated the final bend, there it was, a configuration of immensity, an edifice, which threw upon me not less than an inspiration of awe. I marveled at its lofty height and at the extrusion of the upper portico which extended by some considerable footage over the one on the lower tier. And all of this gilded by an array of vines and shrubberies and flowers that did not in any small way fail to attract my observance. I shall not forget that first glimpse. I have lived for long years and yet it is unalterably distinct in my memory. Sometimes in the night I lie recalling the image and in my dreams relive the moments as we drove slowly forward to that magnificent home, eventually drawing under the pavilion and coming to a halt in front of the double French doors. The driver hastened to let Darya out, while I exited from the other side. The front entrance was but a step away, embellished by three whitish columns on either side that I gathered were of the Romanesque/Grecian age. All the while Darya watched me, she most certainly must have, wondering what soared through my head and I wondering the same of her. She had told me of what to expect, not on our way from the airport, but variously in the past, but all the same I failed to comprehend its immensity both in terms of size and grandeur. Needless to say, as my eyes conducted quick inspection of the visage that I beheld, the home and its surrounding adornments, my fathoming of the cost involved in bringing it to completion drew bead on an astounding sum. And aside from this my brain quickly spun with thoughts that dwelled curiously on its origin. "Is this the result of an inheritance that sprang from relatives long deceased? Or was it built from funds accumulated through shrewd and profitable business ventures by Darya's parents? Which?" But then the swirling of these possibilities suddenly gave way to an impending interruption.

The door quietly opened, a servant or butler leading the way then stepping aside, but yet holding it immovably in place while a youthful attractive woman came charmingly through, taking Darya in her arms. Darya's mother. I saw it in a second. The resemblance was strongly descriptive. She laughed tearfully, rejoicing that her daughter had again returned home, and they were anything but hurried to give one another up. They kissed repeatedly. I do not know how to describe her other than to say that her skin very closely resembled Darya's, pure and vibrant, and that her slender frame told that she subscribed to a meticulous regimen of attending to her physical self. Her eyes were dark and incisive though kind and gentle, her voice soft and happy. She moved with deftness, her carriage erect and trained, an elegance taught to her by her parents, I ventured, a quality of poise that began with long ago kindred, migrating forward through family generations to her and then to Darya whose manner and looks bore the same distinction.

"Ah, who have we here Darya?" she asked with lovely expression that made me adore her at once. By now she and Darya had released one another. She clasped my arm with both her hands and laughed a laugh of softness but with a shade of reserve. There ran a trace of sonorousness in her voice. "Don't tell me. So good to meet you Ramsey," she said, turning to me. "And you are greatly welcome."

I did my best to respond with the proper decorum but she overpowered me with her civility and charm. I struggled for the suitability of an answer. "I'm equally glad to meet you Mrs. Narvanna. Your daughter has said much of you and I find that it is unerringly accurate."

"And how is that? Not negative I hope."

"Not at all. It's in every way complimentary. She said you were lovely and friendly and easy to get to know. And on all three criteria I find her correct."

She smiled with her eyes, as if she were happy and amused at the same time. "Did you say such salutary things of your mother Darya?" She only spoke to Darya a second's worth and then her attention fell again on me. She had not expected Darya to answer. "But I'm afraid Ramsey my daughter has over sold me."

"No I haven't Momma. I under sold you. I didn't say enough."

"Well Ramsey," said Mrs. Narvanna, "you see how we take up for one another." And then there suddenly appeared a shift in her disposition.

"But enough of our trading accolades and so on. Shall we move inside?" She called to the butler who stood within hearing and asked him to have someone help us with our belongings.

After they were set into my room and we had all three exchanged talk a while longer Darya suggested that we go for a walk on the grounds because she terribly missed doing that while away, she said, impatient now to stroll among the many species of flowers, plants, and trees, which at this stage of the season were at the peak of verdure. At the last, Mrs. Narvanna decided to string along with us and with little waste dressed in attire designed to help her deal with the occasional pushing aside of undergrowth from narrow pathways while moving about. She promised her daughter that she wouldn't get in the way or constitute a drag on our enjoyment.

"You won't Momma. Don't say that. You won't in the least, I assure you. Do go with us."

It gladdened me that she did, for as we shifted from place to place, she singled out many specimens which she covered extensively with explanations, among them the vineyards that ran from the eastern sector of the estate to the cliffs overlooking the bay, and the Acacia and Lilac trees, which grew in patterned arrangement throughout the grounds.

"Do you make wine from the grapes you grow in this vineyard?" I asked.

"We do. Or I should say that our butler does. He's Polish born, and quite facile at growing grapes, tending them with tender loving care, and conducting the distillation process himself when they are harvested."

"I'm stunned. I didn't dream I'd encounter something like this when Darya invited me to join her in a short stay at home."

"This is Momma's show case, her toy," said Darya, pridefully alluding to her mother's pastime.

"It's not me but Jeremy who deserves the credit. What I contribute amounts to no more than the miniscule thinness of tissue. If not for him I could do nothing but I greatly enjoy the rewards of working in all this, especially seeing Jeremy do things that are beyond reach of the typical orchard grower."

"What is done with the wine after the distillation?"

"It's stored. Some of it for the longest, for years. The kegs from which we draw wine now were filled by our forebears. We take some of it for ourselves, for dinners and guests and other gatherings, and some we give away."

"You don't sell it!"

"No indeed. That's against our principles. I work hard at replacing that which is used for whatever the purpose, our gift to future generations that they might enjoy it just as we enjoy it. But we don't sell it."

We walked on from there, Mrs. Narvanna appearing as enthused as I when encountering specimens strange to my knowledge. As a lad growing up a thorn tree together with some smaller ones grew on the banks of the animal pond near our barn. The thorns were of finger length, as sharp and pointed as a needle on the end and far more dangerous. My father cautioned me repeatedly never to fail wearing shoes when drawing near or into the midst of these trees. "Thorns are poisonous son. Sometimes people step on them and die from infections if they break off and the doctor can't dig them out. Gangrene can set up and that can amount to a very bad thing." The thorns fell frequently from such trees, or a limb to which thorns were attached, and following the advice of my father I faithfully obeyed his caution when in their vicinity.

"Look Ramsey, over there, see, the Acacia tree; look at its beauty. I call it the Acacia although there are other names for it. Some call it the wattle or the thorn tree."

"Thorn tree! I used to live on a farm where thorn trees grew. We considered them dangerous."

"Oh. I don't know. Your trees might have been a derivation of some sort from the Acacia. Well, perhaps. I might suppose they were, but that is not easily said because there are thirty one species of record. Any of the thirty one are considered as leguminous plants, friendly plants, members of the pea family believe it or not, and the one growing over there is known as the Rose Acacia." She pointed to it a second time to make certain I saw it for sure, not satisfied I had. "It grows beautiful flowers. That's why I asked the grounds keeper to set it out."

Only briefly afterwards she decided to part from us and return to the inside where she said there were some pressing things to which she must attend. I offered that Darya and I would assist her back, especially up the steps to the plaza and into the interior.

"Ah. You are joking. Heavens. How numerous are the times I'm out here by myself. No. I don't need assistance, but thank you just the same Ramsey."

Since she seemed in every aspect youthful and agile, I wasn't sincere with my offer. I did it in that I deemed it a proper display of chivalry.

Darya and I went on, eventually halting at the overlook perched high above the Chesapeake, an enormously expansive and gorgeous scene. The water at this hour seemed of a limpid blue, dotted with sailing craft and frigates. "More fantastic than Lake Michigan," I thought, and then I reasoned further. "But I guess I adjudge as much because I am at this considerable elevation able to enjoy at one and the same time the downward as well as the outward scene stretching before me. I can't look down at Lake Michigan. I can only look across."

We sat for most of the remainder of our outing, engrossed by the lovely water and the boats by focusing through a set of binoculars she'd brought with her. We sat on a settee with little mementos etched and carved into the seating and backing by someone who we guessed must have sat there long ago. She said she used to sit there a lot herself, more so when in her young girl years and with a tease in her eyes said she wished I'd been there with her. We decided to walk around for a while longer then returned to the settee. She asked if I were having a good time. And I answered yes, a very good time. I asked if she felt otherwise.

"No. I don't. But you're quieter than usual."

"I'm just adapting to everything. There's such an avalanche of things to absorb that I'm almost overwhelmed."

"Okay. That's good."

All at once she kissed me. I supposed she'd been thinking she would. I kissed her back and asked if she remembered the first time we kissed. She said she did, that it was when we were sitting in the lobby of the fraternity house. I wished instantly I hadn't asked, for I once asked Nenia the same question. As I trained my eyes on that vast stretch from shore to shore, scanning the sail boats and frigates creeping along on the water, as if they were moving in slow motion, I concluded that whoever held the high ground the opposition forces on the lower elevation were severely imperiled. Darya said the same thoughts often occurred to her. I added that the Civil War was among America's worst wars. She answered that any war, regardless of time or place, is the worst. Since our subject at the moment involved the Chesapeake, Darya reminded me that our plans for sailing the next day were necessarily scuttled. News to her from her mother reported that conditions on the water were too hazardous for light sailing craft to encounter and were to remain largely unchanged for the next day or possibly two. Well on its descent to earth the sun slowly dropped below the western rim and then we began with enlivened pace to return to the mansion. The fiery red runners in the west had yet refused to let the earth swallow them up without struggle. But soon would die away. Mrs. Narvanna stood watching this great scene of nature through her drawing room windows as we approached, at last climbing the steps to the plaza, then crossing from there over the smooth slabs of granite to the doorway. Mrs. Narvanna met us.

"I worried," she said, as we made our way in. "I'm glad you're back. Did you enjoy?"

"You know we did," said Darya, going over to hug her mother.

Mrs. Narvanna glanced at me in quest of my agreement.

"We did. Absolutely. That's a breathtaking scene," I returned.

She said that dinner was not long in the making, at approximately seven she added, far past the usual hour of serving at the fraternity house. I was famished. Excusing myself, I retired to my room with the intent of showering and dressing and sitting around reading until someone announced dinner. Instead, I laid down and though unintended succumbed to sleep, not awakening until shortly after six; then showered and slipped into my black pants and black slippers and my nicest white shirt with a lily flower embroidered over the pocket. After bantering the idea back and forth I felt that I should dress a little more formally and decided on my white summer waist jacket. No tie. Previously, back at the university I especially critiqued my dress for dinner with Darya who said that however I dressed for this occasion was fine and left the final choice up to me. While waiting I was especially attracted to the décor of the room, this time with greater scrutiny, the furnishings delicately chosen and arranged, the walls embellished with portraits of varied tastes and choices and done at the hands of not less than renowned artists I assumed. I liked the one entitled *Portrait of a Man in Armor,* brushed by the artist Paris Bordon, Italian, Venetian, 1506-1571. The man in the portrait, or soldier of high rank, is unknown.

Whoever he was he and his two pages were portrayed with an almost palpable empathy. No longer young he sat in pose with grizzled hair and beard, gazing abstractedly to the side as a young page with a lively expression adjusts his armor plate, while another, who gave off a more serious countenance and subtly defined features, held his helmet. "Did this portrait transfer from some past member of the family? Who selected it for display in this lush home?" I knew. "Who else? Mrs. Narvanna, without question, superbly capable of rendering such a choice, given her widespread travels throughout Europe, the Balkans, and the Mid-East, in those travels surveying hundreds of the finest of foreign exhibits."

Knocking on my door Jeremy did the honor of announcing dinner. When I entered the dining area, a man, Mr. Narvanna, rose from his chair and strode politely over, graciously shaking my hand and welcomed me with warmth both ingratiating and sincere. It was in the likeness of his wife who made me feel profoundly accepted when I met her in the early part of the afternoon. He held on to my hand as he spoke other niceties, finally letting go. "These people are of exquisitely polite society, groomed to entertain and charm" it came to me, and while his efforts to please were muchly gratifying I truthfully felt that his bursting friendliness was by some measure pre practiced. With respect to his appearance, I can say he ranked above average in terms of handsomeness, well built and trim and his suit fit nicely on his frame. His eyes were midnight dark, the origin of Darya's, although her mother's were much the same. On our moving to the dining table for dinner Mr. Narvanna graciously assisted his wife with her seating and before I could perform like chivalry for Darya he crossed over, a slight hurried it seemed, and pulled out her chair, standing erectly beside her until she lowered herself. Unless my eyes had not fallen upon Mrs. Narvanna at this exact second I would have missed her incisive coolness toward her husband for preempting what she expected as my obligation of etiquette. Her eyes flashed. Darya showed anger too. But I deemed that he wasn't deserving of their dissatisfaction, that it was an honest caprice. After all, his daughter was freshly home, a peak occasion for excitement, and without letting protocol take the lead chose whatever means that guided him to convey fatherly affection to her. Realizing his error, he blushed and lowered himself into his chair. The dinner servings were various and overwhelmingly plentiful, thanks to Jeremy who preplanned the food and set the table without assistance which in no way he needed. From that long ago occasion I remember the veal cutlets to this day and I think I remember them because Mrs. Narvanna asked as a matter of conversation if I liked veal cutlets. I said that I did and said it convincingly. Truthfully, I loved veal cutlets. Bertinelli prepared them once a week. Sitting there at that enormous table with just three other people seemed by every description strange, in any event something to which I wasn't very much accustomed. If we had sat end to end from each other, Darya and I on one end and her parents on the other, we would have needed a microphone and amplifier for communicating. As it happened Mr. Narvanna sat at one end with Mrs.Narvanna sitting down table to his right and Darya next to her. I sat on the opposite side straight away from Darya. I liked that. It allowed me to talk to her quite directly and this in the sense that I was a tad nervous afforded a degree of calm. The whole ambience of the room hit me with stunningness, attired in splendid décor, yet the table itself appeared to me as the most singular article. Made of teakwood it shown with a luster. Mrs. Narvanna said she bought it in Vietnam quite sometime before hostilities erupted in that region in which America became an unalterable part. Impressed by the rarity of its beauty I felt the draw of temptation from time to time to slide my fingers across the surface.

My intuition conveyed to me that both Darya and Mrs. Narvanna prior cautioned Mr. Narvanna not to overly interrogate me at dinner, or at any time for that matter. I think he kept his questions within acceptable limits, first beginning with the impending Vietnam War, I presumed, since Mrs. Narvanna had already mentioned it, which lingered fresh in his thoughts.

"What have you to say about the troubles in Vietnam Ramsey?"

The question wasn't bothersome. It called for nothing more than a generality. I could answer it easily. "It's dangerous. It may spread into wider conflict. We've seen enough wars and I'm afraid we're on the threshold of being drawn into another."

He seemed nonchalant. I wasn't sure of what he thought of my answer. After further exchanges but not on the same topic he ultimately uncloaked another. But first led with a preface.

"I'm terribly concerned over the federal income tax structure. It's awfully hard on businesses such as the one I'm part of. Darya says you're into law with a group in New York. As a lawyer, can you say anything regarding favorable legislation in the near future?"

"Not really Mr. Narvanna. Not as a lawyer because I'm not one yet. I'm only in training. I do have some disagreements with respect to the laws that are supposed to regulate big oil. Oil corporations are allowed tremendous depletion and depreciation breaks that in my opinion are harmful to the country as a whole."

Chapter 48

AFTER DINNER we all continued to sit at the table, but only for a limited stretch, with Mr. Narvanna exercising care not to ask a bundle of questions, only slipping once, bringing out that his company, actually a syndicate, manufactured and marketed chemicals worldwide, a business with roots in the old country. "Serbia," he said. Which I knew already, Darya telling me as much soon after I first met her. The business relocated in America shortly after the Civil War.

"My grandfather founded the business, a near genius at forging together men, materials, and money, and the initial investors were richly rewarded for commiting their money to him."

"What an exciting venture! Wish I might fall into the good fortune of something like that. Of course, a person like me stands not even the thinest chance of raising the funds for an opportunity of that magnitude."

"It doesn't always take money to get started at something. As a matter of fact, we have excellent positions for young talented men such as you. We'd hire them in a heartbeat. And there are very lucrative investment opportunities for our staff."

On hearing this, Darya smarted, her eyes narrowing, preferring that her father hadn't introduced for consideration any aspect of the family business with me. I helped him move beyond it, maneuvering skillfully away from the topic with an answer to his implication by identifying other occupational fields high on my list of interests.

"It sounds tempting, it certainly does. But I'm pretty well glued to the idea of college teaching, which is still at a distance. I'll have to finish with my undergraduate studies and then start working on the requirements for teaching at the higher educational level. But I'm dead set on reaching my goal and will stay true to whatever is necessary to gain its achievement. In the meanwhile, I'll stay with the law firm. I'll have to earn a living."

"You don't intend to take up law?"

"No sir. I don't think so."

I expected him to pursue me further on the response I'd given, and I'm inclined to believe he would have provided Mrs. Narvanna hadn't cut in and altered the conversation. It was but a fraction that Jeremy came in, inquiring with courtly politeness if anyone would like more coffee or tea and if not he'd like permission to clear away the dinner residuals, the silverware, the plates, the glasses, and the excess food. Promptly, Mrs. Narvanna gave her approval with a nod and gracious smile. And also, at this moment Mr. Narvanna lifted himself from his chair and leaned to his wife and kissed her and then kissed his daughter too, excusing himself for the evening, citing his need to return a welter of telephone calls that were unforgivably over due. "I'll see you in the morning at breakfast Ramsey," he said, moving to my proximity with a pat on my shoulder. Mrs. Narvanna stayed on for awhile then suggested that we remove to the small nook just off the kitchen, where a little rounded table for accommodating four stayed placed next to the window. It permitted an enticing view of the plaza. We sat down and she ordered coffee, which Jeremy promptly brought. We sat sipping and sipping and sipping, not necessarily enjoying or desiring it, I thought, not nearly as much as when served at breakfast. I really hadn't wanted it. I did not speak aloud of that which came to me next. "What we enjoy is the idea of it, of holding a cup of coffee in our hands irrespective of when or where or whether we even like the drink, something of a habitual thing."

"I spend many hours at this precious tiny relic Ramsey, sitting and feasting my eyes on the beautiful flora out there."

"I can imagine. And I'm sure you enjoy the assemblage of portraits that you have hanging on your walls."

"I do. Almost as much as the out of doors scenery."

"I appreciate the one where the soldier is with his two pages. I almost gazed a hole through it."

"You liked it?"

"Yes indeed."

"I chose that room especially for you, especially because of the portrait. I've been wondering if you liked it."

"I assure you I did."

"Was there anything unique in the scene that tugged at your senses?"

"Well, perhaps not unique, at least not too unique."

"And what was that, if I may chide you into an example?"

"The young boy, the one who holds the helmet. He's African. I have to assume that the people of Europe in that period harbored no views one way or another regarding Africans."

"Of course you have reference to slavery. Oh, I think they did. But I can't say. I'm not well read on the matter. But I gather that you are, since you are aiming at a degree in literature."

I glanced at Darya. Curious. Then she felt prompted to exaplain.

"I told her you're into literature. That's how she knows."

"That's an exciting field, Ramsey," her mother continued, "so rich and rewarding as I see it. Heaven knows I wish I could read an nth of the great books in our university and city libraries," she said, sighing. "I'm afraid by the time I die I will have hardly forged a dent."

I laughed pleasantly, and answered.

"You'll read enough, I'm sure."

She declined to comment other than to ask me to reflect on my current reading pursuits.

"Not literature, not in the literal sense. I'm reading through the tracings of the Russian Revolution of 1918, through the surviving memorabilia that belonged to the royal family of Nicholas II, the Czar, memoirs, letters, communiqués, personal papers, dairies, and numerous other left over fragments."

"The royal family?"

"The Romanoff's. The Romanoff family of Nicholas II. He was murdered, as you know, and the rest of his family as well at the hands of the Bolsheviks."

"Yes. I'm aware of that. I—."

At that very moment Mr. Narvanna apologetically poked his head through the doorway to ask his wife if she might breakaway and help him with an issue of business that absolutely necessitated her presence.

"Forgive me. I must see what this concerns. I hope we'll take up the Romanoff's a mite later. You won't forget, will you?"

"I won't forget."

After she'd stayed gone sufficiently long for Darya to determine that her delay seemed excessively lengthy we opted to remove ourselves to the chairs on the plaza. The outside was quiet and cool, the lights from the frigates shining with a glitter and the insects of the night beginning to sing their discordant song. It was getting late when Mrs. Narvanna came back, past eleven, apologizing for her too lengthy delay and bid us goodnight, saying she simply must retire. I lost track of time. We continued to reminisce and talk, for how long I'm unable to say. In any event, very long. We were milling through a hodgepodge of past moments, starting with when we first met, and shifted from there to the fiery debates and exchanges at mealtimes at the fraternity house, and how she helped me decipher the catalogue when I first enrolled and the speech delivered by the renowned Clement Attlee and the snowball fights, and her, Bertinelli, and Aaron graduating with the advent of June, and how insufferably lonely the lives of those left behind, and her future endeavors and mine and a hundred other snippets until overcome with the need to sleep and called it quits.

That night I climbed into a monstrously large bed, obviously of gilded design, the headboard made of heavy walnut with exquisite carvings meticulously placed, some curlicue, and others patterned in half moon shaping. My imagination worked overtime. "Who has slept in this splendid furnishing before me, a hundred years before me? It has to have been built in the middle part of the century past or perhaps decades before that. I'll ask Mrs Narvanna."

"Whoa. What's this?" Even though in this very room that evening before dinner I somehow had paid trivial attention to a small side table with a cut of the finest marble overlaying the surface, within reach of the bed where I would sleep, I had now begun to study it further. I looked for something. On pulling open the top drawer I found it, a note pad. I had wanted to write a trickle of words to my mother. And I began, starting with a description of the illustrious home and grounds and how the hosts treated me with venerable chivalry but at this point my writing pen instantenously came to a halt, or in other words I stopped it. "I cannot do this." In time I knew my mother would ask why it happened that I was there, and if I told the truth I could not avert explaining Darya's name and twisting as well my story into a lie. I abandoned the idea.

As I turned over a time or two my hand detected something not soft and malleable, not likened to that of a bed linen, but an object stiff and brittle and before I opened the envelope, I knew the exact wording that waited inside. I opened it. "Sleep tight." A broad grin lit on my face. Someone emplaced it there sometime earlier, naturally. I had no idea when but I knew who. Shortly I pulled up the covers and drifted into slumber, though saying to myself in the moments preceding that Mrs. Narvanna was a tremendously suave person, a nice lady who lived and breathed for her daughter. "They're close. I'm glad to see that. I didn't know how they jelled person to person. I have sometimes wondered, considering that Darya is so strong of mind and determination. I've figured, but wrongly, that she might stubbornly contest her mother attendant to certain things. I don't see that in the least. They're like sister angels together." The next morning a knock sounded on my bedroom door. Jeremy's knock. "Nine o'clock," he cheerfully called out. I sat up and rubbed my eyes. Jeremy reported that he had breakfast fast on its way, ready in fact in twenty minutes. I dressed and made my way to the dining room, there intercepting Darya who reached her arm around me and said that we'd breakfast in the nook that her mother used when dining alone or with her husband. When Jeremy set out a platter of meat glaringly familiar, I turned and all three, Mr. Narvanna, Mrs. Narvanna and Darya were on the verge of breaking into laughter. The platter was stacked with pork chops three layers high, once my favorite dish, breakfast or lunch or dinner, when I was but a lad, and still remained so. Of this I had at some time or the other told Darya and she had relayed it to her mother.

"Surprise Ramsey," exclaimed Mrs. Narvanna. "Pork chops fried Southern style. We thought this might make you feel quite at home. And what's more. I want you to know that I love pork chops too. And supplementing our pleasure more so Jeremy in the very near making will serve us hot biscuits."

Their laughter never materialized; they only advanced as far as breaking into mischievous grins, for I had begun to laugh harder and louder than any of them might have done, greatly appreciating the humor. The scheme worked. It did make me feel more at home. Shortly following breakfast Mr. Narvanna stood and said he must leave for his office, excusing himself in the manner that he excused himself the evening past, wishing us all a good and happy day on his way out. "See you tonight Ramsey."

Not more than the pouring of the second cup of coffee Mrs. Narvanna asked me if I minded returning to the Romanoff family of Russia. "You recall don't you that we were approximating the Czar's demise or something to that effect, when my husband suddenly interrupted us."

"I remember."

"Good. Then you'll oblige me with more."

"I think I can pick up where we left off. I'll try to keep it brief without preempting too many of the essentials."

"As you wish."

I realized that in a sense we often left Darya out of the conversation, or else she left herself out, yet felt satisfied to sit and listen, glad that her mother and I were getting to know one another. Mrs. Narvanna's eyes asked, "Why don't you begin?" I then began.

"It's a sad story. It deeply touches my heart every time I read it. The family, the Czar, the Empress, and the four beautiful girls and the young son were shifted from place to place after his dethronement, treated as parcel since his arrest, and moved, and slept, and ate at the behest of the Bolsheviks who'd stormed into power. The last stop of the family took place in Yekaterinburg, a rugged backward city in the Ural region, where they were savagely executed at the order sent by Vladimir Lenin, the devil incarnate, who now sat at the top of the power structure in Russia. A designate read the order to Nicholas as he sat with his family in a crowded six by five meter basement room late at night to which they were herded, with no conception of the hideous end momentarily to befall them."

'Nikolai Alexandrovich, in view of the fact that your relatives are continuing their attack on Soviet Russia, the Ural Executive Committee has decided to execute you.'

'What! What!'

"These were the last words to leave the mouth of Nicholas II, Czar of Russia. The executioners raised their weapons and commenced firing, the Czar killed first from a bullet to the head, and then the Empress. Shots were fired chaotically until the whole of the intended victims had fallen. Several more shots were fired and the doors opened to clear away the smoke. There were yet some survivors, stabbed to death with bayonets, the three beautiful young girls, Tatiana, Olga, and Maria not withstanding who were carrying a certain trifle of diamonds sewn into their clothing, and therefore somewhat protected from the bullets. And on them the bayonets were used. Thus, a horrible and primitive inhuman bloodbath unfolded that night in Mother Russia, which has become famous in history.

I now turn to Maria Feodorovna, the former Empress of Russia, mother of Nicholas, who escaped earlier to the Ukraine to the summer palace in Yalta on the Black Sea.

Warned to leave Saint Petersburg a year in advance of the execution, she now received new warnings that the Bolsheviks posed a danger to her life. For a while it appeared that the great distance from Saint Petersburg to the South assured her of relative safety but with the Bolsheviks edging closer that strategy veered into collapse. Consequently, the King of England, first cousin to Nicholas, and whose wife was Maria Feodorovna's sister, ordered the HMS Marlborough to Yalta to rescue her, as well as others of the Imperial Family; and there were others still, though I am without their names or titles. The Empress objected to boarding the ship at Yalta, so as an alternate, the officer of the ship in charge chose to cruise a few miles along the coast to Koriez to intercept his royal guest. Mappings of the Black Sea show that Koriez is a little cove not far from Harax, the Empress's summer palace, the likely reason she required the vessel to anchor there for her and her entourage to come aboard.

I have copies in my files of some of the letters that the Empress wrote to her loved ones during this indescribably painful time of her stay at Yalta. Here, you can read this one if you wish. I sometimes carry it in my attaché case and last night I dug it out anticipating this very discussion with you. It concerns a terribly agonizing experience for the Empress, this being that her son Nicholas and family were incarcerated by the Bolsheviks, and that he and the entire family were in danger. You will notice the date November 21, 1917, the last letter that ever supposedly made its way to Nicholas from his mother.

> *'My dear Nicky. I have received your letter of October 27 which has filled me with joy. I cannot find words to express my feelings and thank you with all my heart, my dear.*
>
> *You know that my thoughts and prayers never leave you. I think of you day and night and sometimes I feel so sick of heart that I believe I cannot bear it any longer. But God is merciful. He will give us strength for coping with this terrible ordeal. Thank goodness you are all well and that at least you are together and in comfort. A year has gone by already since you and darling Alexei came to see me at Kieff. Who could have thought of all that was in store for us, and what we should have to go through? It is unbelievable. I live only in my memories of the happy past and try as much as possible to forget the present nightmare.'*

The Bolsheviks murdered the family July 17, 1918, the Empress taken aboard the British rescue vessel on the date of April 7, 1919, or near that date. It is supposed by some historians that news transferred to her of the execution much before this date but for the longest, for the rest of her life some have written, she refused to believe that her son and his family were dead. On the other hand, it is said that eventually she faced the grim truth of reality and acknowledged that they no longer were alive."

"I am sorrow for the family; immensely touched, and I am grieved over the suffering of the Empress. I wish so that I could have stood at her side to offer comfort," said Mrs. Narvanna with sinking voice.

That afternoon Darya and Mrs. Narvanna left on a mother and daughter shopping spree, driving to a popular mall on the east side of Baltimore where Mrs. Narvanna did her usual purchases and while on the same trip stopping off to attend to an agenda of business she had forestalled for an inappropriate length she said. Darya saw no need to tell me of the minute particulars of their trip but bought a sweater which over my weakly contrived objections she insisted I accept and had her way. I had stayed behind, circling the lush grounds which fascinated me to no end no matter in which direction my eyes turned and sat on the tiny settee on the edge of the walkway overlooking the Chesapeake, "a grand body of water," I kept thinking. Eventually I decided to return to the mansion a short piece away, first circling the periphery—going from back to front and front to back—and this enabled me to study the structure with the most assiduous scrutiny. As I looked ever closer, I discovered that the building process did not take place all at once, annexes to the original of varying styles constructed at staggered intervals over the years. Up until then, I had not viewed the interior with as much incisiveness as I wished and with voracious interest entered the expansive living room where a magnificent chandelier hung glitteringly from the vaulting, which at its apex measured a great distance from floor level. In this sumptuous space people would gather that evening, friends and relatives of the Narvanna's, invited to partake of a lavish dinner and each enjoy one another and trade subjective opinions of Darya's friend from the university. Already I had begun to dread the occasion, even as early as the previous day.

With every piece of information, from the least word sometimes spoken, I began to weave together why this family had ascended to such opulent heights. Half Jewish blood flowed through the veins of Darya's father, with her mother being pure blooded Serbian, deriving from a family of nobility and old money, who yet considered herself European. Mr. Narvanna's grandmother and her husband were somehow linked to the Oppenheimer families whose inception is traceable to Jewish Germanic strains as far back as the seventeen hundreds. Through the Oppenheimer family chain Mr. Narvanna currently profited from the goldfields of South Africa. Not at all did I surmise that I had anywhere near the full compliment of answers but those that I had woven together were proof that I now strode in the midst of lofty wealth. If I sought to unravel a complexity of this family I merely needed to ask Darya, who freely supplied that which I sought to know, not leaving out the minutest granule unless she wasn't asked. Once I failed to ask and Jeremy filled me in instead, this being something of a happenstance that he brought it up. I had been talking to him with regard to what was surely a profoundly high expense of running the Narvanna household, of which he in guarded voice hardly above a whisper remarked to me that where interior decorations were concerned as well as the purchase of clothes for the two women, the matter of cost never surfaced or in any event he'd never heard it discussed or even slightly mentioned.

"You mean there is no budgetary amount set on refinements of that purpose?"

"I am quite sure of it."

"I'm flabbergasted! That sounds dangerously precarious, terribly disconcerting if it were me, not to know up front the cost of an article that I intended to buy."

The family members referred to the coming evening as the evening of the ball, albeit no ball was to be had, only a dinner, but definitely a lavish beautiful dinner. The guests started to pour in soon after six o'clock, the ladies adorned in colorful evening dresses and the men looking pert and smart in their finest suits. By and large their children were with them. What should I say of this gathering of people? Mixed, of course, the ages ranging from the very young to the old. I noticed an assemblage of girls of Darya's age, a number of them close friends who knew her since grade school days. Mr. and Mrs. Narvanna stood at the doorway greeting. "Good evening Mr. and Mrs.—. We are so glad you are here." Close friends and relatives were extended greetings much less formally. Darya joined her parents sporadically, which made for a good impression on the guests, for after all she existed in their reasoning as the most singular cause of their attending. Suavely clad in a white evening dress Mrs. Narvanna was the epitome of elegance. Darya fitted perfectly in a lovely dress of black, a gorgeous design with a red sash pulled around her waist. Nothing daring. Her locks fell to her shoulders. There is no alternative for describing her: she looked remarkably beautiful. And as the two of them, Darya and her mother, stood side by side people spoke of the striking figures they made.

Foods of great quantity and varying choices weighted the tables, three tables arranged in tandem, each in no manner of ordinary length. At the behest of Mrs. Narvanna, Jeremy ordered in catered food delivered by professionals from the city who depended on him to assist them. In my perception all seemed so easily done, almost effortless, an illusion of course since such undertakings are never easy; but they are made easier if the doers are skilled and experienced and finely trained. The guests filled their own plates, this together with securing their own drink and found a place among many places to sit and eat, the plaza chosen above all others. It appealed to most everyone because of the view from that vantage point of the Chespeake, but also because of the live burning torches emplaced on the rock wall that formed the periphery and the chaise lounges that offered lean to comfort. Some of the guests were uncles and aunts and cousins and they, combined with the other guests, summed to a total of nearly sixty turning up for the affair. The chatter and excitement had risen in proportion to the increasing populace flowing through the doorway. The children flocked to Darya, clasping her hand and kissing her cheeks and lips. You could tell they saw her as a beautiful young woman. Once when she kneeled closely to a little twelve month old the child suddenly touched her face to Darya's and sucked Darya's lower lip in her mouth as if nursing. Darya laughed with exuberance, practically cackling, which wasn't normal for her and squeezed and kissed the child repeatedly with loving tenderness. It touched me. I'd never seen her in this light. I searched for words. "Nothing is as powerful in nature as the mother's instinct to protect and love her young. Lucky is the child who is born one day of her flesh and blood." Once a baby who belonged to her cousin a few years older than herself burst into crying which she lifted from her mother's arms and carried to another room. She must have somehow invented a means for quieting the child's distress, for I heard nothing more. When she reemerged she said the child now slept. "Poor little thing. She was just overwrought from the chatter and buzz."

She stayed close to me as much as protocol allowed, guarding I supposed against my becoming overly used as a target of novelty and exploration. As they came forward from time to time folks introduced themselves, briefly chatting and uttering the conventional niceties, the usual waste words but appreciated, expressing how very glad they were to meet someone so close to Darya at the university in the years since she had enrolled. My temptation stayed silent to weave in a correction that she had beaten me there by a year but deemed it of no use. A band played in the great living room over in an area in proximity to the chandelier and another on the plaza, not large ensembles, merely combos of four or five pieces. They played mainly pop tunes, the same as were played at the Cubs Nest. Darya tugged at me once to dance with her; to a slow tune, the only kind allowed. Since there were older people looking on as well as the children she chose not to lower her face against my shoulder. We stood at arms length. When she smiled it beheld her inner thinking. "I wish it were that you could hold me close but you cannot, darn it." During this same interlude but with a different musical arrangement Mr. Narvanna approached us and led her away. They danced well together. He appeared to have been trained. They were an elegant father and daughter pair. The girls kept begging Darya to play something on the violin, with the band giving support. She shied away until Mrs. Narvanna finally persuaded her to do at least one composition. "The folks here are our guests Darya, you owe it." She played *La Paloma,* talentedly done, and amazed me with her capability, as well as all others viewing us from where they stood, moreso those who were hearing her perform for the first time. Even a novice critic of music would have responded with admiration at the sophistication with which she held the violin with delicate finesse against and under her chin, yet without detracting from the sensuality of her nice neck and the profile of her lovely Semitic face. The night wore on, some of the guests leaving though the majority stayed. The hour hand now approached ten o'clock. After the intermission, the bands again began to play and I found myself suddenly sitting in a Victorian high back implaced in one of the reclusive alcoves sipping a glass of punch when a lady approached whose age I estimated at sixty years. She was graying, well finished, and spoke with cultured distinction. I pictured her as a thoroughly attractive woman in younger years and even presently exhibited a certain quality of good looks. She'd kept her weight down. I knew instinctually that she had selected me as her principal target of interest.

"Will you sit down," I invited, as she stopped in front of me?

"Thank you. I will"

Chapter 49

IMMEDIATELY AFTER we'd introduced ourselves, she as Carlotta Asbury and I as Ramsey Maynard, she uncloaked an impulse that had clung to her all evening to speak with me but said I always seemed occupied with a guest. Right away I decided she wasn't typical of the blend of folks whose acquaintance I so far had met, which is prominently why I recall her.

"I'm sorry for your trouble. But you have caught up with me now. And I am at your disposal."

"You're at Chicago University. I'm an alumnus. I hear you are seeking a degree in literature."

"I am and I don't need to guess that it surely was Darya Narvanna who let you in on the secret."

"She did," she said in proud affirmation. "She's a wonderful girl. I've known her since she was a tot. I'm a distant aunt. My, she has changed."

"I'm sure. But I know nothing of her early period as a tot. So, I don't know to what extent she's changed." I trusted that she interpreted my last line in the context of lightful play.

"No, of course not. You were a tot yourself. When did you meet her?"

"My first year in college. Right on the beginning of the school year."

"She's graduating this June. Are you?"

"No. I'm only a junior. I have a year to go."

"She's older than you."

"No, no. I'm two years older than her, almost three. Well, no, let me see. Maybe four. I commenced my college career a little late."

"Now that she's graduating she has to be spinning around in her head what she is to do with herself over the next year, or further I should qualify." Her eyes narrowed as she peered over at me with a kind of wince in one of her cheeks that bespoke that I knew the answer.

"I presume she might take a position with a corporation of a well known name. She's an ideal for public relations, or even international relations. Or many things. And she's a whiz at math. Her talents are pretty rare. Wherever she lands she'll score near the top."

"Easy to see. Isn't it? But I'm not inclined to side that she'll stand still long enough for steady work. There's a restless seed still inside her. She's yet a young fawn, at least to me she is, and harbors a yearning to spread her wings to somewhere out there, seeing foreign ports and strange lands. She just may well do those things too. She's built of grit and then some. Once I took her to a circus in Baltimore when she stood no taller than a puppy and she fell off the merry go round, badly scuffing her knees, ugly injuries. They had to hurt, and awfully. But she never once cried, even when the doctor sewed them up. That's the way she is. She never cries."

"I'll declare" As I shuttled back to our few years together I concluded that I had never seen her cry either, but that of course by the time she met me she was many years past childhood. I went on.

"Well, going abroad like what you've mentioned is intriguing I must say?"

"It is," she said with a flourish. "I wish I were young again. I'd travel around the world nonstop."

"You can still do that."

"I'm afraid not. I've crossed the Rubicon. Well, not that really. I'm still young enough. The fact is I'd rather do other things. At least for now."

"Where have you traveled? "

"The furthest and best trip I ever took was to Spain, to Granada."

"Ummmm. Spain. Did you like it? Did you stay long?"

"I loved it. I stayed six months. The young Spanish men fascinated me and I fell in love with one for awhile and might have kept it up but I discovered that I must leave and come home."

"Why?"

"I ran out of money."

"Money was stronger than love? Was that it?"

"I didn't say that." While uttering these remarks she dropped her head toward her lap then raised it with a pensive grin. "But I've fibbed to you. Money wasn't the reason I left. He lied to me about another woman or several. I accused him of two timing and he said no that wasn't so but finally admitted the truth. That's when I lit out back here."

She would have kept talking without deceleration and without end I thought, considering the way she now had wound up to a peak of arousal, but Mrs. Narvanna interceded and led her away under the guise that she must speak with her about a matter of which there was absolutely no latitude for delay. The guests at this stage began to bid goodnight in sizeable extractions and very few remained. I took it that Mrs. Narvanna feared Mrs. Asbury would start to indulge in conversation with someone else after finishing with me and prolong the evening. Time now had marched on, time for everyone to leave and it was hopefiul in Mrs. Narvanna's revolving that the party would soon end. She needed to retire and prepare to drive Darya and me to the airport the next morning departing at seven o'clock.

With the last of those to leave that evening there suddenly descended a vast emptiness in the vaccuum which replaced the gaiety of all that just passed. Strangely, in my psyche I likened it to an omen that foretold of something moving to an end which would never pass that way again. That night, with the aid of candle glow, I lay in my bed with eyes roving the décor of the splendid room and wondered of many things. "How awesomely different is this splendid ponderous home from the plain and diminutive one in which my mother lives and the one in which I grew up, what are the expectations of this great and opulent family of me, how could I ever possibly fit into their mores of living, is it at the divination of fate that I am here, how can I someday, not now, but someday not break Darya's heart by revealing to her what she does not know, the revelation of the name Nenia, who irrepressibly lives in my soul."

Not long thereafter, when the hour had slipped past midnight and sleep so far evasive, a knock sounded on my door of the faintest and then the door edged stealthily open. It was Darya, clad in her sleeping gown. The nightlight glowed from across the room, making her easily seen, but the incomprehensible lightness of her footfall wafted to my hearing almost with non existence as she moved toward my bedside. Once there she reached with supple hands that I had held times innumerable, and they mine, and pulled back the covers and lay beside me. She proceeded quickly into why she was there. It wasn't for the usual reason. It happened so unexpectedly.

"Has it been difficult?"

"Difficult?"

"Yes. Your being amidst this strangeness?"

"No not difficult. But I, well, why do you ask?"

"At times you've been so quiet, especially when we're alone. Sometimes open and buoyant but sometimes no more to say than a lamb. You've seemed lost in something with thoughts far away."

"It was nothing." I lied. I wished deep within me that I hadn't had to. But telling the truth would have proved worse.

"Nothing, you say. Be truthful. What did you think this was all about, a contrived sweetening of a love affair, a prelude to marriage? I have feared that a notion of that guise has preyed upon you."

"I don't guess I have thought of that one way or another. My stay has been nothing less than perfect, I can say that, and I'm indebted to you for asking me to join you here in this wondrous setting."

"You're ducking the point," she said with soft tender voice, at the same time touching my shoulder caressingly. "Let me be truthful with you my darling. You were not invited here with a design to bait and trap you as I somehow think you feel you were. I love you without limits, down into my very soul, but I know well that love you cannot force or push or cunningly lure. I only hope that some day I can claim your heart because it wants me to claim it. I realize that I am speaking plainly, too hastily perhaps, but am convinced that better to say what I want to say now rather than later or not at all. And I will add to this that my mother adores you and welcomes you with open arms to take a permanent place in this family." I replied that the stars above did not hold that as likely, not for the present anyway, that now my sights were set on working my way toward something vague, in other words trying to find myself, the same as her, and that time was of essence for determining how it worked out in the end.

After that I don't think I said anything else, nor even tried, choosing to listen to her low sweet musical voice as she turned to other things, but no gain would emerge from what she might additionally say or was saying. The significant things were said already. Laying my hand softly on her bosom I felt the easy rhythm of her breathing and in the nightly glow looked into her face of exquisite beauty and kissed her tresses, luxuriant and fascinating. Sometimes we did not talk at all, during which I silently explained to myself that He up there, in the finality, would work everything out, and then not meaning to slipped and returned to where we had left off. "Let us not make this complex. Neither let us rush. Let us take each day at a time and render thanks for the wonderful few years we've had together. The future for me, as I envision it, will slowly mature, filled with hard work and struggle over the next few years and a goal that I cannot fathom clearly. And I can't begin to know when I'll get there."

"I know that. And you are wise to look at things as you do. I have not meant to overly concern you by coming here tonight but I felt a need to say what I said. It was time."

The night did not end there. But neither did we make love. We talked and spun various ideas and thoughts for the longest and when I awakened dawn had broken, Darya no longer beside me. Jeremy sang and stirred in the kitchen. The clock on the mantle read six thirty. With but minimal pause I left my bed and dressed and went to the nook where the others were waiting. Jeremy served breakfast, asking everyone in advance for an input as to the food he ought to prepare, Mr. Narvanna and myself selecting ham and eggs and coffee, and Darya and her mother ordering toast and coffee and sugar free strawberry jam. Mrs. Narvanna said she had decided not to drive after all, opting after contemplating the negative aspects of it to let the regular chauffer do the driving in order to allow her to better indulge the sights and participate more freely in the back and forth conversational talk. I liked Darya's choice of dress and she knew I liked it. She beamed when I offered a compliment. She had selected a stylish emerald green suit with something of a beret on her head that did not altogether match her suit but sufficed as an approximate. I supposed that the style of her wear and the way she appeared in it would have been called chic by experts of fashion design. She looked executive, actually. I'd never seen her in a suit before and it dawned easily on me, as it often did, that some day she would ascend to the headship of her father's vast enterprise if she but chose. Mrs. Narvanna dressed in clothing the complete opposite of Darya's, perhaps a stitch more on the elegant side, such being a tasteful red suit adorned with a white ruffled collar and a coat that slightly opened in front. The cuffs were trimmed in black. Mr. Narvanna said goodbye to each of us on finishing his breakfast, careful especially to invite me back and assured emphatically that they were terribly gladdened by my presence, then left for his office. Shortly the rest of us would leave as well. The limousine waited, packed already with our belongings, the chauffer with Jeremy's assistance caring for this matter sometime before we were ready to go. Mrs. Narvanna elected to sit up front by the chauffer and Darya and I sat in back. As we pulled away something stirred within me to take one quick glance at the grand home which now began to lie behind us, for I nurtured the feeling that I might never see it again. Upon my taking that glance I knew that Darya saw it and understood it but hoped that she wouldn't ask me why. The chauffer in accord with Mrs. Narvanna's instructions turned onto a route way unlike the one on which we came. Somehow, we averted the towering gate. But all in all everything else unfolded much the same; the abundance of flowers in bloom, the tall oaks and elms and cedars flaunting their majestic beauty, and the buildings as we began to enter the city standing tall and noble, showing off their stately windows of clear and tinted glass. Mrs. Narvanna delightedly observed the pretty sights on the roadway, mainly the flowers, and said if we were going home she'd stop and pick some, enough for making a bouquet at the minimum. The limousine hummed along, moving as softly as a cloud, and I very much enjoyed the ride, except I kept thinking that Darya seemed a little tight, reserved, perhaps emanating from the late hour visit to my room the night before. But I figured in short order that I had led myself wrongly, that I had overconcluded. Mrs. Narvanna seemed not tight but somewhat distant though extraordinarily polite and friendly and once again I premised that my imagination stood purely at fault and certainly that her demeanor, however it came to me, should in no way relate to Darya's late hour visit to my room. I knew that Darya wouldn't have ventured into the subject with her. We reached the airport with time to spare, the chauffer beginning to unload our things. Mrs. Narvanna entered the terminal lobby with us and directly before we crossed through the passenger gate to the plane she pulled me to her and gave me a hug and a pat with words delivered in a tone of sincerity and especial warmth that urged me to come back soon to visit. I assured her I would. As she let go of me my eyes met Darya's, smiling as she witnessed the affinity coexisting between myself and her mother. And then Mrs. Narvanna said in an accent of either playfulness or moderate seriousness, and I could not discern which, "Oh, don't forget to attend Darya's graduation. You won't will you?"

"You can bet your life I won't."

The flight from Baltimore to Chicago amounted to no more than a blimp's worth, but not so swift as to prevent my peering out the window at the checkered fields of the Illinois landscape, at the vast fields of knee high corn with leaves of magnificent green. I nodded to Darya to have a look, which necessitated her leaning against me. She abruptly did as I suggested, supplemented with an "Ahhh, what a scene," almost pushing me over, which I muchly liked in that it meant that we were on the best of terms again and that her discontentedness had gotten resolved, if ever it existed at all.

"Do you like to fly?" I asked shortly in advance of our landing, perhaps as a means of forcing converstion.

"I do. It's the best way to travel. Do you?"

"Not exactly. I fly because I have to. My job you know."

"When you come see me you'll have to drive. It's not very far."

"No, not far at all. Will you meet me at the big gate and let me in?"

A lovely burst of laughter sprang into the open. "Yes indeed."

Naturally, we covered a good many other topics, as many as time allowed, but it allowed very little. The plane soon set down.

The next two weeks transitioned into a period of both euphoria and sadness, where the latter dominated over the former. The students buzzed with excitement over the upcoming graduation, some graduating while others close to them were not but elated to know their friends were. Bertinelli, Aaron, and Darya were among those walking the line and I felt great happiness for them. But I also had to meet the obligations of my own activities, carrying out my assignments for Mr. Yazstremski and immersed in last minute cramming for my final exams of the semester. My trip to Darya's home in Baltimore hadn't entirely faded but I kept it confined to the back of my mind and recalled it in short lived spurts from time to time. I dug hard into my studies and begrudgingly gave time to other things, except for Andrea, who devotedly stuck immovably close to pre test me for my math and physics exams.

At some place in that intermission, I opened a letter from my mother bearing the unexpected news that Melissa's husband not too many weeks past had died suddenly and that the knowledge of it left everybody in shock. She attended the funeral and burial. She said in the same letter that Madeline's health had started to fail and that the doctors had expected she would have left this world long before Melissa's husband. But said further that life worked that way, full of calamities unanticipated as written in Ecclesiastes, and that no one knows when his life is to end.

Since I had to absent myself from the funeral I decided to write Melissa a letter in atonement for my not attending.

"Dear Melissa, I am shocked at your husband's passing. I wasn't aware of his illness until the receipt of my mother's most recent letter. Please accept my sorrow and every kind wish that you will find a way to work through this unfortunate event of your life. I wish I could have been there to offer comfort to you and the rest of the family.

Stay brave and uplifted. The Lord has a way of seeing his people through the dark hours.

With love, Ramsey"

I hoped that I had appropriately offered comfort but wasn't sure I used the right words. Whether I had or not my best reasoning convinced me that I'd expressed myself sincerely and that this was the thing that counted.

And then in addition to my mother's, another letter cropped up within the next few days. It was from Leland.

"See you the last week of June. Is it okay?"

"Splendid. Please do it earlier if you can," I answered in my return and said no more. I knew he would telephone for mapping out the details, or else I would telephone him.

The graduation exercise had dwindled down to two days away when Aaron and Darya cornered me at breakfast, letting me know they were treating me to dinner that evening at a favorite place on lakeside. They'd recently discovered it. "Its old country Italianate, pure native, you'll flip at its décor," said Darya, "and the food is top of the heap and the rich red wine is sweet and tasty, and you'll find it quite private." I found her praise of the place well said, decorous, small, and unbothered by overcrowding. We took a booth near the rear where there were very broad windows that allowed for an unimpeded view of the water and the shoreline lights. Quite small art forms were inscribed near the periphery of the windows which were done in loops and swells and scores of abstract characterizations, none of this making sense but finally I did see one that I understood, an imitation of a sea gull flying over the coastline. We stayed late, until three in the morning, no one wanting to give it up, perhaps me not wanting to more than they. The impending loneliness already had set in.

"Well guy," said Aaron who tried to infuse zest into the party, "you'll have that big old house to yourself this fall, you and a bunch of young bucks."

"Yeah." That's all that rushed to me right then. I'd envisioned for some time the image to which he alluded.

Consolingly Darya reached and squeezed my hand. "But you'll deal with it. Pretty soon you will have developed a whole new company of friends."

"I doubt that. Not like the old ones. I'm showing the immature side of my Freudian complex I have to admit but I don't even like to think of it."

It was here that Aaron asked if Andrea were staying on for summer school, which I wished he hadn't—I think he caught Darya's attention; I thoughtfully didn't look over to see—to which I answered that it was my understanding that she planned to fly directly home after the graduating exercises.

As we left late that night or early morning we promised to write and telephone and visit, but it streamed through me that well intentioned sentiments of this weaving were oft spoken by friends ad infinitum, only to fade over time, particularly a long span of time, and that we might even forget one another's names, provided we lived long enough. They both affirmed more than once what my friendship had meant to them, and when Darya said it there was more than an ordinary inflection.

As I should have seen coming another outing began to unfold for the next evening, which reluctantly I had to postpone. Mr. and Mrs. Narvanna arrived in the city ahead of time and Darya passed on to me that they wanted to treat me to dinner, a sort of goodbye on Darya's behalf. In truth a pre obligation already was on my docket that I felt I should absolutely fulfill for Mr. Yazstremski and plead that I couldn't accept. He had asked me to fly to Atlanta, the first time ever that I had delivered a set of depositions there, and I didn't dare disappoint him. But in as much as I planned to return to Chicago that evening, though late, I'd welcome the opportunity to join them at their hotel for breakfast the next morning as early or as late as pleased them. Darya smoothly attended to the arrangement, relaying that they understood and gladly looked forward to seeing me. She couldn't come with them because her hands were full with graduation preparations.

At breakfast Mrs. Narvanna ate light, which I conjectured a natural tendency or an adopted trait of social etiquette. Her husband ate heartily as did I. She mentioned on the beginning how they delighted at my being with them in their home and said in the same breath of speech that since seeing me she acquired a portrait of medieval vintage that she felt certain I would like. Her husband demonstrated an interest but kept quiet. In questions of art and poetry and definitely music he lacked substantially but held firm opinions, which he kept to himself in deference to his wife whom he heralded as an impresario in these spheres, and I held with not a smidgeon of doubt that she was. Throughout the Baltimore community the people at large recognized her as a force for promoting art displays of variegated themes. On politics her husband was well grounded. But on this morning she had no room on her agenda for the subject of politics. While looking into my eyes with a softened smile she spoke of her impending trip to Wolf Trap in Washington to attend a symphony then turned to an abbreviation of lighter topics in between and then to something else, a venting of despair over the war raging in Vietnam. "Think of it Ramsey. So many beautiful things to see and do in life, for example going to Wolf Trap, and here we are sending our young boys off to fight and die in some country we've only recently learned is on the world map and for a cause that isn't convincingly explained by our leaders. "Ah me," she sighed. "What can we do? We want everything perfect, free of controversy, free of evil, and yes, free of war, don't we, but that is unattainable. The bad is with us as much as the good and the good is with us as much as the bad. Life is made up of light and shade." Likely because I so far had stayed free of the draft owing to my college enrollment, I opened my internals that I felt guilty for not already joining my American compatriots in the struggle. With a voice of convincing opinion Mrs. Narvanna spoke up in my defense. "You're simply going by the law Ramsey. Anyone would do that."

My respect and admiration for the lady towered to even loftier heights that morning as it had continued to tower from the first day I met her. "Not only is she endowed of intellect that draws one's attention quickly to her," it fell upon me, "she is blessed as well with a soul that is as compassionate as it is caring."

Chapter 50

THE SUN rose aloft that morning with a fiery glow of red and gold, evincing the promise of a perfect day. At ten o'clock in the great chapel, the sunrays streaming through the massive windows, the graduates stood in shimmering robes of blue trimmed in gold and one by one proudly stepped forward to receive their diplomas, while their parents sat dotingly in an area distinctly reserved for them and viewed it all with beaming faces. I sat watching with Andrea and Balboni from somewhere in the perimeter set aside for non-graduating students wishing to attend the exercise. I stayed busy taking photographs, while at recurring opportunities Andrea snatched the camera away from me claiming she'd spotted something of rarity she simply must not let escape. After the ceremony the parents flooded the stage to embrace and congratulate their children, such being the case with Aaron's and Darya's, although if my remembrance has not deserted me too terribly Bertinelli's parents weren't there. When the crowd on the stage largely cleared away I hastened forward and hugged all three, Darya, Aaron, and Bertinelli, and gave them my heartfelt congratulations. At that, we rather unconsciously gathered in a circle and held hands as if forming a kind of everlasting bond. It was something of a union between us that is hard to explain. I was sure that their thoughts were very nearly the same as mine, that "never again will we likely gather together like this, so etch the image of it deeply in that place in your brain which governs the functioning of your memory complex." On the last Aaron clowningly nudged me and asked if I captured his best profile when I shot photos with my camera. By and large everyone evinced smiles of happiness but the mood of elation soon would undergo a painful transition and there were certain of us who braced ourselves for it though in vain. That afternoon Darya would leave with her parents for home and at two o'clock, the limousine driven by the Narvanna's chauffer already was stationed in front of the fraternity house. At the time I busied myself helping Darya with the last of her packing. She had sunk to a low ebb and I equally. I hadn't fully realized in advance how dreadfully sad this goodbye would hurt. Lifting her encasement, the very last piece which she decided to carry on her own, she started for the door, and then stopped, and when turning to me set it down and tears began to fall. She could cry after all. Leaning heavily into my breast she sobbed uncontrollably. I think I cried with her. I know I did. I reached to pick up her encasement but never made it.

"No. Don't. Please. I'll take it. I don't want you to come with me to the car. It'll just make things worse."

And with that she picked it up herself and left through the fraternity house doorway and with but few steps climbed into the back seat of the waiting vehicle. Going to the window I watched the limousine roll away, trying to imagine Darya's grief. The lump in my throat I knew was there for awhile. "Damn" I uttered, "is this what college is all about, making friends for three or four years and then saying goodbye. Perhaps forever. Why are things as they are?"

Bertinelli, after stopping by to bid me farewell left late that afternoon for his parents' home in Virginia near Washington D. C., so Aaron was the last of my bosom friends of the fraternity house to whom I would say goodbye. Aaron's father and mother wanted to take us to dinner together, a sentimental sort of token in honor of two young men who'd so tightly entwined over the past three years. They met us where they sometimes did when on visit, an unpretentious but busy little Greek restaurant on lake side that served plates of steamy vegetables and hot soup, a gruel of some concoction, the taste of which seemed more than ordinarily pleasing to Mr. Stylman. "Very good," he said, "it warms the insides"

"Southern talk," I thought, "maybe just to please me."

I'd missed speaking to them at the graduation exercises. Ever the lady, in many ways Mrs. Stylman duplicated Mrs. Narvanna's civilities and grace. Naturally enough it suddenly swept upon me to compare these two gracious women with the haughty Madeline Monett who stood a far cry from attaining to their stature. But as she mingled with the people of our small town, and hers, she nonetheless saw herself as a woman both honored and charming. "What a pity," it alighted on me, "that she missed mingling with these ladies during her life's span, for if she had something valuable might have rubbed off on her."

Seeing the Stylman's precipitated a most gladdened feeling. It had been a while. Mrs. Stylman hugged me and said that next to her son she in her heart claimed me as her favorite boy. Should I have been a girl I think I might have giggled.

"It's sad that you and Aaron are separating from one another," she quietly let out in a veiled affectation of sorrow.

"They're not leaving one another, dear," Mr. Stylman cut in. "They're just starting out on different journeys. No telling what experiences they'll undergo in their lives. Granted, they'll land in different camps because they're not trained in the same fields but they'll stay in touch. They'll keep up with one another."

On this occasion especially Mr. Stylman took front and center stage and Mrs. Stylman in no way minded. She preferred to stay in the shadows. He asked but a minimum of that which had to do with our college careers, hardly any pursuant to Aaron's which now had ended, but a dash more about mine which I would finish in another year. He chose in the main to exude enthusiasm over the firm's plastics business and its growth in the burgeoning port of Hong Kong, China, then under British governance.

"We may just send Aaron over there to head up one of the firm's divisions. That's a good way for him to cut his teeth on the aggravations of management. The direct way of doing it but of course there's wisdom in moving into it slowly. I don't know. We'll see."

"Not the direct way honey, no, no, no," Mrs. Stylman hastily spoke up, angling a glance of sympathy at Aaron. "He's still young, practically a boy. He's in need of seasoning. You must have patience."

"I know, I know. That's what I actually meant," Mr. Stylman spoke softly back. He always spoke softly to her, plainly noticeable the first day I met them. His kindness to his wife impressed me. And then I became the object of his attention. "We might just send you there too Ramsey. We would right now, with Aaron, but you have the completion of your college degree hovering over you, and besides, you're doing too well in the firm. But someday. Who knows?"

Nothing but praise resided in my heart for what was no less than a splendid evening, more likened to a party than a goodbye dinner and it flattered me greatly that they had invited me. But as upbeat as everyone seemed there nonetheless was the presence of a sinking mood that tended to weigh on my spirits. This was the feeling that presided inside despite Aaron's antics of joke telling and reviving funny on campus scenes which helped me maintain a balance between lows and highs. On the last Mr. Stylman embarked on the refreshing idea of an emerging law office in Chicago. And without his mentioning it I put to logic that he might have me high on the list for a position with the new firm. But in his continuation, he left me unsure, for in summary he spoke that the installation of a new office still remained as only a remote possibility and that in the home office staff meeting of late talk did not point with any immediacy toward instituting his plan. I made no inquires. I listened, as I unvaryingly did when he addressed something pertaining to my position or job with his firm. To probe into the depth of what he for certain meant I would bide my time and tactfully approach Mr. Yazstremski for his notion of the plan materializing.

No more than seconds after the Stylman's let me out in front of the fraternity house and drove away my thoughts began to drift to Leland's impending visit, a fortunate thing for me since suddenly I found myself alone, not a soul else around, and the impact landed on me jarringly. The expansive lobby that once echoed with laughter now spoke with an entombed silence. I entertained no intention of attending classes that summer, reserving an opening for Leland in the near term and for Nenia later in August or September when she returned from Europe. I had agreed to watch after the fraternity house for the next few days since Mr. Yazstremski wouldn't need me right away and began to enumerate a list of things around the place that I should get done, on the outset dealing with the question of the availability of the food supply. I checked the kitchen and after discovering there were a goodly quantity of items that needed restocking, I wrote out a list and drove to the supermarket for the purchases. My second task was to inspect the rooms where the students had lived, finding nothing extraordinarily out of line, some messier than I liked, but acceptable. When I entered Darya's room, which I saved for last, I discovered as I expected the bed perfectly made up, the furnishings immaculately in place, and that she bought furniture spray on her own and meticulously shellacked every piece. She'd left a note, not conspicuously placed but enough showing that I detected it with comparative ease because my intuition jogged me that I would find one somewehere if I searched avidly enough. There it was. The corner of it peeped barely from under the tall Grecian vase that she used for maintaining fresh flowers. It read, "Yeah, you're lonely. If it's too much on you try telephoning."

I smiled inside. "And I just might."

I prepared a list to which I wanted the housekeeping corps to attend to right away and drove to the nearby maintenance headquarters where I handed it to the dispatcher. I urged him to see to it that cleaning and other chores were taken care of as soon as possible in that I expected a group of students to shortly arrive who had enrolled for the summer semester, and that they were lodging at the fraternity house.

On the third day, or maybe the fourth, the quietness suddenly imploded from the interruption of a familiar voice that vibrantly sounded from the front door entrance. "Ramsey," Andrea cried out, at the same time bursting toward me. She literally ran to my outstretched arms. She hadn't meant to return to campus until fall. Instantaneously I speculated that divine intervention somehow decided to play its hand, that maybe God in his great invisible sympathy was assuming a role. But in the end I attributed much of it to Andrea with the Lord standing close by. I shouldn't have been surprised in the least. That was just like her.

"My goodness, where did you spring from?" I asked in a vein of astonishment.

"I'm back from Louisiana. When I got there, I discovered that I was lonely, seized by the notion that I just had to spend my summer back here. My grandmother on seeing that something was wrong, and guessing what, took me in her arms and said, 'Child, if that's bothering you, you go on back up there and enjoy your friends.' I flew in thirty minutes ago."

"You were away two days. Only two days!"

"I leaned toward staying longer, all summer as you know, but I didn't. And isn't it a nice thing that I changed my mind. Apparently, you're all alone here as I have sensed."

"All alone. Yes I am. I have to tend the ship. At least for a few days."

"I see. Of course, Bertinelli is gone for good. So, they left it up to you following his departure. Who's to take over after you?"

"I don't know, except it's not me. I'm not enrolling this summer. I'm saving my time for a friend who's flying in from San Francisco for a two weeks stay."

"Leland?"

"Ha. I told you of him."

"Yes you did. More than once. When is he to get here?"

"In two weeks. Give or take."

"Good. I'll take care of you in the meanwhile. It's terribly lonely here with everyone gone."

"It is. And I must say that it's great to see you."

"The same here."

"But tell me. Why did you come back? Are you enrolling?"

"No I'm not. I have a research stipend with the department of physics and math. I didn't really mean to return. But as I said I got itchy and started thinking seriously of the amount the department offered. When I telephoned the department head that I strongly considered reporting for a continuation of my work and would work across the entire summer he said he and the entire staff welcomed me back. It wasn't so much for the money but for the challenge that I've done it, plus giving me something to do."

"Ah. That's fantastic. I'll know where to reach you with ease."

"Easier than that. I live next door, remember."

It showed in her every expression. She brimmed with happiness to see me and I her, but we were always happy to see one another, and it did not fall as a surprise to me, but as an expectation, when she suggested that on that same evening we treat ourselves at some agreeable place for dinner, one already familiar to us, and after that take in a movie. I accepted her suggestion without a second thought. My whole being, I told her, had begun to starve for socialization, particularly hers. It produced a giggle. For the next two weeks we shot here and there as if in a whirl, on the go constantly, to dinner, to a movie, to the beach, for the weather had warmed, to the Cubs Nest, riding the trolley throughout Chicago, on one evening taking in an opera performance, and on the weekend that followed driving a rented car all the way to Green Bay and back, equally caught up in a sensation of joy and exhilaration. I had always enjoyed her presence, it ran through me, but now I liked being with her even more. Now our time was free of constraints of any kind, yet even so, it did not evade my conscious for any length that eventually we'd have to come back to earth. She filled my heart with chatter and laughed at everything I said although what I said wasn't even half funny. She never let a moment escape without excitement. She kissed me whenever she wished, just as naturally as Nenia and Darya, warm lush kisses and I made her laugh with not the least of inhibition when I offered the compliment that her kisses were fantastic. "She is gorgeously beautiful," I said passionately to myself as I gazed upon her, "and infinitely intelligent" and wondered why of all things available to her in this world she saw something in me, yet realized that she did. Love overflowed in her heart for me and I knew that too. I had long known that, and it dawned on me also that if only I had met her first instead of Nenia the impending outcome that seemed uneraseably destined with Nenia would have sustained a reversal, but I did not meet her first and so it was with her as it was with Darya. Nenia had lived inside my heart for a very long while. And Andrea did not know. And I would not tell her, never. It was nowhere in me to tell her.

Glancing at the calendar one day I saw the date approaching for Leland's arrival at the airport, a reminder that wasn't essential. Exactly when his plane would land had revolved in my brain every single day, the date and time set down in his last letter and I kept reciting these particulars with the steadiness of an obsession. In due time I drove to the airport to meet him, though not alone. Andrea went with me. And drove. She insisted on going and I gladly agreed for her to join me. We waited in the lobby as Leland previously requested. I caught sight of him immediately as the escalator lowered to the first floor. I waved and yelled lowly, as lowly as I could without it amounting to a full fledged yell. It was too low for him to hear but on seeing me he vigorously returned the frenetic efforts of my hands to gain his notice and simultaneously broke into an enlarged grin. In something of a slow run or fast step we hastened toward one another in the crowded lobby and when we met enwrapped each other with happy hugging arms. With this ritual over we backed away and in the attitude of a kind of involuntary appraisal began to size one another up from head to toe.

"You've not changed an ounce," I let out, still excited, he echoing close to the same.

"You haven't either Amigo. Still the same guy. But I counted on that." I died laughing, people stopping and staring and Leland looking a tad puzzled until he unraveled what had triggered my outburst. "Oh Amigo. Yeah. Why did I do that? I haven't called you that in a while for sure. Son of a gun." We both just stood there, just laughing giddily, living it up and lost in a fantastic interlude of happiness.

We hugged again a time or two and rained words on one another in such quickened continuance that we struggled to understand them and had to ask for a clarification at times of what the other said. Finally, we settled into a calmer state and I then beckoned to Andrea standing nearby to join us whereon I introduced them. Needless to say, he was instantly drawn unquenchingly to her beauty, unable to keep his eyes off her, while pretending unaffectedness.

"How long will you stay?"

"Two weeks, if you can tolerate me that long, this of course including a run down to spend a day and night with Tatiana and Mr. Carney."

"Yeah. You have to do that. But otherwise, there's much on the plate that awaits us here."

"I know. Uh. Perhaps you would ride down there with me? Maybe."

"I'd love to. We'll see. I might have some flights scheduled for New York. Much depends. We'll see."

"When did you last rub shoulders with the people of our little town?" He spoke with his eyes inundated with a flood of images. I presumed that he mostly wondered of the changes that occurred since his departure, if any.

"It's been a while. I took time off this past Christmas to go and see my mother and brother and sisters, and to meander around and see old friends. But I missed seeing Ozzie and Cavanaugh. Sorry. I just didn't work it in. I did drop in on our beloved friends Tatiana and Mr. Carney. Things are pretty virtually the same. You know how a small town is. It takes a century before anything new can happen. Whenever I visit it's only for a short while and I don't expect to witness anything of significance cropping up. I'm mostly attracted to the old things, the way they were when we were growing up. I took a glance at our old school building when last there. I just happened to drive by and decided to pull over and do a splash of reminiscing, sitting there for a while pondering everything, especially noticing the entrance with its Roman arches, and then my eyes drifted over to the baseball field and guess what?"

"What?"

"I thought of you. And the good times we had playing there."

"I'll declare."

"Yeah. But what grabbed at me most was the memory of something we did as boys that likely didn't sit well with the townsfolk's but I guess they figured they couldn't do much to thwart us."

"I'm not sure I follow you."

"Well, we were short of players, as you recall, not enough to make up one team much less two. And no one to play against as a full team. Using our youthful ingenuity, we recruited some of the young Negro boys our age, boys we'd picked cotton with and fished with. We were revolutionaries Leland, right there in our small town. I recall one really fine player. They called him Fox, his family name. I've forgotten his surname, if I ever knew it. I thought then that if only the Negroes were better accepted he would have no trouble making it to the big leagues, maybe to the Cardinals. Every house hold, black or white, knew of Jackie Robinson but a towering roadblock still stood practically uncrossable; which young Negroes had to surmount in places like ours to make it to the big baseball leagues and while Brown versus Topeka was already incorporated into federal law by that date its impact needed time to take root. I'm proud to say that we sort of pioneered integration even though we hadn't the faintest clue of what we were doing. I'm glad we did it. And I think the young Negro guys very much appreciated our efforts and friendship. We did a good thing."

"We did Ramsey. A really good thing. And it wasn't all that long ago. But for sure and certain some jarring changes have sprung up since then. Who would have dreamed back in that era that black and white kids would soon sit side by side in that school house which gave us our kick off into the future? If the laws had stayed as they were chances are the whites would have walled themselves off from the Negroes forever. All the same, the laws were changed and didn't that turn our social system upside down."

Leland then returned to my earlier jibe that if something happened in our small town a century will have passed in attaining it and then adduced that I was correct, but that the same logic was applicable to any small town. "Not much is inspiring in a small town," he said, "because there's nothing there to produce it. You and I were lucky. We left and landed in a beehive of stimulation elsewhere. If we'd stayed on we might have dried up on the vine by now."

"Yeah."

Then Leland had more, his process of thought suddenly unraveled, giving somewhat of a scholarly treatise on the disadvantage accruing to a people living in a limited domain with a shortage of a variety of things to motivate them; then trouncing from there upon a narrative from his readings which argued that if a man is to acquire knowledge and fruitfulness then he must get born in some famous city, and then averred further that it is also necessary that this man is addicted to liberal arts and live in populations where he may have plenty of all sorts of books and sit among learned others and make inquiry of many particulars that may have otherwise escaped him.

"I like your oration," I asserted, "and to recapitulate, you are saying that should we have stayed put and not reestablished ourselves we might well have turned out like that vine devoid of water. Dried up."

"Ha. My logic says yes. What else is there to say?"

"But if we had stayed fixed and removed ourselves from obscurity by reading books and feasting on movies and attending operas in distant venues—even though facing trouble getting there—we would have not needed the many plusses of which you speak in a large bustling city. We would already have them by another means."

"Of course, my dear friend you are correct, provided steps were taken to supply ourselves with those enrichments which you identify. But the guiding final thought here, or fact, is that we didn't stay put and we both passionately believe we are better off for our choices."

We went to the Cubs Nest one night, Andrea happy and delighted to join us and it pleased me infinitely that she was present in as much as she brought along both diversity and charm so vital, certainly quite helpful, to the flow of conversational exchange. And she danced with Leland at various times throughout the evening, which he liked tremendously. I could tell. She obviously wasn't much excited about dancing with him but knew I wanted her to, a faint but hidden reluctance hiding behind that gorgeous face, which I recognized and she knew I did, but cooperated. While there, toward the last, we devised plans for the next day's agenda, from which an idea sprang from Andrea that boating on Lake Michigan would make for much pleasure and I agreed. Addicted to sailing, she stood ever ready for the excursion. I wasn't sure that Leland was acceptable to the suggestion since he lived in San Francisco, and thus blessed by the convenient access to that vast and popular body of water long known as the San Francisco Bay, and so it seemed to me that venturing onto Lake Michigan to him was not a tempting idea whatsoever. But it struck the guy with great favor, and he expressed that it was a tremendous idea, a tremendous idea because in my interpretation of the term he meant that it set in place a chance for him to spend the day in close proximity to Andrea. We would go sailing, of necessity renting a boat and hiring a middle aged experienced captain as well, since neither Leland nor I were capable of steering the vessel and neither was Andrea. I wished for Bertinelli. Andrea packed lunch and carried along an ice box of drinks. Attired in a bikini she posed a magnificent physique which I venture metaphorically knocked Leland's eyes out. And mine too. She particularly seemed to stand or sit next to me, and sometimes I reached my arm around her and pulled her close. Sometimes she kissed my cheek and I hoped that Leland hadn't seen because I wished it were that he enjoyed her as much as I. But not to the point of her kissing his cheek. In any event all went well enough in the social sense but not in regard to the weather, for when we'd eaten lunch the wind heaved sharply, the waves began to wallow, and we were far from port. Something of a chill surged through my stomach, the situation suddenly turning scary. We were all scared. The captain gave off a display of controllable calm but as I saw into his eyes I knew better, that he too felt anxious and in short order hurriedly started yanking at the sail ropes.

"Suddenly it's bad," I said to him, standing at that juncture on his immediate left.

"More than that. I was afraid of this. The confounded wind has gushed impatiently all morning. I saw it building earlier when I passed the downtown post office. The flag whipped every which way. I thought then that everything would calm down. But it's the opposite that's upon us. We'd better navigate this rig to safety," he muttered to himself while evincing the presence of unmistakable anxiety that he sought with the best within him to quieten.

I'd hoped that Leland and Andrea in no way heard him, anxious that what the captain said didn't upset them, and they didn't seem bothered, but had heard him. A seasoned veteran, the captain with supple maneuvering set the nose of the boat directly toward shoreline, his outward calm reassuring that he had control of the vessel and relieved by a slight I looked over at Leland and Andrea, finding that they were by now for the most part settled. We all had reason for apprehension, for the natives from experience proclaimed that the waters on any of the Great Lakes can unfurl a sudden and ferocious temperament, and were aware that entire freighter crews were known to have been lost, let alone pleasure seekers on the lighter crafts such as ours. I would read in not many years of the *Edmund Fitzgerald,* a freighter carrying a full cargo of ore pellets from Superior, Wisconsin near Duluth enroute to Detroit. It sank in a savage storm and twenty nine men were lost, down to the last one on board.

I kept busy with making the next day's plans for Leland, whose curiosity overflowed, no matter where I took him or whatever we did. I worried that we'd run out of time and therefore spoil his attempt to pay call on Tatiana and Mr. Carney but he assured me that he wouldn't let such a slip up happen. Andrea fretted a pout when I spoke to her that Leland and I were flying to New York the next day. "My usual business trip," I explained. She wished to go along but realized the impracticality of fitting her in. I obtained approval from Mr. Yazstremski for the company to pay Leland's fare yet deemed it imprudent to request the same for her. We were to stay overnight and leave back for Chicago the following day. While in New York Mr. Yazstremski treated us to dinner at a restaurant near the New York Stock Exchange and curious, asked Leland what his work at Kaiser entailed, with Leland providing that within the year past he'd worked mainly in the field of electronics and that it appeared likely he'd soon transfer to Edison. Near the ten o'clock hour of the next day Leland and I caught a taxi to Ellis Island. Since he once lived in New Jersey, very close to New York City, he vividly disclosed many of his memories of the famous island, and aspired to see it again.

"This is where my kindred landed Ramsey. You might say this is where I launched my citizenship papers for my rightful claim as an American."

"Ha. No claim to it. You got born on Americam soil just as I did."

"But my parents didn't."

On our way back to Chicago, the motors of the plane droned quietly with no undulations in flight. We exchanged a raft of thoughts with one another, as usual, some of which dealt with what each of us had done with our lives since last seeing one another, knowing that we'd miss some of the vitals but uncover them on a later try. And there were topics which veered a hundred and eighty degrees from any of those we'd already gone over, the name of Andrea never far away from entering the stream of conversation.

"She's gorgeous Ramsey. Absolutely gorgeous. Does she like you?"

"Ah, so so."

"Naw, naw. More than that. How long have you indulged her acquaintance?"

"Two years."

"I see. And she likes you. More than likes you. That's plain. But what happened to Nenia, the girl back home?"

"She's in France. She's teaching there."

"Is she coming back? That is, I—."

"She is. This fall. She has a job waiting for her in Saint Louis."

"Ah, I see. But are you still interested in her? She's a doll, very gorgeous. She and Andrea remind me of one another. Don't you think?"

"Well, I do. But they're not alike. Their personas aren't I should say. And the truth is I'm crazy over Nenia. I always have been. I plan to marry her some day."

"But you might marry Andrea. Might you not?"

"Not likely. Well, that's the hell of it. She's entangled with my soul and is a wonderful girl in every way as is obvious. But eventually I'll have to let her go, or maybe she'll just walk away. I lie awake at nights wondering of the outcome."

"I think I hear you telling me you're not sure of the outcome. Not entirely sure."

"No. I guess not."

"But Andrea, Ramsey, she's, she's so remarkable; the Good Lord doesn't make them like that anymore, I, I, well enough of that." What was it that he actually wanted to get across I asked myself, but as he had done I let it go at that.

I could have gone on to tell that my situation stirred worsely in my inner complex than I let on, that somewhere out there a beautiful young thing named Darya Narvanna lived and breathed and that I also was muchly interwoven with her but held it back. I figured that it might seem too fantastic for him to digest.

"Hmmm," something untelligible crossed over his lips.

There arose a momentary blankness to his face and words tended to fail him, now busily turning over that which he'd just heard. At last, he answered and I felt unordinarily surprised at how he saw it all as revealed in the unexpected nature of his calm and logical remarks.

"These things happen. That's the nature of our age, the age of relative youth and passion, where in the end there is regrettable heartbreak but in time that peters out and all is forgotten. But Andrea is immovably attached to you, and she's one splendid girl, a knockout, and honestly, I don't fathom that you'll discover it easy to overcome your dilemma."

"I don't either my great friend. But I'll have to."

"I'm no stranger to your quandary Ramsey. I'm sort of in a similar fix myself."

"Oh. How?"

"I've met this girl in San Francisco that I like a lot. We're thick. Yet there's also a charming girl in Sophia, Bulgaria that I met some time ago when I vacationed there. My mother is acquainted with her family and urges me with desperation to marry her. 'You should get married Leland,' she says, 'the next thing you know you'll zoom into your thirties.' She's of the notion that the girl is right for me in all major respects and her interest is whetted most keenly in that the girl is of my Christian faith, or in any event the faith of hers, which is the answer to her prayers. I can't muster up the courage to tell her that I don't want this girl as badly as I do the one in San Francisco."

"Of what faith is the one in San Francisco?"

"Protestant. Presbyterian. "

"The faith aspect shouldn't matter seriously. You can resolve that issue reasonably enough. You're like me. It's the compatibility of the partnership that over rides, not the faith."

"I guess that's pretty well the case. At least from where I stand it is. But for now I don't have to grapple with falling into a predicament. I'm in no hurry to marry and won't for a while."

Leland consumed two days on his visit with Mr. Carney and Tatiana, returning with an exhilarated uplifting and many joyful things to say, and said the same of his time with Ozzie and Cavanaugh. I wasn't able to make the trip. Something cropped up from Mr.

Yazstremski. Leland gave a full report, yet didn't tell it all in one stretch. Eventually, he'd fill me in completely.

"Mr. Carney is considering a relocation to New York, Ramsey, which is wonderful, for I think there's a good chance I'll set up residence there too if the Edison Company is willing to take me aboard."

"Terrific. I hope so. Why we'd see one another once a week. Just like old times. What a life. Do you ever wonder how things might have fared for us had we stayed in the tractor business?"

"Sure I do. Once a day every day at the least. How would we have done? Very well. Things were going convincingly in our favor and would still if we'd stayed the course but we didn't. In truth I'm sometimes sorry we didn't."

"Me too. But I soon set the thought aside. That wasn't meant for us in the long run."

"No it wasn't. But maybe for Ozzie and Cavanaugh, although Mr. Carney thinks not. He's of the opinion they haven't a lot to which they can look forward, that the business is in the throes of folding. He's exploring the landscape for them, checking into their landing a job at a tractor plant in Fort Wayne or Peoria and the opportunity sounds pretty good. I pray that it is."

Chapter 51

LELAND DELIGHTED at sitting with Andrea and I in the lobby in the evenings and it was not unusual for us to stay up late fraternizing with respect to a potpourri of things. He relished the camaraderie, most of all Andrea's presence and it gladdened me that he aspired with obvious delight to have her as a part of us. When quite late and all others fast asleep we'd pop open a bottle of red wine that I'd secretly stored in the back of the kitchen pantry, lucky that earlier no one stumbled onto its discovery. Such togetherness was great fun, yet there were intervals when frivolity waxed into a vein of seriousness and thought, where often each adopted a contrary but inoffensive stance, a mild throw back to the debates that once in the brief past resounded around the dining table of the adjoining room. Once Andrea and Leland squared off over the the most useful invention to mankind, the bulldozer or the hydroelectric dam, which on the one hand Leland argued there was no debate, that irrefutable logic contended in favor of the bulldozer, for without this mechanical no dam could have ever gotten built, whereas, Andrea, while agreeing in part premised that other machinery undergoing certain alterations would have built the dam or that in future advances electricity might well replace heavy machinery or the use of the hydroelectric dam. Sometimes topics arose that were much loftier; sometimes crossing over into the great obscurity of the celestial and it was here in this awesome terrain that our intellect met its severest test. On that evening or on another soon following one or the other asked, "What is the purpose of life?" and this complexity, which transcends us all in understanding, consumed the rest of the evening or far past bedtime to say the least.

"You might as well ask is there a Lord and if there is where is He and when did He get born and how did that happen? And if you can answer these things you will have the answer to your question." Thus spoke Leland.

"You are far out Leland," said Andrea in a scientifically toned voice. "Who can speak intelligently about what you ask? Even faith can't explain it. But it is kindred, I must acknowledge, to other things that are obvious in us as humans which are equally mysterious, if you stop and think of the matter."

"Such as?"

"Such as the unsatisfied tendencies of man, God given I have to conclude, such as seeing; man sees but he wants to see more, such as knowledge; man absorbs knowledge but it's never enough, such as acquisition; man gathers but he strives to gather more, such as the infinite succession of ideas; man never stops proceeding from one idea to another, helplessly unable to cease. And on and on and on and on. Who can answer why these things are as they are? We can't. No more than we can answer what you have posed."

"Agreed. But we are humans. The Lord made us, and we'll keep on wondering and asking and searching for answers which will forever remain elusive. Now, what is the purpose of life? It's asked every second by someone. It's what we make of it, I say. It's to work for the Lord and abide faithfully by his commands as decreed from the very first. And to do our daily chores and enjoy our food and our mate in marriage. That's pretty well the extent of it. The answer I guess, if there is one, is inextricably tied to an examination of the mystery of the universe. And what is that mystery? It's the same as asking when did the beginning occur and when was the Lord born? Wasteful thoughts aren't they. Too much for us. There was no first, no beginning, we are told. But we cannot, can we, strive as hard as we will, give up the conception of a beginning and an end. We think it all has to be measurable."

"Seems so," I let myself in, "and we'll never figure it out. It was meant that we cannot but here I go anyway. Was there a beginning, or did the universe always exist and if it did, I am profoundly too overwhelmed to explain it myself but the noble towering Plato did explain it or gamely attempted."

"And tell me, how did he do that?" asked Andrea.

"Let me get my books."

At once I arose and made my way to my study and lifted a text which somewhere on one of its pages depicted words that I read to my companions and we postulated from these printings that Plato actually said that there was a self existent Divinity, a spirit throughout the universe, without body or form, incorporeal, that is, and that our universe is endowed of endless segments which are mysteriously united together, done so only by an all encompassing Being or Divinity—and we three joined to add by oversimplified example that such is apparent in the anatomy of man himself, for he too is comprised of segments, vital ones, his heart and kidneys and liver and colon and blood vessels and brain, all of which are intricately and timely related. And that there had to be a God to have devised such a creature and given him life and caused his body to function healthily, for at least seventy years give or take a little.

With the days of his visit fast dwindling I decided to inquire of Leland which of the sights we as yet had missed seeing in the city did he now wish to visit the most, receiving that the Chicago Stockyards stood at the peak of his remaining itinerary. I myself had toured the Yards on previous occasions, my first with Balboni who possessed an indepth acquaintance with the outlay of the buildings and the stockades where the animals were quatered until slaughtered. This gave me an introductory footing but in the interim I had gone back by myself to learn more. When I toured Leland through the Yards they were in their waning years, the evidence glaringly visible, and we were lucky that operations had not ceased altogether. He shook his head in astonishment at the magnitude of the complex, massive, sprawling, acres of land and buildings, with board made stockades stretching for what seemed miles.

"What a sight! This is the famous Chicago Stockyards I'm at last seeing, unbelievable," he let out, as we gazed across the expanse.

"No. Not exactly. You're using a misnomer. It's the Union Stockyards, yet you are right in a sense, inasmuch as people coming here for the first time generally use the name you use. Most of the people around here locally just say Yards."

"Interesting place."

"Indeed. Once it was the economic heart and soul of Chicago. I can't pinpoint the heyday of the industry but I can call up a few highlights"

"All right."

"For one thing, at its largest size the Yards covered nearly one square mile, and in 1921 they employed forty thousand people and between 1865 and 1900 about 400 million livestock were butchered here."

"I do say! That's stunning, and probably more stunning were you to equip me with some common measure with which to compare your findings. But I don't ask this of you, although I know nothing at all of this business other than just hearing or reading certain prints of it over the years. All the same, your data is impressive. It whets a person's curiosity. And catapaults him to thinking. Anything else?"

"Yeah, one thing more. The officials won't admit us to the inside but the slaughtering process is mechanically perfected, you would see, an assembly line consisting of conveyors and wheels and lifters and holders, much in the manner of the assembly lines of the car making industry. As a matter of fact, I'm told, believe it or not, that in 1913 the renowned Henry Ford studied this system and adapted it to his car making plant in Detroit. Where here the objective is to disassemble, (the slaughtering of animals) Mr. Ford's objective was to assemble the assortment of car parts into a whole, the two systems the same except done in reverse." Leland wished badly to peek inside to see how the process worked but could not. "Too bad," he said, disappointed and I too felt let down. For whatever the reason, as set by administrative fiat, an observation on that day of the inner operations was not honored.

"Hmmm. I didn't know these things," said Leland, referring to the broad scope of all he had seen and heard. "They're very much revealing. But there's something else. Just let your eyes swish over there. All those corrals, the stockades. They're half empty or worse. Where are the animals?"

"Take a good look my friend, for the days of this famous place are numbered. Slaughtering and packing are swiftly spinning into decline."

And then I began an effort to tell him of its storied past.

"The Union Stockyards, or Yards, have been a meat packing district in Chicago for a century or thereabouts. Starting in 1865, a group of railroad companies operated the district, hence the Union, who acquired a substantial quantity of swamp land and converted it into a centralized meat packing conglomerate. The emergence of the stockyards gained its roots by and large from the railroad movement, railroad funded I must add. By the 1890's the railroad money flowing into the enterprise derived in abundance from the coffers of the famous Cornelius Vanderbilt. It might also interest you to know Leland that the settlement you see right over there," I pointed, "was known as the Back of the Yards community near the 1860's, predating the emergence of the meat packers. When the future meat packers first set foot in Chicago, principally Irish and German immigrants, they moved to the Back of the Yards to live, and from their own front doors, in a manner of speaking, they witnessed the rise and fall of the industry, its vibrant emergence into prosperity and its agonizing decline. I say decline because it's teetering on its last leg now."

Within a minimal passage of years, the Yards closed at midnight on Friday, July 30, 1971 after several decades of irreversible bad years, more specifically during the decentralization of the meat packing industry. Carrying the meat by trucks had caught on, packing plants were seriously beginning to crop up throughout the country, and railroads were no longer significantly vital for shipments. Direct sales of livestock from breeders to packers facilitated by advancement in interstate trucking lowered the cost of slaughtereing. Animals were slaughtered where they were raised. Long hauls were no longer necessary. For awhile the packing companies grittily resisted but Swift and Armour both surrendered and vacated their plants in the nineteen fifties, certainly by the turn of the sixties, and their departure marked an early and definite sign of the beginning of the end for the intermediary Chicago Stockyards.

Leland would leave the next day. He said he gained in abundance from what he referred to as our Plato talk and my touring him through the stockyards, speaking of these phenomena with such an exclamation that he convinced me they were among the best of his experiences while on his visit. On his departure I drove him to the airport; and Andrea would have accompanied us but for the obligations she had committed to fulfill by an appointed hour at the department of physics and math. Conscious of his leaving however she showed up to pay her respects and say goodbye. At one point they began a brief toying of a subject which originated a couple of days before. It regarded electrical theory and the potential variations of this energy source, none of it making a great deal of sense to me. Admittedly, I wasn't interested enough to try to grasp what their subject entailed insofar as it fell far out of my intellectual range. The way he looked at Andrea with passionate infatuated eyes told of his smitteness with her and at the same time showed obvious disappointment that she remained distant and aloof from his attentions. At least she allowed his embrace just before he crawled into the car. While on the way to the airport we talked rapidly, trying to cover anything we might have missed in earlier conversations regarding the old days. We didn't think we had overlooked anything. But then……..

Chapter 52

"AH YES," Leland suddenly exclaimed. "I forgot to bring it up. Mr. Carney mentioned they're working on plans to build a new post office where the old Lebranche house once stood."

"Who's behind it?" I thought I knew.

"I asked him that. He said the government's paying for it as part of a rural improvement package."

"A new one is certainly due." I thought of adding that doubtless Billy Mcvector had wormed his way into the spotlight, taking credit for wooing government money to the enterprise. I walked to the boarding steps with him, and told him in one last gesture that it gladdened me so much to see him again. "Likewise," he said, "it was immeasurable, simply immeasurable Ramsey," and relayed further that it gave him much happiness to see me doing commendably well, which to me meant advancing with good results in my studies. But I asked what he meant exactly.

"Your degree. You're almost there. Keep it up. I predict your next chapter will offer returns far more rewarding and exciting than the one past and I can't wait to learn what it is."

He'd always said that literature grabbed at his heart, citing it as the most fascinating of fields of study and I answered that the Lord equipped him with too great a repository of brain power for him to spend his energies and intellect on literature. He would laugh lightly and shosh it off. Sporadically I recommended a stream of books by mail to him to read, the ancient *Plutarch* heading the list, which I knew he undoubtedly retrieved from the library and searched the pages since he later lifted excerpts from the content and addressed them by way of letter in some detail.

The plane's engines snarled but refused to start then snarled again then roared and leveled off, and then the pilot began to rev them higher, the signal that passengers should hasten aboard. We hugged. He climbed energetically up the steps in long careful strides but suddenly turned as if in after thought and hastened back to me.

"Ramsey, I'm terribly sorry that I didn't make it over to your mother's when I saw in on the Carney's. Will you ask her to forgive me?"

"Ha. Of course. But you don't owe an apology. You'll soon come back this way and if you still feel you owe her one you can speak it to her then."

"I shall. I shall."

As he passed out of sight into the plane's interior I suddenly began to recall a deluge of the various things we'd done with one another since early youth and tried to resist a touch of gloominess not knowing when I'd see him again. "A long while I'm guessing, maybe years." As the plane got airborn it flew straight eastwardly and then circled and passed directly overhead, coursing westward. When it began to fade from view, its silver coating still deflecting tiny glintings in the sun, I waved lethargically after it, as if to say another goodbye.

Near the end of summer Andrea left for Louisiana for a few weeks to join her parents. I asked how she would utilize her time while there.

"A great amount of it with my father. He's aleady docketed a bunch of fishing venues for us."

"What do you catch down there?"

"Grouper."

"Wish I could go with you."

"Oh, why don't you? That's a terrific idea. Please."

"I can't. It's tempting, but I have more than I can handle here."

"Oh phooey."

I spoke correctly. My hands were full. Darya's letter lay waiting for me to answer. I received it a day before Leland left—and I felt obligated to answer and with enough length to my letter to match the length of hers. But with sincerity. And another letter arrived from Nenia as well with a message that she wouldn't arrive in Saint Louis until the middle of September or even in late October. No reason given why. Whatever the reason the officials of her work place supported her decision. During this period I sat down with Doctor Linskie in his office who gave me a piece of uplifting news that a teaching position part time was opening at a junior college in the city within another year and that he'd relayed my name as a top candidate with the assumption that I' d approve of his action.

"Is that all right with you Ramsey? I hope so. It's already done."

"Fine, fine. I'm tickled pink."

My hours were full all right, as I had told Andrea, though were fuller from the assignments which I felt strongly dedicated to fulfill that was placed on my shoulders by Mr. Yazstremski. As yet, my work load with the firm had been in a comparative sense rather lax, which suddenly did an about face. The sky caved in. There resulted a landslide of overtime hours and a preponderance of burned energy working at his side combing through the records of legal rulings that sometime earlier I had extracted from the court house files. Computers and electronics call up systems were not then in common practice; we still searched the records with old fashion tediousness.

While there were more students than usual applying for occupancy in the fraternity house once the semester had gotten underway, I still felt lonely without Darya and Aaron around to keep me company; and to worsen my plight I received a phone call from Andrea that she would not return for the current semester, that her grandmother with whom she shared a heartfelt bond, inseparable she said, had hurt her hip due to a fall and that she must help care for her.

"I owe it to my dear grandmother Ramsey. She's meant everything to me. See you after the turn of the year and if you can break free you should head this way. Please. I'll take you fishing."

I almost acceded to her offer. Afterwards I wished I had. But my work load wouldn't let me. I missed her awfully as the semester moved through one week after another, not only since she wasn't around to help me with my more complicated subjects of physics and math, but honestly, without my realization that it had already happened, the sheer sound of her youthful laughter was now an addicted part of my being.

The owners persisted that I take over as the director of the fraternity house, which I respectfully refused, citing my busy schedule, yet consented to acting in an associate capacity likened to the position I held with Bertinelli. Balboni showed up the day before semester studies commenced, his sight sending a thrill of excitement through me. As the old group had been to me formerly, he now replaced them as a standard fixture in the emotions of my psyche. I went and threw my arms around him. Like me he had dropped out of the summer term, and his absence I had sorely missed.

He fell into laughter. "What's this all about?"

"You can't imagine how good it is to see you. The old gang is gone, Aaron, Bertinelli, and Darya and now Andrea. You're the only one left, besides me."

"Andrea! What's wrong with her?"

"Nothing. But there is with her grandmother. She hurt her hip. Andrea's staying home to care for her for a while."

"I gotcha. But I also have some news. Gerard isn't enrolling either. He called me last night."

I had virtually overlooked Gerard, another of the remnants. But only temporarily. "Not back! Not coming back! That makes no sense. This is his senior year. Did he speak of a reason?"

"None. Said he just didn't intend to return to his studies this fall. He did mention that he had to do something that wasn't delayable. But that's all. Didn't sound too serious."

"Hmmmm. I don't know. It's kind of like he's ducking something, not facing up to whatever it is. Don't they say it's when you're running away you're most liable to stumble? But I guess it's nothing like that. Anyway, I think I'll look into it. He needs to come on back to school."

The schism flashed before me that resulted between the two of us over Darya, where I won. I say won, but that's the wrong way to phrase it. I wasn't competing, not in the least. Gerard simply fell for her and she refused his advances. I was sort of caught in the middle. I know it hurt him some, maybe more than that, to endure the unhappiness and all but not long in the making he recovered and we were again friends. I wished badly at the time that the division amounted to nothing more than a blimp between two young men. I rationalized, in other words explained to myself, that such things sometimes naturally happened. So on with it. I speculated that since she derived from a world of high society and he from a farm background she might have entertained something like a morganatic view of him, that is, to say it another way, he stood at a social level beneath her by some measure. And why not the same of me I asked. My answer was quick. "Ridiculous Ramsey. You know she's never thought that. Never."

After hearing he wasn't returning for his last year, and possibly not at all, his circumstance began to grow ever stronger in my thoughts, to the extreme that I took it upon myself, before it was entirely too late to rectify it to drive to Dewitt, Iowa, where he lived on his parent's farm. I'd do my best to turn him around. I chose not to telephone before hand, gambling that I'd catch him home. Depending on an earlier description that he supplied of his whereabouts I drove on the main highway to where I figured I'd reached the road that led to where he lived. But I had erred. I should have waited and taken the next one. A gracious congenial farmer set me straight when he stopped to inquire if I needed help. Said I looked lost. Following his instructions, I drove a scant further to the next turn off and cut left and kept on for a quarter of a mile in my estimation and then suddenly, swoosh, the Warf home, a fine brick structure, immense in size. I guessed five thousand square feet. Since there were only a sprinkling of trees around it the home loomed larger than the actual footage. When I knocked on the front door his mother answered and left instantly and announced to her son that a guest of his had arrived. I had given her my name, naturally, but wasn't sure she made a connection. I didn't explain. Gerard dashed out at once and before he took one step out the door bore signs of near shock, his mouth at least half open. It was too much. Suddenly, there I stood straight out of the blue facing him with a kind of fantastic happiness in my eyes and a mischievous grin on my face. Breaking into laughter he put his arms around me.

"My goodness. What brings you to this frontier Ramsey? Golly. You could knock me over with a feather."

"Well, I had a few hours to burn and thought I'd use them to check on an old friend. As you know, Darya and Aaron and Bertinelli have graduated and Andrea's postponing her studies for awhile. It's as lonesome as a crypt around there."

He eyed me quizzically, as if wondering why I had showed up and at the same time searching for a choice response. I felt certain that he suspected Balboni as the one to clue me in, and he proved my hunch correct. “Well, I see that Balboni has let you know of my intention. I’ve decided not to come back just yet. Thought I’d stay out for a year and help around here. Then take up my studies again next fall.”

Acting with caution, opining it best not to hint the tiniest objection, I began to talk of something else entirely. Motioning toward the front porch swing he led me over and we sat down.

“Some farm you have here. It looks sprawling, immense. And flat. Just as I figured. Of course, I’m unacquainted with the boundaries. Did you tell me once that you folks own in the neighborhood of a thousand acres?”

“That’s close,” he answered nonchalantly, wishing to sound humble.

“Do the boundaries extend back to the main highway?”

“They do.”

“I can’t imagine. It’s a far cry from that poor piece of clay dirt on which I grew up. Fifty acres of nothing. Exactly that in every sense of the word. Plough mules gave us the source of power for doing our work, the only source besides our bodies. If we’d owned a tractor and such, any fraction of these monstrous machines you folks own and utilize here, I would have thought I’d died and gone to Heaven.”

“Ha. That’s a pretty big thought.” He followed with a laugh of disbelief but tempered it with a tinge of sorrow too for anyone up against hardships as bleak as those just described.

“No, no. It was that bad.” His face grew apologetic and he carefully avoided laughing again when I referred to my beginnings in the work fields.

After we’d talked on a while, he suggested that he show me around the farm, not all I thought, for one thousand acres of land amounted to a far piece if a man took into account the many roadways running helter skelter through it to allow for ingress and egress of heavy machinery. He excused himself for a moment in order to speak with his mother, then we crawled into a new Chevrolet truck, a light blue, and began to drive about over a dirt road that ultimately cut into another dirt road and this pattern kept happening until I lost track of the growing endless roads we crossed or entered. I tried to look at everything at once. Little clouds of dust rose and curled and trailed us. The cornfields drew me most; the stalks towering and there was an immensity of them, which easily overshadowed the corrolary soybean crops that also grew in abundance. But corn was the leading staple he said with emphasis. And thoughtfully talked me through their strategy of harvesting and storing prodigious quantities in the granaries until better prices were offered on the commodities exchange, particularly international prices. “This is the way real farming is done,” it spun in my head. Near the last of what seemed to me the end of the tour he glanced over with a predetermined countenance and said, “of course you’re spending the night. I told my mother you were before we left.

That's why I quick footed back inside. Now don't try to wiggle out of it because I won't let you, and besides, I've lined up a surprise."

I attempted to fake that I hadn't come with that intention, and I hadn't, but before I completed one word of objection, he shut me off.

"No debate Ramsey. It's decided. Now, we have half of the afternoon ahead of us, so I'll show you the rest of the farm, then we'll hightail it to town, which won't do a lot to thrill you I'll guarantee, but it will show you how country folks live."

His mother out did herself in my honor, "she is so gracious I thought," that night throwing no less than a grand feed, with friends and relatives of most favored status invited. His father arrived late to join us, apologizing for his tardiness which he explained he couldn't avoid in that he had to pick up and tow a combine from a nearby town where it had undergone some badly needed repairs. Responding to a subtle cueing from his wife he circled round the table to where I sat, patting me on my shoulder and shaking my hand. Soon after the meal Gerard and some of his associates formed a semicircle in a large room abutting the foyer, which fashioned a spread of shiny hardwood floors together with a dome light in the ceiling, and began to play country music. Suddenly I understood the surprise to which he earlier alluded. Most of them sang, his father as well, supported by a complete musical ensemble, a piano, a base guitar, a rhythm guitar, two or three fiddles and Gerard off and on switched from playing the fiddle to the piano and vice versa. This sudden uncloaking of his abilities hit me with a jolt. I'd heard for the longest that he played here and there in the neighborhood of the campus but hadn't taken in any of the performances, early on forming a skewed opinion that he and his whole band were rag tag.

You'd have to call his mother a pretty woman, attractively pretty, in her early forties, with nice dark hair and no grey seen at any angle. She obviously had resolutely kept herself trim. A perpetual smile stayed affixed to her face, an outward mirror which explained much of her heart inside, kind and gentle and giving and seen in the way she related to me and to her son and husband and all others around her. That was her natural self, I quickly surmised, a splendid person every day of her life. When everyone had gotten into full sway with the entertainment, she found it opportune to ease over to me with a revelation that she knew my purpose in coming, for Gerard had told her. She said that he knew why and that she nestled a grateful place in her heart for my efforts and interest at trying to persuade him to go back to finish his education. I learned then why he said to Balboni that something botherrd him to the extent that he decided not to return to college that fall semester. It was that he felt his father badly needed him to harvest the crops that fall and that he couldn't let him down.

"I talked to him about that," said his mother, "explaining that while his father greatly appreciated his thoughtfulness and loved him for it, there were plenty of hired hands to fill his place. I think he sees I'm right."

That night, following the entertainment and after the guests were gone, Gerard and I sat on the front porch swing in casual exchange, hully gulley talk. He sometimes grew quiet and appeared as if contemplating a vision which I began to comprehend before it worked itself out.

"Ramsey, you and I landed at the university at the same time, and do you know what? What a crying shame if you and I don't walk away from that place together that we have learned so much to love."

I fell into laughter and shook his hand.

"What time are you leaving in the morning?" he asked.

"Pretty early. By eight or earlier. After breakfast, I guess I should say. Your mother's orders."

"I'll ride with you if you don't mind. My car is broke down and they won't have it repaired for another week. I'd drive my truck but my father needs it for hauling hay. He's hiring some day workers to help and needs it for their use."

"Good. Glad to have a traveling companion, but what's more important is my seeing another face around the fraternity house that's familiar to me besides Balboni's."

Chapter 53

THE FUTURE is an elusive entity, never unraveling as one hopes or imagines it will. Even the short term is tricky; you think you have it tied down, yet that is when one should entertain the utmost of caution. My plans for the present and for the ensuing year and the year after were clearly patterned. I would again spend many happy hours with Nenia I envisioned, stay close to Mr. Yazstremski's side in fulfilling his expectations; take up my part time teaching job with the small liberal arts college that Doctor Linskie spearheaded for me; finish my undergraduate studies and begin a limitation of studies in pursuit of my master's degree; trade letters and phone calls with Darya and Aaron; and hang out with Andrea when she returned for the second semester. And begin to pursue my studies in law. "This is a carefully prepared and precise agenda," I assured myself and foresaw no reason why things should develop to the contrary. But there were hidden upheavals that lurked to strike from the blind side, despite careful employment of my crystal ball, the impact of which rearranged the course of my life's sojourn for the next few months and years beyond.

Nenia arrived. But not in keeping with the date she had formerly said she would. She got there in late September, flying in on Braniff Airlines, landing in the early part of day, the sun ablaze after a grueling climb over the eastern horizon. Suddenly there she stood in the opening as the door slid back, only a few feet away. A frosty tinge filled the September air and to allow for its nippy demeanor she had clad herself in a gorgeous brown coat, but properly light for the season, and there was a fashionable hat on her head with a larger than ordinary rim that curled tastefully downward. "She is so stunning in her attire," said an internal whisper, "and is the epitome of health and vitality, and why not. Only a year and a half have expired since she went away." These were my immediate impressions as she descended the passenger steps and as she came to me I with a surge of uplifted heart drew her into my arms, kissing her lips and then her face all over, even her nose, one kiss after another, and with equal animation she showered me with like affections.

"Oh, it's wonderful to see you," she said breathlessly, her dark dazzling eyes alive with excitement. "I can't believe it."

"How beautiful she is. Did I forget how beautiful she was and discover now that she is even more beautiful? No. That cannot happen in so brief a span. She is no more beautiful than she ever was and was never any more beautiful than now. I could never forget anything about her, not even her most miniscule feature. But she has changed; she has some. She seems older and more charming, but she is older only by a shade. She is a little more like woman; in fact, she's a year and a half more like woman. But some of it is due to her hat and her lush long coat and her high heels."

"You look executive in your hat," I said teasingly. But I spoke the truth. "Is that your way of getting ready to impress the folks at the archives?"

"You would say that, wouldn't you? No. Some of the girls I knew, my closest friends, began wearing hats, especially when as a group we would stroll up and down the streets of Paris shopping. I think at first one of them picked up on wearing a hat because she'd seen Ingrid Bergman wearing one in a movie. That's what she said. At first I didn't follow suit but in no time succumbed to the infection. And discovered that I loved wearing hats. Soon it was adopted as a fashionable habit for our entire narrow circle, for everyone."

"It's adorable on you, or shall I say that you are adorable with it on?"

We rode the trolley to her home. She refused the idea of a taxi. "No taxi. The trolley is too romantic to pass up." She said nothing of why Thelma and Claude were not there. As I learned, she suggested that they should not bother, that I would meet her. I pitched in that no force on earth could have diverted me.

The wheels hummed smoothly with unhurried speed upon the rails below. There was a nice familiar feeling resulting from everything, the rise and fall of voices, the squeal of breaks, people scurrying to get on and off. Suddenly it seemed she'd not been away at all, again snuggled lovingly against me as she did on our first trolley excursion, which I recalled with mirror exactness. She had relaxed against the backing of her seat and temporarily closed her eyes. When all at once they opened she smiled as if to say she'd caught me peering into her lovely face. I blushed. She smiled even moreso.

"I thought you'd never make it here" I said.

"Me too. I'll explain if you want me to."

"You don't need to. Just seeing you takes care of everything. You're here now and that's what counts."

She went on to explain nevertheless.

"My plans were to arrive earlier, as you know, since you read my letters I'm sure."

"I read them. Every line many times over."

"Good. I know you did. Now, I'll go on. They'd hired a new teacher to replace me but at the last minute another obligation detained her. I couldn't just desert the children. Well, I could have but that would have been terrible. On the otherhand I could have pressed the officials to hire someone to fill in while waiting on my replacement. I didn't. But here I am now."

"Thanks sweetheart for that. And I'll thank you later too when you fill me in on those wonderful experiences—besides teaching—that filled up your life during your stay abroad. But that can wait."

"Yes it can, if you please. Give me time and I will appropriately gorge you with everything."

When we reached the outskirts and approached the familiar passenger pavilion the trolley abruptly slowed, and the people that were unseated grabbed the silver verticals, rounded tubing or pipes, holding on until the forward motion receded and the trolley stopped. Then we let ourselves off. We were two blocks away from her home. I picked up her clothes encasement in one hand and my suitcase in the other and we began to walk. As I looked around I saw nothing had changed; everything still familiar, even though at least a year and a half had passed since we were there. While away, Nenia retained ownership of her home, leasing it to a college age friend for six months during her absence. And when her friend vacated she did not sell it, with Thelma volunteering to see after the maintenance, watering the grass and flowers not withstanding. When we entered the doorway a scent of fragrance invaded my sense of smell and when going into various rooms it became apparent that such lushness extended throughout. The floors of hardwood, lately polished, literally shone. Fresh flowers adorned the dining room table as well as the bulk of side tables that were set into place by a trained eye. "Thelma has been here all right," Nenia happily said.

Thelma left a note which read that she hoped Nenia found the results of her efforts satisfactory, a very polite inference that she knew Nenia would, and proceeded to inform in the same scribbling that fresh tea awaited in the refrigerator and that she knew how well I liked tea even in cool weather. When she finished reading the lines Nenia suggested that we remove to the outside and sit in the alcove. From where we sat a clear view of a mysterious entanglement of tendrils caught one's eye, appearing to be climbing the trellises of an arbor that connected to the corner of her home. I asked for the name of the specimen, not to my recall ever seeing it before. She answered that she didn't know its name, but that Thelma set out the plant some two years before when small and by now it had grown exponentially to a relatively large size. She guessed that it was kindred to English ivy. And then asked for the length of my stay. I returned that I'd stick around for a limit of two days, to which she exacted a frown of disappointment and said that she'd hoped I might stay long enough to accompany her to see her parents whose physical health was slowly failing.

"I can't make it. I'm sorry. I have some pressing demands that won't let me. But I'll get back in two weeks and will go with you then if you still want me to."

"I will. I will want you to."

That night the air brought with it an unpleasant coolness, appreciably more than during the day. But all the same we sat on the patio and talked, both of us clad in clothes heavy enough for light winter, she in a cloak of crimson with fur lined sleeves and bodice, and I in a hunting coat seldom used, the only occasion that I ever put it on being when I went hunting with Uncle Sanford and John Eric in the savannah swamps back home. It was stored in one of her closets during the time of her absence. She had fished it out for me. When she lit candles and set them near us it triggered an image that Darya always made it practice to light candles. I didn't like myself for the remembrance yet what could I do? The mind behaves as it wishes. But the remembrance soon receded of its own free will. She rose once to retrieve something from the inside. Thelma had bought it and left it for us to enjoy, a canter of red wine, a Swedish import. It tasted wonderful as it touched my lips and palate and seemed to fizz as it flushed coldly across my teeth. Some of my remembrances I felt safe to divulge, for example, my last night out at the small café with the Stylman's on the edge of Lake Michigan, and that Mrs. Stylman nurtured a particular fondness for it since it was of true Italianate architectural style."

"You have sometimes mentioned the Stylman's in your correspondence. How is Aaron, your friend?"

"He's fine. As fun making as ever, or was the last I saw of him. He dined with us at the small café I spoke of just now. He graduated last spring. The parents treated us to dinner out of the realization that we were just before going our separate ways. They felt remorse at seeing us part. We were inseparable for three years and my being his close friend during so long a time was to them enormously touching."

"He graduated. That's good. And you will graduate next spring. You will won't you?"

"If all goes well."

"It will. You know it will. I can't imagine it not."

"Nor can I. My marks are fine. And I must make sure they stay that way. I didn't tell you yet that I'm under consideration for a part time teaching position next fall with a small college in the city. I'll keep my fingers crossed that when they scan my resume they'll see nothing that's anti positive."

"I can understand. Is there a promise, or hope in your appraisal, of it eventuating into a full time position?"

"I feel there is."

"But your work with the law firm. The Stylman firm, I believe it is. Do you expect to give it up?"

"I can't say. I'm in limbo. For awhile I'll stick with both, teaching and doing research with the law firm. The teaching position calls for someone to teach two different night time classes per week, on alternate dates. I can do my work with the law firm in the daytime."

"Don't overdo yourself."

"I won't. Of course, here I am talking as if I'm assured of a job full time with the law firm when I graduate and that Mr. Stylman will establish a law office in Chicago. As of this date he's indefinite on whether he will or will not. We'll have to wait and see."

"Yes we will. But Ramsey, I worry more of something else far more than the essentialness of a job for you."

"What is that?"

"The war. The war is prime discussion at the breakfast tables in Paris. It looks bad. I see no end in sight. It's going to escalate. Does that bother you?"

"Some. But wait a minute. I guess it gnaws on me more than I'm letting on. It does worry me. Sometimes I can't fall to sleep at night with it on my mind, knowing that thousands of soldiers are laying their necks on the line fighting the Viet Cong over there."

"That is a worry, a big one, but there's another aspect of it that bothers me too and I'm sure you spin it around ever so often. You must."

"What do you mean?"

"Your draft status!" Softly placing her hand on my arm she showed in her dark expressive eyes an apprehension that I'd never remotely seen before. "I'm afraid they'll draft you sweetheart as soon as you finish your studies and graduate. I shudder at the thought of your going in."

"I think of that as well but try not to let it evolve into an obsession."

We did very little in the manner of entertainment. Just there together afforded entertainment. We sat in the huge lounge chairs and talked and pounced upon endless topics that one or the other brought up. But she appeared a slight tired. A slight reserved. She had endured long hours since early morning and I assumed she needed a quiet inactive evening for recouping. "I think it wise that I don't talk so much. Just being with her is enough. I love sitting here with her in the quiet lying back in these big soft chairs, its nice, very nice. What else is there that's better? I can't think of a single thing." There was something else. It regarded music. We loved music, both of us, and had since we were young, in our teens, incessantly enthralled with forty-five wax recordings and the hundreds of songs played over the radio. So, on that first night it started all over. She played a new one, new to me, which I had not heard before and I judge I hadn't because I wasn't as classically oriented as she. It sounded heavenly, the voices exquisitely beautiful, the strings of the great orchestra swelling to the vaulting. Its name! *Santa Lucia,* sung as a duet, Italians, a male and female singer, two phenomenally gifted artists or else they wouldn't have been chosen to deliver a performance of international renown. It was not until the passing of some months that Luciano Pavarotti and Giorgia Vermonte Bella sang a televised version. Nenia sat beside me; we viewed it together. Young then, Giorgia featured a perfectly lovely voice, but her facial expressions as well drew one to her irresistibly. Her eyes switched with interesting deftness from one mood to another. Pavarotti. Well, what can anyone say of him? One word. "Perfectionist." He performed as he usually did, by every measure fantastic. Great. There are a plethora of versions of *Santa Lucia* but the version performed by Pavarotti and

Giorgia took the cake, simply wonderful and exquisitely meshed and the strictest of critics would have said without a second of mulling it over that they had just witnessed a great artistic performance. Nenia began to play it again in the quiet of evening when I came to see her. Sometime after the first hearing I grew curious to know why *Santa Lucia* happened to get written, what might have inspired the author, and upon consulting certain files of musical records discovered that *Santa Lucia* is a traditional Neapolitan song, a very old song, published in Naples in 1849, and that the original lyrics were in celebration of the picturesque waterfront district, Borgo Santa Lucia, in the Bay of Naples. In the lines the author has a boatman extending an invitation to someone, or more than one, to ride in his boat and enjoy the cool of the evening and the beauty of the surroundings.

We sat up late that night as we would the next, a kind of ordered attempt to come abreast of everything that escaped our lives together since we'd been apart. Even though a frosty nip presented itself in the evening air we continued to sit outside in the porch swing.

"Isn't it really quiet and peaceful?"

"You too? I have the same thoughts. Takes me back to my boyhood when on a hot sweltering night we couldn't sleep on the inside so we'd gather our quilts and trek out on the back porch and sleep there. Until the dawn."

"You can't do that here. Not now."

"That's too bad. But back then, way off in the countryside where we lived we felt no threat. We thought nothing of leaving our doors unlocked. What is the saying that an ancient patriot once uttered. 'The gates are never shut day or night in the city and a purse of gold may be safely left in the fields'"

"I like that but tonight we'll lock the doors tightly."

When the hallway clock neared the hour of one we embraced and left for our separate bedrooms, though not falling off to sleep, neither of us, and it was but a slight until on little lightsome feet she stole to my bedside. She felt wonderful in my arms and if it failed in the swirls of her imagination to wish that we were married it certainly did not fail in mine.

"I'd love to have you, you know that."

"Of course I know it. And I would love for you to. But my principles still remain as always. In time my sweetheart, but not this time."

"And that time will come when?" I asked with piquancy in my voice with firm knowledge of her answer.

"When we marry, silly boy."

A humorous thought suddenly jogged in my head of someone who once said or penned that you shouldn't ask a woman to let you seduce her, for woman views talk as a waste in the art of making love. But no place for that existed in Nenia's code of values and virtues, or so I believed. She let me embrace and hold her as much as I wanted and returned it, though putting curfew on passion when reaching the place where women of chaste draw the line. We would not make love, such being the moral tenant which seemed forever unalterable in her soul. And I cherished her for it. We lay there for the longest, often in silence, just caught up in the nearness of one another, with me listening to the soft hypnotic rhythm of her breathing. Her kisses, lush and fresh, were as sweet as nectar and I would have relished them until the dawn. But the kisses little by little faded as they began to weaken to the advent of slumber. I listened. Her breathing now virtually silent, the rise and fall of her bosom hardly perceptible; it seemed almost like there existed no space or time between suspiration and expiration, all of it one continuous breath. With lamblike gentleness I lifted her up and carried her in my arms to her bedroom—not once did she awaken—as carefully as a mother's hands tucking her in; and kissing her brow I pulled the covers up over her and there she slept as an unweaned baby until the hour of nine the next morning.

I myself did not fall asleep in a moment. As if a current, a theme kept recurring in my head and finally, unable to free myself from its presence, hurried to write it down lest I let it slip my grasp and never again able to forge it to recall.

"Adam and Eve, our mother and father, are the progenitors of that phenomenon we call sensuality, a force that surges within the passions of man and woman, arguably stronger in man than woman, yet existing strongly in both, invited and approved by Him, for the sake of procreation as well as for pleasure, though with limitations, for if passions were turned loose to fall prey to the primitive urge of man or woman think of the chaos. Nenia once said that desire is natural, is part and parcel of man and woman and to experience the beauty of it could pose no wrong, except for the resulting creation of a life out of wedlock; an infant baby, and shame, but I know her soul. Other restraints guide her too, the scriptures, and marriage. She is right. Marriage is the only legitimate and proper way to live. She is strong, stronger than me. I'm glad she's like she is. But maybe woman by design from the grace of Heaven is stronger than man. However it is, in the long run I'll gladly appreciate that she is of such staunch principle. She wouldn't be Nenia if she were not. I'm not saying that my making love at heightened moments with Darya was entirely wrong either'and I'm not avowing that she's not a good young women because in my heart she is wonderful and if it were in the cards I'd marry her with no hesitation. I guess in the finale I have to accept that both are truly fine and wonderful."

The next morning at nine she came yawning and stretching onto the patio where I sat reading the daily paper. Thelma had allowed for every contingency, ordering delivery no later than the hour of breakfast and on hearing it thump as it landed in the front yard I hastened to retrieve it and brought it inside and began to read. At the rustle of Nenia's gown I looked up. "My! Lazy girl."

"Ha. Lazy yourself. You don't exactly appear industrious. But how did you sleep? Really well I hope."

"Serenely well. But late when I turned in. I commissioned myself to transport someone else to bed before I sank into my own." She tapped my cheek. "And how did your night go?" I asked.

"I died. But I'm so glad to know that I'm alive and back home this morning with that sun raining brilliance down on us, and that you are here with me."

"I'm glad as well. A whole lot glad."

"I guess I don't need to remind you that I missed you awfully while away."

"What did you miss most?"

"Do you have a whole year to listen? Oh, let me see. What did I miss most? How about everything?" she answered coquettishly.

"That's good for a starter, but in addition to the lightsomeness of the moment let me turn to something, something regarding your folks. How are they? You haven't said. And I haven't asked."

"They're doing reasonably well. And your mom. How is she? You haven't said."

"She's all right. Staying busy talking of us or so her letters indicate."

"About us?"

"About us."

"What does she say? Really?"

"A little of this and that. The usual things that a parent says, I guess. But back to your folks?" She wasn't pleased with the shortness of my answer. A frown had lit on her face. But she picked up from there.

"Oh, they don't say much. Whatever mom says goes. She speaks for dad. His mind is determined by her mind. I'm seldom privy to that which is spoken between them that concerns you and me but Thelma is keyed in on the larger of what is said. She's like a sister to mom. Mom shares things with her that she won't dare share with me. Thelma said to me once that my mother once said, 'Now Phillip, Ramsey is turning into a young man and he is no longer the young boy who used to sit and listen to the news with you; he is now young man and that's different, and he is a fine young man, and means the moon and stars to Nenia, so you act nicely toward him and don't let your cantankerous moods upset something that's truly good.'"

I didn't even try to restrain my laughter; it gushed. And I remarked that I regretted causing him undue worry, if I ever did, and intended to try with every vital within me from there on to deserve his trust.

"You already have."

And then breakfast, or the breakfast about to get underway.

"Ah. It's late. You're surely hungry sweetheart and I will see to it that you are not for very much longer. It's something quite terrific that I have in store for you. You can watch if you choose or stay out here. Whichever."

"I'll tag along with you. It's most definitely a rare something that's in the making, considering you are so airy at praising whatever it is."

"Perhaps I've overstated. In any event I have reference to a Bacon Apple Waffle; translated, that equates to three golden brown petite waffles topped with apples, hickory smoked bacon, syrup, and a tint of orange zest."

"Hmmm. Sounds ravenously appetizing. And where did you acquire this knowledge, or recipe, of putting together Bacon Apple Waffle?"

She had begun to stir the batter and laid the bacon already in to fry when she answered.

"At Mimi's, a charming little recluse a step or two off the beaten path where my friends and I ate once a week. Close to that anyway."

"Were they all teachers?"

"No. One worked full time as a flight stewardess and another, Franciose Leblanc, did programming for a stock brokerage firm. I plan to correspond with her and we promised to visit one another."

She returned to the breakfast preparation. "I memorized the ingredients from a recipe sheet the waitress gave me. She'd written them down. 'I'll do better than that,' she added, 'the manager will let you see the chef do his preparations.' He did. But back to that fantastic breakfast. We'd sit eating and laughing and talking out under the giant umbrella in that refreshing Parisian air with people swirling by who seemed not to notice us in the faintest."

"Not even the guys."

"Sometimes they'd stop off."

I felt guilty for asking. But continued.

"Did they know you were an American?"

"In no way. My friends and I conversed entirely in French. They didn't know unless they began speaking slang stuff which necessitated that I speak slang in return, or attempt to, and when I did they wrinkled their brows. But they still didn't know. Guess they thought I was just a teacher and had to enunciate like a teacher and they were right. I was just a teacher. I got to know one of them pretty well during that time, a soldier who said he'd soon leave for the battle front in Vietnam. I felt really sorry for him. I think he feared the future. It really showed. I can't say when it first happened but he started to sit by me at the table and I'd talk to him and do the best I could to urge him to face is dilemma with confidence, that all would turn out well. I accompanied him to the train station when he received his overseas traveling orders and hugged him goodbye. I sort of missed him later when we girls gathered at the same table for breakfast where he sat by me."

I didn't say anything. I just sat and listened and faked an interest. I didn't think much about her treating the young soldier with kindness. I supposed it the right thing to do, that their acquaintance happened on the spur of the moment and that he meant nothing to her. Little did I know then nor could I have guessed in my wildest that she had just given preface to a shock soon to implode and with an effect of long lasting consequence.

Chapter 54

ANOTHER DAY and night passed. I had to leave and return to the campus. Two weeks flew by and then I caught a plane for Saint Louis again. There Nenia and I as preplanned boarded a train for Meadville where Charlie, no longer driving his yellow pick up, stood waiting and then drove us in his newly bought replacement to his and Nenia's parents. In the manner of my itinerary as of late our stay was of necessity hurried and brief. Nenia said up front that she couldn't stay away from her new job for any length. The family received us with jubilance, drunk with happiness at seeing her and at meal times showered her with unrequited affections, endless little delicate touches and adoring glances. Her parents weren't well, but yet weren't ill to any degree, no infections nor suffering from any sort of debilitation as far as I noticed, just showing their old age. Nenia and I walked about sparingly, choosing to stay close to them, but once took the liberty to visit the barn to browse among the horses, on one of these outings saddling up two of the most reliables and riding across the farm, stopping short of the river. We didn't talk much to each othert. Just sort of rode along. She seemed a little quiet. Not normal I took it. After going as far as we cared we reined the horses around and went back. Borrowing Charlie's pickup we drove around our little town—the new post office by then virtually complete—and then over to Meadeville. Thelma rode with us. Nenia and Thelma were as Siamese, endlessly chattering every minute of the trip, alternately bursting into laughter. Thelma said she planned to stay on for a while with her parents and this lent badly needed relief to Nenia inasmuch as she worried endlessly over their not having her or Thelma there to look after them, even though Charlie and Arlene lived nearby. On the two nights we were there I naturally stayed with my mother. She asked me to catch her up on the events of my campus life, more interested in remarks regarding my schooling, rather than law, oddly, which I answered more generally than specifically. The news that she usually relayed to me fell upon a death or deaths in the community, an older person more than not, and on this visit the norm held steady as expected. "Miss Ruby Allison died son; she suffered from leukemia, and by the time she went she'd wasted down to nothing but skin and bones. She was your first grade teacher, wasn't she?"

"Yes mom. My first grade teacher. I hate to hear that she's gone. She was the kindest teacher I ever knew. I once ate my sack lunch at the ten o'clock recess hour and at noon showed that I was still hungry, my mouth salivating, watching the other kids eating and all, but my lunch was already in my stomach. She noticed and brought her sack lunch over and gave it to me, explaining that she wasn't hungry or didn't want it for some other reason. Wasn't that something? I'll never for forget it."

At the end of our two day visit we left, Nenia and Mrs. Stoddard in tears and Mr. Stoddard somber and forlorn, his mouth drooping at the corners, exerting his best to disguise his downtroddeness. Charlie dropped us at Meadeville to catch the train to Saint Louis, its arrival due at four in the afternoon. The trip time summed to a fraction over five hours, and in the course of it she more than once seemed to begin to utter something that weighed upon her more than ordinarily but then cut short the expression. I expected a continuance. None came. I took it that whatever the bother, if any, the essence of it amounted to minor importance and let it drift away. When we pulled into the station she pled with me to stay over and I badly wanted to, but I begged off, giving an honest excuse: "I have to go on; I wish I didn't have to sweetheart but there's no choice. Too many things are stacked up on my agenda and I can't afford to fall further behind. I've missed more classes than acceptable already." She saw me off to the plane, catching the taxi with me to the airport. I tended to object but she refused to listen. I worried that she'd have to go into her home alone when she arrived because darkness will have fallen.

Prior to the beginning of the summer term Doctor Linskie allowed me to enroll in one course by assignment. It saved me a great deal of time. To fulfill the requirements, I'd write a paper of some magnitude on a Roman or Grecian notable of antiquity, or on a figure of the concurrent period with unimpeded latitude of choice. I chose Field Marshall Edwin Rommel of the German military. It was not difficult. The great world war hadn't ceased by many years and the general yet lived on every learned person's lips, admired by international statesman and military leaders alike. A prominent speaker whom the university not long past had invited to speak to the student body and faculty gave a speech which he named, *"Get It While It's Hot."* During the war he reported for a major newspaper on the events of the battles and his boss had directed him to rush to the scene of action as promptly as trucks or jeeps could transport him after the action ceased and set to print what he saw, heard, smelled, and felt and scribble down these stimulants before they began to cool from his senses. The name Rommel still sizzled, in any event in the recordings of historians and journalists.

I wrote ten pages, typewritten, after spending two weeks researching the background material, infusing not one phrase in the work unless deeming it entirely consequential.

Not even arguably the last lines were the best; they said exactly what I wanted the reader to read. It wasn't in me to end my portrayal better. "Rommel is regarded in every aspect as a humane and professional officer. His Afrika Korps was never accused of war crimes, and allied soldiers captured during the African campaign were reported to have been treated humanely. Orders to kill Jewish soldiers, civilians, and captured commandos were ignored."

Once when Doctor Linskie and I took lunch in one of the university cafeterias a young professor who sat at our table overheard us speak of the desperate attempt of the Germans to savage London to the ground with daily and nightly bombings and that despite the relentless attacks of the Lufwaffe the will of the stubborn British refused to collapse. At this the young professor drew a paper from his satchel and read aloud. "Please God, keep the British from getting excited any more than they are for one more year and we'll not bother you again." Doctor Linskie took issue, emphasizing that he realized that the originator of the citation intended it as a pun against the Germans, supposedly implying that they were light minded, which of course was a bad misstatement, but that which pricked him more than anything else, he said, was the negative reflection, or possibly a negative reflection on the great general. "Rommel too was German, young man, a rare military strategist and thinker and a great and humane general and you should set yourself aright by correcting your error." The young professor recognizing his carelessness of judgment puppishly apologized and added that he would instanteously begin to dig into the background of the famous Rommel, which he confessed he knew little of. Some years later I added Dr. Linskie's blistering lines to the orginal ten pages that I used as the main body of a speech that I delivered to the local rotary club.

Nearing the end of the fall semester, my last class with him, Doctor Linskie unleashed a surprise as he strode into the classroom bright and animated. His eyes sparkled, as if he were on the verge of sharing something spectacular. At first, I very much was lost in attempting to decipher the scheme he was about to unravel—but finally, after a few tries I believed I had unscrambled his intent and it happened that I was correct. I determined that he had whipped up something new and unoriginal even before he let out the first word.

"Literature classes ladies and gentlemen are replete with stories which we call novels if the stories are committed to print. But there is only a thread of difference between a novel and a story—they are the same one may logically contend, but with one obvious qualifier. A story precedes the novel; it has to. A novel is not possible unless someone tells it first in his head. But let us for the sake of simplicity say that we are at this moment adopting the story for discussion and are forgetting my allusion to the novel. Now, I ask myself this; who are the greatest users of the story? Our system of public schools? Our universities? I'm saying neither. And if I have said correctly then who perhaps are the greatest users of story telling Ramsey?" he said, angling his eyes over at me. "Will you care to render an opinion?

"The movies. Who else but the movie makers?"

"Ditto. That's my guess too. The movie industry thrives on stories; like us, they'd starve without them, and we profit lavishly from their adventuresome spirit. I love to go see movies. Many are in fact the spawning grounds for still more rich stories or movies that arise from the scenes we see and hear—the thrilling swashbuckling concoctions, some incredibly bizarre and ingenious plots of heroes and heroines who fall in love before our very eyes and when we come out of that theatre we're primed and ready to write our book and have our characters fall in love just like them. Now where is all this leading? It's time I decloaked the mystery. It's leading to something of a game and here is how it works. At a time when I give you a signal you are to choose in silence, without prompting from your classmates, two movies, the best or worst in your opinion you ever saw and tell me what they are. I will assume the role of interrogator and you at my prompting are to answer Why you have given each of your movies such high or low marks. Since however there are more of you than time will permit for participation, I must limit to a number of three those who will take part." I did not feel shocked at his choosing me as one of the three. I somewhat expected it. I'd been with him longer than anyone else. We were asked to stand and begin. He gave his signal by way of gesture for us to select our movies and then assigned each a position of order which signified when we were to step forward in defense of our selections. I ended up in second place. The movies chosen by the person preceding me have faded into the mist, nor do I any longer possess his name; I was too busy internalizing my own choices. When Doctor Linskie turned to me I said *Roman Holiday* before he half way emptied out his question.

"Ha. You are quick today Ramsey. But do go on. Your taste is excellent."

"I liked the plot tremendously; to say it in brief it's where a bored and sheltered princess escapes her guardians and falls in love with an American reporter in Rome, as all of you know. It's an utterly unbelievable tale and if your intellect tells you it isn't believable your heart almost convinces you that it is. I loved the parts played by the actors; Audrey Hepburn was absolutely luminous, as she always is, so much so that I wanted to push her partner aside and take her for my own. Sometimes two people are phenomenally magical when teamed with each other and they were exactly that. Gregory Peck, his usual stoic self came off as lovable and comedic; and as a great gentleman. Though deeply smitten with the princess, in fact very much in love with her, he tried desperately not to show it and on the last when appearing at the palace for the princess's interview with reporters from near and far, dared not let an inkling of it seep through, calling upon every ounce of steely resolve within himself to display a poker face. It hardly sufficed. If you looked closely the faintest of evidence in his countenance gave him away. The story is as funny as it is beautiful and has that special appeal, a fairy tale twist that draws you to it time and again. I never tire of watching it."

"Is that all?"

"Yes sir."

"Now the second."

"Streetcar Named Desire. Brando, Brando, Brando."

"What do you mean by that exclamation, Brando, Brando, Brando?"

"Marlon Brando uncontestably was the most singular powerful figure in the film, dominant, overshadowing all others by far in the casting—the epicenter of the show, in fact was the show—, a hot dark haired young man who looked of danger and wildness and anger, his way off screen as well as on and to whom women, because of his good looks and sensual attractiveness, streamed in droves. They would drop their pants for him in a heartbeat should the opportunity have led the way. Married women and single. Who can forget his portrayal of Stanley Kowalski, that brash young man howling Stelaaaaaaaa, which in time lovers of movies began to regard as a cultural touchstone? As it is with *Roman Holiday,* I never tire of watching *Streetcar Named Desire.*"

When the third student finished Doctor Linskie did not necessarily praise or compliment us but there was a controlled pleasure in his smile that showed his delight with the results. Needless for me to here say that down through the years Doctor Linskie's experiment on that day popped up in my head times inumerable and that I had adopted his technique for use in my endeavors of teaching.

The fall zipped by. The holidays and the turn of the year had come and gone, and January, then February, then March and soon following the spring flowers began to bud, during which I spent appreciably less time with Mr. Yazstremski than ordinarily. Even the minor legal cases and therefore the deposition deliveries were beginning to substantially taper off. For awhile, over the past month, my trips to New York lessened to two days a week, the result of two major corporations selling off, which for years had kept the firm on retainer. In the meanwhile, I continued to receive a weekly check in the same amount. My pay not in the slightest reduced. One day I answered the phone and there was his voice, resonant and peaceable and gentle, which I sensed was attendant to my resuming my regular work load. It wasn't. And I didn't ask. I listened.

"Ramsey, I see that you're due here on Friday. Can you make it earlier, say on Thursday, or Wednesday if at all possible?"

"Yes sir. I can."

"You choose the day."

He meant Wednesday and I wouldn't disappoint him. He further indicated that there were a few items, legal and non legal, that he'd like to explore with me.

"We'll luncheon at Arnos. You'll recall it I'm sure. It's that small Italian recluse over on the back street behind us. A dinge but the food is good. And it's not noisy there."

"I know. We were there together before. And Aaron took me there a time or two also."

"Ah yes. Aaron liked it."

The next day, Tuesday, I boarded a plane in the early afternoon. As it droned along, I looked out the window at the soft white clouds which the plane was parting and pushing aside, then leaned back in my seat and began to ponder what the meeting might involve, besides the legal portion, though quickly set that aside because just being with him I thought was the winner for me, the best thing of all about our meeting. "Uplifting, as it always is." Yet, this one bore a cast of difference from the usual, mainly in the sense that we were going to Arnos, which we hadn't patronized in some time and I knew therefore that whatever we took up would evolve unhurriedly. More social than anything else. Still, there was an air of difference about the meeting that I couldn't put my finger on. I returned to trying to determine the upcoming situation once more but convinced myself of its uselessness and stopped, figuring that we'd for sure take up a slough of narrations before we finished and that I couldn't possibly out guess him in advance. And after this I began to think of him in a personal sense.

"He's wise, a wise man indeed. Like Mr. Carney. I'm blessed that I am showered with his friendship as I've said many times. A very dear friendship. I've learned practically all I know in the parameters of law through him or because of his guidance. He's like a private teacher. Isn't that amazing? A private law teacher. What young squirt in town can claim that advantage?"

"Well, Ramsey. You're here. Good you could come." It was nine o'clock the next day. I chuckled underneath at his remark. It was his custom to greet me with the same unaltered expression, "Good you could come," whenever I flew in and reported to him at his office. "What I have in mind will eat up a couple of hours and if there are more we'll break anyway. I have a table reserved at Arnos for lunch."

"Yes sir. Glad I'm here. And glad we're going to Arnos. Am I too early? We didn't exactly set the time, so I just came on over."

"You're fine. Fine. It's nine o'clock and that's a good hour for us to start." As usual he had checked into his office at seven to attend to other matters in addition to prepping for me. "Pull up a chair and we'll take a look at the agenda, part of it business and part of it social, but more social than business. How does that sound?"

"Sounds good." I dragged over an empty chair bound heavily of fading brown leather which he liked to allude to as his favorite piece. I recalled him once commenting that it belonged to his grandmother. It was old, you could tell that at a glance, but so were the other furnishings in his office, which encompassed his desk with the accordion roll up panel. He loved this room; I honestly thought it contributed heavily to his inveterate passion for work and that it undoubtedly added to his efficiency. I loved it too. Sometimes when catching him away I'd sneak in and carry out my preassigned tasks at his desk but with his permission given in advance.

"You've heard of asset forfeiture laws have you not?"

"Some. Now and then when you mentioned them. But not much. The fact is I'm as green as a gourd relevant to such laws."

"That's all right. I didn't expect that you were a great deal informed. That's why I'm introducing them to you."

He saw that he had my undivided attention, all ears ready for his words, with my note pad laid out before me on the edge of his desk and pen in hand. A pleasant smile lit on his kindly face as his eyes leveled across at me.

"Now, a thing or two on the beginning—a sketch of history. Forfeiture has been practiced literally since ancient times to take property wrongfully used or acquired. The Greeks and Romans were among the first to activate the law, yet the use of it goes back to the Old Testament. The first statute in this country authorizing civil forfeiture was enacted in 1789 as a sanction against ships for customs violations. You see then, that asset forfeiture is not a recent legal device. From time to time it has undergone various amendments and I suspect that will occur again as new elements of society evolve or suddenly spring up. Any questions so far?"

"No sir."

"Then I'll move along"

But he paused, at least for a second or so, thinking I had held back, that I actually did have a question. I didn't.

"Asset forfeiture. What is it? Simply putting the matter it's a system of seizing or confiscating money, or other forms of wealth, by the state or federal government which has been illegally gained. Cases regarding asset forfeiture are either civil or criminal. That's how they're classed. Criminal is one thing and civil is another I restate because that is a key element as far as litigation and prosecution are concerned. Criminal cases are the more serious; and that figures because that's where you get at the drug traffickers and prostitution rings. The government, I must emphasize, likes to seize these monies since the take is sizeable and they can use it to put more cops on the street. And I buy that. It's a good thing. Of course, the government likes to tap or seize this money, but what they don't like is the hard-complex draining rigor of tracking down the drug kingpins and the like. So many go betweens."

"You mean—?"

"As I say, the go betweens, layers of low level cronies that cover for them and I should stress that they are in such numbers and of such complexities that an investigator faces a monstrous ordeal to progress anywhere near the real culprits that pull the strings."

"What can the officials do about it?"

"What can they? Often nothing. The feds can't seize something they can't find."

Acting as if thinking of something else to add he ran his fingers across his chin and winced, meaning that he now bordered on the cusp of an idea but apparently some of it had temporarily slipped his grasp. Whatever it was he decided not to pursue, suddenly rising and crossing over to a side table cluttered with papers with barely enough room left for the emplacement of even one more sheet, if here I am allowed to exaggerate.

"Coffee Ramsey? There's another cup for you."

I answered that I would and thanked him while going over to pour my own. We then returned to his desk and sat down.

"We've dwelled enough on the criminals; now let us concentrate on the civil offenders, the less serious of the two. To begin with, this sphere of the law is troublesome. I'm mixed in my views in regard to the trial cases of record and the laws themselves. What is civil asset forfeiture? It's what the wording says, the seizing of assets. The process has been harshly criticized by liberal and civil liberties advocates for its greatly reduced standards for making it easier to convict, reverse onus, they call it, and they point out that conflicts of interest are tempting when the law enforcement agencies who decide whether or not to seize stand to gain by keeping the assets for themselves."

"The seizing agency can go too far, overstepping its boundaries?"

"I think that is right. In fact, I hold that they do. I'll cite you a case. I didn't quite believe it when I tripped across it for the first time, but when I studied the law more penetratingly, I began to evolve a staunch dislike against the tactics that were employed. A grocery man who had operated his business for forty years reported that the IRS seized in the neighborhood of $30,000 of his store money even though he wasn't charged with a crime. That's scary. His state of affairs was made worse by his shortness of sufficient funds for paying his suppliers. In other words, his suppliers shut him down. Left him helpless. The IRS used an obscure federal anti-money laundering statute to seize his business bank account, alleging that the man frequently deposited store receipts in amounts of less than a certain sum—I can't seem to remember the figure—to hide his profits from the IRS. Whether he did or not is something of a moot question. The grocery man is bringing suit against the government for judgment."

"It seems unfair. How could the man have known of an obscure hidden law, and what's more, suppose he deposited a mite more than whatever that figure was, then what?"

"Ah yes. You have a point and questions like that will arise from the plaintiff's lawyer. I'd like to see him win. Actions like this are beginning to veer out of control."

We kept at it until half past twelve then snapping his finger he suddenly said we'd better leave for Arnos. We were soon on our way, with him continuing to verbalize the subject of asset forfeiture, annoyed with himself over his failure to recall the exact fiscal amount that landed the grocery man into a legal snare. The clump clump of our shoes pounding hard on the cobblestone alleyway muffled his low level of speech so cogently that I strained to catch what he said and moved closer.

"Ramsey if you're puzzled that I've given you a tour through asset forfeiture you need no longer remain that way. And with good reason. We're opening an arm to our firm in Chicago this fall and want you among other things to head up the research on cases of that sort for us. How does that strike you?"

"Strikes me well. But I'll have to bone up on the laws, and that'll take some doing."

"It will. That's a fact. But remember. I'm as as close as the telephone or closer. You know that."

"Yes sir. I do. As you are in all else."

"Any questions?"

"One. That is, one above many others. Will we represent plaintiffs more than defendants?"

"Ha. That depends."

The interior of Arnos appeared muchly a semblance of that which I had expected, granted, I hadn't been there in a couple of years and then only limitedly. I found it nearly the same as when I first set foot in the place with Aaron, the furnishings and décor still as they were but I failed to remember the imponderable conglomerate of pots and pans that hung from the walls, which did not contribute well to the atmosphere. They weren't there before I felt certain. The lighting too had been converted to a pale dim. He said before hand that I shouldn't expect any noise and there wasn't, only the presence of old men talking in low broken mutterings sitting around the tables munching their lunch numbering to no more than fifteen. Someone sitting next to us wore a reddish plaid shirt, while his associate to his right sported a double breasted brown with a bow tie at his neck. Most of the men that day were clad in suits, yet Mr. Yazstremski explained that by and large they dressed in street clothes of an irregular fashion.

"Look at all those guys Ramsey, old codgers, and look at me while you're at it, for I'm just like them, none of us with many years left before we stop breathing air. A bunch have prostate cancer and so do I."

"You do!"

"Yep, I do. I hope the mention of it doesn't bother you excessively and it shouldn't, with your sharp intellect telling you that one day you'll grow old too and if you don't suffer from prostate disease, you will from something else that will eventually put an end to your life's journey."

As my great friend talked and I largely listened, my gaze fell upon his face, entrenched now with furrowed lines and drying skin no longer young. But his mind was young and I had heard him proclaim innumerably in past sittings that he took life one day at a time, not worrying a second of his impending demise, knowing, or believing, that he'd stand another year of existence and that he darn well intended to enjoy it.

"Is your prostate ailment terribly bad?" Concern showed in my voice which I tried to camouflage and regret augured sadly in his eyes that he had brought up his condition to me.

"No. Not now. It's the slow kind, inching up by small creeping gradients, the kind you don't notice, but you know it's hanging around, eating relentlessly at your flesh. But we don't need to dwell on this. You're a young man and you have other things on your mind besides sickness and the eventual struggle with death. I didn't like to think about such things either when young and I didn't unless a relative died.

"When you landed on Ellis Island with your family how old were you if you don't mind?"

"Not at all. A mere fourteen."

"Young. A boy."

"Yeah. I was. And it's been a grand ride ever since. If I wrote you a book or a lengthy letter of my history I wouldn't change one line. I've been blessed, helped by the Lord and then by the people. Lots of them. If they hadn't helped I don't know what I would have done. But they did. And I hope by some generous amount, generous in His eyes, I'm paying them back by helping someone myself. That's the one thing a person can do and should do you know. And it's all so easy if you stop and think about it. A candle loses nothing by lighting another candle."

"You've lit mine Mr. Yazstremski. And you'll never know what that's meant to me. I can't thank you enough."

"Ha. You've thanked me a plenty. I wish I could have a million acquaintances like you around me Ramsey."

The waiter wearing a white apron approached with a pad in hand, and with pleasant face spoke Mr. Yazstremski's name. He knew him well, and asked in corresponding breath if his lunch should consist of the usual.

"You know the answer Alphonse: white beans, slaw, corn bread, a cut of fish, and a piece of cocoanut pie. Coffee to drink. You have it all don't you?"

"I do sir. I knew I didn't need to take it down. It's stayed in my head from the last time."

"Which was last week."

"Yes sir. Which was last week. Ha, ha, ha." It was a meekish submissive laughter I thought, born from his sensing or knowing somehow that he now stood in the presence of a man far superior to himself. Then I thought further: "even the least educated realize when they are facing a man of greatness." Alphonse had begun to turn to me but Mr. Yazstremski supplied the answer before he could form his question.

"My friend here will order for himself."

"I see. What will you have sir?"

I had already decided. "Make mine exactly the same."

"Very good."

Chapter 55

WE BEGAN to eat and more talk followed. The subject he sprang on me soon thereafter turned out as another unpleasant one, more than unpleasant, shocking, and I struggled to recover, unsure of finishing my meal.

"I've been waiting to tell you this Ramsey. I don't think I can break it to you gently, so I'll unload it directly without circling around to land it on you lightly. Aaron has gone into the service, leaving in the realm of a month ago. He asked me to let you know."

"Ah! He has? Ah, my goodness. I'm stiffened. I don't know what to say. Was he drafted?"

"He was. It's happening to a bunch of young men these days. And some actually are not so young." I qualified as the latter but avoided saying it.

"I would have thought he might have told me, written or called."

"Yes. From your stance I would have expected that. But he didn't. He had his reason. Said he wished to avoid bothering you with his troubles in than you were weighted with enough of your own. He really meant that he wanted me to do it for him."

"Where is he?"

"San Luis Obispo, California."

"I'll declare. Boot camp. Way off out there."

"That's right. He said tell you he'd write and poked into the conversation that you were the best of the mass of his friends that were in his midst while in college. And I believe that."

"His best friend. And I believe that too sir. And I can't wait to hear from him and as soon as I do, I'll write back. He shouldn't have tried to spare me. I know the score. All young men our age are subject to the draft. I am, and I know it. But I'm not going to let that bother me. I'll hope for the best, as they say, and take whatever comes. That's all I can do."

"Well, that's a healthy way of looking at things, certainly that's the case when you don't have control over them. I pray that you don't have to go in, but you may and you could fall victim to a bullet—a horrible thought—and I may read of you and grieve like a mother in mourning who's lost a baby child and wish that God had put me in your place, an old aging soul, instead of a youthful man in his prime on the verge of delivering splendid things to the world around him. Let's hope with fingers crossed that the war will soon end or that one of a preponderance of other events intervenes to keep you out and safe. But no man knows what awaits him. That's for sure. He can only march with time and see."

Then he shook his head as if to say that we both were gorged by now with the conversation he'd largely instigated, at least feeling that way about himself. "Ah me. No more of this. It's dejecting. Let's switch to another topic."

The hour at this juncture reached two and I expected Mr. Yazstremski to rise promptly and announce that we'd better get going, an expectation that failed to materialize; for he stayed exactly as he was, relaxed and comfortable, and gave no indication of leaving. Once he motioned to Alphonse to serve more coffee. Along with the coffee Alphonse of his own accord set out another piece of cocoanut pie for each of us, on the house he said. We pursued a miscellany of things, one thing and then another, a good many things in fact without notice of the clock. I hadn't intended in the least to address the names of Darya and Nenia and Andrea, and did not say anything of Andrea but as the conversation progressed, I lowered my guard and opened up my entwinement with the two girls. Aaron had once said a few words to him regarding my closeness to Darya and a girl whom he could not name. That was of course Nenia. Never once did I give Aaron her name, only referring to her as a girl or that girl. When Mr. Yazstremski spoke of Aaron's revealation I owned up to the truth, or rather, provided an accounting of the events as they had transpired to which he sat and partly grinned and countenanced amusement. I explained that once I was infatuated with Darya and still was and in love with both her and Nenia but more in love with Nenia, or thought I was, and that I had been in love with her for years, almost as far back as the beginning of our teens, and that while there were dual affections at play, I knew in the finale what I would do. I said that it surely was Nenia who would win out and that the end of it all was decided a long while ago. My dilemma was, I told him, the severing of the cord with Darya without hurting her and that frankly I couldn't see myself mustering up enough courage to initiate the final dissolution. But that I'd have to.

"Ah yes. You'd encounter a little sorrow in your heart. I'm sure of that. Don't they say that grief is the price you pay for love? But why not look at it this way. You're young. Young people pass through many romantic flings, full of starry notions, that they treat a mite too seriously. Perhaps you shouldn't let a minor fix like that preside over your emotions. You may see many young girls in your early youth that tug at your heart off and on. And the two girls you've spoken of may see some young man that attracts them too. That's a pretty natural tendency of young people, male or female. Young women, like young men, don't always reveal to their current lover or husband the things they've done or thought of doing. Even the daintest most perfect seeming little housewife will fudge in opportune moments. If the truth is uncovered their answer is quite often that they were just kind of innocently drawn in. But you say it's Nenia who has the advantage, the girl of your heart, and that she's the one. That's good. You can't settle on two. You could but you'd regret it. So, it looks like you're on the right course. That's what I did, narrowed down to one. Oh sure you may look at me now, an old fop who's past his prime so long ago he can't even recall when it was, and wonder what mysterious forces merged that led to my getting emotionally mixed up with two different beautiful girls. Well, I did. I was young then just like you. In time it turned out well. I narrowed it down to one and I've stuck by her, no monkey business after that. I wouldn't take all the gold there is for my Ginny. She's my life. A miracle happened the day she came to me. I'm sure that Providence threw its influence on her to do that. But back to you. Don't worry over your dilemma anymore Ramsey. It'll all clear up in the wash."

Yet, I didn't let things stop there. "I never meant to let myself succumb to infatuation for Darya. I really didn't, but I did. My eyes simply could not stop looking at her. She was so beautiful and seemed to take a liking to me and before I knew it we were likened to two peas in a pod. It's as simple as that."

"Ah yes. I know. She looked awfully good to you as many girls do to a young man. You've no doubt heard the common adage that the grass is greener on the other side of the fence. And that's true. It is or else it looks as if it is. The pretty girls are the same as the grass. A young man is always seeing one that he thinks looks a little better than the one he already has."

"But I didn't mean to intimate that Darya is more beautiful than Nenia. I just meant that she's very beautiful. But she's not quite as beautiful as Nenia. Well, not necessarily. They're tied most of the time."

"I understand." His face lit up all over as he laughed, not an outright laugh, more or less subdued, which emanated a kind of grating from deep in his throat. I think I had sounded a bit immature, unaware of it until his laugh playfully suggested that I had amused him. "I only meant to characterize the human male in general. And I'm glad you're taking up for Nenia. I like her and I've not even met the girl." And then, "I don't know that I can explain why a man's behavior is like it is Ramsey other than he is born with a tendency to explore the sight of the opposite sexes. They fascinate him. And even at my age I have to admit that women, so beautiful and all, whom the Lord made that way, are alluring to my eyes. It could be also that it's His strategy of putting man's restraints to a test, teaching him self denial, which he has to learn sooner or later. But it's hard. Man sees and he wants, wants incalculable things he can't have, definitely beautiful women, which he hungers for, that's his nature—but the Lord couldn't afford, with good reason, when He made man to let him have his way entirely, for if He had that would have amounted to absolute chaos and He therefore wisely decreed, 'You can have one and that's enough, so pick out one and if she'll have you let that do,' or so I imagine him saying as much. And that's very good advice as I believe I myself have earlier said or implied."

And then I put in. "But Kings and Sultans and the whole wanton bunch since the beginning of history have blatantly ignored the Lord's precepts, haven't they?"

"They have. That's the consummate truth. But they paid for it at a dear price. Herod, as is said, reputedly laid claim to ten wives and no telling the unnamed concubines and ladies of his court and whether he contracted infectious diseases from these women I suppose remains substantially invalidated, yet it's of record, at least speculatively, that he might have succumbed to a rare degeneration of the genitalia."

Finally, he lifted himself from his chair and stretched, announcing that unbelievably four o'clock now had descinded upon us and that he didn't mean for us to discourse all that while, then apologized for insufferably boring me with endless litany, not in any way the case. It was an honor that he willingly usurped his time and intellect to go into a range of topics with a young man who in comparison to his astounding legal mind hardly could have been worthy of carrying his coat. And I told him as much and that I greatly coveted his presence for the afternoon and the wisdom as usual that he had imparted to me. He sloughed it off. It seemed to embarrass him. "Ah Ramsey. You have it backwards. It was I who benefited. What an afternoon! I wish every afternoon could unfold like this one. I'll remember it always."

On our return to the office the snarl and roar of the commuter traffic echoed loudly on the next street over, a thoroughfare, the taxi drivers impatiently tooting their horns. It hit me that lady fortune had smiled generously on me the day I found an apartment so close by, which permitted the great advantage of walking to work when I came to New York. And there emerged another reflection of cheery uplifting. I recalled that Mr. Yazsrtremski mentioned that I should begin revolving my duties lying in wait for my occupancy of a seat with the law firm in Chicago at the end of summer; and confidently remarked that within two years I'd have my law degree and likely end up as the attorney second in command. These were nice thoughts, uplifting thoughts, and I smiled broadly, but there was another of equal strength which when combined with them made me even happier. It had to do with a burden that had gnawed at me for a lengthy while, whereupon one day he up and suddenly said that it was good that I planned to teach a course or two at the college that fall. "You're young and unmarried Ramsey, so you'll have time and freedom for bearing the extra load. No family obligations. And it will broaden your footing as a lawyer." I cleared my throat in relief, badly needing his blessing. I wasn't sure up until then that he approved of my teaching and working with the law firm simultaneously.

When graduation day rolled around I somehow deluded myself that Bertinelli, Aaron, and Darya will have parked themselves in the crowd, there clapping and waving when I walked the line and even before that meet me at the Cubs Nest for a pre celebration. It almost seemed as a given that they should show up. It wouldn't happen. Fantasies, no matter how hard we wish, seldom come true. Bertinelli telephoned that he couldn't attend, giving a perfectly acceptable reason, but time has washed away the words of his message. Aaron,

I believed I knew, either still remained in boot camp on the West Coast, or now, according to the last letter that I received from him, was on his way to Vietnam and I judged maybe already there. Worse perhaps, more than anything, at least more stunning, was the letter from Darya that arrived at approxuimately the same time.

Dear Ramsey, my sweetheart:

You will find this letter difficult given that you were not forewarned and that it is suddenly sprung upon you. I must not beat around the bush as you sometimes say but speak truthfully and forthrightly. For sometime I have believed that our affections for one another were imbalanced, that I loved you dearly, almost obsessively, while your affections for me began to fade. I believe that is absolutely how it was. My senses did not steer me wrongly. I wish that things had gone some other way.

But do not decide by any measure that my realization of our situation is responsible for what I am here revealing. It's not. Everyday I see by way of television and the evening news our boys dying abroad, too often—which is terrible—no one around to try to help them stay alive and to help in some way relieve their suffering. This has affected me deeply, it has torn at me unceasingly, and the best way to cope with it is what I am doing or have done: I have volunteered for service with the medical corps of the United States Army in the Vietnam Theatre of war. Yes, I am untrained but they will train me. I can learn quickly if I have to.

I would have met you and told you my dear face to face what I have here said but that would have proved enormously trying for the both of us. It is best to let this letter say it all.

Goodbye for awhile.

I love you.

Darya

I should not have felt surprise, should have seen it coming and would have except for my failure to sufficiently decipher the subtle inferences of her earlier letters. I likely showed in mine that I had lost a slight of my usual exuberant self toward her, showing indirectly in the lines that someone else occupied first place in my heart, Nenia of course, which she somehow must have known or sensed. In the lines that she wrote she often said she loved me and I realized that she loved me as only a woman can for whom love outweighs all else that is good in life. I also recalled that in my lines not once did I tell her that I loved her too, although I did. I did very much. But the shadow of Nenia kept me from uttering the sentiment, as well as an impulse in my heart never to use the term unless exclusively given. I didn't opine that Aaron had told her about Nenia. I once mentioned Nenia to him; just as I told Mr. Yazstremski I had, yet only referring to her as "that girl," not by name. Even if I should have mentioned Nenia by name I would have posted great odds that he wouldn't have exposed my secret. But Darya I am convinced guessed the truth. And I knew that she had as surely as I lived and breathed. I believed then as now that there is a mystical strain in women which equips them with insight far superior to that of men in fathoming the deep bottom of a secret. They feel and sense things and interpret little vague signs that men do not.

At last, it happened that I hurt her which I so avidly hoped to avoid. Perhaps she was right; better for her to have refrained from facing me face to face and saying that which she felt she must in print. I silently thanked her for that. It wasn't as easy as my great friend Mr. Yazstremski said it was or should be in matters where young lovers face a moment of severing the umbilical cord that has closely bound them. Or so it was with me. My heart was a mellow heart, not natured to suddenly harden itself in preparation of killing a love affair.

I plumped down on the couch, the big one where we two used to sit and studied the floor. I remembered that first day I met her, a gorgeous Serbian girl with coal dark hair lapping over her shoulders and then some, who a moment before came through the doorway with Aaron. They were out touring the town they said. When she smiled, she did not smile broadly; it was a controlled smile, soft and lovely, and her eyes seemed to survey me from head to toe with such skill of stealth that their designs would have easily escaped the notice of better than the most meticulous observer. I saw then that she liked me and I liked her, not in my wildest however envisioning where our affinities were to lead, but even if I had I doubt that I would have traversed a different course. Such a lovely creature is impossible to disregard. Very soon we fell in love.

Carefully making certain the folds were exact I cupped the letter in my hands as if a precious adornment and went and tucked it in my files as a keepsake.

A sizeable number of those who seriously intended to attend my graduation failed to appear, outnumbering those who actually did; Nenia, for instance, with great enthusiasm counting on attending, buying a new dress for the occasion, but falling ill with a stomach virus which forced her to bed for a solid week; and then my mother who felt persuaded to stay with Lillian Yancey, who still lived in a nearby town, once our landlord, now on the brink of blindness and debilitating feebleness. Her husband no longer lived. My mother called more than once to express her disappointment that she'd have to miss seeing me in the graduation line on this coveted day, "a pivotal moment" she said, pleading that Mrs. Yancey desperately needed her. "Desperately needed her," I echoed with a touch of anger. "Ah yes, Mrs. Yancey. It suddenly gallops back. Mrs. Lillian Yancey. 'Don't!

Don't! Don't put your hands on the car Ramsey, you'll soil it,'" she nearly shrieked when the scrubby little urchin touched her bright shiny new car doors and fenders with his soiled hands which got that way by his playing in the dust of our front yard. I marvel in retrospect at my mother's spirit of forgiveness. Even at my young age I read the woman's flaunting, the vanity in her pride, and that she cared little more than she might a morsel for the sharecropper family struggling to eke out a subsistence on a farm owned by her and her husband, the soil of which seldom if ever previously tasting an ounce of fertilizer enrichment. I realized as well that people even of the same flesh and blood will not think alike and that on this issue my mother and I stood eons apart. But that she was right in her conviction and I wrong. Yet, in my heart I strongly resisted accepting as much, and knew that I would never exonerate myself from the dislike of the vain and overly proud image of Mrs. Lillian Yancey, nor would I forgive her, but would no longer carry a grudge, if for no other reason than if I did so I would hurt only myself.

I promised my mother that I'd see her shortly after graduation, after I'd cared for a growing heap of other obligations.

Among those that attended were Doctor Linskie and Mister Yazstremski, the latter completely unexpected, who said he wouldn't have missed it for anything under God's Heaven. It did me good to see them meet and speak so warmly to one another, both praising in my presence, but giving no name, a fine young man of whom the future should behold for destiny foretold of his making an exalted place for himself. Gerard's parents were there too; Mrs. Warf, his mother, finding her way to me in the crowd after I'd walked the line to hug and kiss me. She was adorably dressed, and beautiful, too young in appearance for one to genuinely believe was Gerard's mother. The glow of her skin lent proof that she spent a goodly tally of hours in the sun ridden fields helping with the harvest. I recalled that she said to me on my visit that she sometimes drove the truck and guided the tractor that pulled the low boy trailer on which the hay and corn were hauled.

"Thank you Ramsey for coming to see us when you were needed. You turned the tide and I'm forever grateful to you."

"It really was nothing Mrs. Warf. I mainly wanted to see him, that's all, and the family farm that he talked so fondly of and loves so much. I enjoyed the trip indescribably and other than that I need not have come. He would have gone back on his own."

"You're nice to say it that way. You will come to see us, won't you?"

"Count on it."

Chapter 56

MY MOOD sailed to a lofty height after seeing and speaking with Mrs. Warf, but soon she faded from conscious when shortly someone else tapped my shoulder and turning, my eyes peered amazed into the gorgeous beaming face of Andrea, who'd not sent one letter or made one telephone call that she planned to attend. She had evaded my sight throughout the graduation exercise. I burst into laughter and reached, then pulled her into my arms and hugged her and delivered a kiss full on her lips. "Mercy," she gasped, then laughed a laugh of euphoria and in return wrapped her arms around my waist, exuding a grunt as she squeezed me with all her might. And kissed me back. We just stood there for a little, then began to hug again all over.

"You're a sight," I said upon our letting one another go and revisiting normalcy, "a sight completely unexpected. But a nice one I must attest. So, you decided to come back after all. I wouldn't have bet a dime on it."

"What? Shame on you. Of course I did. I wouldn't have missed it even if I'd had to walk all the way here from Louisiana."

I chuckled at the extremity and playing the game I said that there would have been no need for that, for I would have driven to Louisiana to pick her up, and then take her back if I'd known she wanted to see me graduate that badly.

"How did you travel?"

"By car."

"How long are you here? At least a few days, I hope."

"Two, maybe three. My grandmother is doing okay and we have a person staying with her that she trusts and so do we."

"You and your parents."

"Yes."

"That's good. Where are you staying? Are arrangements already in place?"

"At the Ritz Carlton. But I'm not yet registered."

"That's good news. Save your money. We'll call over there and tell them to cancel. For a while practically everyone has left the fraternity house and the place is weeping from loneliness in that vacancies are in the high percents."

Within a jiffy she took me up on my suggestion and I walked with her to her car, then we drove from there the four blocks to the fraternity house, together transferring her belongings to a room next to mine. She offered apologies for the excessive trouble that she said she was now causing.

"Don't say that Andrea. It's no bother. It's a good way to keep you close. You've been away far too long and we need to catch up."

"Okay. You win."

"How long did you say you can stay?"

"Three days. I've just changed it from two."

We took lunch at one of the university cafeterias. "The kitchen at the fraternity house is closed, and not to reopen for another two weeks."

"That's all right," she said. "Anyway, we need privacy. Are you sure your preference is the university cafeteria or some little nook downtown?"

"Let's save downtown for later."

"Good."

Following lunch we pursued a miscellany of options—strolling across campus, side tracking now and then into some of the old buildings where she many times attended classes, as well as myself; and going by the department of physics to let her say hello to some of her research professors, who were wild at seeing her again and prodded her to come back soon.

"We have a batch of work for you Andrea, whenever you're ready. You are rejoining us, aren't you?"

"Sure. I'm looking forward to it."

"How is your grandmother?"

"She's doing very well. She's approaching perkiness again."

Afterwards we drove meanderingly throughout the city, even through some of the back alleys which we knew well, despite never really patronizing some of their cafes, and then for awhile up the west shore of the lake, in the interim happily concurring that if the next day showed up as warm as the present we'd spend a few hours on the beach. The activities of that night were predetermined. Whoever mentioned it first gained support from the other that we'd hang out at the Cubs Nest and take dinner and dance a round or two and see old faces. When the hour of eight arrived, it found us there sitting around one of the dwarf size tables, with candles furnishing the usual glow, exchanging hellos with a host of students who knew her, most asking Andrea if she'd returned for good and hoped that she'd made up her mind to because they'd missed her awfully.

"Not yet. But I'm sure I'll enroll in the fall."

Shortly a waiter stole over. A very young person. And good looking. He recognized her, and, his face lighting up, gave off an encompassing smile.

"Glad you're back."

"Same here."

"Like to order?" He looked at her.

"Un unh. Not this minute." But then. "Would you like some wine Ramsey? A small one, a teaser to send us properly into the evening."

"Sure. Why not?"

Right away the waiter returned and poured full our glasses, glasses tall and shiny and with disproportionately long spindles or necks, no bigger round than a girl's little finger.

A quirk within me had forever stood curiously poised to inquire of the brand name of a wine, any wine, for instance likened to the one just poured, but this one varied from the norm, absent of that exotic invention, the label, conspicuously emplaced on the surface of the bottle to give the drink greater salability. The waiter poured from a canter, not from a bottle, so no label was seeable anywhere even though I looked all around the surface for one.

"Crimean white wine," he said.

"Hmmm. Haven't heard of it before. How did it land on these shores?"

"People travel. They buy it and bring it back," said Andrea.

"That's right," chipped in the waiter. "We don't sell it here. The owner only last week flew back from the Black Sea, from Yalta, with a limited supply. He's offering samples to his guests."

A good start to a good evening I thought. Instead of Andrea lifting her glass to her lips for the first sip she extended it outward across the table and I met it with mine, "clink," a dead echoless sound emanating as they bumped together.

"A toast," she quipped.

"Okay. What? Say it."

"No."

"You won't tell me?"

"No. It's secretive. I'll never tell you."

"Well! The complicated kind, are you?"

She closed her eyes as she silently said her toast and to this day I am without knowledge of that which revolved in her private scheme. I guessed, and destiny, I believe, proved that I guessed correctly.

Then time for dancing. While the rest of the girls dressed in casual wear, some in pants, Andrea chose to fit into more formal ware. Upon her person there clung a lovely dress of soft chiffon that fell to her ankles, in the style of the Spanish, speckled with tiny red and yellow flowers running round it as if they were leaves blown haphazardly across an open field. The sleeves foamed and quivered on her pretty arms, a glitzy spangle appended to one of them near the wrist. As was Nenia's and Darya's her hair dangled in extended strands about her shoulders, so enticing to touch that I ran my fingers through it once and lightly tugged, for which I drew a playful sanction. "Naughty." Laughing, she reached and pinched my nose. During our last hour we mainly sat and reminsenced and projected our thoughts into the invisible future, likened to an immovable sphinx lying in wait, vaguely fearing and vaguely trusting whatever promise it held in abeyance.

"It's not the same without Aaron and the others, is it?"

I said it wasn't and then she asked of his whereabouts and if his letters reached me without lengthy delays.

"He's in the Army, in Vietnam. For a while on the West Coast but I'm very sure he's in Vietnam now."

"What!"

"Yep. That's where he is."

"When?"

"A couple of months back. The draft took him."

"Mercy."

"That's what I said."

"Who told you?"

"Mr. Yazstremski."

"I'm flabbergasted. Are, are—?"

"I know. What's my situation you're thinking. I'm not unlike any other guy. I'm squarely in line for the draft, even though I'm a few years older than the average going in. It's only a matter of time."

Then a look of seriousness, if not anxiety, swept unfamiliarly onto her youthful face, which suggested the sudden news caught her off guard, as did Nenia when the discussion of the draft also surfaced.

"Oh Ramsey! You too?"

"Me too. And why not?"

"You take it so casually, with no concern whatever."

"I'm concerned. But I can't do anything about it. It's the God of war I'm up against. He's speaking to all us young men. We're the guinea pigs of his experiment. There'll always exist a God of war irrespective of the era. He's been around since the period of the great Caesar and all time before. But let's not discuss this further. Tonight is a night for pleasure; that's why we're here."

"Yeah. It is. I'll do my best not to bring it up anymore."

She kept her word, not asking anymore questions, not any regarding her fears of the war and the draft, locking these forbiddens inside for keeps, her intestinal grit guaranteeing that there they would stay. I admired her for her exceptional intelligence and beauty but said to myself that her strength of grit equaled or transcended them both.

Looming within me there was something else, something of another nature that I expected sooner or later to disclose itself which she had every right to open for discussion. Did I still have feelings for Darya? Or anyone else? She never asked, appearing to have no interest or speculations in regard to the question, or so I assumed, and wagered that such would remain her attitude of mind so long as she could manage to keep me exclusively for herself, at least for a while. Once she'd been willing to share me with Darya, and that appeared of no bother to her. But I wondered—and concluded; "A mere pretense," I said, "which won't last much longer. No young beautiful woman can claim that degree of tolerance." And in the same breath as well, I imposed strict constraints on myself not to inquire if someone else lived in her life too, which would have come to me disbelievingly if learning of the matter. But still, I couldn't fathom why there wasn't. "She's stunningly beautiful and intelligent and passionately sought after in droves by the males. It's not their fault that they can't win her, for they certainly try. It's hers. What else can I say?"

Chapter 57

I TOOK ON a new job that fall. Not as the office director that Mr. Yazstremski said might pass to me when I finished my law degree in two years, but as the lead researcher for the firm digging into cases of law of the multiple sorts, asset forfeiture among them. Mister Stylman in concert with other power figures of the firm, fractional owners, Mr. Yazstremski a significant part of the cadre, finally decided to proceed with the opening of an office in downtown Chicago which they for several months had explored. The site of the building which housed the office overlooked the waters of the massive lake, the waters sometimes unruly, sometimes placid and friendly, a location with which I couldn't have been more pleased. Admittedly somewhat nervous I started my first job as a lawyer, or a staffer doing a lawyer's work, a tad unorthodox because I hadn't yet earned a law degree, and I entertained a tinge of uneasiness that other young lawyers of the firm might harbor resentment. A consultation visit with the staff by Mr.Yazstremski extinguished once and for all the upshot of that likelihood.

"Now ladies and gentlemen we all have a job to do. Getting the job done is what counts. Do your work well. And recall at all times that team work is at the very core of the principles for which this firm stands. Team work. Working as a team is the utmost of essence. Always keep your consciousness tuned that you are to function as a team member, but simultaneously are to carry out your individual assignment. And never wonder for a moment what the guy or gal in the next office is doing. Or why they are here. Others will assume that responsibility. And if you abide by these tenets you will have made a significant contribution."

To the last person the implications of his address were emphatically understood. And as a result I felt more secure. He would never tell me and I would never ask whether his expressions were designed and delivered for my advantage, which I believed more than not they were. That fall also marked my first experience as a college teacher, albeit part time and at night, teaching only one class, which proved quite enough. Doctor Linskie in his bargaining on my behalf suggested that they use me in literature, my strong suit, and I hit it lucky. I loved teaching literature, I knew I would, and easily developed a wholesome camaraderie with the freshmen, my students, so eager and intelligent and innocent and vibrant and all this I relayed to Mr. Yazstremski, who on witnessing my gush of enthusiasm could have asked if I liked teaching more than the practice of law but didn't, for which I expressed silent thankfulness. I didn't know how it might strike him, my old friend and mentor, if I said teaching, whose heart held passionately that I should become a lawyer, a fine lawyer, perhaps in the semblance of himself, which to me was as impossible as suddenly discovering the outer boundary of the galaxy. But if I had asked him to let me know his feelings: "Well Ramsey, that is a hard one. You say you like teaching better right this minute. But tomorrow you might do a three hundred sixty degree turnaround. Isn't it a fortunate thing indeed to have two from which to choose and I might add an analogy of lightness if you will so allow. It's a whole lot easier than choosing between two young beautiful girls that you like equally or about equally."

For awhile I said nothing to Mr. Yazstremski of my choice of teaching over the practice of law. I did say it to my mother in one or several of the letters I wrote to her. "I'm teaching part time Mom, only one class at night, three times a week, at a small college in the city, a great thrill, more than I ever remotely envisioned, and to my way of thinking this is what I'll end up doing for good—but still dabble in law, a profession that so far has treated me more than well, better than I have deserved. Meeting up with Mr. Yazstremski has resulted in my receiving a lifetime of experience in a mere glimpse of time and I will never forget the things I have learned from him. I thus must say merely that I'll stay close to the profession, and to him, and maybe when all is said and done opt to law altogether. Who knows? But at the moment I dearly love teaching."

With my ambition serving as the drive force, perhaps an ambition a mite too excessive, I enrolled for a graduate class at the university offered each Monday night between the hour of seven and ten, sitting beside students I'd never before seen, none of the old ones, although I did see Andrea who ran into me practically every night I turned up for class. Since I still resided in the fraternity house and she lived next door she frequently dropped in to see me there too. She'd beg me to meet her at the Cub's Nest.

"Come on Ramsey. You need to loosen up. You need a break. Let's meet over there this next Friday night," and not infrequently I took her up on her entreaty. The semester rolled along and suddenly Thanksgiving and then Christmas raced upon us. Andrea pleaded with me to spend a few days with her in Louisiana on either Thanksgiving or Christmas, one or the other or both, a plea I knew I couldn't accept and she knew it too. Still, she asked. I liked the idea, and had liked it ever since I met her, specifically when in the beginning she one day colorfully implanted a picture in my head of the unmatachable fun we'd have together on some backwater secluded bayou in the State of Louisiana, which so far hadn't happened, the wish nonetheless staying alive and it continually dwelled within me that one day I just might find myself out there with her on Lac des Allemands hauling in a mess of large mouth bass. Sometimes I'd tell her of such dreaming to which she'd let out, "yeah Ramsey. And we'd catch those dude's too. I guarantee. I know how it's done."

That Christmas I stayed for two days in our small town, brief to the extreme, for as soon as I arrived it was as if I'd started back. Even in a small town you can't see or do much in a span with so great a limitation. I saw my mother for the larger part of the first day and Nenia for the larger part of the other. Nenia had told me she would catch the train home for the holidays and that she'd arrive several days ahead of me. She frowned when hearing of my shortness of stay.

"It's brief Nenia. I acknowledge that. But there's too much on my plate. I just can't stay longer."

She had to return to work too, given that it wasn't as quickly, which furnished the grounds for making my decision easier.

While there, on my first day, I learned of an incident which badly disturbed the townsfolk, as it did me, this because I knew both people in the involvement and had for years, once attending the same Sunday school that they attended. There was a flare up. Lennie Peyton, the son of Wallace Peyton and Maudine, a pint size dandy in his early thirties with a bantam rooster temperament—and a hustler of young women—attacked his wife Jeanette with a Coca Cola bottle. They'd married when she approached her eighteenth birthday, his age at the time recorded at twenty four years. The old men sitting around on the seed sacks at one of the grocery stores often speculated over who was the best looking woman in town and she usually drew the over all pick.

"He wuz just tired of her, or wuz struck on another woman" one man said to another, "and the cocky little bastard tried to kill her with a Coca Cola bottle."

"Was it jagged?" asked the other. "They said it was."

"Nope. Smooth. If it wuz jagged he might have finished her off, but apt as not he couldn't have done it. She wuz too strong for him, a big stout woman, and fought the son of a bitch off. But he woulda killed her if he could have. At ere is what the prosecutor claimed."

With Wallace's money behind him Lennie avoided incarceration in the penitentiary, from there on the people uttering or mailing nasty threats against his life and rather soon the townsfolk began to report they'd scarcely glimpsed him since they didn't know when. His mother found it strenuous to continue in church to which she'd devoted four decades of her life. In the years that followed a report surfaced that Lennie started peddling dope, driving to somewhere in Mexico where he picked it up and sold to buyers and addicts in the United States. Whether defensible or not the townsfolk spread such darkened news, further alleging that while driving on a mountain road south of the border with a car secretly stuffed with drugs, a band of outlaws, drug dealers, intercepted him and sent him and his car caroming over a cliff of immense height. I looked once to see if they might have buried him in the Mount Pisgah Cemetery, detecting his name nowhere on the headstones in the quadrant where his mother and father lay. John Eric said they never found him in the wreckage, "so how could there have been a burial?" He speculated that if a body of bones were lifted from the carnage there would have been nothing to see but bones, the flames likely melting the flesh to less than a cinder.

Another year came and went. There were interludes when I felt that no war raged anywhere. All seemed too peaceful to adjuge otherwise. I even began to create an illusory ideation that I might dodge the war. After all I'd heard nothing from the draft board. I weighed the possibility that they might have purposely overlooked my name due my being a few years older than the average. Settling in on my graduate studies proved easy enough, let alone the single law course in which I had enrolled and I had done well in my position as the lead researcher for our new Chicago office, research for the New York office in addition, particularly for Mr. Yazstremski. He called me practically everyday, and if he did not I called him. Even sometimes I delivered depositions back and forth for both offices. I kept up with Aaron through his mother, who as thoroughly as practical sent news that I anxiously welcomed, especially news of his status of well being which topped everything else of interest in that heretofore he had averted injury and stayed alive. Mrs. Narvanna wrote letters too; to the effect that Darya had reported her involvement in the Mekong Delta, to whom I wished badly to send a letter and would have except Mrs. Narvanna wasn't absolutely sure of her address base in the war zone. "She moves around constantly, here today and some place else tomorrow" I could tell by her words, a bit veiled, that Dary often was close to the fighting, and that danger lurked for anyone in that sector of the world and that anywhere, wherever in that hell hole, was too close. Her mother said that she served in a medic's role, an associate helper I judged, considering she possessed no degree in medicine, or even in tertiary medicine; but had been well trained, I felt sure.

And then it happened. My draft notice showed up in the mail, sent first to my mother's address, and then seeing the identity of the sender on the face of the plain brown envelope she shrieked, and then fell into chronic worry, but adjusted to the shock and relayed the document onward. I talked to very few of my fast changing situation. The military allowed me ten days for wrap up before reporting for training, too brief I moaned, not nearly enough time, but it never is. So, I pulled myself together and wrote as many as I felt I should, not very many actually, and went to see the rest, my mother, Nenia, Mr. Carney and Titiana, John Eric, Mr. Yazstremski, and Mr. Stylman. Of course mother cried as I left and clung to me as long as time would let her. From there I caught the train to Saint Louis for a last farewell to Nenia, where I would have time enough for a two hour stay before taking another plane to Chicago. When Nenia opened the door I saw she was crying, and evidently for the duration of the afternoon, her face red and eyes in some manner swollen. She kissed me and clung to me and uttered most pitifully that it was near beyond her ability to stand seeing me go. I let her talk. She appeared very much to want to, her words grievious of hurt and sorrow. And then a most unexpected thing happened, a confession, a calamity, an excruciating shocking confession. It blew my mind.

"You will hate me for what I am about to reveal but I cannot secret it any longer."

Any number of possibilities surged into my mind. "What on earth" I asked in silence, stiffened with suspense. Dumbfounded. "Wha, what on earth."

"You're going into the war Ramsey, and may never come back."

With this she at once pressed her face against my chest and started to pour out an array of deep hurtful sobs. But went on after a brief recovery.

"I told you once of a French soldier that I accompanied to the train as he neared his time of leaving for Viet Nahm."

"Yeah. I recall your saying something of him, that you'd just met him and that you went with him to the train to see him off."

She had now hung her head and explained amidst soft convulsive sobs that their seeing one another went further than that.

"I didn't tell you all and now I must, even if it hurts you badly. I did go with him. But I'll have to confess that I misled you. I actually had been seeing him for a month, not just a few days. On his last day he begged me to let him make love to me and I, I,—I did." She now wept remorsefully. "I didn't mean to but it was his last night, and he begged me pitifully. I felt so sorrow for him. I can't explain or defend why I surrendered, that is, why I gave in. You hate me terribly, I know, but I couldn't let you go away without clearing my conscience, which has hounded me relentlessly every since I, I, I."

"Was intimate with the French soldier," I said, finishing for her in the bitterest of tone.

My will to act with patience and civility suddenly collapsed in favor of my other side, my very bitter harsher side, my emotions suddenly beginning to run the gamut; first I stood frozen, in disbelief, then tried to reason why she'd let him break her down—utterly useless, for she'd already said she couldn't explain why, and then a thread of unmanageable ambivalence edged into my stomach. Anger raced through my every being, bitter hateful anger. "Here she is," my other voice cried out, "the girl you've always worshipped, whose virtues were as clear and clean as certainty itself, the girl who declined you time and time again with citations of scripture to back her up."

I stood looking at her but my eyes saw nothing, not at the moment in any event, the form before me only a blur in my state of vehemence. I recall before opening and storming through the front door that she amidst her unstoppable sobs uttered meekly that I could have her now if I wanted.

"Hell no. Keep it. Give it to your French soldier boyfriend."

As I stumbled infuriatingly down the street toward the bus stop she followed as far as the edge of the front yard, crying out, "Don't, don't leave me like this Ramsey. Please come back and talk with me."

Not to her but to myself, I answered, "Talk with me, that's the joke of the century. The sweet girl that for so long I planned to marry and she me, up and let's a Frenchman screw her. Who knows how many times? And wants me to talk it over with her." But in the fog of my cruelest temperament, I asked God to forgive me, cooling enough to feel it beneath my ordinary character to have uttered the rawest form of vulgarity. Despite the awful searing hurt that tore through me I saw myself as a better man than that.

The bus arrived on time, the brakes screeching loudly, and I jumped on and promptly found a seat and began to sort through that which unfolded a short while before. I couldn't think. My mind swirled. I do recall amidst moments of forced calm that it all came about with such sudden swiftness, when an hour before I couldn't have with the aid of angels anticipated the jolting admittance about to descend upon me. I kept whipping up a montage of self consoling words that all of this soon would pass and that the girl wasn't worth the torment that held me in its paralytic grasp. When I boarded the plane I sat down by a Japanese man dressed in an upscale suit that only big money could buy. And we struck up a conversation which touched upon the war. He saw my military bag.

"You going in or are you already there?"

"Give me two days and I can tell you it's the latter." I did my best to display better temperant with the man in furthered conversation which bordered on the edge of impossibility. Nenia's admission to infidelity spun like a cyclone in my head, the state of my bewilderment plainly showing in my eyes. The man apparently saw something amiss in my behavior and arose from his seat and wove his way to the front in search of another place to sit.

Chapter 58

ANDREA DROVE me to catch the bus assigned by the military to transport me and a bunch of other guys from Chicago to Fort Oglethorpe, Georgia, the site of the boot camp where I would intern and train until further instructions directed otherwise.

While the training passed quickly it nonetheless tried my endurance, an ordeal of an incredible grind, and for the first phase, a few weeks, I began to doubt if I had the capacity to withstand the pain and the terrific physical rigor that I must continue to endure. Within two months a transition in the chain of decision making suddenly came into being that drastically placed me in an unexpected circumstance, which made me ecstatically happy. Someone in the chain of command, detecting my educational background, and my proclivity of penmanship, ordered my transfer to communications, a field which to me meant that I was to assume duty as a combat correspondent. Not so. Much to my chagrin I would shuffle papers in a military office in Tokyo, and edit the descriptions of action sent to us from the military officers in the center of battle. That's all. They tried at Fort Oglethorpe to infuse the trainees with the deadly serious notion that all phases of training were designed to win the war and help keep soldiers alive when entering the battlefield campaign, with the addition of one step more, the installation in our young minds that the aim of the war undergirded the high and noble purpose of securing peace for the entire world, "peace at any price," our President had transmitted to the American populace in a nationally broadcast speech, and that we were there for that reason. Yet how many were the times that the same reason got jammed into the ears of scores of young men drafted into the future wars that followed. After my own thought processes took over and I began to cut through the political hype, it dawned on me with an acidic bitterness on my tongue that a long pre-existing adage was never more truly spoken than, "War is a young man's fight and an old man's folly."

Why were we there? Why the Vietnam War? Reams by this stage of history are now compiled of that epochal event and continue to grow.

When attempting to trace these questions to their remotest sources you quickly discover the name Ho Chi Minh, who emerged as an outspoken voice for Vietnamese independence while living as a young man in France during World War I. Inspired by the Bolshevik Revolution, Minh joined the Communist Party and traveled to the Soviet Union for training and indoctrination. He helped found the Indochina Communist Party in 1930 and the League for the Independence of Vietnam, or Viet Minh, in 1941. At World War II's end Viet Minh forces seized the northern Vietnamese City of Hanoi and declared a democratic state of Vietnam (or North Vietnam) with Ho as President, known as "Uncle Ho," occupying that seat of power for the next twenty five years, emerging as a symbol of Vietnamese struggle for unification during a long and costly conflict with the strongly backed anti-Communist regime of South Vietnam and its powerful ally, the United States. The Vietnam War, was also termed as the second Indochina War, and also known by the current Vietnamese citizenry, even to this day, as the Resistance War against America or simply the American War. They called it a cold war, not only played out in Vietnam, but also in Laos and Cambodia and ran from November 1, 1955 to the fall of Saigon on April 30, 1975, twenty long years of strife. Two principal opposing forces lead the conflict, North Vietnam, supported by the Soviet Union, China, and other Communist allies—and the government of South Vietnam, supported by the United States and other anti-Communist allies. The U. S. Government viewed American involvement in the war as a means of preventing a Communist take over of South Vietnam, a containment strategy, the Americans argued, with an aim of stopping the spread of Communism, which if left alone would proliferate into a domino effect—where, if one state fell to Communism, so too would the adjacent others. The North Vietnamese government had its sights set on reunifying Vietnam under Communist rule, viewing the conflict as a colonial war, fought initially against forces from France, in the Indo China war, and then America, and later against South Vietnam, which it regarded as a puppet state. And herein is given the principal reasons why the war erupted.

But there is much more which is significant to say, which is that a mere reading of the conflict as a historian might report may fail to capture the fierceness and inhumanness of the battles, in other words, the savage destruction of man by man.

An allusion to the Vietnam War as an unconventional war by any measure stands as the key place to begin, reminiscent of the jungle combats pitting the Japanese against the Americans in the South Pacific during World War II, a hit and run war exacted by the Japanese on soil with which they were microscopically familiar and which posed a great and difficult disadvantage to the young American soldiers unacclimated to the terrain and the heat and the rain and the mud, not to mention the nature of the fight itself, the unorthodox tactics contrived and employed by the enemy. Endless talks were exchanged among the staff in Tokyo, where I officed, with regard to the Viet Cong, suddenly a strange adversary, a guerilla force fighting for the Communist cause, savage fighters, merciless, suicidal, attacking by surprise from out of nowhere, utilizing a maize of underground tunnels—200 miles of a network of that sort connected to one city alone, some of the staffers said, and this made for easy escape which by and large meant that they simply faded into the population masses, the distinguishing difference between a Viet Cong guerilla and an ordinary citizen virtually beyond the capability of the American soldier. North Vietnamese and South Vietnamese looked indelibly alike, friend or adversary and the South Vietnamese feared with trembling the ensuing penalty should they squeal on a Viet Cong hiding among them. Adding to the Viet Cong's arsenal of warfare devisements was the recruitment of young boys in their teens for joining the resistance, who elatedly entered the fray, and did it with passionate zeal after undergoing a period of carefully controlled intensified brain washing. Severe ridicule or shame fell upon those who hesitated or declined. The North Vietnamese army varied radically from the Viet Cong in tactics and the use of heavy weaponry, tanks and cannons and mortars conveniently supplied for their disposal by the Chinese and Russians. The Viet Cong weren't as effectively prepared to operate such weaponry but yet the implication is not here given that they were completely lacking of its usage. For both the North Vietmanese army and the Viet Cong women were a vital link in the war chain. Unlike the American women the North Vietnamese women enlisted to fight in the combat zone as well as providing manual labor to help keep open the Ho Chi Minh Trail for the soldiers and for the transport of weaponry and munitions. Some served as comfort women, sexual providers, for male Communist fighters.

If you seek to win a battle or the entire war, according to some military tacticians, you must not spare the extremes to realize your purpose; entertaining the view that it is better to annihilate without pity or mercy as was the temperament of Genghis Kahn, and scores of soldier emperors likened to him, before and after his time. The Americans were not of that constitution, yet committed atrocities, it is fair and honest to acknowledge, slaughtering women and children among which the Viet Cong were hiding, the intent to kill rather than the opposite—but on the whole the American soldier wasn't conditioned to commit genocidal murder. It yet flows in the consciousness of the American public, perhaps not as strongly embedded as some tend to believe, that the American military lost the war, which is not the truth. The only war lost occurred on the home front. U. S. forces, most singularly special operations troops, won almost every military battle against the Viet Cong guerillas and the North Vietnamese army. The American politicians are the ones who caved in as protests erupted against the war and spread like wildfire on the college campuses and in the sprawling cities throughout the nation.

Since I viewed the War from my office in Tokyo, distanced far away from the fighting, I only knew it second hand, from the reports pouring in from the front, hideous and horrible, even when described in words, but reports and words only scratched the surface, never coming close to capturing the terribleness of the actual battle—the rampant screams of young men, on both sides, as shells fell one after another upon them, blowing bodies apart, the awful unimagined disorder of both soldiers and officers, confused, in disarray, striving in the madness of it all to find shelter but with none found and yet somehow in the wildness of the furor reaching into the depths of themselves for a way to counter and turn the tide. Only met by more cannon fire and mortar explosions. This was war, hell on earth. I thanked the Lord many times over that I had escaped the fury of the battle front. I thanked Him many times over again when after a stint of two years the military sent me home, a decision unlikely to have been initiated should they have believed I would have functioned as a military correspondent. When I asked the old Commandant in charge why they elected not to try me in this capacity he answered that I lacked sufficient experience, but that mainly they already had good capable men filling the role, and that moreover the cost of training to fit me into such a position would far outstrip the value returned. "It's a matter of economics my boy."

Darya left the armed services long before my own discharge. During my stay of service I went to see her twice, once in Saigon and then after they transferred her to a recovery hospital in Tokyo famed for its therapeutics successes. Her mother a while before conveyed by letter that she lay in medical care at one of the makeshift hospitals in Saigon, wounded from shrapnel in the Mekong Delta where the Viet Cong launched a vicious surprise attack. When I arrived at the airport a soldier drove me by way of jeep to the hospital, a low lying structure, one story in height, constructed of a combination of Southeast Asia soft wood and plastics and some aluminum. As I entered a pretty South Vietnamese nurse clad in American nurse's attire met me and showed me a barely habitable living space, as squeezing as a garret, French for attic or cramping space, where I would reside during my stay, but it would have to do, then I followed her down a maize of ever changing corridors, turning left then right and then the reverse and continued these logistics until getting to where we were going. The smell of hospital odor pervaded the hall ways. It at first tended to engender in me a lightness of balance, a queasy stomach, as hospitals generally did and the moans and cries from the suffering young soldiers in the wards we passed were even more unsteadying. I asked for the direction of the men's room.

"Are you all right sir?" the nurse asked, her brows narrowing.

"I'm fine," I lied. But shortly I emerged and said that we could go ahead. The affectation passed quickly as I knew it would. Then we were at Darya's room.

"Ah, there you are," I said, as I walked in, pretending utter calm, faking the impression that to me she appeared her usual self—rather than pale and gaunt, and strikingly underweight, as I saw on first glance. One or the other of her legs extended upward at an angle of thirty degrees by my approximation, fitted into a cast, held in that position by pulley wires useful for lowering or raising her leg if she asked or if otherwise determined necessary.

"Ramsey," she feebly said with a resonance barely above a whisper. Seeing in her face that it strained her to talk I went over to her, sitting down on the side of the bed that allowed barely enough space for doing as such, and, glancing at the pretty nurse for a gesture that all was okay if I did. I took Darya in my arms and held her, while she sobbed softly. I supposed that she'd nurtured an apprehension that she might not survive but when she saw me her face lighted with happiness and her anxiety appreciably lessened. They said they'd notified her of my visitation but nonetheless she appeared overcome with surprise upon my walking in, so much so that she made an exertion to lift herself but the nurse stepped in with comforting restraints that she'd better not. "You must lie still dear. Don't strain yourself. We need you to help us guide you to wellness." Clasping her face with my hands I kissed her forehead, and then her lips, but only her lips lightly, not a kiss of old. More tender than that, uttering as sweetly as a man can utter sweetness that at last I had come and would have sooner except looking for her wasn't an easy thing. "But I'm here now darling."

"My mother. She let you know," she said weakly.

"Yes."

"I knew she would. She thinks much of you, that you're the finest."

"And I echo the same of her."

She tried to smile but the smile refused to surface. The pretty nurse showed concern, realizing that even though Darya felt a great urge to converse with me further she should nonetheless cease. She couldn't handle the strain. After I held her lovingly in my arms for a little longer I did as the nurse wished, caressingly leaning her back on her pillow.

"Say nothing else sweetheart. I'll let you rest for the time being. We'll talk later." She offered no resistance, her energy spent. Easily and quickly she fell off to sleep.

The nurse left, seeing about a call for her assistance down the hall. But was back abruptly, evincing that we should talk and of the opinion that I wanted to, to anyone willing to give me an appraisal of Darya's condition. I very seriously worried.

"Darya has sustained very bad injuries sir. She's weak."

More than weak I had decided. "I can see that she is. How bad are her injuries?"

"Her leg is riddled with wounds, cuts and gashes and contusions."

"Shattered."

"What do you mean?"

"Torn to pieces, never again useful for walking."

"I don't know sir if she can walk again. I'm not a surgeon. But I've seen the wounds. They're awful, I hate to say. I'd like to spare you. But I have to speak plainly."

"Ah me. Will she live? She looks awfully bad, so frail and lifeless. I'm afraid for her."

"We'll have to see Mr. Maynard. I cannot tell you more."

Chapter 59

HER CALLING me by my family name meant that the hospital administrator received advanced news of my arrival and conveyed it on to his staff. I thanked the nurse, looked at Darya once more lying fast asleep, and asked of the whereabouts of the hospital cafeteria, ravenously hungry all at once. I hadn't eaten since early morning. I found the cafeteria and sat down and ate, ordering from the menu, and after this studiously trained my eyes on the workers scurrying helter skelter. I concluded that the management ran an efficient cafeteria, as good as any in the United States, the staff obviously well trained, the bulk of them South Vietnamese, and the food evenly balanced between American and local South Vietnamese selections. But then. "What am I to do about Darya? I fear for her. I can't fly back to Tokyo in two days; I have to stay with her. She might die any minute, and if she doesn't, she for sure needs me to help pull her through. Her fight is a test of will, I said reassuringly to myself. How badly does she in her deep internal psyche want to survive? It's up to me to help her, to give her strength, to avail myself by her side when she needs me, to give her someone to talk to in the lonely hours of night." It was then that I resigned myself to do what was a must.

"Yes sir, yes sir." I had called the Commandant of our operation in Tokyo and now responded to his questions in broken patches of grammar. "Her life is at risk. She's border line at best. Frankly sir, I'm afraid for her. We were close in college, and remained close until she up and joined the U. S. Military Medics, and after that I lost track, at least temporarily, until her mother very thoughtfully sent word to me that there was a good chance I'd find her here in Saigon."

"Her mother told you that, hunh."

"Yes sir."

"All right. Take a month. I'll personally oversee the handling of your furlough papers."

"You're granting my request?"

"It's done Ramsey. Nurse the young girl back to health."

Each day I sat with Darya, holding her part of the time as she sat propped on her pillows stacked three high or when I did not hold her she leaned against my breast or shoulders. In the first week of my stay I detected no appreciable improvement in her condition, her voice yet low and weak like when I first came and her conversation limited. A few sentences at the most. But she did her best to smile and though brief talk took place between us she reveled in my holding her and I felt that just holding her was as therapeutic as the exchanges of conversation.

The monsoon season had started its perennial drenching, a sign that the life style of the city populace was to undergo drastic alteration for awhile, but which did not deter my slipping on a raincoat now and then and rummaging through the streets. The people were friendly and nodded and smiled, as they recognized me as just another American. Saigon rippled with energy, vastly overcrowded, this happening because of the influx of refugees, and I ventured that it drove the officials to some considerable stress to try to devise a system that assured its smooth and viable functioning as a municipality. Sometimes I ventured as far as the docks that faced the South China Sea, a mile away or more, driven there by means of a man operating a cyclo-pousse, men of his trade pedaling away without rest, day after day, not uncommonly dying young from over work. Under ordinary conditions the boats and ships anchoring further out would have been within easy sighting, but on this day, even with the lessening of the rains, the discharge of steam and mist obscured the harbor. A trifle discouraged, I returned and don't believe that on any other occasion I went back.

"Where did you wander off to," asked Darya, weakly, when I entered her room.

"To the sea front, just a short distance. I'd love to see it in the sunlight. Much more gorgeous then."

"It is. But you worry me. One never knows when the terrorists will strike. You must exercise more caution. Will you promise not to go quite that far again?"

It bothered me that I had brought worry to her. "I promise. I'll limit my strolls to right around close."

The nurse in attendance of Darya soon made it practice to join me in the cafeteria for coffee at the midmorning hour. Her break time. In these sittings I more and more came to know her, the curtain of strangeness between us by tiny but measurable gradients beginning to open and draw away and with minimal time I adapted to her broken English.

"How is she?" I asked one morning, alluding to Darya.

Sipping her coffee she seemed as if debating an answer. Then a bright little twinkle shone in her pretty dark eyes as her lips lifted from the rim of her cup. "Making progress. Slowly but surely. Can't you tell?"

"I'm not sure. But that's what the doctor says anyway. Right?"

"Yes he does. The infection is no longer a threat. And she eats better, as you surely see. Just still weak."

"More time. That's the thing."

"More time."

They called her Luan Wing in the wards and hallways, a nice name. It fit her perfectly. As said, she developed a pattern of joining me every morning on her break, no longer taking up Darya's condition as the sole subject, during which she taught me many things pertaining to the Vietnamese culture, their wants and needs, their likes and dislikes.

"We like Americans," she once said. "We are sorry there is war. I talk to my fiancé about it often. When it's over, or if something should allow it to happen sooner, we will marry."

"He's an American?"

"He is."

"My! Where is he now?"

"Here at the hospital. But wait. I mean he's a medic attached to the hospital. He brings the wounded here from the field of battle."

She did not have to explain that he assumed a formidable undertaking, enormously dangerous. Later in the conversation she mentioned that he came from Atlanta, Georgia and that they would settle there when married.

"You'd leave South Vietnam?"

"We would. Better to raise our children in America."

"How brave and trusting," I pondered, "marrying a guy from such a far off place, going with him into a land of strangers with greatly different customs from those native to her, everything stunningly different except for the children she will give birth to and raise, her common bond, her beacon of strength, Americans, and her salvation for the daring leap she will have taken. May God see after her. I pray that all turns out well."

As time passed my conscience began to urge me to act on something that I determined as a must, and tapped Luan on her shoulder and asked if she'd mind accompanying me to a flower shop to help select a bouquet for Darya. "I should have done this long before, Luan. I'm afraid men are terribly lax in the little niceties that mean so much to a woman." I wasn't sure of her thoughts of my displays of affection but the brightness of her smile assured me that she loved what I had done, and she happily said she'd go with me at lunchtime. The shop had on show literally rows of flower arrangements of countless variations, a sea of them, as one would find in America. Walking around we saw many that were tempting choices but backed out and kept looking. Finally, eyeing one that caught my fancy, I said to Luan, "I think that's it."

"She'll love it Ramsey. Tell them you'll take it."

The teaser advertisement read, "Fuchsia roses are sweetly stunning amongst red matsumoto asters and pink mini carnations and lush patches of greens." The clerk clarified the descriptions and repeated that this included emplacement of the bouquet in a classic Venetian clear vase. "Add that to my bill," I said. I carried the adornment into Dary's room hoping to spring a surprise, only to find her sleeping, which I did not dare disturb, deciding that the suitable option was to set it on a side table adjacent to her bed so that she would notice it upon awakening. As of late I had started taking meals with her, mine taxied in from the cafeteria in response to special order, which she now expected. I left for a brevity for a stroll on the street. When I came back I sat down and sat there until she awakened and looked over and smiled at me. Shortly after we'd begun to eat she stopped and paused, with a peek of frivolity in her countenance as she looked into my face and said that someone had delivered a mysteriously beautiful bouquet to her room while she slept that afternoon, and then unable to hold back burst into laughter.

"You didn't have to do that sweetheart. You really didn't. But it was the sweetest thing. It was touchingly thoughtful."

"Yes I did have to. That laugh that I have just witnessed proves it. It's worth ten doctors and a hundred doses of medicine. I feel like kicking myself for not visiting the flower shop sooner."

"You won't do Ramsey. You say the most adorable things."

Nearing the end of my furlough it became clear that Darya had rallied, had fought well, had won, out of danger the doctor affirmed, a fact that I myself previously established because we'd begun to have long extended talks throughout the day and partly into the night provided she managed to stay awake. Not often but once in awhile she inquired of Aaron, with me answering that I didn't know anything, that I hadn't heard of his whereabouts other than through his mother who in a letter said that he in all likelihood was in the throes of battle somewhere in Vietnam.

"I'll ask the Commandant if he will try to put a finger on where he is."

"That's good. Do that. And then let me hear of his remarks."

"Yeah. I will. I miss the guy," I added with heartfelt lament.

"And I do too Ramsey, awfully much, and all the rest of the old gang."

"The old Cubs Nest gang, I guess you mean."

"Yeah." She smiled softly across at me as I sat in a chair by her bed. "That's what I mean."

The days dwindled down, and one day we knew that I was on my way to leaving the very next day, both hesitant to let it pass over our lips, but at last forced it to surface. I spoke first.

"I'll journey back this way soon. Promise that you'll take extra good care of yourself. Do as the doctor instructs."

"I don't have a choice, do I?" she pitched in, following with a cutely contrived wrinkle of her nose.

"Afraid not. Any speculation of the length of your stay here?"

"Yours is probably better than mine. I am improving, very much. I can tell so much so that I've begun to wonder."

"Wonder what."

"If you'd like to kiss me. I mean a very good kiss. You've not given me one yet."

"I'd like it. I would very much like it. Just been waiting for the invitation."

"Now you have it."

And then taking her in my arms I kissed her, warmly and prolonged, almost like old times, but not quite. Not yet. Luan had done her hair and the natural vibrant color had come back to her cheeks for keeps. She looked almost as beautiful as when I first met her, almost, but not quite. That would happen but in its on good time.

The rain fell in torrents that night, slamming fitfully against the hospital walls and on the roof top, appearing that it would last throughout the next day and not slowing or stopping perhaps for several days in that the temperament of the monsoon season was nearing the peak of cresting. I began to speculate on the dependability of my flight schedule, whether the flight control center might issue a cancellation or alteration. By dawn the clouds lifted and while the sun refused to break through, the signs of the atmosphere were evident that our plane would have sufficient clearing for landing and taking off. It was scheduled to land at ten o'clock and pick me up. After breakfast I went to Darya's room with my baggage encasement strapped across my shoulder and set it down next to the doorway, gathering her in my arms.

"I have something to tell you," she said, sounding an uplifted note, excitement in her eyes.

"What?"

"They're transferring me to a therapeutic hospital in Tokyo for the remainder of my recuperation, not just yet they say, perhaps in two months. I'm overjoyed."

"That's wonderful."

"Tokyo is on my high priority list to see, a fabulous city, with every imaginable novelty, and I'm determined to heal ahead of time because then, with me well and sound, we can explore it together without me tagging along as a hindrance. You'll do it won't you?"

"Are you kidding? I'll jump at the chance. I'm already rummaging through the list of places I'll take you. That's my ordinary bailiwick you know. As efficiently as a map maker I've learned my way around and can navigate with the utmost of ease to any place of your choosing."

After this she began to talk filler talk, a ploy to keep me there until the absolute last minute. But, as I anticipated, the tears started to well. I hugged her one last time and turned abruptly and left, my way of sparing her, and sparing myself. I didn't want her to see me cry either.

But she wasn't the last to whom I would say goodbye. As I made my way up the hallway a nice soft little hand tugged at my sleeve and then turning there she was, Luan, who laughed brightly at my surprise and said she'd walk me to the front door.

"She will miss you Ramsey. Badly. You've been good for her."

"Yeah. I think I have. I really do. Every day, likened to a freshly budding rose opening up and exuding outward, her health by tiny strides gained new heights. I could see it happening. It gladdened my soul that I might have had something vital to do with it."

The soldier waited in a jeep a short distance from the doorway, sent there to drive me to the tarmac where my plane would set down at ten sharp and take off with minimum delay. Crawling in I leaned over and drew her to me. She had stood close. "Goodbye Luan," I called out as we were rolling away, "if I don't see you before, then I'll see you in Atlanta."

"Oh yes! We'll look for you."

After returning to my work in Tokyo by three weeks I guess, I opened a letter from Leland.

Dear Ramsey,

What words can I select for inquiring of your welfare and safety? I won't try. Instead, I'll hope and pray that you are all right. I think of you every day and say a little prayer for you often.

Likely, I would now serve there beside you were it not for my marriage to a girl who will soon become the mother of my son or daughter. My obligation as a married man to a pregnant wife has let me escape the draft, which I view from two different stances: I feel guilty for not being there in the fight, and yet am glad that I'm not.

You won't take it as a great and sudden surprise I know to hear that I'm now linked to Edison Electric, and in the forthcoming months will transfer from San Francisco to Schenectady, New York. When you return home and continue your work with the law firm in New York City that'll put us together again. Of this I am bursting with an apex of excitement. My fingers are crossed that it will happen in the nearest of time.

Take care,

Leland

I almost did a little jig at hearing from him, and began to contemplate the news carried by his letter, namely, that he had married and his wife was with child but that he neglected to explain whether he married the girl in San Francisco, the one he said he truly wanted or the girl from Sophia that his mother preferred.

And I received other letters, from my mother, and one from Nenia, believe it or not, and Andrea, the latter two sending hopes and prayers much in the manner of Leland's letter, and I confess that they gave me a lift, their words dear and touching, even Nenia's, despite my vow that I'd never have anything to do with her again. But my concern and thoughts at that interval clung to Darya, who badly needed me. I telephoned her daily, and decided that I wouldn't return an answer to Andrea just then, unable to perform this obligation without a feeling of betrayal to Darya. I laid Andrea's letter aside with the notion that I'd take up the business of answering her at a later opportunity when Darya's status of health significantly turned upward. I wouldn't answer Nenia's letter in any fashion, though taking a cue from my better side I softened and felt that at least in time I should write a word or two and might get around to doing it.

My mother in her letter indicated her usual self, in other words, caring and worrying, asking first how I had been faring and next letting me know that she prayed every night that He would protect me, and making an otherwise effort to bring me abreast with things in our small town. Billy Mcvector, the mayor, had taken the lead in erecting a plaque with limited names embossed on it in memory of their service to the United States Military during World War II. Arthur Lynn Smith, Claude Wilkins, Horace Landsden and James Warner Buckingham were killed in that war. They were of Melissa's age. The idea had gotten around that it was best to erect the memorial on a rise where the Miss Estonia Lebranche home once stood, not many paces from the new post office and the Monett Bank and Trust Company in clear view of the people passing to and fro on the adjacent sidewalk. She mentioned in her closing passages that now she stayed full time with Lillian Yancey and cooked and ironed and cleaned the house, the news begetting to me an attitude of exasperation, yet eventually I doused my repugnant feelings, as I always did, careful not to let my anger spill over and upset her and believed, leastwise hoped, that the Good Lord looked upon her and smiled because of her goodness.

Darya arrived in Tokyo a month later than she supposed, delivered by helicopter from the plane to the hospital. I met her at front side and stayed with her until the aides checked her in with a nurse and doctor who were to direct her activities of recovery. She would begin her therapies starting on the second day.

Tokyo is the capital of Japan, the center of the greater Tokyo periphery (prefecture) and is the most populated area in the world. The people suffered catastrophically during the Great War past, ending in 1945, and to witness the restoration of a city of its magnificence found me lacking of adjectives, yet in any event the rise from its damage, physical and mental, appeared to me as a feat of monumental amazement.

Darya moved about on crutches reasonably well, but of creeping slowness, a handicap presposterously nettling to a person of her great will, a will to free herself from a dependency on persons and ambulatory devices. She reacted to the wheel chair with passionate dislike.

"So be it," I said. "I'm rolling you anyway." I had brought one in from the staorage commissary down the hallway.

She raised no fuss, other than a pout, when I commenced helping her into it and with this done I pushed her out onto the street, the sun bright and the wind calm, joining the throng of people hastening back and forth. On these excursions we naturally did not travel far from the hospital, but even for a little piece Darya expressed thankfulness. She smiled gaily. Later, when I relayed to him how she took to the joy of being outside in the fresh air among the people the Doctor grinned.

"A good start for the healing process. Keep it up."

Despite her limitations we toured continually and extensively, of necessity hiring a taxi for trips of much length, shops seen everywhere irrespective of where we went. She loved the shops and sometimes I amusedly ventured that had we the time she would have pressed me to take her into every last one throught greater Toyko. It largely became the shops by day, the restaurants at night, beginning at nine. We preferred going late and staying until midnight. The restaurants, glitzy, abuzz with patrons, and colorfully attired waiters and waitresses scuttling in light quick steps here and there served a very rich tasting cuisine which the establishment advertised as a specialty. We could not stay away, always soon coming back. Tokyo was then and is still internationally acclaimed for its fine cuisine, Paris running markedly behind in the ratings. However uncomfortable she might have been from her leg not once did I hear her complain when we were immersed in the ambience of the restaurants, the gaiety of it all immeasureably good for her, psychologically for certain if not somehow physically. But there were other attractions. From a certain angle the snowcapped peaks of Mount Fuji stood proudly and beautifully, but the snow seemed as an anomale, out of place. After all, this was not what people like us would expect to see in a subtropical climate. We did not overlook the Tokyo National Museum nor fail to ride by on a daily basis the Imperial Palace, with Darya, swayed to the point of excitment by the beauty of that inimitable shrine, invariably turned to me with exclamations of astonishment.

Glittering, bustling, vigorously alive, steeped in the culture of a great people, a fascinating metropolis—this was Tokyo, and we did our best to cover every last square mile, reluctantly mindful that soon time would run its course and that we will have missed an enormity of enchantments if we did not hasten. But as said, we did our best.

She improved. But to what degree? Skeptical, I asked the doctor at times for a status report, feeling that his attendance of such a huge count of patients was virtually overwhelming and that to ask for five minutes at the maximum amounted to an imposition. Still, he gave me the time.

"She's coming along nicely Mr. Maynard, and I will add that devoting a perpetual stream of your energies and thoughts to her is an essential contribution. She'll make it physically, well enough to function, possibly with a show of a slight disability for a while, maybe for a long while if you allow me to speak bluntly; and that worries me. How will she turn out over the long haul? That is the question a man of my profession has to ask however uncomfortable the burden it may place on his shoulders. Will the memory of her lively youth, her adventuresome spirit, what she could have had that never materialized, start to weigh upon her at some stage down the road and lead to, to something she can't deal with?"

"You mean depression, despondency. Something in that vein."

"Yes. Something in that vein. But you likely have a better reading of that prospect than me. You are constantly around her, you know, and surely in your moments of privacy you two raise to surface everything under the sun, as young folks do."

"I am with her constantly. And we do go over a lot of things"

And as I said to the doctor we forever did talk about a lot of things, night after night sitting in one of the colorful little cafes nestled off in the shadows where there were infusions of Japanese and American music and pretty burning candles, particularly American music from the era of the 1930's and 40's.

"Would you like to dance?" she once asked with a shade of uncertainty, doubt in herself to go through with it, her eyes trained hopefully into mine.

"Really? I mean we haven't since you know when. We can if you want to."

"With your help."

I didn't want to say that that she'd step right into it, with no difficulty whatsoever, that she could just lean on me and we'd do just fine. But I didn't say that. I said, "Okay. Let's do. It's time we did. Shall I ask one of the singers to perform a special song for us?"

"No. Don't. Let's just let the juke box play it. I'd like to hear *The Music Stopped*, a slow tune sung by Frank Sinatra. Will you?"

Going to the juke box I deposited a quarter and then returned directly to our table where she had risen and stood waiting, her hand pressed flat against the table top, balancing. The pale meek dimness of the lights meshed perfectly with the song and I held her closely while we simply swayed and moved with infinite slowness, inch by inch, toward the center of the dance floor while Sinatra sang the lovely romantic tune.

The music stopped but we were still dancing
Which goes to show that music has charm
The lights were low so we kept on dancing
I felt the glow of you in my arms
The band had left the stand and we were in Heaven
Dancing on a cloud way off in the blue
The music stopped and people were glancing
But we went on dancing, for we didn't know
Because, the lights were low and we were in love

Chapter 60

AT LAST we sat back down, begrudgingly done on her part, the song obviously touching her heart strings she asked me to play it once more, and rising I went to the juke box and deposited two quarters assuming that she would like to hear it not once but twice more. The waiter came and served us coffee. She asked if I liked the décor of the room. "Of course. Just like when we were here last." And then she asked if this seemed like old times at the Cubs Nest. "It does. How could it not? And I was just thinking of that very thing" Her eyes wandered off. I patted her hand and squeezed her arm, curious to know of the inner ideations that now ran through her. "Does she recall the letter she wrote," I asked myself, "where she said she knew I didn't love her as she loved me? Does she still feel the same? I won't ask. I'm here to help her heal, to help her journey through this awful episode of her young life. I won't dare let myself drift into the emotions of that letter. I shouldn't. But I can't help but wonder."

"Do you hear from your mother Ramsey? I haven't heard you mention her."

"Not often. The mail is slow. You understand how it is. For a while no mail of any sort. Then wham. All at once the sky falls and you're deluged with a backlog. It builds up. That's how mail is from folks back home."

"Have you heard from her recently?"

"Last week."

"What does she say is happening in your native town?"

"Not a great amount. Not much ever happens in a hamlet like that. Not anything of importance to me anyway. Wait a minute. There was one thing. She wrote that they're demolishing the junior high school where I finished the tenth grade in favor of building a consolidated high school accommodating the students countywide."

"All that sounds like a progressive idea." Then she suddenly switched, the demolishment of the school building clearly not revealing anything that motivated her.

"Do you hear from Leland?"

"I do. It hasn't been long. He's moving to New York in the fairly near future, in the nearbouts of six months I think he said."

"Ummmm. Well. I'm surprised he's not in the military. Must have something to do with the strategic importance of his job."

"I guess the draft board has the answer to that one. They keep sticky tabs on young guys of draft status." My remarks were evasive and I knew that, intended to skim over the subject, which I envisioned might turn into an awkward exchange and therefore better left alone. Darya said nothing more of Leland and I opted over to something else.

"I guess you've told me before, and if you have, forgive me. My memory might have started to fail." I didn't get to finish.

"Ha. Yeah. Your memory failing. Very likely." She paused and I paused, then we both broke into laughter. "What did you start to say before my distraction my darling guy? Sorry. But we needed a little fun."

"Why did you join the war effort sweetheart, the terrible conflagration that's eaten up so many young lives? You didn't have to."

"You know the answer," the slow but thoughtful explanation starting to leak out. "It's the cause."

"The cause!"

"Yeah. To help young soldiers, to sit with those wounded, or dying, lying flat of their backs breathing their last breath, with only a newly made buddy or stranger around trying to do his best to lend comfort. I saw these scenes from the living room of our home on the television screen. Deeply touched, I up and volunteered, my mother protesting, and begging, and reasoning with me to no avail, as did my father, both intimating that I suffered from vain gloriousness and perhaps affected too by the hippie marchers and protesters everywhere on the big city streets and college campuses. Maybe they were right. Maybe not. But here I am nonetheless."

"Are you sorry for your choice?"

"I have to admit the truth. At times I am. This horrible injury, the wound, my leg battered into disfiguration. Were I to have stayed home I, well, why talk of that. I didn't."

"When will they send you home?"

"Based on the doctor's prognosis they'll release me in two months. Says I'll get even better treatment at one of the superb facilities in Baltimore."

"Two months. In two months you will have gone," I uttered, very much disliking the idea and showing more than a degree of remorse in my countenance.

"Does that sadden you?"

"It does. I'll find myself still hanging out here wondering what you're doing in Baltimore. I don't know what I'll do with myself. But whoaaa. Me! Wait a minute. I don't count in the least. It's your getting well that counts. It's the only thing that counts."

"Thank you sweetheart. But it's not the only thing."

We somehow soon forgot that matter and I turned to something else which had begun to gnaw on my counscious, but I had to exercise care. "How is your leg doing, your wounds?" I asked with tender caution. "You seldom speak of it except just now. Is it still heavily bound? Do you see it often?" And then it fell upon me with a crunch that I had gone too far, carelessly probing into a part of her emotional fabric which I should have scrupulously avoided. If she wanted to speak of it that was all right. But not all right for me to bring it up. For a moment I judged that possibly I hadn't erred. She had not as much as blinked.

"Not often. I did at first. Not any more. It, it—."

Then she began to cry. I wanted to kick myself for the dumbness of my slippage, and then exerting my utmost to compensate reached my arms around her.

"Now, now. Things will work out. All that's needed is a little time."

Pretty soon, after she pulled herself together we left, once reaching the hospital embracing one another and kissing goodnight. She wouldn't take me up on my offer of assistance, making it to her room unaccompanied.

Sleep evaded me the whole night through. I tossed. "How fatefully unkind is life's deliverances. You never can predict, or even sense, that which awaits you in the shadows." I'd like to have seen her leg I thought but further opined that once I laid my eyes on it, I might have seriously wished to the contrary. A memory suddenly came to me not at all strangely of a similar tragedy that occurred on the grounds of the junior high school which I attended when but a boy, say in the third or fourth grade. I now retraced the event in vivid detail which had stayed immovably in the recesses of my mind for years. A charming girl of my age, the epitome of vibrancy, sat next to me in class, out of the way kind to tutor me in my assignments—her brightness seemed to know no bounds—and meant much to me in other endeavors of friendship, scribbling notes on a yellow tablet sheet and dropping the endearments on my desk when catching me absent of slight duration, out of the classroom temporarily for a reason that I have forgotten.

At recess the students scrambled onto the grounds to play. And there, in one awful moment, Elizabeth Johnson met her most fateful and regrettable intermission, a pitiable day, a day inestimably better a thousand times over for her if she had stayed inside. But children must play. A young boy, three grades ahead of us, capriciously, or because of whatever seized him to do as he did picked up a hedge ball from the ground, a green, firm, apple shaped non edible fruit—and threw it aimlessly in the direction of a collection of girls, not intending harm to anyone, just foolishly letting it fly on an unvarying course to Elizabeth's leg, smashing into the muscular region inches above her right knee. One cannot easily envision her scream and the terror on the young boy's face as he raced to her. The doctor's tried, saying for a while that she would recover but slowly, then later that it would take a while longer, longer but assured recovery in time, and then, seeing it futile to continue to hold back gave forth the vaguely worded explanation that they were incapable of providing remedy. My course of reasoning now relays to me that if that time were of the modern time they would have simply replaced the knee and thus given her a life of normalcy.

The dear girl's life had by a fluke fallen into ruin, no longer the vibrant youthful person we earlier enjoyed playing and being with, who gallantly showed no self pity, nor the slightest inkling for our sympathy as she entered the classroom each morning with her book satchel strapped over her shoulder, dragging her right leg as if a heavy weight, forever deformed. It was in the semblance of a broken twig, the middle part tending inward at the knee, bumping into the companion leg, the lower part, the ankle and foot, tending increasingly outward. I see her still, the imprint unerasible. Why did I never go to her when I attained to adulthood? And talk. At least I could have talked to her. That would have helped some. How pitiable. Never did she know love as ordinary woman knows, nor the bearing and rearing of children, nor the gaiety of a Saturday night dance, nor the pleasure of an afternoon on a sandy beach clad in a bikini, nor a thousand other wonders of pleasure. Where is the scripture that explains and justifies a fate so crushingly destructive?

I found myself wishing that my remembrance of Elizabeth hadn't suddenly lunged into my consciousness, bringing with it the pitiable sorrow that I still carried in my heart for her. In that moment I in fantansy substituted Darya in her place and shuddered. "Please Lord. Not her too. See that she heals. Empower the doctors to guide her to wellness. Infuse her with strength to fight and the will to overcome her suffering and her debilities."

From there on I tended to avoid the slightest reference to Darya's leg, or any notion of commenting of it, which I doubted she would have minded in so far as she spoke of it herself with relative ease from time to time. I supposed as much but one night when something pursuant to her leg cropped up she suddenly broke down and cried, with me assuming that she had fallen victim to a mood of downcastness which struck every person sooner or later. I supposed as much, yet on reopening the matter doubted my first supposition. I rephrased. "It's true that many persons suffer from a sunken mood of melancholy but not for the reason that it affects Darya." I guessed underneath that she had envisioned her future and that it portrayed the bleakest of promises for her, such happening far more penetratingly than I surmised. There was nothing that I could say nor did I try. But I knew of one thing to do of which I felt certain. I drew her to me and held her cheek against my breast until she sobbed herself out.

The two months would soon expire and discover her flying home. We kept steadily on pace at seeing the endless shrines of the city, done during the day light hours by and large. As the nightly shadows descended we headed for one of the literally hundreds of cafes where they served dinner and offered old nostalgic songs sung by live on stage singers or from the nickelodeon. Sometimes hillbilly music, which to us was markedly out of date. Relentlessly we switched from café to café. And must have gone to every opera performance that visited the stages of Tokyo, for which she said she was utterly starved. She shot hundreds of scenes with her camera, buoyantly explaining that they were destined for her scrap book or book of mementos. Unfurling a completely unexpected surprise my C'ommandant treated us to a sailboat excursion on the serene blue waters of the Sea of Japan, hiring a seasoned boatsman, a pro, who boasted that he had captained tourist outings for forty years. I knew the Commandant had arranged the excursion for Darya in that he nurtured great compassion for her in her condition. He'd heard of her bravery on the battlefield and aspired to do something to show his appreciation however minimal. This was his first time to meet her. He had said he badly wanted to do something for her when I first told him of her arrival at the treatment hospital. They got along famously, with him monopolizing the dialogue, mostly carrying on in jocular fashion.

"That big lake over there by Chicago, Darya, is big but a mere drop in the bucket if the Sea of Japan is used as a yardstick."

"Correct. But sir I think you're assuming I'm from Chicago. I'm not. It's Baltimore."

"Ah! Baltimore. My error. It's been in my craw that you are a Chicago girl."

"No sir. I only did my college work there."

Mrs. Narvanna flew in a short while later to join her daughter, asking beforehand by way of letter if she might see me, to which Darya replied by telephone that she would do her best to make the arrangements, and I zealously looked forward to seeing her again. Optimistic, as we all were, the plan fell through. The Commandant sent me to Saigon for ten days duty just before her arrival and said that in his careful consideration of granting an exception he found no defense for my request to qualify as an an extenuating cerstumstance. On my return Darya said that her mother calmly expressed disappointment at my inability to see her but understood.

"Where all did you take her for entertainment?"

"Everywhere. The places that you and I went to. Except one."

"Which?"

"The Geisha's. We went to see the Geisha's. And you and I didn't."

"Goodness, I thou—."

"That they're prostitutes. No, no. Far from the truth. I boned up on them at the library. One of my nurses, a young Japanese, also told me a lot about them. A long standing stigma has unfairly accompanied young japanese Geisha girls. When someone thinks of a Geisha they think of a glorified prostitute or call girl. Which is, as I've said, far from the truth. Geisha's are entertainers, refined and finished, trained vigorously and precisely in art and music and dancing. If you translate Geisha into English, you get artist. The Geisha as a prostitute in modern times is a foreign misunderstanding."

"I'm stunned at what you tell. But where exactly did you see the Geisha's?"

"At the festival. In particular, mother wanted to see a Maiko, a certain level or quality of a Geisha, from the Kamishichiken district who serves tea at the plum blossom festival at Katano Tenman-gu. Our Maiko served us tea too. And she was a very beautiful girl, very soft in speech and gentle of nature. Geisha's have led a cloistered existence in the past but they have now risen to a plateau of public acclaim here in Tokyo. Would you like to go see the Geisha's?"

"I would. Set it up," I regret deeply that we never made it.

"What will you do with your time when you have returned home?" I asked her one night when the hour had turned late, shortly before she left Tokyo. "No wait. Let me narrow my question. Actually, I have two questions. What are your plans for further university studies or will you perhaps join your father's business in some capacity?" It took her but a blink.

"I have to say I don't know. I can envision myself for a while doing nothing but sitting out on the veranda in enjoyment of a soft subtle breeze lifting from the waters of the Chesapeake. As to your questions, well, I'll have to heal first of all, and learn to walk without a mechanical support or anyone to lean on. The doctor is working out a regimen that he's sure the doctors at the Baltimore hospital will adopt. I'll get well. I'm determined. I'll get well."

"That's the girl. And you will too"

"When this crazy war is over you'll return home yourself Ramsey. You can't guess when that will happen—but let's wish hard that it's sooner than later."

"I'm for that. We'll see."

"You asked me something. Now it's my turn. What will you take up as an occupation when you're back? Let's see. You've taught some you've told me, and like it, and then there's Aaron's father's law firm. That looks like a pretty bright future. What about it".

"Right now?"

"Sure."

"It shouldn't amount to a hard thing to answer but it is. Teaching has the edge. A slim edge but an edge. But honestly, I can't speak with certainty. Maybe I won't have to decide. That's what I keep thinking. Maybe I can do some of both."

"Not much money in teaching. You may need a second income."

"True. And that worries me. You can't starve and do a very good job of teaching."

I figured she held the view that it was nonsensical to go into teaching with a monthly salary at a preposterously low level in comparison to other fields of choice, law for example or her father's firm. An interlude at this point suddenly invaded our conversation, neither of us uttering a word, just lost in pondering, me taking it that any second she would speak the next lines and she surmising that I was on the verge of following likewise. "Do you ever think of the war much?" I'd often wondered if she did. "If you do, you're very effective at keeping it to yourself."

"I do. Everyone does, I'm sure. You can't help it. Do you have the same thought? I don't hear you saying much in that regard either."

"Some. I haven't experienced the midst of it like you have. So, your reflection I'm sure is a departure from mine altogether. It's much more real to you than to me."

"In what way?"

"To me it's like its almost real and unreal at the same time, coming alive, shall I say, when I choose to turn on the switch that lets it into my head. Or goes away if I turn it off. I don't gather that it's that easy for you."

"I guess not."

"Meaning?"

"Well, for me, your metaphor, the switch, is an over simplification. Sometimes I find it impossible to turn it off, especially in the stillness of the night when doing my utmost to drop off to sleep. In day time the switch stays turned off pretty well, more or less; at night back on and doubly hard to snap off. My sleep is a restless sleep."

"Bad scenes, hunh?"

"Bad. Awful. Mutated, whirling and tumbling, or worse."

"That's graphic enough. But try not to think of them. Please try extra hard not to. Time you had a break from it all. Don't let your mind any longer see what it doesn't want to."

"And how is that done?"

"I don't know. I wish I did. But work at it. And don't forget your mother. I'll wager she can offer tremendous help."

"You're a sweet guy. I know you wish me the best. But let's consider your situation."

"What?"

"You'll leave here sometime soon I trust. Where are your sights for landing?"

"Oh, you know. First, my little home town for a stay with my mother for a while, and afterwards to Chicago with my fingers crossed that I'll still have employment with the law firm. And after that. Let me see. Probably taking up a law course or two. I don't have my law degree yet. I need to push that up on the front burner."

"Good plans. And you'll need to zip right into them. But don't overload yourself with a lot of busy stuff that gets in your way of coming over to see me. You'll find me in tip top shape by then."

Not the last but one of the last was this conversation with Darya in Tokyo, which I remember with unique transparency owing to her attitude toward attaining to a state of complete wellness. While she had undergone serious struggles with her lingering wounds from the war, I felt that she with her bent of purpose would eventually throw them off. Arranged by the military she flew from Tokyo to Stuttgart, Germany and after a two day stopover flew on to the city of Baltimore. I laughed aloud at the playful telegram wording she sent from Stuttgart, not waiting until she settled into her home surroundings in the states. "Hi. I'm staying here for two days for a medical check up. The doctors are playing it safe. Miss you. When you're sitting down to a juicy meal at one of those pixie cafes tonight why don't you order an extra glass of red wine—but don't drink it, don't even sip it; just turn your glass round and round and think of the addicting good times we relished together roving the streets of what now is one of my favorite cities. Love you."

Within a year after she had gone I also was gone, leaving by way of military aircraft, my Commandant the last person with whom I exchanged conversation, who said with the warmest of accolades that swelled my pride, "You're a fine young man Ramsey, capable, a meticulous researcher, your reports and treatment of facts down to the last one right on spot. Your law firm will more than gladly welcome your return to their midst."

"Back to normal," sounded happily in my brain as I landed on American shores but normal is something you should never believe is going to really happen if you've been off at war. You'll never find your way back to the normal that you once knew; as a disproportenant number of our returning soldiers bitterly learned, you merely adjust to the new normal, in my case many of my office associates in slight measure no longer the same, to whom I'd have to acclimate myself, and even the physical outlay of the law firm evinced radical transition, books and journals housed on different shelving's and additional offices designed and constructed. They also had enlarged the suite where I once officed. Virtually all of the former staff were yet intact, and this warmed my heart, each bending over backwards to welcome my return, and meant it, as well as the new young lawyers who warmly shook my hand but without the familial affection demonstrated by my old associates. I'd have to get used to them too. I smiled on my first morning back as I entered my former office, now mine again, which a certain young lady attorney occupied during my absence, and performed admirably the word had gotten about. The lawyers of the firm had seriously started to depend on her research efficiency. I did not anticipate anything but complete solidarity and helpfulness from her in the change over or anything to the contrary from anyone who at first might silently devote their allegiance to her rather than to me. Mister Yazstremski likely entertained some earlier perceptions pursuant to this very thing because he had taken steps to clear the atmosphere of potential disputes and struggles for turf, and flew in from New York to meet with me face to face. "Ramsey," he slyly chirped and laughed lowly in a guise as if it suddenly seemed to him like old times, "you are to pick up exactly where you left off. Janet Sayora has capably exacted your duties and I'm proud of her. She however is not quite up to your speed. But we need her. The firm has grown. I want her to office next to yours and function as your associate, the two of you acting as a team but with you calling the shots. That's the way it must happen and will happen. No slippages. Already I've talked with the young lady, clearing up any questions whatsoever, and there were none, and as you'll find out she'll make a splendid person to work with, affording value to you in indeterminate ways."

With this said he shifted to asking if I had emerged from the conflict unharmed, easily telling by scanning my physique up and down that no defects were visible, and purposely threw in that I couldn't begin to know his gladness at my returning to the firm. Then kept going. "The girl. Darya. Mrs. Stylman has alluded to her as of late, saying that she was less fortunate than you in that she is now confined to her home from an injury sustained in battle. Her mother sees after her with the most thorough surveillance. You knew the girl in college, didn't you? Do you hear from her?"

"I do. I plan to visit with her once I'm settled here"

"Good. Good. She and Aaron were chums in college?"

"They were. The best of chums."

"And while speaking of Aaron I'm sorry to pass on that we are worried, the Stylman's and myself, over the fact that some several months have expired since his last mailing to anyone. The War Department has not issued notice that he's missing or killed which gives us hope that he is all right, or at least there's a chance of his being all right.

"I see sir. I've never heard from him in all this time, the latest and most direct contact coming in a letter from Mrs. Stylman to me in Tokyo. She said he wished me well and sent best wishes."

"Well, let's think positively and nightly say our prayers. But back to you my boy. That dingy old men riddled café on the back street is still there and I'm elated at the idea of our breaking bread there at our favorite corner table again and soon. I have a pending note on my desk that directs you to fly to New York on business in the near weeks ahead."

If the context of my hopes and intentions had held true I would have been going to see Nenia as soon as manageable. But I would not go, only reflecting in my mind that had I gone, and if I could have forgetten the past, I would now discover myself driving down from Chicago, swooping her into my arms as she moved happily to me. Suddenly I will have fallen in love with her more than ever and that from there on would see her on every opportunity, driving from Chicago to Saint Louis every other week. But as said, I would not be going. It was still there, bitter and burning, the leftover embers of a once vibrant love affair living within my heart now shattered by betrayal. "The times, the times," I repeated in reflection, sort of hurtfully. Then finished it out. "The times she said she loved me. The times we'd sit on the edge of the little creek and kiss and do as teenagers do. How pure she seemed. But how camaflouged the untruthfulness that dwelt within her heart, completely hidden? But am I wrong in coming down this rigidly hard on her. After all, the world isn't overflowing with perfect beings, man or woman. You've slept with Darya, you know you have, although you'll argue that she didn't betray you and you'll have many a person to side with your view. In any event, you've learned the hard way that woman too has a weakness if the circumstances are right enough and the temptation is great enough."

"But so much for that. It seems clear that Nenia in the finale is out of your life for good and Andrea and Darya are neck and neck in the running."

Happily, I plunged into work at the law firm and recommenced my legal studies, soon discovering my plate full, if not over flowing. "A good thing," I said. "It'll help me forget" Eventually I picked up again on teaching literature at the small college in the city where I taught prior to my draft into the army.

Time passed. Days turned into months and months into more than a year. Perhaps two or three years. I cannot recall exactly. In any event after I finished with my legal studies and attained to a higher position in the ranks at the firm a yen started to play in my being one day to go see Darya. It gnawed on me that I had behaved neglectfully in this regard. I should have done it long before. We had traded letters but infrequently. She walked much better she exhuberantly reported. But in something of the same perspective a wish had crept into into my psyche urging me to spend a little time with someone else also, Andrea, who no longer resided on campus. She'd taken a position some years before with the military intelligence and parked her coat and hat sporadically in southern Louisiana and at varied outposts around the world. I recalled that she was the last of the two girls that I saw before directly going into the army. I called on the department head of mathematics and physics to verify her exact whereabouts. He knew.

Seldom did I have a glimpse of Melissa when I slipped into to town for a brief stay. But once I caught sight of her walking down mainstreet. She looked fine I thought, far better than the usual woman her age. She had begun to enter the drugstore, this coinciding with the very moment that John Eric and I rode through the heart of town in his pick-up truck. I made certain that she would not recognize me by turning myself at an angle that let her see only my back. John Eric saw her too and spoke of her mother. "Did you hear Ramsey? Madeline Monett died last month. I figured your mother might have passed the news on to you. "

"She didn't. She just forgot. Big funeral I'm supposing?"

"Yeah. It was. Bunch there. I think mainly due to curiosity, just eager to see what she looked like laying there stiff and unmoving compared to her snootiness and flightiness when alive. That's people for you."

"I understand. Glad you let me know."

Chapter 61

AT SOME point, with the Vietnam War evincing signs of winding down—while the North Vietnamese and the Viet Cong were winding up for the finish—I turned to monitoring the news more intensely, on occasions flying over to Darya's to check on her progress, and while there the two of us with peaked interest shedding views of the fiasco. It loomed clear that the American politicians were on the throes of withdrawing our troops. The South Vietnamese army held on until the massive carnage dictated their capitulation. I watched by way of television as the catastrophe unfolded, the collapse of Saigon. It hurt deeply. My mouth flew open and I think I gasped upon glimpsing some of the streets on which I once strolled up and down. Thousands of families were evacuated in the panicked exodus as the South Vietnamese government crumbled, a sizeable many by helicopter on the last day, but many not as fortunate, aware of the terror that lay in store—the torture, the executions—racing in frenzied helplessness toward the aircraft with outstretched arms, as if pleading for a last chance to climb aboard. It was the last flight out, now already lifting off, within minutes coursing across the waters to the naval aircraft carrier anchored in the South China Sea.

As I have said before, I now wish to repeat again something that I have earlier stressed because it is a must in my heart that I should address this episode of history. Numerous Americans felt, sensed, or believed that the American military lost the war, which is not the truth by any way you look at the facts. It was on the home front that the Americans met failure. In the zone of combat the U. S. forces, most singularly special operations troops, won almost every military battle against the Viet Cong guerillas and the North Vietnamese army. The American politicians were the ones who caved in as protests against the war began to spread like wild fire on the college campuses and big cities throughout the nation and sued for peace.

The soldiers came home, not as well appreciated and welcomed as they should have been, various things of a negative sort happening to them, some becoming outcasts of their own choosing, unable to find a comfortable niche in society for themselves, while others couldn't or wouldn't enter the job market. Of those who needed it we should have striven to help and done even more.

I continued regularly to visit my mother on every opportunity that my work calendar allowed, learning on one visit that Mr. Carney and Tatiana at last moved to far away Sophia, Bulgaria where the majority of her folks lived. Tatiana wrote earlier that each day had begun to draw them closer to an imminent farewell, and with this piece of correspondence in my possession the news of their departure did not fall on me with surprise. Not of long duration afterwards my mother wrote that Ozzie and Cavanaugh decided to relocate to Fort Wayne, Indiana, landing a job with a heavy machinery company, a natural for them and I rejoiced at their good fortune. In the meanwhile, Leland reported his transfer to Schenectady, and though not as often as I liked we met periodically in New York City. He hadn't changed significantly, older looking yet still young, but what mattered most was his warmth and affection toward me and his memory of old times when we were fledglings.

Funny how time slips away. Once the war ended the years began to disappear one after the other at high speed. That is the way it is when you notice that you are beginning to age. Suddenly I had zoomed well passed thirty. "Damn! I can't believe it." Sometimes Mr. Yazstremski would embark on the subject, mostly making a brief comment of it and then passing on to something else.

"Ramsey, you're moving on up into your thirties. You say you don't like it. Well, I didn't either. But you're still young and still look out of youthful eyes at the advancement of aging or the passing of time much differently than myself."

"In what way sir?"

"Time to youth and time to people of an older age, say myself, is a phenomenon of opposite poles. To youth, up to a certain level, the years pass awesomely slow. Christmas seems never to come. But spin this around for thought. When you're saddled with the number of years that I carry on my old bent shoulders you'll discover that they don't walk by they fly by, and one day you'll recite these same aphorisms, proclamations if you will, but in the meanwhile don't try to hold the years back, just content yourself that you're still young." Ever mindful that his span could suddenly play out I spent many an hour or whatever he could spare with this grand old man, my mentor, my great friend, not in the best of health, intent on drawing from his rich repository of wisdom all that my mental capacity was able to absorb. Seldom did I react with surprise at what cropped up when we got together. One day all at once—.

"Ramsey, you're earning a few dollars from your job, for which I'm ecstatically glad. But where do you put it?

"Put it? Well, in real estate, a good safe place to invest according to what I read in the journals and hear from agents of the profession."

"Yes it is. I strongly support that claim. Yet, there are other investments besides real estate and as long as you diversify, I personally think you might want to consider them."

"What are they?"

"Hold on. Not just yet. Let's talk first of investment fields or categories. Energy is a good one, maybe slow to yield, but if you stay with it you'll enjoy some pleasing rewards. And then there are the drug stocks, the pharmaceuticals, and I can say the same of them as I've spoken of the energy stocks. Let me see. There's another. Not the last but another. Finance, big banks, the money handlers, equipped with a cogent sniffer that seems magically to lead them to the money pile. Over the long haul they seldom miss. We won't seriously name specific stocks today. I'm simply exposing you to the scent. Do your research then we'll talk of particular companies in which I'm invested personally."

As a consequence, I invested a portion of my holdings in stocks as Mr. Yazstremski suggested, narrowing my determination to Exxon, Walgreen's, and J. P. Morgan, and in a little while sank a small amount in a prestigious apartment complex owned by the law firm. As it turned out these were the wisest, or in any event the most fortunate investments I ever made if the investment is excluded where Leland cut me in as half owner of the tractor company that we sold, with Mr. Carney negotiating the transaction.

The characteristic nature of a small town is perhaps described best in the usual scheme of things as a gossip mill, where the juicy stuff is lapped up hungrily by those ever alert to ingest juicy news of any sort, and this is the description best befitting my small town as I reflect backward. But aside from this characteristic there existed a balancing side too, a side where good things happened because there were good people who resided there. The women of the three churches were the leaders in this regard, not only seeing that the church affairs were properly exacted, cooperating with the minister and such, but promoting community benevolences. Somewhere along the way a town gathering on mainstreet had begun to take place each year in late spring which promoted good will and fellowship among the citizens—picnic on the grounds, horseshoeing, fiddling contests, and the like—and in autumn a memorial celebration of our fallen soldiers in World War II took place, but none from the Korean War and none from the War of Vietnam which struck me as a serious omission. I protested. And as a result, in the year that followed the omissions were justifiably corrected, the proceeding rightfully exhibiting and celebrating our heroes previously left out. I had vowed, with an extra splash of vanity I have to admit, in a release to the county newspaper that until this happened I could not and would not accept the armistic of these two wars as a valid instrument for ending the hostilities. Hardly anyone internalized the meaning of my allusion to the armistinces, believing that long ago the wars had ended. They had, but not officially. As said in my letter a short while thereafter to

Leland my little snippet appearing in the press likely was the most significant thing I ever did for the homefolks other than help him establish the tractor business way back when.

In the whereabouts of this period Mrs. Narvanna flew into the city of Chicago and while there got in touch with me, or attempted to but caught me away from my desk. She had called. I reeled with curiosity. "What could she want? Nothing of importance I'm sure. Merely a social call." Learning of my absence for the afternoon she asked someone handling the incoming telephone messages when I might return, the answer given with the epitome of politeness that I hadn't left a communication pertaining to my return, but gladly suggesting the leaving of a note on my desk that she had called, and asking if there was anything else that she might wish conveyed.

"Not anything else. Just tell him please that this is Perica Narvanna and that yes I would like very much for him to telephone me. And that I am staying at the Ritz Carlton." At this she gave the telephone number.

"I'll lay a note on his desk immediately."

The hour hand pointed to four o'clock when I returned, and on reading the message wasted no time dialing her room, Mrs. Narvanna answering at once.

"Oh Ramsey. I knew that was you. You received my call, or rather to say that one of your associates did."

"Yes. And I'm delighted. How warming to hear your voice."

"Easily I say the same. I'm here on business and wanted to take time out to talk to you. Now don't ask me what about. Let's say it encompasses everything in case you are overly curious. Can I treat you to dinner this evening? Is seven a good hour?"

I needed no time to think. Why in the context of good sense would I decline?

"Perfect. Where?"

"In one of the private dining rooms here at the hotel which you'll discover is quite agreeably pleasant."

"Of course. Fine. Fine. I'll see you at seven and thank you for inviting me."

"Not at all," the obvious cultured voice returned.

I arrived in the lobby earlier than we agreed, but only by minutes, there taking a seat on one of the sumptuous couches and waited until seven then dialed, feeling a touch of nervousness.

"You're right on time. You're in the lobby I presume. I'll come right down." She delayed ten minutes.

"Rich people's protocol. That's the way rich women are, a man is made to wait, a guile of theirs, and tonight as it has been on any occasion when in her company, I'm in for experiencing another lesson in civility and charm. At this she's a master teacher without even knowing it. That's right. Without knowing it? It's all so natural to her. What she has you don't teach. You just have it or you don't. What I'd give for her to join Mr.Yazstremski and myself at lunch someday. He'd take a fantastic liking to her."

Mrs. Narvanna attired herself in what to me was an executive suit, expensive and elaborate but not overdone, and there sat a hat on her head of tasteful size of which I took notice, tilted a slight off balance, and showing of deep dark green in the semblance of the suit that agreeably embraced her frame. She overwhelmed me with her persona; she did everyone. In her beauty there shone her daughter, unmistakably apparent, and once again I easily recognized the source from which her daughter's beauty sprang.

"I have a private dining room reserved for us Ramsey. I'm finicky I suppose. I don't like a room full of chatter pouring into my ears when I'm visiting with a special guest." At her own qualms she smiled a soft light smile and laughed demurely. It was an executive laugh, or so I interpreted it. An escort led us briefly down a hallway and when he turned right and stepped down four steps we followed. We were there, the room richly set, with sconces emulating those of long ago Italian heritage lining the walls, shiny walnut newel posts and balusters flaunting themselves, heavy grained oak chairs and side benches particularily arranged, the dining table over laid with the finest quality of arabesque tapestry. I stood astounded at where I suddenly found myself with hopes that I did not excessively reveal it. When I finished helping her with her seating she spoke.

"I'm here to do a scant of business for the firm, more public relations than anything else, and with spare time on my hands I thought it good to have dinner with you. I'm glad you could free yourself to join me. I trust that I'm not imposing on another of your schedules."

"Goodness. Not at all."

"Darya sends you her best."

"Yes. Tell her that I send mine back to her using you as a carrier." She chuckled a little.

"I will."

"How is she? The last I heard, which came straight from her, she indicated that she's progressing better than expected, really well. She must keep it up."

"Yes. Yes. And she will. I spoke to her doctor just this past week and he reported a very encouraging prognosis."

"What was it?"

"He thinks that within a year or a spec briefer she'll again function normally, with no limp or any slight of handicap showing or hampering her."

"That's exciting." But somehow, she seemed skeptical that she doubted the doctor's glowing report of healing, at least in the entirety. But I sloughed off my suspicion momentarily, taking it that any doubt or doubts of my own probably were without merit.

We talked on. Dinner was suddenly there, served by a young Italian man in his mid twenties dressed in an off-white waist jacket and charcoal black trousers, his hair distinctly pomaded. He flashed a likeable smile as he spoke to us, though his attention stayed rigdly fixed on her, not me. His sense of opulence alertly grasped that she represented a lavish tip at the desk when he left from his day's work. All the while I had begun to gather that Mrs. Narvanna aspired in her sentiments to unleash a wish in regard to her daughter, in fact a wish deep down but unexpressible, that I would marry her daughter some day. Yet none of her words carried this meaning. We talked of a plethora of things; the arts, travel, investments, her charitable endeavors, the past war, and music. Many things, but not marriage.

"I'm so glad you're unscathed by the war Ramsey. You look fine."

"I feel fine. But as you know, and I think you do, I wasn't in the conflict of battle, stationed I should say, well out of the reach of danger in Tokyo occupying a job position which in military jargon they defined as a communications specialist."

"I know that. You weren't in the conflict. But it could have been different, and I'm terribly glad it wasn't."

"That makes two of us."

"Yes. And how is your law work turning out, if I may ask?"

"I'm busy. I enjoy it. It's not entirely smooth sailing every day, always problems, but that's the nature of the job. As with any job one has to learn to retreat from it once in a while, and I do pretty well at that."

"How?"

"Well, the usual things, movies, books, going to New York to the home office to carry out assignments from Mr. Yazstremski who never seems bent out of shape about anything, a splendid man for a younger person like me to learn from."

"I've heard of him. Darya has brought him up. And by the way, since you're in New York at recurring intervals why don't you drop in on some of those wonderful symphonies? You're so much into literature and art that immersing yourself into such entertainment would make for a perfectly natural thing for you. Something you'd greatly enjoy. Just last week I went to a symphony in Baltimore featuring some of the compositions of the great Rachmaninoff. I loved it. His immensity as a composer and pianist are recognized worldwide.

"He's Russian?"

"Indeed."

"I've heard his classical version of *Full Moon and Empty Arms* over the radio. It's beautiful, enchanting. But as for Rachmaninoff himself I'm lacking depth."

"You must catch up. His story is replete with fascination."

"Why not tell me yourself for a starter."

She laughed that demure laugh again as if she were amused. "All right. A shred. You'll have to read his biography yourself if you're interested in grasping the larger background of the man." And then she commenced. "He is of Russian stock as you have observed, his biography alluding to him as a composer, pianist, and conductor, all three, which speaks to his intellect and imagination. Breaking from the influences of earlier composers he gave way to a personal style notable for its long melodicism. At an early age he fell in love with his first cousin and married her in 1917, just as the Bolsheviks were ascending to power, and fearing for their lives, because they were aristocratic, they fled Petrograd for Helsinki in an open sled. Near the end of 1917 he received three offers of American contracts, declining all three, but packed up in November of the following year and moved to the United States. And this is sufficient. You're on your own from here."

I thanked her for her snippet on the great man and committed to her that I would look in on his biography at the earliest opportunity. Nine o'clock now beckoned, or so said my watch. We'd been going for better than two hours. Wondering if she now considered that the visit had neared the end of its course, I began to revolve whether I should suggest adieu to the evening. Or was that her prerogative? And apparently reading my facial language, she in a manner of elegance and dignity announced that she supposed we'd said enough and that likely I must heed to the early alarm of the clock the next morning. She walked me to the lobby and hugged me and bade goodnight.

"She's a marvelous woman, impeccably charming," it played upon me as I drove homeward. "But what did she really want? I'll never know, I'm sure. Did she edge close to asking me if someday I might marry her daughter? There is no doubt that she wishes it. Is it possible that Darya knows of this visit and its purpose? No. That's out of the question. Nor do I believe that Mrs. Narvanna has gone ahead of her daughter in representation of her in a matter of the most intimate nature and thereby forbiddingly awkward to address. I know how they relate. She is anything but a smothering mother of her greatly independent daughter. She could not bring herself to that inclination even if she so desired and she doesn't. Maybe I'm wrong. Maybe it is nothing more than a generous act of kindness that she invited me to dinner. But whatever the purpose it is to my good fortune. She is a rare connoisseur of etiquette and charm and remarkably impressive at conversation."

It was in the realm of this same time, as I recall, that someone or several people back home organized a class reunion of all graduating classes as far back as there were people who once attended my old school. It matured into fruition, the turn out heavy. I went, though saw very few that I recognized, partly due to the time lapse since my class graduated from the twelfth grade and partly because of the innumerable many attending the affair that came after me. When I picked up the program brochure I shouldn't have been shocked, but teetered on the brink of unexpectedness nonetheless, upon reading of a scholarship fund set up in honor of Melissa Monett, her married name unmentioned. It said, "Educator and generous benefactor of many worthy causes in the community and long standing citizen." Expecting to see her I glanced around and after failing to detect her presence anywhere in the masses I asked someone, a girl appearing of high school age, if Melissa happened to have attended.

"No sir. She's ill. We understand that she is suffering from an upset stomach. We're greatly sorry she couldn't come. She's a legend around here. Do you know her sir?"

"Of some time ago. Yes. We're old friends."

"Sorry you're missing her. Shall I tell her your name and relay your warmest regards?"

"I suppose not. I'll catch up with her by letter. How is it that you relate to her?

"Oh. She was my teacher."

Growth had occurred in my small town but only slightly, as is the nature of small rural towns everywhere, hardly any growth from incoming industry. The people talked that this was all right with them for they were doing well enough by holding on to their fifty man work force factory, a ten thousand square foot metal building, which produced clothesware sufficient in volume for putting a pay check in their pockets at quitting time each Friday afternoon, the end result of what they lived and worked for. These same workers filing out of their work place each Friday afternoon possessed no notion whatever that the land on which their plant now rested was once sold by Billy and Melinda Mcvector to its current owners at a hefty profit, and neither were they remotely aware that Billy and Melinda were negotiating presently to buy back the land, and the building too, at an astonishingly cheap price, and that soon following the factory would close. The owners promised to keep the impending sale secretly under wraps for a substantial while, absolutely secret Billy demanded until the property legally changed hands. And for a while the secret stayed intact. But somehow it eventually leaked out, a whisper of news that the plant might shut down, with folks refusing to believe the news flowing into their ears, especially at first, and then starting to believe they were hearing the truth, sensing the approaching reality of what Mr. Carney had mentioned to me a few years before, "Ramsey, the Jews are certain to pull up stakes. The profit's not there and the Jews have put their property, not the business, just the property, quietly on the table for Billy to think about purchasing. And with Melinda egging him on he's chaffing to buy it. But it'll cost him. Talk is Warren Bethune is after a piece of the pie, as well as Wallace Peyton from the Peyton clan, which is not in the stars to happen in either case due to a few obvious reasons: Warren is too old and in bad health, the Peyton guy is lacking entirely in business sense, and Billy and Melinda wouldn't trust either of them as partners no more than they could throw a rock across the Mississippi River and Warren Bethune and Wallace Peyton wouldn't trust Billy and Melinda either. Jackals may gather at the watering hole but each is hesitant to drink for fear of attack on their flanks by one or the other."

When the dealing foamed to a head the townsfolk learned that Billy and Melinda bought the plant and the land, of necessity using some of Melissa's money to own the property outright. Without any preconceived use of the building they began soon after purchase to utilize it as a storage space for a miscellany of sporting goods items, camping tents and guns and fishing gear and motor boats and even land rovers, cunningly releasing preprepared messages that they were in an expansion mode for benefiting their son who one day would take over as manager and owner of the enterprise. Already he actively helped run the hardware store, learning the ins and outs from his father Billy, a gypsy shopper that relentlessly tracked the auction circuit, quick to seize upon merchandise going at shamefully less than bargain basement prices and then cleaning it up and marking it up for sale through Mcvector's hardware outlet. Junk merchandise often proved to have the value of gold to Billy.

The status of Aaron stayed as steady as the doldrums, changeless, though the family persisted: "Where is he? Is he dead, or in a POW camp wounded and slowly dying or starving?" Time had begun to turn into years. No news was released by the War Department and it was interpreted that they possessed not a large amount more than his family, and everyone speculated as to his status. When by chance intercepting Mrs. Stylman at a public restaurant where she and her husband were dining out for dinner, her hurt stood out so pitiably that an urge stirred within me to turn away. I found it painful to face her. Of course, I didn't turn away. Though I judged it a trying effort on her part she did not fail to hug me and pat me on my back, but without making mention of her son. Seized by an impulse to speak his name in some manner or other I found on the attempt that the words deserted my lips. They stayed in my chest. The lingering unknown of Aaron waxed badly on us all, bad on me but monumentally painful to her and her husband who had decided it better to say nothing of their son rather than speak his name or anything pertaining to him and burst into tears in the presence of friends. The days drifted away one by one, still no papers or telegrams, nor letters, from the military. In their suffering the Stylman's seemed as if they were withering away, life no longer yielding up meaning. It sometimes whirled inside me that Mrs. Narvanna and Mrs. Stylman might profitably luncheon together, where they could talk of their children who had suffered through similar experiences, albeit Aaron's experience was not yet known and his status unverified. On second reflection I bent in favor of setting the prospect aside on the rationale that such a rendezvous could easily result in something problematical. "Mrs. Stylman might not handle her emotions suitably well. Better to call the idea off."

Sometimes, I admit, Nenia crept into my awareness. I remember once but not with absolute clarity when I had attained to thirty five years of age, or thirty six, or better, that I began to revolve if ever I expected children in my life I'd better step along and find a wife and marry. Nenia had attained to an age three to fours behind me if I'm not too badly failing. At that stage I had begun to forgive her for her indiscretion, but begrudgingly and only by a scant. "I have to forgive her at least some. I am a great hypocrite if I don't. For I too am guilty of indiscretion. It's illogicaly and abysmally unfair if I don't look at things that way. But I'll never marry her. I know I won't. I guess that's because in my psyche she's tainted. But so am I."

Shortly afterwards I decided to go over certain aspects of wedlock with my most valuable friend, Mr. Yazstremski. But not at lunch. The idea traced through me that what I must bring to surface amounted to a matter best said in private, preferably in his office, a setting richly endowed of vintage furnishings that I had long admired and loved to work amongst.

"As you wish Ramsey. No need to do business over lunch every time there are mutual interests to ply through."

"It's not exactly mutual Mr. Yazstremski. It's something I hold secretly in my heart that I'd like to spread before you which I judge will not strike you with moving interest, but is of great interest to me."

"And it therefore should equaly interest me. Go ahead. Let's have it."

"You may laugh and if you do that's all right. And with this said as a qualifier will you allow me to create a supposition?"

"I do allow it and I won't laugh."

"Suppose sir there are three loves," Nenia one of the three, I had decided, "and that they live deep inside you and have lived there for the longest while, for years I'm disposed to add. All beautiful, all wonderful young women, all of equal merit in most major respects and you are on the brink of marrying one. You would marry them all if you could but the laws of bigamy, among other trifling hindrances, will step in to interfere."

"What a bizarre contrivance. Are you writing a novel?"

"In a sense."

"It sounds as if it's a very serious one."

"It is."

"Ha. Very well. Which am I to marry? And what wisdom am I to employ as a guide to help me decide and proceed with surety beyond a thread of doubt that I have acted with irrefutable certainty. The answer suddenly lands on my brow without a moment's hesitation or torment."

"And?"

"Who is the truest; the truest over the long haul of life, never faltering or failing me in any crisis or in the face of beguiling temptation that seeks to break down her defenses? That is the one I should choose most likely. Surely in your story, if you are writing one, you will penetrate and examine this virtue, this virtue of trueness, or faithfulness if you prefer. Now let me ask you this if you don't mind."

"I don't."

"Good. Then could it stand as a chance that you Ramsey Maynard, my dear young friend, are on the precipice of matrimony and that it is no little task in the selection of one from among the three wonderful girls, young women, that you will give your heart and name to and does it play in your mind that she is not Darya, nor Andrea, but the young lady Nenia that more completely enchains your affections and draws you ever nearer the alter?"

"How, how did you know?" I had affected a falsity and my great friend would have been correct if depending on conditions between Nenia and me some years earlier. There was more.

"How do I know of Nenia? Do not react with shock. I always knew of Darya and Andrea, of course through Aaron, who talked with me as privately as you and I, and learned of Nenia through him, who, born with more than a fair share of tenacity sneaked away to your native place of birth and stumbled upon everything of virtue attached to that splendid lass, which led him straight to the Saint Louis Archives and Library where, most probably jarring to his senses, he met Nenia Stoddard."

"I'll declare."

"You should I suppose. But let me take one step further. It happened rather uncannily, didn't it, that is to say his travel to your small town, the start of catching up with Nenia two weeks previous to his drafting into the military."

"Uncanny is not the word. Wow."

"Yes wow. But he vouched to me, Ramsey, that he intended to share all this with you in time. Now allow me. It's not an easy choice even if you select Nenia, for the other girls are stunningly beautiful, which Aaron affirmed, with genes tied to a strain of remarkably fine pedigree and each, as I envision, patterened splendidly by Him up there to join some young man as his wife. But there is another barometer that I might employ in the determination of choice."

"And what is that sir?"

"The other girls weren't first in your life. Nenia was, and you were the first in hers. Often that makes the difference however thin. Childhood sweethearts mold formidable bonds. Now mind you, longevity of acquaintance should not stand as the sole decision maker and I am not hard set on the notion that it is. It's only a consideration. But in the instance of Nenia it surely comes close to a vital one, for true enough, after all these years, and in view of the luring competition that sought to strip her from you, she has stuck tightly to your heart strings. And held."

"Right for the most part, but he doesn't possess the full page of facts," I murmured inaudibly. "And I don't think I'll have the heart to ever tell him."

Chapter 62

ANDREA HAD once spoken with confidence a few words that now returned and rang invitingly in my head. "If anyone can catch those dudes I can. I know how." A good many years had passed since that moment, that moment being that I promised or indicated that at a date when I could break free from my work obligations, I'd gladly join her on Lac des Allemands. We went over the scheme in some detail. We'd try our luck at catching catfish and crappie we said and lie on the makeshift deck of the outboard in the lazy Louisiana sun and talk and laugh and eat—and after all this finish off with a dive into the moderately still waters for a swim. I remembered that day and the details of the conversation with indelible clarity. I smiled. But that day was so long in the past. Little did I dream or wildly envision that my promise was still alive and stirring in my head after so many years had expired, yet all at once I caught myself leaning back in my chair studying a map of the State of Louisiana. What a wonderful trip and how wonderful to see her again it kept revolving. But something else coarsed through me too; it gnawed at my insides. I could not escape a certain suspicion. "Do I any longer cross her mind, or has she long since formed the notion, which will have been most natural, that I have married and shoved me into the distant corners where she stores fading events and people that no longer mean more than a blink of an eye to her? No. I cannot seriously decide that is so. Somehow, as preposterous as it seems, I just can't envision her married to another man. No matter what. But still, I'll have to see." Sitting at my desk one mid afternoon, with little to do, certainly not an ordinary occurrence, my eyes swept to the upper right hand corner of the Louisiana state map which I had lifted from one of the bureaus, where, written in haphazard penmanship there appeared in bold capital lettering, Lac des Allemands, with a phone number listed beside it. I dialed. When the voice came to me it sounded exactly of the vibrancy which I expected and when I spoke there resulted a pause, brief as it was, and then, "Ramsey, Ramsey," she called out in excited volleys, repeating my name, "Ramsey,

Ramsey," over and over again and then at last letting go with happy loud bursts of extended laughter. I heard myself laughing with her. "I'm thunder struck. I've waited for this call for no telling how long. I'm blown away. You've returned to life."

"Indeed. But I'm going to do better than that."

"What?"

"I'm coming to see you. Once you promised me a fishing excursion on one of your secluded bayou lakes down there and although ridiculously belated, I'm hoping now that you'll let me take you up on it."

"Oh yes! I remember. And how can I refuse. When?"

"Any time. The sooner the better."

"All right. Let me work on it and I'll get right back."

"Please do."

"But for now, I'm so beside myself that I don't know how to handle it. I'd like to drown you with a million questions, starting with are you all right and what have you been doing with yourself, but I can get to such things when we see one another."

"The same here," I said, almost unrestrainedly tempted to call her sweetheart but held back. It seemed so natural to speak that endearment."

"Where did you have in mind fishing, if you really are serious about coming?"

"I'm very serious. No doubt about it. I'm coming. But I'm leaving the where up to you. It's properly your call. You know the territory and the weather conditions. I've never set foot in Louisiana, never."

"What a pity! And it's your fault. But okay. I won't belabor that. Right off the bat I'm suggesting Lac des Allemands, sometimes called merely Lake Allemands by the locals."

We went on for at least a half hour, going over past times and then leaving them for fresher discourses and then getting back. She brought up that we had for the longest traded letters and then dropped off to nothing and I answered yes, we had, the thought springing into my head that we'd start again. At some junction she inquired if any harm in the least came to me during my stint in the war zone of Vietnam, knowing surely by the letters that I sent to her during that ordeal that I got through it unscathed, but when I again assured her of my physical soundness she let out a little sigh. And she asked also if my work presently suited me at the law firm and I answered yes, everything continued to go well for them and me and that moreover I taught some literature classes at a college.

That night I browsed an assortment of tourism materials of the State of Louisiana, leafing through the pages until spotting a montage of photos which showed in dazzling color a lush blue lake of water and wholly agreed with Andrea's suggestion. For awhile I don't think I moved a muscle, my eyes running up and down and across the mass configuration of water that Louisana folks by and large called Lac des Allemands. It was the perfect haven for spending a few days with her trolling here and there in search of catfish and crappie, provided she'd have no trouble sparing the time. From front to back I tenaciously studied the brochure. "Lac des Allemands," it read, "is a 12,000-acre lake about 25 miles west of New Orleans, Louisiana in Lafourche, St. Charles and St. John Baptist Parishes, a segment of a region called the German Coast. The lake name is French for Lake of the Germans, referring to the early settlers who inhabited the lands contigious with it. The lake is shallow, with a maximum depth of 10 feet and an average depth of about five feet, and 5.5 miles in length and 6.5 miles across. Its waters lie at sea level." The weather station reported that the immediate locale should not encounter stormy weather nor even suddenly sprung rain squalls, the days staying sunny and bright and according to the reports originating from the gulf coast weather station the entire lower coast of Louisiana should for the next several days expect sunhine and moderate temperatures. I flew from Chicago to New Orleans, then persuaded a Cajun used car salesman to drive me to the community of Des Allemands, an unanimated small settlement whose people moved at an unhurried pace and gave off an unbelievable impression that their lives were free of worries and things needing completion on time. A few scattered grocery stores and one story brick edifices for other purposes and a wide mainstreet were virtually the extent of everything, which bore faint distinctions to my home town, assuming the boats and boat houses were discounted. Andrea had supplied the instructions that I needed to travel from Des Allemands to Lac des Allemands, every crook and nanny meticulously set down and underscored, which I followed without a bobble and when the driver called out that there was a pretty woman standing on the edge of the boat dock just ahead I knew we had arrived. I looked and there I saw her, clad in a multi flowered skirt of native colors and designs dropping nearly to her ankles, foaming softly in the breeze. I paid the driver and set off my gear, by this time Andrea leaving from where she stood and coming full stride with a face about to burst with happiness. I met her, and picked her up, swinging her round and round. She kept telling me how wonderful it was to see me and I told her the same, both caught up in a cloud of euphoria, and this, prolonged by the kisses and hugs, appeared likely to last for the full afternoon. But it lessened and we returned to earth. The hour neared one o'clock.

"Climb in," she said, with her hand outstretched toward what she referred to as a flat boat, a rectangular shaped craft built in the likes of an elongated wooden box with the motor hemmed in by under water walls which was a means of defending against snags and submerged logs and a hodgepodge of other sub surface impediments capable of rendering serious damage.

"I'll spin us over to where we're staying."

"While we're here?"

"Unh hunh."

"And where is that?"

"My cottage. It's nestled on the edge of a lagoon approximately three miles up the way. I say it's mine. I didn't pay for it. My father deeded it to me. You'll like it Ramsey. It's rustic but decorous—and I cook good too," she signed off, and let out a girlish laugh.

"Ha! Cook good, hunh? I still love your slang. And I'll wager serious money that your cooking is good."

She turned on the ignition switch from which there erupted a sudden snarl, the motor dying and recovering, the sound at its loudest shooting upward and echoing across the waters. As I knew already, she demonstrated masterful skill at operating the motorboat as if she were born doing it. Sitting on the hard plank seating, the hardness partially offset by the cushion appended to the top side, she steered the boat with natural ease to the left a little and to the right a little, while the wind grabbed fiercely at her hair and whipped it into the wildest of contortions, even though she exerted gallant efforts to hold it in place, and at length sighed and more or less gave up and laughed amusedly at herself. The massive spread of water lay calm and agreeable in front of us while Andrea alternated her scan between a certain familiar opening of the shoreline and me, off and on, me then the opening that she knew was there because she lived there. She sat erect, poised, confident, as familiar with the waters and shorelines as any Cajun who earned his living on this lake that locals alluded to as the catfish capitol of the world. The suffusion of sunlight now visited full upon her face, and there, in the midst of open nature, suddenly she seemed as a portrait, more beautiful than ever. About the mid way distance, we tried to resume a semblance of conversation, discovering however that the high drone or sometimes growl of the motor became too much, drowning out any attempt at words. But soon that came to an end. We had arrived. Puttering the boat into an opening, more conventionally labeled an inlet, she navigated it into a niche so small that I quite frankly disbelieved she would succeed; but she did, reversing the motor propellers at the exact right instant and degree to complete the maneuver and jumped ashore with rope in hand to tether it to one of the pier posts jutting upward out of the water.

"We're here. Unless the electricity has gone haywire owing to some fluke beyond my control coffee is almost ready. You recall the coffee drinking days, don't you?" I understood from the gathering on her face that she meant how could either of us ever forget anything of the past of our younger days.

"My! How cozy. It's captivating." It would have been impossible for me to miss as I passed through the doorway that her every space appeared tastefully furnished and decorated with the most assiduous selections, and there exuded an air of freshness throughout, much of it attributable to the flowers she had set out at conspicious places here and there. I loved everything I saw and spoke the best words at my command to let her know of my admiration. She pretended as if she wasn't deserving of the praise but liked it nonetheless.

"I'll pour the coffee. Ready?"

"Anytime."

"And I have croissants. But wait. Are you hungry? It's my thinking you are. How unlike me to slight you so inhospitably. I can have you something in a jiffy."

"No. No I'm not hungry yet. I ate a sandwich, in fact two sandwiches over at the village before we left for here. I'd rather wait."

"Okay. I'll serve an early supper. For now, let's enjoy the coffee and munches and catch up. How is that with you?"

"Good."

I expected chicory coffee—the origin of which is French, bitter enough to turn your mouth inside out—a Louisiana mainstay, but it wasn't chicory; it was a conventional American brand and unbelievably energized my taste buds as it passed across my teeth and over my tongue and afterwards I said I'd have another cup, The croissants, artfully arranged on the serving tray, were just as tasteful, very good in fact, and I asked after consuming a helping of the delicacies, "Did you bake them?" nodding toward those which until then were untouched.

"Yes I did."

"My compliments."

"Thank you."

An overflow of old time reminiences were in store that I'd saved for reflection with her and felt sure she nurtured a bundle that she itched to take up with me but as it happened we were a tad hesitant to rush things. We'd let the past return slowly. I think what coursed through me most was the image of the beautiful bright eyed freshman sitting on the front porch swing of the house next to the fraternity house where I lived. And the circumstances leading to our acquaintance. I almost laughed; I did laugh just enough that Andrea's antenna's were aroused.

"What's funny; why do you laugh?"

"I won't tell."

"Yes you will. Now come on. What's it all about down there in your privately guarded little discrete world?"

"You, and how we met."

"And where and how was that?"

"Let me start with the dance, the dance at the Cub's Nest one night. Darya had consented to a turn with Aaron and you took my hand and tugged me into the fray. Wasting not a second you started telling me that you saw me each day passing the house where you lived and I asked which house and you said the one next to where I lived and I answered with the pretense that I didn't notice. And you asked if it were you or the house that I didn't notice but that it must have been you because you often sat on the front porch swing watching as I strode by."

She seldom laughed loudly, but this time held nothing back, the whole of it likened to a giggle and a laugh of a girl of eighteen. "That's super funny. I think you got it perfectly right. That is exactly how I met you. But do you know something else?"

"Tell me."

"I knew the first time I ever saw you go by that I would like you."

"How soon after that did I find out?"

"Very soon. When we started studying together."

I stayed five fun filled epic days, the two of us indulging in every adventure imaginable from sun up until sunset and sometimes it carried over beyond midnight until as late as two or three in the morning. Some things stand out more prominently than others in my recall, the daily gadding about in the flat boat during which we caught a sizeable count of crappie and catfish, but more crappie than the latter; and sitting on the leather covered oversize couch out on the screened in porch watching the fireflies and the lights from the two man fishing boats skimming up and down Lac des Allemands; and once attending an open air Cajun dance on mainstreet, the musicians, led by the fiddlers and accordionist playing with such speed that I completely lost my timing, with Andrea quickly putting me back in cadence; and then on Sunday next to my last day, we went to church, a Catholic Church, an unpretentious small stucco with a limited flock led through Sacrament by an old priest who clad himself in a cloak of the darkest hue which extended to his ankles, summarily capped off by a broad brim hat with a dome shaped top.

My first night there, we sat on the big leather couch and listened to the radio—she hadn't equipped the cottage with television—and besides the radio keeping us occupied we, as said, watched the fireflies and the twinkling lights emanating from the fishing boats running up and down the waters. Sometimes she leaned against me with me taking her and holding her in my arms.

"It's serenely peaceful out here away from everything," I said.

"You mean here in the bayou country."

"That too. But I really meant here on the front porch."

"I gotcha. Yeah, the front porch is fine. But all this whole big broad bayou is fine. I do love it so much when I'm back here, which is seldom. So free and easy. Pity the folks in the big cities, Ramsey, crammed together like sardines and the crime and all. Just think about it. Suppose there were no cities and that people only lived in places like this. Isn't that a utopian idea? Do you ever think about that?"

"Some. But I guess that wasn't in the grand design. And it wasn't or else the Good Lord would have fixed it that way."

We let it go at that and she left her chair for the kitchen enroute to retrieving a flask of pretty red wine and brought back two very tall glasses already filled and handed me mine. Then the clinking as we tapped them together. And simultaneously, I made up some words that easily popped into my head which to me bode perfectly for the occasion of the moment.

"Here's to us for the next four days. May they prove as fruitful as the first one, which is not even over?"

She leaned against me and kissed my lips, warm and sweet and tender. And there was a little coo that followed. I couldn't resist a tease.

"I didn't realize that wine acted this quickly."

"Clever boy. And as for yourself, do you indulge as much as you used to?"

"I've tapered off. Pretty well quit. I enjoy it mostly on social occasions."

"Really. Why set a limit? The ingestion of wine is good for you. Important to the physical system everyday. Perhaps you've given up the wrong thing, or pretty well quit as you say."

"But not tonight darling. This is pretty delicious stuff."

And then she paused for a brevity, as if contemplating an idea, but soon continued.

"You know Ramsey, seldom do you hear of anyone getting hooked on wine, in other words addicted to it, but that's not the way it is with alcohol. Alcohol is a strongly addicting substance, powerfully resisting one's attempt to break the habit. My uncle once was addicted to wine and alcohol at the same time, at least that's what he said. He decided eventually to break away from both, stopped drinking wine but kept on with alcohol. I asked him why he succeeded in quitting one but not the other. 'Well Andrea, it's like this: good habits are easier given up than bad ones.'"

"Ha, ha, ha. That's hilarious. But he likely wasn't addicted to wine in the first place."

"I'd say that."

"Is he still living around here?"

"No. He died. Suffered a heart attack and fell off his boat into this very lake and drowned or died from the heart attack itself. I miss that old coot. I used to fish with him a lot right out here on these waters."

We did no fishing on the first day, waiting and starting early on the next, with mine beginning when I awoke and smelled coffee and knew that she'd soon have bacon in the skillet. It was seven o'clock. We ate breakfast and headed for the boat dock.

"Will they bite today? Maybe?"

"Sure. They bite every day if you try the right spots."

I didn't ask her where they were, knowing she'd take us there soon enough. When we had pushed off and gotten away from the cottage by a short duration of minutes she swung suddenly into an inlet and began to troll.

"We'll trust our luck over by those dead stumps Ramsey. Crappie just love to hover around old stumps and logs, close to the bottom but not too close to the bottom."

After a while, at mid morning, she opened the thermos she'd stored in her "miscellany pouch," as she called it, and poured a metal cup full of coffee for me and one for herself. "Ah, what a taste," I murmured to myself, "nothing better than coffee and food when you're out in the open, and quick as a streak John Eric and Uncle Sanford and the rabbit hunts flooded into my head.

Andrea's luck began the moment she lowered her hook into water, my luck less, but with her encouragement and suggested techniques I reeled in a better than expected catch. When we shifted to another nesting place a school of crappie began to strike with shark like fierceness, Andrea excitedly dragging in one catch after another, as fast as I managed to help her free them from the viciously stubborn fish hook. Though long seasoned at the sport each catch to her came as a triumph of newness, igniting a shriek to the top of her lungs as she yanked it from the water, flopping, jerking, lunging, spinning, writhing, thrashing, instinctually summoning forth a fantastic cascade of gyrations to help it escape its fateful snag. Andrea proved her magnificence at the sport and were it not for the two or three that got away she would have had a perfect mark.

At lunch we broke, sitting and eating while the listless breeze skimmed across the waters and against us, forcing a tiny quiver to appear in Andrea's loosely clad dress. The urge to dive in for a swim cogently tempted her.

She declined, forcing a pucker of regret. "Let's not. I have no swimsuit with me. Tomorrow."

My eyes swept across the breadth of the lake to the misty shores on the opposite side from where we were, then up and down its length, marveling not only at its size but at its serenity. I still considered taking a dip but wouldn't without her in the water with me. Mostly we sat and ate and basked in the reverie of quietness, thinking, thinking of something, she in her own way and me in mine. It was one of those moments when for some reason two people just stop talking, reveling in one another in silence. The night before she mentioned that her job centerted on war games for the military, and that her knowledge of physics and mathematics played a key role in what she did. She said no more than that, her hesitancy to offer anything additionally suggesting that a huge parcel of her assignment fell into the restriction of classified information. "War games! Very complicated stuff. And that's what she does. She is so capable—and yet so gorgeous too. It's almost unfair that someone can have such an immensity of brain power and beauty implanted together in a single package."

Her neighbors outdid themselves with friendliness, going overboard to do her favors, even when the favor wasn't needed or wanted, this coming of life later in the week when a Cajun fisherman, one of her favorites, waved and pulled his craft alongside ours. He watched after her property during her long stints away at her work for the military.

"Helo Andrea. I has something fo you."

"What is it?"

"Snapping turtle. I got five. Fifty pounders. I don't needs all of em. I want you to hav one. And your friend. I'll dress it fo you."

"I'll take it," she said, without the heart to turn him down, which, if she had, she said, he might have taken as an act of impoliteness. "But I can't use all of it. Will giving some of it to my neighbors sit well with you?"

"Ye, ye."

"You won't get angry with me?"

"No, no. I won't."

"Thank you Lonzo. Meet me at the cottage. You can dress it in the back"

"Okay. I will."

"Snapping turtle," I intruded, talking directly to Lonzo. "I've seen them. I used to fish for turtles with my uncle. He caught them on a trot line. But they weren't nearly as big as the ones you're speaking of."

"Unh unh. Not de same. I'm talking bout alligator snapping turtle. Huge. A beast. Likes to swim crawl on a bottom of the lake, stirring up cloudy looking mud stuff. He's a bad un. But good eatin."

We followed Lonzo to Andrea's cottage and as he'd pledged, he took a fifty pounder out back and in short order finished dressing and washing it. Andrea thanked him and we carried the meat inside and stored it in a second freezer recessed next to the kitchen. "Actually, Ramsey, its good meat and we'll try some of it when it's opportune. But most of it I plan to let the good priest have over at Des Allemands to divide among his flock."

The next day a lady living nearby in a cottage with her husband brought over a quart size fruit jar of coon ass, a strange jargon to me and I showed by the twist of my facial expression that the term had sent me to wondering, but Andrea on seeing my uncertainty began explaining that coon ass for eons had been classic language among the natives and that I should envision the concoction as a first cousin to gumbo.

Chapter 63

ON THE third day we decided on a variation of things to do, thus far able to lay claim to a terrific catch of crappie and catfish, which we stored as much as space allowed in the second freezer, giving the surplus to her friends. We went swimming at mid afternoon, with Andrea lamenting when we got out on the water, she'd forgotten her swim suit, a bikini, then catching me looking the other way slipped off her dress and dove in. But I turned in the nick of time, catching an eye full of her stunning form, as good as when she was in her late teens, if not better. She knew I liked very much what I saw. A phenomenal swimmer, she easily maneuvered all around me when I joined her, darting about as skillfully as a fish, sometimes diving under me and shooting up on my blind side. "Here I am," she'd call out and die laughing. Biding my time, I'd catch her unaware and push her under and hold her there for a little, then finish off with a kiss. Then we'd pop up.

"Devil,"—after squirting out a mouthful of water.

"But you liked it."

"Ha. You jest. Of course I liked it. What a stupendous way to indulge in amour."

On the fifth day, a Saturday, we attended the Cajun dance in Des Allemands, a spirited gathering that she said was a must for us, proclaiming that it was something of a a fandango that everyone in town indulged. "Literally everyone Ramsey, parents, children, and grand folks. Everyone. But I'll tell you what we must do while we're there."

"Yeah."

"The turtle meat. We'll deliver it to the priest at the church. I'll call him before hand to expect us."

"What time does the dance begin?"

"At seven thirty. But we'll lag back until after eight to show up."

As the longest clock hand reached seven, we left for Des Allemands in her pick up truck with the meat boxed in ice and stored in the truck bed closely against the cab. She said she chose to drive the pick up rather than the new Cadillac the military supplied her due to the conditions of the roadway, more bumpy than smooth, and endowed with a raft of convolutions and mud holes. The flowery dress in which she'd attired herself struck me as a style of gypsy wear, foaming like a wave on the ground around her feet. I succumbed to the urge to ask her to say something of it.

"No. It's not supposed to emulate the gypsy style, granted that it may look like that to you. It's purely Cajun, excepting the basque which tries to squeeze the heck out my breasts."

"Are you Cajun Andrea? At least some?" It kind of slid out unintended. But for the longest I had nurtured the temptation to ask her.

"What a question." Her laugh sounded of coquettish amusement. "No. I'm not; I have no Cajun blood flowing through my veins, none that I know of, yet some folks believe I have, if they're non-Cajun. But I love the Cajun folks and they pay me back in kind. They're always inviting me to their fandangos, their outings, and particularly to their dances, or to whatever is going on. And some things are a shade extraordinary I have to admit. Once, if I may, a Cajun friend invited me to her wedding, and I quite contend that that wasn't unusual, but there was an unusual aspect of it that just about bowled me over. I won't soon forget it."

"Tell me."

"Well. The groom, wearing his newly bought wedding suit, showed up at the church driving a John Deere tractor. I swear it. I was there."

The priest accepted the turtle meat with ebullient warmth which sprang lovingly from his heart, evinced by his happy embrace and kiss to Andrea's cheek. His manner, overwhelmingly kind, struck me as somewhat incongruent with the length of his frame, a big man, but I lost no time in scolding myself that a big man's heart is as soft as a small man's and to quit my foolish analogies—but he was big, as I visually measured him for the second time, towering prodigiously over Andrea who looked up with worshipful eyes into her pastor's reverent face.

"The people will like the turtle meat Father, and I trust that you will accept it as if it is a gift from the most generous recesses of my heart."

The priest did not attempt to hold back his voluble laugh and hugged her caressingly. "You amaze me my Angel with your carefulness to present things in an infinitely proper light. But that is who you are, sweet and kind in every manner. I accept, naturally I accept and they will also. You are more than thoughtful to do this." Then he turned to me. "She is a precious thing in my flock Mr. Ramsey. I'm supposing that you can discern as much for yourself. No, she is not Cajun. But the people will contend that she is even when they know that is not the truth. They love her as if she is their very own."

"I know she's not Cajun. But I can tell that they hold her dearly in their most compassionate environs."

"In their hearts. Yes of course and she them. If they possess one complaint pursuant to this dear girl it is that she is not here with us enough. But we understand. Her job takes her far and wide, even abroad as you know."

The accolades beginning to embarrass her Andrea spoke up that if we were going to attend the dance we had best take leave.

"Surely," the priest rejoined. "They were at it pretty heavily some time ago and are now in full commotion as you can adjudge from this whereabouts." As we started off he sent a reminder after us, "Don't forget church tomorrow Andrea, and you too Mr. Ramsey."

The dancers were already assembled in the center of the village, in the middle of the preponderantly wide street, and as we pushed through the gallery of those for the time being not electing to dance we plainly saw the inner whirl of activity, men in blue jeans and women oft as not in shorts, all wearing the most colorful of clothing, happy and laughing. In every way a fandango it dawned on me. The sight convincingly relayed that now I witnessed the socialization peak of their week and it came to me that no where on earth was there a people who enjoyed a frolic more than these. Andrea immediately took my hand, pulling and tugging, and led me into the midst of the excitement, no one paying attention to us as we squeezed through an opening and nudged and bumped those around us and thereby laid claim to our own space.

"They say down here Ramsey that you don't try to dance according to any pre set maneuvering you might have earlier learned about dancing; you just listen to the music and the beat and let that and the sound take care of the rest. That's Cajun music for you."

She earlier fore cautioned that the music would sound louder than the average loudness, which was muchly a fact, the accordion player, the fiddlers, the banjo pickers, and the drummer all "busting a gut" to out do anyone else; and then the lead singer, let me not leave out, whose twisted French and original Acadian dialect tested my ears to understand. Sometimes a local tapped Andrea on her shoulder and stole her away from me for a turn, and most of the time even when I danced with her I stayed half lost with the music, sometimes a Cajun Jig, sometimes a Cajun Jitterbug, sometimes a fais do-do, and another time a music they called Zydeco, troubling, I must assert. The cadences were difficult, but Andrea did better than well with them irrespective of which, and as the evening wore on every Cajun male on the street began to watch for a chance to partner with her.

On the road home after the dance, well past midnight, we began to go over the heritage of these people, with Andrea taking the initiative to explain that they weren't exactly a distinct culture, more a mixture of French and Acadian foremostly, but blended through the species of cross marriages with Spanish American, Indian, and African peoples that climaxed into a potpourri of influences.

"Why are the Cajuns here?"

"All right," she said, stepping right into it. "Cajun is a reshaped name for Acadian, and thus, more pertinently, your question should have to do with why did the Acadians come here. And here is why. Since migrating from Europe the Acadians had lived in Nova Scotia, Canada for a while, a good long while, under French rule and relatively untroubled. But the British drove the French out and the British forged radical change onto the scene. Faced with the refusal of the Acadians to pledge allegiance to the British the governor took action to retaliate. Acting on his own and not on orders from the crown he delivered the edict that led to the expulsion of the whole colony, in 1755 I believe, which is also known as 'Le Grand Derangement.' And there you have it. They're called Cajuns now and have been ever since I remember, but Cajun is a corruption of the original, which over the years has become accepted and standardized."

Getting out of bed early enough to allow us to reach the church before seven amounted to no less than a chore; nonetheless, we made it, and put on an agreeable and cheerful face as we met the priest standing at the doorway.

"Good morning Andrea. Good morning Mr. Ramsey."

We responded with like formality and entered the doorway, taking seats midway of the sanctuary. The priest shortly thereafter appeared before the congregation dressed in purple vestments and a purple cope and I believe a cap set on his head adorned with the presence of a cross. The service began with his citing something from scripture in Latin, followed by an old lady clad in a soft blue, very long dress, with more than a plentiful head of grey hair collapsing to well below her shoulders, who read different scriptures from those cited by the priest. Andrea whispered that all wording, whether read or cited, was delivered in Latin. I had long wondered why Catholic services were given in Latin, yet recalled that I'd picked up, read, or heard—perhaps from being around Darya and Andrea in college days—that the custom dated back to the apostles. I knew this fell far short of a satisfactory answer. My curiosity wouldn't let me rest without learning more.

When it became apparent that the liturgy of sacrament had just started to get underway, I detected an older lady sitting on Andrea's right bending over to say something into her ear that she took quite disagreeably I presumed. The lady asked, as Andrea later let me know, if I were of the Catholic faith. And upon Andrea answering that I wasn't the old lady winced and voiced that I should refrain from that portion of the worship, in retaliation of which there resulted a sharp retort, "You offend me Mrs. So and So. He will do no such thing. The Christ that presides over you presides over him the same." Cornerned that her outburst might have caused a disruption she went straightaway to the priest shortly after the service to offer an apology for flying off the handle in the Lord's Church, "You would have been infinitely ashamed of me Father," but this was met by his caressing arms and assurances, "Don't trouble yourself with that my angel. You had every good reason to take up for your friend. I would have done the same."

When I kneeled at the altar the young server in his surplice, a loose white linen, passed to me first the wafer and then the chalice of wine, both of which I partook of, while the kindly priest with tender redemptive eyes looked down at my efforts to copy with exactitude that which others were doing. Andrea's hand softly gripped my arm, and as I looked over at her, she smiled, and as I glanced up at the priest he smiled too, because my smile and hers had met.

As we left, the priest, standing by the doorway embraced Andrea and kissed her brow, and expressingly hoped that I'd found the people and circumstances most cordial during my stay.

"I've had a wonderful five days. I hate to leave."

"And when is that?"

"Tomorrow."

As we sat on the front porch that evening and into the night I felt the dread in her voice of my impending departure early the next morning. Curious all along with respect to her military connected work I used the subject as a means of steering her away from her mood of sadness, which to a degree appeared effective. She did not shrink from questions when I brought them into conversation but carefully averted revealing a great deal either of her military occupation: yet easily talked of her busy travels to Atlanta, Washington, New York, Miami, San Diego and to a sprinkling of strategic sites and cities abroad. Speaking a slight out of her established bounds she once explained a particle of her involvement in the exercise of military war games, principally that part which dealt with the exploration of the effects of warfare and the creation and testing of strategies. "Simulation of real live warfare is at the base of my work" she further shared, "and is rapidly becoming a common element of computer technology." And then shifted back to her busy travels. "I'm on the go Ramsey. It's a hurried life I'm leading. The military is an organ which is in perpetual motion; they have no choice—security being the thing of essence, and every soul that's tied to them is in nonstop high gear. But let's not carry this too far. Tell me of your stint in Vietnam. You've hardly said anything at all of it in depth."

As she had done, I cut it short, or tried to convince myself that I had, ending up with my experience as a teacher in college, which brought me abruptly back to the debacle of war and its tragic impact on the lives of young people caught up in the draft.

"When I made it back home Andrea, I mean to Chicago, and eventually began to teach college kids I encountered an experience that I would have given anything to have avoided. I don't think I'll ever recover from it."

"For land sakes. What was it?"

"A young student ventured into my office one morning before class began with apparent trouble on his mind. I knew that the moment I glanced up. Of senior status he intended to graduate in the coming May from Loyola. He had opted to enroll in my class at the lower level just to bolster his record in literature. His work would transfer to the university."

'Mr. Maynard,' he said in a vein of apology, 'may I discuss something privately with you?'

"I assured him that he could by all means and motioned to him to proceed. He continued to stand."

'Well sir, I don't know how you feel toward the draft and certain other views about the war.'

'I do have my views I must say.'

'I see sir. As do I.'

'You should, and that is I presume why you are here.'

'Yes sir.'

'All right.'

'I'm a conscientious objector. I don't believe in wars, or in laws that demand a man fight and risk his life against his will and religion and to kill other people that we call our enemies.'

'With certain limitations I'm inclined to adopt your view.'

"At this he revealed the reason for the visit."

'Will you then agree to write a letter to my draft board that I am in your class, that you are well acquainted with me as a person, and that it is your considered judgment that I should in no way qualify for induction into the armed services?'

Before speaking to his request, I remained in silence for at least enough to establish a well conceived answer. I truthfully wanted to do my best.

'Writing a letter of the substance that you request is not an effort of substantial bother and I will consider it; yet, I doubt that my decision will augur favorably on your behalf.'

'Will you tell me why?'

'I will. Think of the other young men who have voluntarily or through the draft fought for their country and have died in the heat of battle for the cause. My sentiments for you flow sincerely from my heart but what you ask of me is close to the level of too much. I will think about it. Come back tomorrow for my answer if you wish. I will need time.'

Andrea sat as quietly as a stone through my brief story, but no longer.

"Oh, that was awful, for both of you. What did you tell him the next day when he returned?"

"Nothing. He left school that afternoon they said and no one produced an account of him afterwards."

"No account afterwards! Oh! What would you have told him should he have come back to see you?"

"Go to Canada, or Mexico. Anywhere. The same advice that many a parent might have passed on to a son after thinking it through."

"My. What a fix you were in. Your answer though throws me off balance. Young men have to fight. They're born with that likelihood, I'm sorry to say. But somebody has to fight. Suppose that everyone suddenly declared it against his moral principle to represent his country as a soldier. We wouldn't have a country very long, would we? But still, I can't blame you for the answer you said you would have given, because likely I would have done it myself."

Then, suddenly, out of the blue. "Do you like teaching?" She figured we'd sufficiently wrung the neck of the current topic.

"Immensely."

"Someday I may quit what I'm doing now and earn a teaching certificate and settle into teaching myself—just like you. Or go into commercial fishing."

"You're kidding."

"Yeah I am."

"You've got a good job, a heck of a job; and whether it's dawned on you or not you're clearing the trail for women to follow. It's a man's world you're in and that's where women aspire to break into."

"Precisely. And I'm aware of where I am and said the same of myself when I filled out the application and undertook the exams. I have liked it from the start. I don't see it as a man's world though; it's a woman's world too as long as she equals the standards."

"How can I logically entertain an otherwise opinion, and for sure and certain you are at the top of the game."

"Hm, hm. You flatter me."

"I don't mean to. I know well who you are. Remember those physics and math tests you helped me pass back there at the university. But allow me. Historically women have been the teachers, more in the elementary grades than in the higher ones, but in either case they're inclined toward change. They'll not content themselves from here on just to teach in the schools; there's law and engineering and finance and medicine, men's positions, it's said, and the time is approaching when with another war or two they'll turn to soldiering. Flying airplanes and navigating ships. True enough, I think, back in my home town they'll wait a long while before fully adopting such modernity but it'll happen. They won't want to settle for teaching, not the young ones. They'll leave out of there for the cities and when they do they won't give a hoot about their elders' opinions. They'll set their sights on what to them are the prestige professions."

"Your hometown. You mentioned it just now. You never talked to me much about it when we were in college. Seldom anyway."

"What would you like to hear?"

"Anything you're willing to share."

"In the first place I would have told you all you wanted to know back then. But I don't recall your asking. Should you have asked I would have gladly taken you down there on a quickie visit for a sight seeing?"

"I'd have liked that."

"As is in the likeness of small towns mine was slow, and still is. Some of the folks live their lives for the church, and subscribe to other sedate styles of living. Slowness of pace, it must be assumed, doesn't bother them. To others it does. They're the ambitious lot, the ones ending up in trouble with their fellow man. Disagreements erupt now and then, or worse, and people are marched off to court for settlement, and some are thrown in jail. The town also has its festivals and recognition ceremonies for persons who've done good deeds, a fine thing. And it has its wealthy too, as well as the less wealthy. The same old story. The haves and the have nots. Yet, the wealthy aren't as wealthy as they think they are, for if you compare them to the sure enough wealthy people of the big cities, for instance Chicago, you'd discover that they're the lowest of the wealthy lowest. It has its share of Negroes, fine folks and I'm closely acquainted with most of them, or once was. Negroes and Whites with few exceptions harmonize very suitably. There is however a tight lipped expression among the Whites that admirable relations among the races have forever existed because the Negroes have stayed in their places, a premise that is by all forms of sensible logic a mite unfair. They didn't need to stay in their places. The evidence begs to vouch that they were almost always in their places, good citizens, good for the town. It's not hard to argue that the Whites get along with the Negroes better than the Negroes get along with themselves and sometimes that is correct and sometimes upheavals occur and no one can unravel who's to blame. Let me tell you of a most fateful misfortune that'll help make this plainer. A man lived there once whose name was Elizar Lebranche, of mixed blood, half white and half black, whose son he had named Czar, a strikingly handsome person, even lighter than his father, and when he attained to adult age moved up North. I can't say where. It got about that he attracted White women to him in droves, an exaggeration I'm confident, though some of it true. He had fairly loose reins with White women in the North apparently but back home in the South the tenor of acceptance ran grossly to the contrary. On one of his returns home he went to a town several times larger than his, and mine, for a shave and hair trim. While sitting in the barber's chair with a steaming towel over his face awaiting the shave a masked man, his face altogether covered, rushed in and shot Czar dead with a shotgun, blood splattering everywhere they said, on the barber's chair, on the floor, on the mirror, on the barber's white shirt. All over. Then the speculation spread wildly. Did a Negro shoot Czar who'd been messing around with his girl friend or wife, or did a White man do it violently outraged because of Czar's intimacy with a White woman? No one ever learned the truth and the tale lingered on, for years, and after I grew up I heard it myself. The general belief had it that a white man did the killing, for it spread among the gossipers that Czar was seen rather recently in a romantic attitude on the back roads of the community with a woman whose skin color reflected shades somewhat lighter than his own, a white woman in other words."

"That's an awful story. Just awful."

We sat beyond the midnight hour pursuing one conversation piece after another, until not completely unexpected the name of Aaron surfaced, of whom she inquired and said that for a substantial while she had not received news of his status in any regard.

"I can't say much to enlightenment you I'm afraid. Mr. Yazstremski timely forwards to me anything noteworthy, but the only news of worth to me I must say weighs heavily on whether he is still alive, and there is nothing to that effect. In fact, there is nothing at all. If something turns up, good or bad, you'll hear from me without delay."

"Thank you. I'll appreciate your doing that."

As the minutes ticked off and the hour edged toward one o'clock, she leaned against me and yawned, with me mentioning that we should turn in because I needed to arrive at the New Orleans airport by eight.

"Oh, that's right. You have. Remember that I'm driving you."

"I do. I told the driver I wouldn't need him to pick me up. But you didn't have to drive me. He could have done that."

"But I do have to," she said a little sadly, but determinedly, looking across at me in the candle glow. "Wish you would stay here a few more days, forever if you just will."

"I wish that too." I did not lie. I wished it in my soul. "What an idyllic place," I said silently. "What an idyllic out of the way place to spend a lifetime with someone like her."

As if she had read what spun inside my head she sweetly kissed my lips and then reached her arms around my neck and kissed my face all over. "Why can't you stay a while longer? You can't imagine my loneliness without you."

In my heart there stirred a murmur of tenderness as if it were a person and I heard it speak to me beseechingly, "How can you do without her, how can you possibly learn not to love her, how can you leave her here once and forever and forget her? As surely as you have a soul within you, you know you cannot."

It rained that night as was the case all week long off and on. I think it had decided to fall usually between midnight and daylight, a soft pitter patter audible on the roof top, and we always perked up when it commenced, then lying in bed, sometimes cutting short whatever we were talking about, just listening, listening, listening.

"Isn't that soothing" she would say and I would answer yes, very soothing, and that the Master created rain for many purposes and that one of them was certainly to provide humans the joy of it dropping softly on the rooftop. She laughed and called me silly. She was so lovely lying there, so tempting, the moonglow at intervals pouring through the half covered windows and settling on her face. I wanted her. I admit that. And while she made me very much want to have her, I must tell the truth and say that I did not. And neither did I ask her to. It was implanted deep within my soul that if I went through with it I might well have defiled my future beautiful wife. What man would have chosen likewise? I do not know. Why dwell on that? I merely say that if the Good Lord had anything to do with the outcome, I pray to Him my grateful thanks. Neither Andrea nor I ever had to look back over our long lives together and suffer regrets.

The rain halted and stayed gone and I quit worrying that my trip of necessity was on the verge of cancellation. Talking but sparingly we drove to New Orleans, starting not a long while after daylight uncloaked itself, her slack in conversation not in any semblance imitating her normal self. There had evolved a misty thickness which formed during the night, rising from the lakes and bayous and now the commuter traffic purposefully creeping ahead of us jammed the highway arteries that coursed into the city, which we hardly noticed. The throbbing pangs of the impending goodbye consumed us. We had to wait a while for the plane. It was late. Standing by me with her arm cradling mine she stayed until it landed and rolled in our direction, racing its motors, beginning to pull toward us for the passengers to load, and then suddenly she stood on tip toes and kissed me, saying words, I love you I presúmed, but couldn't make them out clearly. The pilot revved the motors to a crescendo, the terrible fierce roar insinuating they were on the threshold of exploding. I moved a step closer to the gate, but on turning around with the intent of holding her one last time found her gone. I looked, harder, further, searching, and then saw her vanishing into the crowd. "She didn't want you to see her cry."

Chapter 64

I RETURNED TO my work. Mr. Yazstremski soon summoned me away from the Chicago office to help him with a case that proved wrenchingly complex and time consuming in the extreme, directing that Janet Sayora would have to absorb my load in my absence, which I relayed shortly to my immediate superior who announced it to the staff. That I got called upon by the most powerful and respected man in the New York office to give him a hand might have in the past pricked the staff's tentacles of animosity, a sprinkling of them to say the least, but by now they were accustomed to his closeness with me and had long ago realized and accepted that if a specialty assignment came down from the New York office it would land on my desk. In the main I now was viewed as the heir apparent to managing the affairs of office when the existing director, now aging, retired or else transferred.

All along I stayed in touch with Darya and Andrea by brief visits and by way of letters and telephoning—but only in scattered instances. Nenia wrote now and then, or telephoned, attempting to carry on in the manner that we once did, in effect pleading that she wished deep in her heart that we'd find our way back together. And I deemed that she believed that we eventually might. But too much hurt and anger still lingered. Sometimes I softened in my considerations recalling that I too had made love to Darya and blamed myself for being hypocritical. But unfair as my attitude might have seemed toward Nenia I knew in my heart that reconciliation fell far short of the reach of possibility.

After the expiration of years, I cannot cite the number, the news at last resounded in our hearing. The family heard in full about Aaron, the military belatedly sending a formal document that Aaron died in a POW internment while the war still raged, said Mr. Yazstremski, the first to notify me of the report, and my heart sank with remorse. Running through me with the swiftest speed were the good days with Aaron, beginning with the time that he and Darya bounced gaily through the doorway of the fraternity house where Bertinelli introduced us. There arose an echo of recall in my heart, "Wasn't he such a happy young guy?" I telephoned Darya then Andrea, sure that they'd want to know even if receiving devastating news. My compassion reached out to Mrs. Stylman, who bravely suffered the enormous blow and this on top of the years of waiting, fearing, not knowing, wondering. "Life is sometimes terribly cruel?" it sounded within me, and then ploughing through the whole of everything with not a great deal of delay reached for the telephone, knowing that I must call Mr.Yazstremski for ceremonial and burial details.

"They are shipping the body back, are they not?"

"No Ramsey. There is no body and likely never will be. We only have a brief official transmission from the military and that is final. There is a ceremony planned for paying respects and you are expected to attend. Mrs. Stylman has asked if you will."

"Please tell her yes, by all means. It is in the synagogue, isn't it?"

"Yes. Of course."

"I'm trying to conclude something sir, Darya and Andrea, the girls. They were close to Aaron, confidants of his more or less. Should I tell them that they are invited?"

"Definitely. Will you take care of that?"

"Yes sir."

"Good. I'll supply you with the date shortly. When it's determined."

Prior to the funeral date by one day Darya and myself and Andrea met as agreed at the fraternity house, Andrea and I caught somewhat unsuspecting when Bertinelli showed up too. Darya had tipped him off. With all of us hugging and carrying on with hyper animation we sat down on the giant divans in the lobby, declaring that we could virtually still hear Aaron's voice at the dinner meal elevating above everyone else's, pressing hard for or against an issue of the debate. A young man of management presently zipped over, recognizing us as strangers, and politely asked if we'd like iced tea or coffee, who upon bringing the tea volunteered that he'd chosen political science as his major area of study. We told him we were once students there and that the four of us lived in that very same house. "Well, I'll declare! I'll tell my supervisor." Andrea walked about glancing here and there, peeping into the dining hall as if it generated an extraordinary appeal and from there left for the portico, and there turned left toward the house in which she lived when we were in college. I followed her. Sensing that I had edged close she did an about face. and chuckled. "I can't believe it's been so long." Our group of four, the solid mainstays from yesteryear, sat reminiscing for at least another hour going over the minutest things that were a part of our lives as young students. The reunion was affectedly nostalgic; and wide of range but singularly dominated and presided over by the heartfelt absence of our deceased and beloved friend.

The girls and I flew out of Chicago that afternoon for New York. Since Mr. Yazstremski previously invited me to two Jewish funerals I to a minor degree understood the customs better than they, and emphasized before leaving that each synagogue established its own traditions and therefore, I wasn't knowledgeable of those applying to the synagogue to which we were going, and confessed only partial correctness in what I said. At this, I walked them through the procedures, the traditions, and then again while we were in flight. If you're a Gentile attending a Jewish funeral, I told them, dress in a respectful manner, in dark colors preferably, where a man wears a suit and a woman a dress or skirt. Some synagogues require women to cover their hair and a man to wear a skull cap, yarmulke, which is most likely available at the entrance. Unlike Roman Catholic or Orthodox Christian rites, Jewish funerals are closed casket, but irrelevant of course for Aaron's ceremony. The funerals take place at funeral homes or a temple or a synagogue where special prayers and eulogies are given by family members. And I should not leave out that attendees customarily sign the guest book and take a seat and speak quietly to anyone sitting adjacently. If feeling comfortable in doing so one may participate in the prayer service by standing up or simply sitting in place and responding to the prayers that are read or chanted. And all this I explained to Darya and Andrea.

The funeral did not last long. It was held at a synagogue on New York's west side with which I possessed no familiarity, even though Mr. Yazstremski meticulously explained in advance its whereabouts to me by telephone. The gathering had begun when we arrived, the service in the first phase beginning. As the rabbi read and partly chanted from Hebrew text the people stood, and continued to stand, I myself standing between Darya and Andrea, who were clad in lovely soft dresses of placid colors, with no make up on their faces, strictly abiding by the rules of Jewish tradition. Few of the rabbi's words were meaningful to me, since they were spoken in the Jewish vernacular, but which in most respects I thought I understood, taking my cues from his tone. Mr. and Mrs. Stylman sat on the front row grieving, a terribly sad moment for them and Mr. Yazstremski too who sat nearby, three seats over from me. I'd never seen him that sad.

When my eyes trailed off through the window, I caught the sunlight radiating downward and the wind timidly flicking the leaves in the trees on the synagogue grounds, suddenly attracted to the notion that this was a good day for funerals and then I caught myself. "Good day for funerals! What's wrong with you? There's no such thing as a good day for funerals." I chastised myself harshly for veering away from the text, the funeral ritual, but kept letting things run through my brain, going back to a long while ago when but three or four. I'm pretty sure of my age then. I walked at my mother's side who tugged me along with her en route to a funeral while talking to a friend that the dead man laid in open casket at the church. It scared me quite awfully. "A dead man. Gracious. What is that like?" The mystery, the grotesqueness of what I heard birthed within me a sort of petrified stiffness.

But now I regained the occasion of moment, and cautioned myself to quit those dark macabre images of the past, that this was Aaron's funeral, my best friend, or once was, and that I should feel ashamed for losing a grip on my purpose of being there. But then something else. It came to me comfortingly that I had a long while ago progressed to manhood, much older now, and that older people no longer feared death, not as they did when young, that the older they became the less the fear. But on the other hand, I found this hard to reconcile as fact.

Shaking my momentary comatoseness, my drifting off, I began again to focus on the proceedings of the ritual.

Once Andrea reached and took my hand and held it in hers and didn't let go for the longest. Standing there between her and Darya I suddenly returned to the great cathedral on the university campus where the three of us often attended church on Sunday morning, admiring how beautifully they sang the "old timey" hymns. "Funny," I said in silence, "they are now as they were then, neither showing signs of jealousy. You'd almost think they see me as their brother if you were a stranger."

When the service ended, we passed with the other attendees by the Stylman's who now stood, offering our sympathies, Mrs. Stylman reaching and drawing me to her and holding me for a moment, kissing my cheek and whispering softly that she loved me. Determining beforehand not to let Darya pass through the line without an embrace she motioned for her to come near and with loving affection wrapped her arms around her, letting her know that she knew she meant much to her son. On his thin and frail old legs Mr. Yazstremski short stepped, pitter pattered, his way over and hugged me and the girls, lightly exchanging courtesies with them. As we moved away from the crowd Andrea murmured lowly that this was the saddest thing she had ever gone through and Darya said it too, lending an extra insertion that she felt gladdened to have come but didn't think she'd attend another as long as she lived. The three of us rode to the airport together; Darya's plane the first to arrive, with me escorting her up the stairway to the passenger boarding door, a mere few strides away from the interior. But I did better. I escorted her to her seat and kissed her. Her departure meant that I'd spend a short period alone with Andrea. We took tea in the nearby restaurant just off the hallway not many paces from the boarding gate. She hoped that we would see one another more often and I promised that I'd keep my part of the bargain. She playfully threw in that the fish were still biting. I hugged her dearly as she started to move through the gateway to board her plane. I would be staying for a while in New York, fulfilling an assignment by Mr. Yazstremski. The hour then neared one o'clock and I went to my office hoping to do some work, but no work was done, not even for the entire afternoon, a flood of memories filtering through me of my dear young friend crowding out everything else. "He's the guy who landed me my job with the law firm. Exactly him. No doubt. He'd talked with his father on my behalf. Without it I wouldn't have gotten to where I am right now. It's who you know, is it not? No, not exactly. You have to have ability too. So, it's who you know together with what you know combined with your abilities. Either way I'm ever thankful to him and some day I'll write him a letter and burn it and send to him in Heaven my appreciation for his favor."

By this stage, perhaps a year or two longer, maybe a slight more, my hurt and anger against Nenia had begun to lessen and I leaned a long ways toward forgiving her. How could I not do that? Granted, a faintness of the indiscretion yet lingered but I had begun not to count that as a major hindrance. After all I too bore some measure of committing an indiscretion, I reminded myself. "But I did not betray Darya and neither did she me." I argued with myself, but quickly swept it aside, that there was an inkling of a chance of Nenia and I coming together in wedlock at last. Even so, it was ordained in Heaven, I was of complete belief, that such a union would never materialize into fruition. Time and the events of time had combined to shape the ultimate outcome. For one thing some marriages, imminent as they may appear, and which everyone thinks will happen as surely as the sun rises, play out and fall apart. That we once loved one another neither of us questioned, that we were practically betrothed since the onset of puberty we could both attest, and that in our hearts we acknowledged that it hurt deeply to sever the strand of affection which fought courageously to yet bind us. But if these admissions were the truth why did we let marriage slip away? And I answer by equating our own passionate and long lasting epoch with the romance of two lovers in my home town that I now summon forth.

At the time I occupied either the eighth or ninth grade in school with my friend Leland. We from the beginning watched the affair bud then blossom then reach full bloom. The whole town witnessed and enjoyed their outward adoration of one another. With vivid imagery I recall that they had passed into their early to mid twenties. Not by many weeks after he received an honorable discharge from the armed services the young man was seen donned in his military jacket going about town. It was something of custom for soldiers on furlough or else honorably discharged to sport such ware, especially in vew of the fact that General Eisenhower often wore the jacket while in command of the troops in the European war sector. The son of Jeremy Dodson, the former grocery store owner on the corner, the young man was widely popular in the town even before the war and now had become a figure of even greater popularity, a hero, a handsome figure and a shade cavalier in his distinction, and many a girl on seeing him melted as he appeared tall and erect striding at more than ordinary pace down or up mainstreet. They called him Paul Elgin. She went by the name of Louisa. She taught school at a town close by, the whereabouts of her birthing and parental rearing. They said that her bloodline regressed to a family of olden reputation and erudite distinction. How he and Louisa met I cannot propose to know. But they met and pretty soon were seen regularly at the local basketball games sitting on the lower portion of the bleachers and easily visible to scanning eyes. I recall their entry into the gymnasium, only minutes before the tip off, rather grand and deliberately late, I took it, she with her fashionable very pretty cropped hair freshly done and wrapped in her smart dark brown winter coat looking every bit as beautiful as he looked handsome. They were called the beautiful couple long before the term earned a common place in society. "What a gorgeous pair," a spectator would render to a companion sitting adjacently by, delivered with a sigh that carried the softest of expression. Not only at the basketball games were they seen; they were noticed at other places all over, at dinner in another town or towns where there were bigger and choicer restaurants, but the scene that I most distinctly retain is their showing up at the basketball games, making that grand entry, *noblese oblige* royalty dwelling in our midst—and I am supposing that basketball games were prominent because immediately after the war money wasn't as plentiful as later and cars weren't as available as later and one could not find suitable entertainment other than the events in our own community or in another of limited distance from our own. A few years after moving away, entering college, I returned once and asked someone—because suddenly it dawned fast in my thoughts—whatever happened to Paul Elgin and Louisa, the beautiful couple, the answer following that no one knew. Everyone remembered them as I remembered them but not what happened to them.

"Did they marry?" I asked.

"No. Most peculiar, wouldn't you say. We all figured they would, certain they would. But they never did. That was the oddest thing. They were together a long time."

"Why odd?"

"Because it just seemed that it ought to have happened."

In one sense I couldn't blame Nenia anymore than I blamed myself for the dissolution of our marriage plans. Professional ambition drove her. And as forcibly as she I sought to climb the ladder of success. Attaining to one of the upper echelon positions in the law firm figured in my psyche as a primary goal, an obsession that translated into burning the candle late into the night for sufficiently preparing a law suit, which promised a handsome monetary pay off and an elevation in reputation waiting at the end of the line. Foolish ambition I now contend. It wasn't worth it. It's never worth it. Nenia's ambitions were parallel to mine, only unlike mine in the nature of our work, that of a topflight executive, a chief executive officer of a book conglomerate that paid her in the six figures. We both said that we could not turn down the prospects that seemed to offer opportunities which were immense in terms of professiomal success and monetary gain. Marriage would have to wait, could wait a while longer, a little while anyway, and we put it off and put it off until one day we awakened and realized that it wasn't going to happen. She plead, and I listened believingly, that she wanted desperately for us to stay close, to see each other more frequently, that we should live with each other in secret, and that her parents would never know in that we lived too far away for them to ever find out. And that Thelma would know but wouldn't care. That Nenia loved me in every crevice of her heart I shall forever believe, and she laid out every self devised good reason why I should forgive and forget and that we should hold on. Then suddenly, I must tell it here: suddenly yesterday sprang upon me and there she was, that young beautiful girl sitting with me on the green grassy banks of that gurgling brook. "But that was a while ago" my inner voice reminded. "She's older now, quite older by some years, and the sweetness of her youth does not radiate as glowingly as it did then. But she's still a beauty. Maybe we can work it out." But we did not work it out. I can't begin to identify the year that we more or less decided, without seriously speaking it, that we were going our separate ways; I can only attest that some years had passed. I spoke to John Eric of our circumstance when once I went home on visit, asking him to treat it privately.

"Too bad Ramsey. You two were once the talk of the town around here. We didn't ever see you here very much. You spent a bunch of your time over at Meadeville for a fact but folks here still saw you when they went there and came back and gossiped to the people here about it. Now, whose fault was it that you busted up? That's what you're asking."

"We don't look at it like that. Neither was at fault."

"Well, how do you look at it? Who do you blame?"

"Our jobs. Ambition. The drive to rise to the top, a high place which we didn't dream we'd ever reach."

"That figures. But there ain't nothing wrong with gittin to the top and making money. I hear people say all the time that greed is the baddest thing that ever befell man and that money is at the root of all evil. Chances are they're like me. They don't have a damn thing and never did git anywhere. I'd like to have made some myself, I mean serious money, instead of being a dirt farmer and day laborer that I am. Thank your lucky stars you did what you did. You got the hell out of this mud hole. Got yourself fixed to earn a pile and I'm glad you have my boy. Not many in this town can do what you can do. But I'm drifting off. Back to you and Nenia. Things have changed since my best days. Back then young folks spoke their vows and stuck together. Of course, you and Nenia haven't even got together. Not married anyway. I don't think I should try to say anything of what made you tick but it seems to me that maybe Nenia fell into that trap that nowadays they call women's independence. It seems to me she feels she's better off not getting hooked by marriage and saddling herself with all them responsibilities that'll follow along with it. Babies grasping at her hemline ever time she takes a step. That's how a lot of women are looking at things these days I'm told."

"Yeah, I guess. And I guess also you can't blame them."

"Do you still see her?"

"Some. Precious little."

"And you sleep with her."

"No. I never have."

"Well, I'll be damned. Is that the truth?"

"It is."

"I can't believe it."

And that is how it unfolded for me in that particular time of my life, seeing Darya on occasions, still looking in on her health, and Andrea on occasions and still keeping in touch with Nenia at times but infrequently—still, I saw her, and doubtless it unrequitedly thrilled her whenever we met and said so and kissed me and wanted to make love. I know she did. But I declined; perhaps due to the effect of an old memory that naggingly held on or perhaps because at that stage Andrea lived irretrievably deep in my heart.

Demands on my energy and time from the head office had substantially increased, drawing me to New York for most of my work load, Mr. Yazstremski ever on the phone, "My boy, I need you. Can you check in with me near the middle of the week?" After the call I often rolled back from my desk and peered out the window and mused. "My dear great friend. How does he keep going? But I know the answer. Keeping on going is what keeps him going. It's as simple as that. He's a wonder." Though I saw in him a vigor that amazed me I simultaneously detected a small semblance of giving way, of slowing down, and that soon translated into my assuming a seat beside him in his office where the two of us combined our energies and intellectual capabilities and joyfully took on a greater load than ever before, with me assuming the major portion. And gladly.

And thus, this was the beginning of my promotion up the ranks to near the top of the ladder. But no matter, I began to go over in private silence that vanity now knocked on my door and decided convincingly that I should take care not to lose sight of the target to which I should genuinely guide myself. Teaching kept edging back into my ideations and more and more there evolved an urge within me to ask for a full time position at the small college where I taught part time, a mere one class three times each week. Nonetheless, I elatedly shared my promotional honor at the firm with Andrea, who'd just flown into New York to see me, whom I expected to offer congratulations and shower me with every accolade that she could engender, yet her lips failed to utter that which I hoped to hear and her countenance expressed anything but approval.

"Ramsey, are you sure that isn't too much? Your health. It comes first. Maybe the thing you should do is to start slowing down rather than speeding up."

The words somewhat took me aback. Shook me a bit. But I answered and in the exact way that I felt it. It was now her turn to react with surprise if not with a stronger feeling. "It's an ego booster to visualize sitting near the top. I have to speak the truth. Although, I've thought it through for a while and have begun to consider that living such a life, at high speed, is not what I want at all. And most recently have concluded that it's only for a while, a very limited while from here on, and then I'll opt to something else, at least from what I'm doing now. If it weren't for my dear friend Mr. Yazstremski I think I would have already left."

"Goodness. Are you serious? I'm overwhelmed to hear you say that."

"Absolutely. The question is when, though not before Mr. Yazstremski retires, I'm sure."

Ending this exchange one or the other of us suggested lunch and we happily ended up at one of our favorite niches. I knew then, recalling now, exactly where and when it was, that she had sunk into my skin forever and that I would soon ask for her hand in marriage.

Months passed and then I received a telephone call from Nenia, shortly after the usual exchanges telling me that her mother wasn't doing well and that she worried continually over her condition.

"I'm sorry to hear that. And how is your father?"

"Not well either."

"When they go, when they die, what's to happen with respect to the farm? It's such a massive parcel." On second thought I scolded myself for asking the question, that it shouldn't have been asked at all, for what relatedness to the inheritance did I now have?

"That poses a dilemma,' she first answered. "For the most part the tendency among the heirs is to sell it, Charlie the one exception. He'd like to somehow keep it for himself and his growing sons. The rest of us hope that he can, even if now it seems unlikely of materializing because he hasn't nearly enough money to pay the appraised price. I'm sure we can work something out. Maybe all of us will decide to sign a note. We'll see."

Chapter 65

EVENTUALLY, ANDREA and I married, the decision reaching a culmination when I sat with her one evening on the screened in front porch of her cottage. Twilight had commenced to descend on Lac des Allemands, the lights on the two man fishing boats twinkling and flickering in the semblance of playful fire flies as they sputtered frenziedly in the sunless waters. We had a short while before taken dinner. She had clasped my hand in hers and whispered how much she adored me with her lovely face raised to mine. "How warmly she lives inside me," I thought, "how endearing, how fulfilling. No where on earth will you discover someone to better share your life's rewards and tribulations. She has always loved you, unreservedly. Beginning when you tackled that beautiful young girl in the snow. Remember? What are you waiting for?" What followed flowed generously from the depths of my heart, not from the emotions of the moment, nor from the sweetness of her kisses. It was the right thing to do, the wise thing, an urge as if sent from Heaven, and I felt it in my every being. "She cares for you greatly. No woman can give you as much as she. Ask her to marry you, ask her now." All at once I heard from my own lips these words long ago fated; "Andrea, will you marry me?"

For a tiny second she froze into speechlessness. Then started into tears and began to kiss my face, hungrily, and hugged me as if attempting to break my body into.

"Do you mean it?" she asked, in a voice of unsureness mixed with great joy. "Do you mean it darling?"

"From the depths of my heart. More than I have ever meant anything."

"And that's quite enough. I've prayed for this, I swear I have. Since the day I first met you."

"Who will officiate the wedding?" I asked.

Father Garibaldi over at Des Allemands, naturally. When do you prefer?"

"Tomorrow is not soon enough."

She laughed a laugh of ebullient joy and punched me in my ribs and kissed me yet more, setting the wedding date at two weeks hence. I was beside myself. "I'm lucky beyond human explanation that no one else caught up with her. I remember how all the guys on campus used to chase after her for at least a mite of attention. She always insisted that none of them appealed in the slightest to her, that only one lived in her heart and now I know that one is me. It surely was meant. So, at last this splendid woman will soon pledge herself as my wife and I pray solemnly that I will as her husband live up to all those expectations as written in that Holy Book. I'll work with all there is within me to assure that I do."

Father Garibaldi would marry us in that quaint little Catholic Church with a cross affixed to the frontage gable, and assume the extra responsibility of aiding Andrea in staging the affairs of ceremony. No one of my acquaintance would attend. They were too far away. I exerted no effort to notify acquaintances and relatives, not that I sought to shield anything I thought. But on pursuing it further came to the realization that I actually did. There were those who would have caught their breath if learning of the impending affair, not the least of whom were members of my own blood kin, my mother the foremost. In their hearts such should have been Nenia's wedding.

The priest advised us that the ritual did not have to include mass, adhered to only when a Catholic marries a baptized non-Catholic.

"Are you a baptized Christian?" he asked.

"Yes Father."

"Good. Then there are no troublesome hurdles ahead of us."

Andrea and the Father proceeded with shaping the entirety of the ceremony which was taken from a published standard of the Holy Catholic Church. She walked through the tenets with me two days prior to the wedding date. Among them she stressed that the active role of the marrying couple in the eyes of the Church centered upon the Holy sacrament, that the fact that the wedding was to take place in a Church signified a ceremony of holiness; that the scriptural should or would speak of God's plan for the marriage and of His presence in the lives of the newly weds, that the priest should give the homily, or the deacon, addressing to them the meaning of marriage and that the exchange of rings give their affirmation and promise to create a loving and lifetime union and an openness to children.

Andrea appeared in all respects as familiar with the steps of ritual as the priest and with his blessing happily laid out her requirements.

"It's your wedding my Angel, my Chinita," the latter a Mexican term of endearment as the priest used it. "By all means proceed."

Her sometimes subdued smile played around her pretty lips and she stayed in that reserve without change. "I want an icon of the Virgin Mary set near the altar, as close to Ramsey and myself as is suitable, and I'll have a lady, my neighbor Mrs.Landsbury whom I have known for the longest to serve as maid of honor. Then too, I've chosen a little flower girl. A Cajun band will perform but rest assured in good taste. Some girl with an Angelic voice will perform the hallelujahs. I'm arranging for a choir. My father (Gregorio) is to give me away. I will wear a beautiful dress of conventional style, a jersey silk tunic which I shall insist is unpretentiously done, with flower designs rippling upon the surface. Lonzo will hand the rings over at the appropriate time. I will school him. You know of Lonzo don't you Father?"

A smile of amusement lifted from his face. "Very well. Our dear Lonzo donated the turtle meat as I vividly recall and let me say that my parishioners gave out many good compliments after I distributed it to them. He is a good man and loves you as his own Andrea," and at this she paused while a barely perceptible moistness rose mistily in her eyes.

"And lastly, Ramsey and I will alternate in the reading of the scripture."

"And what is it Andrea, if you don't mind?"

"It was what Ruth said to Naomi."

"Can you recite that portion of verse which you will read?"

"'Do not ask me to abandon or forsake you,' she said, 'for wherever you go I will go, wherever you lodge I will lodge. Your people shall be my people and your God my God. Wherever you die I will die, and there buried. May the Lord deal with me, be it ever so severely, if anything but death separates you and me.'"

"Ah! That is touching. And very fitting for a couple starting out and so in love. Let me see. You say that you and Ramsey will alternate the reading."

"No not exactly. Let me explain. He will read it first and I last."

"Good. Good my child. You have selected wisely. I bless you, as I will again when you are married."

Weddings are beautiful creations, and while I admit biasness, I have to describe this one as ethereally beautiful. The best man and I proceeded to the area of the altar first. When appropriate someone tapped my shoulder that I should ready myself to go in. I had stood on the outside for the past twenty minutes, a tad nervous, patiently waiting, trying to control myself, wondering ahead and trying to visualize the protocol of the wedding, a bit concerned that I wouldn't do as I should, in other words as Andrea had taught me. When notified that I should now commence my entry I gestured to the best man and said the time had come and then we passed through the ponderous double doors and advanced to the altar and there turned and faced the audience in silence and waited. Andrea had introduced me to him the day before. His age nearly approximated mine. She called him Rocco, a more than just a nice looking lad, eye catching handsome, with features resembling a Frenchman I later said to her, who answered, "Why not. About three fourths of the blood flowing through the veins of a Cajun is French anyway." I was dressed in a brand new blue suit. With me tagging along she had chosen it in a New Orleans men's store of recognized elegance, where they all without the slightest pause knew her. It took at least one hour, maybe more, to finalize the selection. Unable to make up her mind she would look at one and then another, not too pleasing a look, handing it back and going to another prospect. But she treated the salesman with the softest of kindness and exuded from her lips the gentlest of apologies. "Sir I'm sorry but I have not seen anything to my liking. Not yet. I wll appreciate your patience."

"Oh, I am Miss Andrea. You take your time."

Soon thereafter she all at once decided on one and upon this moment I virtually rejoiced but didn't dare tell her. Following her around had worn me down. We'd return for the garment when alterations were complete.

Next there proceeded the little flower girl, Cajun by blood, who made her entrance with an arm full of adornments, striving with all the resistance within her to make sure that the beautiful diminished smile now on her face stayed exactly as it was. As she moved abreast of me—her eyes betraying that inside there lived a cascade of great happiness; "I am especially chosen,"—she paused for a moment and then passed on, laying the flowers ever cautiously near the icon of the Virgin Mary, and afterwards crossed over to the proximity of the choir and the Cajun band, there folding her hands and facing the congregation, her smile of angelic sweetness fading into pensiveness.

Next came Mrs. Landsbury, an older woman, the maid of honor, accompanied by the lesser maids; and then next the apex, the entry of Andrea and her father through the massive double doors, thrown open the instant the Cajun band sounded forth with a rising crescendo, promptly lowering into an aura of softness, led by the fiddlers, who performed as if playing for a symphony. It amazed me with virtually a feeling of awe that they had transformed themselves in a split second from Cajun hillbilly to Beetoven or Bach. Andrea, with her father on her right, depicted an incomparably gorgeous image as she approached down the aisle, slowly, quite slowly, looking delightfully a little to the left a little to the right, beaming, fluttering her fingers to the people, a sort of wave, and even threw them kisses, to which they let out a roar that ascended to the vaulting, but shortly settling into silence. When she reached my presence, she stood on her toes and kissed my cheek and took her position beside me, a happy contented countenance on her face. "Isn't she beautiful," I thought. "Isn't she something?" She was not only beautiful; she was spiritually beautiful and that made her more beautiful than ever. "You have given her to me to have and hold Good Lord and I promise to clasp her tightly always."

The priest had officiated weddings in the manner of this one no telling the times, but not quite in the manner of this one, this one being foremostly brief, the same as the language pertaining to the utterance of our vows; "Do you Ramsey Maynard take this woman as your lawful wedded wife in the eyes of the Lord and do you take her to have and hold in happiness and comfort and in sickness and failing health, and Andrea repeated likewise, switching only the gender, and then the priest gestured for the rings. Lonzo proudly stepped forward and the priest took them from him, speaking words of which I don't recall exactly, but whatever they were they conveyed a meaning of inestimable endearment and spirituality. "You are man and wife" he said on the last. "Your lives have just begun. You may now kiss each other."

Gregorio and Felicia Cellus, Andrea's father and mother, who had stood in our midst, now bursting with smiles, rushed hand in hand to compliment and embrace us. She kissed them full on their lips as she always did and they in the same way kissed her back.

When I telephoned Mister Yazstremski that I'd very recently married and would appreciate an extra week of absence from the office he merely chuckled, and asked in the same breath if I landed the right one of the three, with me returning yes but that he'd mispeculated. That it wasn't Nenia.

"Well, then, don't leave me guessing. Which one if not her?"

"Andrea. I met her later than I did the other two girls."

"Ah! Andrea. Fine choice. Andrea is such a melodious name. Congratulations. Now you say you'd like to delay your return to the office for another week. You need more days than that. Think of your fresh beautiful wife and what she may want or expect. Why don't you take a month? We'll do well enough here for that long without you."

"Are you sure? I can avail myself with minimal delay if you feel in the least that I should."

"Nonsense. Stay a whole month. Where can I reach you if I must?"

"Des Allemands, Louisiana." Making certain I didn't garble any of my words I slowly called out Andrea's phone number and address and promised to telephone or write him once each week.

The next thirty days were for me and Andrea a continuous pageant of happiness and joy, and freedom, no going to the office, the weather generously tranquil, except for the rain squalls welling up at noon time, the bulk of our hours spent on Lac Des Allemands fishing and swimming. After dinner when the moon crept over the eastern rim, we'd sit in the chairs of bamboo backing that semi circled a small rounded table, it too made of bamboo, listening to the radio and sipping a glass of wine, at the most not more than two. Still later in the evening as the lovely ballads wafted from the radio we'd dance. Both endowed of superb stamina we kept at it for muchly extended periods before ceasing. Sometimes during the daylight hours, the neighbors paid us visit, bringing a wedding gift, but careful not to stay improperly beyond the limits of common protocol. Careful not to over stay also Andrea's parents drove over from New Orleans with gifts, a one thousand dollar gift certificate and her grandmother's old family Bible that Andrea said dated back through four generations. She protested against accepting it, at least not then, explaining that it yet belonged to her mother, but her mother insisted and had her way. Not by any stretch were the folks in the community entirely Cajun. There was a sizeable tally of non-Cajuns, émigrés, many of whom were from the northeast who chose the near semitropical coastal climate as their home. The traditions and mores of these people, the émigrés, were endowed of a culture widely different from the native stock, yet I treasured them and they clearly harbored the warmest of feelings for me, which touched Andrea's heartstrings with a cord of happiness. At the end of the month she went her way and I went mine, with me reporting to New York and her to various ports of call around the globe. Phone calls flew across the wires, she telephoning me or vice versa. Getting a phone call from her from abroad at any hour became a practice of regularity. Even if we were apart, far apart oft as not, we circled back with minimal delay to her cottage on the lake, she as always racing to my arms as soon I came within reach. "I have been indescribably hungry to see you my darling. Gracious. It seems like a year."

"You took the words right out of my mouth," I answered.

For awhile, perhaps a year I'm supposing, this stayed as our routine, and then a transition in jobs reordered our lives, Andrea quitting hers upon my temporary transfer from New York back to Chicago on the decision of Mr. Yazstremski who determined that the office in Chicago needed me more than he. "Only for the time being," he said. So I went.

Such news Andrea had long hoped for and when learning of it took my arm and happily danced me around the room. "Good darling. I'll quit my job and join you, take a temporary sabbatical anyway, and move to Chicago." I too was carried away. The incessant lapses of not seeing one another was ending. Living apart is not the way that husband and wife should live. She suggested outright that she'd start looking around Lake Michigan, that lady luck might smile on her and help her find a cozy little cottage that some landlord might agree to lease. With the assistance of a real estate lady of exacting familiarity with the city she soon found what she hoped for. It swept back not more than fifty yards from the shoreline.

"Terrific. You work fast. Now how fast can we take possession? I can't wait."

"Two weeks."

"You're a wonder, and I ditto that I can't wait."

We missed the two week target date but came close. She would take a month just decorating, buying and arranging furnishings, a near overlay to the interior stylization of her cottage in Louisiana. Then she began to settle in to house keeping and reading books, lots of books, and viewing television but with a limitation, and with the time left over navigating the alluring streets and shops of the city, notwithstanding the university department of physics and math, the department head with whom she'd stayed in contact attempting to hire her on the spot. She refused, much to my satisfaction. She needed a break from work I told her."

"Ha! Look who's talking."

Gradually she began to drop into the office to help me with whatever the tasks I currently pursued, eagerly volunteering I surmised largely because boredom had begun to creep into her psyche at home. Lightning fast at transposing legal documents and grasping lawyer's legalese she overwhelmed me as well many of the staff who took notice, and upon someone calling her aptitude to the attention of Mr. Yazstremski, he flew to Chicago for the singular purpose of seeing her capability for himself. She fascinated him, at first owing to the quickness with which she grasped even the most legal abstraction and enlarging upon any given topic. He relished talking with her. So far, he'd seen only the surface of her talent but soon would see much more because he meant to. Once Andrea and I sat talking when—.

"Pardon me." He had half appeared in the doorway, giving the notion of hurrying for something. "I think just about everybody is tied up at the moment. Would you mind helping me with something Andrea, I mean—.

"Certainly. Well, I will give it my best."

By noon he made no bones to me about singing her praises. "Lest I offend people around the firm here I'll only whisper it to you. Her ability is colossal. She could run this operation by herself. Why don't you bring her to New York with you? I'd like for her to see the firm there. Indeed, on my next trip to the great city she did it with me. I might have guessed that he'd take us to lunch at the back street diner. We walked. Andrea remarked particularily of the cobblestones which lay intact most of the distance, clip clopping her shoe heels against the surface which yielded a jumble of echoes when bouncing from the adjacent walls of the varied buildings lining both sides of the walkway, and continued to repeat her clip clopping with enlivened playfulness. When we entered the old men at the tables raised their heads and stared, unmistakably gawking, innervated by the beauty of the young woman who suddenly had shown up nestled between us.

"They're getting an eye full Andrea," said Mr. Yazstremski. "Enjoy it. But forgive them. They don't see the likes of you every day."

Chapter 66

WHEN WE retraced ourselves to the office and Andrea had excused herself to go temporarily elsewhere Mr. Yazstremski said to me, "She could greatly serve as a partner with you Ramsey, right here in New York or in Chicago, if you ever decide to venture into private practice, and even now we'd take her on here in a second. Her research acumen is incredible. We'd pay her exponentially."

"She of course speaks for herself. But as for now I don't think she's interested in a job. She's on sabbatical from the military and if she were to return to the work force, I believe she'd go back to that realm of activity. At least I think so." And then he began to digress.

"I think I've slipped a bit Ramsey. Set me straight. She attended Aaron's funeral didn't she, in the company of yourself and that other girl. Darya, you called her. I met both of them there, only talking to them briefly. Now I have met Andrea for real. She possesses such civility and charm. But why were they at the funeral?"

"Friendship. They were at the university when Aaron attended school there. It comes to me that she was of freshman status then, maybe of sophomore classification but I don't think so. Aaron would have given anything if he could have interested her. No such luck. Isn't it ironical? He was my best friend and I ended up marrying the girl of his dreams."

"She went for you?"

"That's about it."

"Well, that is something. I take it that you and he stayed friendly."

"Absolutely. Not ever one waver between us. As a matter of fact, at one time I would have stepped aside and let him have her."

"I'll declare," he let out, which I suspected carried a thread of doubt.

Mr. Yazstremski's interest in placing Andrea with the law firm, either in New York or Chicago, whichever she preferred, she gave prime consideration, and also consideration to a return to a lofty paying assignment with the military, but both potentials suddenly took a back seat. She was with child. She would not stay long in Chicago, though relishing the shoreline bungalow on Lake Michigan, where as students we had gone skiing on many a sunny afternoon. I sensed that Lac des Allemands dwelled formidably in her heart, and naturally much of her bent of mind clung fast to the impending reality of her oncoming new born.

"I would like to give birth to our baby in a place which is native to me. You do understand, don't you?"

On the surface the answer fell out with no complication. Underneath, the transition wasn't nearly as smooth. We moved back to South Louisiana, or she did, with me returning each week end for a three day stay, a trying arrangement for the both of us. Mister Yazstremski approved my schedule, consenting and believing that I could render equally valuable service to the firm by doing much of my work at home, and while I gave myself satisfactory marks, I still felt in my craw that my efficiency dipped below par. The trips to and from were draining and missing her more and more stressful. I brooded. Since she no longer pulled in a hefty paycheck our budget declined below the usual. There shouldn't have been any worry. My earnings were more than ample. Sensing, I took it, that I harbored some concern over the money shrinkage, in comparison to the previous inflow, she of her own accord applied to rejoin the war games department, provided she carried out the work at home and did not have to exceed a stipulated period of work time daily. They confirmed agreement by telegraph and telephone within twenty four hours.

In the meanwhile, I returned to see in on my mother as much as time spared, stopping off when I traveled to Memphis by plane then renting a car and driving to where she lived. Of some months past she had moved to another town, making the transition in that it let her live nearer my brother and oldest sister. I hired a contractor to build her a new house, a simple small frame structure with an exterior of brick, a spacey kitchen, and a front porch. The rest of the family had talked before my house building concept of placing her in a shared living facility, an arrangement that I vehemently opposed and got my way, saying to Andrea once, "You couldn't lure me with a boat load of gold to live in one of those places."

"Don't think about it darling. That's a long way off."

I had in not many days passed attended a conference in the nation's capitol that dealt with aging as a problem of one's decreasing power. I suppose that my mother's situation caused it to resurface. I cued Andrea in on the gist of the conference and she began to prod me for more.

"Everyone ages darling, and it's an advisable thing for a person to gear up for it. Get prepared, just as anyone should prepare for the future when young. Now tell me more. Did you take notes?"

"I'm embarrassed to admit I didn't."

"And you're a lawyer! Ha." She gave off a little chuckle as she sometimes does.

I chuckled too and then went on. "But I can do well enough without the notes, that is if you're seriously intent on hearing some of the highlights, a few at least."

"I am. At least a little more than just a gist of what went on."

I then did my best. "Here's the meat of the whole conference. Because power resources decline with increased age, older persons become more and more unable to enter into balanced exchange relations—that is, talking and listening and hearing and responding and giving and taking and so on—with other individuals and groups with whom they've had good comaraderie for years. As one guy said to me 'that's what happens to you when you start going down hill.' Somebody else spoke of it as the 'process of disengagement,' which at one and the same time, the term hatched up by some slick college professor, he could have said it's the start of going down hill just like the guy said that I've quoted a second ago—yet I don't care what it's called because it all means the same thing, getting old, yeah getting old, that's what it means and that in my vision isn't much fun."

She had listened. I know she had, due to the way she looked when she's immersed in something of particular depth.

"But darling we are all going to get old sometime, and its best in my view not to fight it, but go with it, letting it happen as it naturally will, and may I add the best thought of all—enjoy your old age; there are scores of rewarding things you can do when you are old, and in fact you may discover it's the best part of your life when you get there."

I said nothing more, concluding that she had spoken wisely, more than I, certainly, especially when she laid it out convincingly that in the stages of old age one may discover that it is replete with much pleasure and enjoyment. In the absence of anything else to add, apparently, she walked lightly over to the window and looked out and sighed as if to enjoy the sight of a beautiful day, thinking, thinking, thinking, I supposed, in contemplation of something much in depth as she often did. She just stood there for a brevity, looking across the way, the sun rays falling full upon her. Her pregnancy was now beginning to show. "Isn't she a picture. She looks almost angelic." Then at once she turned, emerging from whatever beheld her, and came back to me and ran her hand softly across my cheek and kissed my lips, gathering me tenderly in her arms, her way of saying silently that she loved me.

"Let us return to the matter of your mother, shall we?"

"Let's do."

"How is she? You don't speak of her physical well being much. How did she look?"

"Not well. It bothers me."

"Did you notice anything in particular?"

"No. I can't say that I did. She just looked thinner, not a lot but some. Well, to say it more directly there was a slightly weakened appearance in her eyes and face."

She started to say something else, perhaps beginning another question, but stopped short, reclining into silence. I wondered what was going on in her intelligent head. I wondered what but declined to ask. "She'll tell me when she gets around to it," I pondered on in silence. "Was she possibly wondering if I have not yet told my mother that I'm married? Of course, I don't know that. But it's something I must attend to. It'll hurt mom to the quick to learn that something happened to split Nenia and me apart but I can't wait much longer to let her know." That chance was soon forthcoming. The news in little time reached me that Maggie Stoddard died suddenly, a heart condition, John Eric telling me this who'd adopted the practice of carrying my whereabouts and phone number on a crumpled envelope pushed down into his billfold.

Hearing of Maggie's death stunned me for a slight, though it should not have landed on me surprisingly. She had sunk into a state of declining health, clearly worsening, but slowly, for the past few years of her life. For a moment I returned to an earlier era with the Stoddards, reminiscing very precisely how I started to get drawn, or how I drew myself, deeper and deeper into the family. "The Stoddards" I recalled, "were old friends with my family dating back to the beginning, when I was but a boy, sitting with Mister Stoddard in early evening listening to the war news and upon Kaltenborn finishing his last sentence Maggie announced with lifted voice from the kitchen that she had supper on the table. It got so that I needed no invitation to eat with them. It was understood that I would. Never failing, Nenia sat by me, taking her place there as if it were long established custom."

It was a must that I attend the funeral and visit with the family, my marriage status posing no impending embarrassment, I imagined, for Nenia in the months past had told everyone about it and emphasized that the fault rested on her shoulders that I did not marry her. She over did her explanations to protect me. She shouldn't have pointed to herself as the full bearer of the blame. I too should have born it equally.

"How am I to tell Andrea? How am I to justify going that far piece to attend a funeral?" I justified it by explaining that the Stoddards were our dear neighbors once upon a time, and that within me there stirred a heartfelt obligation.

"Certainly darling. You must go. If I weren't as far along as I am with my pregnancy, I'd go with you. Besides, I don't even know them. You do. It's settled. You go."

The Stoddard family had gathered at the home place, all of the children there, Gaylon also, who I saw for the first time in my life. Whether he and his father were now on friendly terms stirred in my thoughts as a matter of curiosity. But I wasn't in any manner inclined to ask. Nenia met me at the door when I arrived, still beautiful, reaching her arms around me and kissing me on my cheek. I cannot say that it wasn't touching; it was very touching and I think it was to her. From there she led me into the living room where Mister Stoddard sat, sad and forlorn, as if in a daze, now astonishingly older. I took his hand in both of mine and spoke. Though crevices of old age ran unmercifully in his face his eyes lifted energetically upward and twinkled. He recognized me."

"Ramsey, my boy. How are you?"

"Fine sir."

"You must stop by to see me more often. It's been a year or was it last month? Let me see. I, I, I'm badly forgetful as you can tell."

It hit me with sobering realness that his mind had sunk into misty fogginess, or frequently did, coming and going in the fashion of the outgoing and incoming tides. To expect him to alertly reconcile the past with the present reached far in excess of common judgment. Nenia looked on rather pitifully, taking his condition grieveously hard and struggling to maintain her composure. I left them and drifted about shaking everyone's hand and offering condolences, soon meeting up with Charlie, the two of us taking up old times, and whether or not aappropriate under the conditions I asked of his farming ventures, with him replying that he'd had a good year but that it overloaded him to the gill to keep everything moving productively. His two sons were old enough however to help do much of the work, he said. Pretty soon I visited with Thelma, finding that Nenia sufficiently cleared the way for my continued warm and compatible relationship with her. It was unavoidably embarrassing when she said she hated that Nenia and I did not marry, but that nonetheless she would always consider me as part of the family. Her kindness stole into my heart. I thanked her for her understanding. What else could I have sensibly done, except hug her? Nenia clasped my arm when I moved within reach and mentioned that they were serving food right away and that I must stay, to which I begged off with the legitimate excuse that the obligation to go see my mother simply had to outweigh everything else. I hadn't seen her yet and felt a pressing need to be off without further delay. "I have to get back to Louisiana within two days. I'm quite pushed to use every hour zealously."

"I understand. But before you leave for your mother's let me talk you through the funeral. It's at the church at two o'clock tomorrow. You will attend, won't you?"

"By all means. You say at two? Are there seating arrangements and so forth?"

"Seating. Yes. I'd like for you to sit by me. Will you mind?"

"Not at all. I will gladly." How was I to refuse, and yet with a flash Andrea's loving face with intimate presence coursed through my thoughts, a thread of guilt welling up inside me. "What would she say? How would she advise me?" Nevertheless, in the end I justified my acceptance. "Don't take this to extremes. It's not like you're betraying Andrea, your adorable wife. It's not like that at all. This is a funeral and you're part of the family, and you know how Andrea is, so stay calm and sensible. She'd tell you to realize that you are there especially to pay respects to a great old friend."

It was past mid afternoon when I arrived at my mother's. I would spend the night with her as well as the next half day before attending the funeral, then leave for Louisiana. News had reached her of Maggie's passing, the funeral of which she'd hope to attend if someone would volunteer to take her and I told her I would, but she declined, and gave no other response. She appeared in no way up to traveling and undergoing the stress of making an appearance. When I asked how she had been feeling she said all right but being constituted of a stubborn fortitude she wouldn't admit the truth. Finally, I summoned up nerve enough to address the uncomfortable subject that had pressed me for days to let out. "I have something to tell you mom."

"Oh!"

"Yep. I didn't want to tell you but I know I have to. Nenia and I are no longer to each other as we once were. We decided some time ago that we wouldn't marry."

She remained relatively unaffected on the surface but still I knew my words struck a sensitive place down deeper. A spec of unnatural stillness rushed to her face and stayed for a moment, then, "Why was that?"

"Our work, I want to say. We're ambitious, I suppose. And put our striving first, ahead of marriage which we kept putting off and putting off."

"Well, are you going to marry someone else, sometime, that is?"

"I'm already married. That's what I wanted to tell you."

We were standing up until then. Now she sat down in a nearby chair, kind of slumped down into it actually, and I sat down beside her.

"Who to? Why?"

"She's a beautiful little girl that I've known since college. Her name is Andrea. She's wonderful. I always loved her, even when I loved Nenia."

"Oh son. I so wished that you'd—. But you know and I know that these things happen, even though a person thinks them impossible of occurrence. People break apart, for whatever the reason, and sometimes the reason doesn't make much sense."

"I'm sorry mom. I hope you take this without stress."

"I do. Don't worry. You caught me unsuspecting, but I'm all right."

"I'm grateful for that."

"You're sure you love Andrea? Oh, that's awkward and not well said. Forgive me. What I really ought to say is that I'm sure you do and that you thought carefully through everything when you picked her out."

"I did. Nothing hastily done. She's lived in my heart for years. She's greatly caring for others. She would have made the trip with me to see you if not for her condition. She's pregnant."

No flinch manifested itself, nor startle, nor any show of dishevelment. She now appeared in an aura of calm, more calculating than any other display of internal affectation. "You'll get around to bringing her? When the baby is born?"

"We'll both see to that."

"The funeral is tomorrow at the church, you tell me. And you are counting on being there. Is that right?"

"I am. I visited the family before driving on up here to see you. They were visibly saddened but were taking their grief in stride. Nenia had arrived earlier. I talked with her some. We're on very good terms. All the family is on good terms with me. When I spoke with Thelma, she hugged me and said that she hated that Nenia and I didn't marry, and yet even if it didn't turn out the way she had hoped she still thought of me as part of the family. I found it well nigh impossible to choose words of reply. It was awkward."

"It's wonderful that they still accept you, especially Nenia. "

"It was wonderful that it went so well. But Mom, it couldn't have been expected that they would have treated me as if I were a leper," I said in something of an ironical slip.

She merely smiled. "To that I quite agree."

We let it stop there and embarked on other things, which entailed her mentioning that she'd cooked some that morning, realizing that I would show up sooner or later, and that she hoped I will have worked up a very good appetite for supper. "Joyful is the moment," it suddenly sprang to me, "when the son sits down at his mother's table to a good meal that she has lovingly prepared for him." And I added, "There's hardly a moment in his life anytime that's better."

"Will you be hungry enough by supper time dear if I serve it earlier than usual?"

"Ha. Mom, did you ever see me when I didn't have an appetite, especially for your cookings."

At the church the next day before the funeral proceedings began I met the preacher, whose name sounded familiar though we'd not met face to face. Asking with Christian mildness when Nenia introduced us how as a relative did I fit into the family I replied with a shade of embarrassment that I wasn't a part of the family, merely a close friend that dated back over the years, with Nenia's surveillance keenly beaming down on me. Then taking my hand she led me to where the family would gather, several already in their seats, and briefly the remainder worked their way over and sat down. I of course sat by Nenia, glancing tepidly around in anticipation that certain of the family members were looking curiously at us sitting together. No one seemed to notice, but perhaps if I had been observant at another moment, I might have detected puzzled eyes training upon us. The minister's words were of the usual litany; Maggie was a fine upstanding woman all her life, from youth onward, had raised and nurtured an exemplary family, and that she in all spiritual respects paid homage to the Lord. Citing scripture, he assured that death did not intimate an end but a beginning and that the life and resurrection of Jesus Christ furnished the proof. The funeral over, the hearse transported the body to Mount Pisgah Cemetery, where after carefully selected farewell passages were issued by the minister the casket was lowered into the grave, followed by the summary Amen. At this, the family members fell into weeping and hugging, offering solace and comfort to one another, but after a while one by one, their grievance running its course, they wandered to their cars. Peculiarly, I suddenly realized that Nenia and I were the last to leave, or very nearly the last, and that together we'd begun silently to edge in the direction of our vehicles, just as the others had, soon to depart. When we reached them, and just before she crawled into hers, she clutched my arm. "You can't know what it meant to me that you came, Ramsey. I'll never forget it." Once again, as it happened the day before when Thelma and I intercepted one another, I found myself affected by an inability to speak anything that I deemed fitting. But I knew I should say something. It happened that I didn't have to. She continued. "Here, take this with you. But don't read it right away. Promise me you won't. And make certain that you are alone when you do. You will promise, won't you?"

"With my hand over my heart."

I took the envelope that she handed me, which sent my head flying into a cascade of possibilities, attempting to unravel what on earth it contained, and exactly what purpose did she have in mind. At this, though not entirely unexpected she folded her arms around me and kissed my lips, and without the slightest utterance turned and slid onto the front seat of her car and drove away.

The road ahead of me lay long and difficult, I realized, and that I should expect but few breaks if I were to reach Des Allemands at an hour in the proximity of midnight.

It wore on me by the minute that in my coat pocket there lodged a partially crumpled envelope which contained a letter with lines that I suspected cut straight to my heart and eventually, as dusk descended, my curiosity grew overwhelmingly forceful, so at the next convenient filling station I pulled over and with the aid of the overhead lights of the pavilion peeled open the envelope and read. Her thoughts piled unbrokenly on one another without pause, the way she talked ordinarily. Only once did she switch to the second and only other paragraph.

> *Dear Ramsey, when you were close to me, today and yesterday, it started all over, my unyielding caring for you, which will never go away no matter the length of our lives. It was so very hard to have you near and unable able to touch you. You can't know how affectionately I have thought a thousand times of you in the night, wishing that time were reversible and that somehow the ending, the failure of our intentions of marriage, could have been different. It hurts and even though it does I must find a way to accept it. I try to imagine how your wife must look; most beautiful I am sure, the girl that stole you away. When did you meet her? Was it some time ago? I take it that it was. But I never once suspected. Someday I'd like to see her face to face. I don't know why but somewhere deep down I think I want to.*
>
> *It's too much to expect I know but I cherish the thought of hearing your voice by phone once in a while. But you have your wife to consider and owe her every ounce of faithfulness in you. In any event you will always live near my heart and I will wish that I am close to yours—but that is asking more than I'm sure is reasonable and possible. Still, I'll hope.*
>
> *I love you.*
>
> *Nenia*

For the longest these confessions of heartbtreak shot discomfortingly through me, so sad I thought, and they were in no way easy to repress. She hurt; that's what the letter said and I nurtured sorrow for her. "She's faced with picking up the pieces for the rest of her life and I'll forever wish that she did not have to carry that burden."

But as the miles dissolved one by one I commenced to explain to myself that life is a struggle and unpredictable and that the endings don't always suit our wishes. It wasn't that easy to explain I knew but for wont of a better answer I rationalized it nonetheless, at least for the moment. After a while I set Nenia aside and decided without further pause that I must dispose of the letter, stopping the car and retrieving the envelope and setting it afire, holding to the edges till the flames forced my fingers to let go, the blackened fragments of infinitesmal thiness swooping and then rising and swooping once more on their descent to the grassy shoulders of the roadway. Crawling back in I started on. "What shall I tell Andrea in matters of the funeral? Everything? But not quite everything."

It's lonely driving by yourself, especially on a highway that covers two hundred or three hundred miles in length. I wished that Andrea were with me. But a powerful metallic companion with many faceted accessories served as my accompanist, the car motor, which purred rhymithcally along in its trajectory and I said silent thanks that it behaved with foamy smoothness, showing no signs of faltering, for on a busy interstate at the peak of night an auto breakdown is among the worst of imaginery horribles. I prided myself for my record as a safe and careful driver, and I was now especially diligent, to begin with for my own welfare, but beyond this, and far more importantly, a beautiful wife with child inside her womb now looking for my arrival within the next few hours. The glare from the lights of the traffic streaming in my face was fretting but irrespective of its impact the effect worked in my favor. It kept me awake and alert. Near the end of my journey, I reached and switched on the radio, the voice of a late night news commentator surging through—who summarily spoke of the nation's gas shortage, cars every where backed up at the filling station pumps, and the ignominious departure from office of one of our American presidents. And then, never far removed, there reemerged the image of my Andrea. She was sleeping at this hour, surely. I saw it as if it had already happened, her sweet note affixed to the front door. "Welcome home darling. I've missed you terribly."

Chapter 67

AS THEY say, the earth makes its unvarying revolution around the sun season after season, never failing to return to its starting place, which is another mode of relating that the calendar is ever marking time. Somewhere I had lost track, I musingly said one day, time flown away imperceptively fast, ten years of it I suddenly discovered, my son now half passed growing up—and then I retrieved a finery of literature writ by an obscure poet that sent me into contemplation that if the ten years just passed soared away so quickly, so too would the next ten vanish with twicefold haste. As my old friend Mr. Yazstremski once said, "My boy at my age years run by you faster than a flicker and run still faster as each year gets away from you but you are young and they for you have not yet become acutely noticeable. They will. It will get to where when Christmas makes its annual visit and leaves, you'll say, 'My lands. What magical trickery is this? It has hardly gone and another is fast on its tail.'"

My mother died near the end of this frame of years and too Mr. Yazstremski, my teacher, my confidant, my rock of dependency, then others of my long acquaintance somewhere in the same interlude, these being Mr. Stoddard, as well as the Stylman's, both of them, and Darya's father, but Mrs. Narvanna still lived on and had retained her youthful health and beauty. She yet climbed mountains and perpetually traveled world wide.

Why I chose to singularily isolate my great friend Mr.Yazstremski and my mother from the passing of others, as I have herein mentioned, requires no extension of explanation. In a nutshell, they were the dearest.

Though consoled somewhat by knowing that my mother's death did not bring with it a great deal of pain and suffering I nontheless found myself emotionally crushed shortly after she'd gone, long nights without sleep fixed upon her and the endearing moments we shared as mother and son. The memories are too preponderously many and varied to call forth into written detail. I can only say that months dissolved before I returned to my original self, or in any event returned to my normal functioning. If it were ever contended that the loss of a father is hard to bear the contender should also have said that the loss of a mother is nth times greater. For the longest I kept her letters in an old blackened trunk that my grandmother bequeathed to me and randomly lifted one or two in breaks of stillness to capture an image of her that I yearned to glance just one more time. It was not to my surprise when once I fished out one which carried the lines that she knew aside from my studies at the university I surely now enjoyed the mammoth snowfall which the radio news folks were reporting. "Ah," there suddenly billowed to me an internal impression, "the snowball fights I used to have with Darya and Andrea, but always separately of course."

After taking the phone call that Mr. Yazstremski had fallen victim to a stroke and died shortly thereafter I sat for a while, a very long while, stunned in my chair, then finally rolling over to the office window of quite large proportion my thoughts of easy accord began to journey backwards. I started with college days when he hired me to deliver depositions to New York and how he bent over backwards to bestow kindness. "In him God has blessed me with a second father. Everything that I am up to here I owe to my great friend." I tried not to dwell upon the sadness of his passing but instead on the brightness with which his light shone on those in his midst, especially on me. "I was his pet; I don't doubt it a second. His leanings were apparent and I cannot deny his favor to me over the other staffers, muchly to my advantage." I remembered his affection for Aaron and how he was wrought with forlorn sadness at the funeral but uplifted in his hour of darkness that two young women, Darya and Andrea, were there and emplaced their arms around him and kissed his cheek. It dawns on me too that he especially nurtured a fondness of Andrea, greatly so in his very late years wherein because he badly needed her unique capabilities, he often called impromptu the Chicago office to ask if she might possibly break free for assisting him a bit with some knotty complexities that were currently troubling. "Of course," I said. "You must go. Think of the inestimable trust he has in you. And after all, he personally assisted you in getting your law degree. He gave every free minute of his time to you. And don't worry about me," I said with lightness of fun, "I think I can do without you for at least a few days."

At last, I rolled my chair away from the window, searching for something capable of distracting my immediate obsession, or else tried to, knowing that only time fills such voids—yet never completely. His influences would steadily hover over and guide me for the remaining tenure of my life.

On learning of my misfortunes a few months afterwards Leland out of nowhere came to see me, not in Chicago but at Andrea's cottage on Lake Allemand, his visit, he explained, deriving out of a felt need to comfort and console an old friend in his trial of readjustment. He made the trip unaccompanied by his wife who he said had gotten detained because of the demands of her job. I picked him up at the sleepy little nearby town, Des Allemands, where, I told him, Andrea and I were married in the Catholic Church. It was greatly exciting once again at seeing one another, even if but a short few days. We talked without let up on the way to the cottage with him looking at everything at once,—at the wildlife and the ancient swamps and the trees of Spanish Moss hanging over the bayou landscape, mysterious and charming, not to mention the keenness of his fascination with the casual gait of the locals as they meandered along to wherever they were going.

"They're civil now, good people Ramsey, but hark back to two hundred years ago, when this region wasn't much more than swampland or swampwater. Very few people here then I gather. The land didn't know it then but it was gonna witness one heck of an inmigration of humanity."

I nodded with shortened gesture. "I see it that way too. It had to happen something likened to the manner in which you explain it. Andrea and I often speculate about the history of these people. They're different Leland, eons different from the Yanks in New York, but I'll guarantee you'll like them." He reminded me of myself upon my first ever to come to Des Allemands, affectedly moved by the courtesy and manners and gentleness of the locals. Leland would as well quickly discover there was a genuine tenderness alive in himself for these good folks who at first seemed so strange to his sphere of understanding.

He stayed a week, and made much of the arrangements, as if they were fit for a king, and that was quite so, for thanks to Andrea we did everything that the furtiveness of our minds suggested, fishing and boating and swimming and taking in a Cajun square dance—Andrea danced endless rounds with Leland—and at nighttime decided unanimously to sit out on the screened in front porch, (actually the material wasn't screen but a network of webbing) and partake of more wine than that which was practical—Andrea kept pouring—and we had attained to such looseness and giddiness by midnight that we commenced to talk and ramble through a myriad of disconnected things that on other occasions we might not have taken up in the least. During all this Andrea was clad in a gown like dress, full and flowing below the waist line with a mix of varied colors, the design being of the Spanish culture more than of any other. In it she was a lovely thing. But it compared only as a minature in elegance to the lovely gowns she fashioned when we were out on more formal occasions. Not long before our marriage she trained under a reknowned tutor to master two very exotic dances—the Argentine tango and the salsa—sophisticated dances the world round, indeed graceful and charming, attributed historically to the people of latin origin, demanding of the participants impeccable finesse, performing in exact correlation with the music and cadence. These are beautiful dances. They are perhaps better acknowledged as a form of art more than they are a dance, if there is a difference. She constantly plead with me to learn them, volunteering to teach me and with her wishes I obeyed, sufficiently able in due time to match with her as a respectable partner, but barely, whenver we attended some of the extravaganza ballroom events held in New Orleans or Houston.

But there were other stylizations of her dressware of which I can speak. I meant to explain earlier that when the two of us were home alone Andrea pattered around in denim jeans and a shirt of Panamanian flavor, and that no matter in which attire she had chosen to clad herself during his visit she must have caught Leland's eye, for he outpouringly praised her beauty in his remarking that she hadn't aged a minute since he last saw her. I can say very little of the manner in which Leland and I were dressed excepting that the nights were balmy if not hot and that we made our concessions to the climate by mainly doning ourselves in T shirts and kahkis.

The dining room table where we took our nightly dinners was most exquisitely laid, as one would expect from Andrea, plenished with fresh orchids grown on the periphery of the cottage grounds and the silver shone with an alluring brightness. And I should not omit that folded into very elaborate shapes and coming in varying sizes even the napkins were inviting to see. She served on one evening, one that somehow is especially extant in my memory, a chicken and fish casserole, separately I should emphasize, these dishes augmented by a ponderously large bowl filled with a heaping of colorful salads. I asked why she chose to prepare two casseroles, why more than one, her answer explaining that my mother used to make chicken casseroles for me, knowing that I liked them so well, and this played vividly in Andrea's thoughts, she said, and so therefore wanted to honor my mother by serving on this night such delicacy to her son and his guest. The fish casserole she chose to prepare for the benefit of Leland, to acquaint him with one of the chief dishes that the Cajuns not infrequently spread on their table. But taking precedence over this one perhaps, which she served twice more during his stay, was the Cajun shrimp sausage pasta that Leland voraciously tore into. He asked after the first serving of this dish, "Andrea, am I too bold should I inquire if I might see this one again before I leave?"

"Certainly Leland. You have infinitely graced our table with your generous compliment. Now, how can I not abide generously with your wish?"

Once we strayed into that mysterious thing called change, change in human beings specifically speaking, with Leland deciding to tell of his reading a celebrated work of the inimitable William Shakesphere which had to do with the beginning and the finality of the life of man.

"It's decidedly revealing," he said in a spirit of liveliness, as if he'd discovered something rare, "to penetrate into the definiteness by which we progress from one stage to another."

"And so," Andrea wasted no time at weaving in as if to urge a quickly given continuance.

"Well, if you'd look it up, and you likely have, he wrote a little peace, a play, which featured a character he chose to name Jocques where Jocques did all the talking. Shakesphere did the play as a monologue.

"And the name of the play was?" she asked.

"Sure. *As You Like It*, or *The Stages of Man*. I think they're interchangeable. As I've inferred, it's very interesting." And then he paused, as if he'd finished or else fallen to unsteadiness of intellect resulting from overly ingesting the wine that Andrea had continued to pour and would issue nothing more from his lips.

"Go on." Andrea then squinted her eyes in show that she wasn't sure whether he'd come to a stopping place altogether or would eventually complete his stream of thought. In a moment he again commenced.

"Oh yes. Yes, yes, yes. Sorry. I suddenly drifted off, locking in on something else." He smiled at Andrea in realization that she delighted in picking at him and that she did it with relish. With this exchange between the two over he resumed. "Yeah, Mister Shakesphere points out, or else a translator does it for him, that there are seven stages to a man's life; the first being the helpless infant, then the whining schoolboy, then the emotional lover, then the devoted soldier, then the wise judge, then the old man still in control of his faculties, and at last an extremely aged person, returned to a second stage of helplessness."

"Ah. Gruesome reminders indeed," I cut in, "especially the latter two and and has it ever occurred to you," meaning Leland, to whom I pointedly addressed my remarks, "that we ourselves one day will have grown old, no longer youthful, and that the new generation will look upon us as tiresome old men and women."

"But my dear fellows," said Andrea with a countering in her speech, "some individuals are literally thriving with creativity when they are markedly into old age, witness if you will the venerable Sophocles and Milton who died at their peak, vigorously active and productive despite the calendar years piled on their shoulders."

"Granted. But Shakesphere spoke in the general context when he exemplified the latter two stages of an old man's life. I think he was pretty close to being on target."

"Just a minute," I said, feeling we were not far from bidding goodnight and that there hadn't been much room for injecting my own substance. "I have a word or two. Shaksphere is one of the world's four great playrights, the others, all Greek, living much earlier, creating and producing before the birth of Christ, Sophocles among them and it is proclaimed that he exceeded them all."

"I'm supposing that is correct," said Leland.

The wine had with certainty slowed him. I anticipated a lengthier comeback, maybe a slight alteration or correction, but there was none, Leland simply blinking his eyes as if sleepy and demonstrating a facial shaping which I interpreted to mean that in fact he agreed, but had something else to say.

"By the way Ramsey, if I may shift the subject here, what are you reading in the scriptures these days, you know, like we used to do, when we'd read and then trade our interpretations with one another and go into all sorts of spinoff topics. I wish we still had the time to do that."

"I wish it too Leland. I fervently do. What am I reading you ask? For the present it's Isaiah and for the fifth time. It's a lengthy piece of work, something in the realm of sixty chapters or more."

"I didn't know that," Andrea curiously remarked.

"That's true. Better than sixty. Isaiah was a rigid firebrand and came down wrathfully on his fellow Judeans, preaching the severest of punishment from the Lord if they disobeyed what the Lord had decreed."

"Would you have been a little bit softer on them Leland?" Andrea not surprisingly asked.

"I suppose. Maybe I'm what you'd call a liberal religionist."

"How would you have been softer?"

"Hmmm. Let me see. Well, I guess I'll frame it this way although I'm doubtful that I'm really answering your question. I think I believe that all folks will receive respectful treatment or in any event should receive respectful treatment in the life beyond this one. But in the finality that's up to our Maker, isn't it, not to we poor weak humans."

With this we left off for the evening, all three a mite woozy from the excessive consumption of wine, even Andrea, and we bade Leland good night. The next morning, the coolness of the widespread due giving way to the sultry day, we drove him to the airport in New Orleans to catch his plane. Just before he exited the car door—. "And say. I tell you folks I've had a ball. When you're in my town you'll of course join us for a spell."

"Good. Good. Tell your wife hello for us Leland, and that we send our love," Andrea, ever an example of the art of protocol warmly relayed.

From there we went to the apartment where her parents lived, a visit that Andrea lamented wasn't nearly frequent enough, envisioning in the same breath of wording the fabulous fun filled vacations on which they took her in years past. As part of the general conversation the subject of church arose, Andrea's and my church over at Des Allemands.

"It's but a miniature in size compared to the Saint Louis Cathedral here in New Orleans," remarked Mr. Cellus. "I think I'd like a church such as yours but you're too far away for us to drive."

"Visit at least father, every chance you get," replied Andrea, with hopeful expression in her voice and a countenance of adoration in her eyes.

"We will sweetheart," Mrs. Cellus spoke up, "and you come any time you can and we'll have a ball shopping together. They have some fabulous stores here."

Andrea assured her that she could count on that. We stayed but briefly; we seldom stayed long. Andrea promised that we'd soon drop by again and stay so long that they couldn't stand us.

"Ha! That's a day I'll never see. Ramsey promise me that you and Andrea will soon come back and stay for the longest. You do promise, don't you?"

"With my hand over my heart."

We stayed on at Lake Allenands. We asked for and received approval from the law firm for a sabbatical running six months in time, Andrea pleading the necessity for the sabbatical in that both of us needed a respite from work, and that the fall was more beautiful than she'd ever seen. The water in the lake had sunk to its lowest ebb in a good while, because the rains weren't as plentiful as usual and no storms had appeared to any degree in the Gulf of Mexico, the storms deciding to stay calm and quiet for a change. This meant that the storks and cranes and other birds of prey lavishly helped themselves to the fish. Later in the fall the occasional light showers started to visit more often than usual, in the vicinity of sundown, and this created a very thick gummy fog which enshrouded the lake and most of the shoreline. The leaves had turned to a brilliant gold, then within not many weeks began their slowly paced conversion to a deep chocolate brown. The fog covered the leaves at night. But when daylight pushed through the sun did also, its rays bestowing a magical beauty on and about them. At night we sat on the front porch, rarely missing. We'd set out our chairs soon after dark had fallen. Andrea, just before we turned in, raised the webbing that had kept the mosquitos at bay, thus the falling leaves blown in by the persistent but gentle breeze during the night were scattered in disarray over the flooring. I awoke earlier than she and grabbed a hand broom and swept them away, knowing she'd ask me to if it were not done and I didn't want to put her to the trouble of reminding me of my obligation. Besides, she took it faithfully on herself to make the coffee and cook breakfast. The New Orleans radio station offered pretty music starting at eight o'clock in the evening and sometimes we'd get up and dance to a slow tune when it played. With lights flickering on both ends, front and back, the fishing boats motored up and down the lake continually until sun up though thinned appreciably as daylight drew near. Sometimes after dark had fallen Lonzo dropped by with a mess of crappie that Andrea fried in an open skillet the next day. With the exception of his visit, we'd often sit for hours with no one around but us, and nothing else of non human substance to which we paid notice except the candle glow and the side table on which the candle rested.

"It's like time stands still out here," I said, "but it doesn't. You know that it's always in the shadows creeping up on you." Then I went on—.

"But at my back I always hear,

Time's winged chariot hurrying near."

"From Hemingway's book darling," Andrea enjoined. "Let me see, which one was it?"

"*Farewell to Arms*. The words aren't his. He lifted them from a poem. They're clever. Quite poetic. Aren't they?"

"Beautiful."

Lonzo's boat stood separate and apart from all others on the lake in that when he navigated into the shallow waters leading to the cottage, he gunned the motor up high, thus producing something of an angered snarl which he executed in multiples of five or six or more in rapid succession, sort of triumphantly, an alert that he'd soon arrive at our docking. "Gots a mess uv fish fa ya'll Miss Andrea," he'd let out proudly in what I secretly deemed the poorest of dialect, even for a Cajun. Even inattentive ears would have noticed his raspy asmatic cough too often working up from his chest, yet as I mentioned the affectation to Andrea she answered that according to the medical doctors over at the local clinic he had no asmatic cough, that the disturbance evidently stemmed from his continued sloshing around in the sloughs and swamps, "the gloom," as she sometimes called it, trapping for furry game, foxes and bobcats, where the tree leaves hung suspended in such massive thickness that the dappling of sunlight struggled to break through. I was there with him once. Fallen leaves from far back in time, I guessed, had gathered in layers one upon the other, to a depth of many feet, damp and mossy, thus giving off an ever-present cogent smell of effluvium. The doctors said Lonzo stayed in this atmosphere more than was healthy for him.

"What do the doctors say causes him to cough? I mean specifically what do they say?"

"They say but I doubt them. I don't think they know. They just say it's because he spends too much time in the damp unlighted back marshes and that it's not good for him. I truly worry about Lonzo. I pray that his condition, whatever it is, won't worsen. I'm thinking of flying him to Houston for an examination."

Andrea did all within her to cheer me up, even though months had expired since my mother's passing. "You don't have to do that anymore," I'd mildly protest. "I'm over that now."

"I know, I know. But I want to do it anyway." She once considered it a wise diversion for both of us to go over and meet the new priest. The old one, Father Garibaldi, the one who married us, now served in another parish fifty miles west. She sorely missed him, her mood down more than ordinarily, obviously, the real reason she wanted to go I gathered, but she still felt it would help boost me too. The new priest looked of astonishing youth, twenty five years of age I figured, possibly younger and seemed uncomfortably shy. At first, he showed reluctance to look at my face when talking. I said to Andrea soon after we met him that it puzzled me that they'd appointed him as priest of the parish. It dawned on me however, after we'd grown more acquainted with each other, that inside there resided a brilliant mind and that he possessed a warm and generous tolerance of his flock. At first, we awkwardly addressed him as Father, but we did and it began to happen with naturalness when we again started regularily to attend mass at his church. As we did with respect to the older and former priest, we in time grew attached to Father Casandra. I think Andrea also wanted to go and meet him for another reason. Our son was away in boy's school and she missed him terribly. She didn't outright say it but she did. She'd seen the young priest before at a distance without introducing herself. He reminded her of our son. We had struggled with the idea of sending him to boy's school, Andrea more than me.

"Ramsey, do you think it's a good thing to send Dawson away," she asked? "South Carolina is quite far."

"He'll be all right."

But my words were undergirded with only mild confifence. We finally adjudged it okay to enroll him but only after she had mustered enough courage to go through with it. I wondered at the wisdom of our decision but declined to reveal my internalization to her regarding the matter. So many boys fall into mischief at private schools I envisioned, and franlkly, I debated with myself whether ours was a wise or unwise choice but decided that what is wise in one circumstance is not wise in another, at last making up my mind that it's humanly impossible to tell which is which and soon let the complexity fade into obscurity. We sent him to boy's school.

He joined us in Louisiana for Christmas, joyful for everything we did for and with him, boating everyday and his mother for the first time began to teach him to shoot geese, for food, not for sport. She did everything better than me for the boy and suddenly began teaching him all sorts of out of doors skills. She gorged him with Christmas gifts too, among them a bow and arrow set.

"You'll spoil the child."

"I don't care Ramsey if I do. You only have a child with you but once. Think of it. He's only leased to us for a little while. In a blink it's over. He's gone."

When he left for South Carolina following the holidays he actually didn't leave, not alone in any respect. He went with his mother. She flew with him. "A mother's prerogative Ramsey. Don't pout."

"I'm not pouting. When will you get back?"

"Shortly. You take care of things. Don't forget to feed the pet squirrel. And without fail attend mass."

She stayed a week. Upon her return she opened a letter or telegram from the head of the law firm apologetically asking her if she might fly back to New York to negotiate and take the lead in the legal proceedings which involved an anti-trust suit, noting also that big bucks were at stake and that she should turn the matter over very seriously before declining.

"It's in the closing stages Ramsey. I'll wrap it up in two weeks. I think I'd better take him up on this one."

"Two weeks," I said, sounding disappointment but protesting feebly. I knew she'd remain away for at least a month or more. She just about was. She telephoned every night, never missing a single one. The letter sent by the head of the law firm never once mentioned using me. I saw then that in their eyes she by far and away occupied a position of value a few steps ahead of mine. I laughed aloud when the thought settled in on me. At last she returned. It was as if we hadn't seen one another in a hundred years, or as Andrea phrased it a few days afterwards, "We were as sky high as children going on an adventursome journey." It took an hour at the least for us to regain normalcy. The money remitted to her for successfully leading the team in a very demanding high stakes assignment indeed amounted to a handsome sum.

Not many days had disappeared from the calendar when I received a letter from Darya, not a surprise in the least, for sporadically she sent little social notes, notes containing lines of casual wording. I read it and left it face up on the credenza. It was not within me to conceal anything from Andrea. Darya inquired of my health and that of Andrea's but there was no doubt that she sent the letter to me. Andrea read it. She asked me once if I heard from Darya often, with my comment being that she knew the answer because she always read the mail from her to me. She laughed and said she did and further added that I likely thought her jealous and then said that in no way was she. In that remarkable character of hers she harbored deep and abiding feelings for Darya, I knew that for sure, and talked often of her struggle with her injured leg resulting from the war. In her heart there resided a consummate sorrow for the woman who once as a girl in college competed with her for my affection. Sometimes they exchanged letters that spoke the sweetest caring for one another, and this too was only slightly less than incredible, but it shouldn't have been. They wern't the first women who have risen above the adversity of competition for a man only in the end to anoint one another with love.

"We must vist her Ramsey, see about her. She speaks of such loneliness in her letters, not so much directly but between the lines. She means much to the both of us."

"We should. We will."

Too soon the six months sabbatical faded away, a period in which we'd immersed ourselves in fun and edenian pleasure, and moreover had exacted a superb amount of legal service for the firm, even in absentia. Now we would have to prepare to return to the big city and there join the hectic ebb and flow of daily business. Lake Allemand and the idyllic little cottage were now imprinted in my soul and grievously I found it hard to think of parting from it. I believe that Andrea dreaded leaving even more than I.

"For a little Ramsey I'd toss a coin for deciding whether to go or stay."

"Ho, ho. But heads or tails you'd go in the end."

"Yep. I have to say I would."

Not by accident Lonzo happened by when we were busily packing. "Oh hello Lonzo," I said. Only by an instant afterwards he virtually fought back tears in realization that he would badly miss us, then hugged Andrea and then me."Don't take any wooden nickels Lonzo." That helped.

"Ha, ha, ha. No Mista Ramsey I won't do that," then crawling into his boat he at once pulled the starter cord which ignited the expected fierce snarl of the motor, and set out for the opposite shoreline, moving rapidly away, very quickly becoming smaller and smaller, until eventually he and his boat faded dimly into the mist.

We spent an extra day from that point before leaving and arranged to pay call and express our goodbye to the young priest.

"Dio sia con te," he returned in Italian.

Chapter 68

IT WAS at some time after this, when Andrea and I after a few years were recognized as a very productive team for the firm, that our nation was once again at war, the war that historians and journalists refer to as the Iraqi War or the Persian Gulf War or merely the Gulf War. Not a few Americans questioned why we ended up in that calamitous fiasco, not withstanding Andrea and me, and most of those making up the legal staff of the law firm. The cause of the war led directly down the pathway toward black gold, the synonym for oil. Saddam Hussein, the bully leader of the Iraqi nation, ordered a military invasion and occupation of Kuwait with the apparent aim of usurping that tiny nation's burgeoning oil supply, and therefore, among other things, in a single sweep wipe out the debt that his country owed the Kuwaitis. It is true also that he in no way concealed in this movement his intent to vastly expand Iraqi power in the region. The United Nations coalition of members demanded that Hussein remove his military machinery from Kuwait and upon his refusal an action began that someone named Desert Storm which unleashed a scheme to destroy or disable every facet of the Iraqi resistance structure, the destruction or disabling of its air defenses, communications networks, government buildings, weapons plants, oil refineres, and bridges and roads across the historic Tigris and Euphrates rivers. By mid February the colition army, led significantly by the United States, had shifted from air to ground attacks, soon leaving a sprawling carnage of battered tanks and trucks and dead Iraqi soldiers, armless, legless, faceless, horrible scenes of death, a killing field, grotesque, caught in a merciless bombardment of rocket fire as they attempted escape along the road to Baghdad.

It is said that war is an old man's folly and a young man's fight and that was very much so in so far as Andrea and I were concerned when we heard that hostilities had broken out. We were affected by a most singular reason. Our son was ripe for the draft, which hit us stunningly, to which he proudly and bravely faced, issuing to his parents that gladly he would serve his country and passionately expressed loyalty to it. We were moved that he staunchly supported the land of his rearing, yet when he hugged and kissed us and said goodbye on the day of his departure for boot camp our hearts sank and I secretly nurtured an inordinate regret that I had not advised him to take flight to Canada, or to some other foreign sovereignty, thus avoiding the dreaded field of battle and staying alive. Andrea hurt almost unbearably. The war in a flash ended, mercifully, and our son not many weeks afterwards met us with arms outstretched at the doorway safe and sound. We knelt on our knees and prayed thanks to the Lord.

Time passed. And while I cannot cite a particular calendar date, I do recall the period to which I have reference and the three definite reasons for that recall, the first being that we had just returned to the firm's Chicago office from another stay in the warmth of the Louisana sun and secondly, that Andrea and I approached or had arrived at the top of our game as legalists. The third had to do with the winter, a very cold winter which had just set in. We rode an inner-city bus to work on our second day back, walking a full block from where the driver stopped and let us off near our destination. The temperature had dropped to below freezing, and the icy wind blowing in from Lake Michigan cut to the bone.

"Brrrrrh," a shiver reverberated from Andrea's lips as we entered the doorway to the warmth inside.

"Me too," I replied.

Barely were we settled, within the next few days that is, when a deluge of lawsuits lit on our desks marked for settlement in the courts, a good many of them tagged with a target date for trial just around the corner. Suddenly we were thrown into a maelstrom of pressure laden trial dockets that never softened. For the next few years we were constantly seen in the court rooms of Chicago and New York City litigating an endless flow of cases, many a case, let me stress, of an extraordinary stature, the biggest cases, the name cases, where the deep pockets of the corporate empire were satiated with indescribable wealth. Andrea and I drew assignments that linked us together with few exceptions, the firm's deliberate contrivance, both of us side by side researching the statutes, mapping out strategies, and combining our talents to great advantage, all of which created a formidable team in the practice of law. The firm liked us; we made them money. The firm loved us; we made them rich. And we loved our success. And not withstanding the lucrative size of our paychecks, certainly. Why in a natural sense, I thought, should I assert to the contrary. But then, as if he hovered close over us, the wisdom of his old and raspy voice rang as a caution in our ears. "Now young friends, no one can reasonably accuse you of wrongdoing when you start to earn huge sums, and you will do that, mark my word; but do not let yourselves fall victim to the temptation of greed. Many a lawyer has ended up on the rocks of ruin and despair by becoming prey to that weakness."

He need not have worried. We were reminded of those precautions every single day, in any event in the days that our work led us to New York. You see, we were there quartered in the same office space occupied by that dear one for so many years. He had penned into mandatory print that as long as the firm continued to exist it was his wish that I should enjoy occupancy of his former desk and chair when he had gone on to his Maker, and at my discretion use all other office furniture when and if I desired. Nothing appeared in his memorandum that prohibited Andrea from sharing this coveted environ with me, room and furnishings, and so she did, digging out of storage an old elongated side table of quite some size partially camaflouged with heavy tarpaulin fabric laid over it and using it as her part time work station. At other times she sat by me at my desk, or shall I say his, and did her preparations or used it altogether upon my absence as if it were hers.

At the pace we'd been going it began to foam in our conscious that we were facing burn out, or worse, the awareness of which prompted us to seriously start considering moving ever closer to a change. She spoke of it first. I could tell by the coming and going of the somberness of her face that morning that something was astir. She had asked earlier if I'd like to take her to lunch at Arnos even though we looked ahead at the noon hour with clear understanding that we'd find the vigorously active little place on the corner jammed with hungry patrons. A year had passed since we'd been there. I thought that we definitely should go. My answer was sudden. "Yes indeed. Let's do" Going to lunch with her at Arnos ran in my head as a funfilled delight. Upon our shoving the disheveled stacks of materials on our desks aside we set out a few minutes ahead of schedule hoping to beat the crowd, aiming for the next street over. The cobblestones were still there; they were forever there I embellished, starting with my first trip along this way with Mr. Yazstremski, round and grey in appearance, some large and some small and others of midsize, once embedded deep in a mire of asphalt which now had started on the surface to wear away. Andrea looked over, her pretty eyes flitting with cherished remembrance.

"Isn't this something. The same old clip clop, the same old echo. Always the same."

"Yep. Always the same. Don't you wish he were here with us?"

Soon we were there. The old men there too, as well as the steamy mist pouring out of the kitchen and the raspy gratings coming from the throats of the cooks as they barked out at the waiters to more clearly enunciate an order. We were more drawn to the old men however than to any other attractant, all seemingly immersed in harmony in their low murmured voices, sometimes exuding an unvigorous laugh at something just told or said. I wistfully imagined for a second that these were the same old men I'd seen on my first visit there with my dear friend. But the ones of that vintage were now gone, the ones presently before me relatively young in that time but now in the present time old themselves."

"Lots of memories here Ramsey, hunh," she said, keenly looking around at the pots and pans lining the walls and at other relics, but particularily at the old men."

"Lots."

"Wouldn't you like to live those times over again? Just once."

"Would I. I'd give all for just one minute."

Not to my surprise she let go with a revelation which I had anticipated, and that she couldn't hold in much longer. "I was thinking my darling," she slowly began to release, "that, that—."

"What?" My eyes were glued immovably to hers.

"I'm thinking of this, that we're not getting any younger, you know, and we work so very hard."

I reinforced her. "And you're right on both counts."

"It's time to think about a change. Are you willing to explore that possibility? Maybe?"

"Am I. I could have said just what you said yourself. I've been going over this very thing for a considerable while. And recently too. Just yesterday in fact. And this morning come to think of it. But I'm getting ahead of you here. What do you have in mind my sweetheart?"

"It's this. First, we have to change our life style. To slow down."

"But not yet leave the firm altogether any time soon."

"Right. But I am saying that we should begin to shoulder a much lesser load than we now bear. Doing part time, I should say. Being on call for case assignments now and then. And that only."

"Gads. You have thought it through, not a pebble unturned. But I read you. And you're right. Of course, the firm might not like it when we approach them with our decision."

"But they'd have to," she spoke with a sureness of voice.

"All or nothing you're intimating. In other words, if it came down to where the rubber touches the ground we'd quit if we had to. Our way or it's over."

There was an unexplainable appearance that rushed to her face preceding her smile of happiness, and then,"I love you," and stretched her arm across the table and supplely touched her fingers to my lips. "Yeah. Over" And then she laughed one of those adorable laughs. Then grew serious. "I know. I know. What then, you're asking."

"That's a pertinent question. So, what will we do, if we do anything at all?"

"We'll do it darling. I promise you that. And I do have something in mind, which I've spun in my head over the past year or so at least a hundred times."

"Wow! Something well worth listening to I'm sure. What is it?"

"I know I musn't keep you guessing, no I musn't, so here it is. I, I. I'd like for us to leave this big old city and settle in some little out of the way peaceful place, maybe leaving for good. Starting a new life."

"Sounds as if we're moving back to Lake Allemand?"

"That's a beginner. Or some place else for awhile."

"Where are you exactly leading me to?"

"All right. I'll speak with exactness. It's whirled in my head more than once in recent days, and long before, that I'd like for us to spend a little while in a secluded little hamlet, say a year or so at least, hmmmmm, maybe in the Catskills, you know, that mountainous woodsy back country in lower New York, renting and living in a sort of small log built cottage, and getting to know the good folks there, even shopping on Saturday's at the local grocery with our fingers crossed that we might win a prize at the six o'clock drawing and by all means go to church on Sunday morning. And. And. Well, I think I'd better stop here. Time I signed off. My cup runneth over."

She had but a second to wait for my come back.

"You are a salesman, that's for sure. You've convinced me. I'd like to leave right now. How long will it take us to pack?"

Curling her arms around my neck she let go with a voracious burst of laughter.

"Silly" Then half giggled, half laughed and then grew serious. "No need to rush. But at least I've given you something to think about."

"I'm puzzled. You mentioned the Catskills. I didn't have the least suspicion that some place like that spun around in your secret network.

"That's just another place where my parents took me when I was but a young girl. The truth is I have fantasies now and then of going back there someday. Maybe living there for a spell. But I mean a limited one."

Soon we were on our way back to the office, now coming onto the cobblestones only a few steps removed from Arnos, where the obvious notice of clip clop clip clop once more began, ricocheting sharply from the stone laid walls on both sides of the street, thus producing the effect of hundreds of hard leather shoe soles striking the surface in unpatterned cadence.

Suddenly, unexpectedly, "Let's sit for a moment," she said, sliding onto one of the hodgepodge of settees set about here and there. I gathered she'd decided to delve further into the conversation ending minutes before our departure from Arnos. But it wasn't that.

"You know Ramsey. Cobblestones literally fascinate me." And then commenced to elaborate in detail. "They're so pretty, so artistic, appearing in so many colors—red and brown and gray, not taking into account the many others that presently escape me. As a military man my father was once stationed in Imola, Italy. Cobblestone streets are there everywhere. Even the churches are built of them, and walkways and pools with lavish gurgling fountains. I remember how pretty they were, made up of so many shapes and sizes. It's a beautiful little city and offers much to see but I remember it more for its cobblestones than for any other thing of lure. I've hung on to some snapshots that I took. Remind me to show them to you someday."

"I will. I had no idea they were among your collections."

"They are" And then she went on.

"But America has its share of cobblestone usages too, for example, Savannah, Georgia, where my mother and father carried me once on vacation. A street ran alongside the Savnannah river and somebody a long while ago hit upon the idea of lining the street with cobblestones. Hundreds and hundereds. I asked why they were there and someone explained that they were once in olden times used for providing stability, balance, to the ships sailing back and forth from Europe."

"And?"

"Well. Eventually the shipping business fell into serious decline, with all at once the need cropping up to dump the cobblestones on the shoreline which were later used for constructing the street. What else could they do with them?"

"I see. But take me back a step or two. You said something to the effect that the cobblestones stabilized the shipping vessel. Resay that for me."

"Sure. Cobblestones were placed on the empty side of the ship to match the other side which they'd loaded with cargo, this being necessary or else the vessel might have tipped over."

Chapter 69

THOUGH INTENDING with the staunchest resolve to soon pack up and move to an idyllic cottage setting in the Catskills we hung back for two more years. We'd stay for three months at a time we said. And then we said we'd stay longer, four to five months at a time. We kept going back year after year but only for a few weeks at a time, short vacations, but never moving there permanently. Deep down I personally lacked faith in our settling down in the Catskills for an extended stretch, figuring that after a while we'd regret leaving Chicago and move back, and, Andrea by then, after years of living in it, was emotionally attached to our little cottage on the shore of Lake Michigan to such an extent that she couldn't bear thinking of leasing it out to anyone irrespective of the length. "Ramsey, I can't possibly visualize anyone else living in this enchanting little abode except ourselves." And our son figured in as well, who then lived with his wife and two young children in South Carolina. Andrea said that she'd gotten used to visiting them in South Carolina from Chicago and that if we moved to some other place it might seem terribly far away, whether it was or was not. She, as a doting mother would naturally do—which was a good thing; who could argue that it isn't—flew down to stay a stretch with them as much as her schedule allowed.

The head of the law firm withered easily in face of her submission of notice that she and her husband were going on an abbreviated leave, the man never once objecting or putting up a fuss. She was a gifted negotiator, with a high percentage of getting her way, in this instance assuaging what displeasure he concealed inside by promising to attend to certain legal matters at our vacation residence, provided that such business was subject to a specified limited work load.

The years began to sprint away from us. About ten I judge had expired since our beginnings with the Catskills. We had gained enough determination to leave Chicago, which had been our second if not our first home and return permanently to Louisana.

The thought of leaving was hard in the extreme, Andrea grieving for a month before we decided to really go.

It was the custom. The fine ladies, the wives of the male staffers, had conceived of and coordinated the taxing details of our retirement ceremony. They outdid themselves on every turn, not the least of which was the preparation of a monstrous sized cake of seventeen layers dripping with red and green icing that symbolized the inward and outward gratitude of everyone. In their efforts, as well, they engaged a plushly finished ball room situated in the vicinity of Soldiers Field. It wasn't used often and this helped seal the deal. They rented it for a bargain price. From the appearance of it the whole of the building might have stemmed from the renovation of an older building financed and erected by a once rich and powerful family of the midwest—perhaps by a German family who had hit it lucky by amassing huge tracts of land through homesteading. Infinite care was taken to align the walls with elaborate lighted sconces, exotic relics of an old Europen flavor and extending around the walls also were fresh pretty flowers and dwarf sized shrubberies implanted in urns and pots of miniature volume. The urns were much larger of course with sculptured curlicules and scrolls and a multiplicity of other artistic variants imbibed on their surface. Jarvis Bolinger, the head of the firm flew in from New York City, a jocular guy who delighted at being the center of attention, sallied up to me and whispered lowly that the head of the firm once was mine if I had shown and spoken an interest. I took it as put on, a charge of vanity, and winked at Andrea standing close enough to over hear, her mind the same as mine traveling swiftly back to that day when Mr.Yazstremski called me into his office and sort of advised, sort of plead for me to go after the position, which he could guarantee. Jarvis at the time amounted to no more than a mere fledgling in the ranks, with no one seeing in his crystal ball that this young kid as we all uncalculatingly saw him would elevate so high so fast. But I forgave Jarvis for all his showiness, for after all he now held the reigns as the commander-in-chief and a commander-in-chief must exact a certain amount of pretentious protocol when in a crowd.

A large count of the staff, men and women, cried at the thought of our departure, at least half of them I gather, making it natural for me to call up that day of some years past when we wished to honor Mr. Yazstremski upon his stepping down. Death beat us to him. I asked that we pause for a moment to recall and honor that dear man. An abundance of those in the room had worked under his guise and every one present stood in silence and shed a tear, not just a portion, and every tear shed was a passionate tear. I searched my cerebral archives for his age presently had he lived to take part in the current ceremony, mine and Andrea's.

Andrea and I talked with affable smiles and spoke and acted the part befitting a Shakesphearan charcter in moments of his best behavior as we sauntered about or when the people came to us.

"The very best for you. And may you have many blessed years." Such was the usual message or very nearly the usual message delivered to me or to Andrea or both as we mingled among them.

"Ah. Thank you. You are very kind. We'll remember your kind words always."

The turn out was heavy, substantial in numbers, some of whom retired the previous year, one such person known as Josh Kinard, to whom I'd grown relatively attached over the years, who'd teamed with me and Andrea in a wide mix of cases. I saw him ploughing through the crowd, pushing sometimes, which drew an unfriendly gesture. But as it happened most knew him and ended up shaking his hand and inquiring of his health and how he now kept himself occupied. When he drew abreast we embraced. He spoke first.

"Hi ya old buddy. Remember me?"

"Ha, ha, ha. Are you kidding. Life's been treating you well I hope."

"Great. Great."

"Retirement suits you?"

"Pretty well. But I took a while getting used to it. The worst part of retirement is the monotony I'm supposing, the sameness that is, and then there's something else about equally as aggravating.

"Really?"

"Yeah. You never get a day off." He guffawed with laughter. A loud laugher. People looked around at us.

I Laughed too. And after filtering the essence of what he'd said concluded that not only was it hilariously clever but also true.

Andrea and I kept shaking hands and demonstrating the utmost of chivalry toward our hosts, as of course we should have done. Such diplomacy was a gift of naturalness to her, but somewhat less for me. After we retired to bed that evening I asked her how I'd behaved.

"Pretty good for a country boy."

I started wandering around searching for the men's room. I badly needed to pee. As I closed the door there resulted a sudden blast from a siren on the street below. Instinctively I looked out the window. Nothing, just a police car rushing to somewhere I thought to myself. "I'll be damned. Even on the day of my retirement. Isn't it a wonderful thought that I'll happily miss all this clutter of big city bustle? I'm going to love Lake Allemand."

The music never stopped. It played without let up allowing naturally for breaks. At one point someone in the band strummed a melancholy Gypsy tune on a mandolin. *Golden Earrings.* That's what somebody called it. It sounded a little sad. But I supposed that was just me. All in all, I ranked the gathering as a grand event. No one presently acted as if they wanted to give it up. But it had to reach its climax and as the clock inched toward eleven the crowd began to thin, commencing as a trickle to move toward the doorway. Andrea and I said aloud, when we were asked to give our parting remarks, that we'd be coming back and with some sort of assurance to the idea spoke hopefully that we would, but deep within entertaining the conviction that the odds were against setting our eyes on more than a tiny few ever again.

All the same the space selected for the event was most fitting and at every opportunity, near the last at least, I proceeded to commend the women for their good and efficient work and time in putting things together so perfectlty.

So, we moved on, for awhile taking residence in Andrea's cottage on Lake Allemand. We'd live there only long enough to build a comfortable more standardized dwelling on higher ground on the opposite shore line from her cottage. We could easily see the cottage on a clear day. We'd go there often, unable to stay away. Pretty soon we felt very much at home, well entrenched and living like everyone else. But there was a catch. We discovered little by little that a substantial populace of old faces were gone, replaced by new ones whose lifestyle differed somewhat noticeably from the one to which we were accustomed in former years. Lonzo had died, his son deeded the property as described and required in the wording of the will, and who now energetically skitted up and down the waters in his two man boat in the style of his father. He worked as a mechanic at a government supplemented shipyard operating on the Louisana coastline west of us. He brought us fish in abundance practically every week. I say that he brought us fish, yet not exactly. He brought them to Andrea; "I got ye a mess uv fish Miss Andrea," he would let out just as Lonzo said it, more or less.

I began to teach part time at a large comprehensive high school nearby at a branch of Louisiana State University, New Orleans each Saturday morning. These were graduate students, some I figured on their way to earning the terminal degree. I taught literature, advanced literature more specifically speaking, the students of an approximate age of twenty five to thirty years, well read and well informed already, since they taught literature in high school themselves. I suspected many times that they knew more than me of the subject matter and must admit that I viewed the situation with a certain feeling of intimidation. But my age helped. They respected age, at any event their demeanor relaying as much. The temptation strongly played upon me to tell them of my previous too long ago to matter exposure to such greats as Mr. Yazstremski, Dr. Linskie, and Clement Attlee, yet couldn't right then, but would get around to that in a proper way when I adjuged the time was right. The one thing of primacy that I had going for me centered on my past prolific reading, over and over, of Tolstoy's *War and Peace* and *Anna Karenina* and sufficiently whetted their appetite by exposing their minds to these rich compositions. On the outset I learned that my students knew little of the great Tolstoy, nor were they enlightened on the works of Anton Chekhov, Tolstoy's young confidant and Russia's greatest short story author. When they dug into the lives and fantastic voluminous output of these famous men their spirit of interest skyrocketed. They learned to love Russian stories of far reaching generes and remarked disappointment at missing so much. Dr. Linskie would have expressed heartfelt proudness of his former pupil.

Over in the little town of Des Allemands we set up an office designed to help people in need. The poor folks. We had gained more wealth than we'd ever wisely use we calculated and surmised that that was what we wanted to do for humanity's sake. Andrea first started the office, then in time I joined her. Only once during this phase did we journey to Chicago to assist the firm with a case, simply putting it, a case where a Texas farmer had struck it rich, an oil well suddenly mushrooming up on his farmland overnight, where the big corporate oil monolith stepped in with the argument that they held an airtight lease on the land with the old gentleman entitling them to any and all oil discoveries whatsoever, a claim they argued that ran indefinitely. I'll sidestep the details, but we won. I said to Andrea that the outcome surely was predestined, that this was the last trial case for us, ever, and that the Good Lord let us leave the game of big chips a winner where opulence was the driving force. I shall here have to recant. We did involve ourselves on occasions in other cases, but only to defend the economically disadvantaged, never in anything of appreciable magnitude.

The seasons kept coming and going and it registered with me one day, on my seventieth birthday, that "when you reach seventy you're living on borrowed time, each day a gift." I remember it well, sitting down and drafting a letter to my friend Leland, who'd written me not many weeks earlier. He'd called to my attention that I had a birthday heading my way.

Dear Leland,

Since you are of my age, born a mite before or after me, you very likely have as of late let it slip into your musings that you have weathered seventy seasons of life. Yes sir. We are seventy, which says that we are now old. And so too our friends, or people who once were our friends, Ozzie and Cavanaugh and Mr.Carney and Tatiana for instance. I've not heard from them in a long long while and fear that they are no longer with us. Do you hear from any of them? If you have will you send me their address? Andrea and I live near Des Allemands. You know where that is. For sure you do. I go back to my little town near Memphis once in a while. Mainstreet is the same, as wide as ever and very short and the railroad still passes by the upper portion, the trains transporting as usual their freight loaded box cars and the highway still runs straight through town. The former Sinclair gas station with its towering dinasour gazing down on everyone buying gasoline there is now replaced by a barren piece of land and still talked of by the few survivors who can remember that far back. And I'm adding to my list. Warren Bethune's cotton gin, now gone too, but a monument in its heyday whose fundamental importance to the community was measured in terms of the number of men it employed. But why do I tell you all this? You knew these things anyway. So let me sign off with adios until I pick up my pen again or better still see you in person.

As always,
Ramsey

Andrea and I had begun to live a conventional life, meaning that we went to the supermarket twice each week and paid call on the sick, with me teaching a limitation of graduate classes now and then and Andrea practicing a slight of law simply as a favor to some of the unfortunates who were badly in need of legal assistance. I must not omit Father Casandra who had emerged as my great and indispensable friend, excepting my beloved Andrea, whose friendship and love as my dear wife was immeasureable, only understood by my own heart. In many respects the Father's manner and wisdom was something of a facsimile of the same great qualities possessed by Mr. Yazstremski and Doctor Linskie—I only mean to say somewhat—who were gone but whose memories were woven indelibly into my heart as fixedly as a stone. Andrea and Father Casandra are now my most intimate conversationalists and discussants of ideas and thoughts, of practically every field under the sun, everything, thelogy and philosophy and politics and science and mathematics; or of common every day words and their derivation, such as, "change" and "solution" and "logic" and "mind" and "poetry" and "opinion" and "quality" and "justice." Nothing left out. How, I often asked myself, did all these words evolve? Who created these words? Why? What was the reason? Did God store them back for man to eventually trip across and find a way for their use? There were times when I picked up the phone or conversed by letter with Leland and Darya to enlarge upon these and similar complex and mysterious aspects, doing it in part because it was movingly a thrill to revisit with old friends, but foremostly because in all honesty they were exceedingly deep in ther caverns of intellect.

One year passed and then another and then another and in an about this time, Darya let Andrea and I know of a certain detectable decline in her health, this coming recently from her doctor, the news upping our desire to go visit her. I said we should, my usual comment, and Andrea took the position that we must absolutely make the trip or trips, and began to look in on her with increased regularity, in a sense becoming her nurse during these stays, with some stays stretching to well beyond the length of a month.

"She needed me Ramsey and I could not have afforded to disappoint her. You should have gone with me."

"Oh, I could have. I have to admit that. But I deemed it best if just you two spent time alone with each other. You know, talking women's talk."

"All right. But I assured her that you'll come soon."

Andrea in her remarkable graciousness knew that passions between Darya and I had long ago taken flight from our hearts and that my going to see her only amounted to two old friends coming together to explore the ups and downs of their lives, and to help Darya pass the time a little better.

"It's a good thing Ramsey. You go spend a few days with her. She may not have a lot of time left."

I cannot begin to place my finger on a date, or month, or year, but say five years following my seventy fifth birthday, when Father Casandra and I began to spend what seemed as endless moments in a little flat bottom fishing boat on Lake Allemands, the both of us emptying out innumerable and varied things that had to do with mankind and his unsolvable complexities. Once Andrea asked what on earth did we two talk about during all those times when we were alone out there in that little fishing boat, to which Father Casandra laughed politely and issued, "Good question Andrea. In all truth we talk about everything, or try to, but I'm of mind that the Good Lord feels very sure that we know nothing in depth about any of it." Father Casandra has become a great joy to me in my aging years and they have lasted much longer than I ever expected. Never a day comes when we are together that one or the other of us fails to pop a challenging question, apt as not quite spontaneously. It was my time, apparently.

"Father is life harder than it is easy?"

"Gracious! Right out out of the blue. I could laugh at your unexpected witticism my great friend but I don't. Why do you ask such a thing?"

"Because I ponder it incessantly as I do a myriad of things and because to my mind it's something that every human being thinks about from time to time. They can't help it. It's a pretty natural thing, wouldn't you agree?"

"Ha. You're good at gigging me into tackling the difficult ones. Is life harder than it is easy? Tell you what. This time why don't you go first? "

"Well, in my own instance I have to say it's not been easy. Life is a struggle one famous poet declared. I have to accept his premise. Life is a struggle, hard, not at all easy."

"Why so?"

"It's so rife with pitfalls and suffering. Sometimes, and I'm admitting that this is a trifle on the light side, I think if I were suddenly bestowed the power to reorder my birth I'd say 'whoa, hold up, are you sure you want to try this again?'"

"Well. Hmmmmm. That's hilarious my friend."

"To a degree. But life is indeed hard. Permit me again Father, to ask you why? Why is one's life so filled with trials and tribulations and suffering. Why didn't the Lord draw up a different blueprint? Wouldn't that have made more sense?"

"I can't answer you very well, not to your satisfaction I'm afraid. I can only tell you that our Great and Hallowed Maker in his scheme of the universe had a reason for all things, mankind inclusive, which we weren't suppose to understand and don't."

Father Casandra seemed in some ways enamored with Andrea. Why not. She was most beautiful. Whether or not he was in love with her I can't say and won't. What I can say is that he loved being around her and on many occasions, she went fishing with us. She'd sometimes swim while we fished. For hours she would. While he indulged in but a few out of door pleasures I chided him that I found it easy to believe that he would have taken up fishing as a full time avocation were I to agree to join him. He chirped at the idea, unvaryingly insisting that the Lord had charged him to spread the word and to minimally devote his mind and energy to other things irrespective of what they were. "Lake

Allemands is truly a thing of divine creation Ramsey, certainly it must be, and one will hold firmly that such is true if he only pauses and reflects but a miniscule second on the beautiful scenes of nature that surrounds him out here."

"Who am I to deny it or even shed a speck of light upon it with wisdom and understanding? It must have taken our Diety of greatness—no, more than greatness, I suffer from lack of word power here—to piece all these things together—but I, I, well—."

"What?"

Whatever it was I recall it having to do with one's spiritual belief and the concept of Heaven and eternal life, or something close to that, but pulled up short of going into these misty ventures, telling myself that I found it much more comfortable to converse on the subject at hand with Leland, or even sometimes with Darya. At times Andrea and I did wander into these complexities. But Andrea, though capable of traversing into these deep and complicated spheres beyond the rest of us, Father Casandra included, tended to stay away from such far out rationales, keeping her thoughts simple and in perspective as she put it, an indelible belief in the life of Jesus Christ, "the light," and the resurrection and let it go at that.

"There are those father, as you unremittingly will declare I'm sure, who have troubles with coming to a conclusion that agrees with ours"

"Yes. You are very right."

"And I too sometimes have doubts."

"Doubts?"

"Not that exactly. Infinity, an eternal life. What is eternity? Life has always been here or should I say the universe has always been here? How can we fathom such things? You see what I mean?"

"Readily I do. I've grappled with the question myself over and over."

"I am afraid to utter such thoughts of mind aloud, Father, as foolish and ridiculous as it may seem. I pray that God will forgive me and will not punish me."

"Then what are you to do about it?"

"What am I to do about? Most humbly I am asking you to instruct me."

"There is a God Ramsey, a Presider over all things and is Maker of all things, all of which is beyond our grasp, all of which we thoroughly and completely don't understand. But I accept it, I profoundly do, just as I accept Lord Jesus as my savior and my redeemer. Just as Andrea does, your beloved wife, as you well know. That is all I can offer."

Such was our conversation on that day and many another day. These questions that sprang from my head were questions that have confounded man since time immemorial, and they are questions that shall forever remain unalterable, as thus I said to Father Casandra. But I would learn to look at these mysteries with peace of mind and a heart of trust, perhaps because of Andrea's steadfast Christian belief and her faith in me and her love for me and perhaps the Lord himself began to lend a hand.

"Father Casandra is right, my dearest," said Andrea one night with whom I had taken up the matter as we lay in bed. "A God, our God, presides over us all and loves us all, irrespective of who we are or what we are."

I think another year had escaped us. In any event we were off fishing again or possibly just boating at first then fishing. Andrea had joined us as she often did. As things turned out she surely wished she hadn't and Father Casandra and I in the finale wished we hadn't gone either.

Sometimes the three of us would sit and watch the sunset in the west, the sun seeming to slide slowly below the tree line, "gorgeous, breathtaking," I mused, and we always looked with happy anticipation to seeing another; but the sunsets were not always entirely serene and peaceful; quite the reverse sometimes. I say this because of the ferociousness of a storm that descended upon us during one of these outings, "one of the scariest I'd ever seen in my life," I remarked afterwards.

Andrea looked upon our friendship with Father Casandra with great fondness and made it a point from time to time to suggest that we invite him over for a two or three day stay at the cottage. I arose early that morning, two hours before my usual awakening, the air deathly still and the mist hovering lowly over the waters as far as the distant shore. The geese that customarily foraged for fish quacked nervously and bunched tightly together. "Something is amiss," I said, "a bad omen." But it was just my intiuition I prankishly assured myself and should forget it. The sun burst through the cloud cover at mid morning and the omen left me. At four o'clock Father Casandra arrived and we went fishing, all three, Andrea first choosing to stay home then changing her mind at the last minute. The fish were muchly alive, vigorously attacking the bait, bringing oft recurring smiles to our faces and expressions of unbelievability at what we saw and experienced. Father Casandra smiled gladly that Andrea had decided to join us and said she would have been terribly sorry if she had not. It was the best fishing day in a good long while, maybe the best day ever. But we would find out relatively soon how quickly luck can pivot against you.

The dying of the day was at least an hour and a half away we concluded and leaned back in our boat chairs, waiting for the sun to sink on down and for the descending dusk to come and take its place. All at once the whole surroundings began to roar and tremble, in the distance a cloud, heavy and twisting, engulfing the tree line, moving with obvious speed, the sun turning yellow, and everything else gray. Rushing to the rear of the boat to pull the starter cord I virtually stumbled which prompted cautions from the lips of Father Casandra, "Take it easy Ramsey. Think of your age."

"Hell, I am. And if we don't get our asses out of here neither of us will have any age to think about." In the bluster of the moment he laughed, I'm certain he did, and I know that Andrea frowned at my rankish words uttered at our dear reverened friend.

At that I yanked the cord and the motor surged into life and we were off, trying desperately to beat the storm to the cottage. The rain and wind overtook us but we were then very near the inlet and able to putter quickly to the mooring dock and tie down the boat before the major portion of the storm struck. Andrea, who had dashed ahead of us, now stood holding the door open. Wringing wet we burst through. Within minutes the rain swept upon the cottage and surroundings with a vengeance, driven by powerful horizontal winds the news people later said, with such force that the grass looked all bent over in the front yard.

"Quite a summer squall," said Andrea in playful declaration, although she like us stood in clothes which were wringing wet.

"I mean," replied the Father. "And downright scary. It happened most suddenly."

Now on her way to her bedroom she didn't bother to answer. In a little she had begun to slip into dry clothes, and called out that in no time she'd have a spaghetti dinner ready, which she'd mostly prepared in advance. We at that moment were changing into dry clothing.

"You'd like that wouldn't you Father."

"You know the answer to that Andrea. And I'll lay two to one odds that yours is even better than they serve in the old country."

"The old country," I chimed in. "I almost forgot. You once lived in Italy."

"So I did."

"When were you last there?"

"A long while ago. I'd been cashiered out of the Italian army and began to turn over the possibility of coming to America. My papers were stamped with approval and I'd soon push off. Before I left, I'd spend two weeks with my parents in Genoa.

"I'll declare. So, you were in the army."

"Yes I was."

"What doing?"

"I was a chaplain. And when I landed in America I joined the American Army and served in the same capacity."

"For how long?"

"Less than a year. A short while before taking over the church here."

"We must explore that period of your past sometime. I mean your Italian Army past."

"Yes we must, I welcome it."

"But not at this very moment," said Andrea. "I know that the both of you are famished. Let us take our places at the dining table. The spaghetti is sufficiently microwaved and ready to go."

When Father Casandra had given the blessing, Andrea arose and brought first the wine, red sparkling wine, Lucite she explained, to which the Father nodded that he knew that, and then she went to the kitchen and returned with both hands gripping a garguantan bowl of Italian styled spaghetti. We ate slowly but hungrily while Father Casandra started reliving his life that dated back to his early days as soldier/chaplain in the Italian Army. The wine had begun to loosen his senses and he wasn't stingy about holding back.

"I tell this with the utmost of vividness, merely a blimp of the whole. Only a blimp. Only one instance and I don't especially revere it. I'll tell you everything that I remember in time. We were in the mess hall for the nightly supper. I again sat among the racketyiest of rogues, as I had evening after evening, roughened crude uncultured soldiers, actually officers, but still crudely conditioned and educated, who kept kidding me about girls, winking at one another.

'No, no,' I politely protested.

But they kept on. The head chef aided by two young associates approached with the meal, you guessed it, spaghetti, piled into a huge round deep bowl, and they dug in, grunting primitively with every bite, lifting the spaghetti in huge round balls on a fork, and then bending their heads over sideways slurped or sucked in a mouthful. Pausing only long enough from their most mannerless gorging to seize upon a flask of wine, a gallon, which stayed covered by a metal plate of a sort through which there passed a flexible neck, or hose, something like a water hose, with a stopper passing through it, the removable of which could be done with one's fingers. For the longest they kept at it. Or until unable to hold more or had gotten so drunk that their bellies refused to tolerate another drop. Of those who were still able the chanting began again, 'Priest like girls, Priest like girls.'

'No, no,' I each time repeated.

"Slavs, dirty filthy slavs," Andrea angrily lashed out. "Treating my dear young priest with such disrespect. I am so sorry Father."

"Don't be. They were soldiers. Laying their life on the line. That's war for you. People behave much differently under conditions of war."

"But no war went on then Father, or else I don't think it did."

"I know. But these were old soldiers. Veterans. Career soldiers steeped in wars of the past."

"War," I spoke up. "I know what it is. I got caught up in it. And two dear friends were in it who fared much worse than I"

"Oh yes. They were Aaron and Darya, weren't they?"

"Yes. Aaron and Darya." I had primed myself for an in depth discussion.

"War" said Andrea. "Let's not talk tonight of things that hurt and haunt us. Tonight let's dwell on pleasant things. Of simple and ordinary things. Not of war, and the terribleness it rains upon us. See the lights on the fishing boats going up down the lake out there. Sometimes I sit for hours on end just watching. Not thinking of anything, just watching. Just enjoying. Definitely not letting war encroach on my mind."

"Yes darling. Let's talk of things lovely and good, or of things very ordinary as you put it. That is why we had Father Casandra over."

So, we talked until well after midnight, of a raft of things; of movies, of late model cars, of the trouble with getting adequate house hold help, of the difference between philosophy and religion, of travel abroad, and of one of Leland's visits, and about Leland's visit Andrea did the larger part of the telling.

"Ah Father, that Leland is a character. He flew down to see us once and we sat up late as we're doing tonight. Leland ingested the wine rather heavily, and resultingly forged aggressively ahead in the activity of conversation. He took up Shakesphere at one juncture, which dealt with his description of the stages of man, starting with birth and ending with old age. We all drank more than we should, thoroughly woozy by the time we went to bed."

"Correction Andrea. Leland had bordered on the fringes of getting drunk."

"Yep. I'd have to agree."

Telling one tale after another we finally came to one that involved Andrea when in her teens which the Father pled with her to go over, especially for him, but with Andrea at first balking, until both Father Casandra and myself playfully threatened to stay up for the rest of the night unless she gave in. Laughing loudly at our prankishness she accused us of colluding and at the same time said "all right," then began. It dealt, she said, with when her father carried her with him on a military assignment to Saudi Arabia. He was there at the behest of the state department to officiate a matter of business between the Saudi hierarchy and ARMAMCO. While there, she and her father were passing though one of the marketing quadrants, on a cultural exploration she said, where the Bedouin tribesman spread their wares, when a chieftain, a tribal head, siddled along side and asked her father to put a price on her head, that he wanted to buy her.

"That scared me to death." Andrea let out. "It really did."

'Why do you want to buy my daughter,' my father asked.

The rest I picked up on and spoke myself of what I had retained of the tale from Andrea's own telling during our many nightly chats when this episode suddenly came to her. The answer was that he liked her white skin, and her nice dark fleeces, and the way she carried herself and that she was pretty to see. But done in broken English.

At this Andrea announced that Father Casandra's bed lay ready and that we should turn in.

"Good. Good," the Father enjoined. "I'm ready Andrea. Goodnight. And oh yes. The wine tasted wonderfully well, it did exceptionally, but I'm not drunk."

Chapter 70

ANOTHER YEAR vanished and I recalled Mr. Yazstremski's clever remark that when you attain to a certain age Christmas comes and by the time it has passed another is tight on its heels.

Somewhere along this spectrum I discovered that I had not seen my favorite uncle Eric in an unforgivable lengthy while, too long absolutely not to see in on someone who had been so dear to me throughout my life. Andrea, kind as she eternally was to her friends of the community had committed to fly one such person to Houston for a diagnosis of an illness, whereupon she suggested to me that my obligations to my dear uncle should take precedence and therefore since I intended not to accompany her I should go and spend a couple of days or more with him and that she knew in his loneliness he would joyfully welcome me with open arms.

"You could catch a plane as far as Memphis and ride the bus for the rest of the trip. Promise me you will."

"You mean promise you that I'll go and at the same not drive."

"Precisely dear. You shouldn't allow yourself to drive that long a distance."

At the very base of my reasoning something told me that I should listen to her, that I might just be too damn old to drive way off up there. In the end I stubbornly insisted that I'd drive and I did. She left soon thereafter, flying her friend to Houston, with words spoken that she'd stay two days or for whatever the time required. I left the next day for Memphis, arriving near dusk and spent the night in a motel. The next morning, I drove on to my small hometown, though not right away seeing in on John Eric. "Too early for that," I figured. I chose to ride around, considering in the interim that it seemed a nice idea to drop in on the Stoddard brothers, Charles D. and Bobby, sons of Charlie Stoddard, Nenia's brother, it may be recalled. But abandoned the notion, for it hadn't been much of a while since I saw them, and Nenia was there as well. She had come to go over with them and me a legal document, a legal trust, whereby the brother's children were to appear in the wording as beneficiaries. Nenia wanted it that way. Nenia still owned the land outright, being the only survivor legally holding the title of ownership. At one time she owned it fractionally with her two brothers, Charlie and Gaylon, and her sister Thelma, all now deceased. Pure clear ownership of the trust description she saw as an imperative. She had earlier asked me by phone if I minded coming up to help her ascertain that there were no legal ambiguities whatsoever in the final preparation.

After the conclusion of this work, I spent an hour or more with her driving around her old homeplace. "One last look," she lamented. I don't recall an extensive exhange between us but it was impossible I thought for her not to journey back in her memories to the time of our youth. Most of all it crossed through my psyche, and I assumed hers, that we once sat by that gurgling little brook with her all fitted tightly in a pretty red dress which every once in a while she innocently slid an inch or two above her knees. And then it alighted on me also that she once asked me if I'd like to kiss her, and shocked, or in any event hardly knowing what to do, I said yes. I naturally did what any young boy would do. But these things I declined to summon up for conversational usage. We'd said goodbye forever once upon a time to a love affair that teetered on the brink of marriage. I deemed it best as did she, I feel certain, to let the past remain passed. We were then old friends and that is how it should have been. It was nonetheless very special to see her once again. "That was two years ago," I recalled.

Now, I was once again in my small hometown to see John Eric and him only, not with the least intention of paying call on another old friend, and wouldn't have except while driving around in observation of this or that, old land marks of familiarity, I caught myself nearing the home once built by the rich and powerful Rupert Monett. Suddenly there it was. Looming out at me. And in the same breath of things an impulse broke through. Why not I asked? It's been decades. I'd understood from hearsay that Melissa Monett had resided there for the duration of her life. As the distance lessened, I stopped along the highway, not yet approaching the home on foot. Merely gazing in its direction, speculating that twenty years had passed since I drove by it. What I saw from a streetside inspection made me wish I had driven on. Time and nature had not treated that once proud edifice kindly. "Melissa grew up in that home, a proud and honored dwelling but proud no more, now visibly in a condtion of gradual decline." I pulled over and parked, opting to embark on a more precise study. I got out and went closer. In the whole of everything before me a veritable unkeptness seemed to enshroud it, disarranged foliage of unfamiliar species gnarled together, growing around one another, and leafy vines of abnormal width and length wreathing up the several brick chimneys towering above the roof line. The exterior walls were burdened with very much the same unsightliness. I heard myself utter that the image of an aging old home with a history of a vigorous and prosperous family who once lived inside its walls does not fall upon the seerer without sadness. But this old home was once not old. It was once new, and on a clear day glistened as a jewel in the sun. I stopped and paused, tempted for a moment to return to my car. Yet something inside urged me not to, to go ownward, to the very door steps and then touch the doorbell. I rang. A lady of sixty I judged answered. She didn't know me. Obviously, she didn't. I doubted she'd ever seen me.

"Good afternoon sir. Who did you wish to see?"

"Melissa. Who are you?"

"Her daughter."

For a moment the revelation took me aback. I'd never seen her either, definitely not as an adult. But I recovered.

"Is she home?"

"She's not very well. But I'll get her." Her phrasing did not carry the message that her mother's condition was something to worry over. I plead regret for my intrusion nonetheless.

"I'm sorry. No don't do that. Not if she's sick."

"It's all right. Who shall I say has called?"

"Ramsey Maynard."

It took a while. Melissa came, softly, her footfall barely audible. The door yet stood open, left as such by her daughter. She eyed me cautiously. I saw in a second as I looked into her face every bit of that complexity which besets a human being when they are struggling to fit everything together. She knew my name when her daughter spoke it to her; it had come to her with easy recall, but the person standing straight in front of her appeared as a stranger, not even faintly that young man she once knew. Then in the split of a moment, as if a cloud had lifted, there emerged a subtle faint smile. She brightened.

"Ramsey."

"Yep. I am." A trickle of warmth surged through me.

"I'm terribly glad to see you. It's been a while hasn't it," she said, her last line essentially asking if I agreed.

When she spoke this time, I detected the slur in her speech.

"Too long."

"Join me inside. Let us visit." In her every appearance she seemed radiantly pleased.

We talked for the longest, with nothing in her posture or facial appearance to denote that she had begun to tire, far from it I decided, but not a word emerged from her mouth making mention of our younger days, only a reference of casual vigor that I had neglected to drop a line from time to time. As the clock progressed, I began to study her more intently. She's old I said and likely has lost some of her lucidity. But how can I know what she remembers or has forgotten. And then, as it had not particularily intercepted my gaze before I now noticed it especially, her hair, her hair, oh yes, now appearing in a shade of gray, or perhaps a cold steely shade of gray. "Ah! What age can do to one," I said in silent remorse, "but it shouldn't strike you at all mysterious that those brittle old strands presently stealing your breath away were once lovely and soft and gorgeous and ran to her shoulders, a young beautiful woman at the peak of her verdure who once lay beside you under the tractor until past midnight, the same young woman who on occasions passed erectly and proudly along mainstreet where old men absent of the rules of decorum that only civility can teach gawked imaginatively from their benches scattered hapzardly in front of Jeremy Dodson's grocery store. She saw you and you saw her, and the both of you knew what the other knew and the both of you were sure with irreproachable certainty that no one else in that little town would ever learn your secrets."

As pathetic as it might seem I discovered myself pondering whether or not she still harbored affections for me and I wished in something of a fantasy she might imply that she did. But something held her back, if the urge were there to begin with, maybe because she now saw it as a shameful thing, or an act of immoral behavior, or for fear that her children would sometime learn the truth. These were my thoughts or a few of them to say the least. Suddenly, sitting there with her so close, I wished she would begin to regress to our first encounter and to the other encounters and come forward to the last time I saw her, the last time I saw her when she looked immensely lovely and youthful. That did not happen. She picked her topics cautiously, talking of things in general, her son's success with the bank that he had inherited, that people called him Mac after his grandfather's middle name, and the need for another factory for supplying jobs for the towns people, and that her former students, long after my time, every once in a while memorialized her with commentaries of praise as an august educatior in the county newspaper and at alumni reunions. Of no surprise on my part but of some expectation she turned to praising my family, emphasizing that they were a fine family and that I was birthed from pedigree strain. "They raised you well Ramsey. We all knew you were going somewhere, to the very top. I especially knew that."

For a flicker she seemed lost in something far away, then—,

"Do you ever see John Eric, your uncle John Eric Caldwell? He is the sweetest thing. I've always liked him."

"I will see him tonight. I'm spending the night with him. Perhaps tomorrow night too. He is alone now, surviving his wife as perhaps you know and his two daughters live somewhere near Chicago."

"Ah! You saw them there quite often, when you yourself lived there."

"I didn't, I'm sorry to say. I kept telling John Eric I would and I tried, finding I must say that the girls were like busy little fireflies on a summer night, hardly a moment in one place. They were awful about answering my phone calls."

"Irresponsible it seems to me."

"One could call it that."

"Is John Eric the last of your close relatives living around here?"

"No, no. Not at all. I have a preponderance of kin living here, one that I see often, much in the manner that I used to pal around with John Eric back in my youth. He's Buren Ray Caldwell, my nephew, a farmer over at Gerald Switch and a preacher once a week, a circuit rider. I get a bang out of him. He's got a lot of John Eric in him, most particularily his bent for hunting swamp bucks in the bottom lands abutting the river."

She brought up her daughter, Meg, she called her, her voice sad, low and strained, as she commenced to explain that Meg met a young man once and married him with the marriage shattering after only a few months had passed. About three she said.

"When was this?"

"Shortly after graduating from high school. All along I didn't think it had lasting capability. Meg isn't given to understanding the under currents of people, certainly she lacked it with young men and hadn't the wherewithal to keep the marriage alive. Her husband treated her badly right from the first."

"You say wherewithal. What do you mean by that?"

Glancing around to ascertain that her daughter had gone to another room and therefore out of ear shot she replied.

"She was too timid, still is, to say it frankly, and didn't know how to fight back."

"That's too bad. Sorrow is now in my heart for her. And I take it that ever since her divorce she has lived with you."

"Yes. In this house. Practically all of her adult life."

I had nothing to say of that. But suddenly felt a compulsion to retrace, to cover something that I didn't think I'd misunderstood but wished to make certain. She'd said it so lowly.

"Melissa, a minute ago you referred to your son as Mac. Is that what you call him?"

"It is. Everyone around here does."

"Mac, Mac," I uttered, but let it stay inside. "The third one in the family, if we count Billy."

Time to say goodbye began to settle upon us. I sensed her readiness for it and stood up from my chair. She came to me and fell into my arms, giving off a barely audible sigh. With her daughter holding open the double doors to the frontage we passed through and halted as we neared the steps leading into the yard.

"Don't say this is a final goodbye Ramsey. Please call again. Don't let me take this as the final one."

As time has progressed, I have become more contemplative, more philosophical one might choose to call it, to which I don't necessarily disagree, and my contemplations perhaps go far in explaining the nature of my life. "You are a thinking animal" sometimes Andrea tells me. "You are reminisciet of what I read in a book once where a child said *Tell Me a Story* and the story teller began. In an instant the world of common reality was left behind and a new reality—more captivating, more intense, more vivid catches up the listener on the wings of imagination. You are like that Ramsey."

"And so are you," I replied. And without bothering to say something in response to my accolade she kept going.

"We never, as long as we live, stop saying *Tell Me a Story*. Our hunger is unquenchable; the more we hear and learn the more we want to hear and learn and the richer the feast the hungrier we grow."

I had to laugh. "You are the thinking animal, Andrea. Far more than me."

In actuality we are both thinking animals. We have had such fun and pleasure and stimulation feeding off one another. Not infrequently one or the other opens a matter for elaboration and sometimes rather unexpected, as was the case one night, when suddenly turning off the television set she abruptly said, as if she'd been spinning it around for awhile, "Ramsey, at this age and we are old my love, what is it that you think about most? Dying?"

"Some. I think of it some. Who doesn't? We must face it, all of us. Even if we don't accept such cold reality. I wish in moments of silent pondering that God hadn't made us mortal. Or else let us live for two or three hundred years more. Why must people have to die when they are just beginning to live? When they are just getting started?

But I must go on a bit with what I think cuts more directly and appropriately to your question, then conclude from there. They say that there is one great certainty in life, the absolute of all absolutes, and that is death. We do not know what it is to die, nor do we know that we shall know even at the moment of death, nor what it is to be dead. Man shows that he is endowed however with an inclination to beat it, though futile, by erecting fabulous monuments named after him so that civilizations will long remember his deeds or image as it was with the ancient Greeks whose rulers of high places ordered the sculpting of their own heads for display throughout their native domain and throughout the world to this day. And to these selfish rather vain glorious attributes allow me to stress that better for them to have bestowed their wealth and generosity on those of need in this life than to try to hide in the shadows afraid and ashamed when meeting them again in Heaven."

"Very philosophical and well put my dear. I listened with unbroken attentiveness to your every word."

To have her with me in my aging years is God's blessing. He had to have directed nature to pattern her for me. She is endowed of a mind that gathers in everything, debating me on every turn, and I feel that on most points of worthiness she is ahead of me. She is devoutly religious, sticking to the scriptures immovably. In her character there is great strength and resolve which one quickly senses and sees. I am blessed that He gave her to me. I guess that happened when first I saw that beautiful young girl sitting in the front porch swing of the next door fraternity house who called out my name as I had begun to pass by and from there captured my heart. It is because of her insistence each night when we have retired to bed, just before we go to sleep, that we recite together the Lords Prayer, seldom missing. "Our Father who art in Heaven………." In every aspect she is a person of goodness; she often likes to say that the hightest purpose of living this life is to do good, to be good, that goodness is love and love is goodness and I fervently believe that there is great wisdom in her words. That the morality of the great Socrates has invaded her readings somewhere along the way is apparent. "Socrates was the wisest of teachers," she quite commonly repeats, "who spent his life pursuing goodness. Do you know the story darling?"

"Partly, but I'm open to hearing more."

"All right."

And then she commences—.

"When the prosecutor had concluded his indictment, a friend talked to Socrates of his predicament but said that Socrates had made no mention of the case. His friend then told him that he ought to be pondering his defense, yet found his remarks to be, 'Don't you think I have been preparing for it all my life?' And when his friend asked him how, he said that he had been constantly occupied in the consideration of right and wrong and in doing what was right and avoiding what was wrong, which he regarded as the best means for his defence. Then his friend pleaded, 'Don't you see Socrates that the juries in our courts are apt to be misled by argumrent, so that they often put the innocent to death and acquit the guilty.'

'Ah yes,' he answered, 'but when I did try to think out my defence to the jury, the Diety at once resisted.'

'Strange words,' said his friend, and then Socrates spoke again.

'Do you think it strange if it seems better to God that I die now? Don't you see to this day I never would acknowledge that any man has lived a better or pleasanter life than I? For they live best, I think, who strive best to become as good as possible, and the pleasant life is theirs who are conscious that they are growing in goodness.'"

So I am old, if Shakesphere's postulations are taken literally, and didn't he say according to Leland that a man at about my age is old but still in control of his faculties, but not too well in control of his faculties I think he might have meant, an assertion which calls for a slight of correction to say the least, for in my own circumstance I have attained to that mid point between 85 and 90 years, not by any significant measure slowed or sunken into a state of debility, and not just holding on to my faculties, but lucid and fresh and vigorous, and unwilling to let a single day pass without learning or trying something new. I jostle with Andrea that my next scheduled venture will involve sky diving. I trade letters with Leland and Darya, recently going to see her by way of plane—a stimulating experience I should contend, for we talked of old times when we were amourous toward one another, and Andrea cropped up in the conversation too. Darya said in something of a subdued tonality that her most hurtful regret as she looks back is that "We failed to marry. I wanted badly to but Andrea won you and you were blessed. She is the finest and purest of any that I know. She is a good one Ramsey. Every guy and gal on campus knew that. But you are the finest as well and it was my unique fortune that you loved me once, at least for a while if not endlessly. I have some great memories. But I am lonely too much, I must tell you but not cripplingly lonely. Once my mother said that a person getting old has to learn to discover and accept new memories or else the old ones will kill you. I try to abide by that, and do as well as I can."

There are four things, make it five, that Andrea and I do with regularity, attending church, seeing movies, traveling to a good many places but doing it short range in most cases, and reading and writing, and lastly but definitely not left out. Fishing. A time or two we have flown to Chicago to again stroll across the university campus and have our driver drive us by the adorable little cottage on Lake Michigan where we once lived. Ah! The old fraternity house. It still stands, and in my imagination, I am once again there in the midst of it all, the lively debates as vigorous as ever at the dinner table, Aaron foremost among the participants.

They say you cannot go home again, a misnomer in so far as I am concerned, for you never forget your native domain, in my case a very small town that stands in some ways as a reminder of the hard times endured by my father and his family. Those were hard times, yes, the worst in my memory being the devastating daylight to dark share cropping hours of his tilling the soil and struggling to make ends meet. And praying that no one fell sick because with what would he pay the doctor. In this light I cannot forget banker Monnett, who once refused to my father a meager loan for acquiring badly needed crop seed. When I mention such hurtful remembrances in Andrea's midst, she attempts to cushion them with a citation from the Lords Prayer that beseeches us to forgive those who trespass against us. I try.

And yet there were good times, good memories—for how can I not remember with a smile the tractor business which ascended into remarkable success and therefore gave Leland and me so much joy, the rabbit hunts with my uncle Sanford and John Eric in the savannahs of the Obion, the Saturday afternoon gatherings on mainstreet of the happy rural folks swelling into overflow proportions, the old checker players up by the corner grocery store jaw boning at one another, and my visits with two of the sweetest people I ever had the good fortune to meet, Mr. Carney and Tatiana. All these things among many.

Finally, at last, I have taken my inimitable friend Father Casandra to see my home town, with Andrea doing the driving. We spent the night in Mississippi on our way up. He has without let up expressed his wish to make this visit. Upon noticing the name on the sign situated at the point of entry he exclaimed surprise at my not mentioning it before.

"No Father, I have not. I've always had a much better one in mind."

"And what is that?"

"Mac Town."

"Why on earth?"

"You'll know someday. But there is a very long story behind it which will take more than the usual while to tell."

Epilogue

Now my days have dwindled down to a precious few
I'm in the shadow of my years
I'm likened to those fine old kegs
With seasoned wine from the brim to the dregs
With a taste as sweet as its color is pretty
I have lived but I have lived simply
I've had some triumphs and a share of tears
But it's both together that make life dear
And with this said I will conclude
That every day is still like new
It had to be in His wondrous plan
To give me life with so lengthy of span

www.ingramcontent.com/pod-product-compliance
Lightning Source LLC
Chambersburg PA
CBHW080811020826
48982CB00017B/925
9780998852898